Miss Lenore Lester
would need some convincing about
The Reasons for Marriage

Mr. Jack Lester's secret
was making difficult his pursuit of
A Lady of Expectations

Mr. Harry Lester could not quell his desire
for Mrs. Lucinda Babbacombe, who was proving
An Unwilling Conquest

The Lester Family trilogy
Three captivating Regency romances
by bestselling author

Stephanie
Laurens

Dear Reader,

The Lester family trilogy was not "planned" in the sense of my setting out from the first to write three connected novels. Instead, while I wrote the first book dealing with the unwilling surrender to love of Lenore Lester and Jason, Duke of Eversleigh, and the not-so-comfortable adjustments required of them both, Lenore's brothers, Jack and Harry, tended to swan around in the background, arrogant and contemptuous of love, and oh, so clearly intending never to succumb themselves. Their very resistance made them obvious targets for Cupid to take aim at; exploring their stories became a tantalizing temptation. And that's how the trilogy came about, because I couldn't resist learning what it would take to make two very different, but equally recalcitrant Regency rakes willingly accept that which they'd set their defenses so solidly against—what it would take to make them desire, accept and embrace love.

I had a great deal of fun writing the Lester family trilogy. I hope you, as readers, enjoy it, too.

Stephanie Laurens

Stephanie Laurens

Rogues' Reform

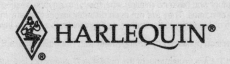
HARLEQUIN®

TORONTO • NEW YORK • LONDON
AMSTERDAM • PARIS • SYDNEY • HAMBURG
STOCKHOLM • ATHENS • TOKYO • MILAN • MADRID
PRAGUE • WARSAW • BUDAPEST • AUCKLAND

ISBN 0-373-83458-6

ROGUES' REFORM

Copyright © 2000 by Harlequin Books S.A.

The publisher acknowledges the copyright holder
of the individual works as follows:

THE REASONS FOR MARRIAGE
Copyright © 1994 by Stephanie Laurens

A LADY OF EXPECTATIONS
Copyright © 1995 by Stephanie Laurens

AN UNWILLING CONQUEST
Copyright © 1996 by Stephanie Laurens

Visit us at www.eHarlequin.com

Printed in U.S.A.

CONTENTS

The Reasons for Marriage

CHAPTER ONE

THE DOOR OF THE Duke of Eversleigh's library clicked shut. From his chair behind the huge mahogany desk, Jason Montgomery, fifth Duke of Eversleigh, eyed the oak panels with marked disfavour.

"Impossible!" he muttered, the word heavy with contemptuous disdain laced with an odd reluctance. As the sound of his cousin Hector's retreating footsteps dwindled, Jason's gaze left the door, travelling across the laden bookcases to the large canvas mounted on a nearby wall.

Expression bleak, he studied the features of the young man depicted there, the impudent, devil-may-care smile and mischievous grey eyes topped by wind-tousled dark brown hair. Broad shoulders were clad in the scarlet of regimentals, a lance stood to one side, all evidence of the subject's occupation. A muscle twitched at the corner of Jason's mouth. He quelled it, his austere, chiselled features hardening into a mask of chilly reserve.

The door opened to admit a gentleman, elegantly garbed and smiling amiably. He paused with his hand on the knob and raised a brow enquiringly.

"I saw your cousin depart. Are you safe?"

With the confidence of one sure of his welcome, Frederick Marshall did not wait for an answer but, shutting the door, strolled towards the desk between the long windows.

His Grace of Eversleigh let out an explosive sigh. "Damn it, Frederick, this is no laughing matter! Hector Montgomery is a *man-milliner*! It would be the height of irresponsibility for

me to allow him to step into the ducal shoes. Even *I* can'
stomach the thought—and I wouldn't be here to see it.''

Pushing back his chair, Jason swung to face his friend as h
sank into an armchair nearby. ''More to the point,'' he contin
ued, stretching his long legs before him, a somewhat grim smil
twisting his lips, ''tempting though the idea might be, if I in
troduced *cher* Hector to the family as my heir, there'd be *
riot—a mutiny in the Montgomery ranks. Knowing my aunts
they would press for incarceration until such time as I capitu
lated and wed.''

''I dare say your aunts would be delighted to know you se
the problem—and its solution—so clearly.''

At that, Jason's piercing gaze focused on his friend's face
''Just whose side are you on, Frederick?''

Frederick smiled. ''Need you ask? But there's no sense i
ducking the facts. Now Ricky's gone, you'll have to wed. An
the sooner you make up your mind to it, the less likely it wil
be that your aunts, dear ladies, think to take a hand them
selves—don't you think?''

Having delivered himself of this eminently sound piece o
advice, Frederick sat back and watched his friend digest i
Sunshine shone through the windows at Jason's back, burnish
ing the famous chestnut locks cut short in the prevailing mod
Broad shoulders did justice to one of Schultz's more sever
designs, executed in grey superfine, worn over tightly fittin
pantaloons. The waistcoat Frederick espied beneath the gre
coat, a subtle thing in shades of deeper grey and mute
lavender, elicited a twinge of envy. There was one man in a
of England who could effortlessly make Frederick Marsha
feel less than elegant and that man was seated behind the des
sunk in unaccustomed gloom.

Both bachelors, their association was bound by many con
mon interests, but in all their endeavours it was Jason wh
excelled. A consummate sportsman, a noted whip, a hardene
gamester and acknowledged rake, dangerous with pistols—an
even more dangerous with women. Unused to acknowledgin
any authority beyond his own whims, the fifth Duke of E

ersleigh had lived a hedonistic existence that few, in this hedonistic age, could match.

Which, of course, made the solution to his present predicament that much harder to swallow.

Seeing Jason's gaze, pensive yet stubborn, rise to the portrait
of his younger brother, known to all as Ricky, Frederick stifled
a sigh. Few understood how close the brothers had been, despite the nine years' difference in age. At twenty-nine, Ricky
had possessed a boundless charm which had cloaked the wilful
streak he shared with Jason—the same wilful streak that had
sent him in the glory of his Guards' captaincy to Waterloo,
there to die at Hougoumont. The dispatches had heaped praise
on all the fated Guardsmen who had defended the vital fort so
valiantly, yet no amount of praise had eased the grief, all the
more deep for being so private, that Jason had borne.

For a time the Montgomery clan had held off, aware, as
others were not, of the brothers' affection. However, as they
were also privy to the understanding that had been forged years
before—that Ricky, much less cynical, much less hard than
Jason, would take on the responsibility of providing for the
next generation, leaving his older brother free to continue his
life unfettered by the bonds of matrimony, it was not to be
expected that the family's interest in Jason's affairs would remain permanently deflected. Consequently, when Jason had re-
emerged, taking up his usual pursuits with a vigour which,
Frederick shrewdly suspected, had been fuelled by a need to
bury the recent past, his aunts became restive. When their arrogantly errant nephew continued to give no hint of turning his
attention to what they perceived as a now pressing duty, they
had, collectively, deemed it time to take a hand.

Tipped off by one of Jason's redoubtable aunts, Lady Agatha
Colebatch, Frederick had deemed it wise to prod Jason's mind
to deal with the matter before his aunts made his hackles rise.
It was at his urging that Jason had finally consented to meet
with his heir, a cousin many times removed.

The silence was broken by a frustrated snort

"Damn you, Ricky," Jason grumbled, his gaze on his

brother's portrait. "How dare you go to hell in your own way and leave me to face this hell on earth?"

Detecting the resigned undertones in his friend's complaint, Frederick chuckled. "Hell on earth?"

Abruptly straightening and swinging back to his desk, Jason raised his brows. "Can you think of a better description for the sanctified institution of marriage?"

"Oh, I don't know." Frederick waved a hand. "No reason it has to be as bad as all that."

Jason's grey gaze transfixed him. "You being such an expert on the matter?"

"Hardly me—but I should think you could figure as such."

"*Me*?" Jason looked his amazement.

"Well, all your recent mistresses have been married, haven't they?"

Frederick's air of innocence deceived Jason not one whit. Nevertheless, his lips twitched and the frown which had marred his strikingly handsome countenance lifted. "Your misogyny defeats you, my friend. The women I bed are prime reasons for my distrust of the venerable bonds of matrimony. Such women are perfect examples of what I should *not* wish for in a wife."

"Precisely," agreed Frederick. "So at least you have that much insight." He looked up to discover Jason regarding him intently, a suspicious glint in his silver-grey eyes.

"Frederick, dear chap, you aren't by any chance possessed of an ulterior motive in this matter, are you? Perchance my aunts have whispered dire threats in your ear?"

To his confusion, Frederick blushed uncomfortably. "Damn you, Jason, get those devilish eyes off me. If you must know, Lady Agatha did speak to me, but you know she's always been inclined to take your side. She merely pointed out that he sisters were already considering candidates and if I wished to avert a major explosion I'd do well to bring the matter to your mind."

Jason grimaced. "Well, consider it done. But having accom

plished so much, you can damn well help me through the rest of it. Who the devil am I to marry?''

The question hung in the calm of the library while both men considered the possible answers.

"What about the Taunton chit? She's surely pretty enough to take your fancy.''

Jason frowned. "The one with reams of blonde ringlets?'' When Frederick nodded, Jason shook his head decisively. "She twitters.''

"Hemming's girl then—a fortune there, and word is out that they're hanging out for a title. You'd only have to say the word and she'd be yours.''

"She and her three sisters and whining mother to boot? No, I thank you. Think again.''

And so it went, on through the ranks of the year's débutantes and their still unwed older sisters.

Eventually, Frederick was close to admitting defeat. Sipping the wine Jason had poured to fortify them through the mind-numbing process, he tried a different tack. "Perhaps," he said, slanting a somewhat peevish glance at his host, "given your highly specific requirements, we would do better to clarify just what it is you require in a wife and then try to find a suitable candidate?''

Savouring the excellent madeira he had recently acquired, Jason's eyes narrowed. "What I want in a wife?'' he echoed.

For a full minute, silence held sway, broken only by the discreet tick of the ornate clock on the mantelpiece. Slowly, Jason set down his long-stemmed glass, running his fingers down the figured stem in an unconscious caress. "My wife,'' he stated, his voice sure and strong, "must be a virtuous woman, capable of running the Abbey and this house in a manner commensurate with the dignity of the Montgomerys.''

Wordlessly, Frederick nodded. Eversleigh Abbey was the Montgomery family seat, a sprawling mansion in Dorset. Running the huge house, and playing hostess at the immense family gatherings occasionally held there, would stretch the talents of the most well-educated miss.

"She would need to be at least presentable—I draw the line at any underbred antidote being the Duchess of Eversleigh."

Reflecting that Jason's aunts, high-sticklers every one, would certainly echo that sentiment, Frederick waited for more.

Jason's gaze had dropped to his long fingers, still moving sensuously up and down the glass stem. "And, naturally, she would have to be prepared to provide me with heirs without undue fuss over the matter." His expression hardened. "Any woman who expects me to make a cake of myself over her will hardly suit."

Frederick had no doubts about that.

After a moment's consideration, Jason quietly added, "Furthermore, she would need to be prepared to remain principally at the Abbey, unless I specifically request her presence here in town."

At that cold declaration, Frederick blinked. "But...do you mean after the Season has ended?"

"No. I mean at all times."

"You mean to incarcerate her in the Abbey? Even while you enjoy yourself in town?" When Jason merely nodded, Frederick felt moved to expostulate. "Really, Jason! A mite draconian, surely?"

Jason smiled, a slow, predatory smile that did not reach his eyes. "You forget, Frederick. I have, as you noted earlier, extensive experience of the bored wives of the ton. Whatever else, rest assured my wife will never join their ranks."

"Ah." Faced with such a statement, Frederick had nothing to do but retreat. "So what else do you require in your bride?"

Leaning back in his chair, Jason crossed his ankles and fell to studying the high gloss on his Hessians. "She would have to be well-born—the family would accept nothing less. Luckily, a dowry makes no odds—I doubt I'd notice, after all. Connections, however, are a must."

"Given what you have to offer, that should hardly pose a problem." Frederick drained his glass. "All the haut ton with daughters to establish will beat a path to your door once they realize your intent."

"No doubt," Jason returned ascerbically. "That, if you must know, is the vision that spurs me to take your advice and act now—before the hordes descend. The idea of being forced to run the gamut of all the dim-witted debs fills me with horror."

"Well, that's a point you haven't mentioned." When Jason lifted his brows, Frederick clarified. "Dim-witted. You never could bear fools lightly, so you had better add that to your list."

"Lord, yes," Jason sighed, letting his head fall back against the padded leather. "If she's to avoid being strangled the morning after we are wed, my prospective bride would do well to have rather more wit than the common run." After a moment, he mused, "You know, I rather wonder if this paragon—my prospective bride—exists in this world."

Frederick pursed his lips. "Your requirements are a mite stringent, but I'm sure, somewhere, there must be a woman who can fill your position."

"Ah," said Jason, amusement beginning to glimmer in his grey eyes. "Now we come to the difficult part. Where?"

Frederick wracked his brain for an answer. "A more mature woman, perhaps? But one with the right background." He caught Jason's eyes and frowned. "Dash it, it's *you* who must wed. Perhaps I should remind you of Miss Ekhart, the young lady your aunt Hardcastle pushed under your nose last time she was in town?"

"Heaven forbid!" Jason schooled his features to a suitably intimidated expression. "Say on, dear Frederick. Where resides my paragon?"

The clock ticked on. Finally, frowning direfully, Frederick flung up a hand. "Hell and the devil! There must be *some* suitable women about?"

Jason met his frustration with bland resignation. "I can safely say I've never found one. That aside, however, I agree that, assuming there is indeed at least one woman who could fill my bill, it behoves me to hunt her out, wherever she may be. The question is, where to start?"

With no real idea, Frederick kept mum.

His gaze abstracted, his mind turning over his problem, Jason's long fingers deserted his empty glass to idly play with a stack of invitations, the more conservative gilt-edged notelets vying with delicate pastel envelopes, a six-inch-high stack, awaiting his attention. Abruptly realising what he had in his hand, Jason straightened in his chair, the better to examine the *ton*'s offerings.

"Morecambes, Lady Hillthorpe's rout." He paused to check the back of one envelope. "Sussex Devenishes. The usual lot." One by one, the invitations dropped from his fingers on to the leather-framed blotter. "D'Arcys, Penbrights. Lady Allington has forgiven me, I see."

Frederick frowned. "What did she have to forgive you for?"

"Don't ask. Minchinghams, Carstairs." Abruptly, Jason halted. "Now this is one I haven't seen in a while—the Lesters." Laying aside the other invitations, he reached for a letter-knife.

"Jack and Harry?"

Unfolding the single sheet of parchment, Jason scanned the lines within and nodded. "Just so. A request for the pleasure, et cetera, et cetera at a week-long succession of entertainments—for which one can read bacchanal—at Lester Hall."

"I suspect I've got one, too." Frederick uncurled his elegant form from the depths of the armchair. "Thought I recognised the Lester crest but didn't stop to open it." Glass in hand, he picked up Jason's glass and crossed to place both on the sideboard. Turning, he beheld an expression of consideration on His Grace of Eversleigh's countenance.

Jason's gaze lifted to his face. "Do you plan to attend?"

Frederick grimaced. "Not exactly my style. That last time was distinctly too licentious for my taste."

A smile of complete understanding suffused Jason's features. "You should not let your misogyny spoil your enjoyment of life, my friend."

Frederick snorted. "Permit me to inform His Grace of Eversleigh that His Grace enjoys himself far too much."

Jason chuckled. "Perhaps you're right. But they haven'

opened Lester Hall for some years now, have they? That last effort was at Jack's hunting box.''

"Old Lester's been under the weather, so I'd heard." Frederick dropped into his armchair. "They all thought his time had come, but Gerald was in Manton's last week and gave me to understand the old man had pulled clear."

"Hmm. Seems he's sufficiently recovered to have no objection to his sons opening his house for him." Jason reread the brief missive, then shrugged. "Doubtful that I'd find a candidate suitable to take to wife there."

"Highly unlikely." Frederick shuddered and closed his eyes. "I can still recall the peculiar scent of that woman in purple who pursued me so doggedly at their last affair."

Smiling, Jason made to lay aside the note. Instead, his hand halted halfway to the pile of discarded invitations, then slowly returned until the missive was once more before him. Staring at the note, he frowned.

"What is it?"

"The sister." Jason's frown deepened. "There was a sister. Younger than Jack or Harry, but, if I recall aright, older than Gerald."

Frederick frowned, too. "That's right," he eventually conceded. "Haven't sighted her since the last time we were at Lester Hall—which must be all of six years ago. Slip of a thing, if I'm thinking of the right one. Tended to hug the shadows."

Jason's brows rose. "Hardly surprising given the usual tone of entertainments at Lester Hall. I don't believe I've ever met her."

When he made no further remark, Frederick turned to stare at him, eyes widening as he took in Jason's pensive expression. "You aren't thinking…?"

"Why not?" Jason looked up. "Jack Lester's sister might suit me very well."

"Jack and Harry as brothers-in-law? Good God! The Montgomerys will never be the same."

"The Montgomerys are liable to be only too thankful to see me wed regardless." Jason tapped the crisp parchment with a manicured fingernail. "Aside from anything else, at least the Lester men won't expect me to turn myself into a monk if I marry their sister."

Frederick shifted. "Perhaps she's already married."

"Perhaps," Jason conceded. "But somehow I think not. I rather suspect it is she who runs Lester Hall."

"Oh? Why so?"

"Because," Jason said, reaching over to drop the invitation into Frederick's hand, "some woman penned this invitation. Not an older woman, and not a schoolgirl but yet a lady bred. And, as we know, neither Jack, Harry nor Gerald has yet been caught in parson's mousetrap. So what other young lady would reside at Lester Hall?"

Reluctantly, Frederick acknowledged the likely truth of his friend's deduction. "So you plan to go down?"

"I rather think I will," Jason mused. "However," he added, "I intend to consult the oracle before we commit ourselves."

"Oracle?" asked Frederick, then, rather more forcefully. "*We?*"

"The oracle that masquerades as my aunt Agatha," Jason replied. "She's sure to know if the Lester chit is unwed and suitable—she knows damned near everything else in this world." He turned to study Frederick, grey eyes glinting steel. "And as for the 'we', my friend, having thrust my duty upon me, you can hardly deny me your support in this, my greatest travail."

Frederick squirmed. "Dash it, Jason—you hardly need me to hold your hand. You've had more experience in successfully hunting women than any man I know."

"True," declared His Grace of Eversleigh, unperturbed. "But this is different. I've had women aplenty—this time, I want wife."

"WELL, EVERSLEIGH?" Straight as a poker, Lady Agatha Colebatch sat like an empress giving audience from the middle of her chaise. An intimidating turban of deepest purple crowned aristocratic features beset by fashionable boredom, although her beaked nose fairly quivered with curiosity. Extending one hand, she watched with impatience as her nephew strolled languidly forward to take it, bowing gracefully before her. "I assume this visit signifies that you have come to a better understanding of your responsibilities and have decided to seek a bride?"

Jason's brows rose haughtily. Instead of answering the abrupt query, he took advantage of his aunt's waved offer of a seat, elegantly disposing his long limbs in a chair.

Watching this performance through narrowed eyes, Lady Agatha possessed her soul with what patience she could. From experience she knew studying Eversleigh's expression would yield nothing; the strong, patrician features were impassive, his light grey eyes shuttered. He was dressed for a morning about town, his tautly muscled frame displayed to advantage in a coat of Bath superfine, his long legs immaculately clad in ivory inexpressibles which disappeared into the tops of glossy tasselled Hessians.

"As it happens, Aunt, you are right."

Lady Agatha inclined her turbaned head regally. "Have you any particular female in mind?"

"I do." Jason paused to enjoy the ripple of astonishment that passed over his aunt's features. "The lady at present at the top of my list is one of the Lesters, of Lester Hall in Berkshire. However, I'm unsure if she remains unwed."

Dazed, Lady Agatha blinked. "I take it you are referring to Lenore Lester. To my knowledge, she has not married."

When his aunt preserved a stunned silence, Jason prompted, "In your opinion, is Miss Lester suitable as the next Duchess of Eversleigh?"

Unable to resist, Lady Agatha blurted out the question sure to be on every lady's lips once this titbit got about. "What of Lady Hetherington?"

Instantly, she regretted the impulse. The very air about her seemed to freeze as her nephew brought his steely grey gaze to bear.

Politely, Jason raised his brows. "Who?"

Irritated by the very real intimidation she felt, Lady Agatha refused to retreat. "You know very well whom I mean, sir."

For a long moment, Jason held her challenging stare. Quite why his transient liaisons with well-born women evoked such interest in the breasts of righteous females he had never fathomed. However, he felt no real qualms in admitting to what was, after all, now little more than historical fact. Aurelia Hetherington had provided a momentary diversion, a fleeting passion that had rapidly been quenched. "If you must know, I've finished with *la belle* Hetherington."

"Indeed!" Lady Agatha stored that gem in her capacious memory.

"However," Jason added, his tone pointed, "I fail to see what that has to say to Lenore Lester's suitability as my duchess."

Lady Agatha blinked. "Er...quite." Faced with her nephew's penetrating gaze, she rapidly marshalled her facts. "Her breeding, of course, is beyond question. The connection to the Rutlands, let alone the Havershams and Ranelaghs, would make it a most favourable match. Her dowry might leave something to be desired, but I suspect you'd know more of that than I."

Jason nodded. "That, however, is not a major consideration."

"Quite," agreed her ladyship, wondering if, perhaps, Lenore Lester could indeed be a real possibility.

"And the lady herself?"

Lady Agatha spread her hands. "As you must be aware, she manages that great barn of a hall. Lester's sister is there, of course, but Lenore's always been mistress of the house. Lester himself is ageing. Never was an easygoing soul, but Lenore seems to cope very well."

"Why hasn't she married?"

Lady Agatha snorted. "Never been presented, for one thing. She must have been all of twelve when her mother died. Took over the household from then—no time to come to London and dance the nights away..."

Jason's gaze sharpened. "So she's...unused to the amusements of town?"

Reluctantly, Lady Agatha nodded. "Has to be. Stands to reason."

"Hold old is she?"

Lady Agatha pursed her lips. "Twenty-four."

"And she's presentable?"

The question shook Lady Agatha to attention. "But..." she began, then frowned. "Haven't you met her?"

His eyes on hers, Jason shook his head. "But you have, haven't you?"

Under the concerted scrutiny of those perceptive silver eyes, Lady Agatha's eyes glazed as memories of the last time she had met Lenore re-formed in her mind. "Good bone-structure," she began weakly. "Should bear well. Good complexion, fair hair, green eyes, I think. Tallish, slim." Nervous of saying too much, she shrugged and glanced at Jason. "What more do you need to know?"

"Is she possessed of a reasonable understanding?"

"Yes—oh, yes, I'm quite certain about that." Lady Agatha drew a steadying breath and shut her lips.

Jason's sharp eyes had noted his aunt's unease. "Yet you entertain reservations concerning Miss Lester?"

Startled, Lady Agatha grimaced. "Not reservations. But if my opinion is to be of any real value, it would help if I knew why you have cast your eye in her direction."

Briefly, unemotionally, Jason recounted his reasons for marriage, his requirements of a bride. Concluding his recitation, he gave his aunt a moment to marshall her thoughts before saying, "So, dear aunt, we come to the crux. Will she do?"

After a fractional hesitation, Lady Agatha nodded decisively. "I know of no reason why not."

"Good." Jason stood. "And now, if you'll forgive me, I must depart."

"Yes, of course." Lady Agatha promptly held out her hand, too relieved to have escaped further inquisition to risk more questions of her own. She needed time away from her nephew's far-sighted gaze to assess the true significance of his unexpected choice. "Dare say I'll see you at the Marshams' tonight."

Straightening from his bow, Jason allowed his brows to rise. "I think not." Seeing the question in his aunt's eyes, he smiled. "I expect to leave for the Abbey on the morrow. I'll travel directly to Lester Hall from there."

A silent "oh" formed on Lady Agatha's lips.

With a final benevolent nod, Jason strolled from the room.

Lady Agatha watched him go, her fertile brain seething with possibilities. That Jason should marry so cold-bloodedly surprised her not at all; that he should seek to marry Lenore Lester seemed incredible.

"I SAY, Miss Lester. Ready for a jolly week, what?"

Her smile serene, Lenore Lester bestowed her hand on Lord Quentin, a roué of middle age and less than inventive address. Like a general, she stood on the grand staircase in the entrance hall of her home and directed her troops. As her brothers' guests appeared out of the fine June afternoon, bowling up to the door in their phaetons and curricles, she received them with a gracious welcome before passing them on to her minions to guide to their chambers. "Good afternoon, my lord. I hope the weather remains fine. So dampening, to have to cope with drizzle."

Disconcerted, his lordship nodded. "Er...just so."

Lenore turned to offer a welcoming word to Mrs. Cronwell, a blowsy blonde who had arrived immediately behind his lordship, before releasing the pair into her butler's care. "The chambers in the west wing, Smithers."

As the sound of their footsteps and the shush of Mrs. Cronwell's stiff skirts died away, Lenore glanced down at the list in her hand. Although this was the first of her brothers' parties at which she had acted as hostess, she was accustomed to the role, having carried it with aplomb for some five years, ever since her aunt Harriet, her nominal chaperon, had been afflicted by deafness. Admittedly, it was usually her own and her aunt's friends, a most select circle of acquaintances, as refined as they were reliable, that she welcomed to the rambling rooms of Lester Hall. Nevertheless, Lenore foresaw no difficulty in keeping her hands on the reins of her brothers' more boisterous affair. Adjusting her gold-rimmed spectacles, she captured the pencil that hung in an ornate holder from a ribbon looped about her neck and marked off Lord Quentin and Mrs. Cronwell. Most of the guests were known to her, having visited the house before. The majority of those expected had arrived; only five gentlemen had yet to appear.

Lenore looked up, across the length of the black and white tiled hall. The huge oak doors were propped wide to reveal the paved portico before them, steps disappearing to left and right leading down to the gravelled drive.

The clop of approaching hooves was followed by the scrunch of gravel.

Smoothing back a few wisps of gold that had escaped her tight bun, Lenore tweaked out the heavy olive green twill pinafore she wore over her high-necked, long-sleeved gown.

A deep male voice rumbled through the open doorway, carried on the light breeze.

Lenore straightened, rising a finger to summon Harris, the senior footman, to her side.

"Oh, Miss Lester! Could you tell us the way to the lake?"

Lenore turned as two beauties, scantily clad in fine muslins, came bustling out of the morning-room at the back of the hall. Lady Harrison and Lady Moffat, young matrons and sisters, had accepted her brothers' invitation, each relying on the other to lend them countenance. "Down that corridor, left through the garden hall. The door to the conservatory should be open. Straight through, down the steps and straight ahead—you can't miss it."

As the ladies smiled their thanks and, whispering avidly, went on their way, Lenore turned towards the front door, murmuring to Harris, "If they don't return in an hour, send someone to check they haven't fallen in." The sound of booted feet purposefully ascending the long stone steps came clearly to her ears.

"Miss Lester!"

Lenore turned as Lord Holyoake and Mr. Peters descended the stairs.

"Can you point us in the direction of the action, m'dear?"

Unperturbed by his lordship's wink, Lenore replied, "My brothers and some of the guests are in the billiard-room, I believe. Timms?"

Instantly, another footman peeled from the ranks hidden by the shadows of the main doors. "If you'll follow me, my lord?"

The sound of the trio's footsteps retreating down the hallway was overridden by the ring of boot heels on the portico flags. With a mental "at last", Lenore lifted her head and composed her features.

Two gentlemen entered the hall.

Poised to greet them, Lenore was struck by the aura of ineffable elegance that clung to the pair. There was little to choose between them, but her attention was drawn to the larger figure, insensibly convinced of his pre-eminence. A many-caped greatcoat of dark grey drab fell in long folds to brush calves clad in mirror-glossed Hessians. His hat was in his hands, revealing a wealth of wavy chestnut locks. The newcomers paused just inside the door as footmen scurried to relieve them of hats, coats and gloves. As she watched, the taller man turned to survey the hall. His gaze scanned the area, then came to rest with unwavering intensity upon her.

With a jolt, Lenore felt a comprehensive glance rake her, from the top of her tight bun to the tips of her serviceable slippers, then slowly, studiously return, coming at last to rest on her face.

Outrage blossomed in her breast, along with a jumble of other, less well-defined emotions.

The man started towards her, his companion falling in beside him. Summoning her wits to battle, Lenore drew herself up, her gaze bordering on the glacial, her expression one of icy civility.

Unheralded, the hall before her erupted into chaos. Within seconds, the black and white tiled expanse had filled with a seething mass of humanity. Her brother Gerald had come in from the garden, a small crowd of bucks and belles in tow. Simultaneously, a bevy of jovial gentlemen, led by her brother Harry, had erupted from the billiard-room, apparently in search of like-minded souls for some complicated game they had in hand. The two groups collided in the hall and immediately emerged into a chattering, laughing, giggling mass.

Lenore looked down upon the sea of heads, impatient to have the perpetrator of that disturbing glance before her. She intended making it quite clear from the outset that she did not appreciate being treated with anything less than her due. The mêlée before her was deafening but she disregarded it, her eyes fixed upon the recent arrival, easy to discern given his height. Despite the press of people, he was making remarkably swift progress towards her. As she watched, he encountered her brother Harry in the throng and stopped to exchange greetings. Then he made some comment and Harry laughed, waving him towards her with some jovial remark. Lenore resisted the urge to inspect her list, determined to give the newcomer no chance to find her cribbing. Her excellent memory was no aid; she had not met this gentleman before.

Reaching the stairs in advance of his companion, he halted before her. Confidently, Lenore allowed her eyes to meet his, pale grey under dark brows. Abruptly, all thought of upbraiding him, however subtly, vanished. The face before her did not belong to a man amenable to feminine castigation. Strong, clean, angular planes, almost harsh in their severity, framed features both hard and dictatorial. Only his eyes, faultless light grey, and the clean sweep of his winged brows saved the whole from the epithet of "austere".

Quelling an odd shiver, Lenore imperiously extended her hand. "Welcome, to Lester Hall, sir."

Her fingers were trapped in a warm clasp. To her annoyance,

Lenore felt them quiver. As the gentleman bowed gracefully, she scanned his elegant frame. He was clad in a coat of sober brown, his cravat and breeches immaculate ivory, his Hessians gleaming black. He was, however, too tall. Too tall, too large, altogether too overwhelming.

She reached this conclusion in a state bordering on the distracted. Despite standing on the step below her, despite the fact that she was unfashionably tall, she still felt as if she risked a crick in her neck as she endeavoured to meet her disturbing guest eye-to-eye. For the first time in living memory, maintaining her mask of calm detachment, her shield, honed over the years to deflect any attack, became a major effort.

Blinking aside her momentary fascination, Lenore detected a glimmer of amused understanding in the grey eyes watching her. Her chin went up, her eyes flashed in unmistakable warning, but the gentleman seemed unperturbed.

"I am Eversleigh, Miss Lester. I don't believe we've previously met."

"Unfortunately not, Your Grace," Lenore promptly responded, her tone calculated to depress any pretension, leaving a vague, perfectly accurate suggestion that she was not entirely sure she approved of their meeting now. Eversleigh! She should have guessed. Curtsying, she tried to ignore the reverberations of the duke's deep voice. She could *feel* it, buried in her chest, a curious chord, thrumming distractingly.

Attention riveted by a welcome entirely out of the ordinary, Jason's gaze was intent as he studied the woman before him. She was long past girlhood, but still slender, supple, with the natural grace of a feline. Her features, fine-drawn and delicate in her pale, heart-shaped face, he could not fault. Fine brown brows arched above large, lucent eyes of palest green, edged by a feathering of long brown lashes. A flawless complexion of creamy ivory set off her small straight nose and determinedly pointed chin and the rich promise of her lips. Her eyes met his squarely, her expression of implacable resistance framed by her gilded spectacles.

Unable to resist, Jason smiled, stepping slightly aside to gesture to Frederick. "And this is—"

"Mr. Marshall." If her tormentor was Eversleigh, then his companion's identity was a foregone conclusion. Belatedly realising that she might well be playing with fire, Lenore retrieved her hand from the duke's firm clasp and bestowed it upon Frederick Marshall.

Smiling easily, Frederick bowed. "I do hope you have saved us rooms, Miss Lester. I fear we had not realised what a crowd there would be and made no shift to arrive early."

"No matter, sir. We were expecting you." Lenore returned his smile, confident in her role. As he was the only duke attending, she had allotted the best guest suite to Eversleigh, with the chamber beside for Mr. Marshall. She turned to Harris on the stair behind her. "The grey suite for His Grace, and Mr. Marshall in the blue room." Harris bowed gravely and started up the stairs. Turning back to Frederick Marshall, Leonore added, "No doubt you'll want to acquaint yourself with your quarters. We'll see you both at dinner. Six-thirty in the drawing room."

With a polite nod and a smile, Frederick Marshall moved up the stairs.

Lenore waited for the large frame on her right to follow, determined not to look up at him until he was safely on his way. The seconds stretched. Eversleigh did not move. An odd nervousness gripped Lenore. Eversleigh stood between her and the crowd in the hall; the sense of being alone with a dangerous companion stole over her.

Having found the novelty of being so lightly dismissed not at all to his taste, Jason allowed the tension between them to wind tight before remarking, in his most equable tone, "I understand, Miss Lester, that you are to be our hostess through this week of dissipation?"

Lenore raised her head, her expression one of remote serenity. "That is correct, Your Grace."

"I do hope you won't be overwhelmed by your duties this week, my dear. I look forward to acquainting myself with what

I have obviously overlooked on my earlier visits to your home.''

Rapidly calculating that if he had visited before, she must have been eighteen and intent on staying out of his or any other eligible gentleman's sight, Lenore met his gaze with one of limpid innocence. ''Indeed, Your Grace? The gardens *are* very fine this year. I dare say you did not get the opportunity to do them justice last time you were here? A stroll about them should certainly prove of interest.''

Jason's lips twitched. ''Undoubtedly,'' he replied smoothly, ''were you to accompany me.''

Trenchantly reminding herself that she was beyond being rattled by rakes, Lenore allowed distant regret to infuse her features, ''I'm afraid my duties, as you call them, frequently keep me from my brothers' guests, Your Grace. However, I doubt my absence is noticed—my brothers' entertainments usually prove *remarkably* engrossing.''

Jason's eyes glinted; his lips curved. ''I can assure you, Miss Lester, that I will certainly notice your absence. Furthermore, I can promise you that the distraction of your brothers' entertainments will be quite insufficient as recompense for the lack of your company. In fact,'' he mused, one brow rising in open consideration, ''I find it hard to imagine what power could deter me from seeking you out, in the circumstances.''

His words rang like a challenge, one Lenore was not at all sure she wished to face. But she was in no mood to permit any gentleman—not even one as notorious as Eversleigh—to disrupt her ordered life. Allowing her brows to rise in cool dismissal, she calmly stated, ''I greatly fear, Your Grace, that I have never considered myself one of the amenities of Lester Hall. You will have to make shift with what comes more readily to hand.''

Unable to suppress a rakish grin at this forthright declaration Jason brought his considerable charm to bear, softening his smile as he said, ''I greatly fear you have misjudged me, Miss Lester.'' His voice dropped in tone, a soothing rumble. '' would rather class you as one of the attractions of Lester Hall—

the sort of attraction that is frequently seen but rarely appreciated.''

If it hadn't been for the odd intensity in his curious grey gaze, Lenore might have taken his words as nothing more than an elegant compliment. Instead, she felt shaken to the core. Her heart, for so long safe beneath her pinafore, thudded uncomfortably. With an enormous effort she dragged her eyes from his.

And spied Lord Percy Almsworthy doggedly pressing through the crowd. He fought free and gained the stairs. Lenore could have fallen on his thin chest with relief. ''Lord Percy! How delightful to see you again.''

''Hello, hello,'' replied his lordship, trying to sound cheery as he tweaked his wilting collars up around his chin. ''Damned crush, what?''

''I'll get a footman to take you to your room immediately.'' Lenore raised her hand, beckoning two footmen forward. ''His Grace was just about to go up,'' she lied, not daring to glance Eversleigh's way.

''The grey suite, I believe,'' came a low murmur from her right. To her surprise, Lenore felt long fingers close about her hand. She swung to face him but, before she could do more than blink, His Grace of Eversleigh raised her fingers to his lips and brushed a light kiss across their sensitive tips.

Jason paused to savour the flush of awareness that rose to his hostess's cheeks and the stunned expression that invaded her eyes before reluctantly conceding, ''Until later, Miss Lester.''

Skittering sensation prickled Lenore's skin. Rocked, she simply stared up at him. To her consternation, a subtle smile twisted his mobile lips before, with a polite nod, he released her hand and, moving past her, ascended the stairs in the footman's wake.

Speechless, Lenore turned to stare at his broad back, wishing she could have thought of some comment to wipe the smug smile from those silver eyes. Still, she reflected as her senses returned, at least he had gone.

Turning back to the hall, she was jolted from her daze by an aggrieved Lord Percy.

"Miss Lester—my room, if you please?"

CHAPTER TWO

"WELL? HOW LONG do you plan to stay, now you've decided Miss Lester will not suit?"

Jason abandoned the view from his windows, his brows lifting in unfeigned surprise. "My dear Frederick, why the rush to so summarily dispense with Miss Lester?"

His expression bland, Frederick strolled forward to sit on the cushioned window seat. "Having known you since seducing the writing master's daughter was your primary aim in life, my imagination does not stretch the distance required to swallow the idea of your marrying a frump. As Lenore Lester is undeniably a frump, I rest my case. So, how soon can we leave without giving offence?"

Taking a seat opposite his friend, Jason looked thoughtful. "Her…er…frumpishness was a mite obvious, don't you think?"

"A matter beyond question," Frederick assured him.

"Even, perhaps, a shade *too* obvious?"

Frederick frowned. "Jason—are you feeling quite the thing?"

Jason's grey eyes gleamed. "I'm exceedingly well and in full possession of my customary faculties. Such being the case, I am, of course, considerably intrigued by Miss Lester."

"But…" Frederick stared. "Dash it—she wore a *pinafore*!"

Jason nodded. "And a gown of heavy cambric, despite the prevailing fashion for muslins. Not just frumpish, but determinedly so. It can hardly have been straightforward to get such unappealing apparel made. All that being so, what I want to know is why."

"Why she's a frump?"

"Why Lenore Lester *wishes* to appear a frump. Not quite a disguise, for she does not go so far as to obliterate reality. However," Jason mused, his gaze resting consideringly on Frederick, "obviously, she has gauged her intended audience well. From her confidence just now, I imagine she has succeeded thus far in convincing those who visit here that she is, indeed, as she appears."

It was all too much for Frederick. "What makes you so sure she is *not* as she appears—a frump?"

Jason smiled, a wolf's smile. He shrugged. "How to explain? An aura? Her carriage?"

"*Carriage*?" Frederick considered, then waved the point aside. "I've heard my mother lecture m'sisters that carriage makes a lady. In my sisters' cases, it definitely hasn't helped."

Jason gestured dismissively. "Whatever. Miss Lester may dress as she pleases but she cannot deceive me."

His confidence set Frederick frowning. "What about those spectacles?"

"Plain glass."

Frederick stared. "Are you sure?"

"Perfectly." Jason's lips twisted wryly. "Hence, dear Frederick, there is no viable conclusion other than that Lenore Lester is intent on pulling the wool over our collective eyes. *If* you can disregard the impression her appearance invokes, then you would see, as I did—and doubtless Aunt Agatha before me—that beneath the rags lies a jewel. Not a diamond of the first water, I'll grant you, but a jewel none the less. There is no reason Lenore Lester needs must wear her hair in a prim bun nor, I'll lay any odds, does she need to wear heavy gowns and a pinafore. They are merely distractions."

"But...why?"

"Precisely my question." Determination gleamed in His Grace of Eversleigh's grey eyes. "I greatly fear, Frederick, that you will indeed have to brave the trials and tribulations of a full week of Jack and Harry's 'entertainments'. For we are certainly not leaving before I discover just what Lenore Lester is hiding. And why.''

NINETY MINUTES later, the hum of drawing-room conversation filling his ears, Jason studied the gown his hostess had donned for the evening with a certain degree of respect. She had entered quietly and stood, calmly scanning the throng. He waited until she was about to plunge into the mêlée before strolling to her elbow.

''Miss Lester.''

Lenore froze, then, slowly, using the time to draw her defences about her, turned to face him. Her mask firmly in place, she held out her hand. ''Good evening, Your Grace. I trust you found your rooms adequate?''

''Perfectly, thank you.'' Straightening from his bow, Jason moved closer, trapping her peridot gaze in his.

The facile words of glib conversation which should have flowed easily from Lenore's socially experienced tongue evaporated. Dimly, she wondered why Eversleigh's silver gaze should have such a mind-numbing effect on her. Then his gaze shifted, swiftly skimming her shoulders before returning to her face. He smiled, slowly. Lenore felt a peculiar tingling warmth suffuse her.

Jason allowed one brow to rise. ''Permit me to compliment you on your gown, Miss Lester. I have not previously seen anything quite like it.''

''Oh?'' Alarm bells rang in Lenore's brain. Impossible not to acknowledge that her novel creation—a silk chemisette, buttoned high at the neck with long buttoned sleeves attached, worn beneath her version of a lustring sack, appropriately named as it fell in copious folds from a gathered yoke above her breasts to where the material was drawn in about her knees before flaring out to conceal her ankles—was in marked contrast to the filmy muslin or silk evening gowns of her contemporaries, cut revealingly low and gathered snugly beneath their breasts the better to display their figures. Indeed, her gown was expressly designed to serve a diametrically opposed purpose.

Eversleigh's allusion, thrown at her on the heels of his unnerving smile, confirmed her dread that, unlike the rest of the
company, he had failed to fall victim to her particular snare.
Disconcerted but determined not to show it, she tiled her chin,
her eyes wide and innocent. "I'm afraid I have little time for
London fripperies, Your Grace."

A glint of appreciative amusement gleamed in the grey eyes
holding hers.

"Strangely enough, it wasn't your *lack* of accoutrement that
struck me." Smoothly, Jason drew her hand through his arm.
"If I was asked for my opinion, I would have to state that in
your case, Miss Lester, my taste would run to less, rather than
more."

His tone, his expression, the inflection in his deep voice, all
combined to assure Lenore that her worst fears had materialised. What mischievous fate, she wondered distractedly, had
decreed that Eversleigh, of all men, should be the one to see
beyond her purposely drab façade?

Deciding that retreat was the only way forward, she dropped
her gaze. "I fear I must attend my father, Your Grace. If you'll
excuse me?"

"I have yet to pay my respects to your father, Miss Lester,
and should like to do so. I'll take you to him, if you'll permit
it?"

Lenore hesitated, fingers twisting the long chain about her
neck from which depended a pair of redundant lorgnettes.
There was no real reason to refuse Eversleigh's escort and she
was loath to cry coward so readily. After all, what could he do
in the middle of the drawing-room? She looked up, into his
eyes. "I believe we will find my father by the fireplace, Your
Grace."

She was treated to a charming smile. With intimidating ease,
Eversleigh steered her through the noisy crowd to where her
father was seated in a Bath chair before the large hearth, one
gouty foot propped on a stool before him.

"Papa." Lenore bent to plant a dutiful kiss on her father's
lined cheek.

The Honourable Archibald Lester humphed. "'Bout time. Bit late tonight, aren't you? What happened? One of those lightskirts try to tumble Smithers?"

Inured to her father's outrageous remarks, Lenore stooped to tuck in a stray end of the blanket draped over his knees. "Of course not, Papa. I was merely delayed."

Jason had noted how Mr. Lester's restless gaze had fastened on his daughter the instant she had come into view. He watched as the old man's washed-out blue eyes scanned Lenore's face before peering up at him aggressively from under shaggy white brows.

Before her father could bark out some less than gracious query, Lenore stepped in. "Allow me to make known to you His Grace of Eversleigh, Papa."

Mr. Lester's steady gaze did not waver. If anything, it intensified. A sardonic gleam in his eye, Jason bowed gracefully, then accepted the hand the old man held out.

"Haven't seen you in some years, I think," Mr. Lester remarked. "Knew your father well—you're becoming more like him with the years—in all respects, from everything I hear."

Standing beside her father's chair, Lenore studiously kept her eyes blank.

Jason inclined his head. "So I have been informed."

Mr. Lester's head sank. For a moment, he appeared lost in memories. Then he snorted. Lifting his head, he looked out across the crowded room. "Remember being in Paris one year your father was there. Group of us, him included, spent quite a bit of time together. Had a rousing six months—the Parisian *mesdames*—now *there* were women who knew how to heat a man's blood." With a contemptuous wave, he indicated the press of bodies before him. "This lot's got no idea. You— m'boys—don't know what you're missing."

Jason's smile grew harder to suppress. From the corner of his eye, he saw Lenore colour delicately. In his own best interests, he decided to forgo encouraging Mr. Lester to recount his memories in more detail. "Unfortunately, I believe Napoleon's comrades have altered things somewhat since you were last in France, sir.''

"Damned upstart!" Mr. Lester ruminated on the emperor's shortcomings for some seconds before observing, "Still—the war's over. Ever think of chancing the Channel to savour the delights of *la bonne vie*, heh?''

At that, Jason smiled. "My tastes, I fear, are distinctly English, sir." As if to include Lenore in their discussion, he allowed his gaze to rise, capturing her eyes with his before adding with calm deliberation, "Besides, I have a particular project before me which bodes fair to absorbing my complete attention for the foreseeable future.''

Despite the quake that inwardly shook her, Lenore kept her gaze steady and her expression serene. Favouring attack as the best form of defence, she countered, "Indeed, Your Grace? And what project is that?''

She had thought to rattle him; although his features remained serious, his expressive eyes warned her she had seriously underestimated him.

"I find myself faced with a conundrum, Miss Lester. A conclusion which, while apparently consistent with the facts, I know to be false.''

Mr. Lester snorted. "Sounds just like the musty old theories you so delight in, m'dear. You should give His Grace a hand.''

Speechless, Lenore looked up, straight into Eversleigh's gleaming grey eyes.

"An excellent idea.'' Jason could not resist a small smile of triumph.

To Lenore, the gesture revealed far too many teeth. Eversleigh was dangerous. His reputation painted him in the most definite colours—those of a highly successful rake. "I really don't believe—''

Her careful retreat was cut off by Smithers, announcing in booming accents that dinner was served.

Lenore blinked, then saw a slow smile light Eversleigh's fascinating features. He had scanned the crowd and now stood, watching her expectantly. Reality hit Lenore like a wave. Eversleigh was the senior peer present. As his hostess, it was incumbent upon her to lead the assembled company in to dinner—on his arm. Aware that, at any moment, the restive crowd would work all this out for themselves and turn to see her, dithering, beside her father's chair, Lenore resisted the temptation to close her eyes in frustration. Instead, her serene mask firmly in place, she walked into the wolf's lair. "If you would be so kind as to lend me your arm, Your Grace?"

She was hardly surprised when he promptly obliged. Harris, the footman, arrived to propel her father's chair. Testily the old man waved them on. "Let's get going! I'm hungry."

Yielding to the slightest of pressures, Lenore allowed Eversleigh to lead her towards the door.

Appreciatively viewing the regal tilt of his hostess' golden head as she glided beside him through the waiting throng, her small hand resting lightly on his sleeve, Jason waited until they had reached the relative quiet of the hall before murmuring, "As I was saying, Miss Lester, I have become fascinated by an instance of what I believe might best be described as artful deceit."

Lenore was having none of it. "Artful deceit, Your Grace? To what purpose, pray?"

"As to purpose, I am not at all sure, but I intend to find out, Miss Lester."

Lenore risked an upward glance, insensibly annoyed at the feeling of smallness that engulfed her. She was used to dealing with gentlemen eye to eye; Eversleigh's height gave him an unfair advantage. But she was determined to end his little game. Elevating her chin, she adopted her most superior tone. "Indeed, Your Grace? And just how do you propose to unravel this conundrum of yours, laying all bare?"

Even as the words left her tongue, Lenore closed her eyes, stifling a groan. Where had her wits gone begging? Then her eyes flew open, her gaze flying, in considerable trepidation, to Eversleigh's hard countenance. Any hope that he would not take advantage was wiped from her mind the instant her eyes met his. Silver gleamed in the grey, white fire under water.

"My dear Miss Lester." The tenor of his voice, velvety deep and heavy with meaning, was a warning in itself. "Would it surprise you to learn that I consider myself peculiarly well-qualified to tackle this particular conundrum? As if my prior existence were nothing more than preparation for this challenge?"

The dining-room loomed ahead, a sanctuary filled with polished oak and silver, crystal goblets winking in the light from the chandelier. The sight gave Lenore strength. "I find that extremely difficult to believe, Your Grace. You must be sure to tell me when you have solved your puzzle."

The smile she received in reply made her giddy.

"Believe me, my dear Miss Lester, you'll be the very first to know when I lay my conundrum bare."

By rights, Lenore thought, she should at least be allowed a gasp. Only her determination not to dissolve into a witless heap under Eversleigh's attack allowed her to keep her head high and her composure intact. "Indeed?" she replied, her voice not as strong as she would have liked. As she assumed her chair at the end of the long table, she tried for dismissive boredom. "You intrigue me, Your Grace."

"No, Miss Lester." Jason stood beside her, one long-fingered hand resting lightly on the back of her chair, his eyes effortlessly holding hers. "*You* intrigue *me*."

Others milled about, taking their places along the polished boards. Noise and chatter engulfed the company. Yet Lenore heard all through a distancing mist, conscious only of the intent in the grey eyes holding hers. Then, slowly, Eversleigh inclined his head and released her, taking his seat beside her.

Shaken, Lenore hauled in a quivering breath. Eversleigh was in pride of place on her right; she had purposely installed young Lord Farningham, an eminently safe young gentleman, on her left.

Watching as the company settled and the first course was brought forth, Lenore felt her nerves flicker restlessly. It was Eversleigh and his disturbing propensity to reach through her defences that was the cause of her disquiet. Quite what it wa he did to her normally reliable senses she did not know, but clearly she would have to cope with the problem for the next few hours.

To her relief, Mrs. Whitticombe, seated beyond Lord Farningham, monopolised all attention with an anecdote on turtle soup as served by a certain Mr. Weekes.

Taking the opportunity to scan the table, Lenore noted her aunt seated a little way away with Gerald beside her to help. In the middle of the table, Jack and Harry, one one either side, kept the conversation flowing. A good deal of laughter and general hilarity was already in evidence as her brothers and their guests settled in. At the distant head of the table, her father and his old crony, Mr. Pritchard, were deep in discussion. Horses or reminiscences of a more ribald sort, Lenore sagely surmised, her eyes on the two grey heads.

"I have heard, Eversleigh, that there's plenty of grouse down your way this year?"

Lord Farningham's question, uttered in the tones of one well aware of the hazards of approaching one of the lions of the *ton*, jerked Lenore to attentiveness.

But Eversleigh's reply, a mild, "Yes, it'll be a good season, so my gamekeeper assures me. You're in Kent, are you not?" relieved her of anxiety. With every appearance of interest, she listened as Eversleigh discussed game and the keeping of coverts with Lord Farningham.

When the subject ran dry, halfway through the first course as the soup was replaced by turbot in cream sauce with side dishes of mushroom florettes and tongue in port wine, Lenore was ready with a blithe, "Tell me of Eversleigh Abbey, Your Grace. I have heard it is even bigger than the Hall."

The look Eversleigh directed at her was unfathomable but he replied readily enough.

"It is rather large. The original abbey dates to just after the Conquest but my family has made numerous additions over the years. What remains might best be described as a semi-Gothic pile, complete with ruined cloisters."

"No ghost?"

Lenore bit her tongue, steeling herself for his rejoinder. A skeleton or two in the cupboard, perhaps?

Manfully, Jason resisted temptation. Sorrowfully, he shook his head. "Not even a wraith, I'm afraid."

Letting out the breath she had held, Lenore inclined her head and opted for caution in the person of Lord Farningham. Lady Henslaw, seated beside Eversleigh, claimed his attention. As the second course was laid before them, Lord Farningham turned the talk to horses. Mentally, Lenore sat back, pleased to see her father and Aunt Harriet both coping well. Taking a moment to cast her eye over the company, she saw that all was proceeding smoothly. Her staff was experienced; the meal was served and cleared and glasses filled with a minimum of fuss.

She was turning back to the conversation when a commotion in the hall drew all attention. Smithers immediately went out, to return a moment later to hold open the door. Amelia, Lady Wallace, Lenore's cousin, hesitantly entered, her companion, Mrs. Smythe, trailing in her wake.

Jack rose. With a murmured, "Excuse me," Lenore put her napkin aside and went forward.

"Hello, Jack. Lenore." Amelia bestowed her hand on Jack and exchanged an affectionate kiss with Lenore. "I'm sorry to arrive so late but one of our horses went lame." Shielded from the table, Amelia grimaced up at them. "And I had no idea this was one of your 'weeks'."

With a brotherly smile, Jack squeezed her hand. "No matter, m'dear. You're always welcome."

Lenore smiled her agreement. "Don't worry. You can keep me company. I'll put you near Papa until you get your bearings."

"Yes, please," Amelia returned, blonde ringlets bobbing as she exchanged nods with those of the company already known to her.

While Jack played the gallant host, Lenore oversaw insertion of another leaf at the head of the huge table. Once Amelia and Mrs. Smythe were installed, Lenore paused to tell Smithers

"Her ladyship in the rose room, with Mrs. Smythe in the room further down the hall."

Smithers nodded and departed.

Lenore returned to her seat, idly wondering what brought Amelia, now widowed, to Berkshire. Picking up her fork, she glanced up to find Eversleigh, his chair pushed slightly back from the table, his long fingers crooked about the stem of his goblet, watching her, an entirely unreadable expression in his eyes. Lenore frowned in what she hoped was a quelling manner.

Jason's pensive attitude dissolved as he smiled, raising his glass in silent toast. He toyed with the idea of informing his hostess that the ability to remain unflustered in the face of the unexpected was a talent he felt certain his wife should possess. His smile deepened as he wondered what she would answer to that.

After one long look at Eversleigh's peculiarly unnerving smile, Lenore determinedly turned to Lord Farningham, irritatingly aware that, if she allowed herself the liberty she could easily spend the entire meal staring at the fascinating face beside her.

Reluctantly, mindful of his true aim, Jason devoted himself impartially to Lady Henslaw and the others about for the remainder of the meal.

At the conclusion of the last course, an array of jellies, custards and trifles interspersed with dishes of sweetmeats, Lenore collected Aunt Harriet and led the ladies from the room. As she crossed the front hall, she made a firm resolution that she would not again allow Eversleigh to unsettle her.

"Shameless hussy! That one dresses in pink silk and thinks we can't see through it. A good deal less than she ought to be, mark my words!"

Her aunt's scathing comments, delivered in a highly audible hiss, shook Lenore from her thoughts. She had no difficulty following Harriet's train of thought—Mrs. Cronwell, thankfully some way behind them, was resplendent in lurid pink silk, the low neckline of her clinging gown trimmed with ostrich feathers. Knowing she was safe, Lenore nodded—it was pointless disagreeing. Virtually completely deaf, Harriet could not be brought to believe that her animadversions, perfectly audible to any within a radius of ten feet, were anything more than the merest whispers. Following her erstwhile chaperon across the room, Lenore helped Harriet, grey-haired and stooped, to settle her purple skirts in her favourite chair a little removed from the fireplace.

Seeing her aunt pull her tatting from a bag beside the chair and start to untangle the bobbins, Lenore placed a hand on her arm and slowly stated, "I'll bring you some tea when the trolley arrives."

Harriet nodded and returned to her craft. Lenore left her, hoping she would not become bored and start musing, aloud, on the guests.

Despite the presence of some women she could not in all conscience call friends, Lenore moved easily through the bevy of bright dresses, scattered like jewels about the large room. She had long ago perfected the art of graciously acknowledging those she did not wish to encourage, leaving them a little puzzled by her serene acceptance of their presence. To those who were her social peers she acted the hostess in truth, listening to their gossip, complimenting them on their gowns. It was in gatherings such as this that she learned much of what was transpiring beyond the gates of Lester Hall.

Tonight, however, once she had done her duty and gone the rounds, she gravitated to her cousin's side, intent on learning why Amelia had so unexpectedly arrived.

"It was Rothesay." Amelia made a moue of distaste. "He's been positively hunting me, Lenore."

Standing by the side of the room, out of earshot of the company, Lenore sent Amelia a commiserating glance. "I take it the viscount is to be numbered among those gentlemen who have difficulty in understanding the word 'no'?"

Amelia frowned. "It's not so much a matter of his understanding as a sad lack of imagination. I do believe that he simply cannot credit the fact that any lady would refuse him."

Lenore swallowed a snort. At sixteen, Amelia had dutifully acceded to her parents' wishes and married a man forty years her senior. Widowed at the age of twenty-three, left with a respectable jointure and no protector, she was ripe game for the wolves of the *ton*. Determined not to be pressured into another loveless union, Amelia spent her days endeavouring to avoid a union of less respectable state. The gentlemen of the *ton*, however, had yet to accept the fact that the widowed Lady Wallace felt in no pressing need of male protection.

Fleeing London and the importunings of Lord Rothesay, Amelia had come first to her relatives in Berkshire. "I'm sure a few months will be sufficient to cool Rothesay's ardour. I had planned to go to stay with Aunt Mary but she won't be back in Bath before the end of the month." Amelia scanned the crowd, swelling as the gentlemen strolled in, forsaking their port for feminine company.

"As Jack said, you're always welcome here." When Amelia continued to consider the gentlemen as they strolled through the door, Lenore asked, "There is none here who has caused you any bother, is there?"

"No." Amelia shook her head. "I was just checking for any potential problems." Linking arms with Lenore, she smiled up at her. "Don't fret. I'm sure I'll manage to survive Jack and Harry's crowd. They all seem to be well-heeled enough not to need my money and well-mannered enough to accept a dismissal. I must say, though, that I'm surprised to see Eversleigh here."

"Oh?" Conscious of a sharp stab of curiosity, Lenore strolled beside Amelia. "Why so?"

"I had heard," Amelia said, lowering her voice conspiratorially, "that he's decided to marry. I'd have thought he'd be playing host to a collection of the fairest debs and their doting mamas at Eversleigh Abbey, rather than enjoying the delights of one of your brothers' little gatherings."

Aware of a sunken sinking feeling, Lenore resisted the compulsion to turn and look for Eversleigh in the crowd. "I hadn't considered him the marrying sort, somehow."

"Exactly so! The story is that he had no intention of succumbing. His brother was to keep the line going. But he—the brother, I mean—was killed at Waterloo. So now Eversleigh must make the ultimate sacrifice."

Lenore's lips twitched. "I wonder if he considers it in that light?"

"Undoubtedly," Amelia averred. "He's a rake, isn't he? Anyway, from everything I've heard and seen, it's the poor soul he takes to wife who deserves our pity. Eversleigh's a handsome devil and can be utterly charming when the mood takes him. It would be hard work to remain aloof from all that masculine appeal. Unfortunately, His Grace is reputed to be impervious to the softer emotions, one of the old school in that regard. I can't see him falling a victim to Cupid and reforming. His poor wife will probably end in thrall and have her heart broken."

Brows rising, Lenore considered Amelia's prediction. "Charming" was not the word she would have chosen to describe Eversleigh; the power he wielded was far stronger than mere charm. Suppressing an odd shiver, she decided that, all in all, Amelia was right. The future Lady Eversleigh was to be sincerely pitied.

Leaving her cousin with Lady Henslaw, Lenore paused by the side of the room. Under pretext of straightening the upstanding collar of her chemisette, she glanced about, eventually locating Eversleigh conversing with her father, ensconced in his chair by the fireplace. The sight brought a frown to Lenore's eyes. Listening to her father's reminiscences seemed an unlikely joy for a man of Eversleigh's tastes. Still, she was hardly an expert on what a gentleman recently determined on marriage might find entertaining. Shrugging the point aside, she embarked on an ambling progress about the room, providing introductions, ensuring the conversation flowed easily, and keeping a watchful eye on some of the more vulnerable ladies. Two such innocents were the Melton sisters, Lady Harrison and Lady Moffat, whom she discovered under determined seige from a trio of gentlemen.

"Good evening, Lord Scoresby." Lenore smiled sweetly at his lordship.

Forced to take her hand, thus relieving Lady Moffat of his far too close attention, his lordship murmured a greeting.

"I hear you have recently set up your town house, Lady Moffat?" Lenore smiled encouragingly at the young matron.

Lady Moffat grabbed her branch like a woman sinking, blithely describing all aspects of her new household. Lenore artfully drew Lady Harrison into the safety of the conversation. Within five minutes she had the satisfaction of seeing both Lord Scoresby and Mr. Marmaluke nod and drift away, vanquished by wallpaper patterns and upholstery designs. But Mr. Buttercombe was only dislodged when Frederick Marshall strolled up.

"I hear the Pantheon bazaar is very useful for all the knick-knacks you ladies enjoy scattering about the place."

Lenore was sure neither young woman noticed the twinkle in Frederick Marshall's eyes, but, seeing the way the sisters responded to his easy address, she was too grateful for his assistance to quibble. He was one of the more easygoing of the gentlemen present and seemed amenable to playing the role of gallant to their ladyships' innocence.

Seeing Smithers pushing the large tea-trolley in, Lenore excused herself and crossed the room to perform her last duty of the evening. Rather than station the trolley by the fireplace, her normal habit, she had Smithers place it between two sets of long windows, presently open to the terrace. With Eversleigh still by her father's chair, the area around the fireplace was likely to prove too hot for her sensibilities.

She had no trouble distributing the teacups, commandeering gentlemen at will. However, she took Harriet's cup herself, not liking to lumber anyone else with the task. One never knew how Harriet would react.

"Thank you, dear," Harriet boomed. Lenore winced and settled the cup on a small table by her aunt's side, confident that by now most of the guests must have realised her aunt's affliction. She turned to leave—and found herself face to face with His Grace of Eversleigh.

"My dear Miss Lester—no teacup?" Jason smiled, pleased that his calculated wait by her father's side had paid the desired dividend.

Lenore told herself she had no reason to quiver like a schoolgirl. "I've already had a cup, Your Grace."

"Excellent. Then, as you've already dispensed enough cups to supply the company, perhaps you'll consent to a stroll about the room?"

The "with me" was said with his eyes. Lenore stared up into their grey depths and wished she could fathom why they were so hypnotic. Perhaps, if she understood their attraction, she would be better able to counter it?

"Just like his father! Forever after lifting some woman's skirts. Not that he'll get any joy from Lenore. Far too knowing, she is." Harriet snorted. "Too knowing for her own good, I sometimes think."

Lenore's cheeks crimsoned with embarrassment. Glancing about, she saw that no one else was close, no one else had heard her aunt's horrendous pronouncements. No one except their primary subject. Drawing a deep breath, she raised her eyes fleetingly to his. "Your Grace, I beg you'll excuse my aunt. She's..." She foundered to an awkward halt.

A rumbling chuckle came from beside her.

"My dear Miss Lester, I'm hardly the type to take offence over such a minor transgression."

Lenore could have wilted with relief.

"However," Jason continued, seizing the opportunity fate had so thoughtfully provided, "I suggest we quit this locality before your esteemed aunt is further stimulated by our presence."

Difficult to counter that argument, Lenore thought, giving conscious effort to maintaining her calm smile as she permitted Eversleigh to place her hand on his sleeve and lead her away from the fireplace. As she fell into step beside him, she saw her aunt's maid Janet and her father's valet Moreton slip into the room. As soon as her father and his sister had finished their tea, it was their invariable custom to retire. Mr. Pritchard would have already gone up. Given what she sensed of the mood of the guests, Lenore felt her own departure would not long be delayed. Catching sight of the Ladies Moffat and Harrison, still under the wing of Frederick Marshall, she decided to drop them a hint.

She attempted to veer in their direction, but her escort prevented her, trapping her hand on his sleeve and raising his brows in mute question.

"I should just like a word with Lady Harrison, Your Grace." Lenore seasoned her request with a smile and was surprised to see her companion shake his head.

"Not a good idea, I'm afraid."

When she stared blankly at him, Jason explained, "I fear I make Lady Harrison and Lady Moffat somewhat nervous."

Lenore decided she could hardly blame them. Waspishly, she replied, "If you were to suppress your tendency to flirt, my lord, I dare say they would manage."

"*Flirt*?" Jason turned his gaze full upon her. "My dear Miss Lester, you have that entirely wrong. Gentlemen such as I never flirt. The word suggests a frivolous intent. My intentions, I'll have you know, are always deadly serious."

"Then you are at the wrong house, Your Grace. I have always considered the theme of my brothers' parties to be *entirely* frivolous." Lenore had had enough. If he was going to use her to sharpen his wit upon, then two could play at that game.

"I see," Jason replied, a smile hovering on his lips. He started to stroll again, Lenore perforce gliding beside him. "So you consider this week to have no purpose beyond the frivolous?"

Lenore opened her eyes wide, gesturing at the throng about them. "My lord, you have visited here before."

Jason inclined his head. "Tell me, Miss Lester. Am I right in detecting a note of disdain, even censure, in your attitude to your brothers' parties?"

Catching the quizzical look in his eyes, Lenore chose her words carefully. "I see nothing wrong in my brothers' pursuit of pleasure. They enjoy it and it causes no harm."

"But such pleasures are not for you?"

"The frivolous is hardly my style, Your Grace." Lenore delivered that statement with feeling.

"Have you tried it?"

Lenore blinked.

"With the right companion, even frivolous pastimes can be enjoyable."

Lenore kept her expression blank. "Really? But no doubt you are an expert on the topic, Your Grace?"

Jason laughed lightly, a smile of genuine appreciation curving his lips. "*Touché*, Miss Lester. Even I have my uses."

Oddly warmed by his smile, Lenore found herself smiling back. Before she could do more than register that fact, he was speaking again.

"But tell me, given your antipathy for the frivolous, do you enjoy organising such events as these, or do you suffer it as a duty?"

Try as she might, Lenore could see no hidden trap in that question. Tilting her head, she considered the point. "I rather think I enjoy it," she eventually admitted. "These parties are something of a contrast to the others we have from time to time."

"Yet you take no part in your brothers' entertainments?"

"I fear my pursuits are in more serious vein."

"My dear Lenore, whatever gave you the idea the pursuit of pleasure was not a serious enterprise?"

Lenore stopped, jerked to awareness by his use of her name. She drew away and he let her, but the fingers of the hand that had rested on hers curled about her hand. "I have not made you a present of my name, Your Grace," she protested, putting as much force into the rebuke as her sudden breathlessness allowed.

Jason raised a laconic brow, his eyes steady on her. "Need we stand on such ceremony, my dear?"

"Definitely," Lenore replied. Eversleigh was too dangerous to encourage.

With an oddly gentle smile, he inclined his head, accepting her verdict. Only then did Lenore look about her. They were no longer in the drawing-room but on the terrace. A darted glance added the shattering information that no one else had yet ventured forth. She was alone, with Eversleigh, with only the sunset for chaperon.

Feeling a curious species of panic stir in her breast, Lenore looked up, but the grey gaze was veiled.

"It seems somewhat odd that you should so willingly organise, yet remain so aloof from the fruits of your labour."

Eversleigh's tone of polite banter recalled her to their conversation. Guardedly, Lenore responded. "The entertainments themselves are not my concern. My brothers organise the frivolity. I…merely provide the opportunity for our guests to enjoy themselves." She looked away, across the rolling lawns, trying to concentrate on her words and deny the distraction assailing her senses. Her hand was still trapped in Eversleigh's; his fingers, long and strong, gently, rhythmically stroked her palm. It was such an innocent caress; she did not like to call attention to what might be no more than absent-minded oversight. He did not appear to be intent on seduction or any similar nefarious endeavour. She strolled with him when he moved to the balustrade and stood, one hand on the stone, her skirts brushing his boots.

About them, the warm glow of twilight fell on a world burgeoning with summer's promise. The sleepy chirp of larks settling in the shrubbery ran a shrill counterpoint to the distant lowing of cattle in the fields. The heady perfume of the honeysuckle growing on the wall below the terrace teased her senses.

Glancing up through her lashes, she saw that Eversleigh's features remained relaxed, hardly open but without the intentness she was learning to be wary of. His gaze scanned the scene before them, then dropped to her face.

"So—you are the chatelaine of Lester Hall, capable and gracious, keeping to your own serious interests despite the lure of fashionable dissipation. Tell me, my dear, have you never felt tempted to…let your hair down?''

Although, as he spoke, his eyes lifted to the neat braids, coiled in a coronet of gold about her head, Lenore knew his question was not about her coiffure. ''It's my belief that what you term fashionable dissipation only results in unnecessary difficulties, Your Grace. As I find more delight in intellectual pursuits, I leave frivolous pastimes to those who enjoy them.''

''And what particular intellectual pursuits are you engaged in at present?''

Lenore studied him straightly but saw only genuine interest. ''I'm undertaking a study of the everyday life of the Assyrians.''

''The Assyrians?''

''Yes. It's quite fascinating discovering how they lived, what they ate and so on.''

Contemplating the fullness of her lips with a far from intellectual interest, Jason assimilated the information that the lady topping his list of prospective brides considered ancient civilisations of more interest than the present. It was, he decided, an opinion he could not let go unchallenged. ''I would not wish to belittle your studies in any way, my dear, but if I might give you a piece of advice, drawn from my extensive experience?''

Warily, half convinced she should refuse to hear him but tempted, none the less, to learn what he was thinking, Lenore nodded her acquiescence.

''Don't you think it might be wise to sample the pleasures that life has to offer before you reject them out of hand?''

For one instant, Lenore nearly succeeded in convincing herself that he could not mean what she thought he did. Then his lids rose; again she found her gaze trapped in silver-grey. Her thoughts scattered, her breathing suspended. A curious lassitude seeped through her limbs, weighting them, holding her prisoner for the warmth that slowly, inexorably rose, a steady tide pouring through her veins from the wellspring where his thumb slowly circled her palm. Dimly, as if it was the only thing that might save her, she struggled to find an answer to his unanswerable question, something—anything—to distract the powerful force she could feel engulfing her. Wide-eyed, she knew she was lost when she saw the grey of his eyes start to shimmer.

With faultless timing Jason drew her nearer. Too experienced to take her into his arms, he relied on the strength of the attraction flaring between them to bring her to him. When her gown brushed his coat he arched one brow gently. When she remained silent, he smiled down into her wide green eyes. "There's a world here and now that you've yet to explore, Lenore. Aren't you curious?"

Held speechless by a timeless fascination, Lenore forced her head to shake.

The lips only inches from hers curved. "Liar."

Against her will, the word fixed her attention on his lips. Lenore swallowed. Her own lips were dry. Quickly, she passed the tip of her tongue over them.

Jason's sudden intake of breath startled Lenore. She felt turbulence shake his large frame, then it was gone. Abruptly, his hands came up to close about her shoulders, setting her back from him.

"The perils of an innocent." His lips twisting wryly, Jason gazed into her confused green eyes. "And you are still an innocent, are you not, sweet Lenore?"

Whether it was his tone or the shattering caress of his thumb across her lower lip that called it forth, Lenore's temper returned with a rush. Clinging to the revitalising emotion, she thrust her chin in the air, her heart thundering in her ears. "Not all women are driven by desire, Your Grace."

She was not prepared for the long, assessing look that earned her. To her fevered imagination, Eversleigh's silver eyes held her pinned, like so much prey, while he decided whether to pounce.

Eventually, one winged brow rose. "Is that a challenge, my dear?"

His voice, softly silky, sounded infinitely dangerous.

Lenore lost her temper entirely. "No, it is not!" she replied, irritated with Eversleigh and his unnerving questions, and with herself, for ever having let him get so far. "I am not here to provide sport for you, my lord. And now, if you'll excuse me, I have other guests to attend."

Without waiting for a reply, Lenore swung on her heel and marched back through the door. Damn Eversleigh! He had thoroughly addled her wits with all his questions. She refused to be a challenge—not for him—not for any man. Stopping by the side of the room to glance over the sea of guests, far more rowdy now than before, Lenore forced herself to breathe deeply. Thrusting the entire unnerving episode from her mind, she looked for Lady Moffat and Lady Harrison. They were nowhere to be seen. Amelia, likewise, had departed.

Unobtrusively, Lenore made her way to the door, appalled at the extent of her inner turmoil. She would have to avoid Eversleigh.

Which was a pity, for she had enjoyed his company.

CHAPTER THREE

SHE WOULD NOT allow him to take command again. Lenore descended the long staircase at ten the next morning, determined that today would see no repetition of yestereve's foolishness. Beneath the smooth surface of her blue pinafore, worn over a beige morning gown, her heart beat at its accustomed pace. With luck and good management it would continue to do so for the rest of the week.

Years before, she had set her face against marriage, the conventional occupation for women of her station. From all she had seen, matrimony had nothing desirable to offer that she did not already have. She preferred life calm and well-organised; a husband, with the duties and obediences that entailed, let alone the emotional complications, could only disrupt her peace. Hence, she had expended considerable effort in establishing a reputation for eccentricity, while avoiding any gentlemen who might prove a danger to her future. To her select band of acquaintances she was the knowledgeable Miss Lester, sure to be engaged in some esoteric study, a lady of satisfactory wealth and impeccable breeding, fully absorbed with her varied interests, with running her household and her father's estates. And, at twenty-four, beyond the reach of any man.

Or so she had thought. Stopping to shuffle the bright flowers in the vase on the upper landing, Lenore frowned. She had encouraged her brothers to invite their friends to Lester Hall, hoping the activity would cheer her father. He was still recovering from his long illness and, she knew, liked the lively bustle and laughter. She had been confident that, now she was an experienced woman, she stood in no danger from exposure to the gentlemen who would attend.

It had taken Eversleigh less than twelve hours to shake the confidence.

Dusting pollen from her fingers, Lenore straightened, forcing her mind to a more positive bent. She was making too much of the situation; she had nothing to fear. Despite his awesome reputation, no one had ever accused Eversleigh of stepping over the line. He was curious, certainly, given that he had seen past her façade. But, until she had declared her lack of interest in fashionable dalliance, he had not been the least lover-like.

Closing her eyes in momentary frustration, Lenore sighed, then, opening them, stared down the main flight of stairs. She should have known that giving vent to her sentiments would have acted on Eversleigh like a red rag to a bull. No rake could resist such a challenge. Certainly not one who, by all accounts, had half the London *belles* at his feet.

Luckily, the reins were still very much in her grasp. Given that she had insufficient defence against him, the only sane course was to avoid him. Absence was a barrier not even he could surmount.

Below her, the house was quiet. All the ladies would still be abed, too exhausted or too timid to have descended to the parlour for breakfast. The gentlemen, she hoped, would have quitted the house by now. Harry had had a long ride planned to show off his racing colts, stabled at a distant farm.

Determined to adhere to wisdom's dictates, Lenore started down the last of the stairs.

The billiard-room door opened.

"Damn your luck, Jason! One day, I vow, I'll have your measure—then I'll exact retribution for all these defeats."

Recognising her brother Jack's voice, and realising that there was only one Jason among the guests, Lenore froze, wildly contemplating retreat. But it was too late. Strolling forward into the hall, Jack glanced up and saw her.

"Lenore! Just the person. Look here—this blackguard has

just taken me for twenty-five guineas and I've no more than five on me. Settle for me, will you, dear sister?''

The request was accompanied by a look of meltingly innocent appeal that Lenore had never been known to resist. She could not do so now, but oh, *how* she wished she could tell her exasperating brother to settle his own debts. At least, those with Eversleigh. With no alternative offering, Lenore descended to the hall. "Yes, of course." Poised, serene, she turned to greet Jack's companion.

Jason took the small hand offered him, noting the nervous flutter of her fingers, like a small bird trapped within his hand. "Good morning, Miss Lester. I trust you slept well?"

"Perfectly, thank you," Lenore lied, retrieving her hand.

"I must off and look at the dogs—Higgs said something about an infection. Papa would have apoplexy if anything serious transpired. I'll meet you at the stables, Eversleigh." With a brisk nod, Jack took himself off.

Viewing her brother's retreating back with uneasy resignation, Lenore murmured, "If you'll come this way, Your Grace?"

Jason inclined his head, falling into step beside her as she led the way down the corridor to a door beyond the billiard-room. It gave on to a small office tucked partly under the stairs. A single window looked out over the lawns behind the house. Ledgers marched, row upon row, along the bookshelves covering one wall. Jason watched as Lenore sat behind the old desk, its surface covered with neat piles of papers and accounts, and drew a key from the small pocket at her waist.

"Is this your domain?"

Lenore looked up. "Yes. I manage the household and the estate."

Propping his shoulders against the window-frame, Jason raised one winged brow. "I've often wondered how Jack and Harry manage. They rarely seem to feel the need to spend time husbanding their acres."

Lenore's lips curved. "As there always seems to be an abundance of entertainments elsewhere to keep them busy and as I find the occupation amusing, we long ago reached an understanding.''

''But it can't be straightforward, not being the one in authority?''

Straightening an account book, left open on the blotter before her, Lenore allowed one brow to rise. ''I've always been here, and everyone about knows who runs Lester Hall.'' From behind her spectacles, she viewed the lean length so negligently displayed by the window. Eversleigh dominated her small room, filling it with an aura of masculine energy. At the moment, however, he seemed reassuringly relaxed. Lenore yielded to the promptings of curiosity. ''Tell me, Your Grace, do you directly manage your own estates?''

One arrogant brow flew. ''Certainly, Miss Lester. That is one responsibility I cannot and would not wish to deny.''

''What, then, do you think of these Corn Laws of ours, sir?'' Eyes alight, Lenore clasped her hands on the desk and leaned forward eagerly.

Jason paused, studying her face, then replied, ''They're not working, Miss Lester.''

What followed was a conversation that, for his part, Jason would never have believed possible. But Lenore had the questing nature of a bloodhound once she realised he understood first-hand the ramifications of the controversial agricultural laws.

Finally, her thirst for knowledge appeased, she sat back with a sigh. ''So you believe they will be repealed?''

''Eventually,'' Jason admitted, his arms crossed over his chest. ''But it will be some time before that's achieved.''

Lenore nodded, her mind still busy cataloguing all she had learned. It was a rare blessing to find a gentleman able and willing to discuss such matters with her. Her father had long since lost touch with the outside world; her brothers cared nothing for the political sphere. And there were few gentlemen among her select circle who held estates large enough to comprehend the negative effects of the reactionary laws.

Recalling what had brought her to her office, Lenore shook

aside her thoughts and sat up. Pulling out a drawer, she fumbled until she found another key, the pair to the first, still warm in her hand. Rising, she crossed to where a cupboard was set into the bookcase. She inserted one key and unlocked the door, swinging it open to reveal a grey metal safe. The second key unlocked the simple safe. Reaching in, Lenore drew out a small pouch. It was the work of a minute to loosen the strings and shake a handful of golden guineas into her palm. She was busy counting them when a large hand closed over hers, curling her fingers about the coins.

"No. Keep them."

"Oh, no." Lenore shook her head vehemently, too well acquainted with male pride to accept such a boon. "Jack would never forgive me." She looked up, into Eversleigh's grey eyes, one brow rising haughtily when she saw his expression harden.

For a long moment, Eversleigh studied her. "I will not accept any coins from you but I'll undertake to tell Jack the debt was paid in full."

Stubbornly, Lenore shook her head, her lips firming in a mutinous line.

Jason held her steady gaze, his eyes narrowed, his fingers tight about her hand. Then, his lips twisted in a wry smile. "Something else, perhaps," he suggested. His smile deepened. He released her hand but not her eyes. "I will not accept any money in payment of Jack's debt. Instead, Miss Lester, I'll settle for the answer to one question."

Lenore frowned up at him. "What question?"

"Ah, no." Jason stepped back to lean against the bookshelves. He eyed her speculatively. "Not until you agree to settling thus."

Lenore's eyes narrowed. Glancing down at the coins in her hand, she debated the wisdom of making any bargain with a rake. But what could he ask, after all. Twenty-five guineas was no great sum, not in her accounting, yet if she saved it she could put it into her special fund for helping their needier tenants.

"Very well." She dropped the coins back into the pouch

and returned it to the safe. Shutting the safe, she locked the cupboard door, all the while reassuring herself that she was the one in charge. Finally, she turned to face Eversleigh. "What is your question, Your Grace?"

Jason smiled. "Why do you persist in hiding your light under a bushel, my dear?"

Lenore blinked. "I beg your pardon?"

The look Eversleigh bent upon her forcibly reminded her of his reputation.

"I asked why you are so assiduous in veiling your attributes from those most likely to appreciate them."

Pressing her hands together, Lenore put her nose in the air. "I have no idea what you mean, Your Grace."

"Let's see if I can explain." Jason straightened, pushing away from the wall. Horrified, Lenore watched, wide-eyed, as two strides brought him to stand directly before her. His hands came up to grasp the bookshelves just beyond each of her shoulders, trapping her between his arms.

Feeling the edges of the bookshelves digging into her spine, Lenore cleared her throat. "I'm convinced you are too much the gentleman to resort to intimidation, Your Grace."

"Believe what you will of me, my dear, but allow me to remove these, before they obscure your very pretty eyes."

Before she could react, Eversleigh had whipped her fogging spectacles from her nose, dropping them on the desk behind him.

Stifling a squeak of sheer outrage, Lenore blinked furiously up at him.

A slow smile was her reward. "A great improvement." For an instant, the silver gaze roamed her face in open appreciation before, with a last unnerving glance at her lips, Jason returned his attention to the matter at hand. "Permit me to inform you, Miss Lester, that, unlike the majority who have visited here, I am neither blind nor gullible. That being so, I wish to know why you insist on purposely hiding your charms."

In the face of such an attack, there was nothing to do but fight back. "My charms, as you are pleased to call them, are my own, I believe? If it pleases me to keep them hidden, then who has any right to gainsay me?'' Lenore felt distinctly pleased with that piece of logic.

"There are many, Miss Lester, who would maintain that a beautiful woman is created for the enjoyment of men. How do you answer the charge of short-changing half the population?''

"*I* am not on this earth to pander to the whims of men, my lord.'' Head back, eyes flashing, Lenore felt her temper take hold. "Indeed, I've discovered that by avoiding the complications engendered by the male of the species, it is tolerably easy to live a calm and well-ordered life.''

Eversleigh's eyes narrowed.

Abruptly realising that she had said too much, Lenore temporised, "That is…''

"No.'' The single syllable stopped her, drying her stumbling words at source. "I think I see the light.''

To her consternation, Eversleigh leaned closer, his narrowed eyes casting a silver net she could not escape. He loomed over her, around her; never in her life had she felt so helpless.

His eyes searched hers. "You don't wish to marry.'' The words were enunciated slowly, quietly, but were all the more definite for that. "You hide your delights beneath heavy cambric and hope no one will see enough to be interested.''

Lenore wished she could shake her head but Eversleigh's compelling gaze prevented prevarication. She summoned a glare. "I see no reason why any man *should* be interested in me, Your Grace.''

The reaction to that was not what she had hoped. A slow smile twisted Eversleigh's lips. He shifted, bringing one large hand up to take a large pinch of her clothing, just above the yoke of her gown. Deliberately, he gave the material a brisk twitch, back and forth.

Lenore's shocked gasp filled the room. Her eyes flew wide at the excruciating sensation of her gown shifting over her tightened nipples. Horrified, she batted his hand away.

"Permit me to inform you, Miss Lester, that you have a severely proscribed understanding of the basis of male interest.

I suggest you extend your studies before you come to any conclusions.''

"As I have *no* intention of marrying, I have *absolutely* no interest in such topics, Your Grace!''

Her declaration focused Eversleigh's attention dramatically. His penetrating gaze bored into her eyes, his expression hardened. Flushed, Lenore held her own, but she could see nothing in the steel of his eyes to give her any clue to his thoughts.

Then, to her considerable relief, he straightened, his hands dropping to his side.

"Miss Lester, has it occurred to you that you have been much indulged?''

Lenore drew breath, determined to keep her chin up. "Indeed, Your Grace. My father and brothers are most supportive.''

"They have been slack, Miss Lester.'' Without warning, he caught her chin on the edge of one large hand, keeping her face turned up to his. The grey eyes once more roamed her features. Lenore could not breathe. His expression was stern, almost forbidding. "Your father and brothers have not done their duty by you. A woman of your intelligence and beauty is wasted outside marriage.''

"That is not my opinion, Your Grace.''

"I am aware of that, my dear. We shall have to see what can be done to change it.''

Paralysed, Lenore stared up at him. Startled conjecture vied with a strange, breathless, senseless yearning, a panoply of thoughts and sensations buffeting her brain. She could think of nothing to say.

The door opened.

"Oh! Excuse me, Miss Lenore, but I've come to do the menus.''

Twisting her chin from Eversleigh's grasp, Lenore peeked around him and saw her housekeeper, Mrs. Hobbs, standing uncertainly in the doorway. "Er...yes. Lord Eversleigh and I were just examining the lock of this cupboard. It was stuck.''

With a warning glance at Eversleigh, Lenore turned towards her desk.

"Ah, well," said Mrs. Hobbs, ambling forward, a large bundle of old menus and receipts clutched to her ample bosom. "I'd better get John to take a look at it, then."

"No, no. It's working now." Lenore cast a desperate glance at Eversleigh, praying he would behave himself and depart.

To her relief, he swept her a graceful bow. "I'm pleased to have been of assistance, my dear. If you have any other difficulties that are within the scope of my poor abilities to cure, pray feel free to call on my talents."

Lenore's eyes narrowed. "Thank you, Your Grace."

Jason smiled, his wolf's smile, and turned to the door. On the threshold, he paused, glancing back to see Lenore close her account book and lay it aside, then draw a pile of menus towards her.

"Miss Lester?"

Lenore looked up. "Yes, Your Grace?"

A long finger pointed at the corner of her desk. "Your spectacles, my dear."

Swallowing a curse, Lenore grabbed the delicate frames and arranged them on her nose, then glanced up, but her tormentor had gone.

"Now. For lunch I'd thought to have…"

Stifling a wholly unexpected sigh, Lenore gave her attention to Mrs. Hobbs.

An hour later, she was staring out of the window, her account book open before her, the ink dry on her nib, when Amelia's head appeared around the door.

"There you are! I'd despaired of finding you."

Lenore returned her cousin's bright smile, laying aside her pen as Amelia crossed the room to subside into the armchair before the desk in a froth of apricot muslin. "I take it last evening passed without incident?"

Amelia waved the question aside. "You were right. They're a perfectly manageable lot. All except Eversleigh. I wouldn't care to have to manage him. But His Grace had taken himself off somewhere. Truth to tell, I retired early myself." She turned to look at Lenore. "I looked for you but couldn't find you anywhere."

Lenore shut her account book with a snap. "I was detained on the terrace."

"Oh? By what?"

"A discussion of the relative merits of present and past civilisations, as I recall."

Amelia grimaced. "One of your dry discussions, I take it?"

Calmly sorting her papers, Lenore did not respond.

"Anyway, you'll be pleased to know I took care of one of your hostessly chores for you."

"Oh?"

"The Melton sisters. They had quite worn down poor Mr. Marshall; I had to rescue him. And that reminds me." Amelia swung about, bright brown eyes dancing. "I've discovered why Eversleigh's here!"

Lenore's hands stilled. "Why?" she asked, hoping Amelia would not detect the breathlessness that had laid siege to her voice.

"Mr. Marshall told me that Eversleigh is dreading the prospect of facing all the matchmaking mamas. I do believe he's here rusticating, recouping his energies before returning to town and facing his fate. He's got *six* aunts, you know."

"Yes, I know," Lenore murmured, her thoughts elsewhere. When Amelia turned an enquiring gaze on her, she added, "They're friends of Harriet's." Lenore cleared her throat. "What sort of woman do you think Eversleigh will marry?"

"A diamond of the first water," Amelia promptly declared. "Whoever of the latest lot fills that description and is suitably connected. It's what's expected, after all. And, for once, Eversleigh seems intent on fulfilling expectations."

Lenore nodded and sank into silence.

After a few moments, her expression pensive, her fingers pleating the ribbons of her gown, Amelia asked, "Tell me, do you know much of Mr. Marshall?"

The question drew Lenore from her own thoughts to gaze in

surprise at her friend. "Just how long did it take to rescue him last night?"

Amelia blushed. "Well, I couldn't just leave the poor man—he was parched for entertainment. Those Melton girls might be very pretty, but *widgeons*, my dear."

Lenore's lips twitched. "I thought you were here to avoid that sort of thing?"

Amelia looked pained. "I came here to avoid being pursued, Lenore. As far as I know, Frederick Marshall has never pursued a woman in his life."

Putting her head on one side, Lenore acknowledged that truth. "I had heard that. Odd, given his association with Eversleigh."

"Yes, but very refreshing." Amelia slanted a glance at Lenore. "Tell me, Lenore, do you still cling to your ideal of a singular existence, without the complications of men?"

Lenore looked down, picking up her papers. "Certainly. It's the only sensible course, given the strictures that rule our lives." She glanced up briefly through her glasses. "I would have thought that you, of all people, would appreciate that."

Amelia sighed, her gaze on the ceiling. "Oh, I know. But, just sometimes, I wonder. If one is not in the marketplace, one cannot buy. And if one is not..." Her brow creased as she sought for words. "If one does not put oneself in the way of love, however will it find you?"

"Love, as you well know, is not for us."

"I know, I know. But don't you sometimes dream?" Abruptly, Amelia swung about in her chair, fixing Lenore with an impish smile. "What happened to those dreams of yours—about being the prisoner of some evil ogre and locked in a tower guarded by a dragon only to be rescued by a tall and fearless knight errant?"

Lenore glanced up from her piles of receipts. "I long since realised that being held prisoner in some musty dungeon was likely to prove quite uncomfortable and that relying on being rescued was a mite risky, given the likelihood of my knight errant's being distracted by a mill, or some such event, and forgetting to turn up."

"Oh, Lenore!" Amelia sat back, pulling a disgusted face. After a moment, she said, "You know, I understand all your arguments, but I've never understood why you're so convinced there's no hope for us."

Lenore paused in her sorting, eyes lifting to the peaceful scene beyond her window as memories of her mother's face always trying to look so brave, filled her mind's eye. Abruptly, she drew a curtain firmly across the vision. Looking down, she said, "Let's just say that love among the *ton* is a sadly mismanaged affair. It afflicts only one sex, leaving them vulnerable to all sorts of hurts. You only have to listen to the tales of Harriet's friends. How they bear such lives I do not know. I could never do so."

Amelia was frowning. "You mean the...the emotional hurts? The pain of loving and not being loved in return?"

Brusquely, without looking up, Lenore nodded.

"Yes, but..." Amelia's brow was furrowed as she wrestled with her meaning. "If one does not take a chance and give one's love, one cannot expect to receive love in return. Which would be worse—to never risk love and die never having known it, or to take a chance and, just possibly, come away with the prize?"

For a long moment, Lenore gazed at Amelia, a frown deeply etched in her eyes. "I suspect that depends on the odds of winning."

"Which in turn depends on the man one loves."

Silence descended in the small room, both occupants sunk deep in uneasy speculation. Then, in the distance, a gong clanged.

With a deep sigh, Amelia stood and shook out her skirts. She looked up and met Lenore's gaze squarely. "Lunch."

THAT EVENING, Lenore entered the drawing-room, her expression serene, her mind in a quandary. Instantly she was aware of Eversleigh, one of a group of guests on the other side of the room, chatting urbanely. Slipping into her accustomed role, she glided from group to group, playing the gracious hostess with effortless ease. Avoiding the group of which Eversleigh was a part, she came to rest beside Amelia, chatting animatedly with Frederick Marshall, the Melton sisters and two other gentlemen.

"Oh, Miss Lester! I did so enjoy this afternoon!" Lady Moffat, blue eyes bright, positively bubbled with innocent enthusiasm.

"I'm delighted you found so much to entertain you," Lenore replied. Lunch, an *al fresco* affair served beside the lake, had been voted a success by all who had attended. This had excluded the majority of the gentlemen, still busy at Harry's stud. Unfortunately, instead of settling to a quiet afternoon, gossiping or punting on the lake, some of the younger ladies had spied the archery butts, stored in the boat-house. Nothing would do but to stage an impromptu archery contest; Lenore had not had a minute to spare.

"I was just explaining that the dancing this evening was to be entirely informal," Amelia said.

Lenore smiled, feeling infinitely more experienced in the face of the younger ladies' overt eagerness. "Just the house guests. The ball on Friday will be a much larger affair."

"How positively exciting! We'll both look forward to the event." Lady Harrison exchanged a bright glance with her sister.

Amelia shot a glance of long-suffering at Lenore, severely trying her composure.

The clang of the dinner gong, and Smithers' stentorian, "Dinner is served," recalled Lenore to an unresolved dilemma. Would Eversleigh take advantage of country party informality to sit elsewhere at table, leaving her to claim whoever she chose for the seat on her right?

Casting a surreptitious glance across the room, she saw her answer crossing the floor, his stride determined, his eyes on her. Quelling a sudden inner flutter, Lenore raised her head. Eversleigh paused by her side, his grey eyes smiling. With a graceful gesture, he offered her his arm. "Shall we, Miss Lester?"

"Certainly, Your Grace." Lenore placed her fingertips upon his dark sleeve. As they headed for the door, her entire concentration was turned inward, to the task of subduing her skittering nerves and overcoming the odd breathlessness that had seized her.

"Would it help if I promised not to bite?"

The soft words, little more than a whisper in her ear, had Lenore looking upward in surprise. The expression in Eversleigh's eyes, a not ungentle amusement, shook her precarious equanimity even more. It was all she could do to return a haughty look, turning her eyes forward, determined not to give him the satisfaction of knowing how grateful she was for his reassurance.

He was as good as his word, conversing amiably with Mrs. Whitticombe, who had claimed the place on his right, encouraging Lord Farningham to such an extent that, to Lenore's experienced gaze, something close to hero-worship glowed in that young man's eyes. His Grace of Eversleigh could be utterly charming when he chose, but, to Lenore's prickling senses, the powerful predator beneath the veneer, the presence that had made Lord Farningham so hesitant initially, was not asleep. He was merely in benevolent mood, watching, patient behind his grey eyes.

That evening, the gentlemen quit their port with alacrity, drawn to the drawing-room by the scrape of the violins, bows wielded with enthusiasm by five musicians installed in an alcove. Lenore was constantly on the move, encouraging the more timid of the ladies to join in, ensuring none of the gentlemen hung back. Despite her real liking for the pastime, she rarely danced herself, knowing how awkward most gentlemen found the exercise. She was too tall for even her brothers, only as tall as herself, to partner adequately in any measure beyond the formal quadrilles or cotillions. She was chatting to Mrs. Whitticombe, slightly flushed after a hectic boulanger, when she felt hard fingers close about her elbow.

A *frisson* of awareness informed her of who stood beside her even before she turned to meet his grey eyes.

Bestowing a charming if fleeting smile on Mrs. Whitticombe, Jason turned his gaze upon his hostess. "You're not dancing, Miss Lester. Can I tempt you to honour me with this waltz?"

The invitation was uttered so smoothly that Lenore had smiled her acquiescence before her mind had analysed his words. Reasoning that dancing with Eversleigh, so tall, was too tempting a proposition to have passed up anyway, she allowed him to lead her to the cleared area of the floor.

"Do you encounter much difficulty finding musicians hereabouts?"

Effortlessly he swept her into the midst of the couples swirling under the light of the chandelier. "N-no. Not usually." With an effort, Lenore focused her wayward wits. Dragging in a calming breath, she added, "There are two market towns nearby. Both have musical societies, so we are rarely at a loss."

After a few revolutions, Lenore became reconciled to the sensation of floating. It was, she realised, simply because Eversleigh was so tall and so strong. As she relaxed, the joy of the dance took hold.

Watching her face, Jason had no need of words. "You dance very well, Miss Lester," he eventually said, struck by the fact. She felt as light as thistledown in his arms, an ethereal sprite. The candlelight set gold winking in her hair; even her odd gown seemed part of the magic.

"Thank you, Your Grace." Lenore kept her lids lowered, her eyes fixed on a point beyond his right shoulder, content to let the dance blunt her senses. Even so, she was supremely conscious of the strength in the arm circling her waist, of the firm clasp of his fingers on hers. "Did you enjoy your tour of Harry's little enterprise?"

"Your brother keeps an excellent stud."

"He has told me your own horses are very fine." Glancing up through her lashes, Lenore watched as a small contented smile softened the lines about her partner's mouth. Then the arm around her waist tightened. The area near the door was congested with couples. As Eversleigh drew her more firmly to him before embarking on the tight turn, Lenore forced her mind to the music, letting it soothe her, blocking out the barrage of unnerving reactions assailing her senses. Only thus could she countenance such unlooked-for delight.

She was thoroughly disappointed when the dance came to an end.

Jason's smile was a little crooked as he looked down at her, her hand still clasped in his. "I feel I should return you to your chaperon, my dear, but I'm not sure I dare."

Recalling Harriet's behaviour of the previous evening, Lenore had no hesitation in stating, "I doubt that would be wise, Your Grace. Luckily, I'm far beyond the age of having to bow to such altars."

To her surprise, Eversleigh's gaze became sharper, his expression more hard. "You are in error, Miss Lester. You may not be a débutante but you are a very long way from being on the shelf."

Lenore would have frowned and taken issue, assuming the comment to relate to their morning's discussion, but to her amazement Mr. Peters materialised before her.

"If you would do me the honour, Miss Lester, I believe they're starting up a country dance."

In consternation, Lenore stared at Mr. Peters' bowing form. Eversleigh's invitation had taken her by surprise; she had accepted without thought for the potential ramifications. As Mr. Peters straightened, a hopeful light in his eyes, the full weight of her role settled on Lenore's shoulders. Pinning a smile to her lips, she looked over Mr. Peters' head to where the sets were forming. With determination, she extended her hand. "It would be a pleasure, sir."

A single glance to her left was sufficient to discern the amused glint in Eversleigh's eyes. "If you'll excuse me, Your Grace?"

As she straightened from her curtsy, Eversleigh's gaze was on her face. He smiled; Lenore felt her heart quiver.

Hand over heart, Jason bowed elegantly. "I wish you noth-

ing but pleasure, my dear Miss Lester.'' His lips curving in
appreciation, he watched as, head high, she glided away.

It was some hours later when he ran Frederick Marshall to
earth. To Jason's shrewd gaze, his friend had developed a predilection for Lady Wallace's company.

"Do you plan to remain for the entire week, Your Grace?"
Reassured by the presence of Mr. Marshall beside her, Amelia
advanced her query, an expression of open innocence on her
face.

Dispassionately, Jason studied the fair features turned up to
him. Languidly, he raised one brow. "That is my intention."
Lifting his gaze to his friend's face, he allowed his expression
to relax. "What say you, Frederick? Do you expect to find
sufficient here to fix your peripatetic interest?"

Frederick shot him a glare before Amelia turned her questioning face to him. "I see no reason why we should not be
tolerably amused for the duration."

"Excellent." Having gained the declaration she sought,
Amelia was all smiles. "I'll look forward to your company,
sirs. But I really must have a word to Lady Henslaw—if you'll
excuse me, Mr. Marshall? Your Grace?'' With an artful nod,
Amelia left them.

Jason followed her progress towards Lady Henslaw, then
turned to see Frederick, similarly engaged. "Let us hope Lady
Wallace does not favour purple."

"What?" Frederick turned to him, then glared as his meaning became clear. "Dash it, Jason. It's no such thing. Lady
Wallace is merely a means to pass the time—a sensible woman
with whom one may have a conversation without being expected to sweep her off her feet."

"Ah." Jason nodded sagely. "I see."

Frederick ignored him. "Speaking of sweeping women off
their feet—that waltz you so obviously enjoyed with Miss Lester? Permit me to tell you, not that you don't already know,
that it fell just short of indecent."

A subtle smile curved Jason's lips as he stood, looking out
over the dancers. "My only defence is the obvious—she en-

joyed it, too. She's unquestionably the most graceful woman I've ever partnered.''

"Yes, and now the whole company knows it. Do you think she'll thank you for the rest of her evening?"

"That, I had not anticipated." Jason glanced at Frederick, a glint in his eye. "Fear not. I shall come about. Apropos of which, I wanted to ask if you have heard any whispers of my impending fate?"

"I have, as a matter of fact." Frederick continued to study the dancers, his gaze following Lady Wallace's bright curls. "From what I can gather, most who have come direct from town have heard something of your intentions."

Beneath his breath, Jason swore.

Frederick turned, surprise in his eyes. "Does that concern you? It was inevitable, after all."

Grimacing, Jason replied, "I would rather it was not common knowledge but I doubt it'll seriously affect the outcome." Narrowing his eyes, he mused, "However, I will, I suspect, have to expend rather more thought on the correct approach to my problem."

Noting the direction of his friend's gaze, Frederick asked, "I take it you have fixed on Miss Lester?"

"Does that surprise you?" Jason murmured, his attention still on her fair head.

Considering that waltz, and all that it had revealed, Frederick shrugged. "Not entirely. But where lies your problem?"

"The lady has set her mind against marriage."

A paroxysm of coughing had Frederick turning aside. "I beg your pardon?" he asked, as soon as he was able.

Jason's eyes narrowed. "You heard. But if you imagine I'll pass over the only woman I've ever met who meets my stringent criteria, you and Miss Lester will have to think again."

A MILL IN THE neighbourhood combined with the after-effects of the evening before relieved Lenore of many of her charges for much of the next day. With the gentlemen absent, the ladies were content to rest and recuperate. After officiating at a light luncheon, Lenore found her afternoon loomed blissfully free. She decided to devote the time to her neglected studies.

The library was a haven of peace in the large house. Located in the oldest wing, the stone flag kept the temperature pleasant even in the hottest of weather. Finding the room empty, Lenore threw open the heavy diamond-paned windows, and let the warm breeze, laden with the scents of summer, dance in. Her large desk, set between two windows, faced the door. Dragging in an invigorating breath, Lenore sat down and drew the tome she had been studying towards her. Hands clasped on the leather cover, she paused, eyes fixed, unseeing, on the far wall.

Ten minutes later, with no wish to examine the thoughts that had held her so easily, Lenore determinedly shook them aside. She opened her book. It took fifteen minutes to find her place. Determined to force her mind to her task, Lenore read three paragraphs. Then, she read them again.

With an exasperated sigh, she gave up. Shutting her book with a snap, she pushed back her chair.

She would go and find Amelia, for she was serving no purpose here.

CHAPTER FOUR

BY THE TIME Lenore learned of her brothers' plans for that evening it was too late to circumvent them. She entered the drawing-room, her usual serenity under threat by the thought of what might occur once the assembled company, growing hourly more relaxed, embarked on an impromptu programme of musical events. Her brothers, she was well aware, could draw upon a large stock of ribald ditties; quite how she was to keep them sufficiently in line cast the shadow of a frown on her face.

Eversleigh noticed. When he came to claim her for dinner, Lenore detected the ghost of a smile and a faint questioning lift to his brows.

"I confess to being curious, Miss Lester, as to what fell occurrence has succeeded in marring your calm."

"It is nothing, Your Grace. Pray disregard my megrims."

Jason threw her a glance of haughty superiority. "Permit me to inform you, my dear, that I have no wish whatever to overlook anything that brings a frown to your fair face."

His bombastic tone had the desired effect. Lenore's lips twitched. "If you must know, I am not entirely at ease over my brothers' plans for us to entertain ourselves with musical renderings."

A chuckle greeted her admission. "Confess that it is not our talents that concern you so much as the possible choice of subject and I'll undertake to quell the high spirits of those of the company inclined to excess. Or," he amended, as they came to a halt beside her chair, "at least keep them within the pale."

Frowning openly, Lenore looked into his eyes, remembering her last bargain with him. "I am not sure that you can do so, Your Grace."

"Doubts, Miss Lester?" Jason allowed his brows to rise in mock offence. Then he smiled. "Relax, my dear, and let me handle the matter." When the footman drew out her chair, Lenore sat and settled her skirts, casting a puzzled glance at Eversleigh. As he moved to take his own seat on her right, Jason cocked a brow at her, his smile impossible to deny. "If you want to muzzle licentious behaviour, who better to turn to than a rake?"

Unable to find an acceptable answer, Lenore gave her attention to her soup.

When the company adjourned *en masse* to the music-room, set at the rear of the house, Lenore found Eversleigh by her side. "Invite the Melton sisters to play." Together, they strolled into the large room. "I take it you play the pianoforte yourself?"

"Yes," Lenore replied, wariness echoing in her voice. "But I *don't* sing." Her escort merely smiled his charming smile and escorted her to a seat in the front row. To her surprise, he sat beside her, stretching his long legs before him, giving every evidence of honouring the proceeding with his full attention. Lenore eyed him suspiciously.

His plan turned out to be simplicity itself. At his urging, Lenore invited one after another of the more youthful of the ladies to play or sing. Lady Henslaw, a matron with a distinctly racy reputation, followed Lady Hattersley. Under Eversleigh's gaze, Lady Henslaw preened, then gave a surprisingly pure rendition of an old country air. The applause, led by Eversleigh, left her ladyship with a smile on her face. Mrs. Ellis followed, with a predictably innocent song. She was supplanted by Mrs. Cronwell, who, not to be outdone in maidenly accomplishment, played a stately minuet with real flair.

From the corner of her eye, Lenore saw her brother Harry shift in his seat. Jason saw it too. "Harry next."

Lenore turned to him, consternation in her eyes. "I do not think that would be wise, Your Grace."

Jason dropped his gaze to her face. He smiled, confidence lighting his eyes. "Trust me, Miss Lester."

With a sigh, Lenore turned and summoned Harry. Her brother stood and strolled forward, his walk just short of a swagger. Taking his stance in front of the audience, he drew breath, his eyes scanning the expectant faces before him. Harry blinked. Shifting his stance, he swept the audience again, then, with a slight frown, he waved at Amelia. "Come accompany me, coz."

Without fuss, Amelia went to the piano stool. The song Harry chose was a jaunty shanty, boisterous but in no way ineligible.

To Lenore's relief, her brother appeared gratified by the thunderous applause that crowned his performance.

"Ask Frederick Marshall." Lenore turned at the whispered command. Raising her brows in question, she was treated to a look of bland innocence. "He sings very well," was all the explanation she received.

That proved to be no more than the truth. With Amelia at the keys, Mr. Marshall's light baritone wended its harmonious way through one of the bardic tales, holding the audience enthralled. The tumultuous applause at the end of the piece was entirely spontaneous. The performers exchanged a delighted smile.

"Try Miss Whitticombe next."

Lenore reacted immediately, no longer doubting her mentor's wisdom. Miss Whitticombe held the dubious distinction of being the only unmarried female guest. A plain girl, she had accompanied her mother, a dashing widow. Miss Whitticombe opted for the harp, proving to be more competent than inspired. Nevertheless, her effort was well received.

"Now Jack."

Lenore had to turn in her seat to locate her eldest brother He stood at the back of the room, shoulders propped against the wall, a look of thinly disguised boredom on his face. Lenore waved to attract his attention. "Jack?" Even from across the room, she saw his eyes narrow as he straightened, then flick from her to Eversleigh and back again.

"No, no, my dear. It's you who should do the honours of the house." A smile Lenore knew boded her no good appeared on her sibling's face. "I suggest a duet. The gentleman beside you will no doubt be happy to join you."

Stunned but far too experienced to show it, Lenore turned to Eversleigh. He met her wide eyes with a charming smile and a graceful gesture to the piano. "Are you game, Miss Lester?"

There was no escape, Lenore saw that instantly. Not sure whose neck she wished to wring, Eversleigh's or Jack's, she allowed Eversleigh to draw her to her feet and escort her to the instrument. A *sotto voce* conference decided the piece, a gentle ballad she felt confident she could manage. Fingers nimble on the keys, Lenore commenced the introduction, distractedly aware of the odd beat of her heart and of Eversleigh standing close behind her.

Afterwards, she could remember little of their performance, but she knew she sang well, her voice lifting easily over Eversleigh's bass. Her contralto was not as well tutored as Amelia's sweet soprano, but, against Eversleigh's powerful voice, it struck the right chord. The final note resonated through the room, their voices in perfect harmony. Clapping burst forth. Eversleigh's fingers closed about her hand. He raised her to stand beside him, his eyes, clear grey, smiling into hers.

"A most memorable moment, my dear. Thank you."

For one long instant, Lenore stared up into his eyes, sure he was going to kiss her fingertips, as he had once before. Instead, his gaze shifted to the watching crowd. Still smiling, he placed her hand on his sleeve.

Deflated, then troubled by the sudden sinking of her spirits, Lenore sighted Smithers with the tea-trolley. She excused herself to Eversleigh, murmuring her thanks for her relief, then forged a determined path through her guests to the relative safety of the teacups. She was grateful to Eversleigh for his assistance, but, in the interests of her own peace of mind, she would be wise to spend much less time in his company.

THE NEXT DAY, Wednesday, dawned bright and clear, with just a touch of mist about the lake. To Lenore's surprise the mild entertainment of the previous evening had engendered a milder attitude among the guests. Everyone seemed more relaxed, ready to trade easy smiles and light conversation in place of the artfully pointed banter and arch looks of the preceding days.

The majority of the ladies had made a pact to attend breakfast in the sunny downstairs parlour. While their appearance initially raised a good many male brows, surprise rapidly faded as the company settled into informal groups about the long board, the ladies, sipping tea and nibbling thin slices of toast, interspersed with the gentlemen, most of whom had made extensive forays among the covered dishes on the sideboard. The talk revolved around possible excursions to fill the afternoon. The gentlemen had already decided on an inspection of the Hall's closer coverts while the morning air was still crisp.

Hovering by the laden side-table, Lenore kept a watchful eye on her charges, ensuring that the younger, less confident ladies encountered no difficulties. Thus far, no contretemps had marred the pleasantry; her hopes were rising that, despite her brothers' inventiveness, the week would pass off more smoothly than she had thought. Assured that all was well, she picked up a plate and helped herself to an assortment of delicacies from beneath the silver domes.

As she was turning away, Amelia came to the sideboard, Frederick Marshall by her side. Her cousin was a picture in a peach-coloured morning gown, her cheeks aglow, her manner slightly flustered. Lenore hesitated, then, with a gracious smile, she nodded her good mornings and left them.

She turned to find a place at the table and was immediately conscious of Eversleigh's grey gaze. He was seated on the opposite side of the table, one long-fingered hand draped over the back of the vacant chair beside him. He was talking to Lord Holyoake but his eyes were on her.

The compulsion to round the table and take the seat she knew would be instantly offered her was strong. With determined calm, Lenore opted to fill the empty place at the foot of the table, smiling at Mrs. Whitticombe and Lady Henslaw on her left, smoothly joining in their conversation. She studiously avoided looking Eversleigh's way but she could feel his gaze, amused, she was sure, rambling openly over the plain brown pinafore she had donned over a long-sleeved white shirt and green cambric skirt.

She told herself she was relieved when he made no move to speak with her. He did, however, catch her eye when she looked up as the gentlemen rose. To her chagrin, she could not wrench her eyes from his smile as he approached and paused by her chair.

"Good morning, Miss Lester." Jason's gaze lifted to include her companions. "Ladies."

With a graceful nod, he acknowledged their ladyships' bright good mornings and Lenore's more subdued greeting before joining the male exodus to the gun-room. Behind him, Lenore frowned at her toast, annoyed that a mere "good morning" should leave her feeling as flustered as Amelia had looked. His Grace of Eversleigh was only being polite.

As the ladies were content to spend the morning ambling about the extensive gardens, gathering their energies for a visit to a nearby folly, the chosen distraction for the afternoon, Lenore took refuge in the library.

The Assyrians, unfortunately, had lost their appeal. She was worrying over her sudden lack of interest in a topic that a week ago had held her enthralled when Amelia came through the door. Her cousin's expression was pensive; with an abstracted smile she came forward to settle with a rustle of skirts on the windowseat close to Lenore's desk. Lenore watched her in silence, swivelling her chair to face her.

Amelia heaved a heavy sigh. "I'm in a fix, Lenore." Frowning, she slanted Lenore a worried glance. "Do you know how to attract a gentleman?"

Lenore's brows flew. "*Attract* a gentleman? I thought your problem was to repel them."

"Precisely," Amelia agreed. "I've experience aplenty in that. Which is probably why I find I haven't the first idea of how to accomplish the other."

"But...why?"

Amelia looked slightly sheepish but, at the same time, quite determined. "It's Mr. Marshall," she confessed. "I've discovered he has no...no *predatory* instincts whatsoever. Oh, Lenore!" Amelia rounded on her cousin, brown eyes alight, her hands clasped before her. "It's so pleasant to be treated as if my wishes were all that mattered. I feel so safe, so *comfortable* with Frederick."

Lenore's eyes widened. "Frederick?"

Amelia waved her hands dismissively. "There's no sense in beating about the bush, Lenore. I want to encourage Frederick to think of me in a more *personal* way. But how does one accomplish such a delicate task without..." Amelia's pert nose wrinkled in distaste. "Well, without giving an impression no true lady would wish to give."

When her cousin looked at her, clearly expecting an answer, Lenore spread her hands helplessly. "I'm the last person to ask such a question, Amelia. I've not the slightest idea how to advise you."

But Amelia was adamant. "Nonsense. You're considered by all to be a most intelligent woman, Lenore. If you would only put your mind to it, I'm sure you'd be able to give me at least a *hint* of how to proceed."

Lenore frowned but dutifully turned her mind to the task. "I suppose," she eventually said, "if you were to encourage him to be with you, by your side as much as possible, he might at least understand that you enjoyed and specifically wished for his company."

"That would certainly be a start." Amelia's gentle features were overlaid by an air of determination. "And the more time I spend talking with him, the more opportunity I'll have to...to nudge his mind in the right direction. But I must make a start immediately or I'll run out of time.''

Lenore looked her question.

Amelia cast her a distracted look. "Rothesay." When Lenore showed no sign of enlightenment, Amelia patiently explained, "Frederick is sure to accompany Eversleigh back to London at the end of the week. Given their friendship, it's only to be expected that Frederick will be on hand to support Eversleigh through the mêlée which is bound to engulf him immediately he sets foot in town. After being held at bay for so long, the matchmaking mamas are bound to descend with a vengeance. So, you see, I expect I'll have to return to town rather than go on to Aunt Mary in Bath. But I would rather not risk Rothesay without knowing there was at least some purpose to the exercise.''

"And if Mr. Marshall shows interest, you'll risk a confrontation with the Viscount?''

Amelia looked out of the window at the sunlight dancing on the smooth surface of the lake. Then she sighed and turned to Lenore, an expression compounded of loneliness and hope on her face. "If Frederick shows any real interest, I believe I'd brave the very fires of hell for a chance of happiness.''

The deep yearning in her cousin's voice shocked Lenore. She felt an echo deep inside, a reverberation, like a heavy gong clanging, the pure sound of the truth she was trying to deny. Abruptly rising, she crossed to put her arms about Amelia. She gave her cousin a quick hug. "I wish you luck in your endeavour, my dear.''

As she looked down at Amelia's determined face, Lenore felt a host of emotions, hitherto steadfastly suppressed, well up and tumble forth into her consciousness where she could no longer ignore them. The bursting of the dam left her shaken but she pinned an encouraging smile on her lips as Amelia rose.

Slipping her arms about Lenore's slender waist, Amelia returned her hug. "I'm going to put your advice into practice immediately. As Frederick will not pursue me, I shall simply have to pursue him." She headed for the door, pausing at the last to add, "In a perfectly ladylike way, of course."

Lenore laughed, wondering just how much encouragement Frederick Marshall would need. Before she had decided the point, her own thoughts claimed her.

She did not get back to the Assyrians.

LUNCHEON WAS A noisy affair, full of chatter and laughter. Almost all the guests had relaxed, letting down the formal barriers. They congregated by the lake, where the meal was laid out on a long trestle, small tables and checkered rugs scattered over the lush grass by the lake's edge. With Smithers and his cohorts in attendance to supply whatever their hearts desired, the company split into transitory groups, the members moving freely from one to the next. The fare was light, as befitted the scene, a succession of delicacies culminating in the season's first strawberries, served with clotted cream.

"A *tour de force*, my dear. Your strawberries were delicious."

Lenore turned to face Eversleigh, ignoring the odd leap of her pulses as she read the appreciation in his eyes. "Thank you, Your Grace. We have an excellent succession house."

"I'm sure it is excellent, if it falls within your sphere."

Lenore let that pass, merely inclining her head gracefully. She moved aside, so that he could join the circle of which she was a member. He did so, standing by her side to listen as the other members discussed the projected trip to the folly.

"Jack said it's quite ancient," Mrs. Whitticombe said.

"And covered with ivy," Lady Henslaw added. "It sounds positively romantic. Harry said there was an old story about lovers using it as a trysting place."

Lenore kept her lips firmly shut. Her brothers' imagination had no limits. The old tower had been built as a lookout in the days of the Civil War. Nothing even remotely romantic had ever occurred there. The lower room, the only one large enough to hold more than one person, had been used as a cow byre until the ivy had claimed the structure. Still, the views from the vantage point were excellent; the company would not be disappointed.

"You must have visited this folly many times, Miss Lester. Are you fired with enthusiasm to see it again?"

Eversleigh's quiet question drew Lenore out of the circle. Glancing up, she saw something in his grey eyes that caused her to inwardly quiver. Calmly she looked away, letting her gaze scan the rest of the company, before deliberately bringing it once more to his face. "I fear I would find the excursion somewhat tame, Your Grace. I think I'll feed the carp in the pond at the centre of the maze."

She dropped her gaze in a bid to appear unconscious, but could not resist glancing up through her lashes. Eversleigh's gaze was on her face, his eyes gleaming silver. As she watched, a slight smile curved his lips. "Undoubtedly a more peaceful place to spend a glorious afternoon."

Her heart skittering, Lenore hung on his next words. To her surprise, Eversleigh looked away.

Following his gaze, Lenore saw Jack approaching, clearly intent on speaking with Eversleigh. Having no desire to meet her eldest brother before he had had time to forget her interference in his plans of the night before, Lenore inclined her head to Eversleigh. With a murmured, "Your Grace," she drifted away.

Jason let her go. The afternoon stretched before them and he had no wish for Jack to divine his interest. Not yet.

"You dog, Jason! What the devil did you mean by assisting Lenore with her little plan last night?"

Jason smiled. "Just to see how you would take it, why else?" His mocking gaze teased Jack. "Besides, your sister was right, if not for the right reasons. Look about you. How relaxed and unthreatened do you think these fair ladies would be feeling today if you and Harry had had your way?"

The comment caused Jack to pause, considering the unfettered gaiety about him.

"You really need to plan your campaigns a little more thoroughly," Jason advised. "Take it from one who knows."

Jack laughed. "Very well. I can hardly argue in the face of your experience. But after last night, I claim the right to another touch at you over the billiard table. Harry'll take this crowd on to the folly. We can have our game, then follow on later."

Jason inclined his head. "An excellent idea."

Ten feet away, ostensibly listening to Lady Hattersley describe the folly on her family's estate, Lenore burned, disappointment, anger and an odd species of shame consuming her. With her usual serene mask firmly in place, she forced herself to wait until Eversleigh's tall figure had disappeared into the house beside Jack before, excusing herself to her guests, she headed for the kitchens. This time, her brother could pay his own debts.

She left the house ten minutes later, a basket of breadcrumbs on her arm. She had considered immersing herself in the Assyrians in an effort to reignite her interest but the day was too glorious to spend indoors and the carp did, in fact, need feeding. Leaving the terrace, she headed for the maze, sited amid a series of informal gardens, designed to lead from one to the other, each with a different feature. The Hall was surrounded by well-tended vistas, with the lake and surrounding lawns before it, the formal parterres and rose garden to one side, the maze with the wilderness and shrubbery on the other. The extensive kitchen gardens and succession houses completed the circle.

As she crossed the first of the trio of gardens leading to the gateway to the maze, Lenore caught a glimpse of peach skirts in one of the interconnecting gardens to the side. A second glance revealed the dark coat of a gentleman hovering protectively. Despite her disgust with her own attempt at encouragement, Lenore sent a wish for success winging her cousin's way before plunging on towards the pool at the centre of the maze.

Once there, she slumped into an untidy heap by the pool's edge, uncaring of her skirts, and settled the basket beside her. As she started flicking crumbs to the ravenous fish, the iniquity of her position engulfed her.

What had possessed her to surrender to the promptings of

her unexpected feelings and issue an invitation to Eversleigh? Admittedly he was no threat to her, given that he would be leaving on Saturday morning to return to town and offer for some simpering ninny, diamond of the first water though she might be. It would undoubtedly be a fitting fate for His Grace. Quite why *she* should feel disillusioned by the prospect eluded her. Beneath her self-imposed calm she was honest enough to recognise a yearning to experience, just once, the thrill other women felt, the thrill to which they became so disastrously addicted. She had felt the first glimmerings, the skittering sensations which prickled along her nerves whenever Eversleigh was near. Instinctively she had clamped down on her reactions; now she longed to set them free, just once, knowing she stood in no danger. Even if she fell under Eversleigh's spell, he would not seduce her. She had seen the stern patriarch behind the rake's mask; she was safe with him.

But was she safe from herself? Would she, too, succumb to love and leave herself open to the hurt that followed inexorably in its wake? Lenore shifted, frowning at the fat fish who rose to gobble her crumbs. Perhaps she should thank Eversleigh, and his liking for billiards, for denying her the chance of finding out?

Twenty minutes later, Jason headed for the maze, his mind entirely focused on the woman he was seeking. He did not delude himself that she had changed her stance on marriage but, given that she must by now know of his need to marry, her transparent invitation to spend time privately with her could only be interpreted as a wish to discuss the matter. He had hoped to make her question her views while at the same time reassuring her she had no reason to fear him; apparently he had succeeded. The small triumph made his steps more determined.

Her wish to remain unmarried was understandable. She had been permitted a great deal of independence and, given her undoubted intelligence, her freedom had become important to her. He intended reassuring her that an independent, intelligent woman need not fear marriage to him.

Indeed, with every passing day he became more certain of

his choice. Lenore Lester would suit him very well. She fulfilled all his criteria and, if there was a deep inclination that could not readily be accounted for on that basis, he felt no pressing need to examine it. The fact was sufficient.

Once he had dispelled her reservations and reconstructed her vision of matrimony along the lines he had in mind, he had no doubt she would find no further reason to cavil.

Emerging from the twisting hedges of the maze, he found himself on a large square of lawn surrounding a rectangular pond. Edged with blocks of stone, the surface of the pool was carpeted with water lilies. Beside it, he sighted his quarry, idly flicking her fingers to the fish, who rose with ponderous dignity to her bait.

An entirely spontaneous smile curving his lips, he went forward to join her.

Lenore knew he was there when his shadow fell across the pool. Instantly her heart soared, all thoughts of stoic safety forgotten as the knowledge that he had, after all, accepted her invitation reverberated through her. Hurriedly she recalled her scattering senses, determined not to let him see how much he affected her. Calmly, she continued scattering crumbs to the gluttonous carp. "Good afternoon, Your Grace."

Jason stopped beside her. "As I surmised, Miss Lester, this is a most peaceful spot." His eyes rose to the high hedges that surrounded them. Given the absence of most of the party, there was little reason to fear interruption. Had he been intent on seduction, he could not have wished for a better setting.

"Would you care to feed the fish, Your Grace?" Lenore turned to look up at him, holding down the brim of her straw hat to shield her eyes against the glare.

"Not particularly." Jason studied her face, then shifted his gaze to the large spotted fish swimming languidly back and forth before his prospective bride. "They look disgustingly over-indulged."

Head on one side, Lenore studied the fish critically. "You're right. Clearly they need no further sustenance." She was dusting her fingers over the basket when Eversleigh's large hand appeared before her. She glanced up, inwardly grimacing for, with the light behind him, she could not see his face.

For a moment, Jason said nothing, then, "Come. Sit with me in the sunshine." Smoothly he drew her to her feet, inwardly assuring himself that she was too innocent to have understood the reason for his momentary silence. A wrought-iron seat graced one side of the lawn. Picking up her basket, Jason led her across the clipped grass.

Settling her skirts as she sank on to the seat, Lenore quelled an unexpected spurt of disappointment that her attire was not more elegant. It was strange enough that she was indulging her dreams, sitting here alone with Eversleigh. Her senses were already running riot, her awareness rising to unnerving heights. Only her conviction that no danger attended her departure from the strict bounds of conventional behaviour allowed her to sit calmly as he took his seat beside her.

"You will no doubt be pleased to learn that I did not vanquish Jack."

"Indeed? You surprise me, Your Grace." Lenore cast a speculative glance his way.

Jason smiled. "I let him win," he admitted.

"Why?"

"It was faster. He has now taken himself off, thoroughly chuffed, to join the rest of the party." He did not add that Jack had been highly suspicious about his stated intention to spend the afternoon practising over the green baize. "Tell me, my dear, do you have any interest in games of chance?"

"None whatsoever," Lenore replied.

"How many games have you tried?"

Looking up, Lenore was forced to face his scepticism and confess to her ignorance. Not to be outdone, she promptly asked which games he favoured. The list was a long one, especially when he had to explain the features of each.

At the end of it, Lenore looked out over the pool and calmly observed, "With such diverse interests, you must spend much of your time in town at your clubs."

Jason laughed. "I dare say it appears that way. But only in

my youth did sitting up all night over the cards hold any temptation.'' Slanting a glance at her profile, he added, ''There are, after all, so many better ways to spend the time.''

''Indeed?'' The face she turned to him was utterly innocent. ''Do you attend the opera, then? Or perhaps the theatre is more to your taste?''

Jason's eyes narrowed. It was on the tip of his tongue to retort that he had, at various times, found elements of interest at both the opera and theatre. Only a firm resolution to remain steadfastly correct in his dealings with his prospective bride kept him from calling her bluff. ''I attend both, on occasion.''

''Have you seen Keane?'' Lenore felt a peculiar thrill at having tempted the wolf and survived.

''Several times. He's an excellent actor provided the part has scope for his talents.''

A discussion of the various theatres and the style of plays produced ensued, followed by a ruthlessly pointed examination of that other source of *ton*-ish entertainment, the Prince Regent.

''A keen mind utterly wasted,'' was Jason's scathing conclusion.

''Particularly given the opportunities he must have had.'' Considering the facilities available to the Prince Regent, Lenore sighed. ''Just being so close to all the bookshops would in itself be a boon to any scholar. I'd dearly love to have Hatchards within reach.''

Her pensive comment drew a searching glance from Jason. He had been patiently awaiting the right moment to introduce the topic of marriage, content to spend some time in idle chatter while she overcame her natural hesitancy. Stretching his long legs before him, he crossed his booted ankles, turning slightly so that he could keep her face in view. ''Tell me, my dear, if you could design your own Utopia, what would you place within it?''

The unexpected question had Lenore turning to study his face, but she could see nothing beyond encouragement in his eyes. A strange recklessness had her in its grip; she felt no reticence in his presence and marvelled at the fact. It was a heady sort of freedom, knowing she was safe. Head on one side, she considered. "Gardens, certainly. Large gardens, like these." With a wave of her hand, she indicated their surroundings. "So soothing to have a large garden to wander in. Tell me, Your Grace, do you wander your gardens frequently?"

Jason returned her smile. "I rarely need soothing. However," he continued, "the gardens at the Abbey are similar to these, though not, I'm sorry to say, in such perfect state."

"Your wife, no doubt, will remedy that." Lenore shifted her gaze to the pool.

"So I sincerely hope," Jason returned. "So, a garden and the staff to tend it. What else?"

"A house, of course. In the country."

"Naturally. Sufficiently large and appropriately staffed. What of town?"

Lenore grimaced. "I admit that I'm curious to visit London, but the idea of living there does not entice."

"Why not?"

"I hesitate to admit to such an unfashionable attitude but the thought of having to suffer society at large, as would be unavoidable should I take up residence in the capital, dissuades me from doing so."

"I protest you do society a grave injustice, my dear. We're not all fribbles and fops."

"But this is *my* Utopia, remember?"

"Just so. So what else takes your fancy?"

"Well," Lenore temporised, caught up in this strange game, "I enjoy acting as hostess at large gatherings—not much use having a large house and well-trained staff if one does not use them, after all."

"Very true," Jason agreed.

"I also enjoy my work among the folk on the estate. However, if this be Utopia, then I would rather not be in charge of the steward and bailiff."

Jason merely nodded, foreseeing no problem there. The reins of his numerous estates were firmly in his grasp; he needed no help on that front. Remembering her studies, he asked, "What of entertainment? What features most in that sphere?"

"My library. I couldn't live without my books."

"The Abbey has an extensive library. My father was an invalid for some time and took delight in restocking it to the hilt."

"Really?"

It was plain to the meanest intelligence that, of all the subjects they had touched upon, this was the one nearest her heart. Jason looked down into her green eyes and smiled. "There's a huge range of classics as well as many newer volumes."

"Have you had it catalogued?"

"Unfortunately not. My father died before he was able to attend to the matter."

The realisation that she would never see his library dimmed Lenore's excitement. "You should have it done," she told him, looking forward once more.

When she remained silent, Jason prompted, "You haven't mentioned people in this Utopia of yours—a husband and children to make your house a home?"

The question shook Lenore. From any other man she would have imagined the query to stem from mere supposition. But Eversleigh knew her mind on that subject. "I see no reason to complicate my life with a husband, Your Grace."

"You're an intelligent woman, Lenore. If a man were able to offer you all your heart desires, would you still not allow a husband into your life?"

Slowly, her heart thudding uncomfortably, Lenore turned to face him. A strange fear had seized her throat, making it difficult to breathe. "Why do you ask, Your Grace?" He was still sitting at his ease beside her, his large frame relaxed, one arm stretched along the back of the wrought iron seat. But the expression in his grey eyes, the unshakeable, implacable determination of a hunter, sent an unnerving combination of fear and yearning spiralling through her.

"I should have thought that was obvious, my dear." Jason

held her gaze. "You have, no doubt, heard rumours that I intended to wed?"

"I never listen to gossip, Your Grace," Lenore said, frantic to deny the scarifying possibility that, moment by moment, gained greater substance.

Exasperation glowed briefly in Jason's eyes. "Just so that you may be assured on the subject, the rumours are correct."

"Everyone's expecting you to marry a débutante—a diamond of the first water." Lenore rushed the words out despite the breathlessness that assailed her. Her mind was reeling in sheer fright at the vision forming with dreadful clarity in her brain.

A supercilious expression infused Jason's features. "Do I strike you as the sort of man who would marry a witless widgeon?"

Lenore forced herself to look at him with some vestige of her customary composure. "No. But I expect not all diamonds of the first water are widgeons, Your Grace." Pressing her hands tightly together in her lap, she desperately sought for a way to hijack the conversation. But her wits had seized, frozen into immobility by what she could see inexorably approaching.

Jason inclined his head. "That's as may be, but I've seen too much of overt beauty not to know its real value." Deliberately, he let his gaze skim her figure as she sat rigidly erect, on the edge of the seat. His voice deepened. "As I said before, you have a very limited understanding of what excites a gentleman's interest, Lenore."

He sensed rather than saw her quiver. Swiftly he moved from that topic. "You have told me what you desire from life, what you consider important. I'm willing and able to provide all that you've named, in return for your hand in marriage."

"And all that that entails." Inwardly aghast, her face registering blank dismay, Lenore pronounced the words as a sentence.

Jason frowned, his gaze fixed on her face. "It entails nothing beyond what you might expect. As we both know, you do not find my company insupportable." He hesitated, then added more gently, "I believe we will deal very well together, Lenore."

Giddiness seized Lenore. His version of her fate was clearly stated in the grey eyes so ruthlessly holding hers. Realisation of the danger she faced, and of how far she had already travelled down the road she had promised herself never to tread, swamped her. Her face drained of all colour. "No," she said, and felt herself start to shake. "I cannot marry you, Your Grace."

"Why?" Jason uttered the question quietly but compellingly. His eyes narrowed. "And why invite me here if not to discuss that very subject?"

Desperate, Lenore retorted, "I did not invite you here."

The long look she received in reply shook her to the core.

Quietly, Jason said, "I suggest, my dear, you take a different tack."

Dragging in a shaky breath, Lenore stated, "Your Grace, I'm greatly honoured that you should consider me as your bride. However, I'm convinced I am unsuited to marriage."

"Why?"

The question had lost nothing of its force in being repeated. Lenore took refuge in remoteness. "That, I fear, is none of your business."

"I'm afraid, my dear, that I disagree." Jason heard his voice gaining in strength, in merciless incisiveness. "In the circumstances, I feel I deserve more than inclination as an excuse. We're both intelligent adults. Despite your aloofness from it, you understand our world as well as I."

Temper, belatedly, came to Lenore's rescue, lending her the strength to defy him. How *dared* he insist she accede to a loveless marriage simply because it was the way of the world? Her green gaze hardened, gold glints appearing in the clear depths. Her lips firmed into a stubborn line. "Permit me to inform you, Your Grace, that you are undoubtedly the most conceited, arrogant, *overbearing* male it has ever been my misfortune to meet." The combination of panic and fury was distinctly unsettling yet Lenore knew no other emotion would serve her now. Imperiously, she rose to her feet, drawing herself up, daring, even now, to meet his silver gaze. "I do not wish to marry. That, for most gentlemen, would be reason enough. Regardless of your thoughts upon the matter, I do not need to explain myself to you."

Jason shifted, his shoulders coming away from the back of the seat, his ankles uncrossing.

Abruptly, Lenore's fury deserted her. Eyes wide, she dropped her defiant stance, taking a rapid step back, panic well to the fore. Her gaze was still locked with his. Nothing she saw in the silver-grey encouraged any belief that she had won her point. With a desperate effort, she dragged in enough breath to say, "If you'll excuse me, Your Grace, I've many important tasks to which I must attend."

Snatching up her basket, she ignominiously fled.

Exasperated, his own eyes narrowed with annoyance, Jason let her go, scowling at the gap in the hedges through which she disappeared. He was, he hoped, too wise to press her now. She could have a few hours to think things through, to tame her wilful ways and acknowledge the appropriateness of his offer. If she didn't, he would do it for her.

To his eyes, the matter was plain. There was, he was now sure, no rational motive behind her wish to remain unwed. Instead, it appeared that his bride-to-be had been allowed to go her independent way for too long. Independence was all very well but in a woman, in their world, there were limits. She had reached them and now looked set on overstepping them. She needed a strong hand to guide her back to acceptable paths. And, as her father and brothers had proved too weak to carry out that charge, it clearly fell to him to accomplish the task.

Abruptly standing, his expression hard and unyielding, Jason stalked back towards the house.

If he was going to dance to society's tune, it would damned well be with Lenore Lester in his arms.

CHAPTER FIVE

No ONE, Lenore was determined, would know that anything was amiss. She entered the drawing-room that evening, a serene smile on her lips, her calm and gracious façade firmly in place. Beneath that mask, dread anticipation walked her nerves. A quick glance about the room confirmed the signal of her senses: Eversleigh was not there. A flicker of relief fed a hope that, perhaps, he had already taken his leave. Lenore squashed the thought. Eversleigh had not accepted her refusal. He would come at her again, nothing was more certain.

Laughing and chatting with the guests occupied no more than half her mind. The rest was a seething cauldron, feeding her tensions, tying her stomach in knots. In the end it was almost a relief to see him enter, just ahead of Smithers. His eyes scanned the room, fixing on her. Lenore stopped breathing. Calmly, he crossed the room, pausing by her side, elegantly offering his arm with a bland, "Miss Lester."

With a cool nod, Lenore placed her hand on his sleeve, subduing by main force the tremor in her fingers. She kept her head high but her lids lowered, unwilling to risk his gaze. As they started for the door, she glanced briefly at his face. No expression lightened his harsh features; the granite planes of cheek and brow gave no hint of any emotion. Nevertheless, that single glance assured her that His Grace of Eversleigh was dangerously intent.

A shiver of apprehension ran through her. She suppressed it, steeling herself for the ordeal she was sure dinner would prove to be.

Beside her, Jason felt the tremor that ran through her. Consciously he tightened his grip on his temper, tried further than it had been in years by the woman gliding elegantly by his side. Despite her peculiar gowns, this evening's a creation in dun-coloured silk, she possessed the power to sway his senses simply by walking beside him. His inclination was to engage her in the most pointedly difficult conversation of her life. He resisted the temptation, knowing she was on edge. His forbearance, entirely out of character, amazed him but he shied away from examining his motives. Time enough for that once he had got her agreement to wed.

Throughout the first course, Lenore was both subdued and unusually nervous as she waited for the axe to fall. Eversleigh, seated on her right, was too large a figure to ignore. But when, in the general conversation, he allowed a comment on marriage to pass untouched, she risked a puzzled glance at him. His eyes met hers. His face was still impassive; Lenore inwardly quaked. Then he asked her a question. Hesitantly, aware of the ears about them, she forced herself to answer. Before she knew what was happening, they were having a conversation of sorts, he asking innocuous questions, she responding. The exchange was stilted, Lenore could not conquer her trepidation, but, to the company at large, all appeared normal.

Lenore led the way from the drawing-room, grateful for the respite even if it was temporary. Eversleigh, for whatever reason, had held off throughout dinner. She held no illusions that he would allow the entire evening to lapse without speaking to her again. Luckily, the consensus had called for a repeat of the dancing held earlier in the week. Thanks to Eversleigh, she would be too busy to spare more than a dance for him. And she had her own plans for surviving that ordeal.

The gentlemen wasted no time over their port. They joined the ladies just as the musicians started up. As Lenore had foreseen, she was promptly solicited for the first dance, this time by Lord Percy.

"Must congratulate you, Miss Lester," his lordship stated, barely able to turn his chin past his collars and the folds of his enormous cravat. "This week's been a great success. A formidable success, yes, indeed!"

Lenore murmured an acknowledgement, her senses focused on Eversleigh. He had entered at the rear of the gentlemen, accompanying Harry. As Harry moved away to claim a partner, Eversleigh paused by the side of the room, scanning the dancers.

Abruptly, Lenore gave her attention to her partner, plastering a bright smile on her lips. "Did you enjoy the folly, my lord?"

"Oh, yes!" gushed Lord Percy. "Such dramatic views. Do you paint landscapes, Miss Lester? Very partial to a sensitive landscape, y'know."

"I'm afraid watercolours are not my forte, my lord."

"But you *sing*, Miss Lester. I was quite moved by your piece with Eversleigh t'other night. Utterly captivating, y'know. I was really much affected."

Lord Percy moved on to describe other duets he had been privileged to hear. Lenore allowed him to ramble on, an attentive expression on her face, her mind elsewhere.

To her surprise, Jack claimed her for the next dance, a country reel which, Lenore recalled, he himself had taught her.

"Well, Lennie? How goes things, m'dear? Everything as calm and peaceful as I told you it would be?"

Lenore returned his smile. "I'll admit that there've been no real difficulties, but I would not go so far as to credit either Harry or you with having made any contribution to my peace."

Jack waved his hand airily. "You mean Tuesday evening. A miscalculation, my dear. Eversleigh set me straight."

"Eversleigh?"

"Mmm. Devilish knowing, is Eversleigh. Well, he was right." A wave indicated the crowd about them. "Had better sport today than we've had all week."

Understanding that the activity her brother was referring to had nothing to do with competitive games, Lenore was not clear on the connection to Eversleigh but decided to leave well enough alone. "Do you see much of Eversleigh in town?"

"Some." Jack twirled her about. "Top of the trees, is His

Grace. Spars with the Gentleman himself, is a darling of Manton's, an out-and-outer of the highest degree.''

"Oh?"

"Gracious, Lennie. You may hide in the country but you ain't blind, m'dear. You've been sitting next to the man for five days.''

"Well, yes," Lenore admitted. "But such things are not entirely obvious, you know." Nevertheless, her memory promptly conjured up the sensation of Eversleigh's arm about her when they had waltzed, of the strength of the muscles beneath his sleeve. She had noticed, certainly, but, used to the vigorous males of her family, she had found nothing remarkable in the fact. Eversleigh was simply slightly taller, his shoulders slightly broader, his chest slightly wider, his muscles slightly harder, his strength that much more compelling.

"But it's not just that, you know." Jack seemed to have taken a notion to widen her knowledge. "Eversleigh's got something of a reputation—not just over women, although there's that, of course. Well—" Jack gestured as they turned with the music. "He's a past master there. But he's a lot more powerful than that. Has connections all over, involved in all sorts of schemes and he's as rich as Croesus to boot." He paused to cast an affectionate glance her way. "He doesn't have to call on his sister to pay his debts.''

Lenore returned his smile. "Does he have a sister?"

Jack shook his head. "Nor brother either, not now. Ricky, his younger brother, was killed at Waterloo." He shot her a glance. "Wouldn't mention it if I was you."

"Of course not."

"Anyway, that's the reason he has to marry. Wouldn't mention that to him, either.''

"I can assure you that marriage is the very last topic I would mention to His Grace.''

"Good. Mind you, it'll be like the passing of an era—Montgomery marrying. He's been a...well, an idol of sorts to us all.''

"He's not that much older than you."

Jack shrugged. "A few years. But it's all that experience, you know." He slanted her a rakish grin. "Dashed if I know how he's fitted it all in."

Lenore let that pass as the dance separated them. When she joined hands with Jack again, he was deep in cogitation.

"All in train for Friday night, then? No problems looming on the horizon?"

The vision of Eversleigh, somewhere in the crowd about them, waiting to pounce, came forcibly to Lenore's mind. But any thoughts of seeking her brothers' or father's aid in dismissing Eversleigh had died with Jack's eulogy. Eversleigh was exactly the sort of gentleman her family would wish her to wed. And no one in all of Christendom would understand her refusal of his suit. He was wealthy, powerful and devastatingly handsome. They would think she had run mad.

"Everything's organised. The whole neighbourhood's accepted, so there'll be quite a crush."

"Excellent." Jack whirled her to a stop, bowing elegantly before her. He winked as he straightened, raising her from her curtsy. "And now I'll leave you to your own devices, m'dear. As the effective host, I'm much in demand."

Laughing, Lenore waved him away but his words rang in her ears. Her own devices. She would have to deal with Eversleigh herself, quickly and decisively.

The opportunity to do so materialised almost instantly. The strains of a waltz drifted over the heads of the dancers. Lord Farningham appeared out of the crowd. Seeing the question in his eyes, Lenore inwardly sighed and smiled encouragingly. He had almost reached her when hard fingers curled possessively about her elbow.

"Our dance, I believe, Miss Lester."

Lenore cast one glance up at Eversleigh's hard face and knew it would be pointless to argue. Besides, this meeting between them had to come. The relative privacy of a waltz, surrounded by other guests, was a safe venue. Summoning an apologetic smile, she held out her hand to Lord Farningham. "I had forgot. Perhaps the next waltz, my lord?"

"Yes, of course." Blushing slightly, Lord Farningham bowed.

Without further speech, Eversleigh led her to the floor, drawing her into his arms as if she was already his. Determined to remain in control, Lenore ignored it, locking her mind against the sensations teasing her senses. "I'm glad to have this opportunity to speak with you, Your Grace, for there is something I wish to say."

"Oh?" Jason looked down at her, his expression forbidding. "What is that?"

Fixing her gaze on the space beyond his right shoulder, Lenore shut her ears to his warning and produced her rehearsed speech. "I am, as I said, sincerely honoured by your proposal. I think, however, that you have not yet accepted my refusal. I wish to make plain to you that my decision in this matter is unalterable, irrevocable. In short, there is nothing you could say or do that would convince me to marry. I would like to point out that this aversion of mine is not personal in nature. I simply do not feel inclined to marriage and, as you must be aware, there is no reason at all for me to wed."

"You are wrong, Miss Lester."

The strength in those words shook Lenore. She blinked, then recovered to ask haughtily, "Which part of my reasoning is at fault, Your Grace?"

"*All* of it."

The conviction in his tone brought Lenore's eyes to his. A will infinitely stronger than hers blazed in the grey depths.

"For a start," Jason said, his accents clipped and definite, "you're not honoured by my proposal in the least, you're scared of it. You know damn well I've not accepted your refusal. There are more reasons than you know why we should wed. And as to there being nothing on this earth that could change your mind, don't tempt me, Miss Lester."

The threat was clear but Lenore was past caring. With a toss of her head she transferred her gaze into space. "I've given you my answer with as much reason as I can, Your Grace. If you chose to ignore it, that is none of my affair. However, I'm sure you can understand that I do not wish to discuss the matter further.''

Lenore felt the arm about her tighten, drawing her closer to his hard frame. Valiantly, she disregarded the hammering of her heart, keeping her head high and her expression untroubled.

''I'm very much afraid, Miss Lester, that I'm not as easily persuaded as other men. You have had your say; now it's my turn.''

His hand was burning her back through the thick silk of her gown. But Lenore managed to infuse her features with an air of supreme indifference as she countered, her voice steady, her gaze tinged with boredom, ''And *I'm* very much afraid, Your Grace, that if you mention the word 'marriage', or any of its synonyms, I—shall—scream.'' The last three words were delivered with emphasis; Lenore allowed her mask to momentarily slip to reinforce them with a glare. Then, smoothly, she looked away, confident he would not call her bluff in the crowded drawing-room.

A long silence followed her threat. When Jason broke it, his voice was even, perfectly controlled. ''Very well, Miss Lester. I shall have to use other means to demonstrate your errors. However, do remember this was your idea.''

Apprehension flooded Lenore.

''Perhaps I should start with the fantasies I have of your hair, loose and flowing in waves about you? Of course, in my dreams, you wear nothing else. Your hair is like silk, is it not? I dream of running my fingers through it, draping it over your charms.''

Lenore's eyes flew wide. A blush rose to her cheeks. She did not dare look at him.

His face calm and impassive, Jason drew her still closer, so that his thighs brushed hers with every step. ''And then there's your eyes. Lucent pools of green, like the hazy green in the summer distance. I dream of how they'll glow when I make love to you, Lenore, of how they'll darken with passion...''

Lenore tried to shut her ears but nothing kept out the tenor of his voice, reverberating through her body. Despite all her efforts, her mind heard his words, his slow, sensual descriptions of her body, of how he would make love to her. His arm about her waist kept her upright, effortlessly whirling her through the turns, the sensation of his thighs against hers emphasising his words.

Inwardly Lenore burned, anger at his strategy melting in the fire his words evoked. Her skin was alive, nerves flickering with anticipation. A self she did not know stretched and purred, luxuriating in the shocking glow of his visions. And still the descriptions rolled on, his voice dropping to a deep caress as explicit as his fantasies.

It was the longest waltz Lenore had ever danced.

When it came to an end and he released her, she felt like sinking to the floor but pride kept her knees functioning. She forced herself to draw breath and turn to him, extending her hand. With a superhuman effort she kept her face as impassive as his. "Thank you, Your Grace, for a most informative dance. I'm sure you'll understand if I decline any further invitations."

With the slightest of curtsies, Lenore headed straight for the tea-trolley, making a timely entrance under Smithers' direction. Her hands shook as she dispensed the cups. Twice she had to stop and drag in a calming breath. Once the chore was completed, she cast a quick glance about. Her father and Harriet were in their servants' care; she had no wish to approach any member of her family in case they sensed her agitation. Amelia would have been a reassuring refuge, but, when she located her cousin's fair curls, she saw Frederick Marshall beside her.

Determined not to give Eversleigh the satisfaction of seeing her run under fire, Lenore settled on Mrs. Whitticombe, joining that lady's circle and remaining there for the rest of the evening.

From the opposite side of the room, Jason watched her, his face impassive, a frown in his eyes.

"MISS LESTER is in the library, Your Grace. Tucked away in the old wing, it is."

"Thank you, Moggs." Jason did not turn from the view

beyond his chamber windows yet his mind was not filled with the shifting green of the canopies nor the rolling hills in the distance. As it had been for the past forty-eight hours, his mind was consumed with thoughts of Lenore Lester.

Moggs, his valet, moved quietly about the room, as self-effacing as ever. Moggs was a creature of silence, capable of so merging with the background that most overlooked his existence. His ability to garner the most surprising information had stood his master in good stead. Jason had frequently used his talents when in pursuit of the numerous mistresses who littered his past. He had, however, felt reluctant to set Moggs on Lenore's trail. But his prospective bride had left him no choice.

It was Friday, the last day of the house party. The afternoon sun was already slanting across the treetops. If he did not gain Lenore's agreement today, certain difficulties would arise. Returning to town without a firm understanding did not appeal, any more than did facing the matchmaking mamas and his aunts with their favourites in tow. But to stay at Lester Hall and continue his strange wooing would mean taking at least Jack into his confidence. That, he was reluctant to do, not least for fear that familial pressure might be brought to bear on Lenore. He was no coxcomb but it was impossible not to acknowledge how society viewed the position of his duchess. And while he had castigated Lenore's family as having been less than effective in their duty towards her, he did not imagine they were fools. They would urge Lenore to accept; he was not prepared to wager on the outcome.

The day before, Thursday, had tried his temper to the limit. He rarely felt moved by the emotion but Lenore prodded it effortlessly. Despite his extensive experience, she had succeeded in avoiding him throughout the long day. He had spent the hours in a fruitless endeavour to come up with her, learning in the process that Lester Hall was extremely large, its grounds more so. He had stumbled on numerous couples in his wanderings, Frederick and Lady Wallace included. That discovery had made him pause, but only for a moment. It was Lenore he wished to find, but he had not found her.

She had entered the drawing-room, serene as ever, and had remained coolly aloof throughout dinner. Hampered by the eyes about them, knowing no one had yet seen anything odd in his attentions to his hostess, he had yielded to the promptings of caution and kept a rein on his tongue. But his plans for her evening had been dashed. When he returned to the drawing-room with the rest of the gentlemen it was to find she had flown. She had pleaded a headache and left her cousin to tend the teacups.

That had been the last straw. He had spent the evening here, in his chamber, examining the reasons for his overwhelming desire to marry her and her alone. They were sound. Aside from satisfying all his needs, he was convinced that marriage to him would be, very definitely, in her best interests too. He had carefully studied the matter from every angle. There was a cloud over her future which she was refusing to see. The idea of leaving her to her fate as an unwed spinster in a household run by her brother's wife was not one he viewed with any favour. What joy would she have then, stripped of the position she presently held, no longer the driving force in the family, the central cog about which they all turned? He was determined to make her face that fact. And allow him to rescue her from her fate.

He had told her she was wasted outside marriage—he had meant every word. She was born to rule a large household, just as he had been born to head a large family. She had the makings of a matriarch, a strength to match his own. And while he was not proud of his behaviour on the dance-floor, the exercise had confirmed his rake's assessment that she was as attracted to him as he was to her. If he had come to Lester Hall with her seduction in mind, he had no doubt he would have attained his goal by now.

Slowly, Jason stood and stretched his long limbs, conscious of the tension rippling beneath his control, determined, today, to keep it suppressed. Her very vulnerability on that front, the quivering response of her slender frame every time he touched her, rendered any further approach by that route ineligible. Not until they were wed. Desire was all very well but it was no acceptable reason for marriage.

She was in the library, alone. He intended to talk with her frankly, show her what her future held in unequivocal terms. She was, first and last, an intelligent woman.

Settling his cuffs, Jason headed for the door and the library in the old wing.

When he reached the library the door was ajar. Quietly, he entered and saw her, standing by the open window, her arms wrapped about her, deep in thought. He considered the door, deciding to close it, the latch making no sound as he eased it home. Then, silently, he crossed the room, pausing before the desk beyond which she stood.

It was pleasant inside the library, the stone flags warmed by the sunshine. She had discarded her pinafore; it lay neatly folded on a nearby chair. A fine silk blouse moulded to her curves; the embroidered waistband of her brown velvet skirt encircled her tiny waist while the skirts fell in soft folds to the floor. Jason studied her face. Her expression was pensive, her fingers picking restlessly at the material of her sleeves. It occurred to him that she was an inherently calm woman—and he had seriously disrupted her peace. An urge to close the space between them and wrap her in his arms, to assure her that he had no thought beyond ensuring her future free of care, rose up, so strong he had to close his eyes to will away the impulse. Opening them, he shifted, as restless as she. The ring on his right hand struck the desk.

Lenore turned with a gasp, her eyes widening as they confirmed the belated warning of her senses. Instinctively, she moved to place the desk between them, struggling to summon her habitual mask to conceal her recent thoughts. They, alone, had left her weak. "Are you interested in a book to pass the time, Your Grace?" To her relief, her voice was steady.

Jason studied her, then shook his head. "I'm interested in

you, Lenore. You and nothing else.'' Slowly, he moved to come around the desk.

Instantly, Lenore drifted in the opposite direction. ''My lord, your pursuit of me is senseless.'' Ignoring the erratic beating of her heart and the dizzying acceleration of her pulse, she glanced at the door. It was too far away. Her fingertips tracing the edge of the desk, she rounded the end, her eyes lifting to his face. The calm implacability she saw there sent a *frisson* of apprehension through her. ''There must be countless women who would welcome the chance to be the next Duchess of Eversleigh.''

''Scores.'' Jason advanced without pause.

''Then why pick me?'' Lenore threw the comment over her shoulder as she hastened past the front of the desk.

''For a host of excellent reasons,'' Jason ground out. ''Which I'm perfectly willing to share with you, if only you'll stand still! For God's sake, Lenore! *Stop*!''

Passing the back of the desk for the second time, Lenore did, swinging to face him. In a single lithe movement, Jason vaulted the desk, landing in front of her. With a stifled shriek, Lenore put up her hands to push him away. Jason caught them in his, taking a single step to swing her back against the desk. Deliberately, he placed her hands, palms flat, on the desk behind her, trapping them under his, leaving her leaning backward while he leaned over her.

It had been his firm intention to discuss the reasons for their marriage with his infuriating bride-to-be, calmly, logically. Instead, as he looked down at her, all logic went winging from his head.

Lenore stared up at the stern face above hers, coherent thought suspended. Her senses were in turmoil. Bare minutes before she had been deep in dangerous dreams, demonstrating to her rational mind just why Eversleigh was such a threat to her. Now that threat had materialised, in the flesh. A frightening anticipation streaked through her. Eyes wide, she shivered.

The silk of her blouse rose and fell with every agitated breath she took.

The sight held Jason transfixed. He had been fighting his inclination for days—he had no reserves left to fight hers as well. Slowly, almost dreading what he would see, he lifted his gaze. To the slim column of her throat, and the pulse that beat wildly at its base. To her full lips, parted slightly. To her eyes, wide, peridot-green, filled with a potent blend of virginal hesitancy and raw desire.

Lenore sensed the struggle he waged but was powerless to help. The tension in the muscles of the arms brushing hers, in his thighs where they pressed hard against hers, told a clear tale. Held by a fascination older than time, she could do nothing to aid her own release. In that instant she did not know if she wished to escape. Instead, she watched, mesmerised, as the eyes holding hers changed from grey to silver, then to a shade that shimmered.

With a strangled groan Jason gave up the unequal fight. And lowered his lips to hers.

It was not a gentle kiss, but in her innocence, Lenore didn't care, held in thrall by the turbulent passion behind it. Her wits, already half seduced by her own dangerous imaginings, were swept away by the reality. Untutored, she sought to appease the hard demand of his lips, her lips instinctively softening, then parting under his.

Any vague idea Jason had possessed of a single, short, salutory kiss—to appease his demons and to demonstrate unequivocally the unwisdom of her looking at him with desire in her eyes—disappeared, drowned beneath the tide of passion her unexpected invitation evoked. He took instant advantage, slanting his lips over hers, confidently taking possession of her soft mouth with a slow, plundering relentlessness that shook him as much as it shook her.

Lenore shuddered, her senses reeling. She felt his hands leave hers, his arms lifting to enclose her, drawing her against him. His strength surrounded her, seducing her more completely than his kiss. Free, her hands lifted, hovering uncertainly before settling on his shoulders. She felt the muscles beneath his coat shift restlessly at her touch. Immediately she splayed her fingers, gripping hard, amazed and then enthralled by the response she drew forth, the tension that wound suddenly tighter, tautening the muscles of his large frame. Hesitantly, she kissed him back, thrilled to feel his soaring response, startled to find a similar reaction coursing her veins.

The sensation was addictive. Her senses, so long reliably content, revelled in the magic they wove. Like pagans, they swirled to the rhythm and demanded more. Wantonly she leaned into his embrace, delighting when his arms tightened, crushing her breasts against the hard wall of his chest. Cast into a realm beyond reality, Lenore had no defence against the power that engulfed her, no reason to fight the tide. Instead, blinded to the tenets of wisdom, her upbringing and society's mores, she followed where her senses led, freely responding, meeting every demand he made of her and wanting more.

Which was considerably more encouragement than Jason's frayed control could resist. He shifted his hold, one hand dropping to the small of her back, drawing her hips against his. Lenore shivered in his arms, her body pressing against his in flagrant invitation. The last vestiges of Jason's once vaunted control cindered. He felt her fingers tangle in the soft hair at his nape. Slowly, he eased her back, bringing one hand up to cup her breast.

Shivery pleasure cascaded down Lenore's spine; heat swelled her breasts. She responded immediately, her kisses more urgent, her mind, her body eager to experience more. Infuriatingly slow and patient, Jason's long fingers caressed her, drawing forth a gamut of sensations she had never felt before. As her nipples tightened to painful little buds, Lenore felt a curious heat unfurl deep inside. Entranced, she made no demur when Jason's fingers slid down the row of pearly buttons closing her blouse. It felt deliciously right when he brushed aside the fine material, searching for the ribbons of her chemise. A gentle tug and the bows were undone. If she had not been kissing him, she would have caught her breath. As it was, she felt her senses slide over some invisible precipice as her silk chemise slithered to her waist. The cool caress of the air on her naked breasts was dispelled by his fiery touch.

Desire streaked through Lenore. She gasped and broke free of their kiss. Her head fell back, her lids fell as pure sensation raced along her nerves. Time and place were no more—her whole being was alive in a world of sensuous pleasure. As Jason leaned nearer, she shifted her hands from his shoulders to thread her fingers through his rich chestnut hair, fascinated by the silky texture and the thick, tumbling locks.

Jason drew a ragged breath, struggling to retrieve his will from the web she had lured it into. But her allure was too strong for even him to break. He could no more stop breathing than deny his fingers the right to caress the creamy mounds bared to his sight. The feel of her satiny skin seared his fingertips, burning itself into his memories. She was even more beautiful than he had imagined, her breasts a perfect fit for his large hands, their peaks pink crests, puckered with passion. Passion he had aroused. The realisation shook him, but her soft murmur as his fingers gently teased, knowingly tantalised, was like a siren's song, dispelling reservations, dispelling all thought. Even as he lowered his head, part of him marveled at that fact.

Trapped in a world of sensual delight, Lenore revelled in all she could feel. His subtle caresses sent her senses spinning. Then his hands left her; one tactile sensation was replaced with another. She gasped, then whimpered with desire as his lips caressed her, his tongue gently rasping one tightly budded nipple. Lenore's fingers tightened convulsively, tangling in his hair as wave after wave of desire crashed through her.

As she felt her bones melt under the onslaught, she was conscious of only one thought. She didn't want him to stop.

Enthralled in desire, neither heard the approaching footsteps nor the click as the latch lifted.

"Here we are! The library. Knew it had to be somewhere. Plenty of books—" Lord Percy came to an abrupt halt as his gaze came to rest, goggling, on the pair behind the desk.

At Lord Percy's first word, Jason disengaged, pulling Lenore to him, crushing her protectively against his chest. As he took in the stunned looks on the faces of the three ladies crowding behind Lord Percy—Mrs. Whitticombe, her daughter and Lady Henslaw—he knew that nothing would erase the image they must have beheld as the door had swung open.

Prevented from seeing what had befallen, her cheek pressed against Eversleigh's coat, his heart thundering in her ear, Lenore struggled to recall her wits from the deep haze still engulfing them.

To everyone's surprise, it was Lord Percy who rescued them all. Abruptly turning, he threw out his arms, flapping to usher the ladies out. "Go and see the succession houses. I'm told they're very fine."

Without a single backward glance, he herded the ladies into the corridor and firmly shut the door.

The sound of the latch dropping home, a cold clang, jolted Lenore back to reality. Slowly, she eased herself from Eversleigh's embrace, aware of a sense of loss as she left its comfort. She steeled herself against it, dragging in breath after breath. Her mind raced, picking up the threads, trying to weave them into a cohesive picture as her fingers automatically fumbled with the buttons of her blouse. Suddenly, she felt very cold.

Wrapping her arms about her, she stepped back, blinking as she fought to regain her composure. Slowly, she brought her head up to stare at Eversleigh's face. The angular planes seemed softer, but she couldn't be sure. He was breathing rapidly. She saw him blink, as if he, too, was as affected as she. But that couldn't be so.

"You tricked me." She made the statement coldly, a deliberate indictment.

Jason blinked again, a frown gathering. Collecting his wits was proving a strain. Not only did he have to shackle his desire, now rampant, and assimilate the shock of their discovery, together with its attendant ramifications, but he had yet to succeed in convincing himself that what had occurred was real. Too much of it seemed like a dream. Never before had any woman undermined his control as Lenore had so effortlessly done. Dazed, he scrambled to catch up with her thoughts.

Unaware of his difficulties, Lenore drifted around the desk, pacing back and forth before it, her features hardening, her entire body stiffening as all that had occurred crystallised in her brain. "I wouldn't agree to marry you, so you arranged *this*!" Her voice gained in force "*This farce*!" Gesturing dramatically, she flung a glance loaded with scorn at the man standing still and silent behind the desk. "When I would not agree willingly, you sought to trap me into marriage. Tell me, Your Grace," she asked with awful disdain, contempt filling her eyes, "did Lord Percy make his entrance too soon? How far were you prepared to go in compromising my honour to gain your ends?" To her horror, her voice broke as a damning self-pity rose beneath her fury.

Abruptly, Lenore swung to face her nemesis over the desk. Head high, she looked him straight in the eye. "You, Your Grace, are undoubtedly the most *despicable* rogue it has ever been my misfortune to meet! Regardless of *what* might transpire, regardless of what whispers and scandal you call down upon me, I will *not* marry you!"

Her denunciation ended on a high, quavering note.

Her fury was nothing to his. With a superhuman effort, Jason forced himself to stand, silent, expressionless, and let her words hit him. His face felt like marble—cold and hard.

When he said nothing, made no attempt to defend himself against her wild accusations, Lenore's composure crumbled. Catching her breath on a hysterical sob, she turned blindly for the door and fled, her heart twisting painfully with every step.

In a feat bordering on the miraculous, Jason succeeded in forcing himself to remain still and silent behind the desk. Inside, his rage, a cold and deadly flame, seared him. As the danger peaked, every muscle in his body clenching in the effort to contain the explosive emotion, he forced himself to recall that Lenore had been upset, hysterical, not in command of herself.

The rationalisation did not ease the sting of her words. Gradually, the danger passed, leaving mere anger in its wake. Even so, Jason refused to give in to the impulse to go after her; he had sufficient knowledge of his own temperament to know that if he found her, her dignity would not survive intact. Instead, dragging in a deep breath, he focused his mind on what needed to be done, first to remove the threat to her reputation, secondly to secure her hand in marriage.

For one fact was now written in stone. Lenore Lester was his. He would not leave Lester Hall without her promise to marry him.

Not after that kiss.

His eyes grey coals, his expression like stone, His Grace of Eversleigh stalked from the room.

CHAPTER SIX

AT FIVE-THIRTY, despite the dull throbbing in her temples and the sickening disillusion that had her in its grip, Lenore entered the drawing-room prepared to greet her father's guests. In honour of the ball, she had allowed her maid to dress her hair high, with large soft curls falling in drifts about her ears and throat. Her lustring sack of magenta silk glowed richly, cream lace filling in the expanse from its square neckline to the base of her throat, her long sleeves fashioned from the same material. She hoped the gown would underline her status; tonight she had every intention of courting the title of ape-leader.

Jack was waiting for her, strikingly handsome in a dark blue coat over ivory inexpressibles. He winked at her. "Ready to greet the hordes?"

"Hardly hordes," Lenore replied absent-mindedly. "If you recall, we agreed to invite only six couples to join us for dinner. The rest won't arrive until eight."

Jack threw her a sharp look, then offered, "Took a gander at the ballroom. Doing us proud, Lennie."

Taking his arm, Lenore summoned a smile. Leading him towards the main doors where they would take up their stance, she tried to deflect the concern she saw in his blue eyes. It was prompted, she knew, by the harried expression she was only just managing to conceal. "I'm sure everything will turn out splendidly, just as long as you and Harry toe the line. The staff have worked like slaves and the guests have thrown themselves into the spirit of things with abandon. There's been such demand for the crimping tongs, the maids are well nigh dead on their feet."

Jack laughed. To Lenore's relief, he said no more.

A bare two hours had elapsed since her dramatic meeting with Eversleigh; she had yet to regain her calm. She had fled the library to immediately fall victim to her hostessly chores. Mrs. Hobbs had caught her in the front hall. After she had given her blessing to the substitution of pheasant pie for the roasted grouse, Smithers had come up, wanting her opinion on the positioning of the heavy épergné in the centre of the table. Next, it had been Harris with a request for guidance in the matter of how many footmen should be stationed in the supper-room. A succession of similar questions and difficulties had kept her from the sanctuary of her room, from giving way to temper and tears in equal measure.

Whenever she thought of what had happened, her emotions threatened to overwhelm her. Knowing she could not afford to be distracted, not tonight, with so many eyes to see, she pushed the jumble of outrage, guilt and hurt betrayal to the back of her mind. With a smile firmly in place, her serenity to the fore, she stood beside her brother and prepared to greet their neighbours.

As the first of the house-guests drifted into the room, chatting easily, Lenore heard the clang of the front doorbell. She turned to Jack. "Papa isn't down yet."

Jack grimaced. "Doubt that he'll show, not till later." When Lenore gazed at him, bewildered, he said, "Never one for doing the pretty, you know that."

Lenore sighed. Retrieving her smile, she turned as Smithers announced Major and Mrs. Holthorpe. Their other neighbours arrived in good time, the ladies making the most of this opportunity to brush shoulders with their London sisters and catch up on both fashion and the latest *on-dits*. Conversation buzzed, punctuated by gay laughter. When the time to announce dinner was at hand and her father had yet to appear, Lenore cast a questioning glance at Harriet. Her aunt shrugged. Wondering if perhaps her father had been taken ill, Lenore started for the door.

She had cleared the crush of the guests and was but a few

yards from the double doors when they swung inwards, propelled by two footmen. Her father entered, Harris pushing his chair. Beside it walked Eversleigh.

Lenore froze, presentiment dropping like a cold cloak about her shoulders.

"Friends!" Archibald Lester, wreathed in smiles, waved a lordly hand at his guests. He saw Lenore, too distant for her face to be properly in focus, and his smile grew brighter still. As the guests, as a body, turned to face him, he continued, his old voice carrying easily over the last shreds of dying conversations. "It's a pleasure to welcome you to Lester Hall. Doubly so for I've an announcement to make!"

Jason, standing alongside, his gaze fixed unwaveringly on Lenore, stiffened. He turned to Archibald Lester, only to hear his host declaim, "I have today given my blessing to a union between my daughter, Lenore, and Jason Montgomery, Duke of Eversleigh."

A buzz of excited comment rolled through the room. Archibald Lester beamed with pride and gratification.

All expression leaching from her face, Lenore stood as if turned to stone.

Two strides brought Jason to her side. His face lit by a charming smile, his eyes filled with concern, he caught her icy fingers in his and smoothly raised them to his lips. "Don't faint." He searched her large eyes, wide and empty, for a glimmer of consciousness.

The warmth of his lips on her fingers tugged Lenore back to reality. Dazed and utterly undone, she blinked up at him. "I never faint," she murmured, her mind completely overwhelmed.

Jason bit his lip and glanced over her head; they had mere seconds before the hordes descended. "Smile, Lenore." His voice held the unmistakable if muted tones of command. "You are *not* going to break down and embarrass yourself and your family."

Vaguely, Lenore's eyes rose to his, slowly focusing as his

words sank in. He was right. Whatever he had done, however hurt she might feel, now was no time for hysterics.

To Jason's relief she straightened slightly, a little of her rigidity falling away. A smile, a travesty of her usual calm confidence, appeared on her lips. But panic shadowed her eyes.

"You can weather this, Lenore. Trust me." His whispered words were loaded with reassurance. Placing her hand on his sleeve and covering it with his, he turned her to meet their well-wishers. "I won't leave you."

He didn't. Strangely, it seemed to Lenore that his support was the only thing that kept her functioning throughout that interminable evening. She should have been too furious to accept his help, to trust him, yet she knew instinctively that he would not fail her. It seemed the most natural thing in the world to lean on his strength.

Luckily, Amelia reached her first, throwing her arms about her and hugging her with joy. As her cousin disengaged, casting a puzzled glance at her weak smile, Lenore dragged and bullied and goaded her wits into action, forcing her features to her bidding. The muscles of her face relaxed into a gay if brittle smile. She got no chance to thank Amelia, nor to respond to her, "Good luck!" as the other guests pressed forward, none wishing to appear backward in congratulating the next Duchess of Eversleigh. She responded as best she could to their felicitations, thankful for Eversleigh's presence, a solid prop to sanity by her side. He kept his fingers entwined with hers, imparting calm strength even as his ready tongue deflected the more ribald comments.

Dinner was delayed. When Smithers eventually interrupted the chorus, Eversleigh drew her free of the throng, leading her in advance of them all as was his right. As usual, he sat beside her, an unnerving but unshakeable protection against any untoward questions. But by that time Lenore had herself in hand. Clamping an iron lid over the turmoil within allowed her to respond to both conversation and organisational queries with something approaching her usual calm grace. As long as she did not allow herself to think of what had occurred, she could cope.

Her father had ordered champagne to be served. As she took an invigorating sip of the bubbly liquid, Lenore caught Eversleigh's eye. To the casual observer his expression was exactly what one would expect—gratified, proud, confident in his triumph. As she studied the concern, the real worry etched in the grey eyes, Lenore wondered if only she could see past his mask. Allowing her lids to fall, she glanced away. Seconds later, she was startled to feel the gentle touch of his fingers on hers, then shocked when her fingers automatically returned the brief caress.

Firmly resettling the iron lid over her treacherous emotions, Lenore threw herself into the conversation.

They rose from the table just before eight, the gentlemen escorting the ladies into the huge ballroom. With long windows and high ceiling, it filled the entire ground floor of one wing. "Oohs" and "aahs" came from all sides as the guests took in the massed spring blooms and the first of the summer roses, tumbling in profusion from every available site. Draped in garlands from the musicians gallery, looped around every pillar, frothing from vases and urns, the flowers scented the warm air and lifted spirits to new heights.

The receiving line was a trial Lenore could have done without. Even though the rest of their neighbours were prompt, there was time enough in between arrivals for her seething emotions to slip loose. One minute she felt like murdering the man beside her, the next, when the touch of his fingers on hers eased her away from disaster, her heart swelled, with reluctant gratitude for his unwavering support, and with something else that she dared not name.

With every passing minute, the turmoil of her thoughts, the tangle of her emotions, intensified. And all she could do was smile and nod and allow her father, in his chair beside her, to introduce Eversleigh as her betrothed.

In her confusion, she did not hear the musicians start up. It was Eversleigh who drew her attention to the fact, smiling down at her father as he settled her hand on his sleeve. "I suspect we should open the ball, sir, if you'll release your daughter to me."

"She's all yours, m'boy." Archibald Lester beamed and waved them to the floor.

Reflecting that her father was definitely to be classed with old dogs—beyond changing—Lenore allowed herself to be led to the edge of the huge area of polished parquetry revealed as the guests drew back.

Smoothly, Jason drew her into his arms, feeling the effortless glide as she matched her steps to his. They waltzed as if they were made for each other, their bodies, his so large, hers slender and tall, natural complements in line and grace.

Lenore let the bright colours of the ladies' gowns whirl into an unfocused blur as they precessed, revolution after smooth revolution, down the long room.

"Your ball has all the hallmarks of success, my dear."

Allowing her gaze to shift to his face, Lenore studied his expression before remarking, her own expression calmly serene, "Particularly after my father's little announcement."

Jason's lips momentarily firmed into a line before he forced them to relax back into a smile. "An unfortunate misunderstanding." He held her gaze, his own steady and intent. "We must talk, Lenore, but not here. Not now."

"Certainly not now," Lenore agreed, feeling her control waver. A misunderstanding? Was it not as she had thought? Abruptly, she looked away, over his shoulder, relieved to see others taking to the floor in their wake.

"Later, then. But talk we must. Don't try to escape me this time." Jason saw her slight nod and was content. Prey to a host of conflicting emotions, the only one he felt sure of was anger. Anger that his wooing of her had gone so disastrously wrong. Anger that such a simple task as offering for a wife had somehow laid siege to his life. But he knew what needed to be done, to reassure her, to smooth away the confused hurt that lingered in her large eyes.

But fate had decreed he would get no chance that night. By

the time the last carriage had rolled down the drive and the last of the house-guests had struggled wearily upstairs, his betrothed was dead on her feet. From the foot of the stairs, he watched as, turning from the main doors, she suffered a hug from each of her eldest brothers and a smacking kiss from Gerald. Lenore received their approbations with a smile that struggled to lift the corners of her lips.

"G'night."

Jason nodded as Harry, stifling a yawn, passed on his way upstairs. With a sleepy smile, Gerald followed.

With Lenore on his arm, Jack approached. "Time for a game before you leave us tomorrow, o, prospective brother-in-law?"

Jason held Jack's gaze for an instant, then inclined his head. "I'll catch up with you in the morning."

"Right-ho! Sleep well." With a rakish salute, Jack left, making no demur when Lenore lingered.

Absent-mindedly, Lenore rubbed a hand across her brow, trying to ease the ache behind. "Now, Your Grace. Perhaps the library—"

"No. You're exhausted. There's nothing that needs saying that won't survive the night."

Numbly, Lenore blinked up at him. "But I thought you said—"

"Go to bed, Lenore. I'll see you tomorrow. Time enough then to sort matters out." When she continued to look blankly at him, Jason reached for her elbow. Gently but purposefully, he urged her up the stairs.

In the end, Lenore went readily, too tired and too grateful to argue further.

She said not a word as they traversed the long corridors. In the dim light, Jason studied her face. She looked so fatigued, so unutterably fragile, now she had laid aside her social mask. When they reached her door, he set it ajar. Taking her hand in his, he raised it to his lips, brushing a gentle kiss across her fingertips. "Sleep, Lenore. And don't worry. We'll talk tomorrow." With a wry smile, he bowed her over the threshold.

She entered, then paused, casting a puzzled glance back at him. Slowly, she closed the door.

"YOU'D BEST BE stirring, Miss Lenore. 'Tis past eleven."

Groaning, Lenore burrowed her face deeper into her soft pillow, hiding from the light that rushed in as her maid Gladys, thrust the bedcurtains aside.

Gladys, a motherly soul, eyed her charge shrewdly. "And there's a note here from that duke."

"Eversleigh?" Lenore turned her head so rapidly her cap fell off. "Where?"

With a knowing nod, Gladys handed over a folded sheet of parchment. "Said you were to have it once you were awake."

Ignoring her cap, Lenore took the note, settling back on her pillows, the folded parchment between her hands as Gladys bustled about the room, shaking out Lenore's evening gown, exclaiming at the way it had been carelessly tossed on a chair.

Lenore eyed the inscription on the front of the note. "Miss Lester" stared back at her in bold black letters.

Despite her conviction that she would fall instantly asleep the moment her head touched the pillow, rest had been a long time coming. As soon as she had settled in the dark, safe and secure in her feather bed, the cauldron of her emotions, simmering all evening, had boiled over. For a while she had let them seethe, shedding frustrated, fearful tears, drawing comfort from the release. Then she had tried to decide where she stood.

One point was clear. The rage that had overpowered her in the library had been misplaced. Recalling her accusations, she squirmed. Eversleigh had deserved none of them. She would have to apologise, an act that would further weaken her position in the necessary negotiations for her release from their unexpected betrothal.

That was as far as she had got in her musings, despite another hour or two's fruitless cogitation. Eversleigh's real concern and care for her, not just that evening, but demonstrated in so many ways now she looked back on their short association, undermined the image she had tried to erect of him, the ruthless tyrant perfectly ready to ride roughshod over her feelings. She had no firm idea of what had transpired between His Grace and her father—until she had the facts in her hands, she would be wise to reserve judgement. And, despite all the shocking revelations of the day before, she still did not know *why* His Grace of Eversleigh was so set on marrying her.

All of which left her in a very uncertain state.

Lenore grimaced, then unfolded the note.

"I'll wait for you in the library," was all he had written.

Her lips twisting in self-mockery, Lenore laid the note aside, along with a childish wish to remain safely in bed, pretending the day before had been nothing more than a bad dream. Downstairs and all about the house, the guests would be preparing to leave. She should be present, lending her aid in a thousand different ways. Today, however, she felt not the slightest qualm in leaving her brothers to their own resources. Her staff were well-trained; her presence was not essential.

With a deep sigh, Lenore sat up. "No," she said, shaking her head at the grey gown Gladys held up. "There's a primrose muslin in there somewhere. See if you can find it—I believe its time has come."

The muslin proved to be more gold than yellow, its scooped neckline perfectly decent although the soft material draped about Lenore's slim figure in a way far removed from her stiff cambrics and pinafores. Harriet had ordered it up from London two years before in a vain attempt to interest Lenore in fashion. Staring at her reflection, Lenore decided it would do. She had coiled her braided hair about her head; to her eyes, her slender neck, now fully revealed, was too long.

Giving herself no time to change her mind, and her gown, she descended to the library.

He did not hear her enter. Seated in the chair before her desk, he had the text she had been studying, a history of the Assyrians, in his hand. Afflicted by a sudden breathlessness, Lenore paused, seizing the rare moment to study him. The planes of his face seemed less angular, his expression less forbidding. There was still a great deal of strength, in his face, in the long body relaxed in the chair, but, to her, now, the impact was more reassuring than threatening, more desirable than dangerous. Slowly, Lenore drew nearer, conscious of her deep fascination. A lingering shadow of the delight she had felt when last in this room touched her.

Jason heard her and turned. His gaze met hers, keenly perceptive, searching for signs of her mood. "Good morning, my dear."

Carefully gliding past the desk, Lenore nodded. "Your Grace."

For a moment, realisation of what she was wearing held Jason still. Then, shutting the book and laying it aside, he stood.

"I must apologise, Your Grace, for my outburst yesterday." Lenore hurried into the speech, desperate to clear that particular hurdle. Rather than take the seat behind the desk, she stopped beside the window, her gaze on the garden, holding herself erect, head high as she recalled her embarrassing behaviour. "I realise my accusations were unfounded and entirely out of order." She inclined her head in Eversleigh's direction, too tense to look directly at him. "I pray you will excuse me."

"I believe you were somewhat overwhelmed at the time," came the smooth reply.

Lenore looked around to find he had come to stand on the other side of the window, negligently propping one shoulder against the frame, his grey eyes oddly gentle as they studied her.

The blush that rose to her cheeks was another irritation. Biting her tongue on the unwise retort that her mind had instantly supplied, she forced her voice to an even tone to say, "At the time, I was not thinking with my customary clarity."

Jason's lips curved. "Granted." His voice retained its even, reassuring tone as he added, "Apropos of that event, you'll be re-lieved to know that neither Lord Percy nor any of the three ladies can recall anything of it. In fact," he mused, "it's doubtful that they recall having been anywhere near this room."

Lenore blinked. She returned his unwavering scrutiny for a

full minute before remarking, "One of the benefits of being born to the purple?"

Jason's smile reached his eyes. "One of the *few* benefits of being born to rule."

A puzzled frown settled over Lenore's brows. "But why?" she eventually asked, curiosity overcoming reserve. "Surely their…interruption strengthened your hand?"

She glanced up to meet a stern, not to say forbidding, frown.

"My dear Lenore, if you imagine I'd allow any breath of scandal to touch my future wife's name—worse, would permit the slightest suggestion that I offered for her to rectify some slight to her honour—you are greatly mistaken."

She had to have imagined it, for he had not altered his stance, yet Lenore was certain he had somehow grown larger, taller, infinitely more intimidating. She felt her eyes grow round. "Oh."

"However," Jason said, letting his sudden tension seep away. He looked down, examining the signet on his right hand. "If we are on the subject of apologies, you have my very humblest, Lenore, for the shock you were subjected to last night. It was not my intention that any announcement be made. I had merely asked your father for permission to pay my address to you in form." He looked up as he spoke, capturing her eyes with his, willing her to understand. "I think, somehow, he misunderstood."

The sincerity in his tone, in the grey of his eyes, the look which was, she suspected, as close to beseeching as he would ever get, shook Lenore. Breathless all over again, she swung her gaze away, out of the window, to the weeping cherry gracing the lawn. "He does that, I'm afraid. He hears only the words he wishes to hear and disregards the rest."

That was the truth. Her father was the worst sort of manipulator—had been for years. But it was the revelation that Eversleigh had not sought to conspire with her sire behind her back that shook Lenore to her very soul. Unfortunately, having her reading of his character thus confirmed did not make the task before her any easier. Drawing a determined breath, she hurried on. "However, even though we might agree that neither of us is to blame for the predicament we now find ourselves in, there is still that very predicament to be faced."

"Which predicament is that?"

Lenore turned to face him only to find his expression improbably bland. Her eyes narrowed. "To all intents and purposes, Your Grace, we are betrothed. Everyone who attended last night believes that to be so."

Jason merely nodded, watching her closely.

Her worries flooding back, Lenore drew herself up, pressing her hands tightly together, crushing the front of her skirt. "My lord, I would ask you to release me from this...this unforeseen contract."

Jason's stern expression returned; Lenore's heart quavered.

"That, my dear, would be very difficult to do."

"But you *could* do it—we could say we were mistaken."

Jason's winged brows rose. "But I'm not mistaken." Lenore allowed her exasperation at that arrogant statement to show. Jason disregarded it, straightening away from the window frame. "Even if I were prepared to allow you to waste your life here—"

"I am *not* wasting my life!"

"With old civilisations?" A contemptuous wave indicated her desk. "You have a life to live, Lenore. You must live it in the present, not the past."

"I have plenty to occupy my present, Your Grace."

"Jason. And if you're referring to your position as chatelaine of Lester Hall," Jason said, advancing to stand in front of her, "how long do you think that will last once Jack weds?"

Her face told him all. Lenore stared up at him, her expression utterly blank. "Jack..." She blinked, struggling to bring the idea more firmly into focus.

"It comes to us all." The statement held more than a hint of irony. When Lenore remained silent, Jason added more gently. "You cannot expect to remain in your position of eminence here, my dear."

It was a major effort to wrench her mind about to view her

life from a different perspective, but, once she had done so, Lenore felt utterly defeated. She had concentrated for so long on getting her present established as she wished, she had overlooked the future. And her brothers, of course, had never encouraged anyone to think of their marrying.

"If you'll consider the matter, my dear, I think you'll see that marriage to me will assure you of the position, the status you deserve."

Jason studied her face, then continued, his words softly seductive. "I need you far more than the Lesters, Lenore." A little staggered by how truthful he was being, he quickly added, "Besides the Abbey, which, God knows, is large enough to house a brigade and frequently does, there's the London houses, as well as minor estates in Leicestershire, Northumberland and Cornwall."

Her gaze abstracted, a frown tangling her brows, Lenore shifted restlessly, casting a troubled glance up at him. "I can understand why your aunts wish you to wed, Your Grace."

"Jason." Jason paused, then carefully played his trump card. "Besides, you wouldn't want to destroy your father's peace of mind." Instantly, he knew he had struck true. Lenore looked up, her expression revealing her suspicions. Relentlessly, Jason pressed his advantage home, his eyes, deadly serious, holding hers. "My offer lifted a great weight from his shoulders. He has worried about you, and your future, for years. From what he let fall, our betrothal will greatly ease your aunt's mind, too. Apparently, she's felt responsible for your state, imagining herself to have failed in imbuing you with suitable sentiments."

"No!" Lenore was appalled. Vehemently, she shook her head. "I decided what I wanted to do. It was no fault of theirs."

"That may be so, but you cannot deny their concern for your welfare."

"But…" Raising a hand to brush back a wisp of hair, Lenore felt the web of her situation closing about her. Distractedly she looked up, into the calm of Eversleigh's eyes.

Moved by an emotion she was not at all pleased to have to

acknowledge, invoked by the helpless look in her eyes, Jason, with the greatest reluctance, chanced his all on one last throw. "My dear, if you can give me one sane, rational reason why we should not wed, I'll do what I can to dissolve our betrothal."

Lenore's mind jumped at the offer, even if her emotions lagged behind. Her eyes brightened, only to dim as the truth of her position sank in. She stared up into his eyes, confirming that the offer was indeed genuine, that he was giving her an opportunity to save her heart.

She couldn't take it.

No lady or gentleman of her class would consider her fear of being hurt, of giving and receiving nothing in return, her very fear of loving, to be a sane and rational reason, not in any circumstances. And how could she dash her father's joy? For she had seen it clearly, had not needed Eversleigh to tell her how proud and relieved her parent had been. There was, as she had feared in the dark of last night, no escape.

Swallowing, Lenore allowed the past to slip away, jettisoning her image of her future and, knowing there was no alternative, she allowed his image to fill the void. Dropping her gaze, she stared at her linked hands. "I have no reason to advance, Your Grace."

She missed the sudden easing of tension in Jason's shoulders as he let out the breath he had been holding. "Jason," he corrected softly. Her reluctance, he knew, stemmed from some peculiar female fear. He would lay it to rest—once she was his.

Lenore looked up, then, slowly, inclined her head, letting her lashes fall. "Jason."

For a moment, all was still. No sound broke the silence bar the cooing of doves from beneath the window and the shrill call of starlings in the cherry tree. Lenore felt the odd tension that held them. Nervous of where it might lead, she shook her shoulders and straightened, raising her head to look out of the window once more. "Given that it seems we are to wed, Your Grace—Jason," she amended, "I would like to know what you expect of me—precisely why you have determined that I am to be the next Duchess of Eversleigh.''

Jason frowned. ''I'm certain you'll fulfil the demands of that role admirably, my dear.''

''Be that as it may, I should like to know precisely what duties you believe that role to encompass.'' Lenore kept her gaze on the cherry tree, knowing without looking that he was wearing his forbidding expression.

Jason eyed her profile. He did not like her question but relief at her acceptance of his suit prompted him to answer. Having considered the matter so frequently in recent days, his reasons for marriage were crystal-clear in his mind. He omitted his first stipulation. After their interlude of the previous afternoon, he needed no further confirmation of her state. Only a virgin could have responded so…so… Abruptly, he hauled his mind away from that track. ''As a wife, I need a woman of breeding who can act as my hostess, someone with the requisite talents and experience to run a large household and to officiate at both formal and large family gatherings.'' Jason forced himself to step back, leaning against the window frame, folding his arms against temptation. ''I do not need a giddy miss, more intent on her own enjoyment than solicitous of her guests' welfare. You, on the other hand, have impeccable credentials in that area.''

Lenore inclined her head. ''What sort of entertainments do you generally hold at the Abbey?''

Jason told her, watching her reactions, elaborating freely when he saw she was inclined to interest. After outlining the huge family gatherings held at Christmas and occasionally in summer, and the numerous estate and country events held in the house or grounds, he described the Abbey in more detail, the number of guest-chambers and reception-rooms, the current levels of staffing, as far as he remembered them. Lenore asked questions, which he answered as best he could, eventually admitting, ''The Abbey has been without a chatelaine for more than ten years. You'll find much that needs your attention.''

Lenore eyed him straightly. "And I'll have a free hand in all household matters?"

A charming smile answered her. "I'll leave all such affairs in your capable hands. My steward, Hemmings, and my secretary, Compton, will assist you as you desire. The management of estate business, however, will remain in my hands."

Graciously, Lenore inclined her head. "I have no wish to interfere in such areas. Tell me, do you have any schemes for assisting your labourers, your tenants and their families?"

Jason shook his head. "As I said, you'll find much to keep you occupied. Without a lady of the house to oversee such enterprises, they tend to be put aside."

"But I'd have your support to institute such measures as I felt were justified?"

"Provided they met with my approval."

Lenore studied him, then decided the caveat was acceptable. Nodding, she broached the subject on which she expected less success. "Will you expect me to spend much time in London?"

Despite her even tone, Jason detected her unease. He remembered their discussion in the maze; she did not expect to enjoy life in London. The fact should have cemented his triumph. Instead, to his surprise, he heard himself say, "I usually spend all of the Season and the Little Season in town. While I would not wish you to remain at Eversleigh House if I was not in residence, I'd urge you to experience life in the capital before you turn your back on it." He saw her eyes cloud and hastened to add, "However, if, after you've tried them, you find the balls and parties not to your taste, I'll raise no demur to your remaining principally at the Abbey, provided you agree to journey to London should I require your presence." He made the concession with reluctance, hoping very much that she would find sufficient interest in the hurly-burly of *ton*-ish entertainments to keep her by his side.

His offer was a great deal more than Lenore had expected. "So—I'm to be your hostess, and take responsibility for the management of your houses. And if I find London unamusing,

I may retire to the country." All in all, the position was not without attraction. For one of her skills, the challenge of rejuvenating Eversleigh Abbey was a potent lure.

Jason nodded. "There is, of course, the matter of the succession."

Lenore switched her gaze away from his, suddenly finding the cherry tree utterly captivating. "I comprehend that you require an heir, Your Grace."

"Jason. And it's *heirs*." Lenore shot him a nervous glance. "Plural," Jason added, just to set the matter straight. "As things stand, if I were to die without issue, the title and all my estates would devolve to a distant cousin. The main line has certainly been sufficiently fecund but, unfortunately, the majority of children have been female. I'm the only duke since the first to have had a brother. At present, the next male in line is many times removed and has had no training in either estate management, in the involved politics of a large and wealthy family nor, I'm sad to say, even in how to comport himself with sufficient dignity to carry the role." He paused, sensing that she was listening intently despite her refusal to look at him. "Consequently, I'm keen to ensure the title remains with my branch of the family."

Not knowing what else to do, Lenore nodded. "I understand." Her voice sounded strained, the relief of moments before clouded by realisation of the other side of the coin. She held severe reservations over her ability to deal with Eversleigh on a personal level without falling in love with him. Yesterday had been an eye-opening experience on more than one front. But she had no choice but to take a chance—to risk falling victim to the vulnerability that afflicted her sex. She would try very hard to keep her distance, but...

"And those are the reasons which prompt you to marry me?" The question was out before she could stop it. Lenore bit her lip and waited.

Jason hesitated, then, his lips firming against an unnerving impulse to say more, he nodded. "Yes."

What had she expected? Lenore suppressed the small, sharp

pang of disappointment that twisted through her. At least he had dealt openly with her; now she knew where she stood.

Clearing her throat, she focused her mind on more concrete problems. "Do you have any strong preference for when we should wed, Your—Jason?"

Greatly relieved to hear that question on her lips, Jason answered without reservation. "As soon as possible, which means in four weeks."

"*Four weeks*!" Lenore deserted the cherry tree to round on him. "We can't possibly be married in four weeks."

One winged brow rose. "Why not?"

Aghast, Lenore stared at him. She had imagined she would have months to come to terms with her new situation. Four weeks was not nearly long enough to strengthen her defences. "Because...because...." Abruptly, she took refuge in anger. "Because you *cannot* simply decide such matters and expect me to meekly agree."

Jason frowned. "'Meek' is not a word I would use in conjunction with your fair self, my dear. If you would come down out of the boughs for long enough to examine my circumstances, you would see why any delay is to be avoided."

Puzzled, Lenore looked her question.

Rapidly, Jason formulated an answer, rejecting out of hand any idea of telling her the truth. "As you know, the notion that I intend to wed is currently circulating among the *ton*. If I return to London without our imminent wedding as protection, I'm likely to be mobbed by matchmaking mamas, seeking to convince me to change my mind and marry their witless daughters instead."

The vision of hordes of matrons, plumes aquiver, lying in wait to pound on him made Lenore's lips twitch. Jason saw it and pounced on her instead.

"It's no laughing matter, I assure you. I was hounded for years when I was younger; you wouldn't believe some of the stratagems the harpies employed."

Lenore arched one brow sceptically. "Why am I so con-

vinced you would survive even their latest manoeuvres un-
scathed?''

Jason threw her a warning look. "Anyway, at our respective
ages, no one will think marrying in four weeks the least odd."

Lenore had her doubts but held her tongue. If marrying
Eversleigh was to be her fate, and as he was so set on it, she
might as well face it in four weeks as four months. Perhaps,
with less time, she would not get so nervous over those duties
she had not before performed.

"Your father has agreed," Jason continued, watching her
more carefully. "We'll be married in Salisbury Cathedral. One
of my father's cousins is the present bishop—my family have
a long association with the bishopric. Jack and I will handle
the arrangements. Harry and Gerald will travel with your aunt
and father to Salisbury."

Struck dumb, Lenore simply stared.

After an instant's hesitation, Jason embarked on his plans
for her. "We assumed you'd wish to use the time to refurbish
your wardrobe. Jack has agreed to stay back until Tuesday.
He'll escort you to town then. As your aunt cannot act as chaperon, my aunt, Lady Agatha Colebatch, will perform that duty.
I believe you're acquainted with her?"

Stunned, overwhelmed, Lenore nodded. "She's one of Aunt
Harriet's oldest friends."

"Good. I don't think she's in town at present. It may take
me a day or two to track her down. She'll know which modiste
to take you to. As I've persuaded your father to allow me to
foot the bill, you may order what you please."

Lenore blinked. "But...but that's not..."

Jason waved one hand dismissively. "Your father and Jack
have agreed."

Beyond amazed, Lenore stared up at him. "Tell me, do you
always organise people's lives for them?"

Cool superiority met her gaze. "When they need organising
and I wish to achieve some goal, yes." Jason watched as she
swallowed that piece of arrogance, hoping he had distracted
her sufficiently from the question of who was financially re-

sponsible for her trousseau. He had had to argue long and hard to wring that concession from the Lester men; only their inability to give him an assurance that Lenore would not appear in London in pinafores had forced them to accede to his odd request.

Unconvinced that he was not engaged in some sleight of hand but unable to see any motive beyond his obvious wish to get their marriage over and done with, an unsurprising reaction given that he had been driven to the altar as it were, Lenore sighed. Slanting him a glance from beneath her lashes, she saw he was waiting for some sign of her capitulation. Inwardly grimacing, she raised her head. "As we have agreed to marry, and as you clearly wish it so, I'll agree to marry you in four weeks, Your Grace."

Jason flashed her a brilliant smile. Lenore felt a slight blush rise to her cheeks. Seeing it, Jason's smile deepened. He straightened and moved closer.

Abruptly, Lenore decided that four weeks were four weeks; she should take advantage of what time was left to her. "And now, if you'll excuse me, Your Grace, I have many tasks awaiting my attention." She bobbed a slight curtsy, rising as he took her hand. He raised it to his lips; she steeled herself to feel his kiss on her fingertips. It came, a tantalisingly light caress. Immediately overpowered by a shaft of pure desire, as, turning her hand, he pressed a far more intimate kiss into her palm.

Lenore's knees shook. She drew herself up, saying the first words that came to her tongue. "I sincerely hope, Your Grace, that you will not regret choosing me as your bride."

Jason's grey gaze sharpened. "Regret? Never, Lenore."

The reverberations of his vow echoed within her as, with a slight nod, Lenore turned and walked to the door.

Jason stood and watched her go, shackling the urge to call her back to reassure her that *she* would never regret marrying *him*.

CHAPTER SEVEN

TUESDAY DAWNED and, as His Grace of Eversleigh had decreed, Lenore, with Jack lounging beside her, headed for London in the Lester carriage. Eversleigh himself had taken his leave of her after luncheon on Saturday; he had promised to meet her at Lady Agatha Colebatch's house in Green Street.

Amelia had left Lester Hall the previous day, also bound for London. Her cousin had been bubbling with plans; Lenore hoped that Frederick Marshall brought her the happiness she deserved. Amelia had been as stunned as she at the news of her betrothal but, unlike herself, had seen nothing to quibble about. Instead, Amelia had enacted the part of rapturous joy for her, praising Eversleigh to such an extent that Lenore had been forced to avoid her for some hours, in case her sharp tongue punctuated the balloon of Amelia's illusions.

She herself had spent the hours since Eversleigh's departure in a state of unaccustomed inertia. While marriage to Eversleigh had seemed a most concrete proposition when he had been standing beside her, once he had gone she had considerable difficulty believing in her fate. In control of her life for so long, she felt adrift, rudderless. Even slightly lost.

With a determined effort, Lenore shifted her gaze to take in the streets of London. They had entered the capital some time before; Green Street could not be far off.

Noise had been her first impression of the seat of the fashionable, an unending cacophony of calls and cries of vendors and street urchins, stridently vying against the constant rumble of carriage-wheels on the cobbles and the brisk clop of hooves. The lilting music of buskers threaded a magical note through the din. Beyond the carriage window, people bustled past on the pavements, hurrying home as twilight approached. In less than the distance of a field, she was sure she had seen more people than she had in her entire life before. Eventually the meaner dwellings gave way to neat brick houses, crammed cheek-by-jowl along the busy road. Then these, too, fell behind, replaced first by larger town houses, handsome with their brightly lit windows, and then by mansions set back from the road.

Their trip had been uneventful, beyond confirming Eversleigh's insight into her family's affairs. Out of the blue, Jack had asked for her help, once she was established as Eversleigh's duchess, in the matter of finding him a bride.

"The old man's been looking so much better since receiving Eversleigh's offer for you, I'll end feeling guilty if I don't." When she had looked her puzzlement, he had explained, "You've been one of his concerns; I've been the other. Now Eversleigh's bitten the bullet, I suppose I should think about getting leg-shackled. Put the *pater*'s mind at rest, y'know."

Leaning her head against the squabs, Lenore quelled a resigned sigh. She was, however reluctantly, going forward into the only life open to her. It was up to her to make of it what she could. Swaying as the carriage lumbered around a corner into a quiet street lined with tall town houses, she allowed herself to wonder, fleetingly, just how much might be possible if she put her heart into her marriage.

The carriage slowed, then rocked to a halt before an elegant townhouse, two rows of handsome windows visible above the pavement with dormers set in under the roof. As Lenore looked out, the doors were thrown wide. Light spilled forth, illuminating the shallow steps.

Jack descended first, then handed her from the coach. Within minutes, they were being ushered into the drawing-room by her ladyship's intimidating butler.

"Lenore, dear child! Welcome to London." Pushing aside the small buhl table on which she had been idly playing cards,

Lady Agatha rose majestically, her haughty features relaxing in sincere welcome.

Lenore glided forward, intending to curtsy before her hostess, but Agatha would have none of it, catching her hands and drawing her into a scented embrace. "Nonsense, my dear. We need not stand on ceremony, you and I." Her gimlet gaze fastened on Jack, watching his sister's reception with an indulgent smile. He caught her ladyship's eye and immediately made his bow.

"I have to thank you, Lester, for bringing your sister to me. Eversleigh said to make his apologies—he had to visit the Abbey on urgent business, something to do with the settlements. Your sister and I will be spending the evening very quietly; Lenore needs to look her best tomorrow. Dare say you'd prefer to dine at your club?"

Hiding a grin at this masterly dismissal, Jack inclined his head. "Indeed, yes, ma'am, if all's well here?"

Lady Agatha nodded imperiously. "You may be content that it is." She held out a hand, watching critically as Jack bowed over it. "You may look in on your sister some time, but I warn you, we'll be busy tomorrow."

Jack nodded. With a brotherly wink for Lenore, he departed.

As the door closed behind him, Agatha waved Lenore to sit beside her on the chaise. "Hope you don't mind, my dear, but men, brothers especially, are devilish in the way sometimes."

Entirely in the dark, Lenore found herself nodding.

Agatha was studying Lenore's gown, a frown in her obsidian eyes. "By the by," she said absent-mindedly. "Eversleigh also intends to drop in on Henry on the way back from the Abbey, just to make sure all's well."

Lenore looked blank. Agatha noticed and explained. "My cousin, the Bishop of Salisbury. He'll be officiating, of course." Relinquishing Lenore's old-fashioned travelling dress to view the far more attractive future, her ladyship sighed. "It'll be the event of the year, of course. We haven't had an Eversleigh wedding for an age, quite literally. The entire town will turn out, mark my words."

Struggling to view the event with something of her hostess's enthusiasm, Lenore felt her confidence waver. But her ladyship was full of revelations. Swivelling to face Lenore, she said, "Can't tell you how pleased we all are, my sisters and I, that you agreed to take Eversleigh on. Didn't think you would, quite frankly."

Faced with the candid query in her ladyship's dark eyes, Lenore blushed slightly as she struggled to find words to explain how her betrothal had come about. "I'm afraid matters became rather tangled. As it transpired, I didn't have a great deal of choice in the matter."

She stopped, halted by her ladyship's disgusted snort.

"Great heavens, Lenore! This really won't do. Don't tell me *you*, of all women, have allowed my arrogant nephew to ride roughshod over you *already*?" Incredulity infused her ladyship's patrician features with an almost comic quality.

Lenore bit her lip and tried to explain. "It wasn't so much that—he did not force me to agree. But it seemed, the way things had fallen out, that there really was no alternative."

With a dramatic gesture, Lady Agatha fell back against the cushions. "Don't tell me—I see it all. I hesitate to disillusion you, my dear, but that's precisely why Eversleigh is so peculiarly successful in getting his own way. Things always fall out so that *his* way seems the *only* way. It's a most trying habit. We're all counting on you to break him of it."

Somewhat startled, Lenore quickly disclaimed. "I greatly fear, Lady Agatha, that I'm unlikely to wield sufficient influence with His Grace to effect any such transformation."

"Nonsense!" Lady Agatha viewed her sternly but not unkindly. "And you may call me Agatha. Eversleigh does, except when he's being difficult. But as for your not being in a position to influence Eversleigh, my dear, I rather suspect you have not entirely comprehended the position you will fill."

"We have discussed the matter," Lenore began diffidently. "Within the bounds of my duties, I see little prospect for a...a closer interaction of the sort needed to...to—"

"*Just* as I suspected!" Agatha reclined more comfortably

and prepared to set her charge straight. "Regardless of whatever..." she waved a hand airily, "*functional* duties my nephew consented to discuss, you may be sure he did not choose you as his duchess, above all others, purely on the basis of your ability to carry out said duties. Jason may be a pragmatist when it comes to matrimony, but I'm convinced he would never offer for a woman he could not deal with on a personal level."

"I believe we will deal very well together, Lenore"...Eversleigh's words echoed in Lenore's mind. Was this what he had meant?

"By personal," Lady Agatha continued, "I do not mean the sort of association a gentleman may form with, for instance, one of the fashionable impures. That, I need hardly tell you, is something quite different." She waved the indelicate subject aside. "No. The sort of relationship a man like Eversleigh will expect to share with his wife is one based on mutual respect and trust. If that is there, and I for one am sure it must be, then you need not fear, my dear. Eversleigh will listen to your arguments, your opinions. If, that is, you choose to tell him."

The prospect her ladyship's words conjured up held Lenore silent.

"That, of course, is why we hoped you'd accept his suit. Jason needs a duchess with character, and the ability to make herself heard, to act as a balancing force. To make him more human, if you take my meaning."

Lenore was not entirely sure that she did, but the opening of the door brought a halt to her ladyship's discourse.

"Yes, Higgson?" Lady Agatha waited while her butler ponderously bowed.

"You wished to be reminded that dinner would be served early, my lady," Higgson stated, his voice as heavy as his movements. "Miss Lester's maid is waiting in her room."

"Thank you, Higgson." Agatha turned to Lenore. "Eversleigh mentioned that your maid at Lester Hall would not be accompanying you to town and suggested I find a suitable girl. Trencher is my sister Attlebridge's dresser's niece. I'm sure she'll know the ropes. But if she's not to your liking, you have only to say and we'll find another.''

Lenore blinked. ''Thank you. I'm sure she'll prove suitable.'' Inwardly, she wondered how far Eversleigh's organisational powers extended.

But, ten minutes later, having been sent upstairs with orders to rest and recuperate before dinner, Lenore found herself thankful her fiancé had had the forethought to solicit his aunt's assistance. Trencher was a treasure. Of about Lenore's age, she was small and deft in her movements, severely garbed in dark brown as befitted her station, her pale face intent under a neat cap. She had unpacked Lenore's trunk, laying her brushes out upon the polished surface of the elegant dressing-table and had ordered a hot bath.

''I hope you'll excuse the liberty, miss, but I thought as how you'd be bone-jarred, having travelled all day.''

Lenore sighed and smiled her approval. She was, in fact, feeling distinctly jolted, but was uncertain as to how much of the effect could be ascribed to her father's well-sprung coach.

After a soothing soak, Trencher urged her to lie down on the luxuriously soft bed. ''I'll be sure to wake you in plenty of time to get dressed for dinner.''

Perfectly certain Trencher would not fail her, Lenore surrendered to what was, for her, a most unusual luxury. It was not, she told herself, as she climbed up on to the feather mattress, that she was tired. Rather, she could use a period of quiet reflection the better to analyse Agatha's view of her marriage. Despite these intentions, she fell deeply asleep the instant her head touched the pillow.

When Trencher woke her an hour later, her maid had no comment to offer on her outmoded gowns. Lenore had packed only the most acceptable and had left her pinafores and her spectacles behind. Her days of concealment, she felt quite sure, were past. Viewing her reflection in the long cheval glass, she grimaced.

Trencher noticed. ''It'll only be for tonight, miss. Her ladyship said as how Lafarge'd be sure to be able to make something up straight away for a customer like you. And there's no company tonight, just you and her ladyship, so you've no need to blush.''

After blinking several times, Lenore decided not to reveal her ignorance by questioning Trencher. She reserved her questions for Agatha, waiting until they were comfortably seated about one end of the dining table, with only Higgson hovering nearby.

''Who, exactly, is Lafarge?'' .

''Ah! Trencher mentioned her, did she?'' Agatha looked up from her soup. ''Quite the most exclusive modiste in London, my dear. She's agreed to do your wardrobe, which, let me tell you, would be a boon to any lady. A positive genius with gowns of all types. We're expected at her salon at ten tomorrow.''

''That's why I have to look my best?''

Recalled to her soup, Agatha nodded, adding, ''The most important person you'll ever have to convince of your beauty.''

Soup spoon suspended, Lenore stared. ''But I'm no beauty.''

Dismissively, Agatha waved the point aside. ''Used the wrong word—attractiveness, style, call it what you will. That certain something that some women have that makes them stand out in a crowd. That's what Lafarge will be looking for. She's agreed to consider taking you on as a client, but she could change her mind.''

Appalled, Lenore considered this unexpected hurdle. She had rather thought that, as the customer, she would choose her supplier. Obviously, in the case of fashionable modistes, this was not the case.

''Don't concern yourself over the matter,'' Agatha said, pushing her plate away. ''No reason she won't see something interesting in you.''

Lenore had no answer to that.

''I'd thought to take this opportunity to fill you in about Eversleigh and the family. Once it's known you're here, we'll be inundated with invitations—unlikely we'll get much chance of quiet nights.''

Lenore noted the satisfied glint in her ladyship's dark eyes. Her hostess was clearly looking forward to being the cynosure of all attention.

"I take it you're aware of Ricky's death?"

Lenore frowned. "Eversleigh's brother?" When Agatha nodded, she said, "Jack told me he was killed at Waterloo."

"Hougoumont," Agatha supplied. "Gloriously tragic. Typical of Ricky, really."

When her hostess did not immediately continue, Lenore hesitantly asked, "What I wasn't clear about was why Jack thought that was the reason Eversleigh had to wed."

"Now that," said Agatha, helping herself to a dish of mussels in white wine, "is a typical piece of Eversleigh organisation." She glanced shrewdly at Lenore before adding, "Always felt you were one young woman I did not need to beat about the bush with, so I'll tell you simply. Eversleigh never intended to marry. Something of a cold fish, Jason, not given to the warmer emotions. At least," she amended, considering her point, "that's what he thinks. Deeply cynical and all that. He and Ricky had a…a pact, so that Ricky was to be the one to marry and his son would ultimately inherit the title."

"And Waterloo dashed that plan?"

"Indeed, yes." Agatha nodded portentously. "And rather more besides." She paused pensively, then shook herself and looked at Lenore. "Jason and Ricky were very close, so Hougoumont smashed more than Jason's plans for a fancy-free future. Even I would not care to mention Hougoumont in Jason's hearing."

"I understand." Lenore stared unseeing at the slice of turbot on her plate.

"Mind you," Agatha continued, waving her fork to dispel the sudden gloom, "I'm beginning to wonder if that wasn't an example of the Almighty moving in strange ways."

Lenore looked up. "How so?"

"Well, I dare say Ricky would have made an acceptable duke—he was trained to it, as was Jason. And the family would have accepted his sons to succeed him." Pushing a mussel about on her plate, Agatha grimaced. "It's just that we would all prefer Eversleigh—that is, Jason—to be succeeded by his own son. Particularly, if *you* were there to ensure said son did not take after his father in absolutely all respects." Agatha waved her knife at Lenore. "Jason's plan was well enough, but he was always one to assume others could perform any task as well as he. But Ricky could never have been as decisive as Jason—no, nor as commanding. He simply wasn't as powerful, as unshakeably strong. And, when it comes to ruling a very large family, and very large estates, it's precisely that quality which makes all the difference."

Lenore raised her brows to indicate her interest but made no other reply. As she had hoped, Agatha rambled on, giving her a sketchy outline of the family estates together with an abbreviated history of the Montgomerys, refreshing her memory of Eversleigh's aunts and their numerous offspring. By the time Agatha waved her upstairs for an early night, Lenore's head was spinning with the effort to store all the information her hostess had let fall.

She rose early the next morning, still attuned to country hours. Trencher was there, bubbling with suppressed excitement at the thought of her mistress's visit to Lafarge's famous salon. As she allowed herself to be gowned in the gold muslin, the most acceptable dress she possessed, Lenore viewed her maid's affliction with a lenient eye, aware that no such emotion had yet touched her. Breakfast was served on a tray in her room, as was Agatha's habit. Afterwards, Lenore strolled in the small gardens behind the house, waiting for her hostess, trying to quell the trepidatious flutter of her nerves and the strange yearning for Eversleigh's large figure to appear, to lend her strength for the coming ordeal—her first crucial step into his fashionable world.

AGATHA'S CARRIAGE pulled up outside a plain door wedged between two shops on Bruton Street. Above the door hung a simple sign—"Mme Lafarge, Modiste".

Handed down from the carriage, Agatha shook out her skirts

and eyed the door shrewdly. "Lafarge only makes for a select few. Hideously expensive, so I've heard."

Joining her hostess on the pavement, Lenore turned to stare. "Isn't she your dressmaker?"

"Heavens, no! I might be well-to-do but I'm not *that* rich." Agatha straightened her straight back and headed for the door. "No—Eversleigh arranged it."

Of course. Lenore's lips tightened momentarily. She permitted herself a frown, then shrugged and followed her mentor up the steep stairs beyond the plain door.

Madame Lafarge was waiting in the large salon on the first floor. The room was elegantly furnished, gilt chairs upholstered in satin damask set in a tight circle facing outwards from the centre of the floor. Mirrors were discreetly placed around the walls, interspersed with wall hangings in a soothing shade of pale green. Madame herself proved to be a small, severely neat, black-haired Frenchwoman who stared unblinkingly at Lenore throughout the introductions.

These completed, she reached for Lenore's hand. "Walk for me, Miss Lester," she commanded in heavily accented English, drawing Lenore clear of the chairs. "To the windows and back."

Lenore blinked, but when Agatha nodded, complied, hesitantly at first, then with more confidence as she returned to where Madame waited.

"*Eh bien.* I see now what *monsieur le duc* means." Stepping close, Madame peered up into Lenore's eyes. "Yes—greens and golds, with nothing pink, white or pale blue. *M'moiselle* is twenty-four, yes?"

Dumbly, Lenore nodded.

"*Très bien.* We do not, then, need to be cramped in our choice." The little modiste's face relaxed into a smile of approval. Her eyes narrowed as she walked slowly around Lenore before nodding decisively. "A *merveille*—we will do very well, I am thinking."

Taking this to mean Madame had found that elusive something in her, Lenore felt some of her tension evaporate.

Abruptly, Madame clapped her hands. To Lenore's surprise, a young girl put her head around one of the wallhangings. A torrent of orders delivered in staccato French greeted her. With a mute nod, the girl disappeared. A bare minute later, the wall-hanging was pushed aside to admit a procession of six girls, each carrying a semi-completed outfit.

Under Madame's supervision, Lenore tried on the garments. Madame fitted them expertly, extolling the virtues of each and the use to which she expected each to be put, gesticulating freely to embellish her words. The ground was littered with pins but her advice could not be faulted. Agatha sat regally on one of the chairs, actively interested in all that went on.

It was not until she was trying on the third outfit, a delicate amber morning gown, that the truth dawned on Lenore. She was unusually tall and slender yet the dresses needed only marginal adjustments. Her head came up; she stiffened.

"Be still, *m'moiselle*," hissed Madame Lafarge from behind her.

Lenore obeyed but immediately asked, "For whom were these dresses made, Madame?"

Lafarge peered around to stare up at her face. "Why—for you, Miss Lester."

Lenore returned her stare, recalling that Madame had not even bothered to take her measurements. "But…how?"

Lafarge's black eyes blinked up at her. "*Monsieur le duc* gave me an…" Her hands came up to describe her meaning. "An understanding of your comportment and your *taille*, you understand? From that, I was able to fashion these. As you see, his memory was not greatly at fault."

A shiver travelled Lenore's spine but she was unsure of the emotion behind it. Agatha had been right—Eversleigh was far too used to organising all as he wished. The idea that her wardrobe would bear the imprint of his hand, rather than hers, was far too much for her to swallow.

Parading before the glass and admiring the way the long amber skirts swirled about her, Lenore made up her mind. "I should like to see these other gowns you've made up."

Besides the three gowns she had already tried on, a green muslin walking dress, a teal carriage dress and the amber creation, Lafarge had made up three evening gowns. Trying on the first of these, Lenore felt a definite qualm. Studying her reflection, the way the fine silk clung to her body, emphasising her height, her slimness and the soft swell of her breasts, she wondered if she would ever have the courage to actually wear the gown. The neckline was cut low, barely avoiding the indecorous. Aside from the tiny puffed sleeves, her arms were entirely bare; she could already feel gooseflesh prickling her skin. The other two gowns were in similar vein.

"You wish to view the rest as well?"

Turning, Lenore stared at Lafarge. "Madame, what, exactly, has His Grace ordered?"

Lafarge spread her hands. "A wardrobe of the very finest—all the materials to be the very best as suited to your station. Dresses, gowns, coats, cloaks, nightgowns, petticoats, chemises, peignoirs." Lafarge ticked the items off on her fingers, then spread them wide. "Everything, *m'moiselle*, that you might need."

Even Agatha looked stunned.

Lenore had had enough. "Have any of these items been made up?"

Sensing that her hopes for the soon-to-be duchess were teetering on some invisible precipice, Lafarge hurriedly summoned her girls with all the items thus far created on His Grace of Eversleigh's orders.

Lenore ran her fingers over the delicate materials. As she held up a chemise, a peculiar thrill went through her. The garment was all but transparent.

Watching her client closely, Lafarge murmured, "All was created at *monsieur le duc*'s express orders, *m'moiselle*."

Lenore believed her but did not understand. Eversleigh had ordered a wardrobe that tantalised—for her. She frowned, laying aside the chemise to pick up a peignoir with a matching nightgown. As the long folds unravelled, her breathing seized. Slowly, deliberately, she turned so that Agatha was granted a full view of the gown. "Surely this is not what other women of the *ton* wear?"

Agatha's face was a study. Not knowing whether to be scandalised or delighted, she grimaced. "Well—yes and no. But if Eversleigh's ordered them, best take 'em." When Lenore hesitated, she added, "You can argue the point with him later."

When I'm wearing them? Lenore quelled another distracting shiver.

"They are not, perhaps, what I would create for all my young ladies, but, if you will permit the liberty, *m'moiselle*, few of my young ladies could appear to advantage in these. And," Lafarge added, a little hesitantly, "*Monsieur le duc* was very definite—he was very clear what he wished to see on you, *m'moiselle*."

Lenore had gathered as much but was still unclear as to his motives. Leaving such imponderables aside, she wondered what to do. As Agatha had noted, Eversleigh's organisational habits left very little room for manoeuvre. More than half the items were at least partly made up; Lafarge must have had her workrooms operating around the clock. Idly fingering a delicate silk chemise, Lenore made her decision. "Madame, did His Grace give permission for me to add to this collection?"

Lafarge brightened perceptibly. "But yes." She spread her hands. "Anything you wished for you were to have, provided it was in a suitable style."

The caveat did not surprise her. Lenore nodded. "Very well. In that case, I wish to double the order."

"*Comment*?" Lafarge's eyes grew round.

"For every article His Grace ordered, I wish to order another," Lenore explained. "In a different style, in a different colour and in a different material."

Agatha burst out laughing. "Oh, *well done*, my dear," she gasped, once she had caught her breath. "An entirely fitting reaction. I had wondered how you would manage it, but that, at least, should set him back on his heels."

"Quite," Lenore agreed, pleased to have Agatha's support. "I could hardly be so insensitive as to not appreciate his gift, but neither will I be dictated to in the matter of my own wardrobe.''

"Bravo!" Clapping her hands, Agatha raised them to Lenore in salute. "Heavens! But this will take an age. Are you free, Madame?"

"I am entirely at your service, my lady." Shaking her head at the incomprehensible ways of the English, Madame summoned her assistants. Far be it from her to complain.

The following hours were filled with lists, pattern cards and fabrics. As she argued the rival merits of bronzed sarcenet over topaz silk, and cherry trim over magenta, Lenore felt some of Trencher's excitement trip her. Agatha encouraged her to air her views. In the end, Lafarge paused to say, "You 'ave natural taste, m'moiselle. Strive to retain it and you will never be anything but elegant."

Lenore beamed like a schoolgirl. The appellation "elegant" was precisely what she was aiming for. It seemed only fitting if she was to be Eversleigh's bride.

At last, having duplicated the long list approved by His Grace, they paused to refresh themselves with tiny cups of tea and thinly sliced cucumber sandwiches.

Suddenly, Lafarge set her cup aside. "*Tiens*! Fool that I am—I forgot the bridal gown."

She clapped her hands, issued a stream of orders and the repast was cleared. The curtains at the back of the shop parted to permit her senior assistant to enter, reverently carrying a gown of stiff ivory silk covered in tiny seed pearls.

Lenore simply stared.

"That's Georgiana's wedding gown—or part of it, if m'memory serves." Agatha looked at Lafarge.

The modiste nodded. "*Monsieur le duc*'s mama? *Mais oui*. He asked for the gown to be re-made in a modern style. It is exquisite, no?"

All Lenore could do was nod, eyes fixed on the scintillating gown. As she climbed into it, she shivered. The gown was unexpectedly heavy. Lafarge had exercised her own refined taste in its design; the high neckline with its upstanding collar and long tightly fitting sleeves met with Lenore's immediate approval. The long skirts fell from just below her breasts straight to the floor, the long line imparting a regal elegance most suitable for a ducal bride.

Once the gown had been adjusted and removed, Lafarge hesitantly brought forward a silk confection. "And this, *monsieur le duc* ordered for your wedding-night."

Resigned, Lenore shook out the shimmering folds and held them up. Agatha stifled a chuckle. "I dare say," was all the comment offered. She handed the scandalously sheer, tantalisingly cut nightgown and matching peignoir back to Lafarge. "I expect you had better send them with the rest."

It was after two when they descended once more to the carriage. The first of the gowns, three day dresses and one evening gown ordered by Eversleigh, would be delivered that evening, along with some chemises and petticoats. As she followed Agatha into the carriage, Lenore heaved an unexpectedly satisfied sigh.

Agatha heard it and chuckled. "Not as boring as you expected, my dear?"

Lenore inclined her head. "I have to admit I was not bored in the least."

"Who knows," Agatha said, settling herself back on the seat. "You might even come to enjoy town pleasures. Within reason, of course."

"Perhaps," Lenore replied, unwilling to argue that point.

"Tell me," Agatha said. "Those gowns you ordered—not in the usual style but not in your usual style, either. Don't tell me Eversleigh has succeeded where your aunt, myself and my sisters all failed?"

A subtle smile played on Lenore's lips. "My previous style was dictated by circumstances. Situated as I was, going about the estates alone, with my brothers bringing their friends to stay, it seemed more practical to wear gowns that concealed rather than revealed, dampened rather than excited. As you know, I did not look for marriage."

Head on one side, Agatha studied her charge. "So you don't mind Eversleigh's choices?"

"I wouldn't go quite so far as *some* of the styles he favours, but…" Lenore shrugged. "I see no reason, now I'm to be wed, to hide my light under a bushel any longer."

Agatha chuckled. "And you wouldn't get any bouquets from my nephew for attempting to do so."

Lenore smiled and wondered how long it would be before Eversleigh came to see her.

HE CAUGHT UP with her the next day. On her way to convey a shank of embroidery silk left in the upstairs parlour to Agatha in the morning-room, Lenore was halfway down the stairs before she heard the rumble of Eversleigh's deep tones below. After a fractional hesitation, she continued her calm descent.

Jason turned as she gained the hall tiles, his grey gaze sweeping from her hair, neatly braided and coiled, over her modish amber morning gown with its delicate fluted chemisette, to the tips of her old-fashioned slippers peeking from beneath the dress's scalloped hem. Seeing his gaze become fixed, Lenore had no difficulty divining his thoughts. She went forward with her usual confident air, her hand outstretched. "Good morning, Your Grace. I trust I see you well?"

With a slight, questioning lift to his brows, Jason took her hand and, without preamble, raised it to his lips. "I apologise for not being here to greet you. Business took me to Dorset and thence to Salisbury, as I hope Agatha explained."

Quelling the now familiar sensation that streaked through her at his unconventional caress, Lenore retrieved her hand. "Lady Agatha has been most kind." Turning to lead him to the morning-room, she added, "You will, no doubt, be happy to know that yesterday she and I visited a certain Madame Lafarge, who is, even now, endeavouring to create a wardrobe fit for the Duchess of Eversleigh. We plan to visit the shoemakers, glovers and milliners tomorrow. Tell me, my lord, do you have any particular makers you wish to recommend?"

The airily polite question was more than enough to put Jason on his guard. "I'm sure Agatha will know who is best," he murmured.

Agatha was delighted to see him, promptly informing him of a ball to be given by her sister, Lady Attlebridge, the following evening. "Mary's agreed to use the event to puff off your engagement. A select dinner beforehand, so you'd best be here by seven. My carriage or yours?"

Jason frowned. "I've sent the main Eversleigh carriages to be refitted, so it had better be yours, I imagine."

Lenore noted his slight constraint and, after years of tripping over her brothers' secrets, wondered if he had intended the refit as a surprise for her.

"I had thought to take Miss Lester for a drive in the Park." Jason smoothly turned to Lenore. "That is, if you'd like to take the air?"

There was, in fact, little Lenore would have liked better. Buoyed by the bracing effect of Agatha's encouragement, she was determined to make a start gaining experience dealing with her husband-to-be while she still had his aunt behind her. "You're most kind, Your Grace. If you'll wait while I get my pelisse?"

Jason merely nodded, sure she would not keep his horses waiting.

Making an elegant exit from the morning-room, Lenore hurried upstairs. The day was unseasonably cool; she was eager to try out the new cherry-red pelisse delivered from Lafarage's this morning. It was an item Eversleigh had ordered; she was determined to give him no warning of her other purchases prior to Lady Attlebridge's ball. Ringing for Trencher, she tidied her hair, fastening it with extra pins given she as yet had no suitable bonnet; she refused to have it cut nor yet to wear a scarf. Shrugging into the pelisse and buttoning it up, Lenore turned this way and that before her cheval glass, admiring the soft merino wool edged with simple ribbon and trimmed at collar and cuffs with grey squirrel fur. The pastel amber of her gown did not clash with the deep cherry. Then she noticed her slippers.

Grimacing, Lenore turned to Trencher. "My brown half-boots and gloves. They'll have to do until I can get something to match. Perhaps tomorrow?"

Descending the stairs busy with the last buttons on her gloves, Lenore did not see Eversleigh at their foot.

"Commendably prompt, my dear."

Lenore looked up, straight into his grey eyes and found them warm with appreciation. She smiled but did not deceive herself that he had not noticed her gloves and boots.

"That shade of red suits you to admiration," Jason murmured as, taking her hand, he led her to the door.

Lenore bit back her impulsive rejoinder, to the effect that it was hardly surprising if his taste found favour in his eyes. Letting her lashes fall, she replied, "It's not a colour I have previously had a chance to wear. I must admit I rather favour it."

The gleam of pride in his eyes as he lifted her to the box seat of his curricle filled her with a curious elation.

The drive to the Park was accomplished swiftly, the traffic in the more fashionable quarters having markedly decreased. It was the first of July and many of the *ton* had already quit the capital. Nevertheless, there were more than enough of the élite left to nod and whisper as His Grace of Eversleigh swept past in his curricle, an elegant lady beside him.

Lenore revelled in the speed of the carriage, bowling along at a clipping pace. She had been driven in curricles before, but never on such smooth surfaces. Jason's matched greys were, she suspected, Welsh thoroughbreds; the carriage, sleek and perfectly sprung, was no great load for them. Above their heads, the sun struggled to pierce the clouds; the breeze, redolent with the scents of summer, whipped her cheeks.

Bethinking herself of the one item she should make a point of mentioning, Lenore leant closer to Eversleigh. "I must thank you for my bridal gown, my lord. It's truly lovely."

Briefly, Jason glanced down at her. "It was my mother's. My parents' marriage was, by all accounts, a highly successful one. It seemed a fitting omen to re-use my mother's gown."

Not quite sure how to take his words, Lenore made no reply, keeping her gaze on the passing trees and the occupants of the carriages about them.

Noting the sensation their appearance was causing, Jason sought to clarify the matter. "The announcement of our betrothal will appear in the *Gazette* the day after tomorrow, after the announcement at my aunt's ball." He glanced down at the fair face beside him, refreshingly open, her complexion aglow. He smiled wryly. "I had to make sure all my major connections, such as my uncle Henry, heard of it first from me, else there'd have been hell to pay."

Lenore returned his glance with a grin. "I can imagine. Your family is very large, is it not?"

"Very! If you were to ask how many could claim kinship I would not be able to tell you. The Montgomerys, I fear, are a somewhat robust breed. While the direct line has dwindled due to accident, the collateral lines continue to increase unabated."

"Will they all be attending our wedding?" Lenore asked, struck by the possibility.

"A large number of them," Jason replied, his attention on his horses. Only when he had successfully negotiated the turn and had the leisure to glance again at Lenore did he perceive her worried frown. "You won't have to converse with them all."

"But, as your wife, I should at least know their names," she countered. "*And* their associations. Great heavens—and you've left me only three weeks to learn them all."

Belatedly perceiving his error, and foreseeing hours spent in recounting his family connections—a topic that had always bored him witless—Jason groaned. "Lenore—believe me. You don't need to know."

Fixing him with a steady gaze, Lenore enunciated carefully, "*You* might be able to wander through a reception ostensibly given by you without a qualm despite not knowing everyone's name. *I* cannot."

Jason glared at her. "Great gods, woman! You'll never get them all straight."

"Am I right in supposing you wish us to marry in three weeks?"

Jason scowled. "We *are* marrying in three weeks."

"Very well," Lenore continued, her tone perfectly even. "In that case, I suggest you lend me your assistance in coming to grips with your relatives. And your friends among the *ton*. Some I know; others I don't. I'll need some assistance in defining those you wish me to acknowledge, and those you do not."

Her careful words reminded Jason that she did, indeed, know some of his "friends" he would not wish her to encourage. And there were yet others who might claim friendship who he would not wish her to countenance.

Considering the task ahead of her, Lenore frowned. "We'll have to prepare a guest-list. Perhaps I could use that?"

Jason felt a sudden chill. "Actually," he replied, "the guest-list has already been prepared."

Silence greeted this pronouncement. While he rehearsed his defence—there was only three weeks, after all—he was well aware that, regardless, she had good cause to feel annoyed. More than annoyed.

"Oh?"

The lack of ire in the query brought his head around. But nothing he could see in her mild green gaze gave any indication of aggravation. Which was impossible. The fact that she was shutting him out, hiding her feelings, and that he could not penetrate her mask if she so wished, rocked him. Abruptly, he focused on his horses. "Your father started the list, Jack and your aunt made some additions and I dictated the whole to my secretary."

Again, a painful minute passed unbroken. "Perhaps you would be good enough to ask your secretary—Compton, is it not?—to furnish me with a copy of this list?"

"I'll call to take you for a drive tomorrow afternoon. I'll bring you a copy and we can discuss it during the drive." Jason heard his clipped accents, quite different from his habitual drawl, and knew his temper was showing. Not that he had any right to feel angry with her, but she threw him entirely with her cool and utterly assumed calm. She had every right to enact him a scene and demand an apology for what was, he knew, high-handed behaviour of the most arrogant sort. Instead, she was behaving as if his transgression did not matter—why that fact should so shake his equilibrium he was at a loss to understand.

Keeping her gaze on the carriages they passed, a serene smile on her lips, Lenore gave mute thanks for her years of training in the subtle art of polite dissimulation. The Park, she was certain, was not the place to indulge in heated discussions. Not that she had any intention of discussing her fiancé's error with him later. He would only use logic and reason to make his actions seem perfectly reasonable, a fact she would never concede. Besides, there were other ways of making her point. His irritated tone had already provided a modicum of balm for her abraded pride. Guilt, she recalled, had always turned her brothers into bears. The thought cheered her immensely.

"Perhaps we could make a start with members of the *ton*. Who is that lady in the green bonnet up ahead?"

Determined not to let another awkward silence develop, Lenore continued to quiz her betrothed on personages sighted until, after half an hour, he turned his horses for Green Street once more.

CHAPTER EIGHT

As THE Colebatch carriage rumbled down Park Lane, Lenore clutched at the edge of her velvet evening cloak, her expression serene, her stomach a hard knot of apprehension. Her silk gown was entirely concealed by the dark green cloak, one Eversleigh, sitting opposite her, had ordered. Although the evening was fine, there was just enough chill in the air to excuse her need for warmth; she had been cloaked and waiting when he had arrived to escort them to Attlebridge House.

Beside her, Agatha was in high gig, resplendent in midnight-blue bombazine with a peacock feather adorning her black turban. Her patrician features were animated, her black eyes alert. It was plain she expected to enjoy the evening immensely. Lenore swallowed, easing the nervous flutter in her throat, and risked a glance at Eversleigh. Superb in severe black, his ivory cravat a work of art, her fiancé was the epitome of the elegant man about town. His heavy signet glittered on his right hand; a single gold fob hung from the pocket of his embossed silk waistcoat.

His features were in shadow but, when they passed a street-lamp, Lenore found his grey eyes steady on hers. Her breath caught in her throat. He smiled, gently, reassuringly. Lenore returned the smile and, looking away, wondered whether she was that transparent.

In an effort to distract herself from the coming ordeal, she reviewed the list of those Montgomerys she was shortly to meet. Thanks to Agatha, she had the immediate family committed to memory. Given that she was already acquainted with Eversleigh's aunts, she felt few qualms about the social hurdles

facing her tonight. It was an entirely different hurdle, one she
had erected herself, that had her nerves in unanticipated disarray.

True to his word, Eversleigh had arrived to drive her in the
Park that afternoon armed with a copy of all three hundred
names on their guest list. She had spared a thought for the
unfortunate Compton, required to produce the copy in less than
twenty-four hours. At Agatha's suggestion she had restricted
her queries to those of his friends included on the list, leaving
the family connections to be later clarified by Agatha. Any
awkwardness that might have existed had been ameliorated by
her shy thanks tendered for the present he had sent her that
morning.

That had been extremely disconcerting. She had returned
with Agatha from a most successful expedition—bonnets,
gloves, slippers and boots had consumed most of their morning,
leaving her with little opportunity to dwell on the iniquitous
behaviour of her fiancé—to discover a package addressed to
herself, left in Higgson's care. Removing the wrappings, she
had discovered a pair of soft kid half-boots in precisely the
same shade of cherry-red as her new pelisse, together with a
pair of matching pigskin gloves. Accompanying these had been
a chip bonnet with long cherry ribbons. There had been no
card.

Agatha had crowed.

Any doubts she had harboured over who had sent her such
a gift had been laid to rest when she had tried on the boots in
her chamber, exclaiming over their perfect fit. Trencher had
giggled, then admitted that a person named Moggs, known to
be in Eversleigh's employ, had materialised in the kitchens the
previous afternoon, asking for her shoe size.

The episode had left her shaken. The idea that Eversleigh
had turned London upside down—or, more likely, kept some
poor cobbler up half the night—just to make this peace with
her was distinctly unnerving. His abrupt dismissal of her
thanks, as if his effort meant nothing at all, almost as if he did
not wish to acknowledge it, had been even more odd.

Throughout their drive, she had kept her eyes glued to his secretary's scrawl and bombarded him with questions. Despite a certain reluctance, she had wrung from him enough answers to satisfy.

The bright lights of Piccadilly swung into view. Lenore quelled a shiver of expectation, drawing her cloak closer.

Ten minutes later, they pulled up outside Attlebridge House in Berkeley Square. Jason descended then turned to assist first his aunt, then his fiancée to the pavement. As Lenore stepped down from the carriage, her cloak parted slightly, affording his sharp eyes a glimpse of silver-green. His lips twitched. Inwardly he sent up a prayer that Lafarge had adhered to her usual standards. After his gaffe over the guest-list, he did not feel sufficiently secure to object even had Lenore donned a pinafore.

Trapping her hand on his sleeve, he detected the tremor in her fingers. Capturing her wide gaze, he smiled encouragingly, trying to banish the lingering memory of the feelings that had swamped him in the Park the day before. The feelings that had sent him home in a savage mood, to give Moggs a most peculiar set of orders. Typically, Moggs had achieved the desired result quietly and efficiently. Yet the fact that he had felt such a compelling urge to prove to his wife-to-be that he was not an ogre was disturbing. She was an intelligent woman—there should be no need to go to such lengths.

As he waited beside her for his aunt's door to swing open, he recalled Lenore's thanks, tendered with a smile of rare sweetness. He had been decidedly brusque, thrown off-balance by the sudden thought that, while he had frequently showered diamonds on his mistresses, he wooed his bride with boots.

And then they were inside the hall, and the moment of revelation was upon them.

Gripped by sudden shyness, Lenore allowed Jason to remove the velvet cloak from her shoulders. Trying for an air of sophisticated confidence, she twitched her skirts straight, then, her head high, fixed her eyes on Agatha's face.

Warm approval shone in Agatha's black eyes. "You look

absolutely *splendid*, my dear." Her peacock feather bobbed with her nod. "Doesn't she, Eversleigh?" This last was uttered pointedly in an attempt to prod her nephew to speech. Agatha glared at him but his eyes were fixed on Lenore.

Lenore knew it. The silence from beside her was complete, but she could feel his gaze roving over her shoulders, bared by the wide neckline of her gown, then moving down, over her breasts, outlined by the high waist, then down, down the long length of her filmy skirts, cut narrow to emphasise her height and slenderness. A slow blush rose to her cheeks. In desperation, she tweaked the delicate cuffs of the long, fitted sleeves over her wrists.

Becoming aware of how long he had stood, gawking like a schoolboy, Jason tried to speak, but had to pause and clear his throat before he could do so. "You look...exquisite, my dear."

At the deep, strangely raspy words, Lenore glanced up, into his eyes—and was content. Then he smiled and she felt a quiver ripple from the top of her head all the way to her toes.

"Shall we go in?" Smoothly, Jason offered her his arm, unable, for the life of him, to take his eyes from her. The silver-green silk clung and slid over her curves as she moved to his side. The gown was more concealing than any he had ordered yet, oddly, it was far more alluring to have such promise so tantalisingly withheld.

Success, Lenore found, was a heady potion. As she placed her fingertips on his silk sleeve her entire body tingled with the thrill of conquest, of having brought the silver light to his eyes. The sensation left her breathless. Side by side, both so tall, she a graceful counterpoint to his strength, they strolled into the large drawing-room.

All conversation halted.

Wide-eyed stares rained upon them; the entire company followed their stately progress to Lady Attlebridge, an imposing figure standing before the fireplace. There was not a shred of doubt who the focus of interest was that night.

And so it proved. To Lenore's abiding relief, Eversleigh remained firmly entrenched by her side, resisting any number of attempts, some subtle, others less so, to either distract him, or displace him. When her memory failed, he prompted or, as happened more frequently, when her memory was blank, because neither he nor Agatha had recalled certain of his connections, he duly filled her in, his charming smile warming her all the while.

From his sudden stiffness when they hove near, she deduced his aunts were his greatest concern, an observation she found particularly interesting. When the fact that she knew them finally registered as they were leaving Lady Eckington, the most redoubtable and unpredictable of the six, he murmured, "They know you, don't they?"

Lenore opened her eyes wide. "I thought you knew," she murmured, turning to smile as one of his cousins passed by. "They often visit Lester Hall. They're all friends of Harriet's. I've known most of your aunts since I was—oh, twelve or so."

Jason raised his brows, surprised yet cynical as realisation dawned. Given the favour of his formidable aunts, Lenore would have no need of his support in establishing her social position. Which was a relief. Nevertheless, his voice held a disgruntled note when he said, "I had thought to have to protect you from them. The next time they come calling with me in their sights, I'll know who to hide behind."

Lenore's eyes widened but she laughed the comment aside. "Never mind that—just tell me who the lady in the atrocious purple turban is. She's been trying to attract our attention for ages. On the sofa by the wall."

Obediently, Jason slowly turned. "That, dear Lenore, is Cousin Hetty. Come. I'll introduce you."

And so it went on. The dinner proved no greater ordeal than the drawing-room; by the end of it, Lenore felt entirely at home among the Montgomerys. An official announcement of their engagement was made at the end of the meal, and their healths drunk in the finest champagne before the company moved to the ballroom, keen to meet the incoming guests and spread the news.

Lenore glided through the throng on Jason's arm, smiling

and nodding, her head in a whirl. She was thankful the long windows to the terrace were open, allowing a gentle breeze to cool the heated room. Despite the time of year, Lady Attlebridge's rooms were full. Bodies hemmed her in, the colours of coats and gowns blending like an artist's palette. As she clung to Jason's arm, grateful for the reassuring pressure of his fingers on hers, her responses to the introductions and congratulations became automatic.

Then the musicians struck up.

"Come, my dear."

As if he had been waiting for the signal, Eversleigh drew her away from the crowd, into the area miraculously clearing in the middle of the floor. As she felt his arm go around her, Lenore remembered. The waltz—their engagement waltz. "Ah," she said, relaxing into his arms. "I'd forgotten about this."

"Had you?" Jason raised one arrogant brow. "I hadn't."

He watched her eyes cloud with delicious confusion.

Lenore blinked, the only way to break free of his spell. Fixing her gaze in convenient space, she prayed he could not hear her thudding heart. "Tell me, my lord. Is Lord Alvanley an accomplished dancer?"

"Accomplished enough," Jason returned, quelling his grin. "But Alvanley's claim to fame is his wits, rather than his grace. Furthermore, given he's half a head shorter than you, I would not, if I was you, favour him with a waltz." He considered the matter gravely. "A cotillion, perhaps. Or a quandrille."

Lenore's eyes narrowed, but, before she could formulate another distracting question, Jason took charge.

"But enough of my friends, my dear—and *more* than enough of my relatives," he added, frowning when she opened her lips. "I would much rather hear about you."

"Me?" The words came out in a higher register and without the languid dismissiveness Lenore had intended, owing to the fact that Jason had drawn her closer as they approached the end of the floor. His hand burned through the fine silk of her gown, his thighs brushing hers as they whirled through the turn.

When they straightened to precess back up the room, he did not relax his hold. Luckily, other couples were crowding on to the floor, obscuring everyone's view.

"You," Jason confirmed. "I sincerely hope you cancelled the gowns I ordered from Lafarge." Lenore looked up, eyes wide. Jason smiled. "Your style is uniquely yours, my dear. I like it far better than any other."

More flattered than she would have believed possible, Lenore stared up at him. "Actually, my lord—"

"Jason."

Lenore felt her fingers tighten around his. She forced them to relax. "Jason, the gowns you had ordered were perfectly appropriate. It's merely that, at least until I get used to such styles, I fear I would find wearing the more revealing gowns unsettling. No doubt I'll get used to such things in time."

"Lenore, I would prefer you to dress as you wish. Your own style is much more becoming and infinitely more appropriate than the current mood. I would be happy to see you always garbed in gowns such as you are wearing tonight."

"Oh." Lenore looked deep into his eyes but could see nothing beyond an unnerving sincerity. She drew a deep breath. "In that case, my—Jason, I suspect I should warn you to expect a very large bill from Madame Lafarge."

A smile of considerable charm lit Jason's face. He chuckled. "I see. What did you do—double the order?"

Eyes on his, Lenore nodded.

For a moment, he could not take it in. Then, the trepidation in her wide eyes, her suspended breathing, registered, confirming the reality. For the first time in a very long while, Jason was at a loss, sheer incredulity obstructing coherent thought. In the end, his sense of humour won through. His lips lifted in an irrepressible grin, breaking into a smile as he saw her confusion grow. Drawing her slightly closer, he sighed. "You will, no doubt, be relieved to know that settling with Lafarge will not greatly dent my fortune. However," Jason continued, his eyes holding hers, "next time you wish to upbraid me for my high-handed ways, do you think, my dear, that you could simply lose your temper? I find your methods of making me sorry rather novel, to say the least." Not to mention effective, but he was not so far lost to all caution as to say such words out aloud.

"I...ah..." Lenore did not know what to say. His grey eyes, gently quizzing her, were far too perceptive to risk any white lie. As the fact that he was disposed to view her actions in an understanding, even conciliatory way sank in, she summoned enough strength to tilt her chin at him. "If you would refrain from acting high-handedly in the first place, my lord, I would not need to exercise my temper in any way whatever. Which would be greatly to be desired, for I find it extremely wearying."

Delighted by her haughty response, Jason could not resist asking, his voice low, "And if I refrained from all high-handed behaviour? Would you be suitably grateful, Lenore?"

Her heartbeat filling her ears as his eyes caressed her face, Lenore struggled to keep her feet on the ground. Her bones felt weak, a sensation that had afflicted her once before. Too concerned with keeping her senses under control, she made no effort to answer him.

The confusion in her eyes was answer enough for Jason.

The music stopped. Reluctantly, he freed her, tucking her hand into his arm, a subtle smile curving his lips.

Released from his gaze, Lenore dragged in a steadying breath.

"Great heavens! Lenore!" Spun about, Lenore felt her hand caught, then she was slowly twirled about. Jack came into view, studying her avidly. Coming to a halt in time to see him shoot a glance loaded with masculine meaning at her fiancé, Lenore tugged to get her brother's attention.

"How is Papa?"

Jack blinked, as if struggling to take her meaning. "Papa? Oh, he's fine. Couldn't be better. And his health will improve no end when he gets a look at you. What happened to your pinafores?"

"I left them at home," Lenore stated with awful deliberation. "Along with my spectacles," she added before he could ask. "Come and dance with me. I need the practice."

Leaving Jason with the mildest of nods, she led the way to the floor.

While circling the floor with Jack, she prised his news from him. He had returned to Lester Hall on Wednesday, to set her father's mind at rest that all was well with her. Apparently all was likewise well at Lester Hall, although Harriet and her father both missed her. However, the arrangements for them to attend her wedding were well in hand; the prospect was the cause of considerable excitement in the household.

"God knows! Some of the servants have asked permission to make the journey, so you might catch sight of some familiar faces in the crowd outside the church."

Lenore was touched, but, already, Lester Hall and its affairs were fading in her mind, overlaid by the more pressing demands of her new role.

Harry came up as Jack led her from the floor. After making comments sufficiently similar to Jack's to earn a stern warning from Lenore, he, too, commandeered her for a dance. At the end of it, however, he insisted on returning her to her fiancé's side, revealing that he had been so instructed by his future brother-in-law and was not about to queer his pitch in that direction.

Lenore did not quite know what to make of that but she was too relieved to be once more in Jason's protective presence to protest.

He was talking to Frederick Marshall when she joined him. Lenore could not miss the stunned look on Frederick's face when he saw her.

"My dear Miss Lester." Coming to himself with a start, Frederick bowed gallantly over Lenore's hand. Straightening, he blinked. "Er…" Appalled by the words that had leapt to his tongue, Frederick struggled to find suitable replacements.

Reading his friend's mind with ease, Jason helpfully explained, "She left her pinafores at Lester Hall."

Bending a glance both haughty and innocent upon him, Lenore asked, "I do hope, Your Grace, that you're not missing them? Perhaps I should send for them, if it would please you?"

Jason was too old a hand to be rolled up so easily. His lips curved appreciatively, his grey eyes gleamed. "I'd be only too pleased to discuss what you might do to please me, my dear. Naturally, I'm delighted that you seek to make my pleasure your paramount concern."

Any possibility that his speech was uttered in innocence was rendered ineligible by the expression in his eyes. Caught in his web once more, Lenore turned hot, then cold, then hot once more. With an effort, she dragged her gaze from his, glancing at Frederick but with little hope of rescue.

She had, however, underestimated Frederick. More used to Jason's ways than she, he sent his friend a stern glance before enquiring, "Have you weathered the Montgomery clan, then? They're somewhat daunting, are they not?"

Lenore grasped the unexpected lifeline, applying herself to a discussion of her fiancé's huge family, thereby, she later realised, punishing him most effectively.

It was not long afterwards that Agatha caught up with them. "If you want my opinion, we should leave now. Best not to give them time to grow too accustomed—keeps their interest up, y'know?"

Jason, his eyes flicking over Lenore's radiant face and seeing the increasing weariness behind her polished mask, inclined his head. "I bow to your greater experience of such matters, dear aunt."

The carriage was summoned; they took their leave of their hostess, Lenore and Agatha receiving an invitation to take tea the following Tuesday.

Ensconced in the carriage, wrapped up in her cloak once more, Lenore sighed as the flambeau lighting the Attlebridge House steps fell behind, her evening's hurdles successfully overcome.

Seated opposite, Jason watched the shadows wreath her face. He smiled. "Well, my dear. Was the ordeal as bad as you had feared?"

Lenore straightened. "Why, no, my lord." She turned to face him fully, rearranging the folds of her cloak. Remembering his requirements of a bride, she added, "I don't believe I will find any real difficulty in either attending or hosting such entertainments."

Jason inclined his head, a frown gathering in his eyes.

"Lady Mulhouse invited us to her rout next week." Lenore turned to Agatha. "And Mrs. Scotridge asked us to tea."

Agatha heaved a contented sigh. "Ah, me! I'd almost forgotten what it's like to be in the eye of the storm. Despite the fact that it's the tag-end of the Season, I dare say life will be hectic for the next few weeks."

Eyes narrowing, Jason watched his aunt stifle a yawn. If nothing else had been achieved at his aunt Attlebridge's ball, the occasion had demonstrated that in her new incarnation Lenore held a potent attraction for the prowling males of the *ton*. No less than five fascinated acquaintances had stopped by his side to remark on her beauty. Placing an elbow on the carriage windowsill, Jason leant his chin on his fist and stared, unseeing, at the passing façades.

After some moments, he shifted his gaze to the object of his thoughts, sitting serene and content only feet away, her face intermittently lit by the street-lamps as she watched the houses slip past. The wheels rang on the cobblestones as he pondered his problem, his gaze fixed, unwaveringly, on the face of his bride-to-be.

As the carriage slowed for the turn into Green Street, Jason stirred. "If tomorrow is fine, perhaps you'd care to drive to Merton with me? My great-aunt Elmira lives there; she's an invalid and will be unable to attend our wedding but she's an avid gossip and will be livid not to have met you."

He ignored Agatha's stunned stare, his attention on Lenore.

Lenore brightened, her spirits lifting at the thought of a drive in the country. Fresh country air was something she was already missing, although she had no intentions of admitting to such weakness. "I'd be delighted to accompany you, my lord." She smiled, feeling as if the final cachet had been added to her evening. "I would not have it thought that we were in any way backward with our attentions to your family."

"You need have no fear of that," Jason returned somewhat ascerbically. "My family, as you will learn, would never permit it."

As the carriage slowed before his aunt's house, Jason allowed himself a small, self-deprecatory smile. The course he had just set his feet upon was not one he would, of his own volition, have followed. However, given that his peace for the rest of his life might depend on the outcome, three weeks of his time seemed a small price to pay.

FOR LENORE, the weeks following the announcement of their betrothal passed in a constant whirl. Visits were crammed between engagements of every conceivable sort—balls, parties, routs, drums. The obligatory appearance at Almack's was accomplished; she was greatly disappointed by the bare rooms and the refreshments she had no hesitation in stigmatising as meagre. Also wedged between *ton*-ish dissipations was a reunion with Amelia; her cousin agreed to act as matron of honour and was duly introduced to Lafarge to be fitted for her gown. Lenore had two fittings of her wedding-gown and the severely cut maroon velvet carriage dress she would wear on her departure from the wedding breakfast, all squeezed into her last hectic week. The only periods of calm in her disordered world were those she spent with Eversleigh.

She had initially been surprised to find him assiduous in his attendance upon her, dutifully escorting his aunt and herself to every evening engagement, frequently taking her driving in the Park, arranging an evening at the theatre to see Keane, always by her side whenever the occasion permitted. He also organised outings which took her out of the bustle of the *ton*, for which she was more grateful than she felt it wise to reveal. They drove in Richmond Park and visited numerous beauty spots. He took her for a tour around London in his curricle, pointing out the sights the guide-books acclaimed, walking with her in St Paul's and along the leafy avenues by the river.

When, however, unnerved by her response to his continuing thoughtfulness, to the sense of protection she felt when he was by her side, she had hesitantly commented to Agatha on the unexpectedness of his constancy, her mentor had dismissed the point with an airy wave. "Hardly surprising. Never a fool, Jason."

The cryptic comment did nothing to ease Lenore's inner wariness; as the days passed, it grew, along with a suspicion that her fears of marriage were well on the way to being realised.

And then, before she had time to come to grips with her affliction, her wedding eve was upon her.

IT WAS PRECISELY three weeks after Lady Attlebridge's ball. In the dim light of a crescent moon, Jason strolled the balcony of the Bishop of Salisbury's palace, looking back over the days of his betrothal, very thankful they were about to end. He would be glad to leave behind the unexpected uncertainty which had prompted him to keep Lenore close, spending as much time with her as propriety allowed. The endeavour had stretched his talents to the full. He had even sent Moggs out for a guide-book.

His admiration for his betrothed had increased dramatically. He was reasonably sure she did not enjoy life in London—she had been right in predicting her dislike. Her transparent enjoyment of the days they had spent out of the capital or in pursuits outside the *ton* had contrasted with her considered appreciation of their evenings' entertainments. However, not even his sharp eyes had detected the slightest crack in the smoothly serene façade she showed to the world. Her performance had been faultless. The subtle change when, alone with him, she laid aside her social mask, was one he had learned to savour.

Smiling, Jason looked up at the stars, diamonds scattered in the black velvet sky. He owed Agatha a debt, not least for refraining from comment on his unfashionable predilection for his fiancée's company. Needless to say, Frederick thought he had run daft.

The end of the balcony rose out of the dark. Jason leaned

on the railing and breathed deeply. Away to the left, beyond
the glow of the town's street-lamps, he could see the pinpricks
of light that marked Ashby Lodge, the home of his cousin
Cyril. The Lester Hall household had been quartered here; Lenore had returned to spend the last night before her wedding
under the same roof as her father.

Tomorrow, they would wed amid the pomp and ceremony
traditional in his family. The town was crammed with members
of the *ton* who, as Agatha had predicted, had returned from all
corners of the land to attend. The wedding breakfast would be
held here, under Henry's auspices, after which he and Lenore
would depart for the Abbey.

Straightening, his lips curving, Jason considered the future,
conscious of nothing more than keen anticipation. No sense of
mourning for his hedonistic freedom, no last-minute hesita-
tions. Casting one last look across the treetops to where his
betrothed was no doubt sound asleep in a high-necked, long-
sleeved nightgown, quite unlike the one she would wear tomorrow night, he grinned and turned back towards the house.

He was well satisfied with the way things had fallen out. Not
just as he had hoped but rather more than he had expected.

REPLETE, lulled into a pleasant daze by the steady rocking of
the coach, Lenore reviewed her wedding with sleepy content.
The event had been remarkable if for no other reason than that
she had had no hand in organising it. Her opinions, certainly,
had been solicited—by Agatha, by Jack and even by Eversleigh, the latter with a pointed care which had set her lips
twitching. Agatha and the reliable Compton, a neat, very serious man of middle age who hid his capabilities behind gold-
rimmed glasses, had borne the brunt of the task; from beginning to end, all she had to do was follow instructions—a novel
and oddly agreeable experience. She had been free to enjoy her
wedding, to savour to the full the fluttering nerves that had
assailed her as she had walked down the aisle, her hand on
Jack's sleeve. Muted whispers over her gown had rippled
through the congregation, bringing a thin frown to the Bishop's

face. She had hardly noticed, her attention commanded by her husband-to-be, standing tall and straight before the steps. Frederick Marshall had stood beside him, a happy coincidence given Amelia's role. When Jack gave her hand into Eversleigh's care, her fingers had shaken; his hand had closed firmly over hers, stilling the movement, steadying her nerves. From that moment on, all had flowed smoothly.

Happily content, Lenore yawned. The only action she had been responsible for that day was the careful aim she had taken when she had paused on the steps of the carriage, surrounded by wellwishers, and thrown her bouquet. If she had not caught it, the large posy of rosebuds and hothouse blooms would have hit Amelia in the face. The memory of Amelia blushing delightfully with Frederick Marshall by her side, his dark head bent as he congratulated her, brought a satisfied smile to Lenore's face.

As the carriage rolled on, the regular beat of the hooves of the four chestnuts drawing it caught her attention. Both horses and carriage were a wedding gift from her husband. She slanted a glance at him, seated beside her on the pale green leather, his long legs stretched out, his hands folded over his waist, his chin sunk in his cravat, his eyes shut. Lenore grinned. Allowing her gaze to roam the carriage, noting the bright brass fittings and velvet cushions and hangings, she recalled the looks of envy it had elicited from the belles of the *ton*. Few could boast husbands who thought of such extravagant gifts; diamonds were easy, individualised carriages and horses required rather more thought. Casting an affectionate glance at her sleeping spouse, Lenore smiled.

Turning her gaze once more to the scenery, flashing past, she wondered how long it would be before they reached the Abbey. Already the sun was starting to slip from its zenith.

"You should try to get some sleep." Jason, far from sleep himself, opened his eyes. "We're still hours from the Abbey."

"Oh?" Lenore swung to face him. "Will it be dark when we get there?"

"Close. But I told Horton to stop at the top of the drive—

from there, you can see the house clearly. There should be light enough to view it.''

Lenore mouthed an, "Oh," noting that her husband's eyes were once more shut. His words focused her mind on the evening, a subject she had thus far avoided. She considered the likely schedule, too nervous to ask for confirmation. She would have to meet the servants, and have a quick look about the main rooms before supervising her unpacking. After that would come dinner. Determined not to let her imagination undermine her confidence, Lenore firmly stopped her thoughts at that point. Eversleigh—Jason—was probably right. A nap would not go amiss. Settling into her corner, warm in her sleek velvet carriage dress, she closed her eyes. Gradually, the excitement of the day fell away. Lulled by the gentle swaying of the carriage, she slept.

She half awoke when a particularly deep rut sent her sliding into Jason. His arms closed about her, stopping her fall. Instead of releasing her, he shifted her, pulling her into a more comfortable position against him, her head on his shoulder. Sleep-fogged, Lenore saw no reason to protest. His body provided a firm cushion against which she could rest, his arms about her ensured her safety. Lenore drifted back into slumber, entirely content in her husband's arms.

Jason was far less satisfied with her position, wondering what form of temporary insanity had prompted him to draw her so close. But he could not bring himself to push her away. She shifted in her sleep, snuggling her cheek into his shoulder, one small hand slipping beneath his coat to rest against the fine linen covering his chest. Jason closed his eyes, willing away his reaction. After a long moment, he squinted down at her, shaking his head in resignation. Then, settling his chin on her coiled braids, he closed his eyes and, fully awake, indulged his dreams.

He shook her gently awake as the carriage rocked to a halt just beyond the main gates of his principal estate. "The light's fading but I think we're in time."

Blinking, Lenore followed as he descended from the carriage, turning to hand her down. Directly before them, the sun was dying in a cloud of bright purple and rose, sinking behind the opposite rim of the valley. Below, gentle slopes surrounded enormous gardens, laid out about a massive pile of stone—Eversleigh Abbey. Stepping to the lip of the bank, Lenore recalled her husband had described his home as Gothic. Towering turrets stood at the four points of the main building, smaller ones marked the ends of the wings. A dome rose from somewhere behind the main entrance, itself an arched and heavily ornamented structure. The broad sweep of the façde faced the drive, the wings at right angles to the main building, enclosed more gardens. Cast in grey stone, Eversleigh Abbey dominated its landscape yet seemed curiously a part of it, as if the stone had grown roots. Her home, Lenore thought, and felt a shivery surge of excitement grip her.

"There used to be a fourth side to the courtyard, of course," Jason said from beside her. "There are cloisters around the inner side of the east and west wings."

"From when it was a monastery?"

He nodded.

"Where is the library housed?"

Jason raised his brows.

Ignoring his supercilious expression, Lenore pointedly lifted one brow and waited.

With a reluctant smile, Jason capitulated. "The main building, west corner." He pointed to two huge arched windows set into the façde. "There are more windows on the west."

As they watched, lights started to appear in the house. Two large lamps were carried out and set in brackets to light the front steps.

"Come. They'll be waiting. We should go down."

Jason took her arm and Lenore turned, consumed by an almost childish eagerness to see her new home.

By the time the carriage pulled up on the broad sweep of gravel before the front steps, twilight had taken hold. Handed down from the carriage, Lenore looked up at the massive oak doors and the soaring stone arch above them. She peered about, trying to discern the features of the gardens before the house.

"They won't disappear during the night," Jason commented drily.

Accepting that truth, Lenore allowed him to lead her up the steps. Long before they had reached them, the doors were swung wide. The hall within was ablaze with light. A chandelier depending from the huge central beams threw light into every corner. Tiled in grey and white, the large rectangular room was filled with a small crowd of people. The butler, at the head of the assembled company, bowed majestically.

"Welcome, Your Grace." Then he bowed again. "Your Grace."

For a moment, Lenore wondered why he had repeated himself. Then she realised and blushed. Jason, an understanding smile on his face, led her forward.

"Allow me to present you to your staff, my dear. This is Morgan, who has been with us forever. His father was butler before him. And this is Mrs. Potts."

Lenore smiled and nodded, acknowledging the greetings of each servant as Morgan and the reassuringly cheerful Mrs Potts conducted her down the line. Behind her, she heard Jason issuing quiet orders to his valet, the one named Moggs. He had been with Jason at Salisbury but had come down ahead of them with Trencher and the luggage. The introductions seemed interminable; Lenore juggled names and occupations, resolving to ask for a list at the earliest opportunity. At the end of the line, Jason took her hand, dismissing the gathering with a nod.

Glancing down at her, his expression resigned, he lifted an enquiring brow. "I suppose I had better show you the library before you set out to discover it yourself and get lost."

Lenore smiled sweetly, gracefully taking his proffered arm as he turned towards an archway. By the time they reached the library door, she was grateful for his forethought. Many of the main rooms were interconnecting; the way far from direct. If left to herself, she would certainly have got lost.

The library was enormous; the small fire burning in the

hearth did nothing to dispel its cavernous shadows. Jason strolled forward and lit a branch of candles. Then he took her hand and led her on a circuit of the room, holding the candlestick high to light their way.

"There must be thousands and thousands of books here." Lenore's hushed whisper drifted into the stillness.

"Very likely," Jason replied. "I've no idea of the number—I thought I'd leave that to you."

"Are they in any order?"

"Only vaguely. My father always seemed to simply know where things were, rather than work to any plan."

Forming her own plans to bring order to what appeared one step away from chaos, Lenore let her eyes roam upwards, to where rows of books seemed to disappear into shadows. Staring up, she realised the ceiling was a very long way away and the wall did not seem to meet it. "Is there a gallery up there?"

Jason glanced upwards. "Yes. It goes all the way around." He turned her about and pointed to where a set of wooden stars led up. "Those lead to it."

Turning about, eyes wide, Lenore realised the gallery ran along above the windows, too. It would be a perfect place to have her desk.

Viewing the total absorption that had laid hold of his wife, Jason, his fingers locked about hers, recrossed the long room. Placing the candlestick down on the table by the fireplace, he snuffed the three candles with the silver snuffer that lay beside the tinderbox.

Only as the light died did Lenore return her attention to him. With a satisfied smile, Jason turned for the door. "You can see the rest of the house tomorrow." He opened the door and ushered her into the corridor. "I've given orders for you to be served supper in your room. Your maid should be waiting upstairs."

"Yes, of course." Quelling her skittering pulse, Lenore glided beside him, a host of impetuous and far too revealing questions hovering on her lips. She was perfectly certain he would have made plans for the evening—she was not at all certain if knowing them would help her.

At the top of the grand staircase, Jason turned her to her right. "Your apartments are along here." He stopped at a polished oak door and opened it, standing back for her to precede him. Lenore went through, into her bedroom.

It was all in greens and golds, soft colours blending and contrasting with the ivory wallpaper. The furniture was of polished oak, gleaming in the light from the candles scattered in candelabra and sconces throughout the room. All the knobs she could see were brass, including those at the corners of the huge tester bed. Drapes of pale green gauze depended in scallops from the frame above the bed; the counterpane was of silk in the identical shade of green. Velvet of a darker green curtained the windows while the stools and chairs were upholstered in amber velvet.

Slowly, Lenore turned, eyes round as she drank in the subtle elegance, her lips parting in wordless approval. Her gaze met her husband's. Jason lifted his brows in mute question.

"It's *lovely*!"

Pleased, more by the delight in her eyes than by her words, Jason smiled. Placing an iron shackle over his inclinations, he shut the corridor door behind him and strolled to a door on the left. "I'll leave you to get settled. The bell-pull's by the mantelpiece." He paused, his hand on the doorknob, his gaze, beyond his control, roving over her. "Until later, Lenore."

With a nod, he went through the door, shutting it firmly behind him.

Slightly breathless, Lenore eyed the door. Presumably, it led to his chamber. She swallowed, her mouth suddenly dry. At least she would not have to endure a formal dinner, facing him over the length of a long polished board with doting servants hovering on their every word. But would that have put off his unnerving "later" for longer?

With a determined wriggle of her shoulders, Lenore shook

aside her silly trepidations. She was hardly a missish deb, fresh from the schoolroom.

Crossing to the mantelpiece, she examined the delicately embroidered bell-pull. Then, with a determined tug, she rang for Trencher.

CHAPTER NINE

"YOU'D BEST COME OUT now, miss—I mean, Y'r Grace, or you'll go all crinkly."

Lazily, Lenore opened her eyes, squinting through the steam still rising off her bathwater. "In a moment." Closing her eyes, she tried to recapture her dozy, carefree mood but Trencher's words had been well chosen. With a resigned sigh, Lenore sat up.

Trencher hurried to tip the extra bucket, left to keep warm by the fire, over her as she stood, water coursing down her ivory limbs. Rinsed, she stepped from the large tub. Once she was dry, Lenore shrugged on the soft silk robe Trencher held out and headed through the door to her bedchamber. Trencher went to the bell-pull, summoning the menservants to empty the bath, then hurried through after her, shutting the connecting door firmly.

Relaxed, Lenore sat before her dressing-table to brush free the long strands of her hair, washed and towelled dry earlier. As she worked through the tangles, she watched Trencher, reflected in the mirror, laying out an ivory silk nightgown and peignoir on the bed. *Ivory* silk? Lenore turned. "Not that one, Trencher."

Trencher cast her an anxious glance. "But Y'r Grace, *His* Grace asked that you wear it tonight."

With an exasperated grimace, Lenore ceased her brushing. What now? Rebel and cause an embarrassing and potentially difficult scene? Or capitulate—just this once? The thought of trying to explain to Eversleigh why she had chosen not to humour him decided the matter.

"Very well." Lenore resumed her brushing, relegating her choice of nightwear to the realms of the unimportant.

Relieved, Trencher hurried to help her with her hair. When the tresses were gleaming like polished gold, sleek and silky on her shoulders, Lenore stood and allowed Trencher to help her into the nightgown. With a distinctly jaundiced eye, she viewed the result in her glass. In Roman fashion, the gown featured a deeply plunging neckline, the two sides of the bodice meeting at the point below her breasts where the raised waistline was gathered in by a silken tie. Sleeveless, with its skirts falling to the floor, the nightgown was otherwise unremarkable. Until she moved. Then, the side slits, from high on her thighs all the way to the floor, became apparent. Studying the effect, Lenore shook her head.

Silently, she held out her hand for the peignoir. Of the flimsiest silk gauze, it hid nothing; rather, seen through its shimmering veil, her long bare limbs took on an even more alluring quality.

Catching sight of Trencher's awed face in the mirror, Lenore reflected that, at least for her maid, the evening was living up to expectations. "Leave me now." As an afterthought, she added, as nonchalantly as she could, "I'll ring for you when I need you in the morning."

Watching the door shut behind Trencher, Lenore shook her shoulders to dispel the panic hovering, waiting to pounce, if only she would let it into her mind.

Dinner, a deliciously delicate meal, had been served to her in the adjoining sitting-room; all that remained now was to wait. Trying not to think, she dispensed with the peignoir and climbed into bed, feeling the soft mattress settle under her, the silk sheets whispering against her skin. A long shiver shook her from her shoulders to her heels. After considering the possibilities, she plumped up the pillows and settled against them, a wary eye on the door to her husband's room. In an effort to distract her mind, she dutifully studied all the pieces of furniture she could see from her perch, mentally cataloguing them, then went about the room again, doing the same with the ornaments. Finally, her eyes fastening on the clock on the mantelpiece, she realised she had no idea when ''later'' was.

And if she sat here for much longer, wondering, she would be a nervous wreck by the time her husband came in. With a disgusted grimace for her inner quaking, Lenore reached for the book on her bedside table.

There was nothing there.

Frustrated, she glanced about. Other items from the trunk which should have carried her current reading had also yet to appear. With a groan, Lenore fell back on her pillows. Condemned to wait in steadily growing nervousness for her husband.

Abruptly, she sat up. An instant later, she was out of bed, grimacing as she hauled on her totally inadequate peignoir. Looking around, she spotted the high-heeled slippers that went with the outfit, placed side by side just under the bed. Lenore looked hard at the heels, then left them where they were.

Easing open her door, she strained her ears but heard nothing. Fervently hoping all the servants were safely behind the green baize door, she tiptoed down the corridor and slowly descended the stairs. Feeling very like a wraith in her filmy garments, Lenore slipped along the corridors and through the unlighted rooms, heading unerringly for the library. Gaining the large room, she closed the door carefully behind her.

The fire had gone out but the curtains had not been drawn, allowing the moonlight to spill in through the large square-paned windows. It was no great feat to kindle a match and light the branch of candles left on the table by the fireplace. Feeling her tension ebb as she looked about her, Lenore started towards the nearest bookcase.

She had only meant to spend a moment selecting a suitable volume, but, as the wavering light of the candle revealed find after exciting find, Lenore ignored her freezing feet and the chill that had started to penetrate her thin gown. The thrill of discovery lured her from shelf to shelf. She was leaving one bookcase to pass to the next, when she walked straight into a large body.

Lenore screamed and recoiled, raising the candlestick high.

Simultaneously, Jason reached for the candlestick. As he took it from her slack grasp, hot wax fell on his hand. Swallowing a yelp, he swore beneath his breath. Glaring at his wife, he transferred the candles to his other hand but before he could tend to the wax, cooling rapidly, Lenore had caught his hand between hers and was brushing the wax away.

"What a silly thing to do!" She examined the small burn, then licked her finger and applied it to the spot. "I wouldn't have burnt the books."

"It wasn't the books I was worried about."

Jason's tone jerked Lenore back to reality with a stomach-seizing thump. "Oh." Carefully, she glanced up through her lashes. Her husband's handsome face bore an expression of unflinching determination. Which was far from reassuring, especially when coupled with the silver gleam in his eyes.

Assuming that realisation of her shortcomings had tied her tongue, Jason hauled back on the reins of his temper. "Would you mind explaining, madam wife, just what you're about?"

"I was looking for a book," Lenore replied warily.

"Why?"

"Well…I usually read before I go to sleep. Trencher has yet to unpack my books so I thought I might borrow one from here." As she tendered her perfectly reasonable explanation, Lenore noticed her husband was fully dressed, a handkerchief knotted about this throat as if he was going riding. Perhaps later was a great deal later. "But don't let me disturb you," she said, a touch of haughtiness creeping into her tone as she wrestled with unexpected disappointment. "I'm sure I can find my way back to my room."

Jason shut his eyes. After a long moment, he opened them, fixed his errant wife with a steely stare and enunciated slowly, "First, as of today, all these books are yours—you don't need to 'borrow' them. Second, you won't need any bedtime reading—not for the foreseeable future. Third, you have *already* disturbed me—*greatly*! And as for my letting you find your way back to your room alone—when pigs fly, my dear."

Stunned, Lenore stared at him.

Reaching out, Jason wrapped his fingers about her wrist. Without more ado he headed for the door, dragging her along behind him. He had entered her room to find her gone. Vanished. Without trace. In the worst panic of his life, he had thrown on his clothes and rushed downstairs, straight out of the morning-room windows heading for the stables, convinced for some reason that she had bolted. In the heat of the moment, he had wondered if insisting she wear that outrageous night-gown had been one arrogant step too many. But, traversing the terrace that ran along the front of the house, he had passed the library windows. And seen the wavering candlelight flitting from bookshelf to bookshelf.

Pausing to thump the candlestick down on a table and snuff the candles with licked fingers, Jason realised he could hear the ring of his boot-heels on the flags but no sound at all from Lenore. Puzzled, he glanced down at her feet. ''Where the devil are your slippers?''

His irritated tone penetrated Lenore's shocked daze. Her chin rose. ''I did not wish to attract the attention of the servants, my lord.''

''Jason. And why the hell not? They're *your* servants.''

Lenore abandoned her attitude of superiority to glare at him. ''I would not feel *the least* comfortable being sighted by the staff in my present state of dress.''

Jason glared back. ''Your present dress was not designed to be worn in a library.'' Her comment, however, focused his attention on what he had been trying not to notice—how very alluring his wife looked in diaphanous silk backlit by moonlight.

''Jason!'' Lenore squealed as she felt herself hoisted into his arms. ''My lord!'' she hissed, as he strode purposefully towards the door. He paid no attention. ''For God's sake, Jason, put me down. What if the servants see us?''

''What if they do? I married you this morning, if you recall.''

He kicked the half-open door wide and strode through. Lenore clung to him, her arms about his neck. It was distinctly unnerving to be carried along so effortlessly.

As Jason passed the front door, he sent a silent prayer of thanks heavenwards. If he had not sighted the candleflame in the library, he would have roused the whole household to look for his wandering bride. The commiserating looks from his footmen would have driven him insane.

She was driving him insane.

Sensing that she had teased his temper to a degree where conciliation might prove wise, Lenore remained silent as she was carried up the stairs. But at the top, Jason turned to the left.

"My lord—er—Jason. My room—it's the other way." Assuming he had simply forgotten, she pointed out this fact without undue fuss.

"I know."

Panic clutched her stomach. "Where are you taking me?" With bated breath, she awaited his answer.

Jason stopped and juggled her to open a door. "I rather thought I'd have you in my bed tonight."

His conversational tone did not convince Lenore that his phrasing was anything other than intentional. But it was too late for panic. The door of his room clicked shut behind them.

And before her loomed the largest four-poster bed she had ever seen.

Jason strode across the thick carpet and, standing her briefly on her feet by the bed, divested her of her peignoir before depositing her on the silken coverlet.

Lenore made no sound—her throat had seized. She watched as Jason stalked to the other side of the bed, whipping off his neckerchief and flinging it aside. As he sat down on the bed to pull off his boots, curiosity got the better of trepidation. "Aren't you going out?"

His second boot hit the floor. Jason turned and stared at her for a moment, then stood and pulled his shirt from his breeches. "I'm not dressed like this for visiting the neighbours. These are my wife-hunting clothes."

The truth dawned on Lenore. She choked, panic and embarrassment laying siege to her tongue. She watched as he peeled off his shirt, dropping it on the floor. Her eyes stretched wide; her heart started to thud. When his hands fell to his waistband, she decided she had seen enough.

Hearing rustling, Jason glanced up to discover his twenty-four-year-old bride had disappeared beneath the bedclothes. "For God's sake, Lenore! You've got three brothers."

"You are not my brother," came distinctly from the lump in the bed.

Jason's sense of humour, sternly suppressed for the past ten minutes, very nearly got the better of him. Quickly, he finished undressing and slid into the bed beside her. She was wrapped in the coverlet, facing the other way. Propped on one elbow behind her, he considered his options.

Frozen, Lenore wondered, with what little mind was left to her, what he would do.

He pinched her bottom.

"Ow!" Incensed, she rounded on him.

And found herself in his arms. Panic flared, only to be submerged by an even more frightening anticipation as he drew her closer. Lenore strove to distract them both. "That hurt!" She tried to glare but, finding his eyes coming closer and closer, she had difficulty focusing.

"Perhaps I should soothe it with a kiss?" Jason murmured, his lips curving as they gently touched hers.

Lenore froze, her wide-eyed stare telling him more clearly than words how scandalous she found his suggestion.

Jason raised a brow. "No?" He sighed dramatically, then bent to feather another kiss across her lips. "Perhaps later."

Later? Regardless of his prowess, Lenore did not think so. She tried to shake her head to deny it all—her feelings, his words, the excitement she could feel rising inside her—but one of his hands framed her jaw. He surged up, leaning over her. Then his lips settled firmly on hers.

Lenore's lids fluttered shut, all thought suspended.

She had not known quite what to expect—more of the magic

she had felt in the Lester Hall library, certainly—but was there anything that could surpass that for sheer delight?

In the long moments of her wedding-night, she learned that, indeed, there was.

To Jason, those same long moments were the culmination of an unusually long courtship—he had never waited for a woman so long. Nor, to his secret amazement, had he ever wanted a woman so much. Introducing his wife to the pleasures of the flesh was a prize he had promised himself, a prize he had actively sought, a prize he had every intention of savouring. To the full. He did not rush her, seeking instead her active participation at every stage along the course he had charted— the longest route he could find to fulfilment. When he slipped her nightgown from her, dropping it over the side of the bed, he was conscious of a sense of wonder, of awe, that all he saw was now his—not conquered but given—a prize beyond price.

She moved sensuously on the sheets, as if savouring the feel of the silk against her smooth skin. He reached his hands into her hair, spreading his fingers and drawing them free, letting the long tresses fall like spun gold across the pillows.

From under heavy lids, Lenore studied his face, recognising the desire and need etched in his shimmering eyes. The realisation fed the flame that burned steadily inside her. She arched lightly, pressing her breast to his wandering hand. He smiled and bent his head. Pleasure streaked through her, leaving her gasping. She heard him chuckle. Lacing her fingers into his hair, she tugged gently, until he looked up, then drew his lips to hers.

He taught her the ways of kissing, how to meet him halfway. He taught her to feel no shame in her wild response to his most explicit caress. His hands were like a conjuror's, roaming her fevered skin, seeking out each secret spot and stroking it to life. His kisses reassured and excited, beckoning her forever onwards, down the path of her desire. She clung to him, seduced by the feel of hard muscle shifting beneath her small hands. And when, after what seemed like an eternity of travelling through a landscape of pleasure, he joined with her to climb the last passionate heights, she learned what it was to soar freer than air, to blaze brighter than the sun before, consumed in the starburst of heightened pleasure, she became selfless, only aware of his heartbeat and hers, mingled, the essence of life.

Slowly, like a vessel refilling, her overloaded senses returned. Sated, sleepy, she returned his soft kisses, barely aware of his murmured praises. When he drew her against him, Lenore smiled to herself, an unconscious self-satisfied smile, then settled, fulfilled and content, by his side.

A CREAK WOKE Lenore. Puzzled, she blinked and tried to sit up, only to find a heavy weight across her waist. Struggling around, she gasped as her eyes met her husband's sleepy gray gaze—and she remembered, simultaneously, where she was, who she was with, how she came to be there and what had happened. A strangled sound, half surprise, half embarrassment, escaped her.

"Hush!"

One large hand came to cradle her head, gently pressing her back to the pillows.

"Moggs—get out."

For an instant, stunned silence greeted this order. Then Lenore heard the bedroom door click quietly shut.

Jason caught his wife's gaze, and tried to keep his lips straight as he explained. "You'll have to excuse Moggs. Doubtless he thought I was alone."

"Oh." That was all Lenore could manage. She did not have her nightgown on. And he did not have a nightshirt on either.

The effect of her discovery was written in her large eyes, palest peridot, bright and clear. Jason read the message, his lips curved in anticipation.

Some vague idea that this was now how things should be—that she should, by rights, have been in her own bed and he in his by dawn—drifted into Lenore's mind. And then out, as his lips claimed hers and the memory of the night's shared pleasures drew her into the sweet vortex again.

It was hours before she rang for Trencher.

THE WEEKS that followed were an idyllic time for Lenore, a period lifted from her deepest dreams—those she had never acknowledged. Her days were filled with laughter and happy enterprise as Jason introduced her to his home. He was never far from her side as the summer days followed each other, sunshine and fair weather mirroring their interaction. The nights brought pleasures of a different sort, an enthralling web of sensation that wrapped them together with its silken strands. And through it all, like a swelling tide, ran a deepening, burgeoning realisation of what she had sensed was possible, what she had feared. But, in that halcyon time, it seemed that no dark cloud could intrude.

AS HE SAT UP and swung his legs over the edge of his wife's bed, Jason aimed a playful smack at her bottom, naked beneath the silk sheet.

"Ow!" Lenore turned to frown direfully at him, rubbing her abused posterior. As he stood and drew on his grey silk robe, her expression turned sulky. Her lips pouted, but her eyes teased. "Didn't I please you, my lord?"

His grey eyes soft as he gazed down at her, Jason laughed. Catching her hand, he leaned over her to raise it to his lips. "You always please me, Lenore, as you very well know. Stop fishing for compliments."

Lenore's smile was dazzling.

Jason ducked his head and planted a kiss on her offended rump. When she merely giggled, he raised a brow at her. "In fact, your progress in your study of certain of the wifely virtues can only be described as remarkable."

Serenely content, Lenore turned to lie back on her pillows. "I had heard you were a very experienced teacher, Your Grace."

Jason's brows rose, his expression coolly superior, but Lenore detected the twinkle in his eyes. "I will admit that in certain disciplines I have been labelled a master. However, natural aptitude and overt enthusiasm are beyond my poor powers to call forth.'' Cinching the tie of his robe, he swept her an elegant bow. "Those talents, my dear, are entirely your own." With a rakish smile and one last lingering look, Jason strolled across the room towards his chamber. The long windows were open; a summer breeze played with the fine curtains. Outside, a bright day beckoned, yet he had to exert all his willpower to leave his wife's bed.

Turning back at the door, he watched as she stretched languorously, like a sleek cat, sated and satisfied. They had been married more than a month yet her allure had not faded. He found her daily more fascinating, more tempting, their mutual passion more fulfilling. Which was not at all what he had expected.

"You have to admit, my dear, that this marriage of convenience has, in fact, been highly convenient for us both." With a slight smile, which did not succeed in disguising the frown lurking in his eyes, Jason turned and left the room.

Lenore returned his light smile with one of her own, yet, when he had gone, her expression slowly sobered. A puzzled frown knitted her brows.

Clouds found the sun. Suddenly chilled, Lenore pulled the coverlet up around her shoulders. Had he intended his last comment as a warning that she should not let herself forget the basis of their marriage?

With a snort, she turned on her side to stare moodily at her nightdress, draped crazily over a chair where it had fallen the evening before. She was in no danger of forgetting their marriage—any part of it. She knew only too well that this was her time in paradise—that soon, this phase would end and he would leave to pursue his life as he had before. She had known how it would be from the start, when they had discussed his reason for marriage in the library at Lester Hall. Her role as he saw it was engraved in stone in her mind, but she had determined to focus on the present, to enjoy each moment as it came and lay up a store of memories, so that when the time came to bid him goodbye, she would be able to do it with dignity.

Grumpily, Lenore pushed aside the coverlet and, shrugging on her robe, rang for Trencher.

THE FIRST HINTS of gold had appeared in the green of the Home Wood on the day Jason and Lenore left its shady precincts to canter in companionable silence across the meadows to the forested ridge beyond.

Holding his grey hunter to a sedate pace, Jason slanted a protective glance at Lenore, beside him on a dainty roan mare. In the last weeks, she had ridden over much of the estate, accompanying him whenever he rode out, eager to learn all she could of the Abbey's holdings. Yet she was a far from intrepid horsewoman, recently admitting, when he had twitted her over her liking for the slowest mount in his stables, that she preferred to drive herself in a gig. His eyes opened, he had, from then on, taken the gig whenever possible. When he had tentatively suggested he buy her a phaeton and pair, she had laughed at him, breathlessly disclaiming all wish to travel faster than the pace of a single, well-paced beast. Jason's lips twitched. His wife, he had finally realised, liked to play safe. She did not take risks; she was happy as she was, content with who she was, and sought no additional thrills. She liked calmness, orderliness—a certain peace.

It had taken him weeks to realise that he had seriously disrupted her peace by uprooting her from Lester Hall. Ever after, he had sought to make it up to her, never entirely sure if he was succeeding, for there was still a side of her that remained hidden, elusive, a part of her he had yet to touch, to claim, to make his own.

The thought brought a frown to his eyes.

As they neared a hedge, Jason drew on his reins, turning his horse's head. "This way," he called and Lenore followed. He led her through a gate, then down a narrow lane, turning aside on to a bridle path cutting deep into the forest slope.

Slightly nervous, as ever, atop a horse, Lenore kept her

placid mare's nose as close as she dared to Jason's gelding's rump. Jason had explained that the lookout he wished to take her to could not be reached by a carriage. She hoped the view would be worth the journey.

As they wended their way upwards, between the boles of tall trees, the smell of damp earth and the tang of crushed greenery rose from beneath their horses hooves. And then they were in the open once more.

Lenore gasped and reined in. Before her, the Eversleigh valley lay unfurled, a patchwork of fields dotted with cottages, the Abbey planted like a grey sentinel in their midst. "How beautiful!" she breathed, her eyes feasting on the panorama.

Jason dismounted and came to lift her down. While he tethered the horses, Lenore looked her fill, then glanced about. The lookout was no more than a natural clearing on the side of the hill. A broad expanse of sun-warmed grass, protected from the winds by the trees about, provided a perfect picnic spot. A small stream bubbled and gurgled through rocks to one side, spreading to form a small pool before tumbling over the lip to disappear on its journey downhill.

It was too late in the day for a picnic, but Lenore saw no reason not to avail herself of the amenities. She sat down, then, feeling the sun strike through her riding jacket, took it off, folding it neatly before laying it down and stretching full-length, her head on the velvet pillow.

With a smile, Jason came up and stretched out beside her, propped on one elbow, a speculative light in his eyes.

Lenore saw it. She struggled up on her elbows and squinted into the distance. "Having brought me here, my lord, you may now proceed to tell me what I am looking at."

Jason laughed and obliged. For the next twenty minutes, prompted by her questions, he described the layout of his tenant farms and gave her a potted history of the families who held them.

When her questions ran out, they lapsed into silence, perfectly content, the afternoon golden about them.

Dulled by his deep satisfaction in the moment, Jason's faculties slowly turned to focus on his contentment—at how odd it was that he should feel so very much at peace, as if he had gained his life's ambition and was now content to lie here, beside his wife, and revel in life's small pleasures.

His gaze dropped to Lenore, lying prone beside him, her eyes shut, a peaceful smile gently curving her lips.

Desire shook him—desire and so much more. A wealth and breadth of feeling for which he was entirely unprepared rose up and engulfed him.

Abruptly, Jason looked away, across the valley, only to have his gaze fall on the Abbey. In the past six weeks Lenore had somehow become a part of it, synonymous in his mind with his home. She was its chatelaine, in spirit as well as fact.

Allowing his mind to lose itself in aspects of his wife he found less confounding, to let the suffocating sensation that had overcome him dissipate, he dwelt on her success in taking up the reins of his household. Not that he had expected anything less. Her confidence in that sphere stemmed from experience and all in his employ had been quick to recognise that fact. He had held aloof, but had watched avidly. His wife had a natural flair for command, for organisation—the entire staff had fallen under her spell, Moggs included. He would not, in future, need to concern himself with matters within her jurisdiction.

Which meant that there was no real reason he could not return to town. September was here, the *ton* would be filtering back to the capital in preparation for the Little Season. The total apathy that filled him at the thought of the social whirl, his milieu for the past decade and more, unnerved him. Why had he changed?

"Penny for your thoughts?"

Startled, Jason glanced down to find Lenore smiling up at him. He blinked, erasing all telltale expression. He shook his head. "They wouldn't interest you."

He would have recalled the words, and his brusque tone, but it was too late. A frown crossed Lenore's brow. Her eyes leached of expression.

"I apologise for having intruded, Your Grace."

Abruptly, Lenore scrambled to her feet, all pleasure in the afternoon shattered. Briskly, she set about brushing down her skirts, shaking out her jacket before shrugging into it and buttoning it up.

Languidly, endeavouring to hide his irritation, Jason rose to his feet. Damn her questions—how could he explain his thoughts when he did not understand them himself? When they might be too dangerous to put into words? They had made an arranged marriage—he had no right to expect more. And no assurance he could get more, even should he make the demand.

What already lay between them was more than he had hoped for—he had no wish to risk it.

Assuming the faintly bored air he used to deflect the curiosity of other women, he turned the matter aside with a superior, "My dear Lenore, it is not the fashion for married couples to live in each other's pockets."

Lenore bit her tongue against the temptation to reply. She went to where her mare was peacefully cropping grass and busied herself untying her reins. Inwardly berating herself for being so foolish as to let his rejoinder bother her—for it was no more than the truth and she knew it—she silently vowed that, henceforth, she would not again fall into error, would never again forget that theirs was an arranged marriage and nothing more. From now on, she would keep her distance, as he, apparently, intended to keep his.

Jason lifted her to her saddle, then swung up to his own. Turning the grey's head back down the track, he led the way down, distracted and abstracted. Through the turmoil of his thoughts one fact stood out, immutable and unchanging. He had stated, clearly and decisively, his reasons for marrying. Lenore had accepted him on that basis, agreeing to leave her sanctuary and brave what he now recognised had been a challenging world. She was succeeding on all fronts—he could ask no more of her than that.

But if he could have his heart's desire—ask and be granted all that he wished—what then?

The grey jibbed.

His expression stony, Jason brought his horse under control and gave his attention to the ride home.

IN THE DAYS that followed, Lenore made a concerted attempt to establish a daily routine that excused her from her husband's side. Telling herself it was no more than what she would need when he was no longer in residence, she organised her day so it was full to overflowing, leaving no time for rides or picnics, or for any moping. And if her household chores were insufficient to fill her time, there was always the library. She had yet to complete a list of the types of books present, let alone consider how best to arrange them.

For his part, Jason endeavoured to respect her transparent wish for her own life, her own interests. How could he not? This was undoubtedly how their lives should be lived, he with his concerns, she with hers. There was no necessity, given the relationship they shared, for any closer communication. He knew it.

Yet, deep down, he didn't like it. At first, he told himself his odd affliction would pass, that it was merely a temporary derangement of his senses, a reaction, perhaps, to taking a wife at his advanced age and so much against his inclination. But, when he found himself propped against the wall of the corridor in the west wing, gazing moodily at the library door, dismissing his present inclinations became that much harder. Fate, he finally decided, was playing games with him.

The surrounding families had not been backward in welcoming Lenore to their circle. She dutifully played hostess to the expected visits; subsequently she and Jason were invited to the parties and dinners at which their neighbours amused themselves. They had dined with the Newingtons, and were descending the long flight of stone steps before Newington Hall, their hosts waiting on the porch above to wave them on their way, when fate sent Lady Newington's fox terrier, escaping from the confines of the house, to nip at the carriage horses' legs.

Chaos ensued.

Both horses reared, then plunged, tangling the traces. The footman, who had been holding the carriage door, swore and dashed after the dog, trying to shoo it from under the frightened horses' hooves.

"Wait here!" Jason left Lenore on the bottom step and ran to the horses' heads. Horton, caught by surprise, was struggling with the reins, trying to calm his charges to no avail. Another minute and one or both of the prize chestnuts Jason had bought to pull his wife's carriage would have a leg over the traces.

Lenore watched as Jason caught the offside horse's harness just above the bit, calming and soothing the panicking beast. But Horton could still not control the wheeler; the horse reared again, dragging on the traces. Lenore heard Lord Newington puffing his way down the steps and waited no longer. She ran to the wheeler, catching its head as she had seen Jason do, crooning soothing nothings to the snorting animal.

Prodded by the footman, the dog scooted from under the carriage and made for the shrubbery.

Slowly, peace returned to the scene before Newington Hall. The horses, sensing the departure of the devil that had attacked them, calmed, still snorting and shifting restlessly but no longer in danger of doing themselves injury.

With a sigh of relief, Lenore let the huge head slip from her grasp. She glanced at her husband—and realised her relief was premature. His lips were a thin line; his grey eyes glinted steel. He was furious and only just succeeding in keeping his tongue between his teeth.

A cold vice closed about her heart. Lenore turned away as Lord Newington reached her.

"I say, Lady Eversleigh! Damned courageous and all that— but dangerous, m'dear—want to watch out for such beasts. y'know."

"Precisely my thoughts," Jason said through clenched teeth. "Perhaps, my dear, you should sit down in the carriage. We'd best be on our way."

Allowing him to hand her into the carriage, Lenore held her

tongue as Jason took his leave of Lord Newington and climbed in after her. Outside, the light had almost gone; in the shadowy carriage, she could not make out his expression.

He waited until they gained the main road before saying, "It's my fervent hope, my dear Lenore—nay, my *express wish*—that in future, when I give you a direct order, you will obey it."

Shaken by the violence of his feelings, Jason did not mute his scathing accents. He turned his head and saw that, far from appearing contrite, Lenore's head was up, her chin tilted at a far from conciliatory angle.

"If that is the case, my lord," Lenore replied, "I suggest you endeavour to instil your orders with more sense. You know per-fectly well the wheeler would have broken a fetlock, if not worse, had I not calmed him." That her husband should so repay her aid hurt more than she would have believed possible. But she was not going to let him see that she cared. "Lord Newington would never have reached him in time, and even then, I doubt his lordship would have had the strength to do the job. I did—and all ended well. I do not in the least understand why you're so piqued. Surely not simply because I disobeyed you?"

Her sarcastic tone proved too much for Jason's temper. "God grant me patience," he appealed. "Has it not occurred to you, my dear, that I might, conceivably, be concerned for your welfare? That I might, just possibly, feel responsible for your safety?"

Lenore's wide stare told him more clearly than words that such a notion had never entered her head. She was appalled by the idea. In her experience, people who felt responsible for one's safety invariably ended by trying to proscribe one's existence. The possibility that her husband harboured such feelings, in a proprietorial way, was alarming. "But why should *you*?" she continued. "We might be married but I can hardly allow that to be sufficient cause to permit you to dictate my actions in such circumstances."

"If your actions weren't so damned foolhardy, I dare say I shouldn't wish to dictate them at all!"

Lenore's temper soared to dizzying heights. Putting her nose in the air, she stated, "I fail to see, my lord, why you should so greatly exercise your sensibilities over my poor self. Given the businesslike nature of our relationship, I really don't see that you need feel *responsible* for me. If I take hurt as a result of my own actions, I do not believe that reflects on you. I consider my life my own concern."

"Until you provide me with heirs you may forget that particular consideration."

Deprived by his chilly words of any of her own, Lenore sat rigid on the carriage seat and uncharacteristically wished her life were over. She felt bereft, struck numb with despair. His tone, cold and hard and utterly uncompromising, confirmed beyond doubt how he saw their union. His only interest in her revolved about whether she could fulfil her role as his wife—giving him the heirs he sought was one part of the contract—a part she had yet to fulfil. Lenore blinked back the moisture welling in her eyes. She had wondered why he had dallied for so long instead of returning to his usual haunts in London. Now she knew. And once she had delivered on that part of her promise, his interest in her would evaporate—his statement implied as much—how much more clearly did she need to have it said?

He had married her for his reasons, there was nothing more to their marriage than that.

Her spine rigid with the effort of preserving her composure, Lenore was grateful for the enclosing dark. Hidden in its shadows, she pushed the hurt deep, reminding herself of the household, the position, the library she had gained through marrying Jason Montgomery.

The carriage was nearing the boundary of his estates before the red haze of temper lifted sufficiently for Jason to realise just what he had said. Appalled, by the fact that she could so overset his reason as well as by his apparent insensitivity, he rapidly cast about for some means to mend his fences. But what could he say?

His fury had been invoked by shock—but he could hardly confess to that. The fact she would do what she deemed right regardless of any danger to herself horrified him. How could he possibly feel confident leaving her if that was the way she might behave, even when he was there to order her otherwise? He had thought her liking for non-hazardous pursuits would have saved him any angst—obviously not so. Lenore preferred playing safe, but if that was not possible, she would do what was necessary. Unfortunately, she was clearly not prepared to take his ridiculous sensitivity into account in so doing.

Even more unfortunately, he felt prohibited from making said sensitivity plain, aware he had limited grounds for feeling so. Worse, she would doubtless see it as an imposition on her rightful freedoms. He had no wish to reward her exemplary efforts to fill the role of the Duchess of Eversleigh by placing what she would see as unwarranted constraints on her behaviour.

But he had to say something. The silence in the carriage had become darker than the night outside.

"Lenore…" For the first time in his entire career, Jason was lost for words. He could not explain what he felt—he did not know himself.

As it transpired, Lenore was not ready for explanations, her struggle not to cry consumed too much of her mind. She put a hand to her temple. "I'm afraid I have a headache. If you do not mind, I would rather we did not talk, Your Grace."

Stiffly, Jason inclined his head in acceptance of her request. Resettling his head against the squabs, he wondered why her headache should hurt him so much.

Lenore managed to hold her head high as Jason handed her down from the carriage before the Abbey. She trod up the steps, her hand on his sleeve, but when they reached the hall, she murmured, "My headache, my lord—I believe I'll retire immediately."

Jason merely bowed, apparently indifferent, and let her go.

For the first time since coming to the Abbey, Lenore slept alone.

CHAPTER TEN

How *COULD* she have overlooked it? Appalled, Lenore stared at the pages of her diary, her mind numb, her fingers trembling.

She had woken early, but had lain, listless in her bed, for hours. Finally rising and ringing for Trencher, she had dressed for the day but had shied from facing her husband over the breakfast-table. Instead, she had sat at the little escritoire by the wall near one window and opened her diary to record the events of the previous evening—depressing though they were.

No words had come. No light comments to record her swelling misery. In an effort to ease her gloom, she had flipped back through the recent pages, filled with glowing happiness and an unstated hope she now knew to be forlorn.

It was then it had struck her.

They had been married in late July. It was now mid-September. August had been a blissful month, totally unmarred by the usual occurrence. For one who had been regularly afflicted ever since she was thirteen, the conclusion was inescapable.

She was pregnant.

With child.

Very possibly bearing Jason's heir.

For one very long moment, she considered not telling him. But that was impossible. Much as she might wish to prolong the time he spent with her—surely last night had simply been his reaction to her supposed indisposition?—she doubted she could keep the news from him and still keep her self-respect. He was waiting for this to occur before he returned to London. He was only doing what his family wished in that respect; the need for an heir was obvious, even she understood that. The requirement had been the principal element in his reason for marrying.

And now she had met it.

Staring, unseeing, at the pale pages inscribed with her flowing script, Lenore called on all her inner strength. She must tell him—and then show a brave face when he took his leave of her. That would be the hardest part. For it had happened much as she had predicted: she had fallen in love with him—when, exactly, she did not know, but weeks ago, certainly. Deeply, totally, irrevocably in love.

And she had known it for weeks, but had tried not to acknowledge it, knowing this day would dawn. Now it had, and she had to carry on, do what she had to and pretend it didn't hurt.

With her usual calm Lenore closed her diary and pushed it into the desk drawer. Then she stood and smoothed down the skirt of her green muslin morning-gown before heading for the door. She had to find her husband and tell him the glad tidings—before she broke down and cried.

But Jason was not at the breakfast-table; when applied to, Morgan informed her he thought his master had gone riding.

There was nothing to do but retreat to the library and try not to think of the black cloud hanging over her.

In the end, Lenore did not set eyes on her husband until dinnertime. Arriving in the drawing-room just ahead of Morgan, he looked so severely handsome that she had to blink rapidly to clear her vision. She accepted his arm into the smaller dining parlour where they sat at either end of the table with space for six between. The presence of the servants made private conversation impossible. Jason seemed abstracted; after casting about and coming up with no subject for inconsequential chatter, Lenore followed his lead and kept silent.

But when it came time for her to leave him to his port, her confidence faltered. What if he did not join her in the drawing-room? Twisting the fingers of one hand in the other, she stood as Morgan pulled back her chair. "My lord," she began hesitantly. "There is something I must discuss with you, if you would be so good as to spare me a few minutes."

Jerked from his thoughts, Jason looked up, frowning as his sharp eyes detected her distress. "Yes, of course, my dear. I'll join you in a moment." God—had it come to this, that his wife needs must make an appointment to see him?

As the door closed behind her, Jason drained his wine and waved aside the decanter a footman proffered. "Leave me."

Alone with his thoughts, he grimaced. What the devil had happened between them? He had spent all day in a fruitless endeavour to define just what had changed—was it him or her or had they both altered in just a month? With a despondent sigh, he pushed back his chair and stood, stretching, trying to shake the tension from his shoulders.

Whatever had happened, he could not concentrate on anything other than the fact that his wife was worried about something. Useless to try to focus on his problem until he had straightened hers out.

Lenore had only just settled in her favourite chair by the hearth when Jason came through the door. She immediately sat up, clasping her hands tightly in her lap. He smiled reassuringly, coming forward to take the chair opposite, stretching out his long legs and crossing his booted ankles.

"Well, madam wife, you perceive me all ears. What has occurred to put you in such serious vein?" In an effort to lighten her mood, Jason tried for a bantering note. "Let me guess—you've discovered that many of the books in the library are fake? No? Don't tell me—you've conceived of a wish to redecorate in the romantic style and want my permission to drape the front hall in yards of pink silk?"

When his ridiculous *badinage* raised not a glimmer of response, Jason became seriously alarmed. He straightened in his chair, his expression sober. "Lenore, what is it?"

"I…" Lenore looked at him helplessly. "I'm pregnant." Despite her best intentions, she could not make the fact sound like anything other than the catastrophic occurrence she felt it was.

As it transpired, Jason did not notice, too bowled over by her news. A streak of pure elation seared through him, followed by a jumbled medley of pride, joy and truly humble thanks to a fate that had given him all this. As the first flush of reaction faded, he realised he was grinning inanely. Then his eyes sought Lenore's only to find that her head was bowed, her gaze on her interlaced fingers, twisting in her lap. "My dear, you've made me the happiest man alive."

Lenore looked up, startled by the sincerity ringing in his tone. "Oh…I mean, yes. That is…" Lenore faltered to a stop, nonplussed. She could hardly tell him it was not entirely her doing—he would laugh at her. Instead, she took a deep breath and, holding her serene mask firmly in place, forced herself to take the next step. "In the circumstances, I expect you'll be returning to London shortly, will you not?"

She had intended to keep her gaze level with his, but could not prevent it falling. Consequently she did not see the frown that passed through Jason's eyes, or the way his jaw clenched as his moment of joy was abruptly curtailed.

For a moment, Jason thought he had not heard her aright. Then his world came crashing down about his ears. She wanted him to leave. He had played his part in fulfilling the expectations of their marriage; he was free to depart. As if from a distance, he heard himself say, "Yes, I rather suppose I will."

An inane response. He did not want to leave but what else was he do do? Stay and make a fool of himself over a wife who did not want him?

He cleared his throat. "There are a few things I should attend to but I expect I'll head back in a day or so."

It was an effort to draw breath but, now the moment was upon her, Lenore found the strength to carry through her charade. Looking up, into his grey eyes, she smiled. "I was wondering, my lord, if you could get me some books from Hatchards? There are one or two studies on cataloguing I would like to consult before I make a start on the library. If you could send them down to me as soon as possible I'd be extremely grateful."

It was not her gratitude he wanted. But, if that was all she was offering, so be it. Stunned, confused, Jason studied her, his expression bleak. "I'd be happy to do so. If you'll give me your list, I'll have my secretary arrange for the matter to be attended to immediately when I reach town."

She managed to keep her mask from slipping even though the thought that her request would be handled by his secretary slipped under her guard and hurt dreadfully. Lenore inclined her head, her smile still in place. "Thank you, my lord. I'll write it down immediately, if you'll excuse me. I would not wish to have you delay for it."

Defeated, Jason stood as she rose. With a regal nod, she passed by him, gliding gracefully to the door.

Lenore paused with her hand on the knob. "Goodnight, my lord."

"Goodnight, madam wife."

His tone was cold, distant, very far from the warmth they had once shared. Stifling her sigh for what she knew she could never have, Lenore closed the door behind her.

Jason slumped back into his chair, covering his eyes with one hand, the other clenching into a fist on his knee. For a long time, he sat motionless, his mind aimlessly scanning the recent past, forming and discarding possible futures. Eventually, he sighed deeply and sat up, running his hands over his face. What to do?

Hours later, he climbed the stairs with no answer to hand. Undressing and donning his robe, he automatically headed for Lenore's room but pulled up short, eyeing the door. She was pregnant—and had all but declared she expected him to leave, his duty done. That was certainly not his inclination but unless he was prepared to stake a claim to something more—to declare his wish that their marriage should be more than the cold-blooded arrangement he had originally sought—did he have the right to demand more of her? If he went in, would she welcome him to her bed? Or simply accommodate him rather than make a scene?

With a smothered groan, Jason turned away from the door,

drifting to the window to stare out at the dark. Lenore had left him with a decision to make and make it he must. What did he really want—of marriage, of life, of Lenore?

He had thought he had known, that his habits were set, yet she had changed him, changed him so much he could not recognise himself. And no longer had any confidence that he knew where he was headed or what was best for him. After thirty-eight years of unmitigated hedonism he felt like a dithering fool, unable to shake free of his confusion and take a firm step forward. His uncertainty paralysed him, destroying his usual decisiveness, making him vacillate when his temperament called for action. The tangled web of his emotions was tearing him apart.

Perhaps he should leave. Lenore clearly did not want him, regardless of whatever he might want of her. He had wanted a bride who would fulfil his reasons for marriage—he had got what he had asked for; he could not complain.

But he could minimise the pain he now felt. There was nothing to prevent him taking her up on her offer to release him from waiting on her here in the country. In London, there would be plenty of women eager to warm his bed—there always had been and, if he knew anything of women, his marriage would only whet their appetites.

Glancing down at the shadows on the floor, Jason thought of the scene when he told her he was leaving. What would she do? Smile brightly and scurry off to get her list of books?

With a smothered curse, he shrugged off his robe and climbed into his bed. He would leave tomorrow morning. Early. Without her wretched list. She could send it on. At least, that way he would not have to endure her smiles as she waved him goodbye.

VACUOUS CHATTER engulfed Jason the instant he set foot in Lady Beauchamp's salon. After two nights in less elevated circles, he was back in the bosom of the *ton*. Wandering aimlessly through the crowd, nodding to acquaintances sighted through the crush, he wondered, not for the first time in the past three days, just what he was doing here. He had arrived at Eversleigh House to find a stack of invitations waiting on the desk in his library; this was the third night of stale air and loud voices he had endured in his search for... His expression hardening, Jason forced himself to continue with the thought, the one he had grown adept at avoiding. He was searching for relief from his fascination with his wife.

He knew no other word for it, the emotion he felt for Lenore. The poets had another, but he was not comfortable with that. Frustrated fascination seemed damning enough to have to admit to.

"Ho! Jason!"

Jason turned to see Frederick pushing through the bodies towards him. They shook hands, Frederick thumping his shoulder.

"Where've you been? Looked to see you long before this."

"The Abbey," Jason replied shortly.

"Oh." Frederick glanced more carefully at him, then looked about. "Where's Lenore?"

Having expected this question, Jason had no difficulty keeping his expression untroubled. "She remained at the Abbey."

"Oh?" Frederick looked worried. After some hesitation, he asked diffidently, "Nothing amiss, I take it?"

Jason opened his eyes wide. "She *prefers* the country, remember?"

"Well, yes, but newly-wed and all that, y'know. Thought she'd have come up with you this once."

"She didn't," Jason replied curtly, feeling his mask slip. Abruptly, he asked, "What's all this I've been hearing about Castlereagh?"

After ten minutes' intense speculation on the latest political scandal, Jason left his friend to move among the brightly clad, exotically scented matrons who had for years provided him with the opportunity for scandal of a different sort. Not that any of his affairs, conducted as they always had been with discretion, had ever been the subject of a duel, nor even much more than speculation. While casting his eye over the field, he met Agatha.

"There you are, Eversleigh. 'Bout time, too." Agatha fixed her nephew with a shrewd eye. "So you've finally managed to drag yourself away from the amenities of the Abbey, have you?"

To his chagrin, Jason flushed and could find nothing to say.

Agatha chuckled. "Where's Lenore? I haven't sighted her yet."

As his aunt glanced about, trying, from her far from sufficient height, to see about her, Jason stated bluntly, "She's not here."

"Oh?" Agatha's eyes gleamed. "Not *indisposed*, is she?"

The prospect of having his wife's condition broadcast to the *ton* stared Jason in the face. His expression hardened. "She stayed at the Abbey."

"Oh." Agatha's face showed clear evidence of her bewilderment. "But..." She frowned, then added, "Dare say you're both old enough to know your own minds, but it would really be much better if Lenore was to come to town now, to be presented as your duchess. Plenty of time later to stay in the country. Best, I would have thought, to get the part of the business she dislikes over with now. Doesn't pay to disappoint the expectations of the *ton*, y'know."

With that sage advice, and looking rather more troubled than she had before she had met him, Agatha nodded and moved on.

Jason returned her nod absent-mindedly, his brain busy with her words. Agatha had her finger firmly upon the shifting pulse of *ton* approbation; no one knew this world better than she. Although he had not previously considered her point, it did not take much thought to suspect her advice was sound. Perhaps he should convey her thoughts to Lenore?

"Eversleigh! It does my heart good to see you back among us, Your Grace."

With a slightly sceptical lift to his brows, Jason turned to bow over the hand of Lady Ormsby, a spectacular beauty whom he had long suspected of having designs on him. Only a few subtle sentences were needed to confirm that fact. Her ladyship gave him to understand that, now that he had provided himself with the additional safety of a wife, a further piece of camouflage for any illicit affair, she felt that nothing now stood in the way of their pursuing a more intimate relationship.

Nothing, Jason mused, his temper stirring at her ladyship's dismissive reference to his wife, beyond his own lack of interest. In days past, he would very likely have accepted Lady Ormsby's invitation. Now, looking into her hard blue eyes, he could not understand what had ever attracted him to her like. They had no softness, no womanly gentleness, none of the spontaneous sensuality he had found in Lenore. The idea of compromising his now much higher standards, of accepting such unattractive liaisons in lieu of his conjugal rights, appalled him. It was not possible.

Extricating himself from Lady Ormsby's clutches without causing undue offence required a not inconsiderable degree of talent. Finally quitting her ladyship's side, leaving her disappointed but not slighted, Jason ruefully reflected that this was the third night he had had need of that particular art. The undeniable conclusion from his three days of distraction was becoming increasingly hard to avoid.

He missed Lenore. During the day, he prowled about town, finding no joy in the pursuits that had filled his life for years. Yesterday, when her brief letter enclosing her list had arrived, he had pounced on it. Compton had not even seen it—*he* had gone to Hatchards and bought her books for her, adding two he thought she might like to the pile before having it wrapped and sent down to the Abbey. For the rest of the day he had wandered about, eschewing his clubs for the fresher air of the parks, his mind filled with imaginings of how his wife was filling her day.

As for his nights, they were lonely and miserable. When it came down to it, he had spent much of his life alone, but now he felt more alone than ever before, cold, as if his arms longed for her warmth.

"Eversleigh! Good God, man, look where you're going! You've trodden on my flounce."

Abruptly called to order, Jason hurriedly removed his foot from his aunt Eckington's purple flounce and nodded in greeting. "My pardon, aunt."

"So I should hope." Lady Eckington fixed her basilisk stare, known to have reduced Hussars to meekness, upon him. "Where's your wife? Haven't seen her yet but that's hardly surprising in this crush."

There was nothing like familial pressure, Jason decided, to force one to acknowledge the error of one's ways. He smiled at his aunt, knowing his imperviousness to her intimidation always annoyed her. "She remained at the Abbey for a few days more—I came up to ensure everything was as it should be at Eversleigh House. I plan to go down tomorrow and bring her back with me."

"Excellent!" Lady Eckington's ostrich feathers bobbed. "A very wise move. She'll no doubt wish to establish herself in society while the leniency extended to a newly-wed wife is still hers."

Jason stored that one up for Lenore, should she prove difficult.

"Must say," her ladyship declared, her gaze fixed on Jason's face, "I'm glad to see you taking your responsibilities seriously, Jason. A workable marriage can make all the difference, y'know. And Lenore's an exceptional choice—getting your marriage on a solid foundation would be well worth your effort."

With a nod, Lady Eckington bustled away. Jason watched her go, a smile on his lips, for once in total agreement with his father's eldest sister.

HAVING MADE his decision, for good or ill, Jason wasted no time. Leaving London the next day, he spent the night at Salisbury, arriving at the Abbey in the early afternoon. Leaving his groom to drive his curricle to the stables, he strode up the steps to where the front doors were propped wide. As he crossed the threshold, his eyes not yet adjusted to the dimmer light, his ears were assailed by a shriek.

"Damnation, Morgan! Oh! It's you, Your Grace. Begging your pardon, m'lord, but we weren't expecting you."

Blinking, Jason saw Mrs. Potts heave herself up from her knees. Glancing about, he met the accusing stares of a gaggle of maids, all on their knees scrubbing the hall tiles. Two scrambled up to mop up the pool of water he had sent across the floor when he had kicked one of their buckets.

"Her Grace decided 'twas time to have a clean-up in here," said Mrs. Potts, drying her hands on her apron as she came forward. "Quite right, too."

"I dare say," Jason replied. "Where is your mistress?"

"In the library, Y'r Grace."

Where else? "Don't disturb yourself, Mrs. Potts. I'll go to her there."

"Yes, Y'r Grace. Er... will you be staying, m'lord?"

Jason halted, frowning. "How long I remain depends on Her Grace. However, we'll both be leaving for town in a few days, at most."

Mrs. Potts beamed. "Yes, of course, Your Grace."

With a benevolent nod, Jason turned and headed for the library. The instant he stepped through the doors, he saw Lenore had made a start on her cataloguing. There were piles of books everywhere, emptied from the shelves and balanced one upon the other in stacks as high as his shoulders. Closing the door gently behind him, he glanced about but could not see her. Carefully he wended his way through the stacks, stepping softly.

Up in the gallery, Lenore was seated on a cushion on the floor, staring out of the large windows before her, a book on the medicinal properties of herbs open in her lap. She had not turned a page for nearly an hour. Despite her efforts to hold back her dismal thoughts, they persisted in trapping her whenever she allowed her mind a moment's respite from the activities she had organised. The first four days following Jason's departure had passed in a dull haze, her mind never really winning free of the aching loneliness that had gripped her on reading his brief note, stating that he had altered his plans and had left early that morning, bidding her a distant adieu until he returned. Yesterday, she had declared "Enough!" and made a determined effort to get her new life back on track. She had her position, her own household to run—it was time she commenced running it again. She had a library to catalogue—she had started in with a vengeance. She had a child, growing within her, and that was what, all too often today, had seduced her mind from the task at hand.

She had not previously given a child much thought—how would a new small person fit into her life? Would a child, their child, ease the empty ache she now felt in that part of her heart that Jason had claimed as his, had filled and now left void? Somehow, she could not quite believe that it would. But she had all that she had been promised—and her memories. She had no cause for complaint.

With a deep sigh, she looked down at the book in her lap, trying to remember why she had been studying it.

"I might have guessed."

Lenore looked up, straight into her husband's grey eyes, and only just managed to keep her joy from bursting forth. He stood a few feet away, one shoulder propped against the window-frame, horrendously handsome, his driving cloak with all its capes hanging from his broad shoulders to his calves. For a moment, her senses swayed, urging her to fly to his arms. With an effort, she shackled them, forcing herself to calm. Serenity intact, she smiled. "Good afternoon, my lord. We did not look to see you return so soon. Is anything wrong?"

Faced with a far calmer reception that he had hoped for, Jason did not return her smile. Her attitude dashed his unacknowledged hopes, making it plain that she had not missed him as he had missed her, that she was perfectly content cataloguing her damned library. "My aunts asked after you," he offered in explanation. "They believe you should come up to town and make your social début as my wife now rather than later. They were quite adamant on the matter and, having considered their arguments, I suspect they're right.''

While listening to this cool recitation of his eminently sensible reasons for returning, Lenore shut the book in her lap and placed it aside. Taking the hand he offered, she rose and brushed down her skirts. "So you wish me to go back to town with you?"

To Jason, her reluctance was obvious. Slamming a door on his emotions to protect them from further hurt, he inclined his head coolly. "I believe it'll be best for you to appear in town at least for the Little Season."

Casting a last, resigned glance at her piles of musty tomes, Lenore allowed him to tuck her hand in his arm and lead her from her sanctuary. The idea of going to town with him—to have to watch from the sidelines as he enjoyed himself in the company of other women, all more attractive to a man of his tastes than she could ever be—filled her with dread. Her feelings, only just soothed after the trauma of his leaving, would be raked raw anew. How could she face it?

She would have to face it, her inner voice noted. He was not asking for anything outrageous; in fact, he was probably doing the right thing in insisting she go to London. If Agatha and the rest of his aunts thought she should, then they were probably right. And she could never explain why she was so very reluctant to leave the secure peace of the Abbey—not to anyone.

Leading her from the library, Jason felt a perverse pleasure in dragging her from her books. Immediately he acknowledged the feeling, he was appalled. What was this fascination of his reducing him to?

As it transpired, having accepted the inevitable, Lenore had too much to do to brood on the fact. On her discovering that her husband intended to dally no longer than was necessary for her to get herself organised, her hours were filled with giving orders—for the household in her absence, to Trencher over which gowns she wanted packed. They departed after luncheon the next day.

As THE CARRIAGE rattled over the cobbles, Lenore put her head back on the squabs and sent up an urgent prayer for deliverance. She could not endure much more swaying. She had never before been so afflicted and suspected the cause was not far to seek. This was what happened to women with child, or so she had read.

The long journey had been uneventful enough. The first stage to Salisbury had not been that long; she had coped quite well, the carriage rattling along at a good pace over the uncrowded roads. They had spent the night with Jason's uncle, taking to the road after breakfast. Breakfast had been a mistake. Luckily, Jason had spent much of the day on horseback. He had decided to take his favourite hunter to town, presumably, Lenore supposed, so that in November he could travel on direct to his hunting box in Leicestershire while she returned to the Abbey. He had elected to ride, allowing Trencher to travel in the carriage with her, leaving space for the groom beside the coachman on the box. Trencher, she had discovered, was a fount of wisdom on childbearing.

"Three of m'sisters have had six of 'em, my lady. Don't you fret. This'll only last a little while. Best try to get your mind off your stomach—think of something nice."

Lenore thought of Jason, and the hours they had shared in her bed at the Abbey. Which had led to her present predicament, which in turn led her thoughts back to the nausea that threatened to overwhelm her.

By the time Jason had displaced Trencher on the outskirts of the capital, she had felt a lot better. As her husband had been unfailingly kind in a highly distant fashion, Lenore was reluctant to attract his somewhat unnerving attention; she had said nothing of her indisposition.

But the slow, rocking progress through the crowded streets of the capital had sorely tried her fortitude.

"We're here." Beside her, Jason sat up. As the carriage rocked to a final halt, he reached for the door. Alighting, he turned to hand her down. Lenore quit the coach with alacrity.

As she walked up the steps by her husband's side, she heaved a sigh of relief to have her feet on solid ground.

Jason heard her sigh but interpreted it quite differently.

Lenore had visited Eversleigh House but briefly in the weeks before their marriage, her only concern then to determine if she wished any of the chambers other than her own to be redecorated. She hadn't. The current vogue for white and gilt had never found favour with her; the solid polished oak with which Jason had filled his house, the deep greens and reds and blues of the upholstery, were much more to her taste. There had been nothing to change; Jason had claimed as his prerogative the redecoration of her rooms. It was, therefore, with a sense of expectation that she allowed him to lead her up the stairs at the conclusion of the traditional servants' welcome in the hall.

"These are your rooms." Jason set the door wide and stood back, his eyes going to her face, keen, despite the continuing hurt that ate at his confidence, to see if she liked what he had had done.

Slowly, Lenore entered, eyes drawn immediately to the bed. Of pale polished oak, it was wide but not overly high, the mattress sunk into the base. High above its centre, a gold ball hung, suspended from where she could not tell. From it depended a tent of green silk, pegged out to the four corners of the bed where four slim columns of turned wood ran upwards to support it. It was an elegant bed of unusual design, the floral carvings that marked the headboard repeated on the footboard. Silks and satins in a melding of pale greens covered the expanse. It looked remarkably comfortable.

Turning, Lenore saw that all the furniture—the large dressing-table, an escritoire, two cheval glasses and three huge wardrobes—as well as a selection of occasional tables, side-tables, chairs and stools scattered about the large room, were all in the same fine wood upholstered in greens and soft golds.

Letting out a long sigh of pure appreciation, Lenore glanced about, locating her husband by the dressing-table. Meeting his watchful gaze, she smiled, utterly unaffected, her mask put aside. "It's absolutely lovely, my lord. Just what I would have wished for."

Her words, she was pleased to note, brought a slight smile to her husband's lips. He had, she had noticed, been rather sombre of late.

"I'd hoped for your approval. And I hope you approve of these, too."

Drawing nearer, Lenore saw that his hand rested on a large, flattish velvet case.

"I had these made up for you," Jason said, lifting the lid of the case. "Using some of the stones in the older pieces of the family collection. The diamonds are in the safe downstairs—I'll show them to you later. But I thought these are probably more your style at present."

Lenore did not answer. Eyes wide, she stared at the range of necklaces, earrings, pendants, rings and brooches revealed within the case. Winking in the last of the afternoon sunlight, emeralds and topazes, pearls and peridots glimmered and shone against the black satin lining. Slowly, Lenore sank on to the stool before the dressing-table, her fingers stealing to the jewels. Her jewels. She had never had much in the way of jewellery—her mother's pearls had come to her, but the rest of the family collection was in keeping for Jack's wife.

As her fingers caressed a delicate peridot and pearl necklace, she glanced up, blinking rapidly, at her husband. She wanted to thank him, but "Oh, Jason," was all she could say, and even then her voice quavered.

Luckily, he seemed to understand, for he smiled, much more his old teasing self, and reached for the necklace.

"Here, try it on."

He fastened the catch at the nape of her neck. Lenore stood and stepped away from the table, the better to view her reflection in the mirror above it. Jason stepped back but remained behind her, watching over her shoulder as she fingered the delicate pearl drops.

Finally, drawing in a shattered breath, Lenore smiled mistily at him in the mirror. "These are truly exquisite, my lord. I don't know how to thank you."

His eyes dropped to her throat, as if studying the necklace. From behind, his fingers came, first to trace the strand as it encircled her neck, then to caress her sensitive nape. "No thanks are required, my dear. You're my wife, after all."

His words were light; not so the expression in his eyes. As his head lowered, his object clearly to place a kiss on her throat, Lenore panicked.

Turning, she blurted out the first thing that came into her head. "Regardless of that fact, my lord, these are the most wonderful gifts I've ever been given. I do thank you, most sincerely."

She could not bear to look into his eyes. The silence stretched, then was broken when he said, "I'm overjoyed that they meet with your approval, my dear."

His tone was distant again, miles away.

"I'll leave you now. No doubt you'd like to rest." Feeling as if someone had landed a direct hit to his stomach, Jason forced himself to stroll to the door. His hand on the knob, he paused. "My aunt Eckington is giving a ball tonight. If you're not too tired, I suspect it would be wise for us to attend."

"Yes, of course," Lenore agreed, desperate to make amends for her rebuff. "I'm sure I'll be perfectly recovered by then." Shyly, trying to read his expression across the slowly darkening room, she added, "I'll take great delight in wearing some of your gifts tonight, Jason."

"I'll look forward to seeing them on you," he replied, coldly formal. With a polite nod, he left the room.

Appalled, Lenore sank on to the stool before her dressing-table, one hand pressed to her lips. She knew perfectly well why she had shied away from that kiss—one kiss was all it would take for him to have her in his arms—and, once that happened, there would be only one end to their embrace. Not that she feared the outcome—oh, no. That, she longed for with all her being. But his leaving her at the Abbey had forced her to acknowledge the depth of her feelings, the totally consuming, all-encompassing love she felt for him.

And she was no longer sure she could keep it secret, certainly not if he surprised her as he had just then. She had no desire to forbid him her bed; she had thought he would come to her at night, when she could keep up her guard, endure her love in silence, protected from his too-perceptive gaze by the dark.

For it would never do to let him know she loved him—not as she did. It would embarrass her and probably him, too, although he would never let her see it. He would be kind and gentle and as caring as could be, but he would not love her.

That had never been one of his reasons for marriage.

CHAPTER ELEVEN

LATER THAT EVENING, Jason, his emotions under the severest control, propped the wall of his aunt's ballroom and watched as his duchess made her bow to polite society. His aunt Eckington's ball was the perfect venue; his senior paternal aunt commanded an awesome position in the *ton*. With Lady Eckington and her sister's support, Lenore's success was assured.

Not that his wife needed any help. She looked superb, all traces of tiredness vanished, her gleaming hair coiled about her head, her ivory shoulders bare. She had worn a pearl and emerald necklace, one he had given her, with her stunning deep green gown. The matching bracelets, worn high on her forearms, caught and diffracted the light. She looked gorgeous; he could not tear his eyes from her.

At the very hub of all attention, Lenore suffered an interminable round of introductions conducted by her hostess, ably seconded by Agatha. They ensured she met all the senior hostesses—to her considerable surprise, all these august matrons seemed only too pleased to exchange words and invitations with her. Then she realised that, as the Duchess of Eversleigh, she herself was now of their group; they were only seeking to establish social connection with the latest member of the highest echelon in the *ton*.

The realisation gave her courage to endure the smiles and nods and arch questions. The danger in admitting to her condition was obvious. Once Jason's aunts learned she was carrying the heir, for so they would see it, they would hem her about, fuss and fume over her—they would drive her mad. So she blithely turned aside all their delicately probing questions.

Her years of experience stood her in good stead; her new awareness of her station allowed her the liberty of distance, if she chose to assume it. Two hours of intense activity saw her feet firmly on the road to social success.

"Phew!" Agatha threw her a heartening glance. "You've done well, my dear. I know it's all a bit trying, especially as you don't look to be in town much. But having the position counts, when all's said and done. It would do you no good to ignore it."

Lenore acknowledged her mentor's words with a smile, inwardly wondering where Jason was. She still felt horrendously guilty over her afternoon's gaucherie. Try as she might, she had not been able to mend her fences, for he had given her no opportunity to do so. In fact, he had been so distant, she had barely found a chance to smile at him, let alone thank him as she ought for his thoughtful gifts. And if he continued as he was, she doubted she would get a chance.

Perhaps that was as well. When he came to her tonight, she would apologise and make him laugh, then thank him as he had wished her to do this afternoon.

"Lady Eversleigh, my dear. A pleasure to see you in Town."

Lenore turned to find Lord Selkirk, a friend of Harry's, by her side. She held out her hand. "Good evening, my lord. Are you here for the duration or merely until the next meeting at Newmarket?"

"Dash it, m'dear. I'm not such a tipster as all that."

"Lenore, dear. How's life with His Grace of Eversleigh?"

Absorbed with turning aside such jocular queries, before she knew it Lenore was surrounded by a small court of acquaintances, friends of her brothers and some of the young ladies she had met in the weeks before her wedding. There was no escape from their chatter. Lenore smiled serenely and bore up under the strain, determined none would be able to say that the Duchess of Eversleigh was not up to snuff.

But she was wilting. In the heat of the ballroom, with the press of bodies all about her, the air close and increasingly stale, she started to feel her senses slide and wondered, in desperation, if she could break free. The conversation about her became a droning buzz in her ears.

"There you are, my dear."

Jason's strong voice hauled her back to reality an instant before faintness took hold. Lenore looked up at him with relief in her wide eyes and a small, tight smile on her lips.

Jason understood. He had crossed the room as soon as he had realised how long she had been standing at the centre of her circle. While no gathering, no matter how large, held the slightest power to overwhelm him, he knew she felt differently. He took her hand in a comforting clasp and, with the briefest of nods to her court, led her to the dance-floor.

Lenore came back to life to find herself held in her husband's arms, slowly circling the room in a waltz. She blinked rapidly. "Th-thank you, my lord. I…didn't feel at all the thing, just then. The lack of air, I expect."

"No doubt." Jason glanced down at her. "We'll leave after this dance."

Lenore was too grateful to take umbrage at his edict.

When she found herself seated beside him in the carriage, she wondered whether now would be a propitious time to thank him for her jewels. She tried to discover some way of introducing the topic, racking her tired brain to yield some innocuous phrase. Unconsciously, she leaned her head against his shoulder. Two minutes later, she was sound asleep.

Realising as much, Jason kept silent. Deep in consideration of his latest discovery on the fascinating topic of his wife, he was thankful she was not awake to further confound him. He had quite enough to deal with with this latest revelation. Standing in his aunt's ballroom, watching his wife smile and laugh at other men's sallies, seeing her attention focused on them, however innocently, he had been racked by a powerful emotion he could only describe as jealousy. He *was* jealous—of the entire *ton*, for the women who claimed her friendship were also included in his sights.

Relaxing back against the leather, he drew a deep breath.

After a moment's hesitation he stretched a protective arm about his sleeping wife, settling her safe against his side. A strong surge of emotion rocked him, but he was getting used to the effect she had on his system and no longer felt surprise at such happenings. This, he knew, was how he wanted things between them, her alone with him, comfortable and secure.

Which was why he had no intention of boasting of her condition. A word to his aunt Eckington as they were leaving had reassured him Lenore had not mentioned the fact. That did not surprise him; his wife was intelligent enough to guess how his aunts would behave once the news was out. His reasons for keeping mum were rather more serious. From his vantage point by the wall, he had seen a number of gentlemen eye his wife speculatively. None had dared approach her; the wolves of the *ton* had a tried and true approach to succulent young matrons who appeared within their orbit—he should know; he had perfected the art. They would not approach a young wife until she was known to be bearing her husband's child. With this point established, most husbands could be relied on to become complacent, keeping to their clubs, leaving their front door unattended. Once it became known Lenore was pregnant, she would become fair game—most tempting game, if he had read the looks on his peers' faces aright. Although he had no intention of ever becoming a complacent husband, he would much rather his wife was not exposed to the lures of the *ton*'s greatest lovers.

He glanced down at her face, what he could see of it, and felt his features relax. She had done well, his duchess. She had appeared exactly as he would have wished, gracious, with just a touch of hauteur in her manner to keep the unintroduced at bay. She would do well in the *ton*—she would succeed there as she had in all the other endeavours she had taken on in marrying him.

When the carriage stopped outside their door, and she did not wake, he carried her inside, soothing her confused murmur when she woke in the light of the hall. To his surprise, she blinked up at him, then smiled and, clasping her arms more tightly about his neck, placed her cheek on his shoulder and allowed him to carry her upstairs.

As he did so, he noted that she did not feel any heavier. It seemed strange that she was carrying his child, that it was growing apace within her, yet there was nothing in her slender figure to attest to the fact. Just as well. With any luck, the Little Season would be over before their news became too obvious to hide.

She was asleep again by the time he reached her room. Trencher, hurrying along the corridor, was taken aback to find her in his arms. At his nod, she opened Lenore's bedchamber door, hanging back as he strode to the bed and gently laid his wife down.

Jason stood by the bed, drinking in the flawless symmetry of his wife's features. Slowly, he let his gaze travel down, over the gentle swell of her breasts, along the slender lines of her body and the long, smooth curves of her thighs. There was nothing he wished for more than to be able to stay here, with her, for the rest of the night. But after this afternoon, he no longer had the confidence to press his claims.

He had thought the desire that had burned between them would never die, even if it had nothing more concrete beneath to support it. After this afternoon, he was not even sure of that. Her rejection, unconsidered though it had been, had been all the more damning for that. He had surprised her and she had reacted automatically—there was no surer measure of a woman's true feelings, he knew that well. Lenore was willing to be his wife—but she had never agreed to be more than that.

He was aware of Trencher, hovering by the door. He beckoned her forward. "Try not to wake her," he whispered. "And let her sleep in the morning."

With that injunction, he headed for his room before his baser instincts could rebel and change his mind.

THE NEXT MORNING, Lenore awoke, stretched, and immediately knew she was alone. Surprised, she swung around—and wished she hadn't. Not only did the smooth pillow beside her bear testimony to the fact that she had not made her peace with her husband as intended, her head was now swimming.

"Oh, dear," she murmured weakly, putting a hand to her brow. It felt slightly clammy.

It was still clammy half an hour later, but by then, she felt slightly better, well enough to stand somewhat shakily and cross to the bell-pull.

"Oh, Y'r Grace! Looks like it's got to you good and proper."

Trencher came bustling up to where Lenore had collapsed in a chair. Chafing her hands, the maid eyed her with concern.

"Now don't you go getting up. I'll just duck downstairs and get some weak tea."

Lenore opened her eyes in alarm.

Trencher saw her horrified look and smiled reassuringly. "Take my word for it—me mam says it works every time."

Ten minutes later, fortified with sweet weak tea, Lenore did, indeed, feel more like herself. "Is that going to happen every morning?"

"For a while, at least. Some, it goes most of the way."

Closing her eyes, Lenore shuddered. Did Jason know, she wondered, what she was going to have to go through to provide him with his heir? She hoped so—in fact, if he didn't, she would make sure she told him.

No, she wouldn't. What could he do about it? She couldn't run from town the day after making her curtsy as the Duchess of Eversleigh—what would all the ladies who had invited her to tea think? If she admitted to this weakness, Jason would feel honour-bound to send her back to the country. He had been so generous—she could not contemplate letting him down. Particularly after yesterday afternoon.

Eyes still closed, Lenore heaved a weary sigh. She had yet to settle her accounts from yesterday afternoon.

Recalling the incident, she frowned. Ever since she had told him of her pregnancy, Jason had not come to her bed. She had explained his absence first on the grounds that he had clearly made the decision to leave early the next morning and had decided not to disturb her, and later, when he had returned to the Abbey but not to her bed, because they were travelling the next day. At Salisbury they had been given separate rooms, of course. But, if he had wished to exercise his conjugal rights, why had he not come to her last night, or at the very least, this morning? Clearly, he had not thought her too tired yesterday afternoon.

Rubbing her fingers across her brow, Lenore admitted to her mind a series of facts she had been staunchly ignoring for the past week. Jason had not been the least reluctant to leave her at the Abbey. He had only come to fetch her to town at the behest of his aunts. Yesterday afternoon had merely been an opportune moment. There was no evidence that he bore any deep-seated wish to maintain a close relationship with her now the business of his heir had been satisfactorily set in train. In short, his interest in her had waned.

Why had she thought otherwise?

Because she loved him and had entertained hopes beyond the possible.

Drawing a shuddering breath, Lenore forced her eyes open. "Perhaps, Trencher, I should lie down again—just for a while." Until I can face the day, she thought, as Trencher helped her to her bed.

Downstairs, in the sunny breakfast parlour, Jason studied the remnants of his substantial breakfast with a jaundiced eye. The fact that his wife had decided to adopt the habit of most fashionable women and stay in bed until noon, and thus would not be joining him, had finally sunk in.

"No, Smythe. No more coffee." Waving his butler away, Jason rose and, picking up the *Gazette*, headed for the library.

Once there, he prowled the room before settling, reluctantly, in the chair behind the desk. He frowned at the correspondence Crompton had neatly stacked by the blotter. With a frustrated sigh, Jason swung his chair about and stared out of the long windows. He could not go on like this.

He had gone down to the Abbey with high hopes, only to have them dashed. What had he expected? He had given Lenore not the slightest indication that his interest went any deeper than the conventional affection a gentleman was supposed to feel for his wife, in the ill-judged expectation that his affliction would pass. It had only grown stronger, until now it consumed his every waking hour, leaving him bad-tempered and generally confused. Leaning his elbows on the arms of the chair, he steepled his fingers and rested his chin on his thumbs. As the long-case clock in the corner ticked on, his grim expression slowly lightened. Eventually, taking his hands from his face, Jason allowed his lips to relax in a small, self-deprecatory smile.

He would have to see the Little Season out; impossible to achieve anything in town—not with every man and his dog, let alone the gossip-mongers, watching. The fact that His Grace of Eversleigh was stalking his wife would make the most sensational *on-dit*. Once they were back, alone at the Abbey, he could lay siege to her sensibilities in earnest, rekindle the embers of passion that had burned so brightly and make her want him as much as he wanted her. Until then, all he needed to do was make sure she came to no harm and that no harm, in the form of the wolves of the *ton*, came to her.

With a decisive nod, Jason turned back to his desk. After a moment's consideration he drew a sheet of paper towards him. Dipping his pen in the inkstand, he wrote a short note to Compton, instructing him to deal with affairs as he thought best until further notice as his employer had weightier matters on his mind. Leaving the note in a conspicuous spot, Jason rose and, feeling as if he was seeing daylight for the first time in weeks, strolled out.

"PASS ME that pot, Trencher."

With a sigh, Lenore held out her hand for the small pot of rouge she had sent Trencher to buy that morning. She had never used the cosmetic before but there was no denying she needed it now. Her cheeks were pallid, her eyes too large. Hesitantly, Trencher handed her the small jar. "Are you sure, Y'r Grace? You've got such lovely skin—seems a shame, somehow.''

''It'll be an even greater shame if Lady Albemarle and her guests see me like this.'' With a grimace, Lenore opened the pot and picking up a haresfoot, dipped it in. Carefully, she brushed the fine red powder across her cheekbones, trying to make the addition as inconspicuous as possible.

It was the end of her first week in London as the Duchess of Eversleigh. She had been fêted and, to her dismay, positively fawned upon by some of the more select of the *ton*'s hostesses. Being Jason's wife, she had realised, made her something of a drawcard, a fact which had left her at the centre of attention for far longer than she liked. Thus far, she had coped.

But her morning sickness was tightening its grip. Not only was she unable to rise much before noon, a fact camouflaged, luckily, by fashionable habit, but in the last two days she had started feeling nauseated in mid-afternoon. Today she had tried not eating at luncheon, taken at Lady Harrison's small town house with a gaggle of other young ladies, and had nearly shamed herself by fainting in the park. How to overcome her increasing problems without absenting herself from a full schedule of visits was a quandary she had yet to solve. But if her illness became any worse, she would have to do something.

Studying the effects of her ministrations, Lenore laid the rouge pot aside and stood. ''My gown, please.''

Trencher hurried over with a gown of silver spider gauze. Once encased in the scintillating folds, Lenore paraded before her cheval glass. It was her fervent hope that her undeniably elegant body would deflect notice from her less than healthy countenance.

Spreading the shimmering skirts wide, she wondered if Jason would be present tonight. She was due to leave shortly for Lady Albemarle's rout, taking Agatha up in her carriage. Like most husbands, Jason did not accompany her on her engagements, not unless they were invited together for a dinner or some special occasion. However, he knew which functions she attended; he might or might not look in on them. Thus far, he had been at every ball and party she had, a fact which had brought her mixed joy.

Mentally shying from the joy her husband brought her, she focused on the far more serious question of whether he would notice her rouge. His eyes were sharp—if he noticed, would he guess her reasons for using it? Deciding there was no point in trying to predict His Grace of Eversleigh's actions if he did, Lenore let her fingers trail over the delicate peridot and diamond necklace, one of Jason's gifts, that she had clasped about her neck. She could never wear any of the pieces without feeling a pang of guilt that she had not, yet, had a chance to thank him as she would wish.

Shaking aside her dismal thoughts, she waved to Trencher. "That small silver fan—and the matching reticule, I think." While Trencher rummaged for the required articles, Lenore fell to considering her social schedule. As yet, she had formed no firm friendships, although there were many who sought her out. Occasionally she ran across Amelia, but her cousin was still consumed by her pursuit of Frederick Marshall; Lenore did not feel comfortable in distracting her attention. Nevertheless, the weeks ahead were rapidly filling with engagements; she herself was hosting a tea party for a select group of ladies next Tuesday.

Every noon she would leave Eversleigh House for some *ton*-ish affair—a luncheon of one description or another. That was invariably followed by an afternoon tea, or a drive in the Park in company with ladies of her circle. At some time after five o'clock she would return home to change for dinner. She and Jason had yet to share a meal over the long table in the dining-room; they had dined, together or separately, elsewhere every day since she had arrived. The dinners would lead to balls or parties—impossible not to attend at least two every night.

She was heartily sick of it all. But she was determined to see the Little Season out, establishing the position of the Duchess of Eversleigh. She owed it to Jason and she had no intention of failing him in however small a degree.

Accepting her fan and reticule from Trencher, along with

her long silver gloves, Lenore disposed these articles appropriately, then stood for Trencher to swing her black velvet evening cloak over her shoulders.

"You look just lovely, my lady."

Bestowing a sceptical look upon her helpful maid, Lenore, head high, swept out of her room and down the stairs to do battle with her particular dragon—the *ton*.

The Albemarles' ball was indistinguishable from the others, all equal, in Lenore's opinion, in their forgettability. She danced with those gentlemen she considered suitable, thankful that the unsuitable had thus far kept their distance. In dispensing with her pinafores, she had expected rather more problems from that direction and could only be grateful if her position as Jason's wife precluded their active interest. And, as had happened for the past seven nights, her husband also attended Lady Albemarle's function. She sighted him through the throng, speaking with the very attractive Lady Hidgeworth and some other gentleman. Her ladyship had placed her hand on His Grace of Eversleigh's black sleeve.

He saw her and bowed slightly. Lenore nodded politely in return, then wished she had not when he detached himself from Lady Hidgeworth's somewhat possessive conversation and strolled, all languid elegance, across the ballroom towards her.

Surrounded by a small coterie of five ladies and three gentlemen, Lenore pretended not to notice her approaching danger. Her heart thumped uncomfortably. Would he notice her rouge?

"Well met, my dear."

At his smoothly drawled comment, Lenore had no option than to turn to him, extending her hand and praying the light of the chandeliers would not reveal her secret. "My lord, I confess I'm surprised to find you here."

Lenore hoped the comment would keep his mind on the company and not on her.

Jason smiled down at her, his mind engrossed with its habitual subject. "Are you, my dear? But how so, when there are so many attractions among Lady Albemarle's guests?"

Lenore blinked. He could not mean her, so presumably he meant Lady Hidgeworth and her like.

Straightening from his bow, Jason kept her hand in his, drawing nearer as his eyes scanned her face. She was looking peaked. And was that rouge on her cheeks? Lowering his voice, he murmured, "Are you quite well, my dear. You look rather tired."

"Do I?" Lenore opened her eyes wide. "I assure you, my lord, I'm thoroughly enjoying myself. Perhaps the wind in the Park has dried my complexion slightly? I must get Trencher to look out some Denmark lotion. Heaven forbid I develop any wrinkles!"

Wondering who it was she was impersonating with such a fatuous response, Lenore kept her expression politely impassive and waited, her breath caught in her throat, to see if she had succeeded in deflecting her husband's dangerous interest.

"Heaven forbid, indeed," Jason murmured, all softness leaching from his expression. There were times when his wife retreated behind a subtle screen beyond which he could not reach. It galled him that such a reserve could exist, that she could keep her thoughts and emotions from him if she so wished. That was something he was determined to change, just as soon as he got her back to the Abbey. "As you are so well entertained, madam, I will leave you to your friends."

With a smile which did not reach his eyes, he bowed and moved away. Turning back to her friends, Lenore felt her heart sink, as if a weight had been attached and let fall as he left.

Contrary to his intimation, Jason went only as far as the nearest wall, where a convenient palm afforded him some respite from the attention of the loose ladies of the *ton*. To his considerable annoyance, they, plural and singular, seemed of the fixed opinion that if he was in London, he was available. Their invitations would have made a whore blush. As he appeared unable to convince them of the error in their assumption, he had been forced to fall back upon a gentleman's last defence—he now ignored them, heartily wishing that they would return the compliment.

His gaze fixed broodingly on his wife's fair head, Jason reviewed the current state of play. He was not at all convinced by his wife's airy reassurance—or was his secret hope that she would soon tire of the bright lights of town and wish of her own accord to return to the Abbey colouring his assessment? If it had been any other woman, he would find no inconsistency with her professed enjoyment—she was surrounded by many, potential friends as well as the inevitable toad-eaters, all vying to excite her interest. She was a social hit on anyone's scale; if she wished, she need never have a moment's peace in her life again. None of which sat well with his knowledge of Lenore—his Lenore—the one who preferred gigs to riding and the company of musty tomes to that of the swells. She, he was quite sure, would not be enjoying herself in Lady Albemarle's ball-room.

Letting his gaze roam the long room, he automatically noted the position of the more dangerous rakes. None had yet braved his wife's circle. Most would have noted his presence at her evening entertainments and drawn the conclusion he wished them to draw.

Jason's lips twitched, then firmed into a severe line as the prospect of Lenore's having an interest in another gentleman swam across his consciousness. Reluctantly, watching her laugh at some sally, he considered the possibility. It did not seem at all likely; there were none of the subtle signs of hyperawareness he was adept at reading present in her manner—only when he hove in sight did she become skittish. Yet he had to acknowledge the unnerving fact that, if she was harbouring any illicit passion, he might not know of it, given that as yet impenetrable reserve she could deploy to conceal her innermost feelings.

As Lenore accepted the arm of gangly Lord Carstairs and allowed him to lead her to the dance floor, Jason grimaced and, straightening, moved away from his protective palm. Convention made it difficult for him to dance frequently with his wife—not when she was so sought after by others.

Lenore's movements in the evenings were easy enough to

follow, given he was prepared to brave any chance observer noting his peculiar pastime. The evenings, however, were not the time of greatest threat. Her afternoons were filled with a succession of entertainments, some for ladies only, but there were others at which the town beaux took care to appear. And where husbands, by and large, were considered *de trop*.

A problem, but not nearly so immediate as Lady Dallinghurst, bearing down on him from the right.

"Jason! I vow it's an age since I've had a chance to speak with you alone, my lord."

"In case it's escaped your notice, Althea, we're surrounded by at least three hundred other human beings."

Lady Dallinghurst made so bold as to put her hand on his sleeve. "And since when has that ever stopped you, Your Grace?"

Jason looked down, into her pretty pink and white face and felt pity for the absent Lord Dallinghurst. Althea Dallinghurst was a Dresden doll who played the game hard and fast. Lifting his brows, his expression nothing if not supercilious, Jason asked, "Dallinghurst in town?"

Lady Dallinghurst's eyes gleamed. Her hold on his arm tightened.

"No. And he won't be back for a month!" She looked up at him, clearly expecting a proposition of the most explicit nature.

"Pity. There's a horse I'd like to see him about. Tell him I'm interested when you see him next, will you, my dear."

With a polite nod, Jason moved into the crowd, leaving a very stunned lady behind him. It was, he decided, time to suggest to his wife that they leave and travel on to Lady Holborn's affair, the next on her never-ending list, before he was provoked into making a wrong move and some slighted madam, with intuition fuelled by fury, guessed just how highly unfashionable was his interest in his wife.

THE NEXT AFTERNOON brought near-disaster for Lenore. She had opted to attend Lady Hartington's luncheon, an *al fresco* affair in the extensive gardens of Hartington House. Because of the distance from town, the luncheon continued all afternoon, with the guests enjoying the amenities of the gardens. To Lenore, it was a welcome relief from the stuffy salons of the capital. All went well, until Lady Morecambe and Mrs. Athelbury, with both of whom Lenore was on good terms, became possessed of the idea of punting on the lake.

"Do come with us, Lenore. Lord Falkirk has offered to pole us about."

Seeing nothing against the venture, Lenore agreed. Together with her friends, she crossed the wide lawn to where a punt was drawn up at the water's edge. Young Lord Falkirk had already assumed his place in the stern, the long pole gripped firmly between his hands. "A quick trip to the fountain and back, ladies?"

They laughingly agreed. In the middle of the shallow lake, an island of stones was crowned by a fountain which fed a small waterfall, the whole, in reality, a disguise for the small waterwheel concealed in the rocks which caused ripples on the otherwise glassy surface of the protected lake.

Mr. Hemminghurst followed them down and gallantly assisted them to board, handing them in with a flourish. Smothering their giggles, they took their seats on the punt's narrow crossboards. There was only just room enough for all three.

"Off we go, then!" With a sturdy heave, Lord Falkirk poled off.

Almost immediately, Lenore had second thoughts. By the time they were halfway to the rocks, she could feel each rolling wave created by the waterwheel as it passed under the punt. Her stomach started to move in synchrony. As they neared the rocks, she pressed a hand to her lips. The nape of her neck was warm and growing warmer—a very bad sign.

"Isn't it delightful!" Lady Morecambe leaned out to pull the boat closer to the island, rocking the boat dreadfully.

Lenore shut her eyes tight, then quickly opened them again. "Yes, quite," she managed, before setting her teeth again. An ominous chill was spreading over the back of her shoulders.

Luckily, the other three occupants of the punt were more interested in the cunning way the waterfall had been created to hide the wheel assembly than in the odd hue she was sure her skin had assumed. Breathing deeply, Lenore told herself that they would head back now, that the rocking would get less with every yard they came closer to the shore. If she could just hold on, she would see this through, without giving her secret away. Agatha, she remembered, was in the crowd on the lawn, and Lady Attlebridge, too. Along with half the female members of the *ton*. This was the last place on earth to fall victim to her affliction.

After declaiming with what Lenore felt to be quite unnecessary long-windedness on the mechanism that drove the wheel, Lord Falkirk turned the punt around. Gradually, Lenore felt her glazed vision improve. The bank, and salvation, were only a few yards away. She blinked, then frowned, as her sight now revealed many of the other guests lining the edge of the lake, laughing and waving at them.

Naturally, Lady Morecambe and Mrs. Athelbury waved back. Perforce, Lenore had to join in, struggling to fix a smile on her lips. But with the increased movement, added to by Mrs. Athelbury leaning out of the punt to flick water at those on the shore, the punt was rocking quite hideously again.

Lenore felt the blood drain from her face. Any minute… She closed her eyes, very close to defeat.

"There we are!"

With a grand gesture, Lord Falkirk ran the punt aground.

Letting out the breath she had been holding in a shuddering sigh, Lenore waited patiently for the other two ladies to clamber out, drawing most of the gathering crowd's attention, before allowing Lord Falkirk to assist her to shore.

Once on *terra firma*, the young man looked at her in concern. "I say, are you all right, Lady Eversleigh? You look dev'lish pale."

Summoning a smile, Lenore plastered it on her lips. "Just a touch of the sun, I suspect, my lord. I think I'll sit down in the shade for a minute. If you'll excuse me?"

Leaving his lordship casting puzzled glances at the light clouds covering the sun, Lenore headed for a wooden seat placed under a willow. The drooping branches of the willow gave her a modicum of privacy in which she could risk hunting in her reticule for the smelling salts Harriet had given her years before. She had never thought to use them, but, sighting the little bottle among the trinkets on her dressing-table, she had added it to the contents of her reticule the week before. Sending a thank-you prayer Harriet's way, Lenore took a cautious sniff then leaned back and closed her eyes.

To her relief, the crowd had moved on in the opposite direction to view the sunken garden. She was left in peace under the willow, a reprieve of which she took full advantage. Only when she was sure she could stand and walk without tempting disaster did she emerge and, finding the first of the guests departing, rejoined the crowd only to say her farewells.

Returning directly home in the swaying carriage, she only just managed to gain her chamber before the inevitable overcame her.

Trencher, tipped off by Smythe, came rushing up to assist her. Finally, with wet cloths laid over her brow, Lenore lay, weak and exhausted, stretched out on her bed. It was nearly five o'clock. Soon, she would have to get up and commence the long process of dressing for the evening.

"You'll feel lots better after a bath, my lady," said Trencher, echoing Lenore's thoughts. "But rest awhile now. I'll call you when 'tis time."

Lenore did not even try to nod. Total immobility seemed the only defence against this particular illness. She drifted into a light doze but all too soon she heard the sounds of her bath being readied in the small bathing chamber next door. The splashing of the water as it poured into the tub pulled her mind back to full consciousness.

This afternoon's near catastrophe could not be repeated—not if she wished to preserve her secret. Luckily, she had devised a plan. A plan that would, she fervently hoped, achieve her twin aims of concealing her indisposition while keeping the

Duchess of Eversleigh circulating among the *haut ton*. A plan so simple, she was confident none would detect her sleight of hand.

With a deep sigh, Lenore removed the cloth from her forehead and slowly, gingerly, sat up. The room swayed gently before settling into its proper place. She grimaced. It was definitely time to put her plan into action.

CHAPTER TWELVE

WITH A PERFECTLY genuine smile on her lips, Lenore whirled down the long ballroom of Haddon House, laughing up at Lord Alvanley as that jovial peer partnered her in a vigorous country dance. It was a week since Lady Hartington's luncheon and, Lenore reflected, her plan had worked wonders.

She laughed at Lord Alvanley's opinion of Lady Mott's latest coiffure, her confidence waxing strong. She had become adept at this charade, projecting the image of blissful enjoyment expected of a new peeress. She could rattle along with the best of them, prattling on about nothing of more serious consequence than their latest bonnets or exclaiming over the monkey Lady Whatsit had got from her latest lover. A charade of the superficial, while beneath her rouge her cheeks were still pale and her mind longed for quieter surrounds and more meaningful pastimes.

But she was determined to preserve her disguise until the Little Season ended and she could retire with honour to Dorset. It was the least she could do to repay her husband's generosity.

"An excellent measure, m'dear," his lordship said as they came to a swirling stop. "Tell me, do you plan to open up that mansion of your lord's down in Dorset?"

While she waxed lyrical about the Abbey and her future plans for its use, Lenore became aware of an odd tingling at her nape, a sensation she associated with her husband's attention. Was he here? She had not seen him that day and was depressingly conscious of an urge to turn about and search the brightly dressed crowd for a glimpse of his elegant form.

Suppressing her highly unfashionable impulse, she nevertheless could not resist turning slightly, scanning the crowd while ostensibly discussing the most acceptable composition of house parties with his lordship.

From the corner of her eye she detected a movement, a black coat detaching itself from the brightly hued background. He *was* here—and was coming to speak with her. Desperately trying to dampen the excitement that swelled in her breast, Lenore realised Lord Alvanley was looking at her, an expectant expression on his good-natured face.

"Er...I do believe you're right, my lord," Lenore hazarded. She heaved an inward sigh when his lordship all but preened.

Then he glanced up. "Here—Eversleigh! I've just had a capital notion—your wife thinks it so, too."

"Oh?" Jason strolled up, favouring Lenore with a nod and an appraising stare. He shook hands with the Viscount. "Just what are you hatching, my friend?"

"Just a little party, don't y'know. A convivial gathering—just the old crew, none of these hangers-on. At the Abbey, old man! Just what your lady wife needs to set her in full trim. We were thinking of just after Christmas—what d'you think?"

One look at Lenore's face, at the way her eyes widened before she blinked, bringing her features under control, was enough to tell Jason the truth. "I think," he replied, taking possession of one of her hands before she could commence wringing it and give herself away entirely, "that you have cast a glib spell over my susceptible wife." Jason calmly switched his smile from his friend to Lenore. "However, we'll certainly consider your 'capital notion', will we not, my dear?"

"Yes, of course." Lenore felt a slight blush warm her cheeks. Glancing up, she met her husband's grey gaze, warm and reassuring, and felt her heart tremble. Abruptly, she conjured a smile and trained it upon Lord Alvanley as he bowed before her.

"Farewell, my dear Duchess," his lordship said, wagging a playful finger her way. "But a last warning. Don't let your reprobate of a husband monopolise your time—not at all the thing, not at all."

With a roguish smile, his lordship departed, merging into the crowd.

Jason quelled an impulse to grimace at his back. Monopolise his wife's time? If only he could. He glanced down; when Lenore persisted in studying his shoes, he calmly raised the hand he was still holding to his lips. She immediately looked up. As his lips caressed the back of her fingers, he felt them tremble. Her eyes, firmly trapped in his gaze, widened. "I'm glad I caught you, my dear. You've been cutting such a swathe through the ballrooms I feared I might not catch you up."

Struggling to keep her voice matter-of-fact, Lenore let her lashes hide her eyes. "Have you been looking for me, my lord?"

"After a fashion." Realising that to remain stationary with his wife was to invite interruption, Jason tucked her hand into the crook of his elbow and steered her towards the side of the room. "I wondered if you might care to ride with me in the Park one morning. My hunters need exercise. I keep a number of mounts suitable for you here in town—you don't need to fear to trust them. Given that you seem to have hit your straps with *ton*-ish entertainments, I thought you might like to savour yet another of London's pleasures."

The elation Lenore had felt on hearing he had been looking for her, and that for the express purpose of requesting her company, sagged dramatically. She could not—dared not—accept. No matter how much her heart longed to do so, her stomach would never permit it. Unconsciously, her fingers tightened on his sleeve. "I...that is..." Desperately, she sought for some acceptable white lie. She could not even get out of bed in the mornings, not at the time he rode. But she had not told him of her indisposition—after all her hard work to avoid doing so, to avoid any possibility of his feeling compelled to urge her to return to the Abbey before she had become established socially, she felt deeply reluctant to do so now. In desperation, she fell back on the fashionable excuse. "I'm afraid, my lord, that I would find it extremely difficult to meet with you at that hour."

That was the literal truth, even though she knew he would

interpret it in an altogether erroneous way. She was hardly surprised to feel his instant withdrawal, although none watching them would have seen anything amiss.

"I see—no need to say more." Jason tried very hard not to feel rejected. He forced himself to smile down at her. "You're bent on taking the *ton* by storm, my dear, making up for your years of absence with a vengeance." Entirely against his will, his smile took on a wistful air. "Don't burn the candle at both ends, Lenore. It never does work."

For one heart-stopping moment Lenore stared up into his eyes, wondering what it was she had glimpsed there.

Simultaneously, both she and Jason became aware of another, hovering before them. She turned and beheld Lord Falkirk, he of the punt, eyeing her, and her husband, uneasily. Having gained their attention, he grew even more nervous.

"The cotillion," he said, as if stating the obvious. When they both continued to stare uncomprehendingly, he blurted out, "My dance, y'know, Lady Eversleigh."

"Oh…yes, of course." With an effort, Lenore gathered her wandering wits. She turned, with the greatest reluctance, to her husband. "If you'll excuse me, my lord?"

"Of course." With consummate grace, Jason bowed over her hand. As she disappeared in the direction of the dance-floor, her hand on Lord Falkirk's arm, he had to fight an almost overwhelming urge to remove her forthwith from this ballroom, London and the *ton* and take her back to the Abbey with all speed. His inexperienced wife had certainly overcome her dislike of *ton*-ish entertainments. In fact, he would not wager a groat she had not changed her opinion entirely on such pastimes. Her enjoyment of the balls and parties seemed all too genuine.

As he settled his cuffs and looked about for the refreshment-room, Jason admitted that he did not wish that last to be so. An unnerving fear that he was losing his wife—the Lenore he had married, the Lenore he now wanted beyond all reason—had started to prey on his mind.

He was turning aside to hunt up a footman when his sleeve was twitched.

"Good evening, Your Grace. Tell me, are you finding this singularly pretentious ball as boring as I am?"

Closing his eyes, Jason prayed for patience. Where were they coming from? It was as if the bored wives of the *ton* had declared open season—on him. Smoothly turning to bow over Eugenia, Lady Hamilton's hand, he allowed his brows to rise. "Do you find this boring, Eugenia?" As if seeing the thronging guests for the first time, Jason lifted his quizzing glass, rarely if ever used except in instances such as this, and scanned the multitude. "Dear me. I believe you may well be right." The glass swung about to focus on Lady Hamilton. For a pregnant instant, Jason viewed her through it, as if examining the pale blonde curls clustered about her sharp face and the voluptuous curves daringly revealed for all to see, before letting the weapon fall. "There do seem to be an enormous number of boring people present. I fear I've been so engrossed in conversation I had failed to remark the fact."

"You were talking to your *wife!*" Lady Hamilton snapped.

Jason's grey eyes, cold and hard, swung down to impale her. "Precisely." He let a measured period elapse, to make sure that barb struck home, before, with the slightest of polite nods, he said, "If you'll excuse me, Eugenia. I'm thirsty."

From her position in the cotillion Lenore saw him turn away and let out the breath she had been holding. They were shameless, every last one. Even had she not come to London with a very accurate idea of her husband's past history, the blatant advances made to him by certain of the so-called ladies of the *ton* would have made all clear to a novice. And she was no novice. She knew all too well what they were offering—it was a wonder he had not yet taken any of them up on their invitations.

As she obediently twirled through the next figure, the idea that he had, but she did not know of it, arose to torment her. In an effort to hold back the tide of sheer misery that welled at the thought, Lenore forced her mind to another puzzling point. What did that odd look mean, the softer light she had seen, quite clearly, just for a moment, in his eyes?

"Lady Eversleigh!"

Just in time, Lenore avoided a collision. Whispering her apologies to Lord Falkirk, she sternly warned herself to keep her mind on the business at hand. That her husband felt some degree of affection for her was no great discovery—witness his many kindnesses. The gentle expression in his eyes owed its existence to that—and nothing more. And his words of concern might just as well stem from an entirely proprietorial interest in her health—and that of his heir. No need to puzzle any longer—there was no mystery there.

She would have to stop her silly yearnings—they could only cause her grief.

"Thank you, my lord." Lenore rose from her final curtsy and gifted Lord Falkirk with a brilliant smile. "Perhaps you could escort me to Lady Agatha?" she suggested. "I think she's near the door."

Perfectly willing to be seen with one of the brightest lights in the *ton* on his arm, Lord Falkirk readily agreed.

Fixing a suitable smile on her lips, Lenore glided graciously by her escort's side, sternly reminding herself of her purpose. She could not simply go home—the night was yet young. But at least she could gain a respite by Agatha's side, before she threw herself once more into the fray—the hurly-burly of being the Duchess of Eversleigh.

It was a difficult task, constantly to perform as if her whole existence revolved about the glib conversations, the innuendo and cynical laughter, the glittering carousel of the *ton* at play. Particularly when her eyes kept straying out over the pomaded heads, searching for elegantly waving chestnut locks atop a tall frame. Now and again, he hove into view, always in the distance. Lenore struggled to shackle her jealousy for those unsighted women who stood before him, warmed by his slow smile.

"I vow and declare, my dear, it's all becoming far too

heated—this argument between Lennox and Croxforth. And all over a horse, would you believe it?''

Nodding her head at Lady Morecambe's assessment, Lenore tried to keep from yawning. She had left Agatha to join her little clique—Lady Morecambe and Mrs. Athelbury, Mr. Merryweather, Lord Selkirk and Mr. Lawton. Miss Dalney, on the arm of Lord Moresby, had just come up. On the outskirts of this inner group, Lord Rodley, Mr. Hemminghurst, Lord Jerry Penshaw and a few other younger gentlemen hung, hopeful of gaining recognition but unsure how to most acceptably make their presence felt. Within the protective confines of her little circle, Lenore knew she would meet no challenge to her equanimity. ''Perhaps they should simply sell the poor animal and halve the proceeds?''

Barely listening to the laughs this produced, Lenore allowed her mind to slide away. Having contributed her mite to keep the conversation flowing, she was woolgathering, her gaze idly scanning the crowd, when her husband again hove into view—but this time much nearer, approaching rapidly and, quite possibly, with intent.

Immediately, Lenore brightened, consciously infusing enthusiasm into her expression, a smile of dazzling brilliance on her lips. ''Will you be attending Lady Halifax's drum tomorrow, my lord?'' With a show of eagerness, she quizzed Lord Moresby. From the corner of her eye, she saw her husband's progress slow. ''I've heard that her gatherings are always a sad crush.''

''Indeed, yes,'' his lordship replied.

''I heard,'' said Miss Dalney, leaning forward to speak across his lordship, ''that at her last ball, part of the balustrade on her stairs was dislodged by the crowd trying to ascend.''

Lenore looked suitably impressed, mentally making a note to put Lady Halifax's affair at the bottom of her list. Lady Morecambe made a comment and Lenore took the chance to cast a surreptitious glance her husband's way. To her relief, he was deep in conversation with Lord Carnaby and seemed no longer interested in her.

In thinking so, she was wrong. While trading information on horseflesh with Lord Carnaby, another amateur of equine bloodlines, a large part of Jason's mind was absorbed in noting how scintillating his wife appeared. She was bright-eyed, radiant. She needed no help in braving the world of the *ton*—she had it at her pretty feet.

"I'll let you know if I hear any more about that bay of Salisbury's." With a nod, Lord Carnaby moved on, leaving Jason to his musings.

They weren't pleasant. A niggle of an entirely unexpected sort had inserted itself into his brain. Was Lenore's effervescent charm, the bloom in her cheeks, the wide starry gaze merely brought on by enjoyment of the *ton*'s offerings? Or was there more to it than that? Could it be that some gentleman, perhaps, was responsible for the transformation in his wife?

Suppressing a low growl, Jason shook off his unsettling thoughts and headed for the card-room. He could not believe Lenore had found a lover—would not believe it. Not Lenore—his Lenore.

Yet such things happened. Every day. None knew that better than he.

Once inside the card-room, Jason halted, dragging in a deep breath. Seeing a footman passing with a loaded tray, he took a glass of brandy. Taking a soothing draught, he calmed himself with the reflection that he was letting his jaundiced view of *ton*-ish wives colour his expectations. As far as his wife was concerned, there was no evidence to support such a notion.

Was there?

ONCE SOWN, the seed would simply not die, no matter how hard he struggled to kill it. Five days later, Jason stood, moodily staring out of the windows of his library and, defeated, considered how to put paid to his suspicions. That such thoughts were unworthy—of himself, of Lenore—he was only too well aware. But he was also aware of the dreams—nay, nightmares—that had come to haunt him.

Despite his very real inclination, he had not returned to his wife's bed. The knowledge that she evinced no real interest in him was depressing; the idea she might yield him his rights out of duty was simply appalling. Sinking into the chair behind his desk, Jason grimaced. Impossible not to admit to a certain measure of cowardice, yet what rake of his extensive experience would not, in the circumstances, feel reticent? Never in his life had a woman turned him down; he had never had to ask for a woman's favours. That the first woman to find him resistible should be his own wife was undoubtedly fate's revenge. Demanding his dues was beyond him, a course entirely repugnant. Once they were alone at the Abbey, he would work on her susceptibilities, draw her to him once again, heal the breach that had somehow developed between them. And rekindle the embers that still smouldered into a roaring blaze from which something more permanent than mere passion would emerge.

Until then, he would have to contain his desire and concentrate instead on retaining his sanity. The first step was to convince himself that his ridiculous suspicions were just that. Leaning back in his chair, Jason focused his mind on his task—how to discover with whom his wife spent her time.

Her evenings were accounted for. Despite her full schedule, she had shown no inclination to deviate from the list Compton left on his desk every morning; no danger there. Her luncheon engagements were rather more hazy, yet, from experience, he knew that was not a favoured time for seduction. Empty stomachs had a way of interfering with carnal appetites. Afternoons, on the other hand, were prime time.

And Lenore's afternoons were veiled in secrecy—at least, from him.

Frowning, Jason reluctantly discarded the obvious solution. He could not set Moggs on her trail, no matter how obsessed he became. Regardless of the truth behind her smiles, regardless of his fears, it would be unforgivable to allow any of his staff to get so much as a whiff of his suspicions.

The steady drum of his fingers on the blotter was interrupted by the click of the door latch.

"Are you receiving?" With a confident air, Frederick entered.

Jason threw him an abstracted smile and waved him to a chair. "What brings you here?"

Subsiding into the chair, Frederick stared at him. "It's Thursday, remember?"

When Jason continued to look blank, Frederick sighed. "Dashed if I know what's got into you these days. You're promised to Hillthorpe and yours truly this afternoon for a round at Manton's."

"Ah, yes." Jason shifted in his chair. "I've been somewhat absorbed with another matter—our engagement momentarily slipped my mind." He flashed Frederick a charming though far from contrite smile and pushed his chair back from the desk. "But I'm only too willing to accommodate you now you've jogged my memory."

"Humph!" As Jason stood and came around the desk, Frederick struggled up out of the comforting depths of the armchair. "Perhaps I should mention your wandering wits to your duchess—saw her just now at Lady Chessington's."

Jason halted in his progress to the door. "Oh?"

"Yes. Luncheon. She was there, along with the usual crowd. Exhausting. Don't know how they all do it. Think Lenore went on to Mrs. Applegate's after that. Gave it a miss, myself."

"An undoubtedly wise move." Jason nodded absent-mindedly as his route to salvation clarified in his brain. As Frederick drew level, he clapped him on the shoulder. "How's Lady Wallace?"

"Amelia? Er…" Trapped, Frederick threw him an irritated glance. At sight of Jason's wide eyes, he scowled. "Damn it, Jason. It's nothing like what you're thinking."

Abruptly assuming his patriarchal persona, Jason raised his brows. "I certainly hope not. I might remind you that Lady Wallace is now a connection."

Frederick looked struck. "So she is. Forgot that."

"Well, I haven't. So I'll take it amiss if you're merely trifling with the lady's affections, dear chap."

Frederick narrowed his eyes. "Jason..." he said warningly.

But Jason only laughed. His interest in the day miraculously restored, he waved Frederick through the door. "Come on. Let's find Hillthorpe. Suddenly, I'm in the mood to take the pips out of the aces."

IT SHOULD, in fact, be child's play to track his wife's movements through the *ton*. Buoyed with confidence, Jason strolled through the crowd at Lady Cheswell's rout, his smile at the ready, his manner easy and urbane, his eyes searching for Mrs. Applegate.

After allowing Frederick to win their round at Manton's, the least he could do to repay his friend for his help, all unconscious though it had been, he had made a brief foray to the Park. From the high perch of his racing phaeton, scanning the fashionable crowds had been simple enough. Lenore had not been there. Presumably, she had spent the afternoon at the Applegates' or some similar function. He was quite sure Mrs. Applegate would be able to confirm his duchess's movements; Lenore had become such a hit, few missed her presence and most, even Frederick, took note of whither she was bound.

The crowd before him shifted, revealing his quarry resplendent in bronzed bombazine. She did not even wait for him to reach her before exclaiming, "Your Grace! What a pleasant surprise."

Suppressing his natural response to such gushing sentiment, Jason kept his most unintimidating smile firmly in place. Taking Mrs. Applegate's chubby fingers in his, he bowed politely. "My dear Mrs. Applegate." Straightening, he considered her with affected surprise. "I confess to being amazed to see you, ma'am. I'd heard your tea this afternoon was positively exhausting."

Flushing with pleasure, Mrs. Applegate fanned her cheeks. "Very kind in you to say so, Your Grace. I'm only sorry Lady Eversleigh was otherwise engaged. Lady Thorpe and Mrs. Carlisle were par-ticularly anxious to make her acquaintance. Perhaps you might drop a word in her ear, my lord? I hold an 'at home' every second week and would be most pleased to have her attend.''

"Yes, of course.'' A sudden chill enveloped Jason's heart. He glanced about. ''If you'll pardon me, ma'am, I've just sighted someone I must catch.''

With an elegant bow, he detached himself from Mrs. Applegate's clinging toils and headed into the crowd. Not the Park, not Mrs. Applegate's. So where had Lenore spent her afternoon?

Seeing the dark head of Lady Morecambe pass before him, he swung into her wake. When she paused by a group of ladies to allow another to pass before her, Jason stopped by her side. "Good evening, Lady Morecambe.''

Theresa Morecambe jumped and swung about. "Oh, Your Grace! You gave me quite a start.''

Looking down into her blue eyes and seeing the relief therein, Jason drew his own conclusions. But he was only interested in discovering *his* wife's afternoon pastimes. Bowing briefly over Lady Morecambe's hand, he fixed her with a cool and somewhat stern gaze. "I believe you spend a great deal of time with my wife, Lady Morecambe?''

There was nothing in the tenor of his words to cause offence, but he was not the last surprised to see Theresa Morecambe's eyes widen. With a visible effort, she pulled herself together, then airily shrugged. "Now and then. But we're not forever in each other's pockets, Your Grace. You must not be thinking so.'' Under his relentless gaze, Lady Morecambe's defences wavered. She rushed on, "In fact, this afternoon I attended Mrs. Marshall's drum. Lady Eversleigh was otherwise engaged—I assume she attended Mrs. Dwyer's musical afternoon—a most rewarding and, er…en-lightening experience, I'm sure.''

Struggling to keep his lips straight, Jason nodded. "I dare say.'' With the curtest of bows, he let Lady Morecambe flee. He gave a minute to consideration of which of his peers was the guilty party in her case, before hauling his mind back to his own unknown. Where had Lenore gone?

The next half-hour went in a vain search for Mrs. Dwyer. Forced to the conclusion that that particular young matron had not featured on Lady Cheswell's list, Jason stood stock-still by the side of the ballroom, a black cloud of suspicion drawing ever nearer.

"Good God, Eversleigh! Stop standing there like a rock. There's a chair behind you, if you haven't noticed. I need it— and you're in the way."

Blinking, moving aside automatically, Jason found himself facing his father's youngest sister. "You have my heartfelt apologies, Agatha." Smoothly, he helped her to the chair.

Settling herself in a cloud of deep purple draperies, Agatha humphed. "No sense trying any of your flummery on me, m'lad."

Jason's lips twitched but he held his tongue.

Looking up at him, Agatha's black eyes narrowed. "But what are you doing here, propping the wall? Watching your wife hard at work?" With a nod, she indicated the set Lenore had joined on the dance floor. "Exhausting ain't it?"

"Exceptionally." Try as he might, Jason could not keep his disapproval from colouring his tone. "I find it hard to believe she is not, now, enjoying what she once professed to abhor."

Agatha chuckled. "Well, if she's convinced you, she needn't fear any other finding her out."

Knowing his aunt harboured a definite soft spot for Lenore, Jason let that remark pass unchallenged.

"Still, at least she escaped Lady Fairford's effort today. I don't know how some of these people find their way into the *ton*, believe me I don't. The most shabby entertainment—nip-cheese from beginning to. end. I went on to Henrietta Dwyer's—timed it well; the singing was over but I didn't see Lenore there. No doubt she went to Lady Argyle's 'at home'. If I'd had any sense, I would have gone there to start with."

Feeling very much like a drowning man making one last desperate attempt to grab hold of a buoy, Jason made his excuses to his aunt and set out on Lady Argyle's trail.

In the centre of the crowd thronging Lady Cheswell's dance

floor, Lenore smiled and chatted, no longer afraid that her mask would slip but rather less sure about her temper. The sheer banality of the exercise was taking its toll; she was bored and rapidly losing patience. "Naturally, my lord," she replied to Lord Selkirk, "I would not favour pink ribbons on such an outfit. I suspect Mr. Millthorpe would only find they tangled in his fobs. He seems to have quite an array, don't you think?" A gale of laughter greeted this purely accurate observation. Lenore converted her grimace to a look of puzzled consideration as she studied the extravagant dandy holding court but paces away. As Mr. Millthorpe seemed to count such attention no more than his due, she did not feel she was committing any social solecism in so doing. Was this all they thought of—silk ribbons and bows?

Behind the solid façade of the Duchess of Eversleigh, Lenore inwardly sighed, hoping that she possessed the fortitude to carry her through the next weeks. Agatha, Lady Eckington and company were all agreed that she should not host any major entertainment until next Season. Which meant that all she had to do was continue to appear at the balls and parties, smiling and dancing, a devotee of all things frivolous. The dreary prospect was enough to make her feel ill. Thankfully, her resistance to indisposition had improved dramatically, at least in the evenings; as long as she adhered to her plan, she was confident her health would see the Season out. It was her temperament that was strained; she had never before had to suffer fools gladly.

"My dear Duchess! Allow me to compliment you on your gown, my dear."

Mentally girding her loins, Lenore turned to exchange polite nods with Lady Hartwell. "How do you do, Lady Hartwell. Madame Lafarge will be delighted to know you approve of her style. Are you enjoying your evening?"

A little taken aback by this forthright response, Lady Hartwell rallied. "Why, yes, my dear. Such a sad crush, is it not? But I wanted to make sure you had received my note about my little gathering tomorrow. Dare I hope you'll be able to attend?''

With the ease born of frequent repetition, Lenore smiled at Lady Hartwell, just the right combination of regret and reluctance in her eyes. "Indeed I got your note, but I regret I'm promised elsewhere for the afternoon. Perhaps next time?"

Fleetingly laying her hand on her ladyship's gloved arm, as if appealing for her understanding, Lenore was not surprised to see resigned acceptance overlay her ladyship's annoyance. She had her routine perfected to an art.

After promising to attend her soirée later in the month, Lenore parted from her ladyship, returning once more to the safety of her own circle. Lady Hartwell's invitation was the sixth she had refused for the following afternoon. The number of ladies desirous of her company over tea would have made Harriet cackle.

Nodding to Lady Argyle as she passed her in the crowd, Lenore banished her boredom, casting herself once more into the fray—the chattering, glimmering, clamouring world of the *ton*.

For her, the time to leave could not come soon enough.

When, at last, the evening was done and she was handed into her carriage by her husband, she merely smiled sleepily at him, then subsided into silence, grateful for the darkness that cloaked her tiredness from his perceptive gaze. It was comforting, the way he was always there to escort her home. At times like this, when her willpower had been sapped by the demands of the ball and her resistance was low, she found it impossible not to admit, to that inner self who knew all her secrets, that she could not imagine any other gentleman giving her the same sense of security, of being protected against all harm. The vibrant strength of him as he sat beside her, his thigh brushing her silken skirts, came clearly to her senses.

Abruptly, blinking back her tears of frustration, Lenore turned to stare out of the carriage window, into the gloom. She had had her taste of paradise; she should be content with her memories—they were more than many others had to warm them.

Beside her, Jason sat, chilled to the marrow, a man condemned. As the carriage ambled over the cobbles towards Eversleigh House, he watched the façades slip past, his hand fisted so tightly his knuckles ached. Long before it had been time to quit Lady Cheswell's ballroom, he had exhausted all avenues of salvation. Lenore had not been at Lady Argyle's; there had been no other entertainments held that afternoon at which a lady of her station would have appeared.

Which left one vital question unanswered, a suffocating cloud of uncertainty pressing down blackly upon him, making it difficult to breathe and even harder to think.

Where *was* Lenore spending her afternoons—*and with whom*?

CHAPTER THIRTEEN

IN THE DAYS that followed, Jason verified beyond all possible doubt that his wife was absenting herself from the *ton*'s afternoon entertainments. His mood vacillated between cold cynicism and the blackest despair. One minute he had convinced himself that he did not need to know who she was dallying with, the next he was overcome by a primitive urge to find the gentleman responsible and flay him to within an inch of his life. In his more rational moments he wondered how it had all come about, why he had been unwise enough to let such a black fate befall him.

It was Agatha who brought the matter to a head.

Pacing restlessly before the fire in his library, the October morning grey beyond the long windows, Jason read for the twelfth time, his aunt's missive. Quite why Agatha had nominated eleven o'clock for a meeting when she rarely rose before noon was a mystery. Likewise, he felt there was some significance in the fact that she had elected to call on him, rather than summoning him to attend her. Unfortunately he could not fathom what it was. Nevertheless, there could be no doubt that she was coming to tell him what he was not at all sure he wished to hear. Presumably Agatha had discovered what he had not—with whom Lenore was trysting.

The sound of the front doorbell halted him in his tracks. Lifting his head, he heard his aunt's tones, unusually muted, in the hall. Squaring his shoulders, Jason braced himself to hear the unwelcome truth.

Smythe held the door open as Agatha swept in.

"Good morning, Aunt." Smoothly, Jason went forward and gave her his arm to the chaise.

"Glad you found the time to see me, Eversleigh." Agatha subsided on to the chaise, settling her heavy green carriage dress and placing her muff beside her. As the door clicked shut behind Smythe, she raised a worried face to Jason, standing by the fireplace, one arm braced against the mantelpiece. "It's about Lenore. Don't know what your plans are, but you should take her back to the Abbey immediately."

Despite the fact that he had expected as much, hearing it said brought the misery that much nearer. His heart a solid lump of cold stone in his chest, Jason steeled himself to learn which sprig had stolen Lenore from him.

All Agatha saw was the hardening of the planes of his face. Already austere, his features took on an intimidating cast. Agatha allowed her own stubbornness to show, wagging a stern finger at him. "Oh, her little deception has been quite clever and entirely successful thus far, I'll grant you, but she won't get away with it forever."

Jason could bear it no longer. "For God's sake, Agatha, cut line. Who the devil *is* the bounder?" He ground the question out, then swung on his heel, restlessly pacing the hearth rug. "That's *all* I want to know. I'll call him out, of course." The last was said with a certain measure of relief, even relish. At last he could do something, strike out at someone, to relieve his frustration and bitter disappointment.

Agatha stared at him as if he had run mad. "Have you lost your wits? If you're to blame any man, it would have to be yourself. And how can you call yourself out, pray tell?"

Jason halted, total bewilderment replacing his look of predatory rage.

Agatha waved him to a chair. "For God's sake, do sit down and stop towering over me. Remind me of your father when you behave like that."

Too taken aback to protest, Jason did as he was bid.

"I'm merely here to bring to your notice the fact that Lenore is not well." Agatha fixed her nephew with a penetrating stare.

"*If* she's breeding, she should be back at the Abbey. You know perfectly well she does not enjoy life here in town. It's my belief the air's not good for her, either. And the strain of supporting her new position, on top of all else, is proving too much."

"Nonsense." Jason had regained his composure. Obviously, his aunt was not as *au fait* with his wife's doings as he had thought. "She's enjoying herself hugely—throwing herself into the fray with the best of them." His tone was dismissive, laced with contempt.

Agatha's brows rose to astronomical heights. "Nonsense, is it? And just how much do you know of your wife's life, sir? It might interest you to know that, when I did not see her at any of the afternoon engagements over the past week, I became suspicious. When she did not appear at Mrs. Athelbury's tea, I stopped by here yesterday at four. And what did I find?"

Transfixed, Jason waited, every muscle tensed. *Here*? In his house?

Agatha's eyes narrowed. "I'd wager my best bonnet she was laid down upon her bed, fast asleep. *That*'s why she looks so much better in the evening than she does at luncheon. Spends her afternoons recouping so no one will see how worn down she is. Doesn't sound like enjoyment to me."

Jason's brain was reeling. "Did you see her?"

"Oh, yes." Agatha sat back. "Those fools of yours woke her before I knew what they were about. Half green, she was— so you needn't tell me I'm not right. She's breeding, is she not?"

Absent-mindedly, Jason nodded. Lenore was not playing him false—had never done so—had never even thought of it.

When her nephew remained silent, absorbed with his thoughts, Agatha humphed. "What the devil is going on between you two? You're head over ears in love with each other, which anyone with eyes in their heads can see, and you're both playing fast and loose—for all the world as if you're trying to convince yourselves, and the *ton*, that isn't so." Agatha paused to draw breath. Seeing the stunned expression on her nephew's face, she rushed on, determined to have her say. "Well—it's not working, so you might as well make the best of it and take off for the country!" She glared belligerently at Jason.

Jason stared back. The idea that the entire *ton* was privy to what he had hitherto believed a deep personal secret left him staggered. Foundering in a morass of relief, consternation and uncertainty, he voiced the first thought that entered his head. "Lenore doesn't love me. We did not marry for love."

"*You* may not have—who said you had?" Agatha opened her eyes wide. "I remember your reasons for marriage quite clearly—you needn't repeat them. But what do you imagine that's got to do with it?" When Jason made no response but, instead, looked set to slide back into melancholy absorption, she added, "And as for Lenore's not loving you—you know nothing about the matter. Well—we all know what rakes are like—and let's face it, dear boy, you're one of the leaders of the pack. Never do know anything of love. Blind, you know. Rakes always are, even when it hits them in the face."

Jason recovered enough to bestow a warning glance.

Agatha was unimpressed. "You aren't going to try to tell me that you don't love her, are you?"

Jason coloured.

"Ah ha! And I'm just as right about Lenore—you'll see. Or you would, if you'd only *do* something about it."

"That, my dear aunt, I think I can safely promise." Feeling that he had allowed his aunt to lead the conversation long enough, Jason straightened in his chair. Agatha frowned, as if recalling some caveat to her deductions.

Glancing up, Agatha found her nephew's grey gaze fixed on her face. "Tell me," she said, narrowing her eyes. "Did you, by any foolish chance, tell Lenore why you wanted to wed her—your 'reasons for marriage'?"

"Of course, I did."

"Merciful heavens!" Agatha declared in disgust. "By all the gods, Jason, I'd have thought you could do better than that. An approach, no better than the veriest whipster."

Jason stiffened.

"Positively useless!" Agatha continued. "No wonder Lenore has been so set on this charade of hers—with no cost counted. She thinks to please you, to give you want you said you wanted—a marriage of convenience—no!—a marriage of *reason*." Her tone scathing, her expression no less so, Agatha gathered her muff and fixed her errant nephew with a stern glare. "Well, Eversleigh! A nice mull you've made of it. Your wife's been endangering her health and that of your heir just to give you the satisfaction of knowing your duchess is accepted by all the best people. I just hope you're satisfied." Imperiously, Agatha rose. "I suggest, now that I've shown you the error of your ways, you take immediate steps to rectify the situation."

Her message delivered, in a most satisfying way, for she had rarely had the pleasure of seeing her intimidating nephew so vulnerable, Agatha bestowed a curt nod upon him and left him to his task. Feeling justifiably pleased with her morning's work, she swept out.

Left to mull over her words, Jason was unsure whether he stood on his head or his heels. Luckily, the numbing sensation did not last, blown away by sheer relief and heady elation. Lenore was still his. Feeling oddly humble, he silently vowed he would take nothing for granted with respect to his wife henceforth. Dragging in what seemed like his first truly relaxed breath in a week, he stood and strode determinedly to the door.

It was time and past he had a long talk with his wife.

Upstairs, Lenore had just staggered from her bed. Unaware of any impending danger, she was engaged in her customary occupation on first rising—contemplating the roses about the rim of the basin left in readiness on a sidetable. She had long ago ceased to fight the nausea that engulfed her as soon as she came upright and took two steps. It was a thing to be endured. So she clung to her bowl and shut reality from her mind, waiting for the attack to pass.

Feeling her legs weaken and her knees tremble, she grasped the bowl more firmly and sank to the carpeted floor. In acute misery, she tried to think of other things as spasm after spasm shook her.

The click of the door-latch penetrated her blanket about her senses. Trencher, no doubt, with her washing water. Lenore remained silent on the floor. She had no secrets from Trencher.

His hand on the door knob, Jason surveyed his wife's room. He had knocked gently but had heard no response. Puzzled, his glance swept the rumpled bed, the drawn curtains. Perhaps she was in the small chamber beyond? Frowning, he took a step into the room and closed the door behind him.

Turning, his vision adjusting to the dimmer light, he looked across to the door that led into Lenore's bathing chamber. And saw her bare feet and the hem of her nightgown on the floor beyond the bed.

"Lenore!"

His exclamation shook Lenore firmly into reality. She lifted her head, barely able to believe her senses. But the heavy footsteps approaching the bed did not belong to Trencher.

"Go away!" The effort to imbue her words with a reasonable amount of purpose brought on another bout of retching.

Jason reached her, his expression grim. "I'm here and I'm staying." Appalled to see her so pale and weak, he sank on to the floor beside her, drawing the long strands of her hair back from her face, letting her slump against him as the paroxysm passed.

Lenore longed to argue but his presence was more comforting than she would have believed possible. His warmth struck through her thin gown, easing her tensed muscles. His hands about her shoulders imparted a strength of which she was sorely in need.

For the next few minutes, Jason said nothing, concentrating on supporting his wife, his hands moving gently, soothingly, over her shoulders and back.

Then the door opened and Trencher came hurrying in. Seeing him, she came to an abrupt halt, only just managing not to slosh the water in the ewer she carried on to the floor.

One look at her face was enough to tell Jason that his wife's maid was well aware of his ignorance of Lenore's indisposition. His eyes narrowed.

Recovering, Trencher came hurrying forward to place the ewer on the washstand. "Oh, Your Grace! Here, I'll take care of her."

"No. *You* can get her a glass of water and a damp towel. *I'll* take care of her."

Even through the dimness shrouding her senses, Lenore heard the determination that rang in his tongue. Despite her present circumstances, despite everything, she felt a ripple of pure happiness that he should be so adamant in his desire to help her, in claiming his right to do so. He was only being kind but she was in dire need of his kindness.

When Trencher returned with the glass and towel, Jason coaxed Lenore to drink, then, ignoring her weak protests, gently washed her face, cradling her in his arms. Handing the towel to the hovering maid, Jason raised a brow at his wife. "Better?"

Suddenly shy, Lenore nodded. Jason's arms slipped from her as he stood. Before she could even sit up, he bent and lifted her into his arms. Lenore clutched at his lapel, her eyes meeting Trencher's awed gaze.

Jason strode around the bed and deposited his wife on her pillows. Anticipating Trencher, he transfixed her with a steely glance and fluffed Lenore's pillows himself, before settling her back on them and tucking the eiderdown about her.

Seeing the maid gather the towel and basin and head for the door, Jason said, his tone coldly commanding, "Your mistress will ring when she has need of you."

Eyes wide, Trencher bobbed a curtsy and withdrew, pulling the door shut behind her.

Making a mental note to have a word—several words, in fact—with his wife's maid, and his valet, on the subject of leaving him in ignorance of such vital matters as his wife's health, Jason turned his attention to Lenore. Smoothly taking her hand in his, he sat on the edge of the bed.

From beneath her lashes Lenore looked up at him, not at all

certain of what would come next. Yet the unconscious movement of his thumb over her knuckles erased any trepidation.

His expression non-committal, Jason looked down at her.
"How long has this been going on, Lenore?"

The concern in his voice tied Lenore's tongue. She looked
down, picking at the lace edge of the eiderdown with her free
hand while considering how much it would be wise to admit.
She wished with all her heart to confess all and return to the
Abbey, but the Season was not yet ended.

When she did not immediately reply, Jason's brows rose.
"Since you arrived in town?"

Looking up, Lenore jettisoned all thoughts of prevarication.
"Virtually," she admitted, her voice low.

Jason sighed and looked down, his fingers interlacing with
hers. "My dear, I wish—very much—that you had told me.
I'm not a monster." His fist closed about her hand, then relaxed
slightly. Mindful of Agatha's words that Lenore had only followed her odd course to achieve what she believed he desired
of her, he added, "There's nothing I can do to relieve you of
your present susceptibility but I would not wish you to tire
yourself further on my account."

"Oh, but I'm perfectly... At least, later..." Eyes wide, Lenore leapt in to avert any decree. But when her eyes met his,
and she saw the comprehension and perception therein, she
faltered to a stop.

One of her husband's brows had risen sceptically.

"Perfectly all right later in the day? *Well*, even? Perhaps I
should warn you, my dear, that I do not take kindly to having
the wool pulled over my eyes."

Under his stern grey gaze, Lenore shifted uneasily but the
affection in his tone, in his expression, gave her the strength
to reply, "But truly, Jason, I *can* manage. I would not wish
the *ton* to think your wife was incapable of carrying her position with credit."

"The *ton* may think what they please. However, in this instance, I think you're making too much of their inconstancy
and too little of their sense. You've succeeded as my duchess

far better than I'd hoped, Lenore. None of those who matter will hold your desertion of their balls against you, certainly not when they learn the cause.'' Entirely unconsciously, Jason's gaze skimmed possessively over his wife's body. When his eyes returned to her face, he saw she was blushing delicately. He smiled, squeezing her hand gently before raising it to his lips. "Who knows?" he murmured, his eyes quizzing her. "They might even be jealous."

Lenore blushed even more. Wishing she possessed the will to retrieve her fingers, for it was exceedingly hard to think with his lips on her skin, she felt obliged to argue for the conservative course, the course she did not wish to follow in the least. "The season will be over in a few weeks, my lord. It will be time enough to return to the Abbey then."

Jason shook his head. "We're leaving for the Abbey tomorrow morning, Lenore. At least—" He broke off, regarding her ruefully. "As early as you can manage it."

They were the words Lenore had both feared and longed to hear. Yet she could not let them pass without challenge. "But—"

"No buts.'' Jason's voice was firm. "You may tell me your engagements and I'll have Compton cancel them."

"But—"

"You'll stay safely in bed until it's time for luncheon. I'll send someone up with a tray—better still, I'll bring it myself.'' Jason rose. "We can remain here all day, or, if you wish, I could take you for a stroll in the square. Tonight, I fear you'll have to continue to bear with my unfashionable company, for I do not plan to go out. We'll have dinner together and then you must rest.'' At the end of this recitation, his gaze dropped to Lenore's face. "Do you have any more buts, madam wife?"

Not sure whether she wished to glare or laugh, Lenore compromised. "I fear there's an impediment to your plans you've overlooked, my lord."

Abruptly eschewing his arrogant stance, Jason asked, "Don't you wish to spend your day with your husband? Or is it that you do not wish, in your heart, to return home to the Abbey with me?''

Lenore's heart turned over. What her heart wished, she was convinced she could never have. But she was a little bemused by Jason in vulnerable vein and was at a loss to know how to word her reply.

Sensing her predicament, Jason smiled, raising the hand he still held to clasp it more securely between his. ''Forgive my levity, my dear. What is it I've overlooked?''

A little relieved, but not entirely at ease for the soft light that glowed in his grey eyes made her heart stand still, Lenore ventured, ''I'm not…entirely sanguine as to how I shall manage in a carriage all the way to the Abbey.''

''We'll travel slowly. No need to rush. We'll only go as far each day as you can manage.'' Jason scanned Lenore's face, noting the circles under her large eyes, the absence of her usual sparkling glance and the frown, born of strain, that haunted her pale green gaze. She had pushed herself hard to fulfil his wishes. ''No more arguments, Lenore. I'm taking you back to the country tomorrow.'' With a smile to soften the absolute nature of that decree, Jason laid her hand down on the quilt. ''Rest now, my dear. I'll wake you for lunch.''

Feeling as if, somewhat against her will, a considerable weight had been lifted from her shoulders, Lenore watched him leave. He had not said what had brought him to her room at such an hour but whatever it had been, the outcome had never been in doubt. She had known all along that Jason was not the sort of inconsiderate husband who would take no interest in his wife's health, even had she not been carrying his child. Given that his concern was real, albeit the sort of emotion a gentleman felt for one in his care, his determination to take her back to the Abbey was not to be wondered at. What she was far less sure about was whether he planned to remain there with her. And whether he had asked, or was thinking of inviting, others to join them in Dorset.

With a deep sigh, Lenore closed her eyes, luxuriating in the knowledge that she did not have to get up, get dressed and attend some luncheon party, pandering to the constant demands of her position.

As sleep hovered near, ready to claim her, she realised she did not know which she feared more—if Jason stayed at the Abbey, alone, in her company, would she be able to maintain the inner mask she wore constantly, the one that hid her love from his sight? Yet, if he invited guests to join them and the ladies, as so many ladies did, made a play for him, would she be able to hide the jealousy that, to her surprise, had started eating at her soul?

Dismissing the answer as one of life's imponderables, Lenore slipped wearily over the threshold of sleep, into that realm where dreams were the only reality.

THEY REACHED the Abbey on the morning of the third day. As she emerged from the carriage and felt the flags of the steps firm beneath her feet, Lenore sighed deeply, relief and appreciation clear in her eyes as they met her husband's. She turned to greet Morgan, thcn sighting Mrs. Potts at the top of the steps, she waved before placing her hand on Jason's sleeve.

"Dare I suspect you are pleased to be home, madam?"

At his soft drawl, Lenore cast him a teasing glance. "Indeed, my lord. I have not forgotten I have yet to get far in my cataloguing of your library."

"Ah, yes." Jason returned her smile, no longer perturbed by her abiding delight in musty tomes.

At the top of the steps, Mrs. Potts sank into a deep curtsy. "Delighted to welcome you home, Your Grace, ma'am."

"I'm delighted to be back, Mrs. Potts."

"I should mention, Mrs. Potts," Jason cut in smoothly, "that Her Grace is in dire need of chicken broth. I believe that's what my mother swore by during her confinements?"

Mrs. Potts' face lit up. "Dear me, yes! Wonderful for picking a lady up when the babe gets you down. Now just you come along, my lady. We'll get you to bed straight away and I'll bring you a bowl. You must be quite worn down with all that gadding about in London."

Swept up by the irresistible force of Mrs. Potts fired with a zeal to tend to the wellbeing of the next generation, Lenore was parted from her husband. When she managed to get a look at him, on her way up the stairs, Mrs. Potts directly behind her, she saw a smugly satisfied smile on his face. Lenore shot him a speaking glance, which dissolved against her will, into a misty and grateful smile, before surrendering to her fate.

Indeed, she had need to recoup. The journey had been painfully slow. Jason had ordered that the carriage, the most well-equipped money could buy, should be driven at a spanking pace. That way, he had explained, the springs and speed took the worst out of the bumps. Even so, they had not been able to cover more than twenty miles without halt. Sunk in the luxury of her tub, filled to the brim with blissfully warm, scented water, Lenore closed her eyes and recalled her husband's unfailing support. He had grown adept at gauging how long she could last, and organising their stops so that she could wander on his arm through delightful little villages, or stroll on a green. Their night-time stops had been at the best inns where her comfort had been assured. Always the best parlour and the biggest bedroom. Her only complaint was that she had spent the nights alone in the big beds, but she had accepted that philosphically. She had his company and his affection—she had no right to expect more.

The day passed swiftly. After the promised chicken broth, Lenore dozed for a few hours. Refreshed, she dressed and descended to the parlour. After an hour reacquainting herself with her household, her husband found her. At his suggestion, they strolled on the sun-warmed terrace. It had been weeks since Lenore had been conscious of the sun on her face; it seemed appropriate that it should shine on her return to her home.

Later, she poured tea for them both. The time flew as they entertained each other with wickedly accurate reflections on the *ton*'s notables. Then it was time for dinner, taken as had been their habit earlier in the year, in the smaller dining salon.

When the covers were finally drawn, Lenore sighed, deeply content, very glad Jason had insisted on bringing her home.

When he raised a brow at her, she said as much, adding, "I already feel very much better."

As she realised her motive in stating that fact, Lenore blushed. Abruptly, she took another sip of wine, hoping the candlelight would hide her reaction. Yet was it wrong for a wife to invite her husband's attentions. Right or wrong, acceptable or not, she just wished she had more of an idea of how to go about it.

Despite her hopes, the candlelight was in no way dim enough to hide her blush from Jason's sight. Her words, and her reaction, sent his hopes soaring. But still he moved cautiously. "We'll have to ensure we do nothing to overtire you."

Her senses at full stretch, Lenore detected the subtle undertones in his deep voice. Hesitantly, she answered, "I don't think anything I do here could overtire me."

Ignoring the clamour of his desire, Jason smiled encouragingly, his eyes holding hers across the length of the table. "Perhaps you should retire early? There's no reason to stay up. I expect I'll come up soon myself."

Finding her lips suddenly dry, Lenore had to pass the tip of her tongue over them before replying, her voice slightly husky, "Perhaps I should."

A footman came to assist her to her feet. Jason stood, then, when she had gone, with one, last, lingering look, he subsided once more into his chair, waving aside the port, indicating instead the brandy decanter. Did she know what she did to him when she looked at him like that? What she would do to any man with the unspoken appeal in her large eyes? Suppressing a shudder of pure desire, Jason took a very large sip of his brandy.

Later, fortified by a large dose of the best brandy in his cellars, Jason eyed the plain panels of the door in front of him. Drawing a breath of purest satisfaction, he turned the handle and crossed the threshold.

From the depths of her feather mattress, Lenore heard him enter and could not quite believe it. Was she asleep already and dreaming? But no. The large male body, warm and hard, that slid into the bed beside her was no dream.

With a sound halfway between a cry and a sigh, Lenore turned to welcome him, only to find herself in his arms. They closed possessively, passionately, about her.

Much later, his wife warm and fast asleep beside him, Jason heaved a contented sigh.

Agatha, bless her heart, had been right.

CHAPTER FOURTEEN

IT WAS PAST NINE the next morning and Jason was deep in yesterday's *Gazette* when the door to the breakfast parlour opened. Assuming it to be one of Morgan's minions come to consult with the butler over some household matter, Jason did not look up. Not until Morgan's voice floated over the top of the pages.

"Perhaps I should clear this all away, Your Grace, and fetch you a fresh pot of tea? And perhaps some toast?"

Jason emerged from behind his newspaper in time to see Lenore subside into the chair Morgan held, a grateful look on her face.

"Thank you, Morgan. Just one slice of toast, I think."

Folding the paper and setting it aside, Jason waited until Morgan and the footman departed, burdened with the remnants of his substantial breakfast, before fixing his wife with a concerned frown. "Should you be up and about so early?"

Lenore smiled, albeit a trifle weakly. "I feel a great deal better this morning." Belatedly realising how that might sound, she rushed on, "Mrs. Potts advised against languishing in bed unless I need to sleep."

"Really?" One of Jason's brows had risen. "I fear I must take exception to such strictures. There are other reasons for languishing in bed, which I hope to have you frequently consider."

Blushing furiously, Lenore shot him a glance she hoped was sternly reproving. Luckily, Morgan appeared with her tea and toast and put an end to such risqué banter.

As she sipped the weak tea, Lenore tried to appear unconscious of the steady regard of her husband's grey eyes. He seemed content to watch her, as if time was of no importance. In the end, she asked, "Do you have much business to attend to down here?"

Jason shook his head. "The harvests are virtually all in. There's not much to be done until early next year." He watched as Lenore nibbled at her toast then grimaced and pushed the plate aside. She was still very pale. "Compton comes down from London every now and then, when there's any business that needs my attention." Remembering that his wife was well acquainted with the workings of country estates, and that she liked going about, seeing work progress, he ventured, "There are some cottages being rethatched in the village. Perhaps, later this morning, we could ride over and take a look at the result? Or would you rather go in the gig?"

Consulting her stomach took no more than a minute. Reluctantly, Lenore shook her head. "I don't think I could. I may be well enough to come downstairs, but I would rather not chance a carriage today. And as for riding, it's perhaps a good thing that I'm not a devotee of the exercise."

She looked up to see a frown on her husband's handsome countenance.

Jason caught her eye. "Is that why you refused my invitations to go riding in town? Because you were too ill?"

Lenore nodded. "The very idea of galloping over the greensward, in the Park, no less, was enough to make me blanch." Laying aside her napkin, she stood.

Recalling the hurt he had felt when she had declined his offer, Jason, rising, too, fixed her with a stern look. "Might I request, madam, that in future, you refrain from keeping secrets from your husband?"

At his mock severity, Lenore chuckled. "Indeed, my lord, I dare say you're right. It would certainly make life much easier." She took the arm he offered and they strolled into the hall. "However," she said, glancing up at him through her lashes, "you must admit you had no real wish to be seen riding in the Park with me. Your aunts told me you never escort ladies on their rides."

"My aunts are infallible on many points. However, while I would not wish to shatter your faith in their perspicacity, I fear predicting my behaviour isn't one of their strengths." Jason glanced down to capture his wife's wide green gaze. "In this case, for instance, while they're perfectly correct in noting that I've never seen any point in accompanying females on their jaunts in the Park, I consider accompanying my *wife* on such excursions a pleasure not to be missed."

Lenore wondered whether the odd weakness she felt was due to her indisposition or to the glow in his grey eyes. Whatever, she wished she had learned to control her blushes, for he was entirely too adept at calling them forth. She no longer had any defence, not when he chose to communicate on that intimate level she shared with no one else.

Raising her hand to his lips, Jason smiled, pleased to see the colour in her cheeks. "I must go and look at those cottages. I'll hunt you up when I return."

With that promise, he left Lenore in the hall and strode to the front door.

When the heavy door had shut behind him, Lenore shivered deliciously. Wriggling her shoulders the better to throw off his lingering spell, she strolled into the morning-room. Jason's behaviour throughout this morning, both before and after he had left her bed, led to only one conclusion. He intended to reinstate their relationship, exactly as it had been in the month following their wedding.

Sinking on to the chaise before the blazing fire, Lenore folded her arms across the carved back and gazed out at the mist shrouding the hilltops. Contented anticipation thrummed, a steady beat in her blood. Things had changed since August. Then, she had been on a voyage of discovery; this time she knew what was possible, knew what she truly wished of life. Coming back to the Abbey and resuming their relationship felt like returning to a well-loved and much desired place, a home.

An acknowledgement that they had shared, and could still share, something that they both now valued.

It was more than she had expected of her marriage—a great deal more.

The only cloud on her horizon was how long it would last— how long Jason would be content with her and country life. Her green eyes darkening, she considered her prospects. The peace of country living had never been his milieu. Her mental pictures had always positioned him against a backdrop of *ton*-ish pursuits. If nothing else, her time in London had convinced her she could never bear more than a few weeks of such distraction; her mind was not attuned to it.

Biting her lips, Lenore frowned. Could his warning that not even his aunts could predict his tastes be a subtle hint, conscious or not, that they were changing? He had denied any plans to invite acquaintances to join them, now or later. Likewise, he had given her to understand that he expected to remain at the Abbey, alone, with her, for the foreseeable future.

With a deep sigh, she stretched her arms, then let herself fall back against the cushions on the chaise. Inside, she was a mass of quivering uncertainty. Despite her determination not to pander to her secret yearnings, hope, a wavering flame, had flared within her. She had his affection and his desire; she wanted his love. That their sojourn here alone would allow that elusive emotion a chance to grow was the kernel of her hope. Unfortunately there seemed little she could do to aid the process.

Her fate remained in the hands of the gods—and those of His Grace of Eversleigh.

"THAT ONE GOES OVER there." Lenore pointed at a stack of leather-bound tomes, precariously balanced near the window.

"How the devil can you tell?" Jason muttered as he lugged an eight-inch-thick, gold-embossed red-calf bound volume to the pile, one of thirty dotted about the library.

Without looking up from the book open in her lap, Lenore explained, "Your father had all of Plutarch's works covered in that style. Unfortunately, he then deposited them randomly through the shelves.'' Closing the book she had been studying, she looked up at her husband. ''This one had best go with the medicinal works. That group by the sofa table.''

She smiled as Jason came up and squatted to lift the heavy book from her lap. Catching her eye, he grimaced as he hefted the volume. ''It escapes my comprehension why you cannot work at a desk like any reasonable being.''

Having already won this argument the previous day, Lenore smiled up at him. ''I'm much more comfortable down here,'' she said, reclining against the cushions piled at her back. ''Besides, the light is much better here than at the desk.'' She had made a thick Aubusson rug just inside one of the long windows her area of operations, lounging on its thick pile to examine the books as each section of the library shelves was emptied. Given that many of the volumes were ancient and heavy, her ''office'' in the gallery was out of the question. Until yesterday, Melrose, a young footman, had helped her unload and sort the tomes. Yesterday morning, after his ride, her husband had arrived and, dismissing Melrose, had offered himself as substitute.

''I'll move your damned desk.'' Jason grumbled, turning to do her bidding.

Her lips twisting in an affectionate smile, Lenore watched as he duly delivered the book on herbs to its fellows. His sudden interest in her endeavours was disarming. Despite being excessively well-read, he did not share her love of books. Quite what his present purpose was, she had yet to divine. She watched him return to her side, his expression easy, his long limbed body relaxed. He carried a small volume bound in red leather in his hand.

Before she could point out the next book she wished to examine, Jason sat down on the rug beside her. Reclining so that his shoulder pressed against the cushions at her back, he propped on one elbow and, stretching his long legs before him, opened the red book. ''I found this amid your stacks. It must have fallen and been forgotten.''

''Oh?'' Lenore leaned closer to see. ''What is it?''

"A collection of love sonnets."

Lenore sat back. Her heart started to thud. Drawing her lists towards her, she pretended to check them.

Jason frowned, flicking through the pages. Every now and then, he stopped to read a few lines. When he paused on one page, clearly reading the verse, Lenore risked a glance through her lashes.

And very nearly laughed aloud. Her husband's features were contorted in a grimace which left very little doubt as to his opinion of the unknown poet.

Abruptly, Jason shut the book and laid it aside. "Definitely not my style."

Turning to Lenore, he reached one large hand to her hip and drew her down, her morning gown slipping easily over the silk cushions and soft carpet.

"Jason!" Lenore managed to mute her surprised squeal. One look at her husband's face, grey eyes shimmering, was enough to inform her he had lost interest in books. Eyes wide, she glanced over his shoulder at the door.

Jason smiled wickedly. "It's locked."

Lenore was caught between scandalised disapproval and insidious temptation. But her fear of revealing the depths of her feelings while making love had receded. She had discovered that her husband was as prone to losing himself in her every bit as much as she lost herself in him. But in the library? "This is not—" she got out before he kissed her "—what you are supposed—" another kiss punctuated her admonition "—to be helping me with."

Having completed her protest, Lenore wriggled her arms free and draped them about his neck. Without further objection, she suffered a long-drawn-out kiss that made her toes curl and the lacings of her bodice seem far too tight. Her husband, luckily, seemed aware of her difficulties.

Raising his head to concentrate on the laces of her gown, Jason's eyes held hers. "I'm sick of handling dusty tomes. I'd rather handle you—for an hour or two."

The laces gave way. His fingers came up to caress her shoulders, slipping her gown over and down. As his head bent, Lenore let her lids fall. An hour or two?

With a shuddering sigh, she decided she could spare him the time.

IN THE DAYS that followed their return to the Abbey, Jason tried by every means possible to break down the constraint, subtle but still real, that existed between himself and his wife. The last barrier. He had come a long way since propounding his "reasons for marriage". Not only could he now acknowledge to himself that he was deeply in love with Lenore, but he wanted their love to be recognised and openly accepted by them both.

And that was the point where he continued to stumble.

Seated astride his grey hunter, he surveyed the vale of Eversleigh, his fields laid like a giant patchwork quilt over the low hills. He had come to the vantage point on the escarpment in the hope that the distance and early morning peace would give him a clearer perspective on his problem.

He had joined in his wife's pastimes, as far as could be excused, working in the library by her side, taking her for gentle walks about the rambling gardens and nearby woods. Mrs. Potts now looked on him with firm approval. And Lenore gladly accepted his escort, his help, his loving whenever it was offered. But she made no demands, no indication that she desired his attentions.

Yet she did. Of that he was convinced. No woman could pretend to the depths of loving intimacy, the heights of passion that Lenore effortlessly attained—not for so long. No woman could conjure without fail the welcoming smiles she treated him to every time he approached. Her reactions came from her heart, he was sure.

The grey sidled, blowing steam from his great nostrils. Leaning forward to pull the horse's ears, Jason looked down on his home, the grey stone pale in the weak morning light. A strange peace had enveloped him since returning to the Abbey, as if for years he had been on some journey and had finally found his way home. *This*, he now knew, was what he had searched for throughout the last decade, a decade filled with balls and parties and all manner of *ton*-ish pursuits. This was where he wished to remain, here, on his estates, at his home, with Lenore and their children. And he owed the discovery and his sense of deep content to Lenore.

However, no matter how hard he tried to show her, his stubborn wife refused to see. He loved her—how the devil was he to convince her of that?

Until he succeeded, she would continue as she was, eager for his company but never showing it, pleased as punch when he elected to stay by her side but frightened of suggesting it, even obliquely. No matter her task, she would never ask for his help, fearing to step over the line of what could reasonably be expected from a conventional spouse.

He had no intention of being a conventional spouse, nor of settling for a conventional marriage. Not now he knew he could have so much more. With a snort of derision Jason hauled on the grey's reins and set the beast down the track for the stables. Agatha had been right—he was a fool beyond excuse for having recited his reasons for marriage. But that was the past; he needed to secure the future—their future.

Thwarted by her reticence, he had attempted, first to encourage, then to entrap her into admitting her love, hoping to use the opportunity to assure her of his. Remembering the scene, Jason grimaced. Unfortunately, his wife was one of those rare women who could, if pushed, out do him in sheer stubborn will. He was powerless to cajole, much less force her to reveal her secrets. She remained adamantly opposed to uttering the very words he dreamed of hearing her say—for the simple reason that he had led her to believe he would never want to hear them.

"Damn it—*why* is it that only women are allowed to change their minds?"

The grey tossed his head. With a frustrated sigh, Jason turned him on to the wide bridle path at the bottom of the hill and loosened the reins.

There was only one solution. He would have to convince her that, against all expectations, he did indeed love her. As the steep roof of the stables rose above the last trees, Jason acknowledged that mere words were unlikely to suffice. Actions, so the saying went, spoke louder.

MOONLIGHT STREAMED in through the long uncurtained windows, bathing Lenore's bedroom in silvery light. Thoroughly exhausted, courtesy of her husband's amorous games, Lenore lay deeply asleep. Beside her, Jason was wide awake, listening for the sounds that would herald Moggs and his surprise. A full week had passed since his visit to the escarpment. It had taken that long to devise, then execute his plan. Tonight was the final stage, for which he had had to enlist Moggs' support.

Eyes wide in the dim light, Jason had time to pray that his valet would, as with most other matters, keep silent on this night's doings. The notion of facing his servants after they had heard of his latest touch of idiocy did not appeal. Quite how he and Moggs were going to conceal the evidence afterwards, he had not yet considered but he would think of some ploy. Unbidden, Frederick Marshall's image floated into his mind. Jason grinned wryly. If Frederick ever heard of this episode, he would cut him without compunction. Recalling his friend's absorption with Lady Wallace, Jason's grin broadened. On the other hand, it was entirely possible that Frederick might need advice on a similar problem someday soon.

A soft click heralded Moggs' arrival. Raising his head, Jason saw his valet's diminutive form glide into the room. Moggs moved about the large chamber, arranging his surprise as directed. Keeping count as Moggs went back and forth, Jason slowly eased from the warmth of his wife's bed and, finding his robe on the floor, shrugged into it. Padding noiselessly across the floor, he joined his redoubtable henchman as Moggs settled the last of his cargoes on the carpet.

"Thank you, Moggs." Jason kept his words to a whisper. Silent as ever, Moggs bowed deeply and withdrew, drawing the door shut behind him and easing the latch back so that it did not even click.

Alone with his sleeping wife, Jason turned and surveyed Moggs' handiwork. Then, reaching into the deep pocket of his robe, he drew forth a stack of white cards. For a moment, he stood silently regarding them, and the words inscribed in his own strong hand upon their smooth surfaces. If this didn't work, Lord only knew what else he could do.

Like a ghostly shadow, Jason circled his wife's chamber, depositing the cards in their allotted places. Finally, with a sigh and a last prayer for success, he slid into bed beside his wife.

LENORE WOKE very early. The muted light of pre-dawn suffused the room, slanting in through the long windows on either side of the bed. It was, she was well aware, anticipation that brought her to her senses thus early in the day. She was facing away from Jason; without turning, she let her senses stretch. His body was relaxed and still, heavy in the bed behind her, his breathing deep and regular. Deciding she could do with a doze before he woke her up, she was about to snuggle deeper under the eiderdown when the outline of something caught her eye.

Something that should not have been there. Raising her head, Lenore blinked through the dimness, waiting for her eyes to adjust. In the grey light she made out the shape of a pedestal placed a few feet from the window, a vase of flowers—were they roses?—atop.

Frowning, she glanced to the right and saw another pedestal, the twin of the first. Slowly easing up until she was sitting, Lenore saw a third and a fourth—in fact, a large semi-circle of pedestals supporting vases of roses surrounded her bed.

They couldn't be roses. It was November.

Propelled by curiosity, Lenore slipped from her bed, shivering as the chill air reminded her of her nakedness. Suppressing a curse, she grabbed up her nightgown from the floor where Jason had thrown it and dragged it over her head. Seconds later, she was standing by the first pedestal, staring through the poor light at the flowers in the vase. They looked like roses—perhaps made of silk? Lenore rubbed a velvety petal between two fingers. Real roses. As far as she could tell in the odd light, golden ones.

Turning to study the display, she counted fifteen pedestals, each vase sporting twenty or so beautiful blooms. Such extravagance would have cost a small fortune. No need to ask from whom they came.

Slanting a glance at the bed, she saw that the large lump that was her husband had not stirred. Looking back at the vase, she noticed a small card propped by the base, overhung by a spray of roses. Picking it up, she held it to the light. ''Dear'' was inscribed upon the pristine surface in her husband's unmistakable scrawl. Nothing more.

Glancing at the next pedestal, Lenore saw it, too, held a card. That one said ''Lenore''.

Faster and faster, Lenore flitted from vase to vase, collecting cards until she stood on the other side of the bed, by the other window and, hardly daring to believe the message they held, forced herself to shuffle them and read it again.

Dear Lenore, I had to do something to convince you I love you. Do you love me?

Her heart in her mouth, Lenore looked up, straight into her husband's grey eyes. He was very much awake, propped on the pillows, his arms crossed, tense, behind his head, watching her. The shadows of the bed hid his expression.

When she simply stood, his painstakingly inscribed cards carrying a message he had sweated blood over in her hands, and said nothing, Jason inwardly grimaced. ''Well, my dear?'' he prompted, as gently as he was able.

Lenore did not know where to start. Struggling to command her voice, she waved at him. ''Come here if you want my answer.''

Slowly expelling the breath he had been holding, Jason sat

up and swung his legs over the side of the bed. Did she have to make this quite so difficult? He was on tenterhooks, more nervous than he had ever been in his life. Reaching for his robe, he stood and shrugged into it, belting it loosely before crossing the few yards to stand before her.

Fingers clutching the white cards she could not yet believe were real, Lenore waited until he towered over her before asking, her voice a shaky whisper, "Do you *really* love me?"

Her throat had constricted; tears were not far away.

Jason's heart stopped. Desperately, his eyes searched her face, trying to discover what she meant by her question, what further assurance it was in his power to give her. From his heart came the answer. Without thinking, he went down on one knee before her, capturing one small hand in his. "Lenore, I arranged our marriage for all the wrong reasons but I never *asked* you to marry me. *Will* you marry me, my dear, not for all my rational reasons, but for the right reason—because you love me—and I love you?"

Tears obliterated Lenore's vision. "Oh, Jason!" she sobbed.

Immediately, Jason was on his feet but before he could do anything, Lenore threw herself into his arms, clinging to him, the white cards scattering like confetti about them.

Bemused, Jason closed his arms about his sobbing wife, burying his face in her golden hair. "Sweetheart, I didn't mean to make you cry."

"It's—" Lenore sniffed, then gulped. "It's just *too* beautiful," she wailed, as a fresh flood threatened. "Oh," she said, struggling to wipe her eyes on his sleeve. "This is *dreadful*. I'm not a watering pot, truly."

"Thank God for that," Jason replied. The fact that, despite her unconventional response, he had got the answer he wanted was slowly sinking in. The relief was enormous. Wrapping his arms about his snuffling wife, he lifted her and carried her back to their bed.

Snuggling back beneath the eiderdown, Lenore wiped her eyes with the lace edge of the coverlet. Her thoughts were whirling, a disjointed jumble of emotions buffeted her. She blinked at her husband as he climbed back into bed beside her, stretching out on his back, his head on the pillows. He shut his eyes, as if worn out. "You really do love me?" she asked, her voice rather small.

Exasperated, Jason groaned. "Lenore—no man in his right mind makes a cake of himself as I have over you without a *bloody good reason.* Now for God's sake come and put me out of my misery and convince me my reason was, in truth, the very best."

He reached for her. Lenore gave a last watery giggle and, without further ado, devoted herself to convincing her arrogant rake of a husband that she did indeed love him.

Beyond all reason.

A Lady of Expectations

CHAPTER ONE

"LADY ASFORDBY, of Asfordby Grange, requests the pleasure of the company of Mr. Jack Lester, of Rawling's Cottage, and guests, at a ball."

Ensconced in an armchair by the fireplace, a glass of brandy in one long-fingered hand, the white card of Lady Asfordby's invitation in the other, Jack Lester made the pronouncement with ill-disguised gloom.

"She's *the grand dame* of these parts, ain't she?" Lord Percy Almsworthy was the second of the three gentlemen taking their ease in the parlour of Jack's hunting box. Outside, the wind howled about the eaves and tugged at the shutters. All three had ridden to hounds that day, taking the field with the Quorn. But while both Jack and his brother Harry, presently sprawled on the chaise, were clipping riders, up with the best of them, Percy had long ago taken Brummel's lead, indefatigable in turning out precise to a pin but rarely venturing beyond the first field. Which explained why he was now idly pacing the room, restless, while the brothers lounged, pleasantly exhausted, with the look about them of men not willing to stir. Pausing by the fireplace, Percy looked down on his host. "Lend a bit of colour to your stay, what? Besides," he added, turning to amble once more, "You never know—might see a golden head that takes your eye."

"In this backwater?" Jack snorted. "If I couldn't find any golden head worth the attention last Season—nor during the Little Season—I don't give much for my chances here."

"Oh, I don't know." Unconsciously elegant, Harry Lester lounged on the chaise, one broad shoulder propped against a cushion, his thick golden locks rakishly dishevelled. His sharply intelligent green eyes wickedly quizzed his elder brother. "You seem remarikably set on this start of yours. As finding a wife has become so important to you, I should think it behoves you to turn every stone. Who knows which one hides a gem?"

Blue eyes met green. Jack grunted and looked down. Absent-mindedly, he studied the gilt-edged card. Firelight glinted over the smooth waves of his dark hair and shadowed his lean cheeks. His brow furrowed.

He had to marry. He had inwardly acknowledged that fact more than twenty months ago, even before his sister, Lenore, had married the Duke of Eversleigh, leaving the burden of the family squarely on his shoulders.

"Perseverance—that's what you need." Percy nodded to no one in particular. "Can't let another Season go by without making your choice—waste your life away if you're too fin-icky."

"I hate to say it, old son," Harry said. "But Percy's right. You can't seriously go for years looking over the field, turning your nose up at all the offerings." Taking a sip of his brandy, he eyed his brother over the rim of his glass. His green eyes lit with an unholy gleam. "Not," he added, his voice soft, "unless you allow your good fortune to become known."

"Heaven forbid!" Eyes narrowing, Jack turned to Harry. "And just in case you have any ideas along that track, perhaps I should remind you that it's our good fortune—yours and mine and Gerald's, too?" Features relaxing, Jack sank back in his chair, a smile erasing the severe line of his lips. "Indeed, the chance of seeing *you* playing catch-me-who-can with all the enamoured damsels is sorely tempting, brother mine."

Harry grinned and raised his glass. "Fear not—that thought has already occurred. If the *ton* stumbles onto our secret, it won't be through me. And I'll make a point of dropping a quiet word in our baby brother's ear, what's more. Neither you nor I need him queering our pitch."

"Too true." Jack shuddered artistically. "The prospect does not bear thinking of."

Percy was frowning. "I can't see it. Why not let it out that you're all as rich as bedammed? God knows, you Lesters have been regarded as nothing more than barely well-to-do for generations. Now that's changed, why not reap the rewards?" His guileless expression was matched by his next words. "The debs would be yours for the asking—you could take your pick."

Both Lester men bent looks of transparent sympathy upon their hapless friend.

Bewildered, Percy blinked and patiently waited to be set aright.

Unable to hold a candle to his long-time companions in the matter of manly attributes, he had long since become reconciled to his much slighter figure, his sloping shoulders and spindly shanks. More than reconciled—he had found his vocation as a Pink of the *Ton*. Dressing to disguise his shortcomings and polishing his address to overcome his innate shyness had led to yet another discovery; his newfound status spared him from the trial of chasing women. Both Jack and Harry thrived on the sport, but Percy's inclinations were of a less robust nature. He adored the ladies—from a distance. In his estimation, his present style of life was infinitely preferable to the racy existence enjoyed by his companions.

However, as both Jack and Harry were well aware, his present lifestyle left him woefully adrift when it came to matters of strategy in handling the female of the species, particularly those dragons who menaced all rakes—the matrons of the *ton*.

And, naturally, with his mild manners and retiring ways, he was hardly the sort of gentleman who inhabited the debutantes' dreams. All the Lester men—Jack, at thirty-six, with his dark good looks and powerful athlete's physique, and Harry, younger by two years, his lithe figure forever graceful and ineffably elegant—and even twenty-four-year-old Gerald, with his boyish charm—were definitely the stuff of which females' dreams were made.

"Actually, Percy, old man," Harry said. "I rather suspect Jack thinks he can have his pick regardless."

Jack shot a supercilious glance at his sibling. "As a matter of fact, I've not previously considered the point."

Harry's lips lifted; gracefully, he inclined his head. "I have infinite confidence, oh brother mine, that if and when you find your particular golden head, you won't need the aid of our disgusting wealth in persuading her to your cause."

"Yes—but *why* the secrecy?" Percy demanded.

"Because," Jack explained, "while the matrons have considered my fortune, as you so succinctly put it, as barely well-to-do, they've been content to let me stroll among their gilded flowers, letting me look my fill without undue interference."

With three profligate sons in the family and an income little more than a competence, it was commonly understood that the scions of Lester Hall would require wealthy brides. However, given the family connections and the fact that Jack, as eldest, would inherit the Hall and principal estates, no one had been surprised when, once he had let it be known he was seriously contemplating matrimony, the invitations had rolled in.

"Naturally," Harry suavely put in. "With all Jack's years of…worldly experience, no one expects him to fall victim to any simple snares and, given the lack of a Lester fortune, there's insufficient incentive for the dragons to waste effort mounting any of their more convoluted schemes."

"So I've been free to view the field." Jack took back the conversational reins. "However, should any whiff of our changed circumstances begin circulating through the *ton*, my life of unfettered ease will be over. The harpies will descend with a vengeance."

"Nothing they like better than the fall of a rake," Harry confided to Percy. "Brings out their best efforts—never more hellishly inventive than when they've a rich rake with a declared interest in matrimony firmly in their sights. They relish the prospect of the hunter being the hunted."

Jack threw him a quelling glance. "Sufficient to say that my life will no longer be at all comfortable. I won't be able to set

foot outside my door without guarding against the unimagin-
able. Debs at every turn, hanging on a fellow's arm, forever
batting their silly lashes. It's easy to put one off women for
life.''

Harry shut his eyes and shuddered.

The light of understanding dawned on Percy's cherubic
countenance. ''Oh,'' he said. Then, ''In that case, you'd better
accept Lady Asfordby's invitation.''

Jack waved a languid hand. ''I've all the Season to go yet.
No need to get in a pother.''

''Ah, yes. But will you? Have all the Season, I mean?''
When both Jack and Harry looked lost, Percy explained, ''This
fortune of yours was made on 'Change, wasn't it?''

Jack nodded. ''Lenore took the advice of one of the pater's
acquaintances and staked a fleet of merchantmen to the Indies.
The company was formed through the usual channels and is
listed in London.''

''Precisely!'' Percy came to a flourishing halt by the fireplace. ''So any number of men with an interest at the Exchange
know the company was wildly successful. And lots of them
must know that the Lesters were one of the major backers. That
sort of thing's not secret, y'know. M'father, for one, would be
sure to know.''

Jack and Harry exchanged looks of dawning dismay.

''There's no way to silence all those who know,'' Percy
continued. ''So you've only got until one of those men happens
to mention to his wife that the Lesters' fortunes have changed
and the whole world will know.''

A groan escaped Harry.

''No—wait.'' Jack straightened. ''It's not that simple, thank
God.'' The last was said with all due reverence. ''Lenore organized it, but naturally she could hardly act for herself in the
matter. She used our broker, old Charters, a terribly stuffy old
soul. *He* has never approved of females being involved in business—the old man had to lean on him to accept instructions
from Lenore years ago. Charters only agreed on the understanding of secrecy all round—he didn't want it known that he took

orders from a woman. Which probably means he won't admit it was us he was working for, as it's fairly well known Lenore was in charge of our finances. If Charters doesn't talk, there's no reason to imagine our windfall will become common knowledge overnight.''

Percy frowned and pursed his lips. "Not overnight, maybe. But dashed if I think it'll be all that long. These things filter through the cracks in the mortar, so my old man says.''

A sober silence descended on the room as the occupants weighed the situation.

"Percy's right.'' Harry's expression was grim.

Glumly resigned, Jack held up Lady Asfordby's invitation. "In more ways than one. I'll send round to Lady Asfordby to expect us.''

"Not me.'' Harry shook his head decisively.

Jack's brows rose. "You'll get caught in the storm, too.''

Stubbornly, Harry shook his head again. He drained his glass and placed it on a nearby table. "*I* haven't let it be known I'm in the market for a wife, for the simple reason that I'm not.'' He stood, stretching his long, lean frame. Then he grinned. "Besides, I like living dangerously.''

Jack returned the grin with a smile.

"Anyway, I'm promised at Belvoir tomorrow. Gerald's there— I'll tip him the wink over our desire for silence on the subject of our communal fortune. So you can proffer my regrets to her ladyship with a clear conscience.'' Harry's grin broadened. "Don't forget to do so, incidentally. You might recall she was an old friend of our late lamented aunt and can be a positive dragon—she'll doubtless be in town for the Season, and I'd rather not find myself facing her fire.''

With a nod to Percy, Harry made for the door, dropping a hand on Jack's shoulder in passing. "I should inspect Prince's fetlock—see if that poultice has done any good. I'll be off early tomorrow, so I'll wish you good hunting.'' With a commiserating grin, he left.

As the door closed behind his brother, Jack's gaze returned

to Lady Asfordby's invitation. With a sigh, he put it in his pocket, then took a long sip of his brandy.

"So, are we going?" Percy asked around a yawn.

Grimly, Jack nodded. "We're going."

While Percy went up to bed and the house settled to slumber around him, Jack remained in his chair by the fire, blue eyes intent on the flames. He was still there when, an hour later, Harry re-entered the room.

"What? Still here?"

Jack sipped his brandy. "As you see."

Harry hesitated for a moment, then crossed to the sideboard. "Musing on the delights of matrimony?"

Head back, Jack let his eyes track his brother's movements. "On the inevitability of matrimony, if you really want to know."

Sinking onto the chaise, Harry lifted a brow. "Doesn't have to be you, you know."

Jack's eyes opened wide. "Is that an offer—the ultimate sacrifice?"

Harry grinned. "I was thinking of Gerald."

"Ah." Jack let his head fall back and stared at the ceiling. "I have to admit I've thought of him, too. But it won't do."

"Why not?"

"He'll never marry in time for the pater."

Harry grimaced but made no answer. Like Jack, he was aware of their sire's wish to see his line continue unbroken, as it had for generations past. It was the one last nagging worry clouding a mind otherwise prepared for death.

"But it's not only that," Jack admitted, his gaze distant. "If I'm to manage the Hall as it should be managed, I'll need a chatelaine—someone to take on the role Lenore filled. Not the business side, but all the rest of it. All the duties of a well-bred wife." His lips twisted wryly. "Since Lenore left, I've learned to appreciate her talents as never before. But the reins are in my hands now, and I'll be damned if I don't get my team running in good order."

Harry grinned. "Your fervour has raised a good few brows.

I don't think anyone expected such a transformation—profligate rakehell to responsible landowner in a matter of months."

Jack grunted. "You'd have changed, too, if the responsibility had fallen to you. But there's no question about it, I need a wife. One like Lenore."

"There aren't many like Lenore."

"Don't I know it." Jack let his disgruntlement show. "I'm seriously wondering if what I seek exists—a gentlewoman with charm and grace, efficient and firm enough to manage the reins."

"Blond, well-endowed and of sunny disposition?"

Jack shot his brother an irritated glance. "It certainly wouldn't hurt, given the rest of her duties."

Harry chuckled. "No likely prospects in sight?"

"Nary a one." Jack's disgust was back. "After a year of looking, I can truthfully inform you that not one candidate made me look twice. They're all so alike—young, sweet and innocent—and quite helpless. I need a woman with backbone and all I can find are clinging vines."

Silence filled the room as they both considered his words.

"Sure Lenore can't help?" Harry eventually asked.

Jack shook his head. "Eversleigh, damn his hide, was emphatic. His duchess will not be gracing the *ton's* ballrooms this Season. Instead," Jack continued, his eyes gently twinkling, "she'll be at home at Eversleigh, tending to her firstborn and his father, while increasing under Jason's watchful eye. Meanwhile, to use his words, the *ton* can go hang."

Harry laughed. "So she's really indisposed? I thought that business about morning sickness was an excuse Jason drummed up to whisk her out of the crowd."

Grimacing, Jack shook his head. "All too true, I fear. Which means that, having ploughed through last Season without her aid, while she was busy presenting Eversleigh with his heir, and frittered away the Little Season, too, I'm doomed to struggle on alone through the shoals of the upcoming Season, with a storm lowering on the horizon and no safe harbour in sight."

"A grim prospect," Harry acknowledged.

Jack grunted, his mind engrossed once more with marriage. For years, the very word had made him shudder. Now, with the ordeal before him, having spent hours contemplating the state, he was no longer so dismissive, so uninterested. It was his sister's marriage that had altered his view. Hardly the conventional image, for while Jason had married Lenore for a host of eminently conventional reasons, the depth of their love was apparent to all. The fond light that glowed in Jason's grey eyes whenever he looked at his wife had assured Jack that all was well with his sister—even more than Lenore's transparent joy. Any notion that his brother-in-law, ex-rake, for years the bane of the dragons, was anything other than besotted with his wife was simply not sustainable in the face of his rampant protectiveness.

Grimacing at the dying fire, Jack reached for the poker. He was not at all sure he wanted to be held in thrall as Jason, apparently without a qualm, was, yet he was very sure he wanted what his brother-in-law had found. A woman who loved him. And whom he loved in return.

Harry sighed, then stood and stretched. "Time to go up. You'd best come, too—no sense in not looking your best for Lady Asfordby's young ladies."

With a look of pained resignation, Jack rose. As they crossed to the sideboard to set down their glasses, he shook his head. "I'm tempted to foist the whole business back in Lady Luck's lap. She handed us this fortune—it's only fair she provide the solution to the problem she's created."

"Ah, but Lady Luck is a fickle female." Harry turned as he opened the door. "Are you sure you want to gamble the rest of your life on her whim?"

Jack's expression was grim. "I'm already gambling with the rest of my life. This damned business is no different from the turn of a card or the toss of a die."

"Except that if you don't like the stake, you can decline to wager."

"True, but finding the right stake is my problem."

As they emerged into the dark hall and took possession of

the candles left waiting, Jack continued, "My one, particular golden head—it's the least Lady Luck can do, to find her and send her my way."

Harry shot him an amused glance. "Tempting Fate, brother mine?"

"Challenging Fate," Jack replied.

WITH A SATISFYING SWIRL of her silk skirts, Sophia Winterton completed the last turn of the Roger de Coverley and sank gracefully into a smiling curtsy. About her, the ballroom of Asfordby Grange was full to the seams with a rainbow-hued throng. Perfume wafted on the errant breezes admitted through the main doors propped wide in the middle of the long room. Candlelight flickered, sheening over artful curls and glittering in the jewels displayed by the dowagers lining the wall.

"A positive pleasure, my dear Miss Winterton." Puffing slightly, Mr. Bantcombe bowed over her hand. "A most invigorating measure."

Rising, Sophie smiled. "Indeed, sir." A quick glance around located her young cousin, Clarissa, ingenuously thanking a youthful swain some yards away. With soft blue eyes and alabaster skin, her pale blond ringlets framing a heart-shaped face, Clarissa was a hauntingly lovely vision. Just now, all but quivering with excitement, she forcibly reminded Sophie of a highly strung filly being paraded for the very first time.

With an inward smile, Sophie gave her hand and her attention to Mr. Bantcombe. "Lady Asfordby's balls may not be as large as the assemblies in Melton, but to my mind, they're infinitely superior."

"Naturally, naturally." Mr. Bantcombe was still short of breath. "Her ladyship is of first consequence hereabouts—and she always takes great pains to exclude the *hoi polloi*. None of the park-saunterers and half-pay officers who follow the pack will be here tonight."

Sophie squelched a wayward thought to the effect that she would not really mind one or two half-pay officers, just to lend colour to the ranks of the gentlemen she had come to know suffocatingly well over the last six months. She pinned a bright smile to her lips. "Shall we return to my aunt, sir?"

She had joined her aunt and uncle's Leicestershire household last September, after waving her father, Sir Humphrey Winterton, eminent paleontologist, a fond farewell. Departing on an expedition of unknown duration, to Syria, so she believed, her father had entrusted her to the care of her late mother's only sister, Lucilla Webb, an arrangement that met with Sophie's unqualified approval. The large and happy household inhabiting Webb Park, a huge rambling mansion some miles from Asfordby Grange, was a far cry from the quiet, studious existence she had endured at the side of her grieving and taciturn sire ever since her mother's death four years ago.

Her aunt, a slender, ethereal figure draped in cerulean-blue silk, hair that still retained much of its silvery blond glory piled high on her elegant head, was gracefully adorning one of the chaises lining the wall, in earnest conversation with Mrs. Haverbuck, another of the local ladies.

"Ah, there you are, Sophie." Lucilla Webb turned as, with a smile and a nod for Sophie, Mrs. Haverbuck departed. "I'm positively in awe of your energy, my dear." Pale blue eyes took in Mr. Bantcombe's florid face. "Dear Mr. Bantcombe, perhaps you could fetch me a cool drink?"

Mr. Bantcombe readily agreed. Bowing to Sophie, he departed.

"Poor man," Lucilla said as he disappeared into the crowd. "Obviously not up to your standard, Sophie dear."

Sophie's lips twitched.

"Still," Lucilla mused in her gentle airy voice, "I'm truly glad to see you so enjoying yourself, my dear. You look very well, even if 'tis I who say so. The *ton* will take to you—and you to it, I make no doubt."

"Indeed the *ton* will, if your aunt and I and all your mother's old friends have anything to say about it!"

Both Sophie and Lucilla turned as, with much rustling to stiff bombazine, Lady Entwhistle took Mrs. Haverbuck's place.

"Just stopped in to tell you, Lucilla, that Henry's agreed—

we're to go up to town tomorrow.'' Lifting a pair of lorgnettes from where they hung about her neck, Lady Entwhistle embarked on a detailed scrutiny of Sophie with all the assurance of an old family friend. Sophie knew that no facet of her appearance—the style in which her golden curls had been piled upon her head, the simple but undeniably elegant cut of her rose-magenta silk gown, her long ivory gloves, even her tiny satin dancing slippers—would escape inspection.

"Humph.'' Her ladyship concluded her examination. "Just as I thought. You'll set the *ton*'s bachelors back on their heels, m'dear. Which,'' she added, turning to Lucilla, a conspiratorial gleam in her eye, "is precisely to my point. I'm giving a ball on Monday. To introduce Henry's cousin's boy to our acquaintance. Can I hope you'll be there?''

Lucilla pursed her lips, eyes narrowing. "We're to leave at the end of the week, so I should imagine we'll reach London by Sunday.'' Her face cleared. "I can see no reason not to accept your invitation, Mary.''

"Good!'' With her habitual bustle, Lady Entwhistle stood, improbable golden ringlets bouncing. Catching sight of Clarissa through the crowd, she added, "It'll be an informal affair, and it's so early in the Season I see no harm in Clarissa joining us, do you?''

Lucilla smiled. "I know she'll be delighted.''

Lady Entwhistle chuckled. "All wound tight with excitement, is she? Ah, well—just remember when we were like that, Lucy—you and I and Maria.'' Her ladyship's eyes strayed to Sophie, a certain anticipation in their depths. Then, with determined briskness, she gathered her reticule. "But I must away—I'll see you in London.''

Sophie exchanged a quiet smile with her aunt, then, lips curving irrepressibly, looked out over the crowded room. If she were asked, she would have to admit that it was not only Clarissa, barely seventeen and keyed up to make her come-out, who was prey to a certain excitement. Beneath her composure, that of an experienced young lady of twenty-two years, Sophie was conscious of a lifting of her heart. She was looking forward to her first full Season.

She would have to find a husband, of course. Her mother's friends, not to speak of her aunt, would accept nothing less. Strangely, the prospect did not alarm her, as it certainly had years ago. She was more than up to snuff—she fully intended to look carefully and choose wisely.

"Do my eyes deceive me, or has Ned finally made his move?"

Lucilla's question had Sophie following her aunt's gaze to where Edward Ascombe, Ned to all, the son of a neighbour, was bowing perfunctorily over her cousin's hand. Sophie saw Clarissa stiffen.

A little above average height, Ned was a relatively serious young man, his father's pride and joy, at twenty-one already absorbed in caring for the acres that would, one day, be his. He was also determined to have Clarissa Webb to wife. Unfortunately, at the present moment, with Clarissa full of nervy excitement at the prospect of meeting unknown gentlemen up from London for the hunting, Ned was severely handicapped, suffering as he did from the twin disadvantages of being a blameless and worthy suitor and having known Clarissa all her life. Worse, he had already made it plain that his heart was at Clarissa's tiny feet.

Her sympathy at the ready, Sophie watched as he straightened and, all unwitting, addressed Clarissa.

"A cotillion, if you have one left, Clary." Ned smiled confidently, no premonition of the shaky ground on which he stood showing in his open countenance.

Eyes kindling, Clarissa hissed, "Don't call me that!"

Ned's gentle smile faded. "What the d-deuce *am* I to call you? *Miss Webb?*"

"Exactly!" Clarissa further elevated her already alarmingly tilted chin. Another young gentleman hovered on her horizon; she promptly held out her hand, smiling prettily at the newcomer.

Ned scowled in the same direction. Before the slightly

shaken young man could assemble his wits, Ned prompted, "My dance, *Miss Webb?*" His voice held quite enough scorn to sting.

"I'm afraid I'm not available for the cotillion, *Mr. Ascombe.*" Through the crowd, Clarissa caught her mother's eyes. "Perhaps the next country dance?"

For a moment, Sophie, watching, wondered if she and Lucilla would be called upon to intervene. Then Ned drew himself up stiffly. He spoke briefly, clearly accepting whatever Clarissa had offered, then bowed and abruptly turned on his heel.

Clarissa stood, her lovely face blank, watching his back until he was swallowed up by the crowd. For an instant, her lower lip softened. Then, chin firming, she straightened and beamed a brilliant smile at the young gentleman still awaiting an audience.

"Ah." Lucilla smiled knowingly. "How life does go on. She'll marry Ned in the end, of course. I'm sure the Season will be more than enough to demonstrate the wisdom of her heart."

Sophie could only hope so, for Clarissa's sake as well as Ned's.

"Miss Winterton?"

Sophie turned to find Mr. Marston bowing before her. A reserved but eminently eligible gentleman of independent means, he was the target of more than a few of the local matchmaking mamas. As she dipped in a smooth curtsy, Sophie inwardly cursed her guilty blush. Mr. Marston was enamoured—and she felt nothing at all in response.

Predictably interpreting her blush as a sign of maidenly awareness, Mr. Marston's thin smile surfaced. "Our quadrille, my dear." With a punctilious bow to Lucilla, who regally inclined her head, he accepted the hand Sophie gave him and escorted her to the floor.

Her smile charming, her expression serene, Sophie dipped and swayed through the complicated figures, conscious of treading a very fine line. She refused to retreat in confusion before Mr. Marston's attentions, yet she had no wish to encourage him.

"Indeed, sir," she replied to one of his sallies. "I'm enjoying the ball immensely. However, I feel no qualms about meeting those gentlemen up from London—after all, my cousin and I will shortly be in London ballrooms. Acquaintances made tonight could prove most comforting."

From her partner's disapproving expression, Sophie deduced that the thought of her gaining comfort from acquaintance with any other gentleman, from London or elsewhere, was less than pleasing. Inwardly, she sighed. Depressing pretensions gently was an art she had yet to master.

About them, Lady Asfordby's guests swirled and twirled, a colourful crowd, drawn primarily from the local families, with here and there the elegant coats of those London swells of whom her ladyship approved. This distinction did not extend to all that many of the small army of *ton*-ish males who, during the hunting season, descended on the nearby town of Melton Mowbray, lured by the attraction of the Quorn, the Cottesmore and the Belvoir packs.

Jack realized as much as, with Percy hovering in his shadow, he paused on the threshold of her ladyship's ballroom. As he waited for his hostess, whom he could see forging her way through the crowd to greet him, he was conscious of the flutter his appearance had provoked. Like a ripple, it passed down the dark line of dowagers seated around the room, then spread in ever widening circles to ruffle the feathers of their charges, presently engaged in a quadrille.

With a cynical smile, he bowed elegantly over her ladyship's beringed fingers.

"So glad you decided to come, Lester."

Having smoothly introduced Percy, whom Lady Asfordby greeted with gratified aplomb, Jack scanned the dancers.

And saw her.

She was immediately in front of him, in the set nearest the door. His gaze had been drawn to her, her rich golden curls shining like a beacon. Even as realization hit, his eyes met hers.

They were blue, paler than his own, the blue of cloudless summer skies. As he watched, her eyes widened, her lips parted. Then she twirled and turned away.

Beside him, Percy was filling Lady Asfordby's ears with an account of his father's latest illness. Jack inhaled deeply, his eyes on the slim figure before him, the rest of the company a dull haze about her.

Her hair was true gold, rich and bountiful, clustered atop her neat head, artfully errant curls trailing over her small ears and down the back of her slender neck. The rest of her was slender, too, yet, he was pleased to note, distinctly well-rounded. Her delectable curves were elegantly gowned in a delicate hue that was too dark for a debutante; her arms, gracefully arching in the movements of the dance, displayed an attractive roundness not in keeping with a very young girl.

Was she married?

Suavely, Jack turned to Lady Asfordby. "As it happens, I have not met many of my neighbours. Could I impose on your ladyship to introduce me?"

There was, of course, nothing Lady Asfordby would have liked better. Her sharp eyes gleamed with fanatical zeal. "Such a loss, your dear aunt. How's your father getting on?"

While replying to these and similar queries on Lenore and his brothers, all of whom her ladyship knew of old, Jack kept his golden head in sight. Perfectly happy to disguise his intent by stopping to chat with whomever Lady Asfordby thought to introduce, he steered his hostess by inexorable degrees to the chaise beside which his goal stood.

A small knot of gentlemen, none of them mere youths, had gathered about her to pass the time between the dances. Two other young ladies joined the circle; she welcomed them graciously, her confidence as plain as the smile on her lips.

Twice he caught her glancing at him. On both occasions, she quickly looked away. Jack suppressed his smile and patiently endured yet another round of introductions to some local squire's lady.

Finally, Lady Asfordby turned towards the crucial chaise.

"And, of course, you must meet Mrs. Webb. I dare say you're acquainted with her husband, Horatio Webb of Webb Park. A financier, you know."

The name rang a bell in Jack's mind—something to do with horses and hunting. But they were rapidly approaching the chaise on which an elegant matron sat, benignly watching over a very young girl, unquestionably her daughter, as well as his golden head. Mrs. Webb turned as they approached. Lady Asfordby made the introduction; Jack found himself bowing over a delicate hand, his eyes trapped in a searching, ice-blue stare.

"Good evening, Mr. Lester. Are you here for the hunting?"

"Indeed yes, ma'am." Jack blinked, then smiled, careful not to overdo the gesture. To him, Mrs. Webb was instantly recognizable; his golden head was protected by a very shrewd dragon.

A lifted finger drew the younger girl forward.

"Allow me to present my daughter, Clarissa." Lucilla looked on as Clarissa, blushing furiously, performed the regulation curtsy with her customary grace. Speech, however, seemed beyond her. Lifting one sceptical brow, Lucilla spared a glance for the magnificence before her, then slanted a quick look at Sophie. Her niece was studiously absorbed with her friends.

An imperious gesture, however, succeeded in attracting her attention.

Her smile restrained, Lucilla beckoned Sophie forward. "And, of course," she continued, rescuing Jack from Clarissa's tongue-tied stare, "you must let me introduce my niece, Miss Sophia Winterton." Lucilla halted, then raised her fine brows. "But perhaps you've met before—in London? Sophie was presented some years ago, but her Season was cut short by the untimely death of her mother." Switching her regal regard to Sophie, Lucilla continued, "Mr. Jack Lester, my dear."

Conscious of her aunt's sharply perceptive gaze, Sophie kept her expression serene. Dipping politely, she coolly extended her fingers, carefully avoiding Mr. Lester's eye.

She had first seen him as he stood at the door, darkly, starkly handsome. In his midnight-blue coat, which fitted his large lean frame as if it had been moulded to him, his thick dark hair falling in fashionable dishevelment over his broad brow, his gaze intent as he scanned the room, he had appeared as some predator—a wolf, perhaps—come to select his prey. Her feet had missed a step when his gaze had fallen on her. Quickly looking away, she had been surprised to find her heart racing, her breath tangled in her throat.

Now, with his gaze, an unnervingly intense dark blue, full upon her, she lifted her chin, calmly stating, "Mr. Lester and I have not previously met, Aunt."

Jack's gaze trapped hers as he took her hand. His lips curved. "An accident of fate which has surely been my loss."

Sophie sternly quelled an instinctive tremor. His voice was impossibly deep. As the undercurrent beneath his tones washed over her, tightening the vice about her chest, she watched him straighten from an ineffably elegant bow.

He caught her glance—and smiled.

Sophie stiffened. Tilting her chin, she met his gaze. "Have you hunted much hereabouts, sir?"

His smile reached his eyes. A small shift in position brought him closer. "Indeed, Miss Winterton."

He looked down at her; Sophie froze.

"I rode with the Quorn only yesterday."

Breathless, Sophie ignored the twinkle in his eye. "My uncle, Mr. Webb, is a keen adherent of the sport." A quick glance about showed her aunt in deep conversation with Lady Asfordby; her court was hidden by Mr. Lester's broad shoulders. He had, most effectively, cut her out from the crowd.

"Really?" Jack lifted a polite brow. His gaze fell to her hands, clasped before her, then rose, definite warmth in the deep blue. "But your aunt mentioned you had been in London before?"

Sophie resisted the urge to narrow her eyes. "I was presented four years ago, but my mother contracted a chill shortly thereafter."

"And you never returned to grace the ballrooms of the *ton*? Fie, my dear—how cruel."

The last words were uttered very softly. Any doubts Sophie had harboured that Mr. Lester was not as he appeared vanished. She shot him a very straight glance, irrelevantly noting how the hard line of his lips softened when he smiled. "My father was much cut up by my mother's death. I remained with him, at home in Northamptonshire, helping with the household and the estate."

His response to that depressing statement was not what she had expected. A gleam of what could only be intrigued interest flared in his dark eyes.

"Your loyalty to your father does you credit, Miss Winterton." Jack made the statement with flat sincerity. His companion inclined her head slightly, then glanced away. The perfect oval of her face was a delicate setting for her regular features: wide blue eyes fringed with long, thick lashes, golden brown as were her arched brows, a straight little nose and full bowed lips the colour of crushed strawberries. Her chin was definite, yet gently rounded; her complexion was like thick cream, rich and luscious, without flaw. Jack cleared his throat. "But did you not yearn to return to the *ton*'s ballrooms?"

The question took Sophie by surprise. She considered, then answered, "No. Indeed, the thought never arose. I had more than enough to occupy myself. And I frequently visited with my father's sisters at Bath and Tonbridge Wells." She glanced up—and laughed at the comical grimace that contorted her companion's face.

"Tonbridge Wells?" he uttered, dramatically faint. "My dear Miss Winterton, you would be *wasted* there, smothered beneath the weight of ageing propriety."

Sophie sternly suppressed a giggle. "Indeed, it wasn't very lively," she conceded. "Luckily, my mother had many friends who invited me to their house parties. However, at home, I must admit I oftimes pined for younger company. My father lived very much retired through that time."

"And now?"

"My aunt—" she nodded at Lucilla on the chaise which by some magic was now a step away "—persuaded Papa to take an interest in an expedition. He's a paleontologist, you see."

From beneath her lashes, she glanced up, waiting.

Jack met her innocent gaze, his own inscrutable. Despite her best efforts, Sophie's lips twitched. With a resigned air, Jack raised a languidly interrogatory brow.

This time, Sophie did giggle. "Old bones," she informed him, her voice confidingly low. Despite the fact he had just sidestepped a trap guaranteed to depress the pretensions of any overly confident rake, Sophie could not stop her smile. As her eyes met his, warmly appreciative, the suspicion that while Mr. Lester might be demonstrably confident, he was not overly so, broke over her. Her breath became tangled again.

His gaze sharpened. Before she could react, and retreat, he lifted his head, then glanced down at her, his brows lightly lifting.

"Unless my ears are at fault, that's a waltz starting up. Will you do me the honour, Miss Winterton?"

The invitation was delivered with a calm smile, while his eyes stated, very clearly, that no feeble excuse would suffice to deflect him.

Nerves aquiver, Sophie surrendered to the inevitable with a suffocatingly gracious inclination of her head.

Her determinedly calm composure very nearly cracked when he swept her onto the floor. His arm about her felt like iron; there was such strength in him it would be frightening if it was not so deliberately contained. He whirled her down the floor; she felt like thistledown, lighter than air, anchored to reality only by his solidity and the warm clasp of his hand.

She had never waltzed like this before, precessing without conscious thought, her feet naturally following his lead, barely touching the floor. As her senses, stirred by his touch, gradually settled, she glanced up. "You dance very well, Mr. Lester."

His eyes glinted down at her from under heavy lids. "I've had lots of practice, my dear."

His meaning was very clear; she should have blushed and

looked away. Instead, Sophie found enough courage to smile
serenely before letting her gaze slide from his. Aware of the
dangerous currents about her, she made no further attempt to
converse.

For his part, Jack was content to remain silent; he had
learned all he needed to know. Freed of the burden of polite
conversation, his mind could dwell on the pleasure of having
her, at long last, in his arms. She fitted perfectly, neither too
tall nor, thankfully, too short. If she were closer, her curls
would tickle his nose, her forehead level with his chin. She
was not completely relaxed—he could not expect that—yet she
was content enough in his arms. The temptation to tighten his
hold, to draw her closer, was very real, yet he resisted. Too
many eyes were upon them, and she did not yet know she was
his.

The last chord sounded; he whirled them to a flourishing
halt. He looked down, smiling as he drew her hand through his
arm. "I will return you to your aunt, Miss Winterton."

Sophie blinked up at him. Could he hear her heart thudding?
"Thank you, sir." Retreating behind a mask of cool formality,
she allowed him to lead her back to the chaise. However, instead of leaving her by her aunt's side, her partner merely nodded at Lucilla, then led her to where her circle of acquaintances
was once again forming. Larger than life, he stood beside her,
acknowledging her introductions with a coolly superior air
which, she suspected, was innate. Feeling her nerves stretch
and flicker, Sophie glanced up as the musicians once more laid
bow to string.

His eyes met hers. Suddenly breathless, Sophie looked away.
Her gaze fell on Lady Asfordby, bustling up.

"Glad to see, Lester, that you're not one of those London
dandies who think they're above dancing in country ballrooms."

Stifling a resigned sigh, Jack turned to his hostess, an amiable smile on his lips.

Her ladyship's gimlet gaze swept the assembled company,

fixing on a bright-faced young lady. "Dare say Miss Elder-bridge will be pleased to do you the honour."

Thus adjured, Jack bent a practiced smile on Miss Elder-bridge, who assured him, somewhat breathlessly, that she would be delighted to partner him in the country dance about to begin. Hearing a murmur to his left, Jack glanced back to see Sophie place her hand on another gentleman's sleeve. They were both poised to move away, their partners by their sides. Jack grasped the moment, trapping Sophie's gaze in his, lowering his voice to say, "Until next we meet, Miss Winterton."

Sophie felt her eyes widen. Lowering her lashes, she inclined her head. As she moved to her place in the set, she felt his words reverberate deep within her. Her heart thudded; it was an effort to concentrate on Mr. Simpkins's conversation.

There had been a wealth of meaning hidden in Jack Lester's subtle farewell—and she had no idea whether he meant it or not.

CHAPTER TWO

HE DID MEAN IT.

That was the only logical conclusion left to Sophie when, poised to alight from the Webb family carriage in the shadow of the lych-gate the next morning, she caught sight of a pair of powerful shoulders, stylishly encased in the best Bath superfine, and then their owner, wending his way aimlessly through the gravestones. As if sensing her regard, he looked around and saw her. White teeth flashed as he smiled. Recalled to her surroundings by Clarissa's finger in her ribs, Sophie abruptly gathered her wits and descended.

In the protective confines of the lych-gate, she fussed with her reticule and the skirts of her cherry-red pelisse while her cousins, Jeremy, George and Amy, as well as Clarissa—at just six years old, the twins, Henry and Hermione, were too young to be trusted in church—descended and straightened their attire under their mother's eagle eye. Finally satisfied, Lucilla nodded and they fell into line, Amy beside her mother in the lead, Sophie and Clarissa immediately behind, followed by the two boys, their boots on the paving stones.

As they ascended the steps leading up from the gate, Sophie carefully avoided glancing at the graveyard to their left, looking up, instead, at the sharp spire that rose into the wintry sky. March had arrived, unexpectedly mild. The chill blue of the heavens was dotted with puffs of white cloud, scudding along before the brisk breeze.

"Good morning, Mrs. Webb."

The cavalcade stopped. Although she could only see her aunt's back, Sophie had the distinct impression that even that redoubtable matron was taken aback by the sight of Jack Lester bowing elegantly before her just yards from the church door. His ambling peregrination had, most conveniently, converged with their route at that spot.

Regardless of her surprise, there was no doubt of her aunt's pleasure. Her "Mr. Lester, how fortunate. We had not looked to see you thus soon" positively purred with satisfaction. "Would you care to join us in our pew, sir?"

"I'd be delighted, ma'am." Until then, Jack had not looked Sophie's way. Now, smiling, he turned to her. "Good morning, Miss Winterton." He briefly nodded at Clarissa. "Miss Webb."

Sophie dipped and gave him her hand.

"Sophie dear, perhaps you would show Mr. Lester the way while I take care of this brood." Her aunt waved an airy hand at her offspring, who, of course, could very well have found their way unaided to the pew they occupied every Sunday.

"Of course, Aunt." Sophie knew better than to argue.

As Lucilla swept her children into the church, Sophie risked a glance upwards, only to meet a pair of dark blue eyes that held a very large measure of amused understanding. Her own eyes narrowed.

"Miss Winterton?" With a gallant gesture, Jack offered his arm. When she hesitated, his brows rose slightly.

Head high, Sophie placed her fingers on his sleeve and allowed him to lead her to the door. As they entered the dim nave, she noted the smothered stir as their neighbours noticed her escort. It was close to eleven and the church was full. Hiding her consciousness behind a calm mask, she indicated the pair of pews, close to the front on the left, where her cousins were already settling. Glancing down as they passed the pew two rows behind, she encountered a malevolent stare from Mrs. Marston and a sternly disapproving one from her son, seated supportively beside her.

Suppressing a sudden grin, Sophie reflected that, as this was God's house, perhaps Mr. Lester was the Almighty's way of assisting her in the difficult task of rejecting Mr. Marston. She had no time to dwell on that unlikely prospect, however, for, gaining the second of the Webb pews, she found herself seated between Lucilla and Mr. Lester. Luckily, the vicar, Mr. Snodgrass, entered almost immediately.

To her relief, Mr. Lester behaved impeccably, as if going to church on Sunday were his normal habit.

Beside her, Jack bided his time.

When the congregation rose for the first hymn, he reached out and touched Sophie's gloved wrist. Leaning closer, he whispered, "I'm afraid, Miss Winterton, that I did not anticipate attending church during my stay in Leicestershire."

She blinked up at him, then glanced down at the slim volume covered in tooled blue leather that she had extracted from her reticule.

"Oh." With an effort, Sophie dragged her mind from the disturbing thought of what, exactly, *had* brought him to the tiny church of Allingham Downs. Her fingers busy flicking through the pages, she glanced up at him and hoped her distrust was evident. "Perhaps, sir, if I hold it between us, we could share my book?"

He smiled, so very sweetly that, if she had not known better, she would have thought his predicament an innocent oversight. Raising her chin, she held her hymnal between them, up and slightly to her right.

The organ swelled into the introduction. Even as she drew breath for the first note of the first verse, Sophie experienced an inner quake. He had moved closer, an action excused by the fine print of the hymnal. His shoulder was behind her, her shoulder close to his chest. She could sense the warmth of his large body, now so near—and feel the dagger glances of the Marstons, mother and son, on her back.

Her hand shook; his came up to steady the hymnal. She quelled the impulse to glance sideways—he was so close, his head bent, his eyes would be very near, his lips a potent distraction. With an effort, she concentrated on the music, only to be thoroughly distracted by the sound of his warm baritone, rich and strong, effortlessly supporting her soprano.

The hymn was one of praise—and an unexpected joy.

At its conclusion, Sophie felt slightly dizzy. She forced herself to breathe deeply.

Her companion hesitated; she knew his gaze was on her. Then he lifted the hymnal from her hand, gently closed it and presented it to her.

"Thank you, Miss Winterton."

It was impossible; she had to glance up. His eyes, darkly blue, warm and gently smiling, were every bit as close as she had imagined; his lips, softened by his smile, drew her gaze.

For a moment, time stood still.

With an enormous effort, Sophie dragged in a breath and inclined her head.

They were the last to sit down.

The sermon brought her no peace; indeed, Mr. Snodgrass would have needed to be inspired to compete with her thoughts, and the subtle tug of the presence beside her. She survived the second hymn only because she now understood the danger; she kept her mind totally focused on the lyrics and melody, ignoring her companion's harmony as best she could. Ignoring *him* proved even more difficult.

It was something of a relief to stroll slowly up the aisle, her hand on his sleeve. They were among the last to quit the church. Lucilla and her children preceded them; her aunt stopped on the porch steps to exchange her usual few words with the vicar.

"Sophia you know, of course." Lucilla paused as the vicar nodded, beamed and shook Sophie's hand. "But I'm not sure if you've met Mr. Lester. From Rawling's Cottage." Lucilla gestured at Jack, immediately behind Sophie.

"Indeed?" Mr. Snodgrass was an absent-minded old soul. "I don't recall ever having met anyone from there." He blinked owlishly up at Jack.

Sophie looked up in time to catch the reproachful glance that Jack bent on her aunt, before, with ready courtesy, he greeted the vicar.

"I'm rarely to be found in these parts, I'm afraid."

"Ah." The vicar nodded his head in complete understanding. "Up for the hunting."

Jack caught Sophie's eye. "Just so."

Sternly quelling a shiver, Sophie turned away. Her aunt had stopped to chat with Mrs. Marston farther along the path. Clarissa stood slightly to one side, cloaked in fashionable boredom. This last was attributable to Ned Ascombe, standing some yards away, his expression similarly abstracted. Noting the quick, surreptitious glances each threw the other, Sophie struggled not to smile. Feeling immeasurably older than the youthful pair, she stepped off the church steps and strolled slowly in her aunt's wake.

Jack made to follow but was detained by the vicar.

"I often used to ride with the Cottesmore, you know. Excellent pack, excellent. Major Coffin was the Master, then." Launched on reminiscence, the old man rambled on.

From the corner of his eye, Jack watched Sophie join her aunt, who was deep in discussion with a country matron, a large figure, swathed in knitted scarves.

"And then there was Mr. Dunbar, of course..."

Jack stiffened as a dark-coated gentleman stepped around the country dame to accost Sophie. Abruptly, he turned to the vicar, smoothly breaking into his monologue. "Indeed, sir. The Cottesmore has always been a most highly qualified pack. I do hope you'll excuse me—I believe Miss Winterton has need of me."

With a nod, Jack turned and strode briskly down the path. He reached Sophie's side just in time to hear the unknown gentleman remark, in a tone that, to Jack, sounded a great deal too familiar, "Your aunt mentioned that she expected to remove to London at the end of the week. Dare I hope I may call on you before you depart?"

Inwardly, Sophie grimaced. "I'm sure, Mr. Marston, that my aunt will be delighted, as always, to entertain Mrs. Marston and yourself. However, I'm not certain of her plans for this week. It's so very complicated, transferring the whole family up to town."

Sensing a presence by her side, she turned and, with inexplicable relief, beheld her late companion. He was not looking at her, however, but at Mr. Marston, with a frown in his eyes if not on his face.

"I believe I introduced you to Mr. Marston last evening, Mr. Lester."

The dark blue gaze momentarily flicked her way. "Indeed, Miss Winterton." Apparently a distant nod was all the recognition Mr. Marston rated.

For his part, Phillip Marston had drawn himself up, his thin lips pinched, his long nose elevated, nostrils slightly flaring. He returned Jack's nod with one equally curt. "Lester." He then pointedly turned back to Sophie. "I have to say, Miss Winterton, that I cannot help but feel that Mrs. Webb is being far too soft-hearted in allowing the younger children to accompany the party." His gaze grew stern as it rested on Jeremy and George, engaged in an impromptu game of tag about the gravestones. "They would be better employed at their lessons."

"Oh, no, Mr. Marston—just think how educational the trip will be." Sophie did not add that 'soft-hearted' was a singularly inappropriate adjective when used in conjunction with her aunt. Lucilla might appear as fragile as glass, but her backbone was pure steel. Sophie knew the combination well; her own mother had been just the same. "The children have been so looking forward to it."

"I should think, Marston, that Mr. and Mrs. Webb are well able to decide the right of such matters."

Sophie blinked. The coldly superior edge of Mr. Lester's deep voice was distinctly dismissive. She turned, only to find an elegant sleeve cloaking an arm she already knew to be steel before her.

"If I may, I'll escort you to your carriage, Miss Winterton. Your aunt has moved on."

Sophie looked up; his expression was not what she had expected. Superficially assured, fashionably urbane, there was an underlying tension, a hint of hardness in the patriarchal fea-

tures; she was at a loss to account for it. However, she was not
about to decline an opportunity to escape Mr. Marston, particularly in his present, officiously disapproving mood. Nevertheless, she kept her answering smile restrained. Mr. Lester, regardless of his mood, needed no encouragement. "Thank you,
sir." Placing her hand on his sleeve, she looked back—and
surprised a look of distinct chagrin on Phillip Marston's face.
"Good day, Mr. Marston."

With a nod, she turned away, and found herself very close
to Jack Lester at the top of the steps above the lych-gate. Sophie's heart hiccoughed. She glanced up.

His dark eyes met hers, his expression mellow. "Helping
you down the steps is the least I can do to repay you for
your...company this morning, my dear."

Sophie did not need to look to know Phillip Marston and
his mother were close behind; all the confirmation she needed
was contained in Jack Lester's smooth, deep and thoroughly
reprehensible tone. Incensed, unable to contradict his subtle
suggestion, she glared at him. "Indeed, Mr. Lester, you are
certainly in my debt."

His slow smile softened his lips. "I'll look forward to re-
paying your kindness, Miss Winterton—when I see you in London."

He made it sound like a promise—one her aunt made certain
of as he handed her into the carriage.

"I would invite you to call, Mr. Lester," Lucilla declared.
"Yet with our departure imminent, I fear it would be unwise.
Perhaps you might call on us when you return to the capital?"

"Indeed, Mrs. Webb, nothing would give me greater pleasure." The carriage door was shut; he bowed, a gesture compounded of strength and grace. "I shall look forward to seeing
you in London, Mrs. Webb. Miss Webb." His blue eyes caught
Sophie's. "Miss Winterton."

Outwardly calm, Sophie nodded in farewell. The carriage
jolted forward, then the horses found their stride. The last view
she had was of an elegant figure in pale grey morning coat,
tightly fitting inexpressibles and highly polished Hessians, his

dark hair slightly ruffled by the breeze. He dominated her vision; in contrast, in his severe, if correct, garb, Mr. Marston seemed to fade into the shadows of the lych-gate. Sophie laid her head back against the squabs, her thoughts in an unaccustomed whirl.

Her aunt, she noticed, smiled all the way home.

SUNDAY AFTERNOON was a quiet time in the Webb household. Sophie habitually spent it in the back parlour. In a household that included five boisterous children, there was always a pile of garments awaiting mending and darning. Although the worst was done by her aunt's seamstress, Lucilla had always encouraged both Clarissa and herself to help with the more delicate work.

Her needle flashing in the weak sunshine slanting through the large mullioned windows, Sophie sat curled in one corner of the comfortable old chaise. While a small part of her mind concentrated on the work in her hands, her thoughts were far away.

The click of the latch brought her head up.

"Melly's here." Clarissa came through the door, followed by her bosom bow, Mellicent Hawthorne, commonly known as Melly.

Sophie smiled a ready welcome at Melly, a short, plump figure, still slightly roly-poly in the manner of a young puppy, an impression enhanced by her long, floppy, brown ringlets and huge, spaniel-like eyes. These were presently twinkling.

"Mama's talking to Mrs. Webb, so I'm here for at least an hour. Plenty of time for a comfortable cose." Melly curled up in the armchair while Clarissa settled on the other end of the chaise. Seeing Clarissa reach for a needle and thread, Melly offered, "Would you like me to help?"

Sophie exchanged a quick glance with Clarissa. "No need," she assured Melly. "There's really not that much to do." She blithely ignored the huge pile in the basket.

"Good." Melly heaved a sigh of relief. "I really don't think I'm much good at it."

Sophie bit her lip. Clarissa, she saw, was bent over her stitching. The last time Melly had "helped" with the mending, at least half the garments had had to be rewashed to removed the bloodstains. And if there was one task worse than darning, it was unpicking a tangled darn.

"Still, I don't suppose Mrs. Webb will have you darning in London. Oooh!" Melly hugged herself. "*How* I envy you, Clarissa! Just imagine being in the capital, surrounded by beaux and London swells—just like Mr. Lester."

Clarissa lifted her head, blue eyes alight. "Indeed, I really can't wait! It will be beyond anything great—to find oneself in such company, solicited by elegant gentlemen. I'm sure they'll eclipse the country gentlemen—well—" she shrugged "—how could they not? It will be *unutterably* thrilling."

The fervour behind the comment made Sophie glance up. Clarissa's eyes shone with innocent anticipation. Looking down at the tiny stitches she was inserting in a tear in one of Jeremy's cuffs, Sophie frowned. After a moment, she ventured, "You really should not judge all London gentlemen by Mr. Lester, Clarissa."

Unfortunately, her cousin mistook her meaning.

"But there *can't* be many more elegant, Sophie. Why, that coat he wore to the ball was top of the trees. And he did look so dashing this morning. And you have to admit he has a certain air." Clarissa paused for breath, then continued, "His bow is very graceful—have you noticed? It makes one wonder at the clumsiness of others. And his speech is very refined, is it not?"

"His voice, too," put in Melly. She shivered artistically. "So deep it reaches inside you and sort of rumbles there."

Sophie pricked her finger. Frowning, she put it in her mouth.

"And his waltzing must just be divine—so…so powerful, if you take my meaning." Clarissa frowned as she considered the point.

"We didn't hear much of his conversation, though," Melly cautioned.

Clarissa waved a dismissive hand. "Oh, that'll be elegant,

too, I make no doubt. Why, Mr. Lester clearly moves in the best circles—good conversation would be essential. Don't you think so, Sophie?"

"Very likely." Sophie picked up her needle. "But you should remember that one often needs to be wary of gentlemen of manifold graces, like Mr. Lester."

But Clarissa, starry-eyed and rosy-cheeked, refused to accept the warning. "Oh, no," she said, shaking her head. "I'm sure you're wrong, Sophie. Why, with all his obvious experience, I'm sure one could trust Mr. Lester, or any gentleman like him. I'm sure they'd know just how things should be done."

Mentally Sophie goggled. She was quite sure Jack Lester, for one, would know just how "things" were done—but they certainly weren't the "things" Clarissa imagined. "Truly, Clarissa, trust me when I say that you would be very much safer with a gentleman *without* Mr. Lester's experience."

"Oh, come now, Sophie." Puzzled, Clarissa eyed her curiously. "Have you taken him in aversion? How could you? Why, you'll have to admit he's most terribly handsome."

When it became clear neither Clarissa nor Melly was going to be satisfied with anything short of an answer, Sophie sighed. "Very well. I'll concede he's handsome."

"And elegant?"

"And elegant. But—"

"And he's terribly…" Melly's imagination failed. "Graceful," she finally said.

Sophie frowned at them both. "And graceful. Yet—"

"And his conversation is elegant, too, is it not?"

Sophie tried a scowl. "Clarissa…"

"Is it not?" Clarissa was almost laughing, her natural exuberance bubbling through her recently acquired veneer of sophistication.

In spite of herself, Sophie could not restrain her smile. "Very well," she capitulated, holding up one hand. "I will admit that Mr. Lester is a paragon of manly graces. There—are you satisfied?"

"And you did enjoy your waltz with him, didn't you? Susan

Elderbridge was in transports, and *she* had only a country dance.''

Sophie didn't really want to remember that waltz, or any other of her interactions with Jack Lester. Unfortunately, the memories glowed bright in her mind, crystal clear, and refused to wane. As for his eyes, she had come to the conclusion that their image had, somehow, impinged on her brain, like sunspots. Whenever she closed her eyes, she could see them, that certain light which she trusted not at all in their deep blue depths.

She blinked and refocused on Clarissa's face, suffused with ingenuous curiosity. ''Mr. Lester is very...skilled in such matters.''

With that global statement, Sophie took up her needle, hoping her cousin would take the hint.

But Clarissa was not finished. Her arms sweeping wide to encompass all they had discussed, she concluded, her voice dramatic, her expression that of one convinced beyond doubt, ''So we are agreed: Mr. Lester is a paragon, a maiden's dream. How then, Sophie can you not *yearn* to find happiness in his arms?''

''Well—his, or someone like him,'' Melly added, forever prosaic.

Sophie did not immediately raise her head. Her cousin's question was, indeed, very like the one she had been asking herself before Clarissa and Melly had entered. Was what she felt simply the inevitable response to such as Jack Lester? Or was it— Abruptly, she cut off the thought. ''Indeed, Clarissa,'' she replied, shaking out Jeremy's shirt and folding it up, ''Mr. Lester is the sort of gentleman of whom it's most unwise to have such thoughts.''

''But why?''

Sophie looked up and saw genuine bewilderment in Clarissa's lovely face. She grimaced. ''Because he's a rake.''

There. It was said. Time and more that she brought these two down to earth.

Their reaction was immediate. Two pairs of eyes went round, two mouths dropped open.

Clarissa was the first to recover. "Really?" Her tone was one of scandalized discovery.

"No!" came from Melly. Then, "How can you tell?"

Clarissa's expression stated that was her question, too.

Sophie stifled her groan. How could she explain? A subtle something in his eyes? An undertone in his deep voice? Something in his suave manner? Then she recalled she had known instantly, in the moment she had seen him framed in Lady Asfordby's doorway. "His arrogant air. He carried himself as if the world were his oyster, the women in it his pearls."

His to enjoy at his whim. Sophie had surprised even herself with her words.

Both Clarissa and Melly fell silent. Then, frowning slightly, Clarissa glanced up. "I don't mean to doubt you, Sophie, but, you know, I don't think you can be right—at least, not in this instance."

Resigned to resistance, Sophie merely raised her brows.

Encouraged, Clarissa ventured, "If Mr. Lester *were* a rake, then surely Mama would not be encouraging him. And she is, you know. Why, she was perfectly thrilled to see him this morning—you know she was. And it was her suggestion he sit with us, beside you."

That, of course, had been the other niggling concern that had been inhabiting Sophie's mind. All Clarissa said was true; the only point Sophie was yet unsure of was what, exactly, her aunt was about. And that, as she well knew, could be just about anything. Given that Mr. Lester was a rake, one of the more dangerous of the species if her instincts were any guide, then Lucilla might just be grasping the opportunity to have her, Sophie, brush up on the social skills she would doubtless need once they were established in London. In the present circumstances, safe in the bosom of her family in their quiet country backwater, there was no real danger involved.

"Anyway," Clarissa said, drawing Sophie from her thoughts, "what I said at first is still undeniably true. Experienced London gentlemen are *much* more interesting than country gentlemen.''

Knowing there was one particular country gentleman Clarissa had in mind, Sophie felt compelled to point out, "But young country gentlemen do grow older, and gain experience in so doing. Even experienced gentlemen must once have been young.''

The comment drew a spurt of laughter from Melly. "Can you imagine Mr. Marston young?''

Clarissa giggled. Sophie knew she should chide them but did not; she agreed far too well to make a rebuke sound sincere. As Clarissa and Melly fell to chattering, comparing various older men of their acquaintance and speculating on their younger incarnations, Sophie tried to visualize a younger Jack Lester. It was, she found, a very difficult task. She couldn't imagine his eyes without that certain gleam. With an inward snort, she banished such foolish thoughts and reached for the next garment to be mended.

Doubtless, Jack Lester had been born a rake.

CHAPTER THREE

FATE WAS DEFINITELY smiling upon him.

Tooling his curricle along the lane to the village, Jack squinted against the glare of the brittlely bright morning sunshine, his gaze locked on the group slowly making its way down the lane on the other side of the narrow valley, also bound for the village. A female figure in a familiar cherry-red pelisse was walking a horse of advanced years, hitched to the poles of a gig. A young girl skipped about, now beside the woman, now on the other side of the horse.

"Looks like a problem, Jigson." Jack threw the comment over his shoulder to his groom, perched on the box behind him.

"Aye," Jigson replied. "Likely a stone from the way he's favouring that hoof."

A tiny track joining the two main lanes across the narrow valley came into sight just ahead. Jack smiled and checked his team.

"Be we a-going that way, guv'nor? I thought we was for the village?"

"Where's your sense of chivalry, Jigson?" Jack grinned as he steered his highly strung pair onto the hedged track, then steadied them down a steep incline. "We can't leave a lady in distress."

Especially not *that* lady.

He should, of course, have left for London by now—or, at the very least, quit the scene. His experienced brother-in-law, for one, would certainly have recommended such a strategic retreat. "Women should never be crammed, any more than one's fences" had been a favourite saying of Jason's. He had, of course, been speaking of seduction, a fact that had given Jack pause. Given that he was, to all intents and purposes, wooing his golden head, he had elected to ignore the voice of experience, choosing instead to take heed of a new and unexpectedly strong inner prompting, which categorically stated that leaving the field free to Phillip Marston was not a good idea.

As he feathered his leader around a tight curve, Jack felt his expression harden.

According to Hodgeley, his head groom at the cottage, Marston was a gentleman farmer, a neighbour of the Webbs. He was commonly held to be a warm man, comfortably circumstanced. Village gossip also had it that he was on the lookout for a wife, and had cast his eye in Miss Winterton's direction.

Jack gritted his teeth. He took the tiny bridge at a smart clip, surprising a startled expletive from Jigson, but not so much as scratching the curricle's paintwork. Frowning, he shook aside the odd urge that had gripped him. For some reason, his mind seemed intent on creating monsters where doubtless none lurked. Fate wouldn't be so cruel as to parade his golden head before him, only to hand her to another. Besides, Jigson, who frequented the local tap, had heard no whispers of Mr. Marston heading south for the Season.

Deftly negotiating the tight turn into the lane, Jack relaxed. He came upon them around the next bend.

Sophie glanced up and beheld a team of matchless bays bearing down upon them. She grabbed Amy, then blinked as the team swung neatly aside, pulling up close by the ditch. Only then did she see the driver.

As he tossed the reins to his groom and swung down from the elegant equipage, she had ample time to admire the sleek lines of both carriage and horses. He strode across the narrow lane, his many-caped greatcoat flapping about the tops of his glossy Hessians, the cravat at his throat as neat and precise as if he were in Bond Street. His smile, unabashed, stated very clearly how pleased he was to see her. "Good day, Miss Winterton."

Stifling her response was impossible. Her lips curving

warmly, Sophie countered, "Good morning, Mr. Lester. Dobbin has loosed a shoe."

He put a hand on the old horse's neck and, after casting an improbably apologetic glance her way, verified that fact. Releasing the horse's leg, he asked, "I can't remember—is the blacksmith in the village?"

"Yes, I was taking him there."

Jack nodded. "Jigson, walk Miss Winterton's horse to the blacksmith's and have him fix this shoe immediately. You can return the gig to Webb Park and wait for me there."

Sophie blinked. "But I was on my way to see my mother's old nurse. She lives on the other side of the village. I visit her every Monday."

A flourishing bow was Jack's reply. "Consider me in the light of a coachman, Miss Winterton. And Miss Webb," he added, his gaze dropping to Amy, who was staring, open-mouthed, at his curricle.

"Oh, but we couldn't impose...." Sophie's protest died away as Jack lifted his head. The glance he slanted her brimmed with arrogant confidence.

Jack looked down at Amy. "What say you, Miss Webb? Would you like to complete your morning's excursion atop the latest from Long Acre?"

Amy drew in a deep breath. "*Oooh,* just wait till I tell Jeremy and George!" She looked up at Jack's face—a long way up from her diminutive height—and smiled brilliantly. She reached out and put her small hand in his. "My name is Amy, sir."

Jack's smile was equally brilliant. "Miss Amy." He swept her an elegant bow, and Amy's expression suggested he had made a friend for life. As he straightened, Jack shot Sophie a victorious grin.

She returned it with as much indignation as she could muster, which, unfortunately, was not much. The prospect of being driven in his curricle was infinitely more attractive than walking. And, after his conquest of Amy, nothing would suffice but that they should travel thus. The decision was taken out of her hands, though Sophie wasn't sure she approved.

His groom had already taken charge of old Dobbin. The man nodded respectfully. "I'll see the blacksmith takes good care of him, miss."

There was nothing to do but incline her head. "Thank you." Sophie turned and followed as Jack led Amy, skipping beside him, to the curricle. Abruptly, Sophie quickened her stride. "If you'll hand me up first, Mr. Lester, Amy can sit between us."

Jack turned, one brow slowly lifting. The quizzical laughter in his eyes brought a blush to Sophie's cheeks. "Indeed, Miss Winterton. A capital notion."

Relieved but determined not to show it, Sophie held out her hand. He looked at it. An instant later, she was lifted, as if she weighed no more than a feather, and deposited on the curricle's padded seat. Sophie sucked in a quick breath. He held her firmly, his fingers spread about her waist, long and strong. In the instant before his hands left her, his eyes locked with hers. Sophie gazed into the deep blue and trembled. Then blushed rosy red. She looked down, fussing with her skirts, shuffling along to make room for Amy.

He had taken up the reins and half turned the curricle before she recalled the purpose of her trip.

"The basket." Sophie looked back at the gig. "For Mildred. It's under the seat."

Jack smiled reassuringly. In a trice, Jigson had the basket out and transferred to the curricle's boot. "Now," Jack said, "whither away?"

Sophie bestowed a smile of thanks on Jigson. "The other side of the village and out along the road to Asfordby, a mile or so. Mildred lives very quietly; she's quite old."

Jack gave his horses the office. "Your mother's nurse, you said. Did your mother's family come from hereabouts?"

"No, from Sussex. Mildred came to Webb Park with Aunt Lucilla on her marriage. My aunt was the younger, so Mildred stayed with her."

Jack slanted a glance at the pure profile beside him—Amy's

head was too low to interfere with his view. "Do you often do the duty visits for your aunt?"

Sophie considered the question. "I've often done so whenever I've stayed." She shrugged. "Aunt Lucilla is frequently very busy. She has twins younger than Amy—they're just six."

Jack grinned. "And quite a handful?"

"That," declared Sophie, "is a description insufficient to adequately convey the full glory of the twins."

Jack chuckled. "So you help out by taking on the role of the lady of the manor?"

"It's hardly an arduous task," Sophie disclaimed. "I've been doing much the same on my father's estate ever since my mother died."

"Ah, yes. I recall you mentioned helping your father."

Sophie threw him a quick frown. "That's not what I meant. Performing one's duty is hardly doing anything out of the ordinary." There had been something in his tone, a note of dismissal, which compelled her to explain. "I acted as his amanuensis in all matters concerning the estate and also for his studies. And, of course, since my mother's death, I've had charge of the house." It sounded like a catalogue of her talents, yet she couldn't help adding, "House parties, naturally, were impossible, but even living retired as we did, my father could not escape some degree of local entertaining. And the house, being so old and rambling, was a nightmare to run with the small staff we kept on." Sophie frowned at the memory.

Jack hid his keen interest behind an easy expression. "Who's running the house now?"

"It's closed up," Sophie informed him, her tone indicating her satisfaction. As the curricle rounded a corner, she swayed closer. "My father would have left it open—but for what? I finally managed to persuade him to leave just a caretaker and his agent and let the others go on leave. He may be away for years—who can tell?"

Jack slanted a curious glance at her. "If you'll forgive the impertinence, you don't seem overly troubled by the prospect."

Sophie grinned. "I'm not. Indeed, I'm truly glad Papa has

gone back to his 'old bones.' He was so abjectly unhappy after my mother's death that I'd be a truly ungrateful wretch were I to begrudge him his only chance at contentment. I think his work carries him away from his memories, both physically and mentally.'' Her lips curved wryly; her gaze swung to meet Jack's. ''Besides, even though I managed affairs for his own good, he could be a crusty old devil at times.''

Jack's answering smile was broad. ''I know exactly what you mean. My own father's in much the same case.''

Sophie grasped the opportunity to turn the conversation from herself. ''Are you his only son?''

''Oh, no.'' Jack turned his head to glance at her. ''There are three of us.'' He was forced to look to his horses but continued, ''I'm the eldest, then Harry. My sister, Lenore, came next; she's now married to Eversleigh. And the baby of the family is Gerald. Our mother died years ago but m'father's held on pretty well. Our Aunt Harriet used to watch over us, but Lenore did most of the work.'' He threw another glance at Sophie. ''My sister is one of those women who shuns the bright lights of the *ton;* she was perfectly content to remain at home in Berkshire and keep the Hall going and the estates functioning. I'm ashamed to confess that, when she married two years ago, I was totally unprepared to take on the burden.''

Noting the wry grimace that twisted his lips, Sophie ventured, ''But you've managed, have you not?''

Jack's lips lifted. ''I learn quickly.'' After a moment, he went on, his gaze still on the road, ''Unfortunately, Aunt Harriet died last year. The estate I can manage—the house…that's something else altogether. Like your father's, it's a rambling old mansion—heaps of rooms, corridors everywhere.''

To Jack's surprise, he heard a soft sigh.

''They're terribly inconvenient, but they *feel* like home, don't they?''

Jack turned his head to look at Sophie. ''Exactly.''

For a long moment, Sophie held his gaze, then, suddenly breathless, looked ahead. The first houses of the village appeared on their right. "The fork to the left just ahead leads to Asfordby."

Their passage through the small hamlet demanded Jack's full attention, his bays taking well-bred exception to the flock of geese flapping on the green, the alehouse's dray drawn up by the side of the road and the creak of the tavern's weatherbeaten sign.

By the time they were passing the last straggling cottages, Sophie had herself in hand. "Mildred's cottage is just beyond the next corner on the right."

Jack reined in the bays by the neat hedge, behind which a small garden lay slumbering in the sunshine. A gate gave on to a narrow path. He turned to smile ruefully at Sophie. "I'd come and lift you down, but these brutes are presently too nervy to be trusted on loose reins. Can you manage?"

Sophie favoured him with a superior look. "Of course." Gathering her skirts, she jumped down to the lane. Collecting her basket from the boot, she turned to Amy.

"I'll stay here with Mr. Lester," her cousin promptly said. "Old Mildred always wants to tidy my hair." Her face contorted in a dreadful grimace.

Sophie struggled to keep her lips straight. She glanced up at Jack, a questioning look in her eyes.

He answered with a smile. "I can manage, too."

"Very well. But don't be a nuisance," she said to Amy, then, unconsciously smoothed her curls, Sophie went to the gate.

The door opened hard on her knock; Mildred had obviously been waiting. The old dame peered at the curricle and all but dragged Sophie over the threshold. Mildred barely waited for Sophie to shut the door before embarking on a catechism. In the end, Sophie spent more time reassuring Mildred that Mr. Lester was perfectly trustworthy than in asking after Mildred herself, the actual purpose of her visit.

Finally taking her leave, Sophie reached the curricle to find Jack busy teaching Amy how to hold the reins. Depositing the empty basket in the boot, she climbed aboard.

Jack reached across Amy to help her up, then lifted a brow at her. "Webb Park?"

Sophie smiled and nodded. Amy relinquished the reins with sunny good humour, prattling on happily as the horses lengthened their stride.

About them, the March morning sang with the trills and warbles of blackbirds and thrush. The hedges had yet to unfurl their buds, but here and there bright flocks of daffodils nodded their golden heads, trumpeting in the spring.

"So tell me, Miss Winterton, what expectations have you of your stay in the capital?" Jack broke the companionable silence that had enveloped them once Amy had run her course. He flicked a quizzical glance at Sophie. "Is it to be dissipation until dawn, dancing until you drop, Covent Garden and the Opera, Drury Lane and the Haymarket, with Almack's every Wednesday night?"

Sophie laughed, and ducked the subtle query in his last words. "Indeed, sir. That and more."

"More?" Jack's brows rose. "Ah, then it'll be three balls every night, the Park and two teas every afternoon and more gossip than even Silence knows."

"You've forgotten the modistes."

"And the milliners. And we shouldn't forget the bootmakers, glovers and assorted emporia, the ribbon-makers and mantua-makers."

"Then there are the intellectual pursuits."

At that Jack turned to gaze at her, his expression one of stunned dismay. "Good heavens, Miss Winterton. You'll show us all up for the fribbles we are. No, no, my dear—*not* museums."

"Indeed," Sophie insisted, tossing her head, "I fully intend to view Lord Elgin's marbles."

"Oh, those. They don't count." When Sophie stared at him, Jack explained, "They're fashionable."

Sophie laughed again, a silvery sound. Jack smiled. He waited for a moment, then asked, "Will you be riding in the Park?"

"I should think nothing's more likely." Sophie glanced at him over Amy's head. "My cousins all rode before they could walk—literally. My uncle is a very keen horseman and I'm sure he'll be sending mounts down for us."

"So you won't be cutting a dash in a high-perch phaeton?"

"Alas," Sophie sighed. "Although I have always yearned to handle the ribbons, I've never had the opportunity to learn." Immediately, the curricle slowed. As it came to a halt, she turned to look at Jack.

His slow smile greeted her. "That sounded like a cry from the heart. Never let it be said that a Lester failed to respond to a damsel's plight."

Sophie blinked.

Jack's smile broadened. "I'll teach you."

"Here?"

"Now." He leaned across Amy. "Here, hold the reins like this."

Bemused, Sophie did as he said, taking the leather ribbons in her gloved fingers, looping them in accordance with his directions. It was a fiddle, with Amy between them.

"This will never work," Jack said, echoing Sophie's sentiments. Leaving the reins in her hands, he sat back, his gaze considering. "Just hold them a moment. They won't bolt as long as they sense some weight on the reins." He swung down from the carriage as he spoke. "They're not particularly frisky now; they've been out for over an hour."

Sophie just hoped he knew what he was talking about. Her heart was in her mouth as the leader tossed his head.

Jack rounded the horses and came up beside her. "Shuffle up, Miss Amy, so I can give your cousin her first lesson."

Startled, Sophie glanced down at him. The leader immediately tugged on the loosened reins.

"Hoa, there."

One strong hand closed about her fingers, tightening the rein, steadying the restive horse.

Sophie knew she was blushing. With no alternative offering, she shuffled over, followed a delighted Amy across the seat, allowing her rakish mentor to sit beside her. Her first lesson—in what?

She risked a glance up from beneath her lashes; his eyes held a mocking gleam.

"Fie, Miss Winterton." His voice was low. One dark brow rose. "If I offered a guinea for your thoughts, would you take it?"

Sophie blushed even more. She abruptly transferred her gaze to the horses, thus missing Jack's smile.

"Now, the first thing to remember..."

To Sophie's surprise, despite the distraction of his nearness, she quickly mastered the reins, keeping the thoroughbreds well up to their bits. Even more amazingly, he kept strictly to his role of tutor; doubtless, she rationalized, he was sufficiently concerned over the welfare of his horses—and their sensitive mouths—to keep his mind on their safety. Whatever, her suspicions proved unfounded; caution evaporating, she quickly dropped her guard, absorbed in practising the skills he imparted.

Webb Park appeared far too soon.

Exhilarated, Sophie tooled the curricle up the drive, slowing to effect a sedate halt in the gravel forecourt. Her eyes were bright, her cheeks pink as she turned to her companion and, with real reluctance, handed back the reins.

"A most commendable first outing, my dear." Jack met her shy smile with a smile of his own, his eyes searching hers.

A groom came running to hold the horses. Recalled to his surroundings, Jack tied off the reins and leapt down. Amy scrambled from her perch on the other side and went to natter to the groom.

Sophie slid to the side of the carriage. She made no demur when Jack reached for her and lifted her down. Her feet touched solid earth; she glanced up, and was overcome by flustered shyness. Sternly subduing the sensation, she accepted her empty basket and held out one gloved hand. "Thank you, Mr. Lester. You have indeed proved yourself a knight errant this day. Not only must I thank you for your timely rescue, but also for your excellent tuition.''

Smiling down at her, Jack took her hand. "On the contrary, Miss Winterton, the gain was mine. I've rarely had the pleasure of an outing with a lady of such manifold talents.''

Squelching the inner glow that rose in response to that compliment, Sophie shot him a sceptical glance. "Indeed, sir, I fear I'm no different from many another.''

Jack's slow smile softened his features. "Now, there you are wrong, my dear.'' He trapped her gaze with his. "You are quite unique.'' Sophie's eyes widened; he felt her quiver.

Letting his lids veil his eyes, Jack lifted her hand, studying the slender palm, the long, slim fingers. Then his lids rose, his dark gaze again holding hers. Smoothly, he raised her hand and placed a kiss on her inner wrist, exposed above the edge of her glove. "You take the shine out of all the London belles, my dear.''

Sophie's skin burned where his lips had touched. Her breathing suspended; light-headedness threatened. It took all the experience she possessed to summon an unaffected smile. "Why, thank you, sir. Will you come in and meet my aunt? I know she'll want to thank you for your help.''

He accepted the dismissal without a blink, although the expression in his eyes was amused. "No, I thank you. I know your aunt will be busy; I will not press my presence on her at this time.''

Holding hard to her composure, Sophie inclined her head. "Then I'll bid you a very good day, Mr. Lester.''

He smiled then, his slow, teasing smile. "*Au revoir,* Miss Winterton.''

Sophie turned and climbed the steps. On the threshold, she paused and looked back. He had climbed to the curricle's seat; as she watched, he flicked the reins. With a last wave, he was away, the carriage sweeping down the drive.

She watched until his dark head was no longer in sight. Then, lowering the hand she had automatically raised in farewell, Sophie frowned and turned indoors. She eventually located Amy in the kitchens, munching on a fresh-baked bun.

"Come, Amy. You should change."

Bustling the exuberant child, full of prattle, up the back stairs, Sophie was jolted from her thoughts by her cousin's bright voice, raised in innocent query.

"Is Mr. Lester courting you, Sophie?"

The breath caught in Sophie's throat. For an instant, she felt as if the world had lurched. She coughed. "Good heavens, Amy!" The dimness of the stairs hid her furious blush. "Of course not—he was just funning." She sought for more words—more convincing words—to deny the possibility; none were forthcoming. In desperation, she flapped her hands at Amy. "Come on now, up you go."

As she followed the little girl up the stairs, Sophie frowned. From the mouth of an innocent babe..?

CHAPTER FOUR

NOT CONTENT WITH her efforts thus far, Fate seemed intent on assisting him at every turn.

As he sat his black hunter in the shadows of a wind-break and watched the small cavalcade come thundering up Ashes' Hill, Jack couldn't keep the smile from his face.

Jigson, ever mindful of his place in the scheme of things, had been assiduous in his visits to the tap. Thus Jack had learned that the junior Webbs, accompanied by Miss Winterton and Miss Webb, were to be found on horseback most afternoons. Weather permitting, they would hack about the lanes and fields, but, according to one of the Webb grooms, the track over Ashes' Hill was currently their favoured route.

As he watched them canter up onto the green swath before him, Jack's smile broadened. His golden head was a delight in moss-green velvet, the long skirts of her habit brushing tan boots. On her guinea-gold curls perched a typically feminine contraption; he knew she'd call it a hat, but to his mind the wisp of fabric anchoring a pheasant's feather hardly qualified for the title. Turning, he lifted a brow at Percy mounted on a bay gelding beside him. "Shall we?"

Percy started; his abstracted gaze, very likely visualizing the rival merits of herringbone and country plaid, rapidly refocused. "What? Oh, yes. 'Bout time."

Jack smiled and led the way forward, out of the shadows of the firs.

Pulling up on the crest of the hill, then wheeling her horse to view her cousins, straggling up in her wake, Sophie did not immediately see him. Clarissa, who had reached the spot some moments ahead of her, had likewise turned to view the vista spread below them. Stone walls and still-dormant hedges divided the brown fields, their colour just tinged with the first hint of green. Jeremy and George, fourteen and twelve respectively, were but yards from the top; Amy, bouncing along on her placid cob, brought up the rear. The twins, yet to graduate from plodding ponies, were not included in these afternoon expeditions.

Reassured that all was well, Sophie relaxed her reins. Eyes bright, cheeks aglow, she drew in a deep breath, savouring the crisp freshness.

"Well met, Miss Winterton!"

The hail brought her head round; the deep voice sent the colour to her cheeks even before her eyes found him. He was mounted on a raking black hunter, sleek and powerful. As the animal walked towards her, neck proudly arched, black withers rippling, Sophie was struck by its harnessed power. Then her eyes lifted to its owner.

Broad shoulders encased in a hacking jacket of soft tweed, his powerful thighs, clad in buckskin breeches, effortlessly controlling the horse, he appeared the very epitome of a wealthy country gentleman. His face, features stamped with that coolly arrogant cast which identified his antecedents more definitively than his name. His eyes were very blue, dark, his gaze intent.

There was power there, too. As he brought his horse alongside hers, Sophie felt it reach for her.

"Good afternoon, Mr. Lester." She forced herself to extend a gloved hand, disconcerted by the warmth that caressed her cheeks and the breathlessness that had assailed her.

He took her hand and bowed over it, a difficult feat he performed with rare grace. His eyes quizzed her. "We saw you riding up and wondered if we might join you?"

"What a splendid idea!" From beside Sophie, Clarissa beamed ingenuously.

Feeling slightly helpless, Sophie could not resist the subtle laughter lurking in the blue eyes holding hers. Very much on her dignity, she retrieved her hand and indicated the track leading on over the hill. "If it pleases you, sir."

The smile she received in reply warmed her through and through.

Jack gestured to Percy, hanging back on his other side. "If you'll permit me to introduce Lord Percy Almsworthy?"

"Pleased to make your acquaintance, Miss Winterton."

Prepared to be wary, Sophie saw at a glance that Lord Percy was sprung from a mould quite different from his companion. Reassured, she smiled and held out a hand.

As he leant from the saddle to shake it, she thought she detected a look of keen appraisal in Lord Percy's mild gaze. "M'father's Carlisle," he said, giving her a peg on which to hang his hat.

Sophie dutifully introduced her cousins, in strict order of precedence. Jeremy and George barely waited for Amy's shy "Hello," before pouncing.

"What a bang-up set of blood and bones, sir!"

"Splendid hocks!"

"What stable does he hail from?"

"Is he a Thoroughbred?"

Jack laughed. "My brother bred him out of Jack Whistle."

"The winner of the Derby?" Jeremy's expression mirrored his awestruck tone.

Jack's eyes touched Sophie's. "The very same."

"Is your brother staying with you?" Gerald asked breathlessly.

Jack couldn't help his smile. "He was, but he's gone on to Belvoir."

"Oh." Both boys appeared crestfallen that they had missed the opportunity to badger a breeder who could turn out such a horse as the black.

"Never mind," Jack said. His eyes again met Sophie's. "I'll mention to him that you're interested in speaking with him, it's perfectly possible you may meet in him in Hyde Park."

"On Rotten Row?" George's eyes were round.

When Jack nodded, Jeremy put their seal of approval firmly

on the plan. He breathed out in a great sigh, his face alight. "Capital!"

Then, with the rapid change of direction that characterised the young, Jeremy turned to George. "Race you to the oak." They were off on the words, thundering down the slope towards the distant tree.

As by unvoiced consent they set their horses ambling after the two boys, Sophie glanced up at Jack. "You'll have to excuse them—they're rather single-minded when it comes to horses."

Jack slanted her a smile. "Harry and I were the same."

Sophie let her glance slide away. She could hear Clarissa and Lord Percy conversing; they were only a step or so behind. It was true they had no real chaperon, yet she could not imagine there was any impropriety in the situation; the presence of the children lent a certain innocence to the gathering.

Jack had only just registered the absence of a groom. He suppressed an instinctive frown. "Tell me, Miss Winterton, do you commonly ride unescorted?"

Glancing up, Sophie caught the frown in his eyes. Her brows rose. "All my cousins are expert riders; there's little chance of calamity in a gentle ride about the lanes."

"The lanes?"

Sophie had the grace to blush. "You can hardly expect such high spirits—" she indicated Jeremy and George "—to be content with such mild entertainment." Somewhat defensively, she added, "Clarissa and I are experienced riders, and Amy's cob is so ancient it rarely gets above a canter."

That last was self-evident as Amy, not content with their ambling progress, was jigging along ahead of them as fast as the cob would go. Barely a canter, much to Amy's disgust.

"Besides, sir," Sophie added, slanting a glance up at him, "I cannot believe that you and your brother—Harry, was it not?—would have been content with the lanes."

To her surprise, Jack's lips firmed into a distinctly grim line. "Indeed, no, Miss Winterton. Which is why I feel peculiarly well-qualified to express an opinion on what disasters are possible—nay, probable—given two high-couraged youngsters on fine horses." He turned from his contemplation of the boys, now circling the oak ahead, to look down at her. "And," he added, "which is why I think you should most certainly have a groom with you."

A trifle nettled, Sophie reached down to pat the proud neck of her own mount, a raw-boned grey stallion. "You need have no fear of them getting away from me. Few horses can outrun the Sheik."

Her action drew Jack's gaze to her horse; until then, despite his frequent preoccupation with the species, he had not really noticed it. As his gaze took in the large head, the long legs and heavy shoulders and rump, he felt the hairs on his nape rise. Despite the fact he had heard the warning note in her voice, despite knowing she would not welcome his question, he cleared his throat and asked it. "Do you normally ride that beast, Miss Winterton?"

His curiously flat tone had Sophie glancing up, searching his face. "No," she admitted, after a moment's hesitation. "My uncle's stables are extensive. We all take turns helping to exercise the hunters."

Jack's jaw firmed. "And does your uncle know you're riding such a dangerous creature?"

Sophie stiffened. "Mr. Lester," she said, her accents precise, "I have grown up around horses—have been riding since my earliest days. I assure you I am perfectly capable of managing the Sheik, or any other of my uncle's horses."

"That horse is too strong for you." His brows lowered, Jack stated unequivocally, "You should not be riding such an animal."

In the sky above them, the larks swooped and carolled. Their horses, displaying a fine equine imperturbability, trotted on down the hill. Sophie, flags of colour in her cheeks, abruptly retrieved her dropped jaw. Wrenching her gaze from the deeply turbulent blue into which it had fallen, she looked ahead.

The froth of white lace covering her breast rose as she drew in a deep breath. "Mr. Lester," she began, her tone icy, her accents clipped, "I believe we would do well to leave this topic of conversation. I am perfectly capable of managing the Sheik. Now, if you don't mind, I think we should join my cousins."

Resisting the impulse to toss her head, she flicked her reins and the Sheik surged forward. She thought she heard an angry snort, then the black moved up beside her, long fluid strides eating up the turf. Irritation, consternation and something even more unnerving rasped her temper; Sophie kept her gaze fixed forward, ignoring the glowering presence beside her.

Through narrowed eyes, Jack viewed her chilly dignity with very real disapproval.

The two boys and Amy were waiting by the oak. Sophie drew rein and looked back. Clarissa and Lord Percy had followed them down. As his lordship drew up, she heard him remark, "The best bonnets are to be found at Drusilla's, in my opinion. Just off Bruton Street. All the crack at the moment." Her cousin and Lord Percy were clearly deep in fashion. His lordship appeared perfectly content; Clarissa was hanging on his every word. With a smothered snort, Sophie turned to her younger relatives.

"We'll walk along the hedge until we come to the ride. Then back beside the woods."

There was a definite edge to her tone. Jeremy, George and Amy cast her swift glances; without a word, they fell in behind her. Jack remained by her side; Sophie did not waste any effort in trying to dislodge him. Clarissa and Lord Percy brought up the rear, barely glancing up from their sartorial discussion.

Sophie slanted a wary and warning glance at Jack. He met it with a coolly inscrutable expression. With determined calm, Sophie lifted her chin and set off along the hedge.

The silence that engulfed them stretched ominously. She could feel the occasional touch of his glance; she knew there was a frown in his eyes. Sophie wondered why her throat felt so tight, why simply breathing seemed so difficult. Suppressing a grimace, she racked her brains for some suitably innocuous topic of conversation.

Behind her, George was idly threshing the hedge with his whip.

Later, Sophie learned that, entirely inadvertently, George had flushed a hare from the hedge. The animal darted out, straight under the Sheik's hooves.

The stallion reared, screaming.

Sophie fought for control. It was all she could do to keep her precarious seat.

Then the Sheik was off.

Like a steam engine, the huge stallion pounded down the line of the hedge. Sophie clung to his back. Mounted side-saddle, she could not exert sufficient strength to rein in the panicked beast. The wind of their passing whistled in her ears and whipped her breath away. Desperate, she peered ahead through the wisps of hair flattened against her face, through the rough mane that whipped her cheeks. The hedge at the end of the field loomed ahead. Whispering a fervent prayer, Sophie dropped one rein and threw all her weight onto the other. Almost sobbing, she hauled back. The manoeuvre worked. The Sheik's head slewed, responding to the drag on the bit. But the stallion did not slow. Sophie felt herself tipping sideways. A scream stuck in her throat as she flung herself forward to cling once more to the Sheik's glossy neck. The ride they had been making for opened out before them; a single tug of the Sheik's powerful head pulled the rein from her grasp. Snorting, the stallion flew down the green turf.

Rattled, jolted, Sophie struggled to regain the reins. The ride eventually entered the woods, narrowing to a bridle track. She had to control the Sheik before that.

But the horse had the bit firmly between his teeth; even when she had the reins back in her hands, he refused to respond to her puny strength.

A flash of black to her left was her first intimation that help was at hand. Then Jack was beside her, the heavier black crowding the grey. He leaned across, one hand closing hard over her fingers as he added his weight to hers. Sophie felt him exert an increasing pressure, not jerking, as less experienced riders might. The Sheik felt the inexorable command.

Gradually, the grey slowed, finally stopping by the side of the ride.

Dragging in a ragged breath, Sophie sat up. Immediately the world tilted and spun. A ripe curse fell on her ears; it seemed to come from a long way away. Then strong hands fastened about her waist and weightlessness was added to the disconcerting sensations buffeting her.

Her feet touched firm earth. Shudder upon shudder racked her; she was trembling like a leaf.

The next instant she was enveloped in a warm embrace, locked against a hard frame. A large hand cradled her head, pressing her cheek against a firm male chest. The earthy scent of tweed and leather surrounded her, inexplicably comforting. With a gasp, stifled against his coat, Sophie clung to him, a solid anchor in her suddenly perilous world.

"*My God!* Are you all right?"

He sounded as shaken as she felt. Her throat was still closed; dumb, Sophie nodded. Dimly recalling the proprieties, she reluctantly drew away.

Hard fingers gripped her upper arms; abruptly Jack put her from him. Gasping, Sophie looked up, only to be subjected to a mercilous shake.

"*I thought you said you could handle that beast!*"

Numb, Sophie stared at him, at the fury that flamed in his eyes. A chill trickled through her veins, then spread; she felt the blood drain from her face. Cold blackness drew in; she blinked groggily.

Jack paled as she drooped in his hands. With a muttered curse, he gathered her to him.

Sophie didn't resist. Supporting her against him, Jack guided her to a fallen log. "Sit down!"

The harshness in his tone brought Sophie's head up. Simultaneously, her legs gave way and she complied with more haste than grace.

Jack stood over her, his face an icy mask. "You're white as a sheet. Put your head down."

Dizzy, disorientated, Sophie simply stared at him.

Jack cursed again.

The next thing Sophie knew her head was descending towards her knees, yielding to the insistent pressure of a large hand. He didn't let up until her forehead rested on her knees. As another wave of black nothingness swept over her, Sophie jettisoned any thought of resistance. She set her mind on breathing deeply, calming the turmoil inside. The world and her senses slowly returned to her. Only then did she become aware of the long fingers that had insinuated themselves beneath the collar of her habit and blouse, pushing aside her curls to gently caress her nape. Cool, firm, they traced sorcerous patterns on her sensitive skin. Faintness threatened again; his touch drew her back, anchoring her to reality, soothing her frayed nerves, promising security and safety.

They remained thus for what seemed like an age. Eventually, Sophie drew in a deep breath and sat up. The hand at her nape fell away. She glanced up through her lashes. His expression was closed, shuttered. Dragging in another breath, she gathered her skirts.

His hand appeared before her. After a moment's hesitation, she placed her hand in his and allowed him to assist her to her feet.

"I have to thank you, Mr. Lester, for your assistance." She managed the words creditably but could not look at him. Instead, eyes downcast, she fussed with her skirts, smoothing down the moss velvet.

"I would infinitely prefer, Miss Winterton, if, instead of your thanks, you would give me your promise not to ride that animal, or any like him, again."

The coolly arrogant tones left no doubt of the nature of that request. Slowly straightening, Sophie met his gaze. Inscrutable, distant, it told her little, as if he had brought a curtain down across his feelings, shutting her out. Lifting her head, she stated, "What befell, Mr. Lester, was purely an accident."

Jack bit back a caustic response. "The fact you were riding that horse, Miss Winterton, was no accident." His accents clipped, he viewed her through narrowed eyes. "He's too strong for you—and you knew it."

Sophie folded her lips, and gave him back stare for stare, her expression as remote as his.

Jack felt his temper slowly slip its leash. His expression hardened from mere flint to granite. "Before we leave here, Miss Winterton," he said, his voice low and commendably even, "I want your promise that you will not, in future, engage in such wanton recklessness." He saw her blink; he kept his gaze on hers. "Furthermore, I give you fair warning that should I ever find you on such a horse's back again, you have *my* promise you'll not sit a saddle for a sennight." He watched as her eyes widened, stunned disbelief in their depths. He raised one brow. "Is that perfectly clear, my dear?"

Sophie suppressed a shiver. Unable to hold his relentless gaze, her own dropped to his lips, compressed to a mere line in his ruggedly handsome face.

There was no more than a foot between them. Luckily, the shock of her recent terror was fading; Sophie felt her strength, her normal independence, returning, flooding back, stiffening her resolve. She raised her eyes once more to his. "You have no right to make such a demand of me, Mr. Lester—nor yet threaten me."

Her words were cool, her composure fragile but intact.

Gazing down at her, Jack made no answer, too engrossed in a ferocious inner struggle to subdue the tumultuous emotions raging through him. Every ounce of determination he possessed was required to keep his body still, his muscles locked against the impulse to sweep her into his arms, to demonstrate the validity of his claim on her.

Sophie sensed his turmoil. The odd flicker of the muscle along his jaw, his tightly clenched fists, the tension that gripped his whole frame bespoke her danger. The dark blue of his eyes had deepened, his gaze compelling, flames flickering elusively in the darkened depths. The hard line of his lips had not eased.

His physical presence was overwhelming; even more than that, she sensed his strength, a tangible entity, emanating from his large, hard, masculine frame, an aura that reached out, surrounding her, threatening to engulf her, to trap her, to conquer her wilfulness and make her his.

"Sophie?" Clarissa's voice cut across her thoughts. "Sophie? Are you all right?"

A shiver slithered down Sophie's spine. She blinked and realized her heart was racing, her breasts rising and falling rapidly. For one last instant, she met that intense blue gaze. Then, with an effort, she looked away to where Clarissa, with the others in tow, was approaching. Struggling to reassemble her disordered wits, Sophie moved, walking the few feet to the side of her horse. "I'm all right. No harm done."

Jack moved with her, not touching her but ready to support her if needed. Sophie was aware of his protective presence. Recalling how much she owed him, for she was too honest not to acknowledge that it had, indeed, been a very near-run thing, she glanced up through her lashes.

Jack caught her gaze. "Are you able to ride home?"

Sophie nodded. His expression was hard, shuttered, concern the only emotion visible. She drew a shaky breath and raised her head. "I do thank you for your assistance, sir."

Her voice was low, soft, a quaver of awareness running beneath her words.

Jack acknowledged her thanks with a curt nod. Holding fast to the frayed reins of his control, he reached for her, lifting her effortlessly to the grey's back.

Unnerved by the streak of sensation that speared through her at his touch, Sophie made a production of arranging her skirts, using the time to draw every last shred of her experience about her.

As the party reformed, she was grateful to find Clarissa, openly concerned, between herself and Mr. Lester. Lord Percy, on her left, proved an unthreatening companion, chatting on a wide variety of subjects as they wended their way homeward through the golden afternoon.

No further words passed between herself and her rescuer, yet all the way back to the gates of Webb Park, Sophie was conscious of the touch of his brooding gaze.

ONCE SHE WAS SAFELY returned to the bosom of her family, circumstance conspired to afford Sophie no peace in which to ponder. As there were no guests that evening, dinner was served at the earlier hour of five o'clock, *en famille*. All the Webbs barring the twins sat down about the long table in the dining room.

Naturally, her aunt and uncle were immediately regaled with the details of her thrilling rescue. It was all Sophie could do to erase the embellishments with which the younger Webbs enthusiastically embroidered the tale. From their glowing faces and excited voices it was clear that Jack Lester, modern-day hero, could have no fault in their youthful eyes.

"Dear Sophie," Lucilla said, her customary calm intact. "You took no hurt of any kind, I hope?"

"None, aunt." Sophie laid down her soup-spoon. "It was an unfortunate accident but I was not in any way harmed."

"Thanks to Mr. Lester!" piped up Amy.

"You should have seen that black go, sir!" Jeremy addressed himself to his father. "A prime 'un—a real stayer."

"Indeed?' From the head of the table, Horatio Webb beamed his deceptively gentle smile upon them all. A shortish, distinctly rotund gentleman, with a face that somehow combined elements of both youth and wisdom, many, at first glance, relegated him to the rank of a genial country squire with few thoughts beyond his fields. Only those who looked closer, into his fine grey eyes, twinkling now as Sophie's delicately flushed cheeks assured him she had taken no hurt but was being made more than a little uncomfortable by the continuing fuss, saw a glimmer of the quick silver intelligence that lurked behind his outward appearance. The very intelligence that had made Horatio Webb a byword in certain rarefied financial circles and was, at some deeper level, part of the reason the beautiful and talented Lucilla Carstairs, capable of landing a dukedom with her smiles, had, instead, very happily married him. Peering at Jeremy over the top of his ever-present spectacles, Horatio replied, "I must say I would not mind getting a look at any horse that could run the Sheik down."

"Mr. Lester is staying in the neighbourhood, I believe," Clarissa volunteered.

Horatio nodded. "Rawling's Cottage, I expect." With bland calm, he picked up the carving implements and fell to carving the roast which had, that moment, been ceremonially placed before him.

To Sophie's relief, the healthy appetites of the younger Webbs thrust her adventure temporarily from their minds.

Dinner was followed by a noisy game of Speculation, after which, feeling positively exhausted, mentally and physically, Sophie took herself off to bed. She had expected to find time, in the quiet of her chamber, to review the afternoon's happenings—not the stirring events her cousins had described, but the far more unnerving moments she had spent alone with Jack Lester, a rescued damsel with her knight. Indeed, with her inner peace in disarray, she climbed the stairs determined to place the episode in proper perspective.

Instead, she fell deeply asleep, her dreams haunted by a pair of midnight-blue eyes.

THE FOLLOWING MORNING was filled to overflowing with the first of the tasks needed to be completed to allow them to remove to the capital at the end of the week as planned. Lucilla had the entire event organized, down to the last bottle of elderflower lotion needed to preserve their complexions against any breeze that might be encountered while being driven in gentlemen's curricles in the Park.

Excused from the first round of packing for a light luncheon, both Sophie and Clarissa were commanded to appear before the family's seamstress for a final fitting of the walking gowns, morning gowns, chemises and petticoats they had all agreed could be perfectly adequately supplied from home. The rest of their wardrobes, Lucilla had declared, must come from Bruton

Street. As, after four years' absence from London, none of the gowns Sophie currently possessed could be considered presentable, she was as much in need of the modistes as Clarissa. Even Lucilla had murmured her intention of taking advantage of their time in the capital to refurbish her own extensive wardrobe.

It was midafternoon before Sophie was free. She had barely had time to wander down to the front hall before the younger Webbs found her. With the single-mindedness of the young, they claimed her for their accustomed ride. With an inward sigh, Sophie surveyed the bright faces upturned to hers, eyes glowing, eager to be off. "Very well," she said. "But I think we'll take a groom with us today. Jeremy, please tell John he's to accompany us. I'll get Clarissa and meet you at the stables."

To her relief, none of them commented on her departure from their established norm. Jeremy merely nodded, and all three departed with alacrity.

Glancing down at her morning gown, Sophie turned and started back up the stairs, refusing to dwell on what had prompted her caution, reflecting instead that, given that her aunt relied on her to ensure her cousins were exposed to no untoward occurrences, it was the least she should do.

When she appeared at the stables, Clarissa in tow, Old Arthur, the head groom, raised a questioning brow at her. Pulling on her gloves, Sophie nodded a greeting. "I'll take Amber out today. She hasn't had a run for some time, I believe."

Arthur blinked. Then, with a shrug which stated louder than words that it was not his place to question the vagaries of his betters, he went to fetch the mare. To Sophie's surprise, Clarissa, busy mounting her own high-bred chestnut, refrained from questioning her choice. Amber was as close to docile as any horse in the Webb stables. Taking her cue from her cousin, Sophie steadfastly ignored the niggling little voice which harped in her ear. Her choice of mount had nothing to do with Mr. Lester—and even less with that gentleman's too strongly stated opinions.

The tenor of his comments, both before and after dragging

her from the Sheik's back, had stunned her. She had not before encountered such arrogantly high-handed behaviour, but she was quite certain what she thought of it. Yet her lingering re-action to the entire episode was equivocal, ambivalent, no help at all in restoring her equanimity.

Setting placid Amber to the task of catching up with the boys and Amy, already well ahead, Sophie frowned.

Until yesterday, she had been inclined to suspect Jack Lester of harbouring some romantic interest in her. Her conscience stirred, and Sophie blushed delicately. Irritated, she forced herself to face the truth: she had started to hope that he did. But his reactions yesterday afternoon had given her pause; whatever it was that had stared at her from the depths of his dark blue eyes—some deeply felt emotion that had disturbed his sophisticated veneer and wreaked havoc on her calm—it was not that gentle thing called love.

Sophie acknowledged the fact with a grimace as, with a wave and a whooping "halloo," Clarissa shot past. Twitching the reins, Sophie urged Amber into the rolling gait which, with her, passed for a gallop. Clarissa, meanwhile, drew steadily ahead.

Trapped in her thoughts, Sophie barely noticed. Love, as she understood it, was a gentle emotion, built on kindness, consideration and affection. Soft glances and sweet smiles was her vision of love, and all she had seen, between her uncle and aunt and her mother and father, had bolstered that image. Love was calm, serene, bringing a sense of peace in its wake.

What she had seen in Jack Lester's eyes had certainly not been peaceful.

As the moment lived again in her mind, Sophie shivered. What was it she had stirred in him? And how did he really view her?

HER FIRST QUESTION, had she but known it, was also exercising Jack's mind, and had been ever since he had returned from Webb Park the afternoon before. As soon as his uncharacter-istically violent emotions had eased their grip on his sanity, he had been aghast. Where had such intense impulses sprung from?

Now, with the afternoon bright beyond the windows, he restlessly paced the parlour of Rawling's Cottage, inwardly still wrestling with the revelations of the previous day. He was deeply shocked, not least by the all but ungovernable strength of the emotion that had risen up when he had seen Sophie's slender figure, fragile against the grey's heaving back, disappear in the direction of the woods and possible death.

And he was shaken by what the rational part of his brain informed him such feelings foretold.

He had innocently supposed that courting the woman he had chosen as his wife would be a mild process in which his emotions remained firmly under his control while he endeavoured, through the skill of his address, to engage hers. A stranger, as he now realized, to love, he had imagined that, in the structured society to which they belonged, such matters would follow some neatly prescribed course, after which they could both relax, secure in the knowledge of each other's affections.

Obviously, he had misjudged the matter.

A vague memory that his brother-in-law had not surrendered to love without a fight glimmered at the back of his mind. Given Jason's undoubted conversion, and his equally undoubted acumen, Jack had always wondered what had made him hesitate—on the brink, as it were.

Now he knew.

Emotions such as he had felt yesterday were dangerous.

They boded fair to being strong enough to overset his reason and control his life.

Love, he was fast coming to understand, was a force to be reckoned with.

A knock on the front door interrupted his reverie. Glancing out of the window, he saw his undergroom leading a handsome bay around to the stables. The sight piqued Jack's interest.

A scrape on the parlour door heralded his housekeeper. "Mr. Horatio Webb to see you, sir."

Intrigued, Jack lifted a brow. "Thank you, Mrs. Mitchell. I'll receive him here."

A moment later, Horatio Webb was shown into the room. As his calm gaze swept the comfortable parlour, warm and inviting with its wealth of oak panelling and the numerous sporting prints gracing the walls, a smile of ineffable good humour creased Horatio's face. Rawling's Cottage was much as he remembered it—a sprawling conglomeration of buildings that, despite its name, constituted a good-sized hunting lodge with considerable stabling and more than enough accommodation for guests. Approaching his host, waiting by the fireplace, he was pleased to note that Jack Lester was much as he had imagined him to be.

"Mr. Webb?" Jack held out a hand as the older man drew near.

"Mr. Lester." Horatio took the proffered hand in a strong clasp. "I'm here, sir, to extend my thanks, and that of Mrs. Webb, for the sterling service you rendered in averting misadventure yesterday afternoon."

"It was nothing, I assure you, sir. I was there and merely did what any other gentleman, similarly circumstanced, would have done."

Horatio's eyes twinkled. "Oh, I make no doubt any other gentleman would have *tried,* Mr. Lester. But, as we both know, few would have succeeded."

Jack felt himself falling under the spell of the peculiarly engaging light in his visitor's eye. His lips twitched appreciatively. "A glass of Madeira, sir?" When Horatio inclined his head, Jack crossed to pour two glasses, then returned, handing one to his guest. "Phoenix is, perhaps, one of the few horses that could have caught your Sheik. I'm just dev'lish glad I was on him."

With a wave, he invited Sophie's uncle to a chair, waiting until the older man sat before taking a seat facing him.

With the contemplative air of a connoisseur, Horatio sipped the Madeira, savouring the fine wine. Then he brought his grey gaze to bear on Jack. "Seriously, Mr. Lester, I do, as you must understand, value your intervention of yesterday. If it weren't for the fact we'll be shortly removing to town, I'd insist you honour us for dinner one night.'' His words came easily, his eyes, calmly perceptive, never leaving Jack's face. ''However, as such is the case, and we will depart on Friday, Mrs. Webb has charged me to convey to you her earnest entreaty that you'll call on us once we're established in Mount Street. Number eighteen. Naturally, I add my entreaty to hers. I take it you'll be removing to the capital shortly?''

Jack nodded, discarding the notion of urging Sophie's uncle to forbid her his more dangerous steeds. The shock she had so recently received should, with luck, suffice to keep her from the backs of murderous stallions, at least until the end of the week. ''I intend quitting Melton any day, as it happens. However, as I must break my journey in Berkshire, I don't expect to reach the metropolis much in advance of your party.''

Horatio nodded approvingly. ''Please convey my greetings to your father. We were once, if not close friends, then certainly good acquaintances.''

Jack's eyes widened. ''You're *that* Webb!'' Blinking, he hastily explained, ''Forgive me—I hadn't realized. With so many Webbs in these parts, I wasn't sure which one had been my father's crony. I understand you and he shared many interests. He has told me of your devotion to the field.''

''Ah, yes.'' Horatio smiled serenely. ''My one vice, as it were. But I think you share it, too?''

Jack returned the smile. ''I certainly enjoy the sport, but I feel my interest does not reach the obsessive heights of my father's.''

''Naturally,'' Horatio acceded. ''You younger men have other obsessions to compete with the Quorn, the Cottesmore and the Belvoir. But the Lester stud is still one of the best in the land, is it not?''

''Under my brother Harry's management,'' Jack replied. ''Our kennels still produce some of the strongest runners, too.''

While their conversation drifted into a discussion of the latest trends in breeding both hunters and hounds, Jack sized up

Sophie's uncle, Horatio Webb, while younger than his own father, had been a long-time acquaintance of the Honorable Archibald Lester. More specifically, it had been he who had dropped that quiet word in his father's ear which had ultimately led to the resurrection of the family fortunes.

Taking advantage of a natural lull in the conversation, Jack said, "Incidentally, I must make you all our thanks for your timely advice in the matter of the Indies Corporation."

Horatio waved a dismissive hand. "Think nothing of it. What friends are for, after all." Before Jack could respond with a further expression of gratitude, Horatio murmured, "Besides, you've cleaned the slate. I assure you I would not have liked to have had to face my brother-in-law, eccentric though he is, with the news that his Sophie had broken her neck on one of my stallions. As far as I can see, the scales between the Webbs and the Lesters are entirely level."

Just for an instant, Jack glimpsed the reality behind Horatio Webb's mask. Understanding, then, that this visit had many purposes, perhaps even more than he had yet divined, Jack could do no more than graciously accept the older man's edict. "I'm pleased to have been able to be of service, sir."

Horatio smiled his deceptive smile and rose. "And now I must be off." He waited while Jack rang and gave orders for his horse to be brought round, then shook hands with his host. His eyes roving the room once more, he added, "It's nice to see this place kept up. It's been in your family for some time, has it not?"

Escorting Sophie's amazing uncle to the door, Jack nodded. "Five generations. All the Lester men have been bred to hunting."

"As it should be," Horatio said, and meant far more than the obvious. "Don't forget," he added, as he swung up to the back of his bay. "We'll look to see you in London."

Horatio nodded a last farewell and turned his horse's head for home. As he urged the bay to a canter, a subtle smile curved his lips. He was well pleased with what he had found at Rawling's Cottage. Aside from all else, the Lesters were obviously planning on remaining a part of the landscape, here as much as in Berkshire.

Lucilla would be pleased.

BY THE TIME she returned from their ride, Sophie had a headache. As she was not normally prey to even such minor ailments, she felt the constraint deeply. As she preceded Clarissa into the back parlour, she massaged her temples in an effort to ease the throbbing ache behind them.

It was, of course, all Jack Lester's fault. If she hadn't spent half her time worrying about how she would respond if he joined them, and the other half scanning the horizon for his broad-shouldered frame, metaphorically looking over her shoulder all the way, she would doubtless have taken her customary enjoyment in the ride. Instead, she felt dreadful.

Throwing her riding cap onto a chair, she sank gratefully into the overstuffed armchair in the shadows by the hearth.

"A pity Mr. Lester and Lord Percy didn't join us." Clarissa dropped onto the chaise, obviously ready to chat. "I was sure that, after yesterday, they would be waiting at Ashes' Hill."

"Perhaps they've already returned to London," Sophie suggested. "The ground's certainly soft enough to send the tail-chasers back to town."

"Tail-chasers" was the family term for those gentlemen whose only purpose in coming to Melton Mowbray was to chase a fox's tail. At the first sign of the thaw, such gentlemen invariably deserted the packs for the more refined ambience of the *ton*'s gaming rooms.

"Oh, but I don't think Mr. Lester and Lord Percy are tail-chasers, exactly. Not when they both ride such superb horses."

Sophie blinked and wondered if her headache was affecting her reason. "What have their horses to do with it?" she felt compelled to ask. "All tail-chasers, *ipso facto,* must have horses."

But Clarissa's mind was on quite a different track. "They're both terribly *elegant,* aren't they? Not just in the ballroom—

well, everyone *tries* to be elegant there. But they both have that indefinable London polish, don't they?''

Sophie openly studied her cousin's lovely face. At the sight of the glowing expression inhabiting Clarissa's clear eyes, she stifled a groan. "Clarissa—please believe me—not all London gentlemen are like Lord Percy and Mr. Lester. Some of them are no better than…than any of the young gentlemen you've met at the local balls. And many are a great deal worse.''

"Maybe so," Clarissa allowed. "But it's an indisputable fact that both Mr. Lester and Lord Percy put *all* the gentlemen hereabouts to shame.''

Sophie closed her eyes and wished she could argue.

Clarissa rose, eyes shining, and twirled about the room. "Oh, Sophie! I'm so looking forward to being surrounded by all the swells—the dandies, the town beaux, even the fops. It will be so *thrilling* to be sought after by such gentlemen, to be twitted and teased—in a perfectly acceptable way, of course.'' Clarissa dipped and swirled closer. "And I know," she continued, lowering her voice, "that one is not supposed to say so, but I can't wait to at least try my hand at flirting, and I positively can't *wait* to be ogled.''

As she squinted against the glare of the late afternoon sun, her narrowed vision filled with Clarissa's svelte form, Sophie didn't think her cousin would have all that long to wait. She should, she supposed, make a push to bring Clarissa back to earth, and defend the local young gentlemen, Ned in particular. If she hadn't been feeling so ill, she would have. But with her head throbbing so, and her mind still tangled in her own confusion, she doubted she could find sufficient words to succeed.

"But what of you, Sophie?" Abruptly, Clarissa turned from rapt contemplation of her rosy future and plumped down on the chaise close by. "After his dramatically chivalrous rescue yesterday, aren't you just a *little* bit taken with Mr. Lester?"

Sophie let her lids fall; Clarissa, when she put her mind to it, could be quite as perspicacious as her mother. "Indeed," she forced herself to say. "Mr. Lester was everything that is gallant. However, that's hardly the only criterion I have for choosing a husband."

"So, what are your other criteria?"

Squinting through her lashes, Sophie studied Clarissa's grin. Her cousin, she reluctantly concluded, was unlikely to be diverted by any prevarication. "A liking for children," she stated. An obvious test; one, she suspected, Jack Lester would pass. He had handled Amy very well, and the boys, too. "And a sense of humour." He had that, too, reprehensible though it might sometimes be.

"And I would want a man who was steady and reliable, not given to fits of temper." Now *that* was a prerequisite her knight in shining armour might have trouble complying with. Rakes, she had always understood, were totally *un*reliable. Becoming absorbed with her catalogue, Sophie frowned. "Sufficiently handsome, although he needn't be an Adonis. Not mean or stingy. And he'd have to be able to waltz. There," she concluded, opening her eyes fully and fixing Clarissa with a mock glare. "Are you satisfied?"

Clarissa laughed and clapped her hands, making Sophie wince. "But that's famous! Mr. Lester might be just the man for you."

Abruptly, Sophie stood, disguising the sudden movement with a little laugh. "I pray you, Clarissa, don't let your imagination fly away with you. Mr. Lester's presence here—and our meetings—have been occasioned by nothing more than coincidence."

Clarissa looked slightly surprised by her vehemence but, to Sophie's intense relief, she forbore to argue. "I expect something must have detained them today." Clarissa's tone suggested she could see no other likelihood. As she fell to neatly folding the ribbons of her hat, she added, "I wonder when next we'll meet?"

AS HE SAT DOWN to dinner that evening in the dining room of the cottage, Jack could have answered Clarissa's question without further thought. He was leaving Leicestershire on the morrow. Early.

He said as much to Percy, taking his seat on his right hand.

"What brought that on? Thought you were fixed here for another few weeks?"

"So did I," Jack returned. "But something's come up." Before Percy could ask what, he added, "And the weather's turned, so I think I'll do better to look in at Lester Hall before hying up to town."

"There is that," Percy agreed knowledgeably. "Ground's softening up. Not many good runs left in the season."

Jack nodded, unexpectedly grateful for the thaw. As he rode very heavy, the going for his mounts would become noticeably harder in the coming weeks.

"Think I'll take a look in on the old man," Percy mused, his expression distant. "Gets a bit obstreperous if we forget him. I'll go and do my filial duty, then meet you in town."

Jack nodded again, his mind busy with his plans. There was no need to hurry up to town. The Webbs would not be receiving for at least another week.

His decision to quit the field in Leicestershire was prompted by a firm conviction that such a scene as had occurred when he'd hauled Sophie from her stallion's back could not be repeated. However, thanks to the incident, he was now on good terms with the Webbs and had been all but commanded to call, once in town. Assuming Mrs. Webb approved, there would, he felt sure, be no impediment placed in his path should he desire to further his interest with Sophie in the usual way.

It was his first, albeit small, advance.

However, given his turbulent and presently unpredictable reactions, it seemed the course of wisdom to suspend all further activity until his golden head was safe in the bosom of the *ton*. His home ground, as it were.

The strictures of Society reached a pinnacle of stringency in London—the strict mores and unwavering practices would undoubtedly prove sufficiently rigid to ensure his wooing followed acceptable paths.

So, for her sake, and, he reluctantly admitted, his own, he had determined to forgo the sight of Sophie's fair face until she appeared in London.

It would be safer for everyone that way.

CHAPTER FIVE

CLIMBING THE STAIRS of Entwhistle House, Sophie looked
about her, at the silks and satins, the jewels and curls, and knew
she was back in the *ton*. About her, the refined accents and
dramatic tones of the elite of society, engaged in their favourite
pastime, drowned out the plaintive strains of a violin, struggling through from the ballroom ahead. Immediately in front
of her, Lucilla, clad in an exquisite gown of deep blue silk
overlaid with figured lace, forged steadily onward, stopping
only to exchange greetings with the acquaintances, both close
and distant, who constantly hailed her.

Close beside Sophie, Clarissa frankly stared. "Isn't it *wonderful?*" she breathed. "So many beautiful gowns. And the
men look just as I imagined—precise to a pin. Some are very
handsome, are they not?"

As she whispered the words, Clarissa caught the eye of an
elegant buck, who, noticing her wide-eyed stare, ogled her
shamelessly. Clarissa blushed and retreated behind her fan.

Following her gaze, Sophie caught the gentleman's eye, and
raised a coolly superior brow. The man smiled and bowed
slightly, then turned back to his companions. Sophie slipped
an arm through Clarissa's. "Indeed, and you look very handsome, too, so you must expect to be ogled, you know. The best
way to deal with such attentions is to ignore them."

"Is it?" Clarissa sent a cautious glance back at the gentleman, now fully engaged with his friends. Relieved, she relaxed
and looked down at her gown, a delicate affair in palest aqua-
marine muslin, a demure trim of white lace about the neckline

and tiny puffed sleeves. "I must admit, I did wonder at Madame Jorge's choice, but it really does suit me, doesn't it?"

"As that gentleman has just confirmed," Sophie replied. "I told you you should never argue with Madam Jorge. Aside from anything else, it's wasted breath."

Clarissa giggled. "I never imagined she would be like that."

Looking ahead, Sophie smiled. They had quit Leicestershire on Friday, spending two nights on the road in a stately progress that had delivered them up in Mount Street on Sunday afternoon. The rest of that day had gone in the predictable chaos of unpacking and installing the family in their home for the Season. Lucilla had shooed them all off to bed early, warning both Sophie and Clarissa, "We'll be out first thing, off to Madame Jorge. I refuse to permit either of you to step into a *ton* ballroom unsuitably gowned. We shall have to hope Jorge can come to our aid, for we're promised to Lady Entwhistle tomorrow night if you recall."

And so, that morning, immediately after breakfast at the unheard-of hour of ten, they had arrived before the small door on Bruton Street that gave on to Madame Jorge's salon.

"I only hope she can help us at such short notice," Lucilla had said as she led the way up the stairs.

Her aunt needn't have worried; Madame Jorge had fallen on her neck with unfeigned delight.

Madame Jorge was the modiste who for years had been her mother's and aunt's favourite; her own wardrobe for her ill-fated first Season had come from Madame Jorge's salon. But Madame Jorge was definitely not what one expected of a modiste who made for a very select clientele amongst the *ton*.

For a start, she was huge, a massive bosom balanced by immense hip and brawny arms. But her small hands and thick, short fingers were remarkably nimble. She had almost no neck that one could see; her neat grey hair was perennially coiled in a tight bun upon her round head. Small blue eyes twinkled in a rosy-cheeked face. Only the shrewd gaze and the determined set of Madame Jorge's mouth gave her away.

"And Miss Sophie, too!" she had exclaimed, once she had

finished greeting Lucilla. "*Ma pauvre* little one, how good it is to see you again."

Jorge had hugged her to her massive bosom, neatly covered in black bombazine, and then held her at arm's length, the better to survey her. "But, yes! This is wonderful—*wunderbar!*" Jorge had never settled entirely into any one language. She was a polyglot and spoke at least three, often all at once. She took a step back, eyes narrowing, then whipped the tape measure which always hung about her neck into her hands. "For you, my *liebschen*, we will have to retake the measurements." Jorge's eyes had gleamed. "You will turn the gentlemen on their heads, no?"

She had murmured that she hoped not, but was not sure Jorge heard. The modiste had spied Clarissa, hanging back, a little overwhelmed. Her cousin had promptly been even more overwhelmed by Jorge's bear-like embrace.

"Oh—the *petit chou!* You are your mother's daughter, but yes! Very young—but the bloom is worth something, *hein?*"

Utterly bewildered, Clarissa had glanced at her mother. Lucilla had taken Jorge in hand, rapidly explaining their requirements and the need for haste.

Jorge had understood immediately. "*Quelle horreur!* To go to the ball without a gown—it is not to be thought of! No, no, somehow we will contrive."

Contrive she certainly had.

Glancing down at her own silk skirts, in a delicate pale-green hue that was the perfect foil for her colouring, making the blue of her eyes more intense and setting off the true gold of her curls, Sophie felt more than content. The long lines of the skirts, falling from the high waist beneath an unusual square-cut neckline, displayed her slender figure to perfection. Jorge, as always, had come to the rescue; she was a wizard and had waved her magic wand. Their new ball gowns had been delivered at six that evening, the first of their day gowns would be on the doorstep by nine the next morn.

"Sophie! Look!"

Following Clarissa's gaze, Sophie beheld another young girl, weighed down by a gown in frothy pink muslin, a heavy flounce about the neckline repeated twice about the hem making her appear wider than she was tall. The gown was precisely what Clarissa had gone to Madame Jorge's salon determined to have for her first ball.

"Oh, dear." Clarissa viewed the apparition with empathetic dismay. "Would I have looked like that?"

"Very likely," Sophie replied. "Which all goes to show that one should never, ever, argue with Madam Jorge."

Clarissa nodded, carefully averting her gaze from the unfortunate young lady to study, somewhat nervously, the crowd still separating them from their hostess. "I'd never imagined to see so many elegant people in one place at one time."

Sophie felt her lips twitch. "I hesitate to mention it, but this is only a small gathering by *ton* standards, and an informal one at that. There could only be a hundred or so present."

The look Clarissa sent her did not exactly glow with anticipation. They had gained the top of the stairs and were now slowly shuffling across the upper foyer. Then the curtain of bodies before them parted and they found themselves facing Lady Entwhistle.

"Lucilla dear, so glad you could come." Her ladyship and Lucilla touched scented cheeks. Casting a knowledgeable eye over Lucilla's gown, Lady Entwhistle raised a brow. "Dashed if you aren't capable of giving these young misses a run for their money."

Lucilla's eyes flew wide. "*Run,* Mary? Gracious heavens, my dear—*so* enervating!" With a smile that was almost mischievous, Lucilla passed on to greet the young gentleman next in line—Lord Entwhistle's cousin's boy, Mr. Millthorpe—leaving both Sophie and Clarissa to make their curtsies to her ladyship.

Rising, Sophie once more found herself subjected to her ladyship's lorgnette. As before, no item of her appearance escaped Lady Entwhistle's scrutiny, from the green ribbon in her curls to her beaded satin dancing slippers.

"Hmm, yes," Lady Entwhistle mused, her expression

brightening. "*Excellent,* my dear. No doubt but that you'll have a truly *wonderful* Season this time."

Her ladyship's tone left little doubt as to what, in her mind, constituted a "wonderful" Season. Having known what to expect from her mother's old friends, Sophie smiled serenely. Together with Clarissa, she moved on to Mr. Millthorpe.

A young gentleman of neat and pleasant aspect, Mr. Millthorpe was clearly overawed at finding himself thus thrust upon the notice of the *ton.* He replied to Sophie's calm greeting with a nervously mumbled word; she saw him fight to keep his hand from tugging his cravat. Then he turned to Clarissa, who was close on her heels. Mr. Millthorpe's colour promptly fled, then returned in full measure.

"Indeed," he said, his bow rendered awkward by his determination to keep Clarissa's face in view. "I'm very glad to meet you Miss…Miss…." Mr. Millthorpe's eyes glazed. "Miss Webb!" Triumph glowed in his smile. "I hope you won't mind…that is, that you might have a few minutes to spare later, Miss Webb. Once I get free of this." His expression earnest, he gestured ingenuously at his aunt.

A little taken aback, Clarissa sent him a shy smile.

That was more than enough encouragement for Mr. Millthorpe. He beamed, then was somewhat peremptorily recalled to his duties.

Bemused, Clarissa joined Sophie where she waited at the top of the shallow flight of steps leading down into the ballroom.

Poised above the room, Sophie resisted the impulse to send a questing glance out over the sea of heads. Looking down, she raised her skirts and commenced the descent in her aunt's wake. Beside her, Clarissa was tensing with excitement, her eyes, bright and wide, drinking in every sight. The sensation of tightness about her own lungs informed Sophie that she, too, was not immune to expectation. The realization brought a slight frown to her eyes.

The odds were that Mr. Lester would not be present. Even if he was, there was no reason to imagine he would seek her out.

With an inward snort, Sophie banished the thought. Jack Lester was a rake. And rakes did not dance attendance on young ladies—not, that is, without reason. She, however, was in town to look for a husband, the perfect husband for her. She should devote her thoughts to that goal, and forget all about engaging rakes with dark blue eyes and unnerving tempers.

Determination glimmered in her eyes as she lifted her head—only to have her gaze fall headlong into one of midnight blue.

Sophie's heart lurched; an odd tremor shook her. He filled her vision, her senses, tall and strong, supremely elegant in black coat and pantaloons, his dark locks in fashionable disarray, the white of his cravat a stark bed on which a large sapphire lay, winking wickedly.

Jack watched as, her surprise at seeing him plainly writ in her large eyes, Sophie halted on the second-last stair, her lips parting slightly, the gentle swell of her breasts, exposed by her gown, rising on a sharp intake of breath.

His eyes on hers, he slowly raised a brow. "Good evening, Miss Winterton."

Sophie's heart stuttered back to life. Large, dark and handsome, he bowed gracefully, his gaze quizzing her as he straightened. Giving her wits a mental shake, she descended the last step, dipping a curtsy, then extending her hand. "Good evening, Mr. Lester. I had not expected to see you here, sir."

His brow lifted again; to her relief, he made no direct reply. "Might I request the pleasure of a waltz, my dear? The third, if you have it to spare."

She had not even had time to look at her dance card. Shooting him a cool glance, Sophie opened it, then, meeting his eyes briefly, she lifted the tiny pencil and marked his name in the appropriate spot.

The answer to the question in her mind came with his smooth, "And, perhaps, if you're not already bespoken, I might escort you to supper at the conclusion of the dance?"

Blinking, Sophie found she had unthinkingly surrendered her hand to his. Her gaze flew to his as he drew her gently to his side. Her heart leapt to her throat and started beating erratically there. "That will be most pleasant, Mr. Lester," she murmured, looking away.

"It will, you know."

His tone was gently teasing, on more levels than one. Elevating her chin, Sophie drew her composure more firmly about her. Ahead of them, her aunt was strolling through the crowd, Clarissa by her side.

To Sophie's surprise, having escorted her as far as the chaise where her aunt finally deigned to rest, Mr. Lester exchanged a few pleasantries with Lucilla, then, with an elegant bow, excused himself, leaving her to weather a spate of introductions as a small host of gentlemen gravitated to her side.

Despite the nature of Lady Entwhistle's little ball, despite the fact that the *ton* was only just beginning to desert its winter playgrounds to return to the capital, there were sufficient eligible bachelors present to fill her card long before the first dance began.

Clarissa, by her side, proved a potent attraction for the younger gentlemen. She was soon casting anxious glances at Sophie.

Keeping her voice firm and clear, Sophie calmly apologized to Mr. Harcourt. "Indeed, sir, I'm most sorry to disappoint you but I fear my card is full."

Minutes later, she heard Clarissa copy her words, prettily turning Lord Swindon away.

As her equilibrium, momentarily undermined, returned, Sophie became conscious of a niggling disquiet, a sense that something was not entirely right. Only when, for the third time, she found her gaze scanning the room, searching automatically, did she realize just what it was she felt.

Feeling very like muttering a curse, she instead pinned a bright smile on her lips and, with renewed determination, gave her attention to her court. "Will your sister be coming up to London, Lord Argyle? I should be delighted to meet her again."

She was here to find a husband, not to fall victim to a rake's blue eyes.

By dint of sheer determination, Jack managed to keep himself occupied until the country dance preceding the supper waltz was in progress. He was, he kept reminding himself, far too experienced to cram his leaders. Instead, he had forced himself to circulate, artfully sidestepping subtle invitations to lead other young ladies onto the floor. Now, as the last strains of the music died, he threaded his way through the crowd to come up by Sophie's side. Fate was smiling on him again; she had just finished thanking her partner, Lord Enderby.

"Miss Winterton." With a slight bow, Jack reached for Sophie's hand. "Evening, Enderby." A nod was enough to distract her recent partner.

"Eh?" Squinting slightly, Lord Enderby switched his near-sighted stare from Sophie to Jack. "Oh, it's you, Lester. Surprised to see *you* here. Thought you'd be at Newmarket."

Jack smiled—into Sophie's eyes. "I discovered that, this Season, there was to be an unlooked-for distraction in London."

"Really?" Lord Enderby's eyes were too weak to appreciate the action taking place before them. "What's that?"

Feeling the warmth rise to her cheeks, Sophie held her breath, her gaze daring her next partner to say anything untoward.

Jack's gaze grew more intent. "Far be it from me to reveal any secrets," he said. "You'll learn the truth soon enough." His gaze remained on Sophie's face. "But I'm come to steal Miss Winterton from you, Enderby. My dance is next, I believe, my dear?" With a calmly proprietorial air, Jack tucked Sophie's hand into the crook of his elbow and, with the barest of nods for Lord Enderby, now thoroughly bemused, turned her down the room.

Sophie blinked and grabbed her wandering wits. "I believe you're right, Mr. Lester. But shouldn't we return to my aunt?"

"Why?"

She glanced up to find an improbably mild expression inhabiting her companion's patrician features as, undeterred by her remonstrance, he led her further and further from her aunt. "Because it's expected," she replied.

He smiled then, a slow, devilish smile, and looked down, meeting her gaze. "You're not a deb, my dear." His voice had deepened; she felt as well as heard it. Then his intent look softened and he looked ahead. "And, despite the throng, the room is not so crowded your aunt cannot keep you in view, if she's so inclined."

That, Sophie realized as she calmed her leaping heart, was true. A quick glance over her shoulder revealed Lucilla, with Clarissa beside her, almost at the other end of the room. There were many bodies between, but the crowd was not so thick it blocked them off.

"I don't intend to kidnap you, you know."

The soft statement pulled her gaze back to his face.

Jack smiled and tried his best to make the gesture reassuring. "I merely thought you might like to see who else is here tonight."

Her "Oh," was there in her eyes. Then, with a last, still-suspicious glance, she gave up her resistance, her hand settling on his arm.

He did as he had indicated, embarking on a gentle perambulation of the room. "Lady Entwhistle's lucky to see so many here so early in the Season. Lord Abercrombie," Jack indicated that well-known huntsman. "Have you met him before?" Sophie nodded. "He, for one, rarely leaves Northamptonshire until late April. The thaw must be extensive to have driven him south this early."

Sophie had, indeed, been surprised to find so many of the *ton*'s more mature yet eligible bachelors present. "I hadn't realized that the weather was to blame."

Again, she was aware of his gaze. "For some," he said, his voice low. Sternly quelling a shiver, Sophie pretended to look about.

"So, how do you find Society after four years away? Does it still hold some allure?"

Sophie glanced up at the question; a cynical ripple in his smooth tones gave her pause. "Allure?" she repeated, putting her head on one side. "I do not know that that is the right term, Mr. Lester." She frowned slightly. "There's glamour, perhaps." With one hand, she gestured about them. "But any with eyes must see it is transitory, an illusion with no real substance." They strolled on and Sophie smiled wryly. "I have long thought the Season society's stage, where we all come together to impress each other with our standing before summer draws us back to our true professions, to the management of our estates."

His gaze on her face, Jack inclined his head, his expression enigmatic. "You are wise beyond your years, my dear."

Sophie met his gaze; she arched a sceptical brow. "And you, sir?" She let her gaze slide away. Greatly daring, she continued, "I find it hard to believe that your view of the Season agrees with mine. I have always been told that gentlemen such as yourself pursue certain interests for which the Season is indispensible."

Jack's lips twitched. "Indeed, my dear." He let a moment stretch in silence before adding, "You should not, however, imagine that such interests are behind my presence here in town this early in the year."

Resisting the urge to look up at him, Sophie kept her gaze on those surrounding them. "Indeed?" she replied coolly. "Then it was boredom that fetched you south?"

Jack glanced down at her. "No, Miss Winterton. It was not boredom."

"Not boredom?" Determination not to allow him to triumph, Sophie swung about and, disregarding the crazed beating of her heart and the constriction which restricted her breathing, met his blue gaze. "Indeed, sir?"

He merely raised an arrogant brow at her, his expression unreadable.

She met his gaze coolly, then allowed hers to fall, boldly taking in his large, immaculately clad frame. The sapphire glinted in the white folds of his cravat; he wore no fobs or other ornament, nothing to detract from the image created by lean and powerful muscles. "Ah," she declared, resisting the urge to clear her throat. Settling her hand once more on his sleeve, she fell in by his side. "I see it now. Confess, sir, that it is the prospect of your mounts having to wade through the mire that has driven you, in despair I make no doubt, from Leicestershire."

Jack laughed. "Wrong again, Miss Winterton."

"Then I greatly fear it is the lure of the gaming rooms that has brought you to town, Mr. Lester."

"There's a lure involved, I admit, but it's not one of green baize."

"What, then?" Sophie demanded, pausing to look up at him.

Jack's gaze rose to touch her curls, then lowered to her eyes, softly blue. His lips lifted in a slow smile. "The lure is one of gold, my dear."

Sophie blinked and frowned slightly. "You've come seeking your fortune?"

Jack's gaze, darkly blue, became more intent. "Not my fortune, Miss Winterton." He paused, his smile fading as he looked into her eyes. "My future."

Her gaze trapped in his, Sophie could have sworn the polished parquetry on which she stood quivered beneath her feet. She was dimly aware they had halted; the crowd about them had faded, their chattering no longer reaching her. Her heart was in her throat, blocking her breath; it had to be that that was making her so lightheaded.

The midnight blue gaze did not waver; Sophie searched his eyes, but could find no hint, in them or his expression, to discount the wild possibility that had leapt into her mind.

Then he smiled, his mouth, his expression, softening, as she had seen it do before.

"I believe that's our waltz starting, Miss Winterton." Jack paused, then, his eyes still on hers, his voice darkly deep, he asked, "Will you partner me, my dear?"

Sophie quelled a shiver. She was not a green girl; she was twenty-two, experienced and assured. Ignoring her thudding heart, ignoring the subtle undertones in his voice, she drew dignity about her and, calmly inclining her head, put her hand in his.

His fingers closed strongly over hers; in that instant, Sophie was not at all sure just what question she had answered. Yet she followed his lead, allowing him to seep her into his arms. With a single deft turn, he merged them with the circling throng; they were just one couple among the many on the floor.

Time and again, Sophie told herself that was so, that there was nothing special in this waltz, nothing special between them. One part of her mind formed the words; the rest wasn't listening, too absorbed in silent communion with a pair of dark blue eyes.

She only knew the dance was over when they stopped. They had spoken not a word throughout; yet, it seemed, things had been said, clearly enough for them both. She could barely breathe.

Jack's expression was serious yet gentle as he drew her hand once more through his arm. "It's time for supper, my dear."

His eyes were softly smiling. Sophie basked in their glow. Shy yet elated, off balance yet strangely assured, she returned the smile. "Indeed, sir. I rely on you to guide me."

His lips lifted lightly. "You may always do so, my dear."

He found a table for two in the supper room and secured a supply of delicate sandwiches and two glasses of champagne. Then he settled back to recount the most interesting of the past year's *on-dits*, after which they fell to hypothesizing on the likely stance of the various protagonists at the commencement of this Season.

Despite her blithe spirits, Sophie was grateful for the distraction. She felt as if she was teetering on some invisible brink; she was not at all sure it was wise to take the next step. So she laughed and chatted, ignoring the sudden moments when breathlessness attacked, when their gazes met and held for an instant too long.

Her elation persisted, that curious uplifting of her spirits, as if her heart had broken free of the earth and was now lighter than air. The sensation lingered, even when Jack, very dutifully, escorted her back to Lucilla's side.

With what was, she felt, commendable composure, Sophie held out her hand. "I thank you for a most enjoyable interlude, sir." Her voice, lowered, was oddly soft and husky.

A small knot of gentlemen hovered uncertainly, awaiting her return.

Jack eyed them, less than pleased but too wise to show it. Instead, he took Sophie's hand and bowed elegantly. Straightening, for the last time that evening he allowed his gaze to meet hers. "Until next we meet, Miss Winterton."

His eyes said it would be soon.

TO SOPHIE'S CONSTERNATION, he called the next morning. Summoned to join her aunt in the drawing-room, she entered to find him, garbed most correctly for a morning about town in blue Bath superfine and ivory inexpressibles, rising from a chair to greet her, a faint, challenging lift to his dark brows.

"Good morning, Miss Winterton."

Determined to hold her own, Sophie bludgeoned her wits into order and plastered a calm, unflustered expression over her surprise. "Good day, Mr. Lester."

His smile warmed her before he released her hand to greet Clarissa, who had entered in her wake.

Aware that her aunt's deceptively mild gaze was fixed firmly upon her, Sophie crossed to the chaise, cloaking her distraction with a nonchalant air. As she settled her skirts, she noted that susceptibility to Mr. Lester's charms appeared strangely restricted. Despite her inexperience, Clarissa showed no sensitivity, greeting their unexpected caller with unaffected delight. Released, her cousin came to sit beside her.

Jack resumed his seat, elegantly disposing his long limbs in a fashionably fragile white-and-gilt chair. He had already excused his presence by turning Lucilla's edict to call on them to good account. "As I was saying, Mrs. Webb, it is, indeed, pleasant to find oneself with time to spare before the Season gets fully under way."

"Quite," Lucilla returned, her pale gaze open and innocent. In a morning gown of wine-red cambric, she sat enthroned in an armchair close by the hearth. "However, I must confess it took the small taste of the *ton* that we enjoyed last night to refresh my memories. I had quite forgotten how extremely fatiguing it can be."

From behind his urbane facade, Jack watched her carefully. "Indeed." He gently inclined his head. "Coming direct from the country, the *ton*'s ballrooms can, I imagine, take on the aspect of an ordeal."

"A very stuffy ordeal," Lucilla agreed. Turning to the chaise, she asked, "Did you not find it so, my dears?"

Clarissa smiled brightly and opened her mouth to deny any adverse opinion of the previous evening's entertainment.

Smoothly, Sophie cut in, "Indeed, yes. It may not have been a crush, yet the crowd was not inconsiderable. Towards the end, I found the atmosphere positively thick."

It was simply not done to admit to unfettered delight, nor to dismiss a kindly hostess's entertainments as uncrowded.

Jack kept his smile restrained. "Just so. I had, in fact, wondered, Miss Winterton, if you would like to blow away any lingering aftertaste of the crowd by taking a turn in the Park? I have my curricle with me."

"What a splendid idea." Lucilla concurred, turning, wide-eyed, to Sophie.

But Sophie was looking at Jack.

As she watched, he inclined his head. "If you would care for it, Miss Winterton?"

Slowly, Sophie drew in a breath. And nodded. "I…" Abruptly, she looked down, to where her hands were clasped in the lap of her morning gown, a concoction of lilac mull-muslin. "I should change my gown."

"I'm sure Mr. Lester will excuse you, my dear."

With a nod to her aunt, Sophie withdrew, then beat a hasty retreat to her chamber. There, summoning a maid, she threw open the doors of her wardrobe and drew forth the carriage dress Jorge had sent round that morning. A golden umber, the heavy material was shot with green, so that, as she moved, it appeared to bronze, then dull. Standing before her cheval-glass, Sophie held the gown to her, noting again how its colour heightened the gold in her hair and emphasized the creaminess of her complexion. She grinned delightedly. Hugging the dress close, she whirled, waltzing a few steps, letting her heart hold sway for just a moment.

Then she caught sight of the maid staring at her from the doorway. Abruptly, Sophie steadied. "Ah, there you are, Ellen. Come along." She waved the young girl forward. "I need to change."

Downstairs in the drawing-room, Jack made idle conversation, something he could do with less than half his brain. Then, unexpectedly, Lucilla blandly declared, "I hope you'll excuse Clarissa, Mr. Lester. We're yet very busy settling in." To Clarissa, she said, "Do look in on the twins for me, my love. You know I never feel comfortable unless I know what they're about."

Clarissa smiled in sunny agreement. She rose and bobbed a curtsy to Jack, then departed, leaving him wondering about the twins.

"They're six," Lucilla calmly stated. "A dreadfully *imaginative* age."

Jack blinked, then decided to return to safer topics. "Allow me to congratulate you on your daughter, Mrs. Webb. I've rarely seen such beauty in conjunction with such a sweet disposition. I prophesy she'll be an instant success."

Lucilla glowed with maternal satisfaction. "Indeed, it seems likely. Fortunately for myself and Mr. Webb, and I dare say Clarissa, too, her Season is intended purely to—" Lucilla gestured airily "—broaden her horizons. Her future is already all but settled. A young gentleman from Leicestershire—one of our neighbours—Ned Ascombe."

"Indeed?" Jack politely raised his brows.

"Oh, yes," his redoubtable hostess continued in a comfortably confiding vein. "But both my husband and I are firmly of the opinion that it does no good for a young girl to make her choice before…surveying the field, as it were.'' With every appearance of ingenuousness, Lucilla explained, ''The chosen suitor may be the same as before she looked but she, certainly, will feel much more assured that her choice is the right one if she's given the opportunity to convince herself it is so.'' Lucilla's pale eyes swung to Jack's face. ''That's why we're so keen to give Clarissa a full Season—so that she'll know her own mind.''

Jack met her level gaze. ''And your niece?''

Lucilla frowned delicately but approval glimmered in her eyes. ''Indeed. Sophie's first Season was cut so very short it hardly signified. She was presented, and had her come-out and even braved the trial of Almack's, but it was barely three weeks in all before my sister succumbed to a chill. So very tragic.''

Her sigh was sorrowful; Jack inclined his head and waited.

''So, you see, Mr. Lester,'' Lucilla continued, raising her head to look him in the eye. ''Both Mr. Webb and I hope very much that any gentleman who truly appreciates dear Sophie will allow her to have her Season this time.''

Jack held her coolly challenging gaze for what seemed like an age. Then, reluctantly, he inclined his head. ''Indeed, ma'am,'' he replied, his tone even. ''Your arguments are hard to deny.'' When it became clear his hostess was waiting for more, he added, his expression impassive, ''Any gentleman who valued your niece would, I feel sure, abide by such wisdom.''

Gracious as ever, Lucilla smiled her approbation, then turned as the latch lifted. ''Ah, there you are, Sophie.''

Smoothly, Jack rose and went forward, his eyes feasting on the vision hovering on the threshold. She had donned a forest green half-cape over her carriage dress, which was of a strange bronzy-gold shade with piping of the same dark green at collar and cuffs. Green gloves and green half-boots completed her outfit. Jack felt his lips soften in a smile; his Sophie was fashionable elegance incarnate.

Reassured by his smile, and the appreciative light in his eyes,

Sophie smiled back and gave him her hand. Together, they turned to Lucilla.

"I will engage to take all care of your niece, Mrs. Webb." Jack sent an arrogantly questioning glance across the room.

Lucilla studied the picture they made, and smiled. "I trust you will, Mr. Lester. But do not be too long; Lady Cowper is to call this afternoon, and we must later attend Lady Allingcott's at-home." With a graciously benevolent nod, she dismissed them.

It was not until they reached the Park and Jack let his horses stretch their legs that Sophie allowed herself to believe it was real. That she was, in truth, bowling along the well-tended carriageway with Jack Lester beside her. The brisk breeze, cool and playful, twined in her curls and tugged little wisps free to wreath about her ears. Above and about them, arched branches were swelling in bud; the sky, a clear, crisp blue, formed a backdrop for their nakedness. Slanting a glance at her companion, she wondered, not for the first time, just what he intended.

He had, most correctly, escorted her down the steps of her aunt's house, then blotted his copybook by ignoring her hand and lifting her instead to his curricle's seat. On taking his own seat beside her and being assured she was comfortable, he had smiled, a slow, proudly satisfied smile, and clicked the reins. The bustle in the streets had made conversation unwise; she had held her peace while they travelled the short distance to the gates of the Park.

Now, with the first fashionable carriages looming ahead, she said, her tone merely matter-of-fact, "I had not looked to see you so soon, sir."

Jack glanced down at her. "I couldn't keep away." It was, he somewhat ruefully reflected, the literal truth. He had fully intended to allow the Webbs reasonable time to settle in the capital; instead, he had not been able to resist the compulsion to take Sophie for a drive, to show her the *ton*, and display her to them, safely anchored by his side. Staking his claim—and in such uncharacteristically blunt fashion that Sophie's aunt had seen fit to metaphorically wag her finger at him. Even the weather was conspiring to make him rush on with his wooing, the bright sunshine more redolent of April and May than chilly March.

He had expected some confusion in response to his forthright answer. Instead, to his delight, Sophie raised her chin and calmly stated, "In that case, you may make yourself useful and tell me who all these people are. My aunt has had little time to fill me in, and there are many I don't recognize."

Jack grinned. It was close on noon, a most fashionable time to be seen driving in the Park. "The Misses Berry you must recall," he said as they swept down on an ancient landau drawn up by the verge. "They're always to be found at precisely that spot, morning and afternoon throughout the Season."

"Of course I remember them." With a gay smile, Sophie nodded to the two old dames, bundled up in scarves and shawls on the seat of the landau. They nodded back. As the curricle swept past, Sophie saw the gleam in their bright eyes.

"Next we have Lady Staunton and her daughters. You don't need to know them, although doubtless your cousin will make the younger girls' acquaintance."

Sophie bestowed a distant smile on the bevy of girlish faces turned to stare in open envy as she went by. Despite Jorge's undoubted expertise, she doubted it was her new carriage dress that had excited their interest.

As she looked ahead once more, she saw a tall woman, modishly gowned in bright cherry-red, strolling the lawns just ahead. Her hand rested on the arm of a rakishly handsome buck. Both looked up as the carriage neared. The woman's face lit up; she raised her hand in what appeared, to Sophie, a distinctly imperious summons.

The reaction on her right was immediate; Jack stiffened. As it became clear the carriage was not about to stop, nor even slow, Sophie glanced up. Chilly reserve had laid hold of Jack's features; as Sophie watched, he inclined his head in the most remote of greetings.

The carriage swept on, leaving the couple behind. Relaxing

362   A LADY OF EXPECTATIONS

against the padded seat, Sophie forced her lips to behave. "And that was?" she prompted.

The glance she received was dark with warning. She met it with a lifted brow—and waited.

"Harriette Wilson," came the answer. "Someone you definitely do *not* need to know."

His repressive tone evoked a gurgle of laughter; Sophie swallowed it and airily looked around. Lady Cowper's barouche was drawn up in a curve of the carriageway; Sophie waved as they passed, pleased to note her ladyship's answering smile. Lady Cowper was yet another old friend of her late mama's.

They passed many others; Jack knew them all. His running commentary kept Sophie amused and distracted. She was content to enjoy his company and his apparent liking for hers; she would dwell on what it might mean later. So she smiled and laughed up at him, basking in the glow of his very blue eyes.

"Jack!"

The hail jolted them from their absorption.

It emanated from a young, dark-haired gentleman, clearly of the first stare, who, together with his similarly well-turned-out companion, was perched on the driving seat of a swan-necked phaeton, approaching at a clipping pace. Jack reined his horses to the side of the track; the elegant equipage executed a neat turn and came to a swooping stop beside them.

"Been searching for you forever," the young gentleman declared, his eyes, also deeply blue, passing from Jack to Sophie. He smiled with cheery good-humour. "Dashed if I'd thought to find you here!"

Glancing up at her escort's face, Sophie saw a whimsical smile soften his hard features.

"Gerald." Jack nodded to his brother, his knowledgeable gaze roving over the finer points of the pair of high-bred horses harnessed between the long shafts of the phaeton, itself spanking new if its gleaming paintwork was to be believed. "Where'd you get this rig?"

"The phaeton's fresh out of old Smithers's workshop. The nags are Hardcastle's. He'll let me have them for a tithe their true value—five hundred the pair. The phaeton'll be full price, though, and you know what Smithers is like."

Brows lifting, Jack nodded. With a deft twirl of his wrist, he looped his reins and offered them to Sophie. "Will you do me the honour, my dear?"

Scrambling to hide her surprise, greatly pleased for she well knew that few gentlemen would entrust their horses to a mere female, Sophie graciously nodded and took the reins. With a reassuring smile, Jack climbed down. The horses shifted slightly; determined to keep them in line, Sophie kept her eyes firmly on them, her brow furrowing in concentration.

Hiding his grin, Jack paced slowly around Gerald's carriage and horses, his blue eyes shrewdly assessing. Gerald and his friend watched with bated breath, their eagerness barely suppressed. Then, rejoining Sophie and retaking possession of the reins with a warm smile, Jack nodded at his brother. "Not a bad set-up."

Gerald grinned delightedly.

"But allow me to make you known to Miss Winterton." Jack paused to allow Gerald to bow, lithely graceful. "My youngest brother, Gerald Lester."

Having had time to note the similarity between Jack and the youthful gentleman, also dark-haired, blue-eyed and broad-shouldered, but without the heavy musculature that characterized her escort's more mature frame, Sophie showed no surprise.

While his brother introduced Lord Somerby, his companion, Jack cast a last glance over the phaeton and pair. His lips quirked. Turning to Gerald, he smoothly said, "And now you'll have to excuse us. I'm overdue to return Miss Winterton to her home."

"Jack!" Gerald's pained exclamation was heartfelt. "Dash it all—don't tease. May I have them or not?"

Jack chuckled. "You may. But make sure you get an account from Smithers. Drop by this evening and I'll give you a draft." Although it was his own money Gerald would be spending, as his trustee until his twenty-fifth birthday, Jack had to approve all his youngest brother's transactions.

Gerald's smile was ecstatic. "I'll be around at seven." With an insouciant wave of his whip, he touched his horses' ears. As the phaeton disappeared along the avenue, his gay carolling rolled back to them.

Smiling at Jack's exuberance, a sort of boundless *joie de vivre*, Sophie glanced up at her companion.

As if sensing her regard, Jack's smile, distant as he contemplated his brother's delight, refocused on her face. "And now, I fear, I really should return you to Mount Street, my dear."

So saying, he whipped up his horses; they took the turn into the main avenue in style. As they bowled along, a stylish matron chatting idly with an acquaintance in her carriage, glanced up, then waved them down. Jack politely drew in beside the lady's barouche.

"Sophia, my dear!" Lady Osbaldestone beamed at her. "I take it your aunt has finally arrived in town?"

"Indeed, ma'am." Sophie leant from the curricle to shake her ladyship's hand. "We'll be here for the Season."

"And a good thing, too! It's entirely more than time you were amongst us again." Her ladyship's eyes gleamed with a fervour to which Sophie was innured.

Jack was not so fortunate. He exchanged nods with Lady Osbaldestone, wryly resigned to being ignored for at least the next ten minutes. Lady Osbaldestone's lack of concern in finding a young lady with whom she clearly claimed more than a passing acquaintance alone in his presence registered—and made his inner smile even more wry. There had been a time, not so very far distant, when she would not have been so sanguine. However, over the past year, his acknowledged search for a wife had gained him, if not immunity from all suspicion, then at least a certain acceptance amongst the *grandes dames*. He suspected they viewed him as a leopard who, at least temporarily, had changed his spots.

That much, he was willing to concede, might be true. Nevertheless, the underlying temperament remained.

As he heard her ladyship's plans for Sophie's future unfurl, his instincts rose to shake his complacency.

He waited until they had, at last, parted from his ladyship and were once more rolling towards the gates before saying, "Lady Osbaldestone seems quite determined to see you well wed."

Totally unconcerned by her ladyship's grand schemes, which had even stretched as far as the Duke of Huntington, Sophie smiled gaily. "Indeed. They are all of them busy hatching schemes."

"All of them?"

There was something in his flat tones that made her glance up but her companion's expression was inscrutable. Light-hearted still, even light-headed, the aftermath, no doubt, of an uninterrupted hour of his company, Sophie grinned. "All of my mother's old friends," she explained. "They all look upon me as a motherless chick—one and all, they're determined to see me 'properly established'." She uttered the last words in a passable imitation of Lady Osbaldestone's haughty accents.

She glanced up, expecting to see him smiling, laughing with her at the prospect of so many matrons busily scheming on her behalf. Instead, his face remained stony, devoid of expression. Jack felt her glance. His emotions straining at the leash, he looked down.

Sophie met his dark gaze, and felt a vice slowly close about her heart. Avid, eager to find the reason, for that and the force that held them in a curious hiatus, out of time, she searched his face and his deeply glowing eyes. Jack watched as her smile slowly faded, to be replaced with puzzlement—and a clear query.

"Sophie—" He drew in a deep breath and glanced ahead, just in time to avoid colliding with a natty trilby, swung through the gates far too fast.

Jack swore. In the ensuing chaos as he calmed his own horses, then received the shrill and abject apologies of the trilby's owner, a young sprig barely old enough to shave and, in Jack's pithily offered opinion, of insufficient experience to be entrusted with the reins, the purport of Lucilla's words returned to him.

As the trilby crept away, Jack turned to Sophie, his expression carefully blank. "Are you all right?"

"Yes." Sophie smiled brightly up at him, while inwardly she wondered if that was strictly true. The instant before the trilby's advent had left her nerves stretched and quivering.

Jack forced his lips into an easy smile. "I'd better get you back to Mount Street forthwith, or your aunt will doubtless forbid me your company. It's well past our allotted hour."

Sophie kept her own smile light. "My aunt is very understanding."

That, Jack thought, as he eased into the traffic, was undoubtedly the greatest understatement he had ever heard. He made no effort to break the silence until they reached Mount Street. Even then, relinquishing the reins to Jigson, whom he had left awaiting his return, he eschewed comment, reaching up to lift Sophie down to the pavement in what was rapidly becoming a charged silence.

As he expected, she showed no signs of fluster. Instead, she stood before him, her face turned up to his, her query contained in the gentle lift of her delicate brows.

Despite himself, Jack smiled—his slow, sensuous smile, the one he was usually careful to hide from well-bred young ladies.

Sophie didn't disappoint him; she studied his face, openly gauging his smile, then, lifting her eyes to his, merely raised her brows higher.

Jack laughed softly but shook his head. "The time is not yet," was all he dared say. Holding her eyes with his, he raised her gloved hand and, most reprehensibly, placed a kiss on her bare wrist. Then, placing her hand on his sleeve, he covered it with his and strolled with her up the steps. As the door opened to admit her, he bowed. "Once again, my dear—until next we meet."

CHAPTER SIX

FOR SOPHIE, the rest of Tuesday and all of Wednesday passed in a rosy-hued blur. As expected, Lady Cowper called, promising vouchers for Almack's and her most earnest endeavours. Lucilla and her ladyship spent a full hour with their heads close together; Sophie stared absent-mindedly at the window, her expression distant. Recalled to the present when her ladyship rose, she flashed a bright smile and bade Lady Cowper farewell. The smile lingered, muted but nevertheless present, long after her ladyship's carriage rattled away down the street.

"Well then, my dears." Lucilla swept back into the drawing-room. Clarissa followed with Sophie trailing in the rear. "In the light of Lady Cowper's remarks, we had best reconsider our strategy."

Closing the door, Sophie made for the chaise, a slight blush tinting her cheeks. "How so, aunt?" She could not, in truth, recall all that much of Lady Cowper's conversation.

With a long-suffering air, Lucilla raised her brows. "Because, my dear, if the *ton* is already in town then there's no reason not to steal a march on those who have planned their entertainments to coincide with the usual start of festivities and already sent out their invitations." Reclaiming her seat, she gestured to the pile of white cards upon the mantelshelf. "The list grows every day. I have it in mind to make our mark with a tactical manoeuvre, if I have the phrase correctly."

Sophie tried to concentrate on her aunt's meaning. Yet at every pause, her mind slid sideways, to ponder the subtleties in a certain deep voice, and the light that had glowed in his eyes. Frowning, she struggled to banish her distracting fascination. "So you mean to bring Clarissa's come-out forward?"

Deep in thought, Lucilla nodded. "It seems strategically imperative—if she's not out, she cannot be present at the rush of balls and parties which, as dear Emily pointed out, are this year going to precede the usual commencement." Lucilla pulled a face. "Yet it's not the sort of decision one takes lightly." She pondered a moment, one elegant fingernail tapping on the chair arm. Then she straightened. "We have Lady Allingcott's at-home this afternoon and Lady Chessington's little party tonight, then Almack's tomorrow—even they have started early this year. I pray you both to keep your ears open. Depending on what we all hear, I think we might start with an impromptu party, just for the younger folk, next week. And plan Clarissa's ball for the week after that. My ideas are already well advanced; it will simply be a matter of bringing them forward a trifle." Nodding to herself, Lucilla turned to Clarissa. "What say you to that, my dear?"

"It sounds *wonderful!*" Clarissa's eyes radiated excited relief. "Indeed, I wasn't looking forward to missing the balls in the next weeks."

"And why should you?" Lucilla spread her hands wide. "This is your Season, my love; you're here to enjoy it." She smiled her subtlest smile. "As Madame Jorge said; we will contrive."

Sophie had nothing to say against her aunt's plans. Mr. Lester, of course, would not be present at the small, informal parties and dances held by the families with young girls making their come-out, to help the young ladies gain their social feet. Until Clarissa was officially out, the Webb ladies would be restricted to such tame affairs, which were all very well if there was nothing else on offer. But this year, this Season, was going to be different—and it wasn't only the weather that would make it so for her.

They attended Lady Allingcott's and Lady Chessington's entertainments, and on Wednesday called on Lady Hartford and the Misses Smythe, then danced at Almack's, all the while listening to what their peers had to say of projected entertainments.

Over breakfast the next morning, Lucilla called a council of war. "Now pay attention, Sophie."

Thus adjured, Sophie blinked. And endeavored to obey the injunction.

"I've consulted with your father, Clarissa, and he's in full agreement. We will hold your come-out ball at the end of the week after next."

Clarissa crowed. Her younger brothers pulled faces and taunted.

"In the meantime, however," Lucilla raised her voice only slightly; as her eagle eye swept the table the din subsided. "We'll hold a dance at the end of next week—on Friday. An informal affair—but we need not restrict the guest list solely to those making their come-out. I see no reason not to invite some of those amongst the *ton* with whom you are already acquainted."

Sophie knew her smile was almost as bright as Clarissa's. Her aunt's gaze, pausing meaningfully on her, sent her heart soaring. Ridiculous—but there was no other word for it—the exhilarating excitement that gripped her at the mere thought of seeing him again. She lived for the moment but, given he had not appeared at Almack's—faint hope though that had been— it had seemed likely they would not meet again until Clarissa was out and they could move freely in society's mainstream.

Unless, of course, he called to take her driving again.

She spent all morning with one ear tuned to the knocker. When the time for luncheon arrived and he had not called, she put her disappointment aside and, her smile still bright, descended to the dining-room. She was determined none of her cousins would guess her true state. As for her aunt, she had directed one or two pointed glances at her niece and once, she had surprised a look of soft satisfaction upon Lucilla's face. That, of course, was inevitable.

It was at Mrs. Morgan-Stanley's at-home later that day that her bubble of happiness was punctured.

On entering the Morgan-Stanleys' large drawing-room, Lucilla immediately joined the circle of fashionable matrons gathered about the fireplace. Clarissa drifted across to the windows, to where the youngest of those present had shyly retreated to trade dreams. With a confident smile, Sophie joined a small group of young ladies for whom this was not their first Season. She was taking tea with them in their corner when, in the midst of a discussion on the many notables already sighted in town, Miss Billingham, a thin young lady with severe, pinched features, cast her an arch glance.

"Indeed! Miss Winterton, I fancy, can testify to the fact. Why, we saw you in the Park just the other morning, my dear, driving with Mr. Lester."

"Mr. Lester?" Miss Chessington, a bright, cheerful soul, short, good-natured and of an indefatigably sunny temperament, blinked in amazement. "But I thought he *never* drove mere females."

"Not previously," Miss Billingham conceded with the air of one who had made a thorough study of the matter and was unshakeably certain of her facts. "But it's clear he has, at last, realized he must change his ways. My mama commented on the point, even last Season." When the others, Sophie included, looked their question, Miss Billingham consented to explain. "Well, it's common knowledge that he must marry well. More than well—real money—for there are his brothers, too, and everyone knows the Lesters have barely a penny to bless themselves with. Good breeding, good estates—it's the blunt that's wanting."

Sophie was not the only one who blinked at the crude term and the hard gleam in Miss Billingham's eyes but, in her case, the action was purely reflex. Her mind was reeling; a horrible sinking feeling had taken up residence in the pit of her stomach. Her features froze in a polite mask, and a sudden chill swept through her.

"My mama has long maintained," Miss Billingham declaimed, "that he'd have to come about. Too high in the instep by half, he spent all last Season searching for some goddess

Likely he's come to the understanding that he cannot look so high.''

Miss Billingham looked at Sophie. The others, following her lead, did the same. Caught on a welling tide of despair, Sophie did not notice.

"I suppose, it being so early in the Season, he thought to amuse himself—get his hand in at the practice in safety, so to speak—by squiring you about, Miss Winterton.''

It was the rustling of skirts as the others drew back, distancing themselves from the snide remark, that shook Sophie from her trance. As Miss Billingham's words registered, she felt herself pale. A cattish gleam of satisfaction flared in Miss Billingham's eyes. Pride came to Sophie's rescue, stiffening her spine. She drew in a steadying breath, then lifted her chin, looking down at Miss Billingham with chilly hauteur. "I dare say, Miss Billingham." Her tone repressively cool, Sophie continued, "I can only assume that Mr. Lester could find no other to suit his purpose, for, as you say, I hardly qualify as a rich prize.''

At first, Miss Billingham missed the allusion; the poorly suppressed grins of the other young ladies finally brought Sophie's words home. Slowly, Miss Billingham's sallow complexion turned beet-red, an unhappy sight. She opened her mouth, casting a glance around for support. As she found none, her colour deepened. With a few muted words, she excused herself to return to the safer precincts close by her mother, a woman of battleship proportions.

"Don't pay any attention to her," Miss Chessington advised as their little circle closed comfortably about Sophie. "She's just furious Jack Lester paid her no heed whatever last year. Set her cap at him, and fell flat on her face.''

Valiantly, Sophie struggled to return Miss Chessington's bright smile. "Indeed. But what of your hopes? Do you have anyone in your sights?''

Belle Chessington grinned hugely. "Heavens, no! I'm determined to enjoy myself. All that bother about a husband can come later.''

Reflecting that, a few months ago, she, too, would have been as carefree, Sophie dragged her thoughts away from what had focused her mind on marriage. She clung to Miss Chessington's buoyant spirits until it was time to depart.

Once enveloped in the quiet of her aunt's carriage, cool reason returned to hold back the misery that threatened to engulf her. Sophie closed her eyes and laid her head back on the squabs.

"Aren't you feeling quite the thing, my dear?"

Lucilla's calm voice interrupted Sophie's thoughts. Sophie tried to smile, but the result was more like a grimace. "Just a slight headache. I found Mrs. Morgan-Stanley's drawing-room a trifle close." It was the best she could do. To her relief, her aunt seemed to accept the weak excuse.

Lucilla reached over and patted her hand. "Well, do take care. I hope you'll both remember that one never appears to advantage while a martyr to ill health." After a moment, Lucilla mused, "I don't think our schedule is overly full, but if you do feel the need, you must both promise me you'll rest."

Together with Clarissa, Sophie murmured her reassurances.

As the carriage rolled steadily onward, she kept her eyes closed, hiding her frown. Despite her often outrageous machinations, Lucilla was ever supportive, always protective. If Jack Lester was, indeed, totally ineligible as a suitor for her hand—or, more specifically, if, as a mere lady of expectations, *she* was ineligible to be his bride, then Lucilla would not have allowed him to draw so close. Her aunt was as clever as she could hold together. Surely she could trust in Lucilla's perspicacity?

Perhaps Miss Billingham had it wrong?

That possibility allowed Sophie to meet the rest of her day with equanimity, if not outright enthusiasm. Until the evening, when Lady Orville's little musical gathering brought an end to all hope.

It was, most incongruously, old Lady Matcham who squashed the bubble of her happiness flat. A tiny little woman, white-haired and silver-eyed with age, her ladyship was a kindly soul who would never, Sophie knew, intentionally cause anyone harm.

"I know you won't mind me mentioning this, Sophia, my dear. You know how very close I was to your mother—well, she was almost a daughter to me, you know. So sad, her going." The old eyes filled with tears. Lady Matcham dabbed them away with a lace-edged handkerchief. "Silly of me, of course." She smiled with determined brightness up at Sophie, sitting beside her on a chaise along the back wall of the music room.

Before them, the very select few whom Lady Orville had invited to air their musical abilities along with her two daughters were entertaining the gathering, seated in rows of little chairs before the pianoforte. Now, to the sound of polite applause, Miss Chessington took her seat at the instrument and laid her hands upon the keys.

Expecting a comment on the colour of her ribbons, or something in similar vein, Sophie smiled reassuringly at Lady Matcham, returning the squeeze of one birdlike claw.

"But that's why I feel I have to say something, Sophia," Lady Matcham continued. "For I would not rest easy thinking you had got hurt when I could have prevented it."

An icy hand closed about Sophie's heart, all expression leached from her face. Numb, paralyzed, she gazed blankly at Lady Matcham.

"I must say," her ladyship went on, her washed-out eyes widening. "I had thought Lucilla would have warned you but, no doubt, having only just returned to the capital, she's not yet up with the latest."

The chill creeping through Sophie had reached her mind; she couldn't think how to interrupt. She didn't want to hear any more, but her ladyship pressed on, her soft, gentle, undeniably earnest tones a death-knell to all hope.

"It's about Mr. Lester, my dear. Such a handsome man— quite the gentleman and so very well-connected. But he needs a rich wife. A very rich wife. I know, for I am acquainted with his aunt, dear soul—she's passed on now. But it was always understood the Lester boys would have to marry money, as the saying goes.'' Lady Matcham's sweet face grimaced with distaste. ''Such a disheartening thought.''

Sophie could only agree. Her heart was a painful lump in her breast; her features felt frozen. She couldn't speak; she could only gaze blankly as Lady Matcham lifted her wise old eyes to her face.

Lady Matcham patted her hand. ''I saw you in the Park, in his curricle. And I just had to say something, my dear, for it really won't do. I dare say he's everything a gal like you might wish for. But indeed, Sophia dear, he's not for you.''

Sophie blinked rapidly and sucked in a quick breath. Her heart was aching; all of her hurt. But she could not give way to her pain in the middle of Miss Chessington's sonata. Sophie swallowed; with an effort, she summoned a weak smile. ''Thank you for the warning, ma'am.'' She couldn't trust herself to say more.

Her ladyship patted her hand, blinking herself. ''There, there. It's not the end of the world, although I know it may feel that way. Such unfortunate happenings are best nipped in the bud— before any lasting damage can be done. I know you're too wise, my dear, not to know that—and to know how to go on. Why, you've all the Season before you. Plenty of opportunity to find a gentleman who suits you.''

Sophie would have given the earth to deny it, all of it, but nothing could gainsay the sincerity in Lady Matcham's old eyes. With a wavering smile, Sophie gave the old lady a brief hug, then, with a mute nod, rose. Dragging in a steadying breath, she drifted to a corner of the room.

By dint of sheer will-power, she did not allow herself to dwell on Lady Matcham's revelations until, together with her aunt and Clarissa, she was enclosed in the protective shadows of the carriage and bound for home.

Then misery engulfed her, tinged with black despair.

As they alighted in Mount Street, the light from a street flare fell full on her face. Lucilla glanced around; her eyes narrowed.

"Sophie, you will lie in tomorrow. I will not have you coming down with any ailment at this time of year."

Fleetingly, Sophie met her aunt's gaze, sharp and concerned. "Yes, Aunt," she acquiesced, meekly looking down. Ignoring Clarissa's concerned and questioning glance, Sophie followed her aunt up the steps.

THE NEXT DAY dawned but brought with it no relief. From behind the lace curtain at her bedchamber window, Sophie watched as Jack Lester descended the steps to the street. He climbed up into his waiting curricle and, as his groom scrambled up behind, deftly flicked his whip and drove away. Sophie watched until he disappeared around the corner, then, heaving a heavy sigh, turned back into the room.

He had called to take her for a drive, only to be met with the news of her indisposition.

Sophie sniffed. Aimless, she drifted across the room towards her bed, her sodden handkerchief wadded in her fist. As she passed her dressing-table, she caught a glimpse of her face in the mirror. Dark shadows circled her eyes; her cheeks were wan, her lips dry. Her head felt woosy and throbbed uncomfortably; her limbs seemed heavy, listless.

Lady Matcham's warning had come too late. In the dark hours of the night, she had faced the dismal fact: the delicate bud rooted in her heart, influenced by the weather and the warmth of his smile, had already flowered. Now it lay crushed, slain by the weight of circumstance. Soon, she supposed, it would wither.

She was not a wealthy catch, a bride who would bring as her dower the ready cash necessary to rescue a gentleman's estates. Nothing could change that cold, hard fact. She was her father's heiress, a lady of expectations, possessed of no more than moderate fortune, and even that was prospective, not immediately accessible as capital.

Sophie sniffed again, then determinedly blew her nose. She had spent too much of the night weeping, not an occupation she had had much experience of, not since her mother's death.

Now, she felt emptied, desolate, as she had then. But she knew she would recover. She would allow herself one day in which to mope, and by tonight, she would be back on her feet, her smile bright. As the Season unfolded, she would devote herself to her search for a husband with all due diligence. And forget about a handsome rake with dark blue eyes.

That was the way things were in her world; she knew it well enough. And after all Lucilla's and Clarissa's kindnesses, she would not allow her unhappiness to cloud Clarissa's Season. She would do her best to ensure it did not sink her own, either.

Feeling oddly better to have such clear goals before her, Sophie perched on the end of her bed. Her fingers pulled at her wrinkled handkerchief; her gaze grew abstracted. There was one point she had yet to consider: how best to deal with him when they met, as, inevitably, they would.

After deep and lengthy cogitation, she had absolved him of all blame. She could not believe he had sought to cause her pain. She it was who had misread his purpose; she was, in reality, no more experienced in such matters than Clarissa. It was, very likely, as Miss Billingham had said—to him, she was a safe and agreeable companion, one with whom to pass the time until the Season was fully under way and he could set about choosing his bride. Indeed, Lady Matcham's observations left little room for any other interpretation.

There were, admittedly, his curious words when he had last left her. *The time is not yet.* She had thought he had meant.... Abruptly, Sophie cut off the thought, setting her teeth against the pain. What he *had* probably meant was to propose some outing, some excursion which their present early stage of friendship would not stretch to encompass. She had read more—much more—into his innocent words than he could ever have intended.

Which meant that, given his innocence, she would have to treat him as if nothing was wrong. Pride dictated she do so. Any awkwardness she felt must be suppressed, hidden, for she couldn't bear him to know what she had thought—hoped.

Somehow, she would cope. Like Madame Jorge, like Lucilla, she could contrive.

With a sigh, Sophie climbed onto her bed and tugged the covers over her. She snuggled down, settling her head on the pillows; calmly determined, she closed her eyes. She forced herself to relax, to allow the furrows in her forehead to ease away. If she was going to contrive, she would need some sleep.

The days ahead would not be easy.

CHAPTER SEVEN

EVEN PICCADILLY was crowded. Jack frowned as, leaving the shady avenues of the Park behind him, he was forced to rein in his horses by the press of traffic, vehicular and pedestrian, that thronged the wide street. Manoeuvring his curricle into the flow, he sat back, resigned to the crawling pace. To his right, Green Park luxuriated in the unseasonable heat, green buds unfurling as the fashionable strolled its gentle paths. Its calm beckoned, but Jack ignored it. The clamour of the traffic more suited his mood.

Grimacing at his inching progress, he kept his hands firm on his horses' reins. Just as he did on his own. He supposed his wooing of Sophie Winterton was progressing satisfactorily, yet this snail's pace was hardly what he had had in mind when he had exchanged the informality of the country for the *ton*'s structured delights. Lady Entwhistle's small ball had raised his hopes; at its conclusion he had felt decidedly smug. Thus, he felt sure, should a lady be wooed.

That success had been followed by his admittedly precipitous invitation to go driving, prompted by the unexpectedly tempestuous feelings which lay beneath his reasoned logic. He could justify to his own and anyone else's satisfaction just why Sophie Winterton would make him an excellent wife but, underneath it all, that peculiarly strong emotion which he hesitated to name simply insisted she was his.

Which was all very well, but Sophie's aunt, while not disputing his claim, had made it clear she would not assist him in sweeping Sophie off her feet.

Which, given his present state, was a serious set-back.

His horses tossed their heads impatiently, tugging at the reins. Reining them in, Jack snorted, very much in sympathy.

That drive in the Park, that gentle hour of Sophie's company, had very nearly tripped him up. If he was to obey her aunt's clear injunction and allow her to enjoy her Season unencumbered by a possessive fiancé—he had few illusions about that—then he would have to keep a firmer grip on himself. And on his wayward impulses.

Not that that was presently proving a problem; he had not set eyes on Sophie since that morning nearly a week ago. After her aunt's warning, he had held off as long as he could—until Friday, when he had called only to learn she was ill. That had shaken him; for an instant, he had wondered if her indisposition was real or just one of those tricks ladies sometimes played, then had dismissed the thought as unworthy—of Sophie and himself. He knew she liked him; it was there in her eyes, a warm, slightly wary but nonetheless welcoming glow that lit up her face whenever they met. Chiding himself for his ridiculous sensitivity, he had dispatched his man, Pinkerton, to scour the town for yellow roses. As always, Pinkerton, despite his perennial gloom, had triumphed. Three massive sprays of yellow blooms had duly been delivered in Mount Street with a card, unsigned, wishing Miss Winterton a speedy recovery.

He had looked for her in the Park, morning and afternoon, on both Saturday and Sunday but had failed to come up with the Webb carriage.

So, feeling distinctly edgy, all but champing on his metaphorical bit, he had called in Mount Street this morning—only to be informed that Miss Winterton had gone walking with her cousins.

Fate, it seemed, had deserted him. Despite the bright sunshine, his view of the Season was growing gloomier by the minute.

Lord Hardcastle, driving his greys, hailed him; they spent a few minutes exchanging opinions on the unusual press of traffic before said traffic condescended to amble onward, parting them. An organ-grinder, complete with monkey, was playing

to an attentive crowd, blocking the pavement, much to the disgust of merchants and those less inclined to dally. Jack smiled
and returned his attention to his horses. As he did so, a flash
of gold caught his eye.

Turning, he searched the throng bustling along the pavement—and saw Sophie with Clarissa beside her, the two boys
and Amy reluctantly following, casting longing glances back
at the organ-grinder. As he watched, the little cavalcade halted
before a shop door, then, leaving the maid and groom who had
brought up the rear outside, Sophie led the way in.

Jack glanced up and read the sign above the shop, and
smiled. He pulled his curricle over to the kerb. "Here—Jigson!
Take charge of 'em. Wait here." Tossing the reins in Jigson's
general direction, Jack leapt down and, threading his way
through the traffic, entered the door through which Sophie had
passed.

The door shut behind him, abruptly cutting off the noisy
bustle outside. Calm and well-ordered, the refined ambience of
Hatchard's Book Shop and Circulating Library enfolded him.
No raised voices here. A severely garbed man behind a desk
close to the door eyed him, disapproval withheld but imminent.
Jack smiled easily and walked past. Despite its relative peace,
the shop was quite crowded. He scanned the heads but could
not find the one he sought. An eddy disturbed the calm; Jack
spotted Jeremy, George and Amy huddling in a nook by the
window, noses pressed to the pane, gazes locked on the entertainment on the pavement opposite.

Glancing around, Jack discovered that the disapproving man
had been joined by an equally severely garbed woman. They
were now both regarding him askance. With another urbane
smile, he moved into the first aisle and pretended to scan the
spines until he was out of their sight.

At the end of the third aisle, Sophie frowned up at the novel
she most expressly wished to borrow. It was wedged tightly
between two others on the topmost shelf, barely within reach.
She thought of summoning the clerk to retrieve it for her, and
grimaced; he was, she had discovered, quite cloyingly admir-

ing. Sophie smothered a snort. She would make one last effort
to prise the book loose before she surrendered to the attentions
of the clerk.

Sucking in a breath, she stretched high, her fingers grappling
to find purchase above the leather-covered tome.

"Allow me, my dear."

Sophie jumped. Snatching back her hand, she whirled, her
colour draining then returning with a rush. "Oh! Ah…" her
eyes widened as they met his. Abruptly, she dropped her gaze
and stepped back, determinedly shackling her wayward wits.
"Why thank you, Mr. Lester." With all the calm she could
command, Sophie raised her head. "This is quite the last place
I had thought to meet you, sir."

Tugging the book free of its fellows, Jack presented it to her
with a bow. "Indeed. Not even *I* would have thought to find
me here. But I saw you enter and was filled with an unquench-
able desire—" Jack trapped her gaze, a rakish smile dawning
"—to view such apparently attractive premises. Strange, was
it not?"

"Indeed." Sophie sent him a cool glance. "Most strange."
She accepted the volume, reminding herself of her sensible
conclusion, and her determination to view him as he viewed
her: as a friendly acquaintance. "I do, most sincerely, thank
you for your assistance, sir. But I must not keep you from your
business."

"Rest assured you are not doing so, my dear." As he fell
in beside her, Jack slanted her a glance. "I have what I came
in to find."

The tenor of his deep voice tightened the vice about Sophie's
heart. She glanced up, meeting his blue gaze, and abruptly realized that her vision of a "proper distance" might differ considerably from his. A sudden revelation of what that might
mean—the effect his warm regard and teasing ways would inevitably have on her—set her chin rising. With commendable
hauteur, she bestowed a repressively chilly glance on him. "Indeed? I take it you are not particularly fond of reading?"

Jack grinned. "I confess, my dear, that I'm a man of action

rather than introspection. A man of the sword rather than the word.''

Sophie ignored his subtle tone. ''Perhaps that's just as well,'' she opined. ''Given you have large estates to manage.''

''Very likely,'' Jack conceded, his lips twitching.

''There you are, Sophie. Oh, hello, Mr. Lester.'' Clarissa appeared around the corner of the aisle. She smiled blithely up at Jack and dropped a slight curtsy.

Jack shook her hand. ''Have you found sufficient novels to keep you entertained, Miss Webb?'' He eyed the pile of books Clarissa carried in her arms.

''Oh, yes,'' Clarissa replied ingenuously. ''Are you ready, Sophie?''

Sophie considered replying in the negative, but was convinced that, rather than leave, Jack Lester would insist on strolling with her up and down the aisles, distracting her from making any sensible selection. She glanced about; her gaze fell on her younger cousins, glued to the prospect outside. ''I suspect we *had* better leave before Jeremy falls through the window.''

While Sophie and Clarissa went through the process of borrowing their chosen novels, Jack smiled smugly at the disapproving assistant.

To her relief, Sophie found the assistant disinclined to conversation, a fact for which she gave mute thanks. Clarissa summoned her brothers and sister and they all started for the door. As she stepped over the threshold and paused to get her bearings, Sophie felt her packaged novel lifted from her hands.

''Allow me, my dear.'' Jack smiled as Sophie glanced up, consternation in her wide, slightly startled gaze. Puzzled, Jack inwardly frowned. ''If you have no objection, I'll escort you to Mount Street.''

Sophie hesitated, then, her lids veiling her gaze, inclined her head. ''Thank you. That would be most kind.'' With a determinedly light air, she surrendered her hand into his warm clasp and allowed him to settle it on his sleeve. While she waited beside him as he dismissed his groom and, with a simple admonition, succeeded in convincing Jeremy, George and Amy to leave the crowd about the organ-grinder, Sophie prayed that her momentary dismay had not shown; she did not wish to hurt him any more than she wished him to guess how much her heart had been bruised. As their little party got under way, she flashed Jack a bright smile. "Did you see Lady Hemming-hurst's new carriage?"

To her relief, his rakish smile appeared. "And those nags she insists are high-steppers?"

With Clarissa beside them, they chatted easily, more easily than she had hoped, all the way back to Mount Street. Indeed, the steps leading up to her uncle's door appeared before them far sooner than she had expected. Jeremy and George bounded up the steps to ring the bell, Amy close behind. With a cheery smile, Clarissa bade their escort farewell and followed her siblings as they tumbled through the door.

Acutely conscious of the gentleman before her, of Ellen and the groom, still standing decorously a few steps behind, and of Minton, the butler, holding open the door, Sophie held firm to her composure and, receiving her book, presented with a flourish, calmly said, "Thank you for your escort, Mr. Lester. No doubt we'll run into each other at the balls once they start."

Jack's slow smile twisted his lips. "I fear, my dear, that I'm not endowed with as much patience as you credit me." He hesitated, his eyes narrowing as he searched her face. "Would you be agreeable if I called to take you driving again?"

Sophie held her breath and wished she could lie. When one dark brow rose, a gentle prompt, his gaze steady on hers, she heard herself say, "That would be most pleasant, sir." His smile was triumphant. *"But,"* she hurried on. "My time is not always my own. My aunt has decided to start entertaining and I must assist her if required."

Jack's smile did not fade. "Indeed, my dear. But I'm sure she'll not wish you to hide yourself away." With smooth authority, he captured her hand. His eyes met hers; he raised her fingers, then turned them.

"No!" As surprised as he by her breathless denial, Sophie stared up at him, her heart thudding wildly. Abruptly, she

dropped her gaze, quite unable to meet the startled question in his. Head bowed, she withdrew her hand from his and dropped a slight curtsy. "Good day, Mr. Lester."

The words were barely audible.

Jack felt as if he'd taken a blow to the head. He forced himself to execute a neat bow. Sophie turned and quickly climbed the steps, disappearing inside without a backward glance.

Finding himself standing stock-still, alone in the middle of the pavement, Jack drew in a ragged breath. Then, his expression stony, he turned and strode briskly away.

WHAT IN THE NAME of all creation had gone wrong?

The question haunted Jack through the next three days and was still revolving incessantly in his brain as, the evening chill about him, he climbed the steps to knock on the Webbs' oak-panelled door. Despite his initial intentions, it was the first time he had called in Mount Street since his unexpected expedition to Hatchard's. He had returned home in a most peculiar mood, a mood that had been only slightly alleviated by the white and gold invitation he had discovered awaiting him.

"Mrs. Horatio Webb takes great pleasure in inviting Mr. Jack Lester to an impromptu dance to be held on Thursday evening."

The words had not dissipated the cloud that had settled over him, but had, at least, given him pause. Thus, he had not pressed the, albeit minor, intimacy of a drive on Sophie but had waited instead to come up with her in her aunt's ballroom, where, surely, she would feel more confident, less likely to take fright at his advances.

Quite clearly he had been too precipitate. He had put a foot wrong somewhere, although he wasn't entirely sure where.

From now on, he would woo her according to the book, without any subtle deviations. He would simply have to conceal his feelings; he would not risk panicking her by heeding them.

Admitted by the butler, who recognized him well enough to

greet him by name, Jack climbed the stairs, slightly mollified by the man's cheery demeanour. Not what one was accustomed to in a butler but probably inevitable, given the junior Webbs. They would undoubtedly give any overly stuffed shirt short shrift.

Entering the salon on the first floor, Jack paused on the threshold and glanced around. A warm, welcoming atmosphere blanketed the room; it was not overly crowded, leaving adequate space for dancing, yet his hostess was clearly not going to be disappointed by the response to her summons. He discovered Sophie immediately, talking with some others. To his eyes, there was none to match her, her slim form sheathed in silk the colour of warm honey. With an effort, he forced his gaze to travel on, searching out his hostess. As he sighted her, Lucilla excused herself from a small knot of guests. She glided forward to greet him, regally gowned in satin and lace.

"Good evening, Mr. Lester." Lucilla smiled benevolently. She watched approvingly as he bowed over her hand.

"Mrs. Webb." Jack straightened. "May I say how honoured I was to receive your invitation?"

Lucilla airily waved her fan. "Not at all, Mr. Lester. It is I who am very glad to see you. I've been a trifle concerned that dear Sophie might be finding our present round of engagements somewhat stale. Dare I hope you might feel inclined to relieve her boredom?"

Jack forced his lips to behave. "Indeed, ma'am, I would be happy to do whatever I may in that endeavour."

Lucilla smiled. "I knew I could rely on you, Mr. Lester." With an imperious gesture, she claimed his arm. "Now you must come and speak with Mr. Webb."

As she led him into the crowd, Jack suppressed the thought that he had been conscripted.

On the other side of the room, Sophie chatted with a small group of not-so-young ladies. Some, like Miss Chessington, her aunt had invited specifically to keep her company, while others, like Miss Billingham, had younger sisters making their come-out this year. Gradually, they had attracted a smattering of the gentlemen present. Most of these were either carefully vetted Webb connections or unexceptionable young men who were the sons of Lucilla's closest cronies. There was no danger lurking among them.

Stifling an inward sigh, Sophie applied herself to keeping the conversation rolling; not a difficult task, supported as she was by the ebullient Miss Chessington.

"I had heard," that ever-bright damsel declared, "that there's to be a duel fought on Paddington Green, between Lord Malmsey and Viscount Holthorpe!"

"Over what?" Miss Billingham asked, her long nose quivering.

Belle Chessington looked round at the gentlemen who had joined them. "Well, sirs? Can no one clear up this little mystery?"

"Dare say it's the usual thing." Mr. Allingcott waved a dismissive hand, his expression supercilious. "Not the sort of thing you ladies want to hear about."

"If *that's* what you think," Miss Allingcott informed her elder brother, "then you know *nothing* about ladies, Harold. The reason for a duel is positively *thrilling* information."

Discomfited, Mr. Allingcott frowned.

"Has anyone heard any further details of the balloon ascension from Green Park?" Sophie asked. In less than a minute, her companions were well launched, effectively diverted. Satisfied, Sophie glanced up—and wished she could tie a bell about Jack Lester's neck. A bell, a rattle, anything that would give her warning so that her heart would not lurch and turn over as it did every time her gaze fell into his.

He smiled, and for an instant she forgot where she was, that there were others standing only feet away, listening and observing intently. An odd ripple shook her, stemming from where his fingers had closed over hers. She must, she realized, have surrendered her hand, for now he was bowing over it, making every other gentleman look awkward.

"Good evening, Mr. Lester," she heard herself say, as if

from a distance. She sincerely hoped her smile was not as revealing as her thoughts.

"Miss Winterton."

His smile and gentle nod warmed her—and made her suspect she had been far too transparent. Taking herself firmly in hand, Sophie turned and surprised an avid gleam in Miss Billingham's eyes. "Have you made the acquaintance of Miss Billingham, sir?"

"Oh, yes!" Augusta Billingham gushed. "Indeed," she said, her expression turning coy. "Mr. Lester and I are *old* acquaintances." She held out her hand, her smile sickly sweet, her eyes half-veiled.

Jack hesitated, then took the proffered hand and curtly bowed over it. "Miss Billingham."

"And Miss Chessington."

Belle's bright smile had nothing in common with Augusta Billingham's. "Sir," she acknowledged, bobbing a curtsy.

Jack smiled more naturally and allowed Sophie to introduce him to the rest of the company. By the time she had finished, he was feeling a trifle conspicuous. Nevertheless, he stuck it out, loath to leave Sophie's side.

When the musicians struck up, he bent to whisper, "I do hope, Miss Winterton, that you'll return. I would be quite overcome—utterly at a loss in such company as this—if it weren't for the reassurance of your presence."

Sophie lifted her head and looked him in the eye. "Gammon," she whispered back. But her lips quirked upward; Jack let her go with a smile.

While she danced the cotillion and then a country reel, he endeavoured to chat to some of the younger gentlemen. They were slightly overawed. His reputation as a devotee of Jackson's and one of Manton's star pupils, let alone his memberships in the Four-in-Hand and Jockey Clubs were well-known; their conversation was consequently stilted. It made Jack feel every one of his thirty-six years—and made him even more determined to bring his dazzling career as a bachelor of the *ton* to a close as soon as might be.

The prospect was still too far distant for his liking. A quadrille had followed hard on the heels of the reel; Sophie had been claimed for it before she had left the floor. With a brief word, Jack excused himself and wandered over to the musicians. The violinist was the leader; a few quick words were all that was needed, and a guinea sealed their bargain.

When the music stopped, Jack was passing the point where Sophie came to rest. She turned towards the end of the room, where her small group was once again gathering, her youthful partner at her side; she was laughing, her expression open and carefree. Her eyes met his—and a subtle change came over her.

Sophie forced a laugh to her lips, denying the sudden tightening about her lungs, the sudden constriction in her throat. She shot Jack a quizzical glance. "Have you survived thus far, sir?"

With a single, fractionally raised brow, Jack dispensed with her companion. Flustered, the young man bowed and murmured something before taking himself off.

Turning from thanking him, Sophie frowned a warning at her nemesis. "That was most unfair, taking advantage of your seniority."

Jack hid a wince. "I fear, my dear, that my…ah, experience marks me irrevocably." Making a mental note to be more careful in future, he took her hand and settled it in the crook of his elbow. "I feel very much like the proverbial wolf amongst the sheep."

His glance left Sophie breathless. Coolly, she raised a brow at him, then fixed her gaze on her friends. He led her in their direction but made no haste. Nor did he make any attempt at conversation, which left her free, not to regain her composure, as she had hoped, but, instead, to acknowledge the truth of his observation.

He did stand out from the crowd. Not only because of his manner, so coolly arrogant and commanding, but by virtue of his appearance—he was precise as always in a dark blue coat over black pantaloons, with a crisp white cravat tied in an intricate knot the envy of the younger men—his undeniable elegance and his expertise. No one, seeing him, could doubt he was other than he was: a fully fledged and potentially dangerous rake.

Sophie frowned, wondering why her senses refused to register what was surely a reasonable fear.

"Why the frown?"

Sophie looked up to find Jack regarding her thoughtfully.

"Would you rather I left you to your younger friends?"

There was just enough hesitation behind the last words to make Sophie's heart contract. "No," she assured him, and knew it was the truth.

A flame flared in his eyes, so deeply blue.

Shaken, Sophie drew her eyes from the warmth and looked ahead to where her friends waited. In her eyes, the younger gentlemen were no more than weak cyphers, cast into deep shade by his far more forceful presence.

After a moment, Jack bent his head to murmur, "I understand there's a waltz coming up. Will you do me the honour of waltzing with me, my dear?"

Sophie fleetingly met his gaze, then inclined her head. Together, they rejoined her little circle, Jack withdrawing slightly to stand by her side, a little behind. He hoped, thus, to feature less in the conversation himself, commendably doing his best not to intimidate the younger sparks who, he kept telling himself, were no real threat to him.

Twenty minutes of self-denial later, he heard the musicians again put bow to string. Sophie, who knew very well that he had not moved from his position behind her, turned to him, shyly offering her hand.

With a smile of relief and anticipation both, Jack bowed and led her to the floor.

His relief was short-lived. A single turn about the small floor was enough to tell him something was seriously amiss. True, there was a smile on his partner's face; now and again, as they turned, she allowed her gaze to touch his. But she remained stiff in his arms, not softly supple, relaxed, as previously. She was tense, and her smile was strangely brittle.

His concern grew with every step. Even the cool glance her aunt directed at him as they glided gracefully past, held no power to distract him.

Eventually, he said, his voice gentle, "I had forgot to ask, Miss Winterton—I sincerely hope you've fully recovered from your indisposition?"

Momentarily distracted from the fight to guard her senses against his nearness, Sophie blinked, then blushed. Guilt washed through her; his tone, his expression, were touchingly sincere. "Indeed," she hastened to reassure him. "I…" She searched for words which were not an outright lie. "It was nothing serious, just a slight headache." She found it hard to meet his eyes.

Jack frowned, then banished the notion that once more popped into his brain. Of course she had been truly ill; his Sophie was not a schemer.

"And indeed, sir, I fear I've been remiss in not thanking you before this for your kind gift." Sophie's words died as she stared up at his face, strangely impassive. "You did send them, did you not? The yellow roses?"

To her relief, he nodded, his smile real but somehow distant. "I only hope they lightened your day." His gaze focused on her face. "As you do mine."

His last words were whispered, yet they clanged like bells in Sophie's head. She suddenly felt absolutely dreadful. How could she go on pretending like this, trying to hide her heart? It would never work. She was not strong enough; she would trip and he would find out…

Her distress showed very clearly in her eyes. Jack caught his breath. He frowned. "Sophie?"

The music came to an end. He released her only to trap her hand firmly on his sleeve. "Come. We'll stroll a little."

Sophie's eyes flared wide. "Oh, no, really. I'd better get back."

"Your friends will survive without you for a few minutes."

Jack's accents were clipped, commanding. "There's a window open at the end of the room. I think you could do with some air."

Sophie knew fresh air would help, yet the fact that he was sensitive enough to suggest it didn't help at all. She murmured her acquiescence, not that he had waited for it, and told herself she should be grateful. Yet being so close to him, and cut off from ready distraction, her senses were being slowly rasped raw. His effect on them, on her, seemed to get worse with every meeting.

"Here. Sit down." Jack guided her to a chair set back by the wall, not far from where a set of fine draperies billowed gently in the breeze.

Sophie sank onto the upholstered seat, feeling the cool wood of the chair back against her shoulders. The sensation helped her think. "Perhaps, Mr. Lester, if I could impose on you to get me a drink."

"Of course," Jack said. He turned and snapped his fingers at a waiter. With a few terse words, he dispatched the man in search of a glass of water. Sophie hid her dismay.

"And now, Sophie," Jack said, turning to look down at her. "You're going to tell me what's wrong."

It was a command, no less. Sophie dragged in a deep breath and forced herself to meet his gaze calmly. "Wrong?" She opened her eyes wide. "Why, Mr. Lester, nothing's wrong." She spread her hands in a gesture of bewilderment. "I'm merely feeling a trifle…warm." That, she suddenly realized, was the literal truth. He stood over her, his dark brows drawn down, and she was violently reminded of their interlude in the glade in Leicestershire. That same something she had glimpsed then, behind the intense blue of his eyes, was there again to-night. A prowling, powerful, predatory something. She blinked and realized she was breathing rapidly. She saw his lips compress.

"Sophie…"

His eyes locked with hers; he started to lean closer.

"Your glass of water, miss."

Sophie wrenched her gaze away and turned to the waiter. She dragged in a quick breath. "Thank you, John." She took the glass from the man's salver and dismissed him with a weak smile.

It took considerable concentration to keep the glass steady. With her gaze fixed, unfocused, on the couples now dancing a boulanger, Sophie carefully sipped the cool water. An awful silence enfolded them.

After a few minutes, Sophie felt strong enough to glance up. He was watching her, his expression utterly impassive; he no longer seemed so threatening. She inclined her head. "Thank you, sir. I feel much better now."

Jack nodded. Before he could find words for any of his questions, his attention was diverted by a group of younger folk who descended amid gusts of laughter to cluster not ten paces away.

Sophie looked, too, and saw her cousin surrounded by a group of young gentlemen, each vying for Clarissa's attention. Noting the frenetic brittleness that had infused Clarissa's otherwise bright expression, Sophie frowned. She looked up, and met an arrogantly raised brow.

She hesitated, then leaned closer to say, "She doesn't really like having a fuss and flap made over her."

Jack looked again at the fair young beauty. His lips twisted wryly as he watched her youthful swains all but cutting each other dead in an effort to gain her favour. "If that's the case," he murmured, "I fear she'll have to leave town." He turned back to Sophie. "She's going to be a hit, you know."

Sophie sighed. "I know." She continued to watch Clarissa, then frowned as a particularly petulant expression settled firmly over her cousin's features. "What...?" Sophie followed Clarissa's gaze. "Oh, dear."

Following Sophie's gaze, Jack beheld a well-set-up young man, unquestionably recently up from the country if his coat was any guide, bearing determinedly down on the group about Sophie's cousin. The young man ignored the attendant swains as if they didn't exist, an action that won Jack's instant respect.

Directly and without preamble, the youngster addressed Clarissa; to Jack's disappointment, they were too far away to hear his words. Unfortunately, the young man's grand entrance found no favour in Clarissa's eyes. As Jack watched, Clarissa tossed her silvery curls, an indignant flush replacing the sparkle of moments before.

"Oh, dear. I do hope he didn't call her 'Clary' again."

Jack glanced down. Sophie was watching the unfolding drama, small white teeth absent-mindedly chewing her lower lip. "Whatever," he said. "It appears that his embassy has failed."

Sophie sent him a worried frown. "They've known each other since childhood."

"Ah." Jack glanced back at the tableau being enacted but yards away. A wisp of remembered conversation floated through his mind. "Is that young sprig by any chance Ned Ascombe?"

"Why, yes." Sophie stared up at him. "The son of one of my uncle's neighbours in Leicestershire."

Jack answered the question in her eyes. "Your aunt mentioned him." Glancing again at the young couple, Jack felt an empathetic twinge for the earnest but callow youth who was, quite obviously, under the impression he held pride of place in the beautiful Clarissa Webb's heart. As he watched, Ned gave up what was undeniably a losing fight and, with a galled but defiant expression, retired from the lists. Looking down at Sophie, Jack asked, "I take it he was not expected in London?"

Sophie considered, then said, "Clarissa didn't expect him."

Jack's brows lifted cynically. "Your aunt gave me to understand that their future was all but settled."

Sophie sighed. "It probably is. Clarissa does not really care for racketing about and she has never been one to enjoy being the centre of attention for very long. My aunt and uncle believe that, by the end of the Season, she'll be only too happy to return to Leicestershire."

"And Ned Ascombe?"

"And Ned," Sophie confirmed.

Considering the colour that still rode Clarissa Webb's cheeks, Jack allowed one brow to rise.

Sophie finished the last of her water. It was time and more to return to the safety of her circle. "If you'll excuse me, Mr. Lester, I should return to my friends."

Jack could have wished it otherwise but he was, once more, under control. Without a blink, he nodded, removing the glass from her fingers and placing it on a nearby table. Then he held out a hand.

Steeling herself against the contact, Sophie put her hand in his. He drew her to her feet, then tucked her hand into his elbow, covering her fingers with his. Hers trembled; with an effort, she stilled them. She glanced up and saw him frown.

Jack studied her face, still pale. "Sophie, my dear—please believe I would never knowingly do anything to cause you pain."

Sophie's heart turned over. Tears pricked, but she would not let them show. She tried to speak, but her throat had seized up. With a smile she knew went awry, she inclined her head and looked away.

He escorted her to her friends, then, very correctly, took his leave of her.

Jack did not immediately quit the house. Something was wrong, and Sophie wouldn't confide in him. The unpalatable fact ate at him, gnawing at his pride, preying on his protective nature, prompting all manner of acts he was far too experienced to countenance. His restless prowling, disguised beneath an air of fashionable boredom, took him by the alcove where Ned Ascombe stood, keeping a glowering watch over his prospective bride.

His gaze on the dancers, Jack propped one broad shoulder against the other side of the alcove. "It won't work, you know."

The laconic comment succeeded in diverting Ned's attention. He turned his head, his scowl still in evidence, then abruptly straightened, his face leaching of expression. "Oh, excuse me, sir."

Jack sent the youngster a reassuring grin. "Boot's on the other foot. It was I who interrupted you." Briefly scanning Ned's face, Jack held out his hand. "Jack Lester. An acquaintance of the Webbs. I believe I saw you at Lady Asfordby's, as well."

As he had expected, the mention of two well-known and well-respected Leicestershire names was enough to ease Ned's reticence.

Ned grasped his hand firmly, then blushed. "I suppose you saw…" He abruptly shut his mouth and gestured vaguely, his gaze once more on the dancers. "You were with Sophie."

Jack smiled, more to himself than Ned. "As you say, I saw. And I can tell you without fear of contradiction that your present strategy is doomed to failure." He felt rather than saw Ned's curious glance. Straightening, Jack extricated a notecase from an inner pocket and withdrew a card. This he presented to Ned. "If you want to learn how to pull the thing off, how to win the blond head you've set your eye on, then drop by tomorrow. About eleven." Very used to younger brothers, Jack ensured his worldly expression contained not the slightest hint of patronage.

Taking the card, Ned read the inscription, then raised puzzled eyes to Jack's face. "But why? You've never even met me before."

Jack's smile turned wry. "Put it down to fellow-feeling. Believe me, you're not the only one who's feeling rejected tonight."

With a nod, very man-to-man, Jack passed on.

Left by the alcove, Ned stared after him, his gaze abstracted, Jack's card held tight in his fingers.

"WELL, M'DEAR? Did Jack Lester disappoint you?" Propped against the pillows in the bed he most unfashionably shared with his wife, Horatio Webb slanted a questioning glance at his helpmate, sitting sipping her morning cocoa beside him.

A slight frown descended upon Lucilla's fair brow. "I don't expect to be disappointed in Mr. Lester, dear. I really should have organized that waltz myself. However, matters do seem to be progressing along their customary course." She considered, then banished her frown to cast a smiling glance at her spouse. "I dare say I've just forgotten how agonizingly painful it is to watch these things unfold."

Lowering the business papers he had been perusing, Horatio peered at her over the top of his gold-rimmed spectacles. "You haven't been meddling, have you?"

The slightest suspicion of a blush tinged Lucilla's cheeks. "Not to say *meddling*." She dismissed the notion with an airy wave. "But I really couldn't allow Mr. Lester to sweep Sophie into matrimony before the child had even had a taste of success. Not after her last Season was so tragically curtailed."

"Humph!" Horatio shuffled his papers. "You know how I feel about tampering with other people's lives, dear. Even with the *best* of intentions. Who knows? Sophie might actually *prefer* to have her Season curtailed—if it were Jack Lester doing the curtailing."

Head on one side, Lucilla considered the idea, then grimaced. After a moment, she sighed. "Perhaps you're right. When did you say the horses will be here?"

"They're here now. Arrived yesterday." Horatio had gone back to his papers. "I'll take the troops to view them this morning if you like."

Lucilla brightened. "Yes, that *would* be a good idea. But we'll have to give some consideration to escorts." She touched her spouse's hand. "Leave that to me. I'm sure I can find someone suitable."

Horatio grunted. "Wonder if Lester brought that hunter of his up to town?"

Lucilla grinned but said nothing. Finishing her cocoa, she laid her cup and saucer on the bedside table and snuggled down beneath the covers. Smiling, she reached out to pat her husband's hand. "I'm really quite in awe of your far-sightedness, dear. So clever of you to help the Lesters to their fortune. Now there's no impediment at all to concern you, and you may give Jack Lester your blessing with a clear conscience." An expression of catlike satisfaction on her face, Lucilla settled to doze.

Horatio stared down at her, a faintly astonished expression on his face. He opened his mouth, then abruptly shut it. After a long moment of staring at his wife's exquisite features, Horatio calmly picked up his papers and, settling his spectacles firmly on the bridge of his nose, left his wife to her dreams.

CHAPTER EIGHT

AT PRECISELY ELEVEN the next morning, the doorbell of Jack's townhouse in Upper Brook Street jangled a summons. Jack looked up, his brows lifting. "I believe that will be a Mr. Ascombe, Pinkerton. I'll see him here."

Here was the parlour; Jack sat at the head of the table, Pinkerton, his gentleman's gentleman, had just finished clearing the remains of Jack's breakfast and was lovingly glossing the mahogany surface.

"Very good, sir," Pinkerton returned in his usual sepulchral tones.

Jack nodded and returned to his perusal of the latest edition of the *Racing Chronicle*. "Oh—and bring a fresh pot of coffee, will you?"

"Yes, sir." A sober individual who considered it a point of professional etiquette to carry out his duties as inconspicuously as possible, Pinkerton slipped noiselessly from the room. As the sounds of voices penetrated the oak door, Jack folded the *Chronicle* and laid it aside. Easing his chair back from the table, he stretched, trying to relieve the tension that seemed to have sunk into his bones.

The door latch lifted; Pinkerton ushered Ned Ascombe in, then departed in search of more coffee.

"Good morning, sir." Feeling decidedly awkward, not at all sure why he had come, Ned surveyed his host. Jack Lester was clearly not one of those town beaux who considered any time before noon as dawn. He was dressed in a blue coat which made Ned's own loosely-fitting garment look countrified in the extreme.

Jack rose lazily and extended a hand. "Glad to see you, Ascombe—or may I call you Ned?"

Grasping the proffered hand, Ned blinked. "If you wish." Then, realizing that sounded rather less than gracious, he forced a smile. "Most people call me Ned."

Jack returned the smile easily and waved Ned to a chair.

Dragging his eyes from contemplation of his host's superbly fitting buckskin breeches and highly polished Hessians, Ned took the opportunity to hide his corduroy breeches and serviceable boots under the table. What had Clary called him? Provincial? His self-confidence, already shaky, took another lurch downwards.

Jack caught the flicker of defeat in Ned's honest brown eyes. He waited until Pinkerton, who had silently reappeared, set out a second mug and the coffee-pot, then, like a spectre, vanished, before saying, "I understand from Miss Winterton that you would wish Miss Webb to look upon you with, shall we say, a greater degree of appreciation?"

Ned's fingers tightened about the handle of his mug. He blushed but manfully met Jack's gaze. "Sophie's always been a good friend, sir."

"Quite," Jack allowed. "But if I'm to call you Ned, I suspect you had better call me Jack, as, although I'm certainly much your senior, I would not wish to be thought old enough to be your father."

Ned's smile was a little more relaxed. "Jack, then."

"Good. With such formalities out of the way, I'll admit I couldn't help but notice your contretemps with Miss Webb last night."

Ned's face darkened. "Well, you saw how it was," he growled. "She was encouraging an entire company of flatterers and inconsequential rattles."

There was a pause, then Jack asked, "I do hope you didn't tell her so?"

Ned fortified himself with a long sip of coffee and nodded darkly. "Not in those precise words, of course."

"Thank heaven for small mercies." Jack fixed his guest with

a severe glance. "It seems to me, my lad, that you're in desperate need of guidance in the matter of how to conduct a campaign in the *ton*."

"A campaign?"

"The sort of campaign one wages to win a lady's heart."

Ned glowered. "Clarissa's heart has always been mine."

"I dare say," Jack replied. "The trick is to get her to recognize that fact. From what I saw last night, if you continue as you are, you're liable to go backwards rather than forwards."

Ned frowned at his mug, then glanced up at Jack. "I'm not really cut out to shine in town. I don't know how to do the pretty by the ladies; I'm more at home in the saddle than in a ballroom."

"Aren't we all?" At Ned's questioning look, Jack elaborated. "The vast majority of gentlemen you'll see at any evening's entertainments would rather be somewhere else."

"But why attend if they don't wish to?"

"Why were you at Mrs. Webb's little affair?"

"Because I wanted to see Clarissa."

"Precisely. The only inducement capable of getting most of us across the threshold of a ballroom is the lure of the ladies. Where else do we get a chance to converse, to establish any connection? If you do not meet a lady first at a ball, it's dashed difficult to approach her anywhere else, at least in town. So," Jack concluded, "if you're set on winning Clarissa Webb, you'll have to accept the fact that you'll be gracing the *ton*'s ballrooms for the Season."

Ned wrinkled his nose. "My father was against my coming up to town—he thought I should just wait for Clarissa to come back. Mr. and Mrs. Webb are very sure she'll not appreciate the racketing about and will want to return to the country."

"I have inestimable faith in the senior Webb's perspicacity. However, don't you think you're extrapolating just a little too far? Taking Clarissa just a little too much for granted?"

Ned flushed again. "That's what worried me. It's why I came to town."

"And your instincts were right." Jack eyed him straitly. "From what little I've seen, I would predict that, whatever her inclinations, Clarissa Webb is sure to be one of the hits of the Season. That means she'll have all the puppies fawning at her feet, eager to paint unlikely pictures of a glowing future should she bestow her hand on them. And, despite the fact she may remain at heart a country miss, one should not lose sight of the fact that there's no shortage of gentlemen who are also inclined to the country. Such men would not baulk at taking a wife who dislikes town life. Most, in fact, would consider her a find."

Ned's brow furrowed. After a moment's cogitation, he looked Jack in the eye. "Are you telling me Clarissa will be sought after by other gentlemen who would wish to retire to the country?"

Jack nodded decisively.

"And if I don't make a…a push to fix her interest, she may accept one of them?"

Again came a definite nod.

Ned looked slightly shaken. After a long silence in which he studied the coffee at the bottom of his mug, and during which Jack sat back, at ease, and waited patiently, Ned raised his head, his jaw set, and regarded Jack with determined honesty. "I thank you for your warning, Jack. You've given me a great deal to think about." Despite his efforts, Ned's features contorted in a grimace which he immediately hid behind his mug. "Dashed if I know what I'm to do about it, though," he mumbled from behind the mug.

"No need to panic." Jack waved a languid hand. "I've loads of experience I'm perfectly willing to place at your disposal. I dare say once you learn the ropes, you'll find the whole business a challenge."

Surprised, Ned looked up from his mug. "Do you mean…" he began, then took the bull by the horns. "Are you suggesting you'd be willing to help me?"

"Not suggesting. I'm *telling* you I'm prepared to stand your mentor in this."

Ned's open face clouded. "But...why?" He flushed vividly. "I mean..."

Jack laughed. "No, no. A perfectly understandable question." He viewed his guest with a quietly assessing eye. Then he smiled. "Let's just say that I can't bear to see one so young so tangled in the briars. And, of course, I, too, have an interest in the Webb household." He made the admission with easy assurance and was rewarded by Ned's instant comprehension.

"Sophie?" His eyes growing round, his gaze openly speculative. Ned considered Jack—and his revelation.

Jack inclined his head.

"Oh."

As Jack had hoped, Ned seemed to accept that his interest in Sophie was sufficient excuse for his interest in him. While he was certainly drawn to Ned's open earnestness, it was Sophie's transparent concern for her cousin that had prompted him to take Ned under his wing. It formed no part of his own campaign to have Sophie in a constant fidget over her cousin, always keeping one eye on the younger girl. It was natural enough that she do so; to one who was himself imbued with a strong sense of sibling responsibility, Sophie's concern for Clarissa demonstrated a highly laudable devotion. Nevertheless, Sophie's cousinly concern could rapidly become a distraction.

. And Jack was quite certain he did not wish to share Sophie's attention—not With Clarissa, nor anyone else.

Ned was frowning, clearly still uncertain.

"Consider my offer in the light of one doing his damnedest to ensure his lady is not distracted by unnecessary ructions amongst her family," Jack suggested somewhat drily.

Ned glanced up, struggling to hide a grin. "I suppose that's true enough. Sophie's always been like an elder sister to Clarissa."

Jack inclined his head. "I'm so glad you see my point."

Ned nodded. "If that's the way it is, I have to admit it wouldn't sit well to walk away from a fight. But I do feel totally at sea.'' He grinned at Jack. ''Do you think you can turn me into a dandy?''

Jack grinned back. ''Not a chance. What I'm sure we *can* do is to turn you out as a gentleman of the *ton*.'' Sobering, he fixed Ned with a meaningful glance. ''You should never forget, nor attempt to hide, your origins. There is, if you'll only stop to consider, no taint attached to being a husbander of acres. Most of the highest in the *ton* are also the largest landholders in England and I can assure you they're not the least apologetic for the fact. Many spend considerable amounts of time managing their estates. Drawing one's fortune directly from the land is nothing to be ashamed of.''

Ned coloured slightly. ''Thank you. I don't know how you knew but that's exactly what I felt.''

''I know because I've been there before you. I, too, have an estate to manage. That, however, has never stopped me from feeling at home in London.''

''Oh.'' The revelation that Jack, too, had firm links with the country eased Ned's mind of its last doubt. ''So, what do I do first?''

''A tailor,'' Jack declared. ''Then a barber. You can't do anything until you look the part. And then we'll see about introducing you to some of the necessary establishments a gentleman of the *ton* must needs frequent—like Manton's and Jackson's Boxing Saloon. After that, we shall plan your campaign in more detail.'' Jack smiled. ''You're going to have to learn that finessing the feminine mind takes the wiles of a fox and the devotion of a hound.''

''I'll do whatever I need to,'' Ned averred. ''Just as long as I can make Clarissa stop looking at those trumped-up popinjays as she was last night.''

Jack laughed and rose. ''Onward, then. No time like the present to make a start.''

WHILE NED WAS sipping coffee in Upper Brook Street, Horatio Webb was busy introducing his children and his niece to the mounts he had had brought down from the country.

"These should be just the ticket for jaunts in the Park," he said as he ushered his charges into the stables. "Quite the thing, I hear, to be seen riding in the morning."

"Golly, yes!" returned Jeremy, eyes aglow. "All the crack."

Horatio's eyes twinkled. "Now these two, you two should recognize."

"By Jupiter! They're the ones you bought from Lord Cranbourne, aren't they, sir?" George, together with Jeremy, stared round-eyed at the two glossy-coated chestnut geldings their father had indicated.

Horatio beamed. "I thought they needed a little exercise. Think you can handle them?"

A garbled rush of words assured him that they could.

"We'll cut a dash on these," Jeremy declared.

With both boys absorbed, Horatio smiled down at Amy, clutching his hand. "Now for you, my miss, I've brought down Pebbles. Old Maude wouldn't have appreciated the traffic, you know."

Struck dumb at the thought of advancing beyond Old Maude's plodding gait, Amy stared at the placid grey mare who ambled up to look over the stall door. "Look!" she piped, as the mare reached down to nudge hopefully at her pockets. "She knows me!"

That, of course, took care of Amy. Leaving her to get properly acquainted with the mare, Horatio smiled at his two remaining charges. "Now, my dear," he said, beckoning Clarissa forward. "I fear I couldn't improve on Jenna, so I brought her down for you. I do hope you're not disappointed."

Clarissa smiled delightedly as she reached up to stroke the velvety nose of her beautiful chestnut mare. "How could I possibly be disappointed with you, my pet," she crooned softly as the mare nudged her cheek. "I was afraid you would want to spell her for a bit," she told her father. "I rode her all winter."

"Old Arthur seemed to think she was moping, missing all

her rides. You know how soft-hearted he is.'' Horatio patted Jenna's nose, then turned to Sophie.

"And now for you, my dearest Sophie.'' Taking her arm, he led her to the next stall, where an elegant roan mare was bobbing her head curiously. "I hope Dulcima here suits you. Not as powerful as the Sheik, of course, but rather more suited to the confines of the Park.''

Sophie was staring at the beautiful horse. "But...she's new, isn't she?''

Horatio waved dismissively. "Found her at Tattersall's. She's well broken and used to being ridden in town. Quite a find.''

"Well, yes. But I would have been quite happy with one of your other horses, uncle. I do hope you didn't buy her just for me?''

"No, no. Nonsense—of course not.'' Under Sophie's disbelieving gaze, Horatio looked down and tugged at his waistcoat. "Besides,'' he said, looking up, a sudden impish twinkle in his eye. "Dare say Mr. Lester will be riding in the Park on the odd occasion. Never do for him to think I don't take all care of you, m'dear.''

The comment cut off Sophie's protests. Taken aback, she frowned, opened her mouth, then closed it again.

"Leave you to get acquainted.'' With a farewell pat for the mare, Horatio strode back to see how his sons were faring.

Sophie looked after him, her eyes narrowing. Then she snorted disgustedly and turned back to the mare. As if in argument, the mare shook her head, then snorted once, ears pricking forward. Sophie grinned. "Aren't you a clever creature?'' she crooned.

The mare nodded vigorously.

When, at length, they were ready to leave their equine partners, they strolled together back along the mews and around to the house, Horatio with them.

In reply to Jeremy and George's eager question, Horatio replied, "You should give them a day or two to get over their journey, and for those not used to the noise to become more accustomed, before you take them out.''

The boys whooped. ''Monday, then!''

''However,'' Horatio smoothly continued, cutting across their transports. ''You cannot, I'm afraid, simply take off with a groom here in town.'' He glanced first at Sophie, then at Clarissa, walking on either side of him. ''Neither your aunt nor I would be happy with that.''

''But Toby will be here soon, will he not?'' Clarissa ventured.

Horatio nodded. His eldest son, presently at Oxford, was expected to join the family any day. ''True. But even so, you must remember that Toby is barely twenty. It would hardly be fair to foist the responsibility for all of you onto his shoulders. Indeed, although your mother and I have no doubt of his willingness to act as your escort, he is not yet experienced enough to adequately guard against the dangers which might face you here in the capital. This is not Leicestershire, as you know.''

''What, then?'' Sophie asked, knowing he was right. ''Where will we find a suitable escort?''

Horatio smiled his most inscrutable smile. ''Your aunt has promised to see to it.''

TUESDAY AFTERNOON saw the Webb ladies taking the air in the Park. The weather continued unseasonably mild; everyone was out to take advantage. Bright walking gowns splashed colour across the lawns. One or two ladies had even felt the need for parasols.

From her perch in the barouche beside her aunt, with Clarissa gaily smiling from the opposite seat, Sophie nodded and waved greetings, determined thus to keep her mind on noting any newcomers, rather than allowing her gaze to wander farther afield, searching for one she would do well to forget.

After completing a leisurely circuit, her aunt directed her coachman to pull up alongside Lady Abercrombie's carriage.

Her ladyship, as sociable as her husband was not, was all

smiles. "Lucilla, dear! How positively delightful! Do you intend to remain all Season?"

While Lucilla exchanged gossip with her ladyship, both Sophie and Clarissa did what young ladies were supposed to do on such occasions: they responded to any query directed their way but otherwise allowed their gaze to idly roam the passing scenery, which was to say, the passing crowd.

Engaged in this necessary occupation, Sophie greeted any acquaintances who passed, exchanging commonplaces all but automatically, while her wandering gaze became gradually more intent. When it finally occurred to her what she was doing, she frowned and shook herself.

With a determined air, she looked about for distraction. And discovered Mr. Marston, waiting, sober and serious as a judge, to greet her.

"Oh, good day, sir." Annoyed at her awkwardness—she was surely more experienced than this!—Sophie summoned a smile. "I did not know you had intended to come to London."

Phillip Marston took her hand and bowed. He shook hands with both Clarissa and Lucilla, who, on hearing his voice, had turned, brows flying upward. After exchanging a few words, Lucilla turned back to Lady Abercrombie, leaving Mr. Marston to gravely tell Sophie, "Indeed, Miss Winterton, it was not my intention to join the frivolity." A disdainful glance at two young gentlemen who came up to speak to Clarissa declared his opinion very clearly. "Nevertheless, I felt that, in this case, my presence was necessary."

Sophie was mystified. "Indeed, sir?"

"I flatter myself that I am fully cognizant of the inherent sensibility of your mind, Miss Winterton. I greatly fear that you will find little to entertain a lady of your refined nature here in the capital." Phillip Marston cast a glance at Lucilla, once more deeply engrossed with Lady Abercrombie, and lowered his voice. "As your aunt was determined to bring you to town, I felt that the least I could do, as I assured my dear mama, was to journey here to do what I may to support you through this time."

Utterly dumbfounded, Sophie silently searched for the pre-scribed reply to that revelation, and discovered that there wasn't one. In fact, as the full implication of Mr. Marston's declaration impinged on her mind, she decided she did not approve—of him or it. Drawing herself up, she fixed him with a distinctly frosty gaze. "I must inform you, sir, that I find the entertainments to which my aunt escorts me quite fascinating."

A condescending smile lifted Mr. Marston's thin lips. "Your loyalty to your aunt does you credit, my dear, but I feel I must point out that the Season has not yet begun. The entertainments thus far are doubtless mild enough. You will understand my concern once the more…rackety gentlemen are included. Then, I venture to say, you will be only too glad of my escort."

Sophie struggled for words. She dragged in a deep breath, glanced up—and felt a surge of inexpressible relief. Her heart leapt. She promptly tried to dampen her reaction, only to see the corners of Jack Lester's lips lift.

With determined calm, Sophie coolly extended one hand. "Good afternoon, Mr. Lester."

"Miss Winterton." With suave grace, Jack bowed. "I had hoped to discover you here." He ignored Mr. Marston beside him.

Mr. Marston, Sophie noticed, was not ignoring him. He drew himself up, his nostrils pinched as if Mr. Lester's appearance was offensive. Just what he could find amiss with that su-premely elegant figure Sophie was at a loss to guess. "Ah…I believe you have met Mr. Marston before, Mr. Lester? He's down from Leicestershire. I was just commenting on what a surprise it was to see him here." Sophie watched as the two men exchanged glances, Marston visibly bristling.

"Marston." With a brief nod, Jack dismissed the fellow from his thoughts and turned to Clarissa as her two admirers withdrew. "Miss Webb." Jack shook her hand, then indicated the figure beside him. "I believe Mr. Ascombe is known to you both?"

Sophie blinked, then smiled delightedly. From the corner of her eye, she saw Clarissa's jaw drop. Ned had been to a tailor—

a good one. His coat of Bath superfine now hugged his shoulders, doing far more justice to his lean frame than his previous suiting ever had. And he had had a haircut—his crisp brown locks were now in fashionable disarray. His breeches, his boots—all were new and all contributed to a remarkable transmogrification. Taking it all in with one comprehensive glance, Sophie retained sufficient wit to respond to the subtle prompt in Jack's steady blue gaze. She held out her hand and smiled warmly. "Indeed, yes. It's good to see you, Ned."

Some of Ned's stiffness faded. He slanted Sophie a grin. "You look ravishing, Sophie. Determined to cut a swath through the *ton?*"

Sophie was impressed by the clear confidence in Ned's tone. A quick glance to her right showed that she wasn't alone. Clarissa was staring at Ned, confusion clearly writ in her large blue eyes. "I'm certainly determined to enjoy myself this Season," Sophie responded. "Will you be in town for the duration?"

"I expect so," Ned replied, his gaze fixed on Sophie. "I hadn't realized before just how many distractions there were to be found in the capital."

"Hello, Ned."

At Clarissa's somewhat tentative greeting, Ned turned to her with an easy but in no way especial smile. "Good afternoon, Miss Webb. You're looking quite splendid. Have you been enjoying your stay thus far?"

Sophie bit her lip. The quick glance she sent Jack was a mistake. The devilish light in his blue eyes very nearly overset her control.

Clarissa, clearly bemused by the change in her childhood companion, mumbled a disjointed response, lost as Mr. Marston cut in.

"Afternoon, Ascombe." Phillip Marston eyed Ned's new finery with a critical eye. "Your father, I suspect, would be quite surprised to see you thus decked out."

Used to Phillip Marston's sober declarations, Ned merely grinned and shook his hand.

Sophie smothered a giggle. Jack caught her eye; she looked away, her jaws aching.

Then Lucilla joined the fray. She greeted Jack as an old acquaintance, complimented Ned on his good sense, and, under cover of a rapid-fire monologue on the varied entertainments to be found in the capital, managed to divulge that her charges would dearly like to ride in the Park in the mornings but lacked suitable escorts. "For even when Toby arrives," she declared, "I would not be happy to allow a group of such innocents to brave the Park without someone more experienced to handle the reins, as it were."

Stunned, Sophie directed a look of pointed reproof at her aunt. Lucilla pretended not to notice. Predictably, a deep voice answered.

"Mr. Ascombe and I would be only too happy to be of assistance, Mrs. Webb. Would you be content to release your charges to our care?"

Impotent, Sophie watched as Lucilla bent a look of shining approval on Jack. "Indeed, Mr. Lester. I cannot think of anyone I'd trust more."

Jack very nearly winced but inclined his head in acceptance of her commission. In this instance, her stipulation that he was being entrusted with her charges and therefore, as a gentleman, expected to respect her confidence, was no handicap.

And there was hay yet to be made from the situation. "Perhaps Miss Winterton and Miss Webb would care to stroll the lawns while we discuss the most appropriate time to meet?"

Lucilla's eyes widened slightly.

Sophie was not at all certain of the wisdom of strolling beside Jack Lester, even in the middle of the Park. Maintaining an appropriate distance was imperative; closing the physical distance between them was unlikely to help her cause.

"What a perfectly splendid idea!" Clarissa turned to Lucilla, her eyes bright and eager.

With a sigh and a lifted brow, Lucilla relaxed against the squabs. "By all means—but only for fifteen minutes. I'll await you here."

To Sophie's immense relief, Phillip Marston said nothing, merely frowning into the distance in an abstracted fashion. Then, rather abruptly, he bowed and took his leave of them.

Jack barely noticed. He handed Sophie down from the carriage, his satisfaction implicit in his smile. She was a picture in muslin the colour of old gold, a fairy princess with a touch of rose in her cheeks.

With her hand snugly tucked in his arm, they strolled across the broad expanse of clipped grass. Beside them, Clarissa, on Ned's arm, kept shooting shy glances up at him. Very correctly, the party remained together, clearly within sight of Lucilla in the barouche.

Aware, again, as she paced beside him of that strength that seemed an integral part of Jack Lester, impinging on her senses as if she had no defence, Sophie struggled to remain calmly aloof. Just friends—only friends. To her surprise, her companion proved to have a ready line of patter to meet even this occasion, one she doubted he had had much previous experience of.

"The *ton* seems uncommonly eager to commence this Season." Jack commented, idly scanning the host dotting the lawns. "I don't think I've seen such a turnout this early for years."

"My aunt was commenting on that fact," Sophie returned, keeping her gaze firmly on their surroundings. "I believe that a number of ladies are considering holding coming-out balls next week."

"My own ball will be held on Friday," Clarissa volunteered, suppressed excitement quivering in her tone. "Mama says there's no reason not to get into the swing of things."

"Your mother is indeed very wise, Miss Webb." Jack smiled down at Clarissa's delicately flushed face. A few days of Ned's company had more than sufficed to bolster his instinctive liking into solid support. He was quite determined that, come the end of the Season, Ned would retire from the lists with Clarissa's favour firmly in his possession. "I suspect there are few subjects on which you would not be wise to heed your mother's advice.''

"Have you been on an excursion to the Royal Exchange, Miss Webb? I'm told the wild beasts are a fearsome spectacle.'' Ned's tone was commendably even, devoid of overeagerness.

Hearing Clarissa, still warily suspicious but too unsure of this new Ned to risk any airs, answer with unaffected openess, Sophie was hard put to hide her grin.

Seeing her lips quirk, and deciding he had done enough to-day in furthering Ned's enterprise, Jack slowed his pace.

Sophie noticed. Her head came up. Looking her escort firmly in the eye, she raised a brow at him. When he merely smiled back, maddeningly, she surrendered to temptation. "Am I right, sir, in supposing you are helping Ned to adjust to town life?''

Jack smiled and leaned closer, lowering his voice. "Ned's a likeable chap. But having come up fresh from the country, he was facing opposition of unfair proportions. I thought it only fair to even the odds a little.''

Sophie felt her lips soften. "Indeed?'' she replied, her eyes on his. "So your actions are prompted by nothing more than a passing interest in righting an inequity?''

"I'm very keen on righting inequities,'' Jack informed her, his brows rising arrogantly. Then, abandoning his haughty attitude, he added, his tone deepening, "Not that I don't have reasons of my own to wish Clarissa settled.''

"Oh?'' Sophie held his gaze, warmly blue. Caution went winging. "And what might those be, sir?''

"Jack.'' Glancing ahead, Jack asked, "Do you think I'm succeeding?''

Although his glance had taken in Clarissa and Ned immediately ahead of them, his gaze had swung back to her on his question. Sophie, her heart increasing its tempo, was not sure how to reply. With a determined effort, she switched her gaze forward to where Clarissa was still viewing Ned curiously, like some specimen she did not yet understand. "My cousin certainly seems enthralled by Ned in his new guise.''

A heartfelt sigh came from beside her. "Perhaps I should

take a leaf out of his book? Mayhap Percy could give me some hints.''

At his defeated tone, Sophie swung about, her eyes automatically travelling the length of his elegantly accoutred frame before, realizing she had fallen into his trap, her gaze snapped up to meet his. Warm amusement, and a clear invitation to play this game—with him—glowed in the deep blue. Abruptly, Sophie dropped her gaze and murmured, ''Time is flying; we should return to my aunt, sir.''

A gentle, somewhat wry smile softened Jack's lips. ''I dare say you're right, Miss Winterton.'' So saying, he drew her hand once more through his arm. A few quick strides brought them up with the younger couple.

Ned turned, a glimmer of relief showing briefly in his eyes. But before they could retrace their steps to the barouche, they were hailed from the nearby carriageway.

''Jack!''

They all turned. Sophie recognized Gerald Lester—and his new phaeton. Ned had noticed the phaeton, too—and Gerald had noticed Clarissa. Naturally, they had to pause while introductions were performed and accolades on the phaeton and pair duly exchanged.

''No doubt but that I'll see you at one of the balls,'' Gerald said, impartially addressing them all. Then he flicked his whip and waved. ''Tally-ho!''

''Puppy!'' Jack snorted, but he was grinning.

Sophie watched the expensive carriage roll away, then turned towards the barouche.

One more reason why Jack Lester would have to marry well.

She risked a glance up at him; he was scanning the couples between them and the barouche. With Ned and Clarissa in tow, he steered her clear of any interference, making directly for the carriage where Lucilla sat awaiting them. Sophie bit her lip and looked down.

Gerald Lester was clearly a young gentleman unaccustomed to habits of economy. Jack's elegance declared that he, too, was not one to count the cost in presenting himself to the *ton*.

The Lesters, at least those she had thus far encountered, knew their place, knew to a nicety how to behave within the circles into which their birth and estates elevated them. Equally obviously, they thought nothing of financing their expensive style of life on tick.

Well, she amended moodily, perhaps not on tick—but there was little doubt that Jack needed a rich wife.

It was not, Sophie reflected dourly, an uncommon occurrence in the *ton*—families innured to living well beyond their means. She could only curse the fate that had made the Lesters one of them.

Then the barouche was before them and it was all she could do to behave normally, agreeing to ride the next morning in the Park, then acknowledging the farewells, smiling as he bowed over her hand, as if there were no black cloud lowering on her horizon, about to deprive her of the warmth of his gaze.

CHAPTER NINE

RESIGNED to the inevitable, Sophie was the first of the Webb contingent to appear in the hall the next morning. As she came down the stairs, buttoning her gloves, a wary smile twisted her lips. She should have expected Lucilla to seize the opportunity to throw Ned and Clarissa together, especially now that Ned had captured Clarissa's attention in what was, for her cousin, a wholly novel way. And Jack Lester, of course, was an undeniably capable escort. The children, for some mystical reason, had accorded him favoured status; he had only to speak and they tumbled to obey. Sophie grimaced. Descending the last flight, she tried to ease the knot of nervous tension that was tightening within her. The situation, she told herself, could have been worse. Mr. Marston might have spoken first.

Busy with her thoughts, her gaze abstracted, she did not see the young gentleman who emerged from the library.

"Sophie! Just the person! How are you?"

Before she could answer, Sophie was engulfed in a hug which owed more to enthusiasm than art. "Toby!" she gasped, recognizing her assailant. "Watch my hat, you clunch!"

"That wispy thing ain't a *hat,* Sophie." Toby flicked her riding hat, composed of a pheasant's feather and a scrap of velvet, with one finger. "Wouldn't keep the rain off you for a moment."

"As I should hope you are by now aware, Tobias Webb, having attained the years of wisdom, the importance of a modish hat lies not in its ability to protect one from the elements." Sophie's severity was belied by the affectionate twinkle in her eyes. "How was the trip down?"

"Enjoyable enough." Toby assumed a nonchalant air. "Peters and Carmody and I all came down together."

"I see." Sophie hid her smile. "Have you seen your father and mother yet?"

Toby nodded. "Papa told me you were planning to ride this morning with Ned Ascombe and a Mr. Lester. Thought I might join you."

"By all means," Sophie replied, only too glad of another distraction to counteract Jack Lester. "But they should be here with the horses any moment."

"I've already sent around to the stables for mine, so I shouldn't keep you. I'll just change my coat."

As Sophie stood in the hall watching Toby briskly climb the stairs, pausing at the top to greet Clarissa, about to descend, the clop and clash of many hooves on the cobbles beyond the massive oak door heralded the arrival not only of their mounts, but also of Jeremy, Gerald and Amy, who had been keeping watch from a window upstairs.

After whooping in greeting about their eldest brother, who admonished them with mock severity, the tribe descended to whirl about Sophie, eager to be off on this, their first excursion in the Park.

Thus it was that, admitted by a benignly beaming Minton, Jack, with Ned behind, came upon his golden head knee-deep in commotion. However, the expression of resigned calm on Sophie's face assured him she was not about to succumb to the vapours, despite the din.

"Quiet, you vexatious imps!" His firm greeting immediately transformed said imps into angels.

Sophie struggled to keep her lips straight. Jack's eyes lifted to meet hers and she lost the battle, her lips curving in a generous smile. "Good morning, sir. You see us almost ready."

"Almost?" Taking her hand, Jack lifted an eyebrow, then turned to nod to Clarissa.

"My eldest cousin, Toby, has rejoined the family. He's just gone to change." Nodding to Ned, Sophie wondered if it would be possible to tug her fingers free of the warm clasp which held them trapped. Despite her firm intention to remain aloof, her heart, unreliable organ that it was whenever he was near, was accelerating. "Toby's a keen rider and would not wish to miss our outing."

"Naturally not," Jack agreed, his gaze touching the children's eager faces. "Not when we've such an august and intrepid company as shall make all the *ton* stare."

He smiled as he made the statement, which was greeted with hoots from the younger Webbs. Sophie, however, was suddenly visited by a vision of how their cavalcade would appear to others in the Park. With a sudden sinking feeling, she realized that Lucilla, in her usual cryptic manner, had made no mention of the children.

As the children fell to fitting on their hats and gloves and swishing their skirts, Sophie lowered her voice to say, "Indeed, Mr. Lester, I would understand if you feel my aunt was not sufficiently open with you—she did not mention the children, and I dare say you will not care to be seen with such an entourage in the Park."

Jack turned to regard her in genuine surprise. Then he smiled. "If I were a Tulip of the *ton,* I might be concerned. However, such as I am, I feel sure my standing is sufficient to weather being seen with the Webbs, *en famille.* Besides which, my dear, I like your cousins."

Gazing up into his face, and seeing the gentle amusement therein, Sophie could not doubt his sincerity. It eased her mind and brought a calm smile back to her lips.

Which, to Jack's mind, was a perfectly satisfactory recompense for the trouble he could see looming before him.

Then Toby came bounding down the stairs, his enthusiasm only slightly less than that of his younger siblings. Introduced to Jack, he wrung his hand good-naturedly, nodded to Ned with easy familiarity and suggested they be off.

By Jack's side, Sophie was the last to quit the house. Standing at the top of the steps, she beheld a scene of veritable pandemonium. Luckily, her uncle's grooms had come to hold the horses; used to their master's children, the grooms did not blink as the youngsters rowdily mounted. As Jack drew her protectively closer, Sophie quieted her misgivings with the reflection that, once on horseback, she would not have to deal with her apparently inevitable reactions to his nearness. Riding, when all was said and done, should be safe enough.

It was not until they paused beside Dulcima that Sophie realized that there were hurdles, even when riding in London. Hurdles such as gaining her saddle atop the tall mare.

Jack, of course, saw no obstacle before him. He placed his hands about Sophie's slim waist and easily lifted her up.

Gently deposited in her saddle, Sophie tried to hide her blush, vowing to make a special effort, as of today, to stop reacting that way to his touch. Her heart was thudding madly; the tension within her had twisted tight. She felt the warmth of Jack's blue gaze upon her face but refused to meet it. By the time she had settled her skirts, he had swung up to the saddle of his black and the party was ready to depart.

Determined to appear unaffected by his proximity, she forced herself to look up and smile. She watched as Jack brought his sleek black alongside her mare; with the others ranged neatly before them, they brought up the rear of the procession as it clattered, eager but restrained, down Mount Street, towards the leafy precincts of the Park.

Grateful to feel her cheeks cool once more, Sophie kept her gaze fixed ahead. Jack's black swung his head towards Dulcima's, then snorted and shook his mane, setting his harness jingling. Dulcima calmly trotted on. The black repeated the manoeuvre, this time nudging Dulcima's shoulder. Sophie frowned. Four paces on, as the black turned to her mare again, Dulcima whinnied and tossed her head.

"Mr. Lester." Sophie felt compelled to support her mare's protest. She turned to Jack, gesturing to the black. "Your horse, sir."

Jack's expression turned rueful. He obligingly tightened his reins, leaning forward to pat the black's glossy neck. "Never mind, old boy. Delicately reared ladies are always the hardest to win over. Pretend they don't even see one. I know just how you feel.''

For an instant, Sophie's mind went quite blank. Finding her gaze locked with Jack's, she glared at him. Then, with a toss of her head that came perilously close to mimicking her mare, she looked straight ahead, thereby proving Jack's point.

To her immense relief, the gates of the Park appeared ahead. They entered and proceeded down a ride at a leisurely pace, glorying in the sunshine that continued to defy all predictions. About them, the rich smell of warming earth spiced the air, while birds trilled in the branches arching high overhead.

Glancing at Sophie, Jack inwardly smiled. Prey to an unnerving uncertainty, he had not again called to take her driving. But their stroll in the Park had reassured him, even though she had pulled back the instant he had drawn closer. Feminine nerves—that was the problem. He would just have to bide his time, and give her time to grow accustomed to his interest, to become more at ease with him.

So, holding his restless black to a sedate walk, he ambled beside her, his thoughts filled not with the joys of burgeoning spring, but with resigned acceptance of the tales that would no doubt be told in his clubs that night. He consoled himself with the reflection that, as his pursuit of Sophie would keep him in the ballrooms for most of the Season, he would not be spending much time at his clubs.

And if his pursuit of his bride did not keep him sufficiently busy, there was always his self-imposed task of keeping Ned Ascombe from doing himself an injury.

''I dare say the preparations for your coming-out ball must be exercising your imagination, Miss Webb.'' Jack cut across Ned to put a stop to what, to his experienced eyes, had been all too much like backsliding.

Caught out, reminded of the role he had been instructed it was in his best interests to play, Ned looked guilty.

''Yes, indeed,'' Clarissa readily replied. ''But Mama had taken care of all the details. The theme is to be classical, although personally I would rather have had the Rites of Spring.

But Mama held that that has been quite done to death these last years.''

Clarissa glanced at Ned.

"I'm sure Mrs. Webb knows what's best" was his verdict.

Sophie bit her lip.

After a moment's blank astonishment, Clarissa stiffened slightly. When no expression of empathetic understanding joined Ned's bare statement, she pointedly looked ahead.

Jack grinned and drew back, sure Ned would not again lapse into his habitually easy relationship with Clarissa. At least, not today.

"Are we allowed to gallop in the Park sir?" Toby brought his bay hunter up alongside Jack's black.

At twenty, brown-haired and blue-eyed with the same innate elegance that characterized Lucilla, Toby struck Jack as the sort to be up to all the usual larks, yet wise enough to avoid the grief that often overtook his peers. There was a glimmer of wisdom already detectable in his blue-grey eyes. No doubt, Jack mused, he had inherited his parents' brains. "You and your younger brothers and sister could conceivably do so. However, neither Miss Webb nor Miss Winterton would be wise to attempt the feat."

Toby wrinkled his nose. "The usual stuffy notions?"

Jack nodded. "As you say."

Lifting a brow at Sophie, and seeing her smile, Toby grinned ruefully. "Sorry, Sophie." Then, turning to his younger siblings, he waved his quirt and challenged, "Last to the oak at the other end of the turf gets to tell Mama what happened today!"

His three juniors responded immediately. All four thundered off.

Exchanging an indulgent smile, Jack and Sophie set their horses into a mild canter in their wake. Ned and Clarissa fell in behind. As they broke from the cover of the long ride and slowed, Sophie noticed their presence was attracting considerable interest. She did her best to appear unaware, until she realized that surprise was the predominant emotion on the faces of the gentlemen they passed.

Turning, she lifted a brow at her companion.

Jack smiled. "I fear I'm not noted for escorting boisterous families on jaunts through the Park."

"Oh." Uncertain, Sophie blinked up at him.

"I don't regret it in the least," Jack supplied, his smile somewhat wry. "But, tell me, my dear Miss Winterton, if you had to make the choice, would it be town or country for you?"

"Country," Sophie immediately replied. "Town is pleasant enough, but only…" she paused, putting her head on one side, "as a short period of contrast." After a moment, she shook herself free of her thoughts and urged Dulcima into a trot. "But what of you, sir? Do you spend much time in the country?"

"*Most* of my time." Jack grinned. "And, although you might not credit it, quite willingly. The estates, of course, need constant attention. When my sister left, she bequeathed me a list as long as my arm of all the improvements required." His brow darkening as a subject that, now, was very close to his heart claimed him, Jack continued, "I'm afraid, before Lenore left, I had not paid as much attention as I should have. She kept us together financially, which was no small feat. Consequently, my brothers and I left the decisions on what projects the family could afford to undertake to her. Although she was not to blame in any way, I should have realized that she did not have an extensive grasp of the estate as a whole, but was entirely familiar with all matters pertaining to the Hall itself. Hence, our ancestral home is in very good repair, but, for my money, I would have given some, at least, of the improvements necessary on the estate a higher priority."

Glancing down at Sophie's face, Jack added, "I fully intend to resuscitate the estate. I know what's needed; now it's simply a matter of getting things done."

A steel vice closed about Sophie's heart. She let her lids veil her eyes. Her features frozen in an expression of rapt attention, she inclined her head.

Encouraged, Jack briefly described those improvements he

felt most urgent. "I think it has something to do with being the one to inherit the land," he concluded. "I feel an attachment—a responsibility—now that it's virtually mine. I know Harry feels the same about the stud farm, which will one day be his."

Woodenly Sophie nodded, clutching her reins tightly. From her experience of her father's estates, she knew the cost of Jack's dreams. His words settled, a leaden weight about her heart.

Distraction arrived in a most unexpected form. A brusque hail had them drawing rein; turning, they beheld Mr. Marston astride a showy dun trotting quickly towards them. As he approached, Sophie inwardly admitted that Phillip Marston looked his best on horseback; his best, however, had never been sufficient to raise her pulse. Now, with her expectations conditioned by the likes of Jack Lester, she knew it never would.

"Good day, Mr. Marston." Her expression calmly regal, Sophie held out one hand, refusing to embellish the brief greeting with any hypocritical phrases.

"My very dear Miss Winterton." Phillip Marston attempted the difficult feat of bowing over her hand, but was forced to release it quickly as his horse jibbed. Frowning, he restrained the restive animal and, with obvious reluctance, nodded at Jack. "Lester."

Jack returned the nod with a perfectly genuine smile. "Marston."

The dun continued to jib and prance.

Phillip Marston did his best to ignore it—and the fact the dun was no match on any level with the even-tempered black Jack Lester rode. He nodded gravely to Ned and Clarissa, then fixed his pale gaze on Sophie. "I thought I'd take the trouble to find a mount and join you, my dear. I have not, as you know, previously had much experience of town, but I felt sure you would feel more easy in the company of one with whom you share a common background."

Inwardly bridling, Sophie refrained from glancing heavenwards and searched for some acceptable response. She was delivered from her unenviable predicament by the arrival of her younger cousins, whooping gleefully, their faces alight with exuberant joy.

Phillip Marston frowned bleakly. "Really, you young barbarians! Is this the way you behave when out from under your parents' eye?"

Their transports abruptly cut short, their joy fading, Jeremy, George and Amy instinctively looked not to Sophie, but to Jack.

He reassured them with a smile. "Nonsense, Marston," he said, his tone equable but distant. "The Park at this hour is a perfectly acceptable venue for the young to let off steam. Later, perhaps, such behaviour would be frowned upon, but now, with mainly young people and families about, there's nothing the least untoward in such high spirits."

The crestfallen trio were miraculously revived. They shot Jack a grateful glance and fell in beside him, as far as they could get from Mr. Marston. For a moment, Sophie allowed herself to envy them, before regretfully banishing the thought.

Phillip Marston received Jack's wisdom with a stiff little bow. His pinched lips and the slant of his brows left little doubt of his feelings. A charged moment passed in which Sophie bludgeoned her brains for some safe topic—not an easy task with Mr. Marston on one side and Jack Lester on the other—before Marston's particular devil prompted him to say: "I dare say, Lester, not being a *family* man, you don't realize the importance of discipline in handling the young."

Jack controlled his countenance admirably, bending a look of blandly polite enquiry on Marston. As Jack had hoped, Phillip Marston continued, airily declaiming, apparently unaware of Sophie's stunned silence.

"Natural enough, of course. After all, discipline's hardly your style, is it? I mean to say," he hurried on, "that doubtless, having little need for such in your own life, it's hard for you to understand that others live by a different code."

"Indeed?" Jack lifted a brow, his expression remote and

slightly bored. "I hadn't, I confess, thought my life so very different from that of the rest of my class."

Phillip Marston laughed condescendingly. "Oh, but it is." He waved airily. "Why, I dare say you'd be stunned to know that some of us spend months on our estates, grappling with such matters as tenants and bailiffs and crop rotation." Oblivious to the flags flying in Sophie's cheeks, Marston continued, "Not all of us can spend our lives in London, frittering away our money at the tables, sipping, unrestrained, from the bowl of life's pleasures."

That was far too much for Sophie. *"Mr. Marston!"* She regarded him with icy indignation. "I'm surprised, sir, that you even know of such things as life's pleasures." The words—so uncharacteristically sniping—shocked her, but she had no intention of recalling them. However, it immediately became clear Mr. Marston stood in no danger of being crushed.

He inclined his head, smiling unctuously. "Quite so, my dear. Such pastimes hold no allure for me. However, I am aware that others find them much more to their taste." He lifted his pale gaze to Jack's face. "No doubt, Lester, you find this squiring of innocents not at all to your liking. Playing nursemaid to a pack of brats is hardly your style, after all." Marston leant forward and spoke across Sophie. "I heard Mrs. Webb trap you into this little jaunt. Dare say you'd rather be anywhere but here. However, as I've nothing better to do with my time, I'll be only too happy to take the responsibility off your hands."

Ned and Clarissa had drawn closer; along with Toby, who had silently rejoined the company, they held their breath and looked, slightly stunned, at Jack. Indeed, every eye in the party was fixed upon him.

They all saw his slow smile.

"On the contrary, Marston," Jack drawled. "I believe you're labouring under a misapprehension. Believe me, there's nothing I would rather be doing than squiring this particular party of innocents. In fact," he went on, his expression growing pensive, "I believe if you consider the matter more closely, you'll see that one such as I, to whom the…ah, pleasures of life are well known, is precisely the most suitable escort."

The relief that swept the party, all except Marston, was palpable.

Jack's smile broadened as he met the other man's gaze. "Indeed, Marston, I wouldn't have missed this morning's jaunt for the world."

Confounded, Phillip Marston glanced at Sophie. Her glacial expression awoke the first inklings of understanding in his brain. His hand tightened on his reins.

The dun, having behaved reasonably for all of ten minutes, reacted predictably, jibbing, then twisting, prancing sideways. Marston struggled to subdue the animal, muttering perfectly audible curses beneath his breath.

Sternly quelling her laughter, Sophie grasped the opportunity. "Mr. Marston, I believe you would be wise to return that horse to the stables forthwith. I confess its antics are making me quite nervous." She managed to imbue her tones with perfectly specious feminine fear.

Which left Phillip Marston with little choice. His expression grim, he nodded curtly. He left, heading straight for the gate.

"Phew!" Toby came up beside Sophie, a grin lighting his face. "I wouldn't want to be the stableman when he returns that horse."

The comment drew laughter all round, banishing any lingering restraint. Restored to their usual high spirits, the youngsters were soon off again. By mutual consent, the party ambled slowly in Mr. Marston's wake.

Summoning the children, coercing them into an orderly retreat, then supervising them through the traffic kept Sophie fully occupied. But when they turned the corner into Mount Street and the youngsters drew ahead, she glanced up at her companion. His features were relaxed; he looked every bit as content as he had claimed. "I feel I must apologize for Mr. Marston's behaviour, sir."

Jack looked down at her. "Nonsense, my dear. It was hardly

something you could control. Besides," he continued, his blue gaze holding hers, "I have yet to see you encouraging him."

"Heaven forbid!" Sophie shuddered, then, seeing the calm satisfaction that infused Jack's expression, wished she'd been rather more circumspect. It was, after all, no business of Jack Lester's whom she encouraged. Taking refuge in the banal, she said, "So the balls are starting at last."

With a slow smile, Jack inclined his head. "Indeed. And your cousin's come-out will be one of the first. Your aunt seems set to steal a march on her peers."

Thinking of Lucilla and her careful scheming, Sophie smiled. "As you say. She's quite determined to make the most of this Season."

Clarissa nudged her horse up beside Jack's. "Indeed," she declared, unusually pert. "Mama is quite set on my come-out being an *unenviable crush.*"

Sophie exchanged a wry smile with Jack.

Turning to Clarissa, Jack raised a laconic brow. Obviously, Ned had been faithfully adhering to instructions. "Is that so?" Jack asked. "And what do you know of crushes, Miss Webb?"

Clarissa coloured, then waved a dismissive hand. "Sophie told me all about them."

"Ah." Lips quirking, Jack turned back to Sophie as they halted their mounts before the Webbs' steps.

The junior Webbs had already gone in, leaving the grooms with their hands full. Sophie steeled herself and managed to survive the ordeal of being lifted down to the pavement by Jack Lester with commendable composure.

She looked up—and beheld his slow smile.

"Well, my dear?" Jack lifted a brow. "Was it bearable, riding with me?"

Sophie blushed rosily but was determined to give no ground. Lifting her chin, she looked him in the eye. "Indeed, sir. It was most enjoyable."

Jack chuckled. "Good. Because from what I understand, your cousins wish it to be a frequent event."

With an inclination of her head, Sophie indicated her acquiescence.

Her hand in his, Jack looked down at her, his smile a trifle crooked. "Until your aunt's crush, then, Miss Winterton. Rest assured that, despite the sea of humanity that will no doubt be thrown up between us, I will endeavour to win through to your side." With a rakish grin, he bowed over her hand.

And let her go.

With a very correct nod, Sophie escaped up the steps, refusing to give in to her heart and look back.

At the corner of the street, two horsemen sat their mounts, apparently discussing the weather. In actuality, their interest was a great deal more focused.

"Well, that's a relief! It's the older one Lester's got his eye on—fancy that." Hubert, Lord Maltravers, blinked blearily up at his companion. "A hard night followed by an ungodly early start may have taken its toll on my wits," his lordship mused. "But stap me if I can see why."

Captain Terrence Gurnard's lips lifted in a sneer. "Tarnished his image, that's why. The Webbs are a deal too downy to let their chick fly too close to his snare. But obviously the cousin has enough of the ready to satisfy Lester."

"Odd." His lordship frowned. "Thought she had nothing more than the usual. You know what I mean—expectations but no more. Would've thought Lester needed rather more than that."

"Obviously not. The point, thank Heaven, doesn't concern me. As long as he's *not* got his eye on that juicy little plum, he can have the rest of London for all I care. Come, let's get moving. We've seen all we need."

Side by side, they steered their mounts through the streets in the direction of Hubert's lodgings, the slightly rumpled figure of Lord Maltravers slumped in his saddle, the handsome, broad-shouldered guardsman towering over him.

"Y'know, Gurnard, I've been thinking."

"I thought you didn't do that until after noon."

Hubert snorted. "No. I'm serious. This start of yours—sure

there isn't a better way? I mean, you could always try the cent per cents—doesn't hurt to ask.''

"In this case, I fear it could hurt." Gurnard winced. "A very great deal."

Realization was slow but it eventually broke on Hubert. "Oh," he said. "You're already on their books?"

"Let's just say that one or two moneylenders could scrape an acquaintance."

"Hmm." Hubert grimaced. "That does rather cut down on your options." As they turned into Piccadilly, he ventured, "No chance this last opponent of yours would consider holding your vowels for latter payment?"

Slowly, Terrence Gurnard turned his head and looked his friend in the eye. "My last opponent was Melcham."

Hubert blanched. "Oh," he said. Then, "Ah." Switching his gaze to the traffic, he nodded. "In that case, I quite see your point. Well, then—when's the wedding?"

CHAPTER TEN

HER AUNT, Sophie mused, was not to be trusted. At least, not when it came to Jack Lester. Although she had expected to see Mr. Lester at her cousin's come-out ball, Sophie had had no inkling that he would feature among the favoured few who had been invited to dine before the event. Not until he walked into the drawing-room, throwing all the other gentlemen into immediate shade.

From her position by the fireplace, a little removed from her aunt, Sophie watched as Jack bowed over Lucilla's hand. His coat was of midnight blue, the same shade as his eyes at night. His smallclothes were ivory, his cravat a minor work of art. His large sapphire glowed amid the folds, fracturing the light. Beyond the heavy gold signet that adorned his right hand, he wore no other ornament, nothing to distract her senses from the strength of his large frame. After exchanging a few words, Lucilla sent him her way.

Stilling an inner quiver, Sophie greeted him with a calm smile. "Good evening, Mr. Lester."

Jack's answering smile lit his eyes. "Miss Winterton." He bowed gracefully over her hand, then, straightening, looked down at her. "Sophie."

Sophie's serene expression did not waver as she drew her gaze from his; she had had practice enough in the past few days in keeping her emotions in check. Seeing Ned, who had followed his mentor into the room, turn from Lucilla to make his way to Clarissa's side, Sophie glanced up at her companion. "Ned has told me how much you have done for him, even to the extent of putting him up. It's really very kind of you."

Having drunk his fill of Sophie's elegance, Jack reluctantly looked out over the room. Tonight, his golden head appeared warm yet remote, priestess-like in a classically styled ivory sheath, draped from one shoulder to fall in long lines to the floor. Forcing himself to focus on his protégé, Jack shrugged. "It's no great thing. The house is more than large enough, and the proximity increases the time we have to...polish his address."

Sophie arched a sceptical brow. "Is that what you term it?"

Jack smiled. "Polish is all Ned needs."

Sophie slanted him a glance. "And that's the secret of gentlemanly success—polish?"

Jack looked down at her. "Oh no, my dear." His gaze grew more intent. "Such as I, with more sophisticated game in sight, often need recourse to...weapons of a different calibre."

Sophie tilted her chin. "Indeed, sir? But I was thanking you for helping Ned—and must also convey all our thanks for your assistance this morn. How we would have coped had you not removed Jeremy, George and Amy from the house, I simply do not know."

Meeting his eyes, Sophie smiled serenely.

Jack smiled back. "As I've told you before, your cousins are the most engaging urchins; playing nursemaid, as Marston had it, is no great undertaking. I trust all came right in the end?"

With Ned in tow, Jack had arrived on the Webbs' doorstep that morning, as he had for the past two, to find the house in the grip of the usual mayhem coincident with a major ball. Knowing neither Sophie nor Clarissa would be free, he and Ned had nevertheless offered to take the youngsters to the Park—a boon to all as, with the house full of caterers, florists and the like, and the servants rushed off their feet, the youthful trio had been proving a severe trial. They had already caused havoc by pulling the bows on the sheaves of flowers the florists had prepared all undone, then been threatened with incarceration when they had discovered the pleasures of skidding across the newly polished ballroom floor.

"Yes, thank Heaven," Sophie replied, watching further arrivals greet her aunt. "I don't know how Aunt Lucilla manages to keep it all straight in her head. But the storm and tempest did eventually abate, leaving order where before there was none."

Jack's grin was wry. "I'm sure your aunt's order is formidable."

Sophie smiled. "I rather suspect the ball tonight ranks as one of her more spectacular undertakings."

"With both your cousin and yourself to launch, it's hardly surprising that she's pulled out all stops."

Sophie blinked, her smile fading slightly. Then, with determined brightness, she inclined her head. "Indeed. And both Clarissa and I are determined she will not be disappointed."

A subtle reminder that she, too, was expected to find a husband. Just as he would have to find a wife. Sophie was all too well aware that, through shared moments, shared laughter and some indefinable attraction, she and Jack Lester had drawn far closer than was common between gentlemen and ladies who remained merely friends. Nevertheless, that was all they could be, and the time was fast approaching when their disparate destinies would prevail. She was steeling herself to face the prospect.

"Sophia, my dear!" Lady Entwhistle bustled up, her silk skirts shushing. "You look positively radiant, my dear—doesn't she, Henry?"

"Set to take the shine out of the younger misses, what?" Lord Entwhistle winked at Sophie, then shook her hand.

"And Mr. Lester, too—how fortunate." Her ladyship presented her hand and looked on with approval as Jack bowed over it. "A pleasure to see you again, sir. I hear Lady Asfordby's in town; have you run into her yet?"

Jack's eyes briefly touched Sophie's. "I have not yet had that pleasure, ma'am."

"A deuced shame about the hunting, what?" Lord Entwhistle turned to Jack. "Not that you younger men care—just change venues, far as I can see.'' His lordship cast a genial eye over the room.

"As you say, sir," Jack replied. "I fear there are few foxes to be found in London, so naturally we're forced to shift our sights."

"What's that? Forced? *Hah!*" His lordship was in fine fettle. "Why, I've always heard the tastiest game's to be found in the capital."

Sophie struggled to keep her lips straight.

"Really, Henry!" Her ladyship unfurled her fan with an audible click.

"But it's true," protested Lord Entwhistle, not one whit abashed. "Just ask Lester here. Few would know better than he. What say you, m'boy? Don't the streets of London offer richer rewards than the fields of Leicestershire?"

"Actually," Jack replied, his gaze returning to Sophie, "I'm not sure I would agree with you, sir. I must confess I've recently discovered unexpected treasure in Leicestershire, after a year in the *ton*'s ballrooms had yielded nothing but dross."

For an instant, Sophie could have sworn the world had stopped turning; for a moment, she basked in the glow that lit Jack Lester's eyes. Then reality returned, and with it awareness—of the conjecture in Lord Entwhistle's eyes, the startled look on her ladyship's face, and the role she herself had to play. Smoothly, she turned to Lady Entwhistle. "I do hope Mr. Millthorpe has found his feet in London. Will he be here tonight?"

The surprise faded from her ladyship's eyes. "Yes, indeed. Lucilla was kind enough to invite him for the ball. I'm sure he'll attend. He was very much taken with Clarissa, you know." She glanced across the room to where Clarissa was surrounded by a small coterie of young gentlemen. "Mind you, I expect he'll be in good company. As I told your aunt, fully half the young men in town will be prostrating themselves at Clarissa's feet."

Sophie laughed and steered the conversation towards the social events thus far revealed on the *ton*'s horizon. She was somewhat relieved when Jack chipped in with the news of the balloon ascension planned for May, thus distracting Lord Entwhistle, who declaimed at length on the folly of the idea.

His lordship was still declaiming when Minton entered, transcending the impression conveyed by his severe grab to announce in jovially benevolent vein that dinner was served.

Lord and Lady Entwhistle went together to join the exodus. Jack turned to Sophie. ''I believe, dear Sophie, that the pleasure of escorting you in falls...to me.''

Sophie smiled up at him and calmly surrendered her hand. ''That will be most pleasant, sir.''

With her hand on his arm, Jack steered her into the shuffling queue.

Laughing chatter greeted them as they strolled into the dining-room. The surface of the table, polished to a mellow glow, reflected light fractured by crystal and deflected by silver. A subtle excitement filled the air; this was, after all, the first of the large gatherings, and those present were the chosen few who would start the ball of the Season rolling. Horatio, genially rotund, took his place at the table's head; Lucilla graced the opposite end, while Clarissa, sparkling in a gown of fairy-like silvered rose silk, sat in the middle on one side. Ned beside her. Jack led Sophie to her place opposite Clarissa, then took the seat on her right.

As she glanced about, taking note of her neighbours, Sophie took comfort from Jack's presence beside her. Despite his apparently ingrained habits, he always drew back whenever she baulked—smoothly, suavely, ineffably rakish, yet a gentleman to his very bones. She now felt confident in his company, convinced he would never press her unduly nor step over that invisible line.

There was, indeed, a certain excitement to be found in his games, and a certain balm in the warmth of his deep blue gaze.

The toast to Clarissa was duly drunk; her cousin blushed prettily while Ned looked on, a slightly stunned expression on his face.

As she resumed her seat, Sophie glanced at Jack. He was

watching her; he raised his glass and quietly said, "To your Season, dear Sophie. And to where it will lead."

Inwardly Sophie shivered, but she smiled and inclined her head graciously.

On her left was Mr. Somercote, a distant Webb cousin, a gentleman of independent means whom her uncle had introduced as hailing from Northamptonshire. While obviously at home in the *ton*, Mr. Somercote was reserved almost to the point of rudeness. Sophie applied herself but could tease no more than the barest commonplaces from him.

The lady on Jack's right was a Mrs. Wolthambrook, an elderly widow, another Webb connection. Sophie wondered at the wisdom of her aunt's placement, but by the end of the first course, her confidence in Lucilla had been restored. The old lady had a wry sense of humour which Jack, in typical vein, recognized and played to. Sophie found herself drawn into a lively discussion, Mrs. Wolthambrook, Jack and herself forming a nexus of conversation which served to disguise the shortcomings of others in the vicinity.

It was almost a surprise to find the dessert course over. With a rustle of silk skirts, Lucilla rose and issued a charming directive sending them all to the ballroom.

While ascending the stairs on Jack's arm, Sophie noticed the glimmer of a frown in Lady Entwhistle's sharp eyes. It was, Sophie decided, hardly to be wondered at: installing Jack Lester as her partner at dinner had clearly declared her aunt's hand. Lucilla was playing Cupid. It was inconceivable that, after nearly three weeks in the capital, her aunt was not *au fait* concerning Jack Lester's state. But Lucilla was not one to follow the conventions in matters of the heart; she had married Horatio Webb when he was far less well-to-do than at present, apparently without a qualm. Sophie's own mother, too, had married for love. It was, in fact, something of a family trait.

Unfortunately, Sophie thought, casting a fleeting glance at Jack's darkly handsome profile, it was not one she was destined to follow. Hiding her bruised heart behind a serene smile, she crossed the threshold of the ballroom.

Under the soft flare of candlelight cast by three huge chandeliers, the efforts of the florists and decorators looked even better than by day. The tops of the smooth columns supporting the delicately domed ceiling had been garnished with sprays of white and yellow roses, long golden ribbons swirling down around the columns. The minstrels' gallery above the end of the room was similarly festooned with white, yellow and green, trimmed with gold. Tall iron pedestals supporting ironwork cones overflowing with the same flowers filled the corners of the room and stood spaced every few yards along the long mirrored wall, with chaises and chairs set between. The opposite wall contained long windows giving onto the terrace; some were ajar, letting in the evening breeze.

The guests dutifully oohed and aahed, many ladies taking special note of the unusual use of ironwork.

Jack's blue eyes glinted down at her. "As I said, my dear, your aunt's efforts are indeed formidable."

Sophie smiled, but her heart was not in it; it felt as if her evening was ending when, with a graceful bow, Jack surrendered her to her duty on the receiving line.

He had bespoken a waltz, she reminded herself, giving her emotions a mental shake. Conjuring up a bright smile, she dutifully greeted the arrivals, taking due note of those her aunt introduced with a certain subtle emphasis. Lucilla might be encouraging Jack Lester, but it was clear she was equally intent on giving Sophie a range of suitable gentlemen from which to make her choice.

Which was just as well, Sophie decided. Tonight was the start of her Season proper; she should make a real start on her hunt for a husband. There was no sense in putting off the inevitable. And it would no doubt be wise to make it abundantly plain that she was not infected with Lucilla's ideals. She could not marry Jack Lester, for he needed more money than she would bring. Embarking on her search for a husband would clarify their relationship, making it plain to such avid watchers as Lady Entwhistle and Lady Matcham that there was nothing to fear in her friendship with Jack.

Stifling a sigh, Sophie pinned on a smile as her aunt turned to greet the latest in the long line of guests.

"Ah, Mr. Marston," Lucilla purred. "I'm so glad you could come."

Sophie swallowed a most unladylike curse. She waited, trapped in line, as Mr. Marston greeted Clarissa with chilly civility, his glance austerely dismissing the enchanting picture her cousin made.

Then his gaze reached her—and Sophie privately resolved to send a special thank-you to Madame Jorge. Mr. Marston's distant civility turned to frigid disapproval as he took in her bare shoulders and the expanse of ivory skin exposed by the low, slanting neckline of her gown.

Sophie smiled sunnily. "Good evening, sir. I trust you are well."

Mr. Marston bowed. "I…" He drew himself up, his lips pinched. "I will look to have a few words with you later, Miss Winterton."

Sophie tried her best to look delighted at the prospect.

"Lady Colethorpe—my niece, Sophia Winterton."

With a certain relief, Sophie turned to her aunt's next guest and put Mr. Marston very firmly from her mind.

Down in the ballroom, Jack wended his way through the throng, stopping here and there to chat with old acquaintances, constantly hailed as the *ton*, one and all, found their way to the Webbs' ball. Percy, of course, was there. He greeted Jack with something akin to relief.

"Held up with m'father," Percy explained. "He was having one of his turns—convinced he was going to die. All rubbish, of course. Sound as a horse." Smoothing down his new violet silk waistcoat, Percy cast a knowledgeable eye over Jack's elegance, innate, as he well knew—and sighed. "But what's been going on here, then?" he asked, raising his quizzing glass to look about him. "Seems as if every squire and his dog have already come to town."

"That's about the sum of it," Jack confirmed. "I just met Carmody and Harrison. The whole boiling's in residence al-

ready, and raring to get started. I suspect that's what's behind
the eagerness tonight. Lucilla Webb's gauged it to a nicety.''

"Hmm. Mentioned the Webbs to m'father. Very knowing,
he is. He had a word for Mrs. Webb."

"Oh?" Jack looked his question.

"Dangerous," Percy offered.

Jack's lips twitched. "That much, I know. To my cost,
what's more. Nevertheless, unless I'm greatly mistaken, the
lady approves of yours truly. And, dangerous or not, I fear I'm
committed to further acquaintance."

Percy blinked owlishly. "So you're serious, then?"

"Having found my golden head, I'm not about to let her
go."

"Ah, well." Percy shrugged. "Leave you to it, then.
Where'd you say Harrison was?"

After sending Percy on his way, Jack looked over the heads,
curled and pomaded, and discovered that Sophie and her family
had quit the doorway to mingle with their guests. He located
Sophie on the other side of the room, surrounded by a small
group of gentlemen. Eminently eligible gentlemen, he realized,
as he mentally named each one. Jack felt his possessive instincts stir. Immediately, he clamped a lid on them. He had
already claimed a waltz and the right to take Sophie to supper;
Lucilla would frown on any attempt to claim more.

With an effort, Jack forced himself to relax his clenched jaw.
To ease the strain on his temper, he shifted his gaze to Clarissa,
a little way along the wall. Sophie's cousin was glowing, ra-
diating happiness. As well she might, Jack thought, as he
viewed her not inconsiderable court. Puppies all, but Clarissa
was only seventeen. She was unquestionably beautiful and, to
her and her mother's credit, blissfully free of the silly affec-
tations that often marred others of her calibre. Whether she was
as talented as her mother, Jack had no notion—he had seen no
evidence of it yet.

Seeing Ned holding fast to his place by Clarissa's side despite all attempts to dislodge him, Jack grinned. As long as
Ned circulated when the dancing began, there was no harm in

his present occupation. His protégé was maintaining a coolly distant expression, which had made Clarissa glance up at him, slightly puzzled, more than once. Ned was learning fast, and putting his new-found knowledge to good use.

Making a mental note to drop a word of warning in Ned's ear, to the effect that any female descended from Lucilla Webb should be treated with due caution, Jack allowed his mind to return to its preoccupation.

Was Sophie like her aunt, capable of manipulation on a grand scale? Jack shook aside the silly notion. His Sophie was no schemer—he would stake his life on that. To him, she was open, straightforward, all but transparent. As he watched her smile brightly up at the Marquess of Huntly, Jack's satisfied expression faded. Abruptly executing a neat about-face, he strolled deeper into the crowd.

The first waltz was duly announced, and Clarissa, blushing delicately, went down the floor with her father, a surprisingly graceful dancer. At the conclusion of the measure, Horatio beamed down at her. "Well, my dear. You're officially out now. Are you pleased?"

Clarissa smiled brilliantly. "Indeed, yes, Papa," she said, and meant it.

The crowd parted and she looked ahead. To see Ned leading another young lady from the floor. Clarissa's smile faded.

Horatio noticed. "I had better return you to your court, my dear." Blandly, he added, "But do spare a thought for your old father. Don't line up too many suitors for your hand."

Apparently unaware of Clarissa's startled glance, Horatio guided her back to her circle, then, with a blithely paternal pat on her hand, left her to them.

"I say, Miss Webb." Lord Swindon was greatly smitten. "You waltz divinely. You must have been practising incessantly up in Leicestershire."

"May I get you a glass of lemonade, Miss Webb? Thirsty work, dancing." This from Lord Thurstow, a genial red-haired gentleman whose girth explained his conjecture.

But the most frightening comment came from Mr. Marley.

a young sprig who considered himself a budding poet. "An ode…I feel an ode burgeoning in my brain. To your incomparable grace, and the effect it has on your poor followers who have to watch you take the floor in another's arms. *Argh!*"

Clarissa eyed the flushed young man in alarm. Gracious, were they all so unutterably silly?

As the evening wore on, she decided that they were. This was not what she had come to London to find. Being mooned over by gentlemen she classed as barely older than Jeremy and George was hardly the stuff of her dreams. Stuck with her court, surrounded on all sides, Clarissa met their sallies with guileless smiles, while inwardly she considered her options.

When Ned reappeared and rescued her, leading her into the set forming for a country dance, the truth dawned. Smiling up at him, Clarissa shyly said, "It's such a relief to dance with someone I know."

Mindful of his instructions, Ned merely raised a brow. "Is it?" Then he smiled, a touch of condescension in his manner. "Don't worry, you'll soon get used to all the attention."

Stunned, Clarissa stared at him.

"Not a bad ball, this," Ned cheerily remarked. "Your mother must be pleased at the turnout. Don't think I've seen so many young ladies all at once before."

It was, perhaps, as well for Ned that the dance separated them at that point. When they came together again, Clarissa, her nose in the air, treated him to a frosty glance. "As you say," she said, "I'm sure I'll learn how to respond suitably to all the compliments the gentlemen seem so intent on pressing on me. I must ask Mama how best to encourage them."

Again the dance averted catastrophe. By the time the music finally died, Ned, chilly and remote, led Clarissa, equally distant and frigid, back to her circle. After perfunctorily bowing over her hand, Ned quit the vicinity, leaving Clarissa to deal with her importunate followers, her cheeks flushed, a dangerous glint in her large eyes.

A little distance away, Sophie had started to compile a list of potential suitors. The task was not difficult, for they promptly presented themselves before her, all but declaring their interest. The basis for their attraction had her mystified until Lord Annerby confessed, "The young misses are not really my style." When the movements of the quadrille brought them together again, he admitted, "Been hoping a lady like you would hove on my horizon. Not just in the common way, and not likely to giggle in a man's ear, if you take my meaning."

After that, Sophie paid a little more attention to her would-be swains, and discovered that many were, indeed, like his lordship: gentlemen who had been waiting for a lady such as she, not in the first flush of youth but yet young, presentable and altogether acceptable, to appear and walk up the aisle with them. With their reasons explained, she turned her attention to their attributes.

"I understand your estates are in Northamptonshire, Mr. Somercote. I hail from that county myself."

"Do you?" As they glided through the steps of the cotillion, Mr. Somercote made a visible effort to produce his next statement. "Somercote Hall lies just beyond the village of Somercote in the northwesternmost corner of the county."

Sophie nodded and smiled encouragingly, but apparently that was the full extent of Mr. Somercot's loquacity. As they returned through the crowd to where her admirers were waiting, she mentally crossed his name off her list.

The Marquess of Huntly was her next partner. "Tell me, Miss Winterton, do you enjoy the amenities of London?"

"I do indeed, my lord," Sophie replied. The marquess was Lord Percy's elder brother and, despite his bluff appearance and a tendency to stoutness, was unquestionably eligible.

"I've heard that you ride in the Park. Mayhap we'll meet one fine morning."

"Perhaps," Sophie returned, her smile noncommittal.

As they left the floor, Sophie decided the marquess could remain on her list for the present. Perhaps a meeting in the Park, with her younger cousins in tow, would be useful? She was pondering the point when a deep voice cut across her thoughts.

"I believe our waltz is next, Miss Winterton." Jack nodded to the marquess. "Huntly."

"Lester." The marquess returned his nod. "Seen Percy about?"

"He was chatting with Harrison earlier in the evening."

"Suppose I should go and have a word with him. M'brother, you know," the marquess confided to Sophie. "M'father's been at death's door—should see how he is. If you'll excuse me, m'dear?"

Even as she stared at Lord Huntly's retreating back, Sophie's mental pencil was scrubbing out his name. Such callousness was appalling.

Seeing her shocked expression, Jack abruptly shut his lips on the explanation he had been about to make. He did not consider Huntly a rival—but why make a whip for his own back? Appropriating Sophie's hand, he laid it on his sleeve. "Perhaps we could stroll about the room until the waltz commences?"

Sophie blinked, then frowned. "I really should return to my aunt."

His own frown hidden behind an urbane smile, Jack inclined his head and dutifully led her to where her court was waiting.

An unwise move. He was not impressed by the small crowd of eligibles who apparently could find nothing better to do at the first major ball of the Season than congregate about his Sophie. His temper was not improved by having to listen to them vie to heap accolades upon their compliments. For their part, they ignored him, secure in the knowledge that Sophie's expectations were insufficient to permit him to woo her. The thought made Jack smile inwardly. The smile turned to a suppressed growl when he heard Sophie say, "I do indeed enjoy the opera, Lord Annerby."

She then smiled serenely at his lordship.

"I'll be sure to let you know when the season begins, my dear Miss Winterton." Lord Annerby all but gloated.

Jack gritted his teeth. He had avoided the opera for years—a fact that owed nothing to the performances but rather more to those performing. To his immense relief, the strains of the waltz heralded his salvation. "Miss Winterton?"

Surprised, Sophie blinked up at him even as she put her hand in his. His fingers closed tightly about hers. His words had sounded like a command. An inkling of a difficulty she had not previously considered awoke in Sophie's brain.

Without further speech, Jack led Sophie to the door, drawing her into his arms with an arrogance that bespoke his mind far too well. He knew it, but did not care. The relief as she settled into his arms was balm to his lacerated feelings.

As they joined the swirling crowd on the floor, Jack considered closing his eyes. He would wager he could waltz round any ballroom blindfolded, so accustomed was he to the exercise. And with his eyes closed, his senses would be free to concentrate solely on Sophie—on the soft warmth of her, on how well she fitted in his arms, on the subtle caress of her silk-encased thighs against his.

Stifling a sigh, he kept his eyes open.

"Are you enjoying the ball, Mr. Lester?"

Sophie's calm and rather distant comment drew Jack's eyes from contemplation of her curls. He considered her question, simultaneously considering her invitingly full lips. "I'm enjoying this waltz," he replied.

Raising his eyes to hers, Jack watched a frown form in the sky-blue orbs. Puzzled, he continued, "But when are you going to call me Jack? I've been calling you Sophie for weeks."

He had never before seen a lady blush and frown simultaneously.

"I know," Sophie admitted, forcing herself to throw him a disapproving glance. "And you know you should not. It's not at all acceptable."

Jack simply smiled.

Sophie shot him an exasperated glance, then transferred her gaze to the safe space above his shoulder. As always, being in his arms had a distinctly unnerving affect on her. A fluttery, shivery awareness had her in its grip; breathless excitement threatened her wits. His strength reached out and enfolded her, seductively beckoning, enticing her mind to dwell on prospects she could not even dream of without blushing.

She blushed now, and was thankful to hear the closing bars of the waltz.

Jack saw her blush but was far too wise to comment. Instead, he smoothly escorted her into supper, adroitly snaffling a plate of delicacies and managing to install plate, glasses of champagne and Sophie at a small table tucked away near the conservatory.

He had reckoned without her court. They came swarming about, sipping champagne and, to Jack's mind, making thorough nuisances of themselves. He bore it stoically, repeatedly reminding himself that Lucilla would not consider the first major ball of the Season a suitable venue for him to declare his intentions. When the light meal was over, he insisted on escorting Sophie all the way back to her aunt's side.

The look he bent on Lucilla made her hide a grin.

With Sophie and Clarissa both claimed for the next dance, Lucilla turned her large eyes on Jack. "I must say, Mr. Lester, that you're doing a very good job on Ned."

Somewhat stiffly, Jack inclined his head. "I'm glad the transformation meets with your approval, ma'am."

"Indeed. I'm most grateful. *Immensely* grateful."

Seeing Lady Entwhistle fast approaching, clearly intent on having a word in Lucilla's ear, Jack bowed briefly and drifted into the crowd. As he passed the dancers, he heard a silvery laugh. Glancing up, he saw Sophie, smiling brightly up at Lord Ainsley, a handsome and very rich peer.

Muting his growl, Jack swung into an alcove. What numbskull had invented the practice of wooing? Lucilla's comment, which he felt confident in interpreting as open encouragement, was welcome enough. However, the last thing his passions needed right now was further encouragement, particularly when the object of said passions was behaving in a manner designed to enflame them.

Suppressing his curses, he set himself to endure. He could have left, but the night was yet young. Besides, he was not sufficiently sure of Ned to leave his protégé unsupported. At the thought, Jack drew his gaze from Sophie's bright curls and scanned the dancers for Clarissa.

Predictably, Sophie's cousin was smiling up at an elegant youth as she went down the floor in the dance. Jack silently harrumphed, then switched his gaze back to Sophie. Clarissa was clearly absorbed with her partner.

In so thinking, Jack erred.

Although Clarissa smiled and nodded at Mr. Pommeroy's stilted conversation, her attention was far removed from that blameless young gentleman. From the corner of her eye, she could see Ned dancing with Miss Ellis in the next set. The sight filled Clarissa with a sort of quiet fury she had never before experienced. Regardless of its import, it was quite clearly time to refocus Ned's attention on that which had brought him to town.

Her eyes narrowing, Clarissa herself refocused—on Mr. Pommeroy. She grimaced. Startled, Mr. Pommeroy stumbled and almost fell. Guiltily, for she had not meant to grimace openly, Clarissa applied herself to soothing her partner's ruffled feathers while looking about her for inspiration.

Her court, unfortunately, had little to offer. They were so young; not even in her wildest dreams could she cast them in the role she was rapidly becoming convinced she needed filled. Back amongst them, responding to their quips with but half her mind, Clarissa grimly watched as Ned joined the crowd about two sisters also making their come-out this year. Inwardly sniffing, Clarissa shifted her gaze—and saw Toby coming towards her, a positive Adonis in tow.

"Ah, Clarissa?" Toby came to an uncertain halt before his sister. "Might I make known to you Captain Gurnard? He's with the Guards." Toby was unsure how his sister would react, but the captain had been keen to gain a personal introduction, something Toby could see no harm in.

Clarissa's wide eyes took in every detail of the tall, broad-shouldered figure bowing before her. The captain was clad in scarlet regimentals; his tightly curled hair gleamed like fool's gold in the candlelight. As he straightened, Clarissa caught the hard gleam in his eyes and the cynical tilt of his mouth before unctuous gratification overlaid them.

Clarissa smiled brilliantly and held out her hand. "How do you do, Captain? Have you been with the Guards long?"

Blinking, Toby inwardly shrugged and took himself off.

Dazzled, Captain Gurnard saw nothing beyond Clarissa's guileless china-blue eyes and her delicately curved lips. He could only conclude that Fate had taken pity on him. With a consciously charming smile, he reluctantly released Clarissa's hand. "I've been with my regiment for some years, my dear."

"Some years?" Clarissa's expression was all innocent bewilderment. "But—" She broke off and shyly put one hand to her lips. "Indeed," she whispered, half-confidingly. "I had not thought you so old as all that, Captain."

Gurnard laughed easily. "Indeed, Miss Webb. I greatly fear I must admit to being quite in my dotage compared with such a sweet child as yourself." His expression sobered. "In truth," he added, his voice low, "I fear I cannot compete with these young pups that surround you. The blithe and easy words of youth have long ago left me."

Ignoring the rising hackles of said pups, Clarissa smiled sweetly and leaned towards the captain to say, "Indeed, sir, I find a little of such blithe and easy words is more than a surfeit. Honest words are always more acceptable to the hearer."

The smile on Captain Gurnard's face grew. "Perhaps, my dear, in order to hear such honest words, you would consent to stroll the room with me? Just until the next dance begins?"

Plastering a suitably ingenuous smile on her lips, Clarissa nodded with apparent delight. Rising, she placed her fingertips on the captain's scarlet sleeve.

As he led her into the crowd, Captain Gurnard could not restrain the smugness of his smile. He would have been supremely disconcerted had he known that Clarissa's inner smile outdid his.

Sophie, meanwhile, had run into a problem, an obstacle to her endeavours. Large, lean and somehow oddly menacing, Jack had left his retreat, where he had been propping up the wall, to gravitate to her side, a hungry predator lured, she suspected, by the smiles she bestowed on the gentlemen about her.

Under her subtle encouragement, her potential suitors preened.

Jack looked supremely bored. Having by dint of superior experience won through to her side, he towered over her, his expression rigidly controlled, his eyes a chilly blue.

Sophie felt distinctly irate. He was intimidating her suitors. She did not *like* her current course, but it was the only one open to her, a fact she felt Jack should acknowledge, rather than get on his high ropes because... Well, the only conclusion she *could* reach was that he was jealous of the attention she was paying the other men.

But it was from among *them* she would have to chose a husband, and she felt increasingly annoyed when Jack continued to make her task more difficult. When Sir Stuart Mablethorpe, a distinguished scholar, met Jack's gaze and promptly forgot whatever lengthy peroration he had been about to utter, Sophie shot her nemesis a frosty glance.

Jack met it with bland imperturbability.

Thoroughly incensed, Sophie was only too ready to smile at Lord Ruthven, a gentleman she suspected had much in common with Jack Lester, in all respects bar one. Lord Ruthven did not need a wealthy bride.

One of Lord Ruthven's dark brows rose fractionally. "Perhaps, Miss Winterton," he said as he straightened from his bow, "you might care to stroll the room?" His gaze flicked to Jack, then returned to Sophie's face.

Ignoring the glint in Ruthven's eyes, Sophie replied, "Indeed, sir. I'm becoming quite fatigued standing here."

Ruthven's lips twitched. "No doubt. Permit me to offer you an escape, my dear." Thus saying, he offered her his arm.

With determined serenity, Sophie placed her hand on his lordship's sleeve, refusing to acknowledge the charged silence beside her. She was too wise to even glance at Jack as, with Ruthven, she left his side.

Which was just as well. Only when he was sure his emotions were once more under control did Jack allow so much as a muscle to move. And by then, Sophie and Ruthven were half-way down the room. His expression stony, Jack considered the possibilities; only the glint in his eyes betrayed his mood. Then, with his usual languid air, he strolled into the crowd, his course set for a collision with his golden head.

By the time she reached the end of the room, Sophie had realized that Ruthven's green eyes saw rather more than most. All the way down the room, he had subtly twitted her on her keeper. She suspected, however, that his lordship's indolent interest was more excited by the prospect of tweaking Jack's nose than by her own inherent attractions. Which was both comforting and a trifle worrying.

Together, she and Lord Ruthven paused beneath the minstrels' gallery and turned to survey the room.

"Ah, there you are, Ruthven." Jack materialized out of the crowd. He smiled easily at his lordship. "I just saw Lady Orkney by the stairs. She was asking after you."

Sophie glanced round in time to see an expression compounded of chagrin and suspicion flit across his lordship's handsome face. "Indeed?" One brow elevated, Ruthven regarded Jack sceptically.

Jack's smile grew. "Just so. Quite insistent on speaking with you. You know how she is."

Lord Ruthven grimaced. "As you say." Turning to Sophie, Ruthven said, "I fear I must ask you to excuse me, Miss Winterton. My aunt can become quite hysterical if denied." Again one of his lordship's brows rose, this time in resignation. "I dare say Lester will be only too happy to escort you about." With a wry smile, he bowed gracefully over her hand and departed.

Sophie eyed his retreating back through narrowed eyes. She had not seriously considered Ruthven as a suitor but she would certainly not consider a man who aggravated a lady's position, then deserted her, leaving her to face the consequences alone.

As Jack's fingers closed about her hand, she glanced up at his face. His impassive expression didn't fool her for a moment. Then he looked down at her, his eyes hard and very blue.

"Come with me, Miss Winterton." Her hand trapped on his sleeve, Jack headed towards the windows leading onto the terrace.

Sophie dug in her heels. "I have no intention of going anywhere private with you, Mr. Lester."

"Jack." The single syllable left Sophie in no doubt of his mood. "And if you would rather air our differences in public…" he shrugged. "…who am I to deny a lady?"

Looking up into his eyes, and seeing, as she had twice before, the dark brooding presence that lurked behind them, Sophie felt her throat constrict. But her own temper was not far behind his—he was behaving like a dog in a manger. "Very well, *Mr. Lester,*" she replied, holding his gaze. "But not on the terrace." From the corner of her eye, Sophie could see the rippling curtains that sealed off the music room, built out at the end of the ballroom under the minstrels' gallery. Half-concealed as it was by the gallery above and a row of ironwork urns, it was doubtful anyone else had thought to use the room. They could be private there while still remaining in the ballroom. Her lips firming, Sophie nodded to the curtain. "This way."

Jack followed her into the shadows beneath the gallery, then held back the curtain as she slipped through. He followed her. The heavy curtain fell to, deadening the noise from the ballroom. Candelabra shed ample light about the room, casting a mellow glow on the polished surfaces of the pianoforte and harpsichord. It was a comfortable little nook furnished with well-stuffed chaises and two armchairs. Sophie ignored its amenities and stode to the middle of the Aubusson rug in the centre of the floor.

Chin high, she swung to face Jack. "Now, Mr. Lester. Perhaps we may speak plainly."

"Precisely my thinking," Jack replied, strolling forward until he stood directly before her, no more than a foot away.

Mentally cursing, Sophie had to lift her head higher to meet his eyes.

"Perhaps," Jack suggested, "we could start with what, precisely, you think to achieve with all the gentlemen you've been so busily collecting?"

"A most pertinent point," Sophie agreed. She took a moment to marshall her thoughts, then began, her tone calm and quietly determined. "As I believe I told you, my first Season, four years ago, was cut very short."

Jack nodded curtly.

"As you also know, not only my aunt, but all my mother's friends are very keen..." Sophie paused, then amended, "Positively *determined* that I should wed. Indeed—" she met Jack's gaze challengingly "—I can see no other alternative."

A muscle shifted in Jack's jaw. "Quite."

"Thus," Sophie continued, "I must set about...er, gathering suitable suitors." She frowned slightly. Put like that, it sounded decidedly cold.

Jack frowned too. "Why?"

Sophie blinked. "I beg your pardon?"

Jack gritted his teeth and hung onto his temper. "Why do you need a whole *pack* of eligibles? Won't one do?"

Sophie frowned again, but this time at him. "Of course not," she answered, irritated by what could only be deliberate obtuseness. She drew herself up, her own eyes glittering. "I refuse to marry a man who does not have at least *some* of the attributes I consider appropriate."

Jack's frown intensified. "What attributes?"

"Attributes such as having estates in the country and a willingness to spend most of the year there. And being fond of children." Sophie blushed and hurried on, "And who can... can...well, who likes riding and..."

"Who can waltz you off your feet?" Jack's expression relaxed.

Sophie shot him a wary glance and saw the taunting gleam

in his eye. She put up her chin. "There is a whole *host* of attributes I consider necessary in the gentleman I would wish to marry."

Jack nodded. "Nevertheless, coming to appreciate the attributes of the gentleman you're going to marry does not, for my money, necessitate gathering a small crowd with which to compare him."

"But *of course* it does!" Sophie glared. "How *do* you imagine I'm going to know that the one I accept is the right one if I do not—" she gestured with one hand "—look over the field?" Her tone was decidedly belligerent.

Jack frowned, recalling Lucilla's words. Did Sophie really need to compare him with others to be sure?

"And how," Sophie demanded, "am I supposed to do *that*, other than by talking and dancing with them?"

Jack's lips compressed into a thin line.

Sophie nodded. "Precisely. And I have to say," she continued, her nose in the air, "that I consider it most unfair of you to get in my way."

A moment's silence followed.

"Sophie," Jack growled, his voice very low, his eyes fixed on Sophie's face. "Believe me when I say that I have no intention *whatever* of letting you loose amongst the *ton*'s bachelors."

Sophie very nearly stamped her foot. Dragging in a portentous breath, she fixed him with a steely glare. "You are behaving *outrageously!* You do understand that I must marry, do you not?"

"Yes. But—"

"And that I must therefore choose between whatever suitors I may have?"

Jack's expression darkened. "Yes. But—"

"Well, then—with all your remarkable experience, perhaps you'd like to tell me *how* I'm to learn enough about each of them to discover which one will make the best husband?"

Jack's eyes narrowed. "It's very easy."

"Indeed?" Sophie's brows flew. "How?"

Jack focused on her lips, lushly full and all but pouting. "You should marry the man who loves you the most."

"I see," Sophie said, her temper still in alt. "And *how*, pray tell, am I supposed to identify him?" Her tone stated very clearly that she expected no sensible answer.

Very slowly, Jack's lips curved. His eyes lifted to Sophie's. "Like this," he said. Bending his head, he touched his lips to hers.

Sophie shivered, then went quite still. Her lids lowered, then shut as a wave of sweet longing swept through her. His lips were warm, smooth and firm against the softness of hers. His fingers found hers and laced through them; her fingers curled about his, clinging as if to a lifeline. She knew she should draw back, but made no move to do so, held, trapped, not by his desire, but her own. The realization made her tremble; his hands left hers to gently frame her face, holding her still as his lips teased and taunted, soothed and sipped.

Another wave of longing swept through her, keener, sweeter, more urgent. Sophie felt her senses start to slide into some blissful vale; she raised her hands and gripped his lapels as she leant into the kiss, offering her lips, seeking his.

Jack shuddered as his passions surged. Ruthlessly he quelled them, refusing to rupture the magic of the moment by allowing them free rein. Sophie's lips were warm and inviting, as sweet as nectar, just as he had imagined they would be. She drew nearer, her breasts brushing his chest. Her lips softened under his, she shivered delicately—and he knew he had been right from the start. She was his.

He felt his passions swell, possessively triumphant; he stood firm against their prompting, even though his arms ached to hold her. Unable to completely resist the beguiling temptation of her lips, he allowed the kiss to deepen by imperceptible degrees, until he had to struggle to shackle the need to taste her passionate sweetness.

Reluctantly he drew back, bringing the kiss to an end, his breathing sounding harsh in his ears. He forced his hands from her face, willing them to his sides.

Slowly Sophie's eyes opened. Her wise, starry gaze searched his face.

Bemused, bewildered, Sophie eased her grip on his lapels and lowered her hands. But she did not step back. She stared up at him and struggled to understand. She was teetering on the brink of some abyss; her senses pushed her on, urging her into his arms. Dimly she wondered what magic it was that could so overset her reason.

She wanted him to kiss her again. She needed to feel his arms close about her—even though she knew it would only further complicate an already difficult situation.

Jack read her desire in her eyes, in the parting of her full lips. He tensed against his instincts, against the building urge to sweep her into his arms.

Sophie saw the dark prowling beast that raged, caged, behind his eyes. And suddenly she understood. She caught her breath, fighting the excitement the welled within her, an unknown, never-before-experienced longing to meet his passion with her own. To fling herself into the dark depths of his gaze.

Jack saw the spark that lit her eyes, the glow that softened her face. The sight shredded his will. His control wavered.

The curtain cutting off the ballroom lifted and the noise of the ball rushed in.

As one, Sophie and Jack turned to see Phillip Marston holding the curtain back. His expression could only be described as severely disapproving.

"There you are, Miss Winterton. Permit me to escort you back to your aunt."

Sophie did not move. She drew in a breath, then slanted a glance at Jack. He met it, his expression arrogantly distant. Sophie held her breath; she thought she saw one brow lift slightly. Then, to her relief, he offered her his arm.

"You're mistaken, Marston; Miss Winterton needs no other escort than mine."

A delicious little thrill coursed down Sophie's spine; sternly, she suppressed the sensation and placed her hand on Jack's sleeve.

"Miss Winterton was overcome by the heat in the ball-room," Jack glibly explained. "We retired here to allow her to recover." He glanced down at Sophie's slightly flushed cheeks. "If you're feeling up to it, my dear, I'll take you back to your circle."

But not willingly, said his eyes. Sophie ignored the message and graciously inclined her head. "Thank you, sir." At least he wasn't abandoning her to Mr. Marston.

Jack allowed Marston to hold back the curtain as they emerged into the cacophony of the ball, now in full swing.

Sophie held her head high as they slowly wended their way through the crowd. Phillip Marston kept close by her other side.

Jack bided his time until Sophie's little group of would-be suitors, vaguely at a loss having misplaced their focus, loomed large before them. Then he adroitly lifted Sophie's hand from his sleeve and, stepping behind her, interposed himself between her and Phillip Marston. "We have not yet finished our discussion, Sophie."

His words were muted as he raised her hand.

Sophie, her expression once more calm and remote, lifted her chin. "Indeed, sir, I urge you to believe that we have had all the discussion we are ever likely to have on that particular topic."

Jack's expression remained impassive but his eyes held hers. Very deliberately, he lifted her hand and, turning it, pressed a brief kiss to her palm. "I'll speak with you later."

Sophie snatched her hand back, grateful that his bulk shielded them from almost everyone. She opened her mouth to protest—only to find him bowing gracefully. The next thing she knew, she was surrounded on all sides by gentlemen trying to claim her attention. By the time she had smoothed over her absence, Jack had disappeared.

But he hadn't left.

From an alcove by the steps, shielded by a potted palm, Jack kept a brooding watch over his golden head until the last note had sounded and the last of her would-be suitors had been dismissed.

CHAPTER ELEVEN

WITHIN TWENTY-FOUR HOURS, Jack had come to the conclusion that Fate had decided to live up to her reputation. He had fully intended to pursue his discussion with Sophie, rudely interrupted by Phillip Marston, the very next morning. Fickle Fate gave him no chance.

True, they went riding as usual, a mere ball being insufficient to dampen the Webbs' equestrian spirits. The children, however, prompted, Jack had no doubt, by Sophie, hung about him, bombarding him with questions about the projected balloon ascension. When Percy hove in sight, Jack ruthlessly fobbed the children off on his friend, who, by pure chance, was an amateur enthusiast. But by that time, the gentlemen who had discovered Sophie and Clarissa the night before had caught up with them.

Jack spent the rest of the ride po-faced by Sophie's side.

And there was worse to come.

As Jack had predicted, Clarissa Webb's come-out ball became the de facto beginning of the Season. It had been voted an horrendous crush by all; every hostess with any claim to fame rushed to lay her own entertainments before the *ton*. The days and evenings became an orgy of Venetian breakfasts, alfresco luncheons, afternoon teas and formal dinners, all crowned by a succession of balls, routs, drums and soirées. And beneath the frenzy ran the underlying aim of fostering suitable alliances—an aim with which Jack was, for the first time in his career, deeply involved.

Indeed, as he leaned against the wall in an alcove in Lady Marchmain's ballroom, his gaze, as always, on Sophie, presently gliding through a cotillion, the only thing on Jack's mind was a suitable alliance. He had come to town to use the Season as a backdrop for his wooing of Sophie. By his reckoning, the Season was now more than a week old. Then how much longer did he have to hold off and watch her smile at other men?

"I wonder…need I ask which one she is? Or should I make an educated guess?"

At the drawled words, Jack shifted his gaze to frown at Harry. Observing his brother's interrogative expression, Jack snorted and returned to his occupation. "Second set from the door. In amber silk. Blond."

"Naturally." Harry located Sophie by the simple expedient of following Jack's gaze. His brows slowly rose. "Not bad at all," he mused. "Have I complimented you recently on your taste?"

"Not so I've noticed."

"Ah, well." Harry slanted Jack a rakish smile. "Perhaps I'd better converse with this paragon before I pass judgement."

"If you can shake the dogs that yap at her heels."

Harry shook his head languidly. "Oh, I think I'll manage. What's her name?"

"Sophie Winterton."

With a smile which Jack alone could view with equanimity, Harry sauntered into the crowd. His lips twisting wryly, Jack settled to watch how his brother performed a feat he himself was finding increasingly difficult.

"Thank you, Mr. Somercote. An excellent measure." Sophie smiled and gave Mr. Somercote her hand, hoping he would accept his dismissal. He was, unfortunately, becoming a trifle pointed in his interest.

Mr. Somercote gazed earnestly into her face, retaining her hand in a heated clasp. He drew a portentous breath. "My dear Miss Winterton…"

"It is Miss Winterton, is it not?"

With abject relief, Sophie turned to the owner of the clipped, somewhat hard tones, beneath which a certain languidness rippled, and beheld a strikingly handsome man, bowing even more elegantly than Jack Lester.

This last was instantly explained.

"Harry Lester, Miss Winterton," the apparition offered, along with a rakish grin. "Jack's brother."

"How do you do, Mr. Lester?" As she calmly gave him her hand, Sophie reflected that in any contest of handsomeness, it would be exceedingly difficult to decide between Jack and Harry Lester, not least because they were so unalike.

The gentleman currently shaking her hand, then appropriating it in a manner she recognized all too well, was fair where Jack was dark, with green eyes where Jack's were blue. He was as tall as Jack, but leaner, and there hung about him an aura of dangerous elegance that was distinctly more sharp-edged than Jack's easy assurance. This Lester possessed an elegance that was almost extreme, an aesthetic's adherence to Brummel's dictates, combined with a well-nigh lethal grace.

Harry's glance flicked to Mr. Somercote, then returned to Sophie's face. "Perhaps you would care for a stroll about the rooms, Miss Winterton?"

The arrogant smile that curved his fatally attractive lips assured Sophie that, despite their physical dissimilarity, the Lesters were certainly brothers beneath the skin. "Indeed, sir. That would be most pleasant." He had already settled her hand on his sleeve. With a gentle nod for the deflated Mr. Somercote, Sophie allowed Harry to lead her along the floor.

"You've come to town with your aunt and cousins, have you not?"

Sophie glanced up to find a pair of green eyes lazily regarding her. "Yes, that's right. The Webbs."

"I'm afraid I've not had the pleasure of making their acquaintance. Perhaps you could introduce me if we meet?"

Sophie quickly discovered that Harry, like his brother, had a ready facility for filling in time in a most agreeable, and surprisingly unexceptionable, manner. As they chatted, threading their way through the crowd, she found herself relaxing, then laughing at a tale of a most hilarious excursion in the Park when he and Jack had first come to town. It was only the arrival of her next partner, Mr. Chartwell, that put an end to their amble.

Jack's brother yielded her up with a flourish and a wicked smile.

Smiling herself as she watched him disappear into the crowd, Sophie wondered at the steely danger so apparent in him. It contrasted oddly with Jack's strength. Not that she had felt the least threatened by Harry Lester—quite the opposite. But she did not think she would like to lose her heart to him.

Her mind had little respite from thoughts of Lesters; Jack claimed her immediately the dance with Mr. Chartwell concluded, barely giving that gentleman time to take his leave. However, having detected an expression of chagrin in Mr. Chartwell's mild grey eyes, Sophie was too grateful for her rescue to remonstrate.

Her gratefulness diminished markedly when it became apparent that Jack's difficulties in accepting their fate had not yet been resolved.

"Sophie, I want to talk to you. Privately." Jack had given up trying to manoeuvre such an interlude subtly. Sophie had proved the most amazingly stubborn female he had ever encountered.

Sophie lifted her chin. "You know that would be most unwise, let alone inappropriate."

Jack swallowed a curse. "Sophie, I swear…" The music for the waltz started up; Jack shackled his temper long enough to sweep Sophie into his arms. Once they were whirling slowly down the room, hemmed in on all sides, he continued, "If I have to put up with much more of this, I'll—"

"You'll do nothing that would force me to cut the connection, I hope?" Sophie kept her eyes wide and her expression serene; they might have been discussing the weather for all anyone could see. But her chest felt tight and her heart had sunk. She held Jack's gaze and prayed he'd draw back.

A savage light lit his eyes. Then, with a muttered curse, he looked away. But the tightening of his arm about her told Sophie the argument was far from over. He was holding her far too tight. Sophie made no demur. She had long ago given up hypocritically protesting his transgressions—such as his insistence of using her first name.

She felt a quiver run through her, felt her body respond to his nearness. That, she supposed, was inevitable. He wanted her—as she wanted him. But it wasn't to be; their world did not operate that way. They would both marry others, and Jack had to accept the fact gracefully. If he did, then perhaps they could remain friends. It was all she could hope for, and she was selfish enough to cling to his friendship. He shared so many of her interests, much more so than any of the gentlemen vying for her hand. Indeed, she was loweringly aware that not one of them measured up to Jack Lester and that whenever they gave signs of wanting to fix their interest, she felt an immediate aversion for their company. Her heart, no longer hers, was proving very difficult to reconquer.

Sensing an easing in the tension surrounding her, Sophie slanted a glance at Jack's face.

He was watching her, waiting. "Sophie…I'll accept that you need time to look about you. But I'm not an inherently patient man." The muscle along his jaw twitched; he stilled it, his eyes never leaving hers. "If you could find some way to hurry up this phase, I'd be eternally grateful."

Sophie blinked, her eyes widening. "I…I'll try."

"Do," Jack replied. "But just remember, Sophie—you're mine. *Nothing,* no amount of pretty phrases, will *ever* change that."

The possessiveness in his expression, intransigent, unwavering, stunned Sophie even more than the essence of his arrogant demand. A slow shudder shook her. "Please, Jack…" She looked away, her whisper dying between them.

Jack shackled the urge to haul her into his arms, to put an end to this wooing here and now. Instead, as the music ceased, he drew her hand through his arm. "Come. I'll escort you back to your aunt."

At least she had called him Jack.

"SOMETHING'S WRONG."

It was two nights after Lady Marchmain's ball. Horatio, already propped amid the pillows, turned to study his wife as she sat at her dressing-table, brushing out her mane of silver-blond hair. "What makes you say that?" he asked, unperturbed by her intense expression.

Lucilla frowned. "Sophie isn't happy."

"Isn't she?" Horatio blinked behind his glasses. "Why not? I would have thought, with a horde of would-be suitors, Jack Lester to the fore, she'd be as happy as a young lady could be."

"Well, she's not—and I think it has something to do with Jack Lester, although I cannot, for the life of me, imagine what it could be. Why, the man's positively eaten by jealousy every time she so much as smiles at another. Anyone with eyes can see it. I really don't know what more Sophie wants. Jack Lester will be the catch of the Season."

"Hmm." Horatio frowned. "You're quite sure it's Jack Lester she wants?"

Lucilla snorted. "Believe me, my dear, there's no man Sophie wants even a tenth as much. Indeed, if I was intent on doing my job by the book, I should have warned her long ago not to be so blatant in her preference."

"Ah, well." Horatio shuffled his ever-present documents and laid them aside as Lucilla stood and came towards the bed. "I dare say it'll work itself out. These things generally do."

Lucilla slipped beneath the covers and snuggled down. She waited until Horatio had blown out the candle before saying, "You don't think I should...well, find out what the problem is?"

"You mean *meddle?*" Horatio's tone made his opinion quite clear even before he said, "No. Let the young make their own mistakes, m'dear. How else do you expect them to learn?"

Lucilla grimaced in the dark. "Doubtless you're right, dear." She reached under the covers and patted Horatio's hand. She waited all of a minute before saying, "Actually, I was thinking of organizing a short respite from town. The circus of the Season can become a mite tedious without a break. And I wouldn't want Sophie or Clarissa to become jaded just yet. What say you to a little house party at Aunt Evangeline's?''

Protected by the dark, Horatio slowly smiled. ''Whatever you think best, m'dear.''

It wouldn't hurt for the young people to have a little time together—time enough to correct their mistakes.

BUT FATE HAD NOT yet consented to smile again on Jack. And as for Sophie, she was finding it hard to smile at all.

The thought that Jack wanted her to marry as soon as possible was depressing enough. The idea of what he imagined would happen after was even more so. Her dreams were in tatters; Sophie found it increasingly hard to support her serene façade. She had made a habit of joining circles with Belle Chessington, relying on her friend's unquenchably cheery constitution to conceal her flagging spirits. But her glow was entirely superficial. Inside was all deepening gloom.

She had just returned to her circle on the arm of Mr. Chartwell, who was becoming more assiduous with every passing day, when a deep voice set her heart thumping.

''I do hope, Miss Winterton, that you've saved me a dance.'' Jack smiled into Sophie's eyes as he took her hand and drew her away from her court. ''I've been teaching Ned how to tie his cravat, and it took rather longer than either of us expected.''

Sophie felt her nerves knot and pull tight. Was this, she wondered, as they strolled down the room, how it was going to be later? Would he simply arrive and appropriate her at will? Tensing, she lifted her chin. ''I'm afraid my card is full, Mr. Lester.''

Jack frowned slightly. ''I had rather supposed it would be. But you have kept a dance for me, haven't you?''

They both nodded to Miss Berry, ensconced on a chaise, then continued onward in silence. Sophie struggled to find words for her purpose.

Somewhat abruptly, their progress halted and her escort drew her to face him.

"Sophie?" Jack's frown was gathering force.

Sophie's eyes met his, cloudy, turbulent, intensely blue. Her heart thudding uncomfortably in her throat, she slid her gaze from his. "As it happens, I have not yet accepted anyone for the second waltz."

"You have now." Smothering the dark, almost violent passion that had threatened to erupt, Jack trapped her hand on his sleeve and continued their stroll.

He pointedly returned Sophie to her aunt, some little way from her cloying court. Surrendering her up for their delectation was presently beyond him. His expression somewhat grim, he bowed over Sophie's hand. "Until the second waltz, Miss Winterton."

With that, he left her, his mood even more savage than when he had arrived.

For Sophie, the second waltz arrived far too soon. She had not yet regained her composure, seriously strained by the events of the past weeks and now close to breaking. Jack's arm about her whirled her effortlessly down the floor; Sophie held herself stiffly, battling the impulse to surrender to his strength.

So absorbed was she with her struggle that the first she knew of their departure from the ballroom was the cool touch of the night air on her face.

"Where…?" Distracted, Sophie glanced about and discovered they were on a terrace. But that, apparently, was not their destination, for Jack, his arm still hard about her waist, urged her on. "Jack!" Sophie tried to dig in her heels.

Jack stopped and looked down at her. "You were obviously finding the waltz a trial. I thought you might need some air."

Sophie relaxed slightly, and found she was moving again. "Where are we going?"

The answer was a garden room, built onto the house beyond the end of the terrace. Walls of windows let the moonlight pour in, silvering everything in sight. A few padded cane chairs and two little tables were scattered about the small room, which was, Sophie realized as she heard the door click behind them, mercifully empty.

Which was just as well, for Jack demanded without preamble, "How much longer, Sophie?"

Sophie swung about and found him advancing on her.

"How much longer are you going to make me suffer?"

Her hand rose as if to ward him off; it came to rest on his chest as he halted directly before her. Feeling the warmth of his body through his coat, Sophie shivered. She looked up into his shadowed face, the planes hard and unyielding, and a small spurt of temper flared inside. How did he think *she* felt, having to give up the man she loved—and having that man urge her to do it? Her chin lifted. "I'm afraid the decision is not that simple. In fact, I find the attentions of my present admirers not at all to my taste."

That admission went a long way towards easing the tension that held Jack in its grip. He could feel it flowing from him, the muscles of his shoulders and back relaxing.

Still considering her suitors, Sophie frowned. "I'm afraid I would not be happy accepting any of my present suitors."

An icy chill stole over Jack's heart. It beat three times before he asked, "None?"

Sophie shook her head. "I don't know what to do. I must accept *someone* by the end of the Season."

The chill was slowly spreading through Jack's veins. He touched his tongue to his lips, then asked, "Why not me?"

Startled, Sophie glanced up at him. "But..." She frowned. "I can't marry you—you know I can't." She could see very little of his expression through the shadows veiling his face. And nothing at all of his eyes.

"Why not?" Sight wouldn't have helped her; Jack's expression was hard, impassive, all emotion suppressed. "We both know I've all the attributes you seek in a husband: a country estate, a wish to reside in the country, a desire for children, to have a family about me. That's what you want, isn't it?"

Sophie stared up at him.

"And, of course," Jack continued, his lips twisting in an uncertain smile, "we have something else between us." Raising a hand, he delicately drew the tip of one finger from the point of Sophie's shoulder, exposed by her wide neckline, across to the base of her throat, then down to where the deep cleft between her breasts was visible above her gown. Sophie shivered and caught her breath.

"A…compatibility," Jack said, "that makes all the rest fade into insignificance." His eyes rose to trap Sophie's stunned gaze. "Isn't it so, Sophie?"

Sophie swallowed. "But I have no fortune. Nothing but expectations."

"That doesn't matter." Jack's gaze sharpened. He drew a deep breath. "Sophie—"

In a sudden breathless rush, Sophie put her fingers over his lips. "No!" she squeaked, and cursed her quavering voice. At last she understood—and knew what she must do. Drawing in a determined breath, consciously steeling herself, she drew back, forcing herself to hold his gaze. "I'm afraid you don't understand, Jack. I've never been wealthy in my life—I came to London determined to marry well." The lie came out so easily. Her eyes falling from his, Sophie searched for more words to shore it up. "I know I didn't say so, but I thought you understood. Nothing…" She paused to make sure her voice would not waver. "Nothing I've seen in London has changed my mind; I require that my preferred suitor has considerable wealth."

The words came out more than creditably. Sophie heard them; her heart thudded painfully in her breast but she held herself erect, head high. Far better he think her lost to all sensibility than that he offer to marry her, mortgaging his future, turning his back on those responsibilities that were so very important to him. He was just like Lucilla—ready to sacrifice all for love. She wouldn't allow it.

"But…" Jack couldn't have felt more stunned had she slapped him. His brain reeled, grappling with the fact that Sophie did not know of his true circumstances. He had assumed Horatio would tell Lucilla, who in turn would have told Sophie.

Obviously not. The facts were on his lips. Chill reason froze them there.

He looked down at Sophie's face, calm and serene in the moonlight, the face of the woman he had thought he understood. But she was intent on marrying for money—so intent she would happily put aside what was between them, turn away from his love, and hers, in exchange for cold hard cash. Fate was playing games with him; his golden head had gold on her mind. Did he really want to win her by revealing his disgusting wealth? How would he feel when she smiled and came to his arms, knowing that it had taken money to get her there?

There was a bitter taste in his mouth. Jack drew a sharp breath and looked up, over Sophie's head. He felt cold. A steel fist had closed about his heart, squeezing unmercifully.

He took a jerky step back. "I regret, Miss Winterton, if my…attentions have been unwelcome. I will not trouble you more. I realize my actions must have complicated your search for…a suitable suitor. You have my apologies." With a curt bow, Jack turned to leave. And hesitated.

His face in profile, Sophie saw his lips twist in the travesty of a smile. Then he turned his head to look down at her. "I can only hope, my dear, that when you find your pot of gold at the end of the rainbow you're not disappointed." With a curt nod, he strode away, opening and shutting the door carefully.

Leaving Sophie in the centre of the empty room.

For a long moment, she remained as she was, proudly erect, then her shoulders slumped. Sophie bowed her head, drawing in an aching breath, squeezing her eyes tight against the pain that blossomed inside.

Ten minutes later, she returned to the ballroom, no trace of misery on her face. Coolly composed, she joined her little circle, brightly responding to Belle Chessington's quips. A quick glance about revealed the fact that Jack's dark head was nowhere to be seen. Sophie crumpled inside. She had done the right thing. She must remember that.

If this was what it took to ensure he prospered and lived the life he should live, so be it.

From an alcove by the card room, almost at the other end of the floor, Jack brooded on Sophie's ready smiles. If he had needed any further proof of the superficiality of her feelings for him, he had just received it. Raising his glass, he downed a mouthful of the golden liquor it contained.

"There you are. Been looking all over." Ned ducked round the palm that blocked the opening of the alcove. His eyes fell on Jack's glass. "What's that?"

"Brandy," Jack growled and took another long sip.

Ned raised his brows. "Didn't see any of that in the refreshment room."

"No." Jack smiled, somewhat grimly, across the room and said no more. Ned didn't need to drink himself into a stupor.

"I danced the last cotillion with Clarissa," Ned said. "Her blasted card was virtually full and that bounder Gurnard's taking her in to supper. Should I hang around here or can we leave?"

His gaze on Sophie, Jack considered the point. "I don't advise leaving until after supper, or it'll be said you only came to dance with Clarissa."

"I *did* only come to dance with Clarissa," Ned groaned. "Can we just cut and run?"

Very slowly, Jack shook his head, his attention still fixed across the room. "I told you, this game's not for the faint-hearted." For a long moment, he said no more; Ned waited patiently.

Abruptly, Jack shook himself and straightened from the wall. He looked at Ned, his usual arrogant expression in place. "Go and join some other young lady's circle. But whatever you do, don't be anywhere near Clarissa at suppertime." At Ned's disgusted look, Jack relented. "If you survive that far, I don't suppose it would hurt to talk to her afterwards—but no more than fifteen minutes."

"Wooing a young lady in the *ton* is the very devil," Ned declared. "Where do all these rules come from?" With a disgusted shake of his head, he took himself off.

With his protégé under control, Jack leaned back into the

shadows of the alcove, and kept watch on the woman who, regardless of all else, was still his.

FOUR DAYS LATER, Sophie sat in the carriage and stared gloomily at the dull prospect beyond the window. Lucilla's little excursion, announced this morning, had taken the household by surprise. In retrospect, she should have suspected her aunt was planning something; there had been moments recently when Lucilla had been peculiarly abstracted. This three-day sojourn at Little Bickmanstead, the old manor belonging to Lucilla's ancient Aunt Evangeline, was the result.

Despondent, Sophie sighed softly, her gaze taking in the leaden skies. In perfect accord with her mood, the unseasonably fine spell had come to an abrupt end on the night she had refused to let Jack offer for her. A rainstorm had swept the capital. Ever since, the clouds had threatened, low and menacing, moving Lucilla to veto their rides.

Glumly, Sophie wondered if Jack understood—or if he thought she was avoiding him. The miserable truth was, she did not think she could cope with any meeting just now. Perhaps Fate had sent the rain to her aid?

Certainly Jack himself seemed in no hurry to speak with her again. Perhaps he never would. He had been present at the balls they had attended over the past three nights. She had seen him in the distance, but he had not approached her. Indeed, once, when they had passed close while she had been strolling the floor on one of her would-be suitors' arms, and their gazes had met, he had merely inclined his head in a distant fashion. She had replied in kind, but inside the ache had intensified.

Sophie closed her eyes and searched for peace in the repetitive rocking of the coach. She had done the right thing—she kept telling herself so. Her tears, perforce, had been shed discreetly, far from Lucilla's sharp eyes. She had stifled her grief, refusing to dwell on it; suppressed, it had swelled until it pervaded her, beating leaden in her veins, a cold misery enshrouding her soul. A misery she was determined none would ever see.

Which meant she had to face the possibility that Jack might take up the invitation Lucilla had extended to join them at Little Bickmanstead. The guest list numbered some twenty-seven souls, invited to enjoy a few days of rural peace in the rambling old house close by Epping Forest. But Jack wouldn't come, not now. Sophie sighed, feeling not relief, but an inexpressible sadness at the thought.

The well-sprung travelling carriage rolled over a rut, throwing Clarissa against her shoulder. They disentangled themselves and sat up, both checking on Lucilla, seated opposite, her dresser, Mimms, by her side. Her aunt, Sophie noted, was looking distinctly seedy. A light flush tinted Lucilla's alabaster cheeks and her eyes were overbright.

Touching a lace-edged handkerchief to her nose, Lucilla sniffed delicately. "Incidentally, Clarissa, I had meant to mention it before now—but you really don't want to encourage that guardsman, Captain Gurnard." Lucilla wrinkled her nose. "I'm not at all sure he's quite the thing, despite all appearances to the contrary."

"Fear not, Mama." Clarissa smiled gaily. "I've no intention of succumbing to the captain's wiles. Indeed, I agree with you, there's definitely something 'not quite' about him."

Lucilla shot her daughter a narrow-eyed glance, then, apparently reassured, she blew her nose and settled back against the cushions.

Clarissa continued to smile sunnily. Her plans were proceeding, albeit not as swiftly as she would have liked. Ned was proving remarkably resistant to the idea of imitating her other swains; he showed no signs of wanting to prostrate himself at her feet. However, as she found such behaviour a mite inconvenient, Clarissa was perfectly ready to settle for a declaration of undying love and future happiness. Her current problem lay in how to obtain it.

Hopefully, a few days in quieter, more familiar surroundings, even without the helpful presence of the captain to spur Ned on, would advance her cause.

The carriage checked and turned. Sophie looked out and saw

two imposing gateposts just ahead. Then the scrunch of gravel announced they had entered the drive. The house lay ahead, screened by ancient beeches. When they emerged in the forecourt, Sophie saw a long, two-storey building in a hotchpotch of styles sprawling before them. One thing was instantly apparent: housing a party of forty would not stretch the accommodations of Little Bickmanstead. Indeed, losing a party of forty in the rambling old mansion looked a very likely possibility.

Drops of rain began spotting the grey stone slabs of the porch as they hurried inside. A fleeting glance over her shoulder revealed a bank of black clouds racing in from the east. The other members of the family had elected to ride from town, Horatio keeping a watchful eye on his brood. Minton and the other higher servants had followed close behind, the luggage with them. The forecourt became a scene of frenzied activity as they all hurried to dismount and stable the horses and unpack the baggage before the storm hit.

The family gathered in the hall, looking about with interest. The rectangular hall was dark, wood panelling and old tapestries combining to bolster the gloom. An ancient butler had admitted them; an even more ancient housekeeper came forward, a lamp in her hand.

As the woman bobbed a curtsy before her, Lucilla put out a hand to the table in the centre of the room. "Oh, dear."

One glance at her deathly pale face was enough to send them all into a panic.

"My dear?" Horatio hurried to her side.

"Mama?" came from a number of throats.

"Mummy, you look sick," came from Hermione, gazing upwards as she held her mother's hand.

Lucilla closed her eyes. "I'm dreadfully afraid," she began, her words very faint.

"Don't say anything," Horatio advised. "Here, lean on me—we'll have you to bed in a trice."

The old housekeeper, eyes wide, beckoned them up the stairs. "I've readied all the rooms as instructed."

Minton was already sorting through the bags. Sending Clarissa ahead with Mimms and the housekeeper, Sophie came to her aunt's other side. Together, she and Horatio supported a rapidly wilting Lucilla up the stairs and along a dim and drafty corridor to a large chamber. Mimms was in charge there; the bed was turned down, the housekeeper dispatched for a warming pan. A fire was cracking into life in the grate.

They quickly helped Lucilla to bed, laying her back on the soft pillows and tucking the covers about her. Once installed, she regained a little colour. She opened her eyes and regarded them ruefully. And sniffed. "This is terrible. I've organized it all—there are twenty-seven people on their way here. They'll all arrive before dinner. And if the rain persists, they'll need to be entertained for the next two days."

"Don't worry about anything," Horatio said, patting her hand. But even he was frowning as the ordeal before them became clear.

"But you haven't a hostess." Lucilla put her handkerchief to her nose, cutting off what sounded like a tearful wail. She blinked rapidly.

Sophie straightened her shoulders. "I'm sure I can manage, with Uncle Horatio and Great Aunt Evangeline behind me. It's not as if you were not in the house—I can check any details with you. And it's not as if there were no chaperons. You told me yourself you've invited a number of matrons."

Lucilla's woeful expression lightened. Her frown turned pensive. "I suppose…" For a moment, all was silent. Then, "Yes," she finally announced, and nodded. "It just might work. But," she said, raising rueful eyes to Sophie's face, "I'm awfully afraid, my dear, that it will be no simple matter."

Relieved to have averted immediate catastrophe, for if Lucilla broke down, that would certainly follow, Sophie smiled with totally false confidence. "You'll see, we'll contrive."

Those words seemed to have become a catchphrase of her Season, Sophie mused as, an hour later, she sat in the front parlour, off the entrance hall, the guest list in her hand.

After assuring themselves that Lucilla was settled and resigned to her bed, she and Clarissa and Horatio had gone to pay their respects to Aunt Evangeline. It had been years since Sophie had met her ageing relative; the years had not been kind to Aunt Evangeline. She was still ambulatory, but her wits were slowly deserting her. Still, she recognized Horatio, even though she was apparently ineradicably convinced that Clarissa was Lucilla and Sophie her dead mother, Maria. They had given up trying to correct the misapprehension, concentrating instead on explaining their current predicament. Whether or not they had succeeded was moot, but at least Aunt Evangeline had given them a free hand to order things as they wished.

Nevertheless, the prospect of having to keep a weather eye out for an old dear who, so the housekeeper had gently informed them, was full of curiosity and prone to wandering the corridors at all hours draped in shawls that dragged their fringes on the floor, was hardly comforting.

A sound came from outside. Sophie lifted her head, listening intently. The wind was rising, whistling about the eaves. Rain fell steadily, driving in gusts against the windows, masking other sounds. Then came the unmistakable jingle of harness. Sophie rose. The first of her aunt's guests had arrived. Girding her loins, she tugged the bell-pull and went out into the hall.

From the very first, it was bedlam. The Billinghams—Mrs. Billingham and both of her daughters—were the first to arrive. By the time they had descended from their carriage and negotiated the steps, their carriage dresses were soaked to the knees.

"Oh, how dreadful! Mama, I'm *dripping!*" The younger Miss Billingham looked positively shocked.

Mrs. Billingham, if anything even damper than her daughters, was not disposed to give comfort. "Indeed, Lucy, I don't know what you're complaining about. We're all wet—and now here's a to-do with Mrs. Webb ill. I'm not at all sure we shouldn't turn round and return to town."

"Oh no, Mama—you couldn't be so cruel!" The plaintive wail emanated from the elder Miss Billingham.

"Indeed, Mrs. Billingham, there's really no need."

Smoothly, Sophie cut in, clinging to her usual calm. "Every-thing's organized and I'm sure my aunt would not wish you to withdraw purely on account of her indisposition."

Mrs. Billingham humphed. "Well, I suppose with your uncle present and myself and the other ladies, there's really no im-propriety."

"I seriously doubt my aunt would ever countenance any," Sophie replied, her smile a trifle strained.

"We'll stay at least until the morning." Mrs. Billingham cast a darkling glance out of the open door. "Perhaps by then the weather will have eased. I'll make a decision then."

With that declaration, Mrs. Billingham allowed herself to be shown to her chamber.

Hard on the Billinghams' heels came Lord Ainsley. His lord-ship had unwisely driven out in his curricle, and he was soaked to the skin. He tried hard to smile, but his chattering teeth made it difficult.

Sophie was horrified, visions of guests catching their deaths whirling through her mind. Issuing orders left and right—for hot baths and mustard to ward off chills, for the staff to make sure all the fires were blazing—she turned from the sight of Lord Ainsley's back disappearing up the stairs to behold a be-draggled Lord Annerby on the doorstep.

And so it went, on through the afternoon, while outside a preternatural darkness descended.

Belle Chessington and her equally cheery mother were amongst the last to arrive.

"What a perfectly appalling afternoon," Mrs. Chessington remarked as she came forward with a smile, hand outstretched.

Sophie heaved an inward sigh of relief. The Marquess of Huntly, another who had unwisely opted to drive himself, was dripping all over the hall flags. Her little speech now well re-hearsed, Sophie quickly made Lucilla's indisposition known, then smoothed away their exclamations with assurances of their welcome. Horatio had retreated to the main parlour to play host to those gentlemen who had already descended, looking for something to warm themselves while they waited for the dinner gong.

The Chessingtons and the marquess took the news in their stride. They were about to head upstairs when a tremendous sneeze had them all turning to the door.

Mr. Somercote stood on the threshold, a pitiful sight with water running in great rivers from his coattails.

"My dear sir!" Belle Chessington swept back along the hall to drag the poor gentleman in.

His place in the doorway was immediately filled by Miss Ellis and her mother, closely followed by Mr. Marston, Lord Swindon and Lord Thurstow. Of them all, only Mr. Marston, clad in a heavy, old-fashioned travelling cloak, was less than drenched. Sophie left the marquess; she tugged the bell-pull twice, vigorously, then hurried forward to help the others out of their soaked coats.

Mentally reviewing the guest list, she thought most had now arrived.

Mr. Marston moved to intercept her, unwrapping his cloak as he came. He was frowning. "What's this, Miss Winterton? Where is your aunt?"

His question, uttered in a stern and reproving tone, silenced all other conversation. The latest arrivals glanced about, noting Lucilla's absence. Suppressing a curse, Sophie launched into her explanation. Mr. Marston did not, however, allow her to get to her reassurances. He cut across her smooth delivery to announce, "A sad mischance indeed. Well—there's nothing for it—we'll all have to return to town. Can't possibly impose on the family with your aunt so gravely ill. And, of course, there are the proprieties to consider."

For an instant, silence held sway. The others all looked to Sophie.

With an effort, Sophie kept her smile in place. "I assure you, Mr. Marston, that my aunt has nothing more than a cold. She would be most unhappy if such a trifling indisposition were to cause the cancellation of this party. And with my great-aunt, my uncle and Mrs. Chessington and the other matrons all present, I really don't think the proprieties are in any danger of being breached. Now," she went on, smiling around at the others, "if you would like to retire to your chambers and get dry—"

"You'll pardon me, Miss Winterton, but I must insist that you fetch your uncle. I cannot be easy in my mind over this most peculiar suggestion that the party proceed as planned." Supercilious as ever, Phillip Marston drew himself up. "I really must insist that Mr. Webb be consulted at once. It is hardly a minor matter."

An utterly stunned silence ensued.

It was broken by a stupendous thunderclap—then the night outside lit up. The blaze in the forecourt threw the shadow of a man deep into the hall.

As the brilliance beyond the door died, Sophie, along with everyone else, blinked at the newcomer.

"As usual, Marston, you're mistaken," Jack drawled as he strolled forward. "Mrs. Webb's indisposition undoubtedly is, as Miss Winterton has assured us, entirely minor. Our kind hostess will hardly thank you for making an issue of it."

A most peculiar *frisson* frizzled its way along Sophie's nerves. She could not drag her gaze from the tall figure advancing across the floor towards her. The long folds of his many-caped greatcoat were damp, but it was clear he, alone amongst the gentlemen invited, had been wise enough to come in a closed carriage. Beneath the greatcoat, his dark coat and breeches were dry and, as usual, immaculate.

With his usual grace, he bowed over her hand. "Good evening, Miss Winterton. I trust I see you well?"

Sophie's mind froze. She had convinced herself he wouldn't come, that she would never see him again. Instead, here he was, arriving like some god from the darkness outside, sweeping difficulties like Mr. Marston aside. But his expression was impassive; his eyes, as they touched her face, held no particular warmth. Sophie's heart contracted painfully.

Glancing about, Jack bestowed a charming smile on the other, much damper, guests. "But pray don't let me detain you from giving succour to these poor unfortunates." His smile robbed the term of any offence.

Gently, he squeezed Sophie's hand.

Sophie dragged in a sharp breath. She retrieved her hand and pinned a regal smile to her lips. "If you and Mr. Marston don't mind, I shall see these others to their rooms."

Still smiling, Jack politely inclined his head; Phillip Marston hesitated, frowning, then nodded curtly.

Determinedly calm, Sophie moved forward to deal with the last of her aunt's guests. As she did so, Ned slipped in through the door. He grinned at her. "Shall I shut it? Jack was sure we'd be last."

Sophie smiled and nodded. "Please." As she helped Minton ease Lord Thurstow from his sodden coat, she wondered whether Jack Lester had purposely arrived last for greatest effect—or whether his lateness was a reflection of reluctance.

The heavy door clanged shut on the wild night; to Sophie, it's resounding thud sounded like the knell of an inescapable doom.

CHAPTER TWELVE

SHE BARELY HAD TIME to scramble into an evening gown and brush out her curls before the dinner gong sounded, echoing hollowly through the long corridors. The meal had already been put back twice to accommodate the travellers and their recuperation.

With a last distracted glance at her mirror, Sophie hurried out. The corridor was dark and gloomy, the ubiquitous wood panelling deepening the shadows cast by the candles in the wall sconces. Feet flying over the worn carpet, Sophie turned a corner only to find a cordon, formed by two determined figures, across her path.

Jeremy frowned, threatening sulky. "We can come down to dinner, can't we, Sophie?"

Sophie blinked.

"It's not as if we'd cause any ruckus," George assured her.

"It's *boring* here, Sophie. Having dinner with Amy and the twins—well, it's just not fair." Jeremy's jaw jutted pugnaciously.

"It's not as if we're children." George fixed his blue eyes on her face and dared her to contradict him.

Sophie swallowed a groan. With all the trials of the afternoon, and those yet to come, she had precious little patience left to deal with the boys' prickly pride. But she loved them too well to fob them off. Draping an arm about each, she gave them a quick hug. "Yes, I know, loves—but, you see, we're a bit rushed this evening, and although the party's informal, I don't really think it's quite the same as when we're at Webb Park."

They both turned accusing eyes on her. "I don't see why not," Jeremy stated.

"Ah—but if you don't get an early night, you won't be up in time to go shooting tomorrow."

Sophie jumped. The deep, drawling voice brought goose-bumps to her skin. But both boys turned eagerly as Jack strolled out from the shadows.

"Shooting?"

"You mean you'll take us?"

Jack raised a brow. "I don't see why not. I was discussing the outing with your father earlier. If the rain eases, we should have tolerable sport." Jack's blue gaze flicked to Sophie, then returned to the boys' glowing faces. "But you'd have to get an early night—and that, I fear, means dining in the nursery. Of course, if that's beneath you..."

"Oh, no," Jeremy assured him. "Not if we're to go shooting tomorrow."

George tugged his brother's sleeve. "Come on. We'd better let Jack and Sophie get to dinner and go find ours before the twins scoff all the buns."

Restored to good humour, the boys hurried off.

Sophie breathed a sigh of relief, then glanced up at Jack. "Thank you, Mr. Lester."

For a moment, Jack's gaze rested on her face, his expression impassive. Then he inclined his head. "Think nothing of it, my dear. Shall we?"

He gestured towards the stairs. With a nod, Sophie started forward. As they strolled the short distance in silence, she was excruciatingly aware of him, large and strong beside her, her skirts occasionally brushing his boots. He made no move to offer her his arm.

They descended the stairs and turned towards the drawing-room. Minton was hovering in the hall. "Could I have a word with you, miss?"

Sophie's heart sank. "Yes, of course." With a half smile for Jack, she glided across the tiles. "What is it?"

"It's the footmen, miss. That's to say—there aren't any."

Looking supremely apologetic, Minton continued, "The old lady apparently didn't see the need and Mrs. Webb didn't imagine we'd need more. Even with old Smithers—that's the old lady's butler—there'll only be two of us and that'll make service very slow. Naughton—Mr. Webb's man—said as he'd help, but still…"

Minton didn't need to spell it out; Sophie wondered what next the evening had in store. Where on earth could she find footmen to wait at table at a minute's notice "I don't suppose the coachman…"

Minton looked his answer. "I'd rather have the maids. But you know how it'll look, miss, having women wait at table."

She did indeed. Sophie's shoulders slumped.

"If I could make a suggestion?"

Sophie turned as Jack strolled forward. He glanced at her, his expression merely polite. "I couldn't help overhearing. I suggest," he said, addressing Minton. "That you ask my man, Pinkerton, to assist. Huntly's man, too, will be well-trained, and Ainsley's and Annerby's. The rest I can't vouch for, but Pinkerton will know."

Minton's worried expression cleared. "Just the ticket, sir. I'll do that." He bobbed to Sophie. "All under control, miss, never fear." And with that, Minton hurried off.

Sophie knew a moment of blessed relief, superceded by the knowledge that more hurdles doubtless awaited her. She glanced up at Jack. "I have to thank you again, Mr. Lester. I would never have thought of such a solution; I only hope it serves." The last was uttered softly, a slight frown playing about her brows.

Not a glimmer of expression showed on Jack's face as, looking down, he studied hers. "Don't worry. Such arrangements are not uncommon—no one will remark on it."

From beneath her lashes, Sophie glanced up. "Thank you," she murmured, a tentative smile touching her lips.

Jack's hand closed about the knob of the drawing-room door. "After you, Miss Winterton."

Sophie entered to find most of the company already assembled. She moved among the guests, seeing that all had everything they needed. Most had recovered from their soaking and regained their spirits. Only Mrs. Billingham and Mrs. Ellis, a delicate lady, had elected to take trays in their rooms. Clarissa was surrounded by her usual little band, Ned included. Her cousin had drawn the other younger ladies into the charmed circle; the sound of shy laughter now ran as a counterpoint to more sober conversations. Her uncle, together with the more mature gentlemen, was deep in discussion of the sport to be found in the vicinity.

Great-Aunt Evangeline provided an unexpected distraction. She had come down to examine the guests who had invaded her home. Blithely calling Sophie "Maria" and Clarissa "Lucilla," she happily chatted with the ladies, her remarkable shawls threatening to trip her at every step.

When Minton announced dinner, the old lady squeezed Sophie's arm. "I'll take mine in my room, dear. Now remember, Maria—you're in charge. Keep an eye on Lucilla, won't you?" With a motherly pat, Great-Aunt Evangeline retired.

Dinner, as it transpired, posed no further problems. As one course was smoothly followed by the next, Sophie gradually relaxed. She had led the way into the dining-room on the Marquess of Huntly's arm. He was now seated on her right with Lord Ainsley on her left. A hum of good-natured conversation hovered over the table; everyone was reasonably well acquainted and, so it seemed, determined to enjoy themselves. Further down the board, Belle Chessington had taken on the challenge posed by Mr. Somercote; she was bending his ear unmercifully. Sophie smiled and let her gaze travel on, to where Clarissa and Ned, together with Lord Swindon and Mr. Marley, were deep in discussion of some passingly serious subject. Beyond them, Jack Lester was devoting himself primarily to Mrs. Chessington. Sophie had seen him offer that lady his arm in the drawing-room even as she herself had placed her hand on the Marquess's sleeve.

Rousing herself from her thoughts, Sophie conjured a smile

and beamed at the marquess. "Do you intend to make one of
the shooting party tomorrow, my lord?"

Once the covers were removed, Sophie led the ladies back
to the drawing-room. The gentlemen were disposed to linger
over their port, yet there was still an hour before the tea trolley
was due when they strolled back into the room.

As ladies and gentlemen merged, then fractured into the inevitable smaller groups, Sophie wondered how to keep them
amused. She hadn't had time to organize any of the fashionable
little games that were so much a part of country-house parties.
She was cudgelling her brains for inspiration when Ned
stopped by her chair.

"We thought we might try charades, Sophie. Jack mentioned
it was all the thing for the younger crowd."

Relieved, Sophie smiled. "By all means; that's an excellent
idea."

She watched as Ned and Clarissa rounded up the younger
members of the party and cleared an area of the large room.
Many of the matrons seemed disposed to look on indulgently.
Rising, Sophie glanced about—and found her uncle approaching.

Horatio beamed and took her hand. "You're doing magnif-
icently, my dear." He squeezed her fingers, then released them.
"Lester's taken Huntly, Ainsley and Annerby off to try their
luck at billiards. I'll just go and have a word with Marston."
Horatio glanced about the drawing-room. "The rest I fear I'll
have to leave to you—but I'm sure you can manage."

With Mr. Marston off her hands, Sophie was sure of it, too.
Belle Chessington seemed reluctant to let Mr. Somercote escape, which left only Mr. Chartwell, Miss Billingham and a
few relaxed matrons for her to take under her wing. Sophie
smiled. "Indeed, Uncle, it seems we've contrived amazingly
well."

"Indeed." Horatio grinned. "Your aunt will be delighted."

To SOPHIE'S RELIEF, the rain cleared overnight. The morning
was damp and dismal, but sufficiently clement to allow the

shooting party to proceed. By the time the ladies descended to the breakfast parlour, the gentlemen had taken themselves off. Even Mr. Marston had seized the opportunity to stretch his legs.

The ladies were content to stroll the gardens. Sophie went up to check on the twins and Amy. She eventually ran them to earth in the attics; their nurse, who had been with the Webbs for many years, had had the bright idea of turning them loose in such relatively safe surrounds. The trio were engaged in constructing a castle, later to be stormed. Great-Aunt Evangeline was with them. Sophie left them to it and went to look in on her aunt. She found Lucilla sleeping, which of itself spoke volumes. Mimms confirmed that her aunt's indisposition had eased, but she was still very weak.

The gentlemen returned in time for luncheon, an informal meal at which their prowess with their guns was discussed and admired, the ladies smiling good-naturedly at claims of prizes flushed from coverts or taken on the wing.

Listening to the genial chatter, Sophie spared a thought for Lucilla's expertise. Her aunt had selected her guests with a knowing hand; they had melded into a comfortable party despite the presence of such difficult elements as Mr. Marston and Mr. Somercote.

But by the end of the meal, the rain had returned, gusting in from the east in leaden sheets. By unvoiced consensus, the gentlemen retired to the library or billiard room, while the ladies took possession of the morning-room and parlour, to chat in little groups ensconced in the comfortable armchairs or wander in the adjoining conservatory.

With everyone settled, Sophie went to the kitchens to confer with Cook. Belowstairs, she stumbled on an army, the depleted ranks of Aunt Evangeline's aged servitors swelled beyond imagining by the maids, coachmen and valets of the guests, as well as the doyens of the Webb household. But all seemed to be cheery, the bulk of the men gathered about the huge fire in the kitchen. Minton, beaming, assured her all was well.

Climbing back up the stairs, her chores completed, Sophie

decided she could justifiably seize a moment for herself. The conservatory had proved a most amazing discovery; it was huge and packed with ferns and flowering creepers, many of kinds Sophie had not before seen. She had had time for no more than a glimpse; now, she pushed open the glass door and slipped into the first avenue, half an hour of peace before her.

As the greenery surrounded her, Sophie closed her eyes and breathed deeply. The humid scent of rich earth and green leaves, of growing things, tinged with the faint perfume of exotic flowers, filled her senses. A smile hovered on her lips.

"There you are, Miss Winterton."

Sophie's eyes flew open; her smile vanished. Swallowing a most unladylike curse, she swung round to see Mr. Marston advancing purposefully upon her. As usual, he was frowning.

"Really, Miss Winterton, I cannot tell you how very displeased I am to find you here."

Sophie blinked; one of her brows rose haughtily. "Indeed, sir?"

"As you should *know*, Miss Winterton." Mr. Marston came to a halt before her, giving Sophie an excellent view of his grim expression. "I do not see how your uncle can reconcile this with his conscience. I knew from the first that continuing with this affair was unwise in the extreme. Unconscionable folly."

Sophie straightened her shoulders and looked him in the eye. "I fear, sir, that I cannot allow you to malign my uncle, who, as everyone knows, takes exceptional care of me. In truth, I cannot follow your reasoning at all."

Mr. Marston appeared to have difficulty restraining himself. "What I mean, Miss Winterton," he finally replied, his tones glacially condemnatory, "is that I am *shocked* to find you—a young lady whom I consider of sound and elevated mind and a naturally genteel manner—here." He paused to gesture about them. "Quite alone, unattended, where any gentleman might come upon you."

Sophie hung onto her patience. "Mr. Marston, may I point out that I am in my great-aunt's house, within easy call not only of servants but many others whom I consider friends? Is it not all the same thing as if I had chosen to walk the pavements of Covent Garden unattended?''

Mr. Marston's grey eyes narrowed; his lips were set in a thin line. ''You are mistaken, Miss Winterton. No lady can afford to play fast and loose with her reputation by courting—''

''Really, Marston. No need to bore Miss Winterton to tears by reciting the Young Ladies' Catechism. They all have to learn it by heart before being admitted to Almack's, you know.'' Jack strolled forward, green leaves brushing his shoulders. His expression was easy and open, but Sophie saw a glint of something harder in his eyes.

The sudden rush of mixed emotions—relief, nervousness and anticipation among them—on top of her rising temper, left her momentarily giddy. But she turned back to Mr. Marston, lifting her chin challengingly. ''Mr. Lester is correct, sir. I assure you I need no lectures on such topics.''

She made the comment in an even voice, giving Mr. Marston the opportunity to retreat gracefully. He, however, seemed more intent on glowering at Jack, a futile gesture for, as she shifted her gaze to her rescuer's face, Sophie found he was watching her.

She would have given a great deal, just then, for one of his smiles. Instead, he simply bowed, urbanely elegant, and offered her his arm. ''I came to collect you, my dear. The tea trolley has just been brought in.''

Sophie tried a small smile of her own and placed her fingers on his sleeve.

Phillip Marston snorted. ''Ridiculous! Taking lessons in comportment from a—'' He broke off as he met Jack's gaze.

One of Jack's brows slowly rose. ''You were saying, Marston?''

The quiet question made Phillip Marston glower even more. ''Nothing, nothing. If you'll excuse me, Miss Winterton, I find I am not in the mood for tea.'' With a curt bow, he turned on his heel and disappeared into the greenery.

Sophie didn't bother to stifle her sigh. ''Thank you again,

Mr. Lester. I must apologize for Mr. Marston. I fear he's labouring under a misapprehension.''

As they strolled towards the parlour, Sophie glanced up at her knight-errant. He was looking down at her, his expression enigmatic.

''No need for apologies, my dear. Indeed, I bear Marston no ill-will. Strange to say, I know just how he feels.''

Sophie frowned, but she got no chance to pursue his meaning; the tea trolley and the bulk of her aunt's guests were waiting.

WHEN SOPHIE AWOKE the next morning, and tentatively peeked out from under the covers, she was met by weak sunshine and a pale, blue-washed sky. She relaxed back against her pillows, feeling decidedly more confident than she had the morning before.

The previous evening had passed off smoothly, much in the manner of the first. The only exceptions had been the behaviour of her suitors, who, one and all, had recovered from the dampening effects of their arrival and were once more attempting to pay court to her. That and the behaviour of the elder Miss Billingham, who had all but thrown herself at Jack Lester.

Sophie grimaced, her eyes narrowing. After a moment, she shook herself. And rose to meet the day.

She looked in on Lucilla on her way downstairs. Her aunt was sitting up in bed sipping her morning cocoa. ''Indeed, I would love to see how things are progressing, but I still feel quite weak.'' Lucilla pulled a face. ''Maybe this evening?''

''You will remain abed until you are well,'' declared Horatio, coming through the door with a laden tray.

Leaving her aunt to her husband's fond care, Sophie descended to the breakfast parlour. There, her suitors lay in waiting.

''This kedgeree is quite remarkable, m'dear,'' offered the marquess. ''Quite remarkable.''

''Perhaps you would care for some bacon and an egg or two,

Miss Winterton?'' Mr. Chartwell lifted the lid of a silver platter and glanced at her enquiringly.

Sophie smiled on them all, and managed to install herself between Mr. Somercote, engaged in silent communication with Belle Chessington, who was chattering enough for them both, and Mrs. Chessington, who smiled understandingly.

Further down the board, Jack was apparently absorbed with Mrs. Ellis and her daughter. Beside him, Ned was chatting to Clarissa, Lord Swindon and Mr. Marley openly eavesdropping. Sophie hid a smile at her cousin's rapt expression.

She escaped the breakfast parlour unencumbered, using the pretext of having to check on her younger cousins. Jeremy and Gerald had been tired out by a day in woods and fields; they had happily eaten with Amy and the twins the night before. When she reached the nursery she was greeted by an unnatural silence, which was explained by Nurse when she hunted that worthy down. The children had been taken on a long ride by the grooms; peace, therefore, was very likely assured. Smiling with both relief and satisfaction, Sophie descended—into the arms of her suitors.

The marquess took the lead. ''My dear Miss Winterton, may I interest you in a stroll about the gardens? I believe there are some early blooms in the rose garden.''

''Or perhaps you would rather stroll about the lake?'' Mr. Chartwell directed a quelling look at the marquess.

''There's a very pretty folly just the other side of the birch grove,'' offered Lord Ainsley. ''Nice prospect and all that.''

Mr. Marston merely frowned.

Sophie resisted the urge to close her eyes and invoke the gods. Instead, she favoured them all with a calm smile. ''Indeed, but why don't we all go together? The gardens, after all, are not that large; doubtless we can see the rose garden, the lake and the folly before lunch.''

They mumbled and shot frowning glances at each other but, of course, they had to agree. Satisfied she had done what she could to improve the situation, Sophie resigned herself to an hour or two's insipid conversation. At least she would get some fresh air.

As they wandered the lawns and vistas, they came upon little groups of their companions likewise employed. They nodded and smiled, calling out information on the various sights to be found, then continued with their ambles. In the distance, Sophie saw the unmistakable figure of Jack Lester, escorting Mrs. Ellis and Mrs. Doyle. Neither lady had her daughter with her, but Miss Billingham the elder had attached herself to the group. Viewing the gown of quite hideous puce stripes that that young lady had donned, along with a chip bonnet from under which she cast sly glances up at Jack Lester, Sophie gritted her teeth and looked elsewhere. To her mind, her own walking gown of pale green was far superior to Miss Billingham's attire, and she would never cast sheep's eyes at any man—particularly not Jack Lester.

Swallowing a humph, Sophie airily remarked, "The light is quite hazy, is it not?"

Her court immediately agreed, and spent the next five minutes telling her so.

Nevertheless, the brightness seemed to have gone out of her day. Not even the spectacle of her suitors vying for the right to hand her up the steps could resuscitate her earlier mood. She forced herself to smile and trade quips throughout luncheon but, as soon as the meal was over and it became clear that the guests were quite content, she escaped.

Donning a light cloak, she gathered her embroidery into a small basket and slipped out of the morning-room windows.

IN THE SMALL summer-house at the very end of the birch grove, hidden from the house by the shrubbery, Jack paced back and forth, his expression decidedly grim. He wasn't all that sure what he was doing at Little Bickmanstead. He had taken refuge in the summer-house—refuge from Miss Billingham, who seemed convinced he was just waiting to make her an offer.

Not a likely prospect this side of hell freezing over—but she did not seem capable of assimilating that fact.

It was another woman who haunted him, leaving him with a decision to make. A pressing decision. Sophie's suitors were becoming daily more determined. While it was clear she harboured no real interest in them, she had declared her requirement for funds and they each had plenty to offer. It could only be a matter of time before she accepted one of them.

With a frustrated sigh, Jack halted before one of the open arches of the summer-house and gripped the low sill; unseeing, he gazed out over the wilderness. He still wanted Sophie—regardless.

A movement caught his eye. As he watched, Sophie came into view, picking her way along the meandering path that led to the summer-house.

Slowly, Jack smiled; it seemed for the first time in days, Fate had finally remembered him, and his golden head.

Then he saw the figure moving determinedly in Sophie's wake. Jack cursed. His gaze shifted to the left, to the other path out, but the thought of leaving Sophie to deal with Marston alone occurred, only to be dismissed. Besides, Horatio had had to leave for Southampton on business immediately after lunch; it was, Jack decided, undoubtedly his duty to keep watch over his host's niece.

Glancing about, he noticed a small door in the back wall of the summer-house. Opened, it revealed a small room, dark and dim, in which were stored croquet mallets, balls and hoops. Shifting these aside, Jack found he could stand in the deep shadow thrown by the door and keep the interior of the summer-house in view. Propping one shoulder against a shelf, he settled into the dimness.

On reaching the summer-house, Sophie climbed the stairs, listlessness dogging her steps. With a soft sigh, she placed her basket on the small table in the centre of the floor. She was turning to view the scene from the arch when footsteps clattered up the steps behind her.

"Miss Winterton."

In the instant before she turned to face Phillip Marston, Sophie permitted herself an expressive grimace. Irritation of no mean order, frustration and pure chagrin all had a place in it. Then she swung about, chilly reserve in her glance. "Mr. Marston."

"I must protest, Miss Winterton. I really cannot condone your habit of slipping away unattended."

"I wasn't aware I was a sheep, nor yet a babe, sir."

Phillip Marston frowned harder. "Of course not. But you're a lady of some attraction and you would do well to bear that in mind. Particularly with the likes of Mr. Lester about."

Her accents frigid, Sophie stated, "We will, if you please, leave my aunt's other guests out of this discussion, sir."

With his usual superior expression, Mr. Marston inclined his head. "Indeed, I'm fully in agreement with you there, my dear. In fact, it was precisely the idea of leaving your aunt's other guests entirely that has prompted me to seek you out."

Sophie felt her spirits, already tending to the dismal, slump even further. She searched for some soothing comment.

Mr. Marston fell to pacing, his hands clasped behind him, his frowning gaze fixed on the floor. "As you know, I have not been at all easy in my mind over this little party. Indeed, I did not approve of your aunt's desire to bring you to town. It was quite unnecessary. You did not need to come to London to contract a suitable alliance."

Sophie cast a pleading glance heavenward. Her mind had seized up; no witty comment occurred to her.

"But I will say no more on what I fear I must term your aunt's lack of wisdom." Phillip Marston pursed his lips. "Instead, I have resolved to ask you to leave your aunt and uncle's protection and return to Leicestershire with me. We can be married there. I believe I know you too well to think you will want a large wedding. Such silly fripperies might be well enough for the *ton* but they are neither here nor there. My mother, of course, fully approves—"

"Mr. Marston!" Sophie had heard quite enough. "Sir, I do not know when I have given you cause to believe I would welcome an offer from you, but if I have, I most sincerely apologize."

Phillip Marston blinked. It took him a moment to work through Sophie's words. Then he frowned and looked more severe than ever.

"A-hem!"

Startled, both Sophie and Marston turned as first the marquess and then Mr. Chartwell climbed the steps to the summerhouse. Sophie stared. Then, resisting the urge to shake her head, she drifted to the table, leaving her three most eager suitors ranged on the other side.

"Er, we were just strolling past. Couldn't help overhearing, m'dear," Huntly explained, looking most apologetic. "But felt I had to tell you—no need to marry Marston here. Only too happy to marry you myself."

"Actually," cut in Mr. Chartwell, fixing the marquess with a stern eye. "I was hoping to have a word with you later, Miss Winterton. In private. However, such as it is, I pray you'll consider my suit, too."

Sophie thought she heard a smothered snort, but before she could decide who was responsible, Mr. Marston had claimed the floor.

"Miss Winterton, you will be much happier close to your family in Leicestershire."

"Nonsense!" Huntly exclaimed, turning to confront his rival. "No difficulty in travelling these days. Besides, why should Miss Winterton make do with some small farmhouse when she could preside over a mansion, heh?"

"Chartwell Hall is very large, Miss Winterton. Fifty main rooms. And of course I would have no qualms in giving you a free hand redecorating—there and at my London residence." Mr. Chartwell's attitude was one of ineffable superiority.

"Marston Manor," Phillip Marston declaimed, glaring at Huntly and Chartwell, "is, as Miss Winterton knows, a sizeable establishment. She shall want for nothing. My resources are considerable and my estates stretch for miles, bordering those of her uncle."

"Really?" returned the marquess. "It might interest you to know, sir, that my estates are themselves considerable, and I make bold to suggest that in light of my patrimony, Miss Winterton would do very much better to marry me. Besides, there's the title to consider. Still worth something, what?''

"Very little if rumour is to be believed," Mr. Chartwell cut in. "Indeed, I fear that if we are to settle this on the basis of monetary worth, then my own claims outshine you both.''

"Is that so?'' the marquess enquired, his attitude verging on the belligerent.

"Indeed.'' Mr. Chartwell held his ground against the combined glare of his rivals.

"Enough!" Sophie's declaration drew all three to face her. Rigid with barely suppressed fury, she raked them with a glinting, narrow-eyed gaze. "I am *disgusted* with all of you! How *dare* you presume to know my thoughts—my feelings—my requirements—and to comment on them in such a way?''

The question was unanswerable; all three men shuffled uncomfortably. Incensed, Sophie paced slowly before them, her glittering gaze holding them silent. "I have never in my life been so insulted. Do you actually believe I would marry a man who thought *I* was the sort of woman who married for *money?"* With an angry swirl, Sophie swung about, her skirts hissing. "For wealth and establishments?'' The scorn in her voice lashed at them. "I would draw your attention to my aunt, who married for love—and found happiness and success. My mother, too, married purely for love. My cousin Clarissa will unquestionably marry for love. *All* the women in my family marry for love—and I am no different!''

Sophie blinked back the tears that suddenly threatened. She was not done with her suitors yet. "I will be perfectly frank with you gentlemen, as you have been so frank with me. I do not love any of you, and I will certainly not marry any of you. There is no earthly use persisting in your pursuit of me, for I will not change my mind. I trust I make myself plain?''

She delivered her last question with a passable imitation of Lucilla at her most haughty. Head high, Sophie looked down her nose and dared them to deny her.

Typically, Phillip Marston made the attempt. As startled as

the others, he nevertheless made an effort to draw his habitual superiority about him. "You are naturally overwrought, my dear. It was unforgivable of us to subject you to such a discussion."

"Unforgivable, ungentlemanly and totally unacceptable." Sophie wasn't about to quibble. Mr. Chartwell and the marquess shuffled their feet and darted careful, placating glances at her.

Heartened, Mr. Marston grew more confident. "Be that as it may, I strongly advise you to withdraw your hasty words. You cannot have considered. It is not for such as us to marry for love; that, I believe is more rightly the province of the *hoi polloi*. I cannot think—"

"*Mr.* Marston." Sophie threw an exasperated glance at the heavens. "You have not been listening, sir. I care not what anyone thinks of my predilection for love. It may not be conventional, but it is, I should point out, most fashionable these days. And I find I am greatly addicted to fashion. You may think it unacceptable, but there it is. Now," she continued, determined to give them no further chance to remonstrate, "I fear I have had quite enough of your company for one afternoon, gentlemen. If you wish to convince me that you are, in fact, the gentlemen I have always believed you, you will withdraw and allow me some peace."

"Yes, of course, my dear."

"Pray accept our apologies, Miss Winterton."

Both the marquess and Mr. Chartwell were more than prepared to retreat. Phillip Marston was harder to rout.

"Miss Winterton," he said, his usual frown gathering, "I cannot reconcile it with my conscience to leave you thus unguarded."

"*Unguarded?*" Sophie barely restrained her temper. "Sir, you are suffering from delusions. There is no danger to me here, in my great-aunt's summer house." Sophie glanced briefly at Mr. Chartwell and the marquess, then returned her gaze, grimly determined, to her most unwanted suitor. "Furthermore, sir, having expressed a desire for your absence, I will feel perfectly justified in requesting these gentlemen to protect me—from you.''

One glance was enough to show Phillip Marston that Mr. Chartwell and the marquess would be only too pleased to take out their frustrations on him. With a glance which showed how deeply against the grain retreat went with him, he bowed curtly. "As you wish, Miss Winterton. But I will speak with you later.''

Only the fact that he was leaving allowed Sophie to suppress her scream. She was furious—with all of them. Head high, she stood by the table and watched as they clattered down the steps. They paused, exchanging potent looks of dislike, then separated, each heading towards the house by a different route.

With a satisfied humph, Sophie watched them disappear. Slowly, her uplifting fury drained. The tense muscles in her shoulders relaxed. She drew in a soft breath.

It tangled in her throat as she heard a deep voice say from directly behind her,

"You're wrong, you know.''

With a strangled shriek, Sophie whirled round. One hand at her throat, she groped with the other for the table behind her. Eyes wide, she stared up at Jack's face. "Wh—what do you mean, wrong?'' It was an effort to calm her thudding heart enough to get out the words.

"I mean,'' Jack replied, prowling about the table to cut off her retreat, "that you overlooked one particular danger in assuring Marston of your safety.'' He met Sophie's stare and smiled. "Me.''

Sophie took one long look into his glittering eyes and instinctively moved to keep the table between them. As the truth dawned, she lifted her chin. "How *dare* you eavesdrop on my conversations!''

Jack's predatory smile didn't waver. "As always, your conversation was most instructive, my dear. It did, however, leave me with one burning question.''

Sophie eyed him warily. "What?''

"Just what game are you playing, my dear?''

The sudden flare in his eyes startled Sophie anew. "Ah—you're a gentleman, Mr. Lester." It seemed the time to remind him.

"Gentleman *rake*," Jack replied. "There's a difference."

Sophie was suddenly very sure there was. Eyes wider than ever, she took a step back, then smothered a yelp as, with one hand and a single shove, Jack sent the table shooting over the floor.

Sophie's gaze followed it, until it came to a quivering halt by the wall, her basket still balanced upon it. Then she looked round—and jumped back a step when she found Jack directly in front of her. He advanced; she retreated another step. Two more steps and Sophie found the wall of the summer-house at her back. Jack's arms, palms flat against the wall, one on either side, imprisoned her. She eyed first one arm, then the other. Then, very cautiously, she looked up into his face.

His expression was intent. "Now, Sophie—"

"Ah—Jack." Any discussion was potentially dangerous; she needed time to consider just what he had heard, and what he might now think. Sophie fixed her gaze on his cravat, directly before her face. "I'm really quite overset." That was the literal truth. "I—I'm rather overwrought. As you heard, I just turned away three suitors. Three offers. Not a small thing, after all. I fear my nerves are a trifle strained by the experience."

Jack shifted, leaning closer, raising one hand to catch Sophie's chin. He tipped her face up until her wise gaze met his. "I suggest you steel yourself then, my dear. For you're about to receive a fourth."

Sophie's lips parted on a protest; it remained unuttered. Jack's lips closed over hers, sealing them, teasing the soft contours, then ruthlessly claiming them. Head whirling, Sophie clutched at his lapels. She felt him hesitate, then his head slanted over hers. Sophie shuddered as he boldly claimed her warmth, tasting her, teasing her senses with calculated expertise. Her fingers left his lapels to steal upwards, to clutch at his shoulders. He released her chin; he shifted, straightening, pulling her against him, one large hand gripping her waist. The kiss deepened again; her senses whirling, Sophie wondered how much deeper it could go. Then his hand swept slowly upward to firm about her breast, gently caressing even as he demanded her surrender.

Sophie tried to stiffen, to pull away, to refuse as she knew she should. Instead, she felt herself sink deeper into his arms, deeper into his kiss. Her breast swelled to his touch, her body ached for more.

Jack drew her hard against him, then lifted his head to breathe against her lips, "Will you marry me, Sophie?"

Sophie's heart screamed an assent but she held the words back, hanging on to her wits by her fingernails. Slowly, she opened her eyes, blinking up into the warm blue of his. She licked her lips, then blushed as his gaze followed the action. She tried to speak, but couldn't find her voice. Instead, she shook her head.

Jack's blue eyes narrowed. "No? Why not?" He gave her no chance to answer but kissed her again, just as deeply, just as imperiously.

"You said you would only marry for love," he reminded her when he again consented to lift his head. His eyes rose to hers. satisfaction flaring at her dazed expression. "You're in love with me, Sophie. And I'm in love with you. We both know it."

His head lowered again; Sophie realized she was in desperate straits. Faced with another of his kisses, and their increasingly debilitating effect on her wits, she seized the first word that crossed her mind. "Money," she gasped.

Jack stopped, his lips a mere inch from hers. Slowly, he drew back, enough to look into her eyes. He studied them for a long moment, then slowly shook his head. "Not good enough this time, Sophie. You told them—your three importunate suitors— that you would never marry for money. You said it very plainly. They had money, but not your love. I've got your love—why do I need money?"

His gaze did not leave hers. Sophie could barely think. Again, she shook her head. "I can't marry you, Jack."

"Why not?"

Sophie eyed him warily. "You wouldn't understand if I explained."

"Try me."

Pressing her lips together, Sophie just shook her head. She knew she was right; she also knew he wouldn't agree.

To her dismay, a slow, thoroughly rakish smile lit Jack's face. He sighed. "You'll tell me eventually, Sophie."

His tone was light, quite unconcerned. Sophie blinked and saw him look down. She followed his gaze—and gasped.

"*Jack!* What on earth are you doing?" Sophie batted ineffectually at his hands, busy with the buttons of her gown. Jack laughed and drew her closer, so that she couldn't reach his nimble fingers. Then the gown was open and his long fingers slipped inside. They closed about her breast; Sophie's knees shook.

"Sophie—" For an instant, Jack closed his eyes, his hand firming about her soft flesh. Then he bent his head and caught her lips with his.

For a giddy moment, a tide of delight caught Sophie up and whirled her about. Then Jack drew his lips from hers and the sensation receded, leaving a warm glow in its wake. Desperate, Sophie clung to reality. "What are you doing?" she muttered, her voice barely a whisper.

"Seducing you," came the uncompromising reply.

Sophie's eyes flew open. She felt Jack's lips on her throat, trailing fire over her suddenly heated skin. She shuddered, then glanced wildly about the room—what she could see of it beyond his shoulders. "Here?" Her mind refused to accept the notion. The room was bare of all furniture, no chaise or daybed, not even an armchair. He had to be teasing.

She felt rather than heard Jack's chuckle. "The table."

The *table?* Sophie's shocked gaze swung to the innocent wooden table, now standing by the wall. Then she looked back at Jack, into his heated gaze. "No," she said, then blushed furiously at the question in her tone.

Jack's gaze grew warmer. "It's easy," he murmured, bending his head to drop wicked little kisses behind her ear. "I'll show you."

"No." This time, Sophie got the intonation right. But her eyes closed and her fingers sank into Jack's shoulders as he continued to caress her.

"But yes, sweet Sophie," Jack whispered in her ear. "Unless you can give me a good reason why not."

Sophie knew there had to be hundreds of reasons—but she could think of only one. The one he wanted to hear. She opened her eyes and found his face. She tried to glare. His fingers shifted beneath her bodice; Sophie sucked in a breath. She didn't have the courage to call his bluff. He probably wasn't bluffing. "All right," she said and felt his fingers still. She leaned against him, seeking his strength as she sought for her words. "I told you I'm a lady of expectations, nothing more," she began.

"And I've told you that doesn't matter."

"But it does." Sophie glanced up, into the warm blue eyes so close to hers. She put all the pleading sincerity she could into her eyes, her voice. "Your dreams are mine: a home, a family, estates to look after. But they'll remain nothing but *dreams* if you don't marry well. You know that."

She saw his face still, his expression sober. Sophie clung to him and willed him to understand.

Her heart was in her eyes, there for Jack to see. He drank in the sight, then closed his eyes against the pain behind. He dropped his forehead to hers and groaned. "Sophie, you have my heartfelt apologies."

Sophie felt like sagging—with relief or was it defeat?

"I should have told you long ago." Jack pressed a soft kiss against her temple, hugging her to him.

Sophie frowned and pushed back to look up at him. "Told me what?"

Jack smiled crookedly. "That I'm horrendously wealthy—disgustingly rich."

Sophie's face crumpled; her eyes filled with tears. "Oh,

Jack,'' she finally got out around the constriction in her throat. ''Don't.'' Abruptly, she buried her face in his shoulder.

It was Jack's turn to frown and try to hold her away. ''Don't what?''

''Don't lie,'' Sophie mumbled against his coat.

Jack stiffened. Thunderstruck, he stared down at the woman in his arms. ''Sophie, I'm not lying.''

She looked up, her eyes swimming, softly blue, her lips lifting in a heart-rending smile. She raised a hand to his face. ''It's no use, Jack. We both know the truth.''

''No, we do not.'' Jack withdrew his hand from her breast and caught her hand, holding it tightly. ''Sophie, I swear I'm rich.'' When she simply smiled, mistily disbelieving, he swore. ''Very well. We'll go and ask your aunt.''

The look Sophie sent him made Jack grimace. ''All right, not Lucilla. Horatio, then. I assume you'll accept your uncle's word on my finances?''

Surprised, Sophie frowned. Horatio, she well knew, was a man of his word. Not even for love would he so much as bend the truth. And Jack was suggesting Horatio would bear out his claims. ''But my uncle's just left. We don't know when he'll return.''

Jack swore some more, distinctly colourfully. He considered his options, but the only others who knew of his recent windfall were relatives, friends or employees, none of whom Sophie would believe. ''Very well.'' Grimly, he surveyed Sophie's doubting expression. ''We'll wait until he returns.''

Her mind reeling, Sophie nodded, struggling to see her way forward. She glanced down, and blushed rosily. Tugging her fingers from Jack's clasp, she drew back enough to do up the buttons of her gown. Whatever the truth, she would have to keep Jack at arm's length until Horatio returned—or it wouldn't matter what her uncle said.

''Sophie?'' Jack sensed her withdrawal. He had half a mind to draw her back to him, back into his arms where she belonged.

From under her lashes, Sophie glanced up at him almost

guiltily. "Ah, yes." She tried to step back but Jack's arm was firm about her waist. "Now, Jack," she protested, as she felt his arm tighten. She braced her hands against his chest. "We've agreed, have we not?" The light in his eyes left her breathless. "We'll wait until my uncle returns."

Jack's blue eyes narrowed. "Sophie…" His gaze met hers, full of breathless anticipation, yet, for all that, quite determined. Jack heaved a disgusted sigh. "Very well," he bit out. "But *only* until your uncle returns—agreed?"

Sophie hesitated, then nodded.

"And you'll marry me three weeks after that."

It was not a question; Sophie only just stopped her nod.

"And furthermore," Jack continued, his blue gaze holding hers, "if I'm to toe the line until your uncle gets back, then so shall you."

"Me?"

"No more flirting with your suitors—other than me."

"I do not flirt." With an offended air, Sophie drew back.

"And no more waltzing with anyone but me."

"That's outrageous!" Sophie disengaged from Jack's arms. "You don't know what you're asking."

"I know only too well," Jack growled, letting her go. "Fair's fair, Sophie. No more going to supper with any gentleman but me—and certainly no driving or going apart with anyone else."

Smoothing down her skirts, Sophie humphed.

Jack caught her chin on his hand and tipped her head up until her eyes met his. "Are we agreed, Sophie?"

Sophie could feel her pulse racing. Her eyes met his, intensely blue, and she felt like she was drowning. His face, all hard angles and planes, was very near, his lips, hard and finely chiselled, but inches away. "Yes," she whispered and breathed again when he released her.

With his customary grace, Jack offered her his arm.

Drawing her dignity about her, Sophie picked up her basket and placed her hand on his sleeve. She allowed him to lead her down the steps and back towards the house, all the way struggling to cope with the sensation of being balanced on a knife-edge. Determined to give the reprobate by her side no inkling of her difficulty, she kept her gaze on the scenery and her head very high.

Jack viewed the sight through narrowed eyes. Then he smiled, slowly, and started to plan.

CHAPTER THIRTEEN

THE PARTY broke up the next morning. By then, everyone was aware that something had changed, that Jack stood, in some unspecified way, as Sophie's protector. Despite her disapproval of his tactics, Sophie could not help feeling grateful, especially when he helped shoulder the responsibility for their return to the capital. Even with Lucilla all but fully recovered, with her uncle absent, she had not been looking forward to travelling with all her cousins, Toby the only adult male in sight.

But by mid-morning, when she emerged from the door of her great-aunt's home, all was under control. Her younger cousins were to ride as before, much to their delight. With Jack, Toby and Ned to keep them in line, Sophie had no residual qualms. The carriage stood waiting, Clarissa already aboard. Her arms full of rugs and cushions, Sophie glanced back.

Lucilla came slowly through the hall, leaning heavily on Jack's arm. Although still wan, her aunt showed no signs of faintness. Sophie turned and hurried down the steps to prepare Lucilla's seat in the carriage.

At the top of the steps, Lucilla paused to breathe in the crisp morning air. Blue skies had returned; fluffy white clouds held no lingering menace. With a small, highly satisfied smile, she glanced at Jack beside her. "I'm very glad you did not disappoint me, Mr. Lester."

Recalled from his study of Sophie's curvaceous rear, neatly outlined as she stood on the carriage step and leaned in, Jack looked down at Lucilla, one brow slowly rising. "That was never my intention, ma'am."

Lucilla's smile broadened. "I'm so glad," she said, patting his arm. "Now, if you'll give me your arm...?"

Jack got his revenge by lifting her easily and carrying her down the steps. As he settled her amid Sophie's cushions and rugs, Lucilla favoured him with a dignified glare. Then her lips twitched and she lay back on the seat, waving him away.

His own lips curving, Jack handed Sophie up, resisting the temptation to bestow a fond pat on her retreating anatomy. And then they were away.

FIVE NIGHTS LATER, under the glare of the chandeliers in the Duchess of Richmond's ballroom, Sophie dimly wondered why she had imagined awaiting her uncle's return in the bosom of the *ton* would be safer than at Little Bickmanstead. Mere hours had sufficed for Jack to make it patently clear that he had meant every word he had uttered in Great-Aunt Evangeline's summer-house. Twenty-four hours had been enough for her to realize that, that being so, the possibility of ever denying him receded even further with every successive day.

Casting a glance up at him as he stood, planted immovably by her side, starkly handsome in severe black and white, Sophie stifled a sudden tremor.

Jack caught her glance. He bent his head to hers. "There's another waltz coming up."

Sophie shot him a warning glance. "I've already danced one waltz with you."

His rakish grin surfaced. "You're allowed two dances with any gentleman."

"But not two waltzes, if I'm wise."

"Don't be wise, my Sophie." His eyes gently teased "Come dance with me. I promise you no one will remark unduly."

Resistance, of course, was useless. Sophie allowed him to lead her to the floor, knowing any show of reluctance would be pure hypocrisy. She loved being held in his arms; at the moment, waltzing was the only safe way to indulge her senses.

As they circled the floor, she noted the looks of resignation many of her mother's old friends turned upon them. In contrast, Lady Drummond-Burrell, that most haughty of Almack's patronesses, smiled with chilly approval.

"Amazing," Jack said, indicating her ladyship with an inclination of his head. "Nothing pleases them more than the sight of a fallen rake."

Sophie tried to frown but failed. "Nonsense," she said.

"No, it's not. They'll all approve once the news gets out."

Sophie did frown then. Jack had told her how the change in his fortune had come about. "Why hasn't it got out by now? Presuming it's real, of course."

The arm about her tightened, squeezing in warning. "It's real," Jack replied. "But I confess I purposely neglected to mention it to anyone."

"Why?"

"You've met the elder Miss Billingham; just imagine her sort, multiplied by at least a hundred, all with yours truly in their sights."

Sophie giggled. "Surely you weren't afraid?"

"Afraid?" Jack raised an arrogant brow. "Naturally not. I merely have an innate dislike of tripping over debs at every turn."

Sophie laughed, the delicious sound teasing Jack's senses, tightening the tension inside him until it was well-nigh unbearable. He metaphorically gritted his teeth. The wait, he promised himself, would be worth it.

At the end of the dance, he escorted Sophie back to her aunt and took up his position—by her side.

Sophie knew better than to argue. Lord Ruthven stopped by, then Lord Selbourne joined them. With practised ease, Sophie laughed and chatted. While there were many gentlemen who still sought her company, her suitors, not only the three she had already dismissed but all the others who had viewed her with matrimony in mind, rarely hove in sight. Jack's presence, large and dark by her shoulder, was more than enough to make them think twice. Their rides in the Park every morning continued, but with Jack by her side, she found herself blissfully free of encumbrances. It was impossible to misinterpret his interest; as he was so tall, whenever he spoke with her, he bent his head to hers, and she, motivated by her instincts, naturally turned into his strength, reinforcing the image that they were one, wanting only the official announcement. Horatio's absence explained their present hiatus; none doubted the announcement would eventually come, as her mother's old friends' attitudes clearly showed.

She was his, and every passing day made her more aware of that truth. And that much more nervous of her uncle's return. She still doubted Jack's story; she had seen the passion in him and knew his love to be strong enough to motivate the most enormous lie. Regardless of what he said, it was possible. Only Horatio could lay her doubts to rest—and none knew when he would return.

With an inward sigh, Sophie mentally girded her loins. She glanced across at Clarissa, holding court on the other side of her aunt's chaise. Her cousin looked radiant, charming her many youthful swains yet, as Sophie had noticed, careful to give none any particular encouragement. Beside her, Ned occupied a position that had much in common with Jack's. Sophie's lips twitched; she returned her gaze to Lord Selbourne. There was a light in Ned's eyes that she did not think Clarissa had yet noticed.

Ned, in fact, was almost as impatient as Jack. But both his and Clarissa's parents had agreed that no formal offer should be considered until after Clarissa's Season. Which meant he had a far longer wait ahead of him; and, to his mind, far less assurance of gaining the prize at the end.

Which left him feeling distinctly uneasy. His silver princess still smiled on her court; he had even heard her laugh with that bounder Gurnard.

"This wooing business seems to drag on forever," he later grumbled to Jack as they both kept watch over their ladies, presently gracing the floor in other men's arms.

Jack shot him a sympathetic glance. "As you say." After a

moment, he continued, "Has Clarissa let slip any information as to when they might retire to Leicestershire?"

"No," Ned replied. He cast a puzzled glance at Jack. "But I thought they were staying until the end of the Season. That's more than a month away, isn't it?"

Jack nodded. "Just a thought." As Sophie whirled past in Ruthven's arms, Jack's easy expression hardened. "As you say, this business of wooing is an ordeal to be endured."

While Jack, Ned and the ladies of his family were thus engaged, Toby had embarked on amusement of a different kind. At that moment, he was strolling along the pavement of Pall Mall, along the stretch which housed the most notorious gaming hells in town, in company with Captain Terrence Gurnard.

The captain stopped outside a plain brown door. "This is the place. A snug little hell—very exclusive."

Toby smiled amiably and waited while the captain knocked. After a low-voiced conversation with the guardian of the portal, conducted through a grille in the door, they were admitted and shown into a sizeable room, dimly lit except for the shaded lamps which shed their glow onto the tables. There were perhaps twenty gentlemen present; few raised their heads as Toby followed Gurnard across the room.

With his usual air of interested enquiry, Toby glanced about him, taking in the expressions of grim determination with which many of the gentlemen applied themselves to their cards and dice. There was a large table devoted to Hazard, another to Faro. Smaller tables attested to the hell's reputation for variety; there were even two older gentlemen engaged in a hand of Piquet.

This was the third night Toby had spent with Gurnard, and the third hell they had visited. He was, as usual, following one of his father's maxims, that which declared that experience was the best teacher. After tonight, Toby felt, he would have learned all he needed of gaming hells. His real interest tonight lay in the play. Gurnard had allowed him to win for the past two nights; Toby had begun to suspect the captain's motives.

Initially, Gurnard had brushed against him with apparently

no particular intent; they had subsequently struck up an acquaintance. It was after their sojourn at Little Bickmanstead that the captain had sought him out and, being apparently at a loose end, had offered to show him the sights. Toby had accepted the offer readily; he had not previously spent much time in the capital.

Now, however, he wondered whether the captain had taken him for a flat.

By the end of the evening, which Toby promptly declared once his losses had, almost mysteriously, overtaken his current allowance, he was quite sure the captain had done just that. Comforting himself with the reflection that, as his father was wont to say, there was no harm in making mistakes just as long as one didn't make the same mistake twice, he frowned slightly as he looked across at Gurnard. "I'm afraid I won't be able to meet that last vowel until the pater returns to town—but he should be back any day."

He hadn't expected to outrun his ready funds. However, as his father had settled a considerable sum on him two years before, and managed it for him under his direction the better to teach him the ways of finance, Toby had no real qualms about asking Horatio for an advance. "I'll speak to him as soon as he returns."

Gurnard sat back, his face flushed with success and the wine he had steadily consumed. "Oh, you don't want to do that." He held up his hand in a fencer's gesture. "Never let it be said that I caused father and son to fall out over the simple matter of a few crowns."

Toby could have set him straight—he fully expected his father to have a good laugh over his adventure—but some sixth sense made him hold back. "Oh?" he said guilelessly. There were rather more than "a few crowns" involved.

Gurnard frowned, his face a mask of concentration. "Perhaps there's some way you can repay the debt without having to apply to your pater?"

"Such as?" Toby asked, a chill stealing down his back.

Gurnard looked ingenuous. He frowned into space. Then his

face cleared. "Well, I know I'd count it a blessing to have a few minutes alone with your sister."

He leant across the table and, with just the slightest hesitation, conspiratorially lowered his voice. "Your sister mentioned that your party are planning to attend the gala at Vauxhall. Perhaps, in repayment of your debt, you could arrange for me to meet with her in the Temple of Diana—just while the fireworks are on. I'll return her to you when the show's over, and no one will be any the wiser."

Not only a flat—a foolish flat. Toby hid his reaction behind a vacant expression. The poor light concealed the steely glint in his eyes. "But how will I get Clarissa to agree?"

"Just tell her you're taking her to meet her most ardent admirer. Don't tell her my name—I want to surprise her. Women like the romantic touch." Gurnard smiled and waved a languid hand. "Dare say you haven't noticed, but your sister and I are deeply in love. You needn't fear I'll take advantage. But with all the attention that's focused on her we've found it hard to find the time to talk, to get to know each other as we'd like."

Concluding that the captain was the sort of gentleman he should hand over to higher authorities, Toby slowly nodded. "All right," he agreed, his tone bland. He shrugged. "If you'll be happy with that instead of the money...?"

"Definitely," Gurnard replied, his eyes suddenly gleaming. "Ten minutes alone with your sister will be ample recompense."

"TOBY, is anything wrong?"

Bringing up the rear as his exuberant siblings tumbled back into the house after their morning ride, Toby jumped and cast a startled glance at Sophie. Seeing the conjecture in her cousin's open face, she nodded.

"I thought so." With a glance at the horde disappearing up the stairs, Clarissa trailing absent-mindedly behind, she linked her arm with Toby's. "Come into your father's study and tell me all."

"It's nothing really dreadful," Toby hurried to assure her as they crossed the threshold of his father's sanctum.

"Then there's probably no reason for you to be so worried about it," Sophie returned. Sinking into one of the armchairs by the hearth, she fixed Toby with a commanding if affectionate eye. "Open your budget, my dear, for I really can't let this go on. Doubtless I'm imagining all sorts of unlikely horrors; I'm sure you can set my mind at rest."

Toby grimaced at her, too used to Lucilla to take offence. He fell to pacing before the hearth, his hands clasped behind his back. "It's that bounder Gurnard."

"Bounder?" Sophie looked her surprise. "I know Ned's been calling him that for ages, but I thought that was just Ned."

"So did I—but now I know better. Dashed if Ned wasn't right."

Sophie looked pensive, then cast a glance up at Toby. "I've just remembered. Your mother said she didn't trust the man, and Clarissa agreed."

"Did she?" Toby brightened. "Well, that makes it easier, then."

"Makes what easier?" Sophie stared at Toby, consternation in her eyes. "Tobias Webb, just what is going on?"

"No need to get into a flap. At least, not yet."

When Toby said no more but continued to pace the hearthrug, Sophie straightened her shoulders. "Toby, if you don't tell me what this is all about immediately, I'll feel honour bound to speak to your mother."

Toby halted, his expression horrified. "Saints preserve us all," he said. And proceeded to tell Sophie the story.

"That's *iniquitous!*" Sophie was incensed. "The man's worse than a mere bounder."

"Undoubtedly. He's a dangerous bounder. That's why I want to wait until Papa gets back to lay this before him. I think it would be best for all concerned if Gurnard is stopped once and for all."

"Unquestionably," Sophie agreed. After a moment, she added, "I don't think it would serve any purpose to tell Clarissa. She doesn't like the man as it is; I can't see her doing anything rash."

Toby nodded.

"And I really don't think telling your mama would be a good idea."

"Definitely not." Toby shuddered at the thought.

"I suppose," Sophie suggested. "We could seek professional assistance."

"The Runners? And risk a brouhaha like they made over Lady Ashbourne's emeralds?" Toby shook his head. "That's not a decision I'd like to make."

"Quite," Sophie agreed. "Still, at least we know Gurnard's unlikely to make a move before the gala."

"Precisely." Toby's blue gaze rested consideringly on Sophie. "All we really need do is hold the fort until then."

An hour later, Jack sat in his chair in his parlour in Upper Brook Street, the table before him spread for an early luncheon, and attacked the slices of sirloin on his plate with an air of disgruntled gloom. "Permit me to warn you, brother mine, that this wooing business is definitely plaguesome."

Harry, who had looked in on his way down to the country, raised an amused brow. "You've only just discovered that?"

"I cannot recall having wooed a lady—nor any other kind of female—before." Jack scowled at a dish of roast potatoes, then viciously skewered one.

"I take it all is not proceeding smoothly?"

For a full minute, Jack wrestled with a conscience that decreed that all matters between a lady and a gentleman were sacrosant, then yielded to temptation. "The damned woman's being noble," he growled. "She's convinced herself that I really need to marry an heiress and is determined not to ruin my life by allowing me to marry her."

Harry choked on his ale. Jack rose to come around the table and thump his back but Harry waved him away. "Well," he said, still breathless, "that was the impression you wanted to give, remember."

"That was then, this is now," Jack answered with unshakeable logic. "Besides, I don't care what the *ton* thinks. My only concern is what goes on in one particular golden head."

"So tell her."

"I've already told her I'm as rich as Croesus, but the witless woman doesn't believe me."

"Doesn't believe you?" Harry stated. "But why would you lie about something like that?"

Jack's expression was disgusted. "Well might you ask. As far as I can make out, she thinks I'm the sort of romantic who would marry a 'lady of expectations'—her words—and then valiantly conceal the fact we were living on tick."

Harry grinned. He reached for the ale jug. "And if things had been different? If we hadn't been favoured by fortune and you'd met her—what then? Would you have politely nodded and moved on, looking for an heiress, or would you do as she suspects and conceal the reckoning?"

Jack shot him a malevolent glance. "The subject doesn't arise, thank God."

When Harry's grin broadened into a smile, Jack scowled. "Instead of considering hypothetical situations, why don't you turn that fertile brain of yours to some purpose and think of a way to convince her of our wealth?"

"Try a little harder," Harry offered. "Be your persuasive best."

Jack grimaced. "Can't be done that way; believe me, I've tried." He had, too—twice. But each time he resurrected the subject, Sophie turned huge eyes full of silent reproach upon him. Combined with a brittlely fragile air, such defences were more than enough to defeat him.

"I need someone to vouch for me, someone she'll believe. Which means I have to wait until her uncle returns to town. He's off looking over the Indies Corporation's next venture at Southampton. The damnable situation is that no one has any idea of when he'll be back."

Viewing his brother's exasperated expression, evoked, so it seemed, by the prospect of having to wait a few days to make a certain lady his, Harry raised a laconic brow. Everything he had heard thus far suggested that Jack was poised to take the final momentous step into parson's mousetrap and, amazing though it seemed, he would have a smile on his face when he did so. Love, as Harry well knew, was a force powerful enough to twist men's minds in the most unexpected ways. He just hoped it wasn't contagious.

The sound of the knocker on the door being plied with determined force disrupted their peace.

Jack looked up.

Voices sounded in the hall, then the door opened and Toby entered. He glanced at Jack, then, noticing Harry, nodded politely. As the door shut behind him, Toby turned to Jack. "I apologize for the intrusion, but something's come up and I'd like your opinion on the matter. But if you're busy I can come back later."

"No matter." Harry made to rise. "I can leave if you'd rather speak privately."

Jack raised a brow at Toby. "Can you speak before Harry?"

Toby hesitated for only an instant. Jack had spent all the Season at Sophie's feet, concentrating on nothing beyond Sophie and her court. Harry Lester, on the other hand, was by reputation as much of a hellion as Jack had been and had not shared his brother's affliction. Toby's gaze swung to Harry. "The matter concerns a Captain Gurnard."

Harry's eyes narrowed. "Captain Terrence Gurnard?" The words sounded peculiarly flat and distinctly lethal. When Toby nodded, Harry settled back into his seat. "What, exactly, is that bounder up to?"

Jack waved Toby to a seat. "Have you eaten?" When Toby shook his head, his eyes going to the half-filled platters still on the table, Jack rang for Pinkerton. "You can eat while you fill us in. I take it the problem's not urgent?"

"Not that urgent, no."

While he fortified himself, Toby recounted his outings with Gurnard and the ultimate offer to discount his losses against an arranged clandestine meeting with Clarissa.

"So you won for the first two nights but lost heavily on the third?"

Toby nodded at Harry. "He was setting me up, wasn't he?"

"It certainly sounds like it."

Jack glanced at his brother. "I've not heard much of Gurnard—what's the story?"

"That, I suspect, is a matter that's exercising the minds of quite a few of the man's creditors." Harry took a long sip of his ale. "There are disquieting rumours doing the rounds about the dear captain. Word has it he's virtually rolled up. Fell in with Duggan and crew. A bad lot," Harry added in an aside to Toby. "But the last I heard, he'd been unwise enough to sit down with Melcham."

"Melcham?" Jack tapped a fingernail against his ale mug. "So Gurnard's very likely up to his eyebrows in debt."

Harry nodded. "Very possibly over his head. And if Melcham holds his vowels, as seems very likely, his future doesn't look promising."

"Who's Melcham?" Toby asked.

"Melcham," Jack said, "is quite a character. His father was a gamester—ran through the family fortune, quite a considerable one as it happened, then died, leaving his son nothing but debts. The present earl, however, is cut from a different cloth than that used to fashion his sire. He set out to regain his fortune by winning it back from those who had won it from his father. Them and their kind, which is to say the sharps who prey on the susceptible. And he wins. Virtually always."

"The sharps can't resist the challenge," Harry added. "They line up to be fleeced, knowing Melcham's now worth a not-so-small fortune. The catch is that he's also won a lot of powerful friends—and paying one's debts is mandatory."

"In other words," Jack summed up, straightening in his chair, "Gurnard is in a lot of trouble. And once the news gets out, he'll no longer be the sort of escort wise mamas view with equanimity."

"But not yet," Harry said. "The news hasn't hit the clubs.

That was privileged information, courtesy of some friends in the Guards.''

Jack nodded. ''All right. So Gurnard has decided that the most sensible way to get himself out of the hole he has nearly buried himself in is to marry an heiress—a very wealthy heiress.''

''Clarissa?'' asked Toby.

''So it appears.'' Jack's expression was as grim as Harry's. ''And time is not on his side. He'll have to secure his heiress before his pressing concerns become public knowledge.'' Jack turned to Toby. ''Exactly how did he want this meeting arranged?''

Toby had started to repeat the directions Gurnard had been at pains to impress upon him when the door opened and Ned walked in. Toby broke off in midsentence. Ned's amiable smile faded as he took in Toby's expression and Harry's grim face. He looked at Jack.

Jack smiled, a predatory glint in his eye. ''What did Jackson say today?''

Drawing a chair up to the table, Ned dropped into it. ''I have to work on my right hook. The left jab's coming along well enough.'' Ever since Jack had introduced him to Gentleman Jackson's Boxing Saloon, Ned had been taking lessons, having uncovered a real aptitude for the sport. His eyes slid around the table once more.

''Excellent.'' Jack's gaze was distant, as if viewing some invisible vista. Then he abruptly refocused on Ned. ''Strangely, I believe we may have found a use for your newly discovered talents.''

''Oh?'' Jack's smile was making Ned uneasy.

The smile grew broader. ''You want to consolidate your position in Clarissa's affections, don't you?''

''Yes,'' Ned admitted, somewhat cautiously.

''Well, I'm pleased to announce that a situation has arisen which calls for a knight-errant to rescue a fair damsel from the unwanted attentions of a dastardly knave. And as the fair damsel is Clarissa, I suspect you had better polish up your armour.''

"What!"

It took another ten minutes to explain all to Ned's satisfaction and by then Jack had been sidetracked. "You told all this to Sophie?" he asked, fixing Toby with a disbelieving stare.

Toby looked guilty. "I couldn't avoid it—she threatened to speak to Mama."

Jack looked disgusted. "Meddlesome female," he growled, and he didn't mean Lucilla.

"I pointed out that we needn't worry until the gala. If Papa returns before that, there'll be no reason for Sophie to worry at all."

Jack nodded. "Well, don't tell her anything more. We can take care of it—and the fewer complications the better."

Toby nodded, entirely in agreement.

"But how, exactly, are we to take care of it?" Ned's expression was grimly determined.

Succinctly, assisted by helpful suggestions from his inventive brother, Jack laid their campaign before them.

By the time he'd finished, even Ned was smiling.

"ARGH!" Jack stretched his arms above his head, then relaxed into his chair. "At last I think I see the light."

Harry grinned. "Think Ned can pull it off?"

The brothers were once more alone, Ned and Toby having taken themselves off with some vague intention of keeping a watchful eye on Clarissa during her afternoon's promenade in the Park.

"Think?" Jack replied. "I know it! This performance should land Clarissa firmly in his arms, relieving Sophie of further anxiety on the point and myself of the charge of overseeing that youthful romance once and for all."

"Has it been such a burden?" Harry drained his tankard.

"Not a burden, precisely. But it hurts to watch one of us succumb so young."

Harry chuckled. "Well, at least neither of us fell young, and I don't think you need worry about Gerald."

"Thank God. At least I have the excuse of being the head of the family—it's expected, after all."

"Rationalize it any way you want, brother mine; I know the truth."

Jack's blue eyes met Harry's green ones across the width of the table. Their gazes locked, then Jack sighed. "Well, at least with Ned safely settled, I'll be able to give my full attention to a certain golden head. And with Horatio Webb's help, I'll conquer her stubbornness."

"Let me be the first to wish you happy."

Jack glanced at Harry and realized his brother was serious. He smiled. "Why thank you, brother mine."

"And I'll give you a warning, too."

"Oh?"

"The news is out."

Jack grimaced. "Are you sure?"

"Put it this way." Harry set his tankard down. "I was at Lady Bromford's affair last night, and lo and behold, Lady Argyle made a play for me. Not a blush in sight, what's more. She had her daughter in tow, a chit just out of the schoolroom." Harry wrinkled his nose. "Her ladyship was as clinging as Medusa. Totally unaccountable, *unless* she'd heard rather more than a whisper of our affairs."

"And if she's heard, others will, too." Jack grimaced even more.

"Which means it won't be long before we're the toast of the tea parties. If I were you, I'd secure your golden head with all speed. An announcement in the *Gazette* should just be enough to buy your escape. As for myself, I've decided to run for cover."

Jack grinned. "I did wonder over your sudden penchant for the lush green fields."

"In the circumstances, Newmarket looks considerably safer than London." Harry's grin was crooked as he rose. "Given the danger, I feel confident I'll find enough in the country to keep me amused for the rest of the Season."

Jack shook his head. "You won't be able to run forever, you know."

Harry raised an arrogant brow. "Love," he declared, "is not about to catch me." With a last, long look, he turned to the door. His hand on the knob, he paused to look back, his grin distinctly wry. "Good luck. Just don't get so distracted by the excitement at the gala that you forget to keep your back covered. Until your golden head says yes, you're no safer than I."

Jack had raised his hand in farewell; now he groaned. "God help me! Just when I thought I was home and hosed."

HARRY'S DIRE PREDICTION was confirmed that evening at Lady Summerville's ball. Jack bowed gracefully over her ladyship's hand, disturbingly aware of the relish in her gimlet gaze. Luckily her duties prohibited her from pursuing him immediately, but her promise to look him up later left little doubt that his news was out. Fully alert, Jack artfully avoided two ostriched-plumed matrons, as imposing as battleships, waiting to ambush him just yards from the ballroom steps. He was congratulating himself on his escape when he walked straight into Lady Middleton's clutches.

"My dear Mr. Lester! I declare, Middleton and I have not seen much of you this year."

Biting back the retort that, if he had had his eyes about him, her ladyship would have seen even less of him, Jack bowed resignedly. On straightening, he was subjected to the scrutiny of her ladyship's protuberant eyes, grotesquely magnified by lorgnettes deployed like gunsights. "Indeed, ma'am, I fear I have been greatly occupied thus far this Season."

"Well! I hope you're not going to be too *occupied* to attend my niece's coming-out ball. She's a sweet thing and will make some gentleman an unexceptionable wife. Your Aunt Harriet was particularly fond of her, y'know." This last was accompanied by a pointed glance. Jack looked politely impressed. Her ladyship nodded, apparently satisfied. "Middleton and I will expect you."

With a snap, she shut her lorgnettes and used them to tap him on the sleeve.

Choosing to interpret this as a dismissal, Jack bowed and slid into the crowd. It was, indeed, as Harry had foreseen; despite his efforts to make his intentions crystal clear, he was not yet safe. Doubtless, nothing less than the announcement of his betrothal would convince the matchmaking mamas that he had passed beyond their reach. Yet another good reason to add to the increasingly impressive tally indicating that the speedy curtailment of Miss Sophia Winterton's Season was a highly desirable goal.

Looking about him, he spotted his quarry, elegant as ever in a gown of pale green figured silk, her curls glowing warmly in the candlelight. His height was both advantage and disadvantage, allowing him to scan the crowds but making him far too conspicuous a target. By dint of some rapid tacking by way of evasive action, he gained Sophie's side without further difficulty.

As always, his appearance coincided with a thinning of the ranks about her. Sophie no longer noticed. She gave him her hand and a warmly welcoming smile. "Good evening, Mr. Lester."

"Actually," Jack said, straightening and scanning their surroundings. "It probably isn't."

"I beg your pardon?" Sophie stared at him.

"As an evening, I've probably faced better," Jack replied, tucking her hand into his arm. "Ruthven, Hollingsworth—I'm sure you'll excuse us." With a nod for those two gentlemen, Jack led Sophie into the crowd.

Hearing Lord Ruthven chuckle, Sophie glanced back to see his lordship explaining something to a puzzled Mr. Hollingsworth. "What is it?" she asked, looking up at Jack.

"I've been pegged up for target practice."

"Whatever do you…" Sophie's words trailed away as she noticed the simpering glances thrown Jack's way—mostly by debutantes who, two days ago, would certainly not have dared.

She shot a suspicious glance at Jack. "You've put the story of your fortune about?"

Under his breath, Jack growled. "No, Sophie. I have not *put* the news about. It *got* out—doubtless from the other investors involved in the Indies Corporation." He cast an exasperated glance down at her. His temper was not improved by the wary frown he saw in her eyes. "Devil take it, woman!" he growled. "No rake in his right mind, having declared his intention to wed, would then call the dragons down on his head by *inventing* a fortune."

Sophie swallowed her giggle. "I hadn't thought of it in quite that way."

"Well, do," Jack advised. "It's the truth—and you're not going to escape it. And speaking of escape, I do hope you realize that, until your uncle returns and our betrothal can be announced, I expect you to assist my cause."

"In what way?" Sophie asked.

"By lending me your protection."

Sophie laughed, but the smile was soon wiped from her face. A succession of cloying encounters set her teeth on edge; some of the warm hints directed at Jack left her positively nauseous. Somehow, he managed to keep a polite expression on his face and, by dint of his quick wits and ever-ready tongue, extricated himself from the ladies' clutches. She admired his address, and was more than ready to acquiesce to his unvoiced plea. She remained fixed by his side, anchored by his hand on his sleeve, and defied all attempts to remove her. That she managed to do so while restraining her comments to the realms of the acceptable was, she felt, no reflection on the provocation provided. Indeed, on more than one occasion she found herself blushing for her sex. Miss Billingham proved the last straw.

"My mama was quite bowled over to hear of your windfall, sir," she declared, batting her sparse lashes and simpering. "In light of our time spent together at Mrs. Webb's house party, she has charged me to ask you to call. Indeed," she went on, dropping her coy smile long enough to shoot a venomous glance at Sophie, "Mama is very keen to speak to you immediately." Greatly daring, Miss Billingham placed her hands about Jack's arm and smiled acidly at Sophie. "If you'll excuse us, Miss Winterton?"

Sophie stiffened, then smiled sweetly back. "I greatly fear, Miss Billingham," she said, before Jack would speak, "that I cannot release Mr. Lester. There's a waltz starting up." With calculated charm, Sophie smiled dazzlingly up at Jack. "Our waltz, I believe, Jack."

Jack's slow smile was triumphant. "Our waltz, dear Sophie."

They left Miss Billingham, open-mouthed, staring after them.

Sophie was seething as they took to the floor. "How *dare* she? How can they? They're all quite shameless. I thought it was only rakes who were so."

Jack chuckled and drew her closer. "Hush, my sweet Sophie." When she glared in reply, her full breasts swelling with indignation, he brushed a most reprehensible kiss across her curls. "It doesn't matter. You're mine—and I'm yours. When your uncle returns, we can tell the world."

Sophie took comfort in the warmth of his gaze, and in the delight she saw behind it. Did he really find it so surprising that she would fly to his aid?

Whatever the case, she thought, as she felt the waltz, and him, weave their accustomed magic, Horatio had better return soon. In such difficult circumstances, there was no telling what scandalous declaration she might feel obliged to make.

CHAPTER FOURTEEN

GALA NIGHT at Vauxhall was a treat few among the *ton* cared to miss. With their party, swollen by the presence of Jeremy and Gerald, who had been included by special dispensation, Sophie strolled beside Jack down the Grand Walk. She saw many familiar faces, all bright with expectation of the night's revelries. None were as bright as hers.

She glanced up at Jack and smiled, feeling her brittle tension tighten. Horatio was due back tonight; her uncle had sent word that despite the business that had delayed him, he would return this evening to join them at the Gardens. Jack smiled back, his hand warm over hers where it rested on his sleeve. He said nothing, but the expression in his eyes left her in no doubt of his thoughts.

Determined at least to appear calm, Sophie gave her attention to their surroundings, duly exclaiming at the brightly lit colonnade, which had been added since her last visit. Jeremy and George, and, to a lesser extent, Toby, Ned and Clarissa, looked about with avid interest, speculating on the age of the elms lining the gravelled promenade and eyeing the dense shrubbery separating the walks.

"I think the booth your uncle has rented is this way."

Jack steered her to the right of the section of promenade known as the Grove. Toby followed with Lucilla on his arm, Ned and Clarissa behind with the two boys bringing up the rear. In the centre of the Grove, a small orchestra was setting up. Arranged about the perimeter were a large number of wooden booths, many already filled with patrons come to enjoy the night's entertainments.

Their booth proved to have an excellent view of the orchestra.

"Ah, yes." Lucilla settled herself on a chair by the wide front window. "A most satisfactory location. From here, one can see almost everything."

Sophie noticed her aunt's gaze was not on the musicians. Indeed, it seemed as if all of fashionable London were a part of the passing scene. Gentlemen and ladies of all degrees strolled upon the paths; many stopped to exchange pleasantries with her aunt before moving on. Then there were the bucks and their ladybirds, the bright lights of the *demi-monde*. Sophie found herself fascinated by one particular redhead—or rather her gown, a wispy concoction of silk and feathers that barely concealed her charms. Until she noticed the interest the lady evinced in return, and realized it was not for her. A frown threatening, Sophie glanced at her companion—the focus of the red-head's attention—only to find he was watching her. A slow smile lifted his lips; one dark brow rose.

Sophie blushed vividly, and pointedly transferred her gaze to the orchestra. As if sensing her need, they promptly laid bow to string, filling the night with their magic. Soon, a bevy of couples was whirling in the light of the Chinese lanterns, suspended high overhead.

Jack rose. "Come," he said, holding out his hand, a smile and an invitation in his eyes. "No one counts the dances at Vauxhall."

For an instant, Sophie met his gaze. Then, with a calm decisiveness that surprised even her, she lifted her chin and put her hand in his. "How accommodating."

Her uncle had better arrive soon; she couldn't bear to wait much longer.

Luckily, Jack proved most efficient at distracting her, until her mind was filled with nothing beyond thoughts of him, of his teasing smile and the beckoning warmth behind his blue eyes. He danced with her twice, then relinquished her to Ned, who in turn passed her to Toby before Jack once more drew her into his arms.

Sophie laughed. "I find myself quite breathless, sir."

Jack smiled down at her, a slow crooked smile. "Jack," he said.

Sophie looked into his eyes; her breath vanished altogether. "Jack," she whispered, letting her lashes fall.

Jack's arm tightened about her; he swept her into the waltz.

Supper was provided in the booth, laid out on a narrow trestle table at the rear, along with a jug of lemonade and another of the famous Vauxhall punch. When they lifted the linen cloths from the dishes, they found delicate cucumber sandwiches, a selection of pastries and a large platter of the fabled wafer-thin ham.

"Exactly as I recall," Lucilla declared, holding up one near-transparent slice. She looked at Sophie. "When your mother and I were debs, we were always famished after a night at Vauxhall." Nibbling the ham, she added, "I told Cook to lay out a cold collation for when we get back."

Jack, Ned and Toby looked relieved.

Somewhere in the gardens, a gong clanged. The music had stopped some minutes before and the heavy note vibrated through the twilight.

"Time to view the Grand Spectacle!"

Jeremy's shout was echoed from all around. There was a surge of bodies as people left their booths to join the throng flocking to where a looming mountain, now brilliantly lit, rose craggily from amidst the otherwise unremarkable landscape. Fifteen minutes were spent in oohing and aahing at the various elements, some mechanical, others purely decorative, artfully placed within the alpine scene. Then the lights were doused. Chattering and exclaiming, the patrons returned to the walks, the booths and the dancing.

The last of their company to return to their booth, Sophie and Jack strolled through the twilight, her hand on his arm. She could feel the tension that gripped him, lending steel to the muscles beneath her fingertips.

"Sophie?"

Wreathed in shadows, Sophie looked up.

Jack stared at the pale oval of her face, the wide eyes and slightly parted lips. For a moment, he was still, then, concealed by the shadows, he bent his head and swiftly kissed her.

Sophie's lips met his, her heart leaping at the brief caress. Her hands fluttered; her arms ached to hold him.

Jack caught her hands. "Not yet, sweetheart." His smile was decidedly crooked. "Just pray your uncle's carriage doesn't break an axle."

Sophie sighed feelingly and allowed him to resettle her hand on his sleeve.

Covering her hand with his, Jack gently squeezed her fingers. "We'd better get back to the booth." As they strolled out of the shadows, he added, "The fireworks come later."

Puzzled, Sophie looked up. "I hadn't imagined fireworks to be one of your abiding interests."

Jack glanced down at her, then his slow, rake's smile curved his lips. "There are many kinds of fireworks, my dear."

For an instant, Sophie glimpsed the dark, powerful passions behind his blue eyes. A distinctly delicious sensation slithered down her spine. But further discovery was denied her; they were caught up in the dancers and dragged into the heart of the revels once more.

The orchestra was now accompanied by a vocalist, a tenor whose pure notes drifted high over the booths to disappear into the increasing darkness. Stars speckled the sky as night slowly enfolded the scene. The Chinese lanterns came into their own, shedding their rosy glow over dancers and musicians alike. Laughter and the mellow murmur of conversation, softer now, muted by the effects of good food and fine wines, rippled through the shadows.

Throughout the evening, again and again, Sophie's eyes met Jack's. A magical web held them bound; neither was aware of those about them. And what passed between them was magical, too, carried in the weight of shared glances and the lingering touch of lovers' hands.

Their surroundings were part of the magic. At the conclusion of the musical interlude, the tenor embarked on a solo perfor-

mance. Breathless, conversing softly, the dancers headed back
to their booths. As she strolled on Jack's arm, Sophie noticed
Belle Chessington on the arm of Mr. Somercote—surely a most
unlikely Vauxhall patron. Belle waved and smiled hugely, her
eyes sparkling. Mr. Somercote, too, smiled broadly, clearly
both pleased and proud.

"Well, well," Jack murmured. "You'll have to tell your
aunt she's achieved a minor miracle. Somercote's silence has
been tripping the matchmakers up for years. It looks as if he's
finally found his tongue."

Sophie laughed. "Indeed, you have to admit he won't need
many words, not with Belle on his arm."

Jack smiled, then looked ahead.

And tensed. Sophie felt it, and followed his gaze to see the
rotund figure of her uncle clearly visible in their booth.

"Just in time." Jack quickened his pace.

As they entered the booth, Lucilla beckoned to Sophie.
"Mrs. Chessington just stopped by. Wonder of wonders!"

From the corner of her eye, Sophie saw Jack greet Horatio.
They exchanged a few words, Jack very serious, then both
turned and left the booth.

Subsiding onto the chair beside her aunt, Sophie forced herself to concentrate enough to follow Lucilla's discourse. It
proved a supremely difficult task. Her hands clasping and un-
clasping in her lap, she was acutely conscious of every little
sound, every movement in the booth.

She jumped when the gong rang again.

"The fireworks!"

Once more, the patrons poured from the booths and from
the shadowy walks, heading for a small arena surrounded by
lawns. Smiling indulgently, Lucilla allowed Jeremy and George
to tug her to her feet. Sophie rose uncertainly, glancing about.
Ned offered Clarissa his arm; together with Toby they joined
the exodus. Jack was nowhere to be seen.

"There you are, m'dear." Horatio materialized outside the
booth. "Come along now or you'll miss the fun."

Sophie stared at him, her heart sinking all the way to her

slippers. Hadn't Jack asked? Why wasn't he here? Did that mean…? Forcing her shaking limbs to function, she picked up her half-cape. Swinging it about her shoulders, she left the booth.

Horatio offered her his arm. They started to stroll slowly in the wake of the others, now far ahead. But instead of joining his family, Horatio stopped in the shadows, well to the rear of the crowd.

"Now, my dear Sophie, I understand you have had some reservations about Jack's financial situation."

Slowly, Sophie turned to face her uncle, her heart thudding in her throat. She held herself proudly, a silent prayer on her lips.

Apparently oblivious, Horatio rattled on. "It really was quite remiss of him, I agree. He should have told you much earlier. But you'll have to excuse him—not but what, with his experience, you might have expected a little more than the usual impulsive rush. But men in love, you know, tend to forget such minor matters as money." Smiling genially, he patted Sophie's hand.

Sophie drew in a slow, deep breath. "Uncle, are you telling me that Jack is truly wealthy? That he doesn't need to marry a rich bride?"

Horatio's grey eyes twinkled. "Let's just say that for him, expectations alone will be a more than sufficient dower."

A golden rocket burst in a flurry of brilliant stars, gilding Sophie's face. Her eyes shone, reflecting the glory.

"Oh, Uncle!" Sophie flung her arms about Horatio's neck.

Horatio chuckled and reciprocated her, then gently turned her. "Come, let's join the festivities."

Sophie was only too ready to do so. She peered into the darkness, eagerly searching the crowd every time another rocket lit up the scene. They found Lucilla and the boys in the front ranks. The boys pounced on Horatio, bombarding him with questions.

Then a large wheel lit up the night, hissing and spitting as the force of the rockets tied to its spokes whirled it round. In the midst of the crowd, Sophie stood very still, her face slowly draining of expression. The steadier illumination confirmed beyond doubt that Jack, Ned and Toby were not present. Neither was Clarissa.

The memory of Gurnard's plan rushed into Sophie's mind, thrusting all other considerations aside. This was the time Toby was to have taken Clarissa to meet the dastardly captain. Yet Ned had been with them—he wouldn't let any harm come to Clarissa. But where were they? If Jack, Ned and Toby had gone to warn off the captain, where was Clarissa?

Sophie blinked in the glare of a set of coloured flares; elation, guilt and sheer frustration poured through her in a dizzying wave.

Horatio would know. She looked to where her uncle stood, Lucilla beside him, George's hand in his. Jeremy was throwing questions at his father in a never-ending stream. There was no possibility of speaking to Horatio without alerting Lucilla and, potentially worse, the boys.

Everything was probably all right; Jack would surely have the matter in hand.

But maybe Jack was elsewhere, ignorant of Gurnard's threat? Perhaps Toby and Ned had decided to handle it on their own? And Clarissa had followed?

Sophie turned and quietly made her way back through the crowd.

The majority of the patrons were viewing the fireworks, leaving the walks sparsely populated. Here and there, a couple or a small group still wandered, having seen the fireworks too many times. But the crush of revellers that had filled the walks earlier had given way to empty shadows.

Just beyond the booths, Sophie slowed. The Dark Walk, with the Temple of Diana, lay furthest afield, the narrowest and most heavily shaded of the Gardens' promenades. And the most secluded.

Grimacing, Sophie halted. It would be the height of folly to risk the length of the Dark Walk at night, alone. But if she went back up the Grand Wall, wide and well lit, she could take a side path across to the Dark Walk, emerging just a little above the Temple. It was longer, but she was far more certain to reach her goal by that route.

Clutching her cape about her, she turned and hurried up the Grand Walk.

At the Temple of Diana, deep in the shadows of the Dark Walk, Jack waited with Toby, concealed in thick bushes by the temple's side. A small structure in the Ionic style, the temple was little more than a decorative gazebo. The surrounding bushes had grown close over the years, filling the side arches until the space within resembled a room with green walls.

Jack peered through the shadows. Toby had delivered Clarissa to the temple at the appointed time. Ned had earlier hidden himself on the other side of the main archway, awaiting his moment of glory. Gurnard, however, was late.

The scrunch of heavy footsteps on gravel brought Jack's head up. Out on the path, the figure of a man came into view, heading purposefully towards the temple. He made no attempt to conceal his approach; a guardsman's red cape was thrown over one shoulder.

"Here he comes," hissed Toby.

They waited, frozen in the shadows, as Gurnard climbed the short flight of steps and disappeared into the temple.

"So far so good," Jack whispered.

Inside the temple, however, all was not going as either they, or Captain Gurnard, had planned.

Clarissa, delivered by a strangely serious Toby to the dim temple with a promise that her most ardent suitor—Ned, of course—would shortly join her, had entered the shadowy hall with high hopes. It was clear that Sophie would shortly receive the offer she desired; Clarissa, having expended considerable effort in encouraging Ned, expected that he would, tonight, at least take a more definite step in his wooing of her. With any luck, he might kiss her. Why else had he asked her here?

As the minutes ticked by, she had fallen to pacing, hands clasped behind her, her brow furrowed as she wondered how fast she could urge things along. A marriage in September, assuming Sophie did not opt for a long betrothal, seemed a distinct possibility.

She had reached this point in her cogitations when firm footsteps approached and ascended to the temple.

Starry-eyed, Clarissa turned.

And beheld the unmistakable outline of Captain Gurnard.

"What are you doing here?" she demanded, not the least bit pleased at the prospect of having her tryst with Ned interrupted or—even worse—postponed.

Terrance Gurnard blinked. "Why, I'm here to meet you, my dear."

"I'm afraid, sir, that my time this evening is spoken for." If nothing else, Clarissa was Lucilla's daughter. She delivered the captain's dismissal with an affronted dignity that would have done justice to royalty.

For a moment, Gurnard was bewildered. Where was the youthful, wide-eyed innocent he had arranged to meet? Then he shook himself. The hoity young miss was just playing hard to get. "Nonsense, my dear," he purred, advancing on Clarissa. "We all know you're besotted with me. But fear not, for I'm equally besotted with you."

Even in the dimness, Gurnard could not misinterpret the icy rigidity that laid hold of Clarissa's slim frame. She drew herself up and, somehow, succeeded in looking down her nose at him. "My dear Captain, I believe you have lost your wits." The cool incisiveness in her tone bit deep. "If you will but consider, the notion that I, with suitors such as Mr. Ascombe, could consider you, who have nought but your uniform to commend you, is highly insulting, sir!"

Rocked by the strident vehemence in her tone, Gurnard blinked. Then he sneered. "You were ready enough to encourage me to dangle after you—do you deny it?" Abruptly, he closed the gap between them. He did not have all night to accomplish what he must.

"That was because you were being useful." Clarissa, her own considerable temper in orbit, continued with undisguised relish, "Useful in ensuring that *Mr. Ascombe's* attention did not wander."

"Useful, was I?" Gurnard ground out. "In that case, my dear, you'll have to pay the piper." Roughly, he grasped her arms, intending to pull her to him.

Used to wrestling with her brothers, Clarissa anticipated the move enough to wrench one arm free. "Let me *go,* sir!"

Her furious shriek jolted Ned from the dazed stupor into which he had fallen. He shot up the steps, only just remembering their plan in time to change his automatic. "Unhand her, you fiend!" to a relatively normal, if slightly strangled, "Clarissa?"

He saw her immediately, one arm held by Gurnard. With an heroic effort, assisted by the calming effects of the cold rage that poured through him, Ned strolled lazily forward. "There you are, m'dear. I apologize for my tardiness, but I was held up." Commandingly, he held out his hand to Clarissa, his gaze, coldly challenging, fixed on Gurnard's face.

In order to take her hand, Clarissa chose to use the arm Gurnard was holding. She did so without in any way acknowledging Gurnard's grasp, much less his presence.

The action snapped Gurnard's patience. He had no time to play games, nor to brook interference of any sort. He waited until, as Clarissa's fingers slipped into Ned's palm, Ned glanced at her. Then he attacked.

And was immediately sent to grass—or marble, as was the case—by a punishing left jab.

In the bushes to the side, Jack allowed the battle-ready tension that had instantly gripped him to fade. "He said his left jab was coming along."

Inside the temple, Ned frowned, attempting to shield Clarissa from the sight of the captain stretched out on the marble floor. "I'm sorry, Clary. Not the sort of thing one should do in front of a lady, I know. You aren't feeling faint or anything, are you?"

"Good heavens, no!" Clarissa, eyes alight, both hands clutching one of Ned's forearms, peered around him at the captain's prone form. Satisfied that the captain was, at last temporarily, beyond further punishment, she turned her glowing eyes on Ned. "That was *marvellous*, Ned! How *thrillingly* heroic. You rescued me!"

And with that, Clarissa promptly hurled herself into her knight errant's arms.

The watchers in the bushes heard Ned mutter something that sounded like a weak disclaimer but his heart was clearly not in it. Then came silence.

Jack sighed and relaxed, looking up into the night sky, considering, with a certain rakish satisfaction, the prospect of the immediate future. Beside him, Toby shifted restlessly.

Then they heard Ned's voice, and Clarissa's replying; the pair turned, still hand in hand, Clarissa's head against Ned's shoulder, and made slowly for the steps.

"We'll follow," Jack said. "They may be almost betrothed but they're not betrothed yet."

They followed Clarissa and Ned at a distance; it was questionable whether either was aware of their presence.

When they reached the booth, it was to find Horatio beaming benevolently, and Ned standing, proud but a trifle hesitant, as Clarissa poured the details of her rescue into her mother's ear. Jeremy's and George's eyes were wide as they drank it all in. Seeing Jack, Lucilla smiled and asked, "Where's Sophie?"

Ned and Clarissa looked blank.

Toby blinked.

Jack froze—and looked at Horatio.

Suddenly serious, Horatio frowned. "I spoke with her, then we joined Lucilla and the boys. At the end of the fireworks display, Sophie had disappeared. I thought she was with you."

"She must have gone to the temple," Toby said, genuinely horrified.

"Gurnard's still there," Ned pointed out.

"I'll find her." Jack kept his expression impassive, despite the emotions roiling within. He exchanged a look with Horatio, who nodded. Striding to the door, Jack spared a glance for

Lucilla. "Don't worry," he said. The smile that accompanied the words held a certain grim resolution.

Somewhat subdued, the rest of the party settled to listen to the last of the music.

"You know," Lucilla murmured as Horatio took the seat beside her. "I'm really not sure we've done the right thing."

"How so?"

"Well, I'm quite sure Sophie can handle Captain Gurnard. But can she handle Jack Lester?"

Horatio smiled and patted her hand. "I'm sure she'll contrive."

ON GAINING the Dark Walk, Sophie paused to catch her breath. Peering through the shadows, she could just make out the distant glimmer of the temple's white pillars, set back in a small grove. The path leading to the water-gate lay nearby; somewhere beyond the temple lay one of the less-used street gates.

Dragging in a deep breath, Sophie quit the shadows. There was no one about. Her soft slippers made little sound on the gravel as she neared the temple steps. Standing at the bottom, she peered in but could see nothing but shadows. Surely Clarissa could not be inside?

For a full minute, she vacillated, then, holding her cape close about her, Sophie mounted the steps. If there was no one inside, it couldn't hurt to look.

The shadows within enveloped her. Sophie glanced about, then stifled a shriek as a dark shape loomed beside her.

"Well, well, well. Come to look for your cousin, I take it?"

As the shape resolved itself into Captain Gurnard, Sophie gave an almost imperceptible gasp. Straightening, she nodded. "But as she isn't here—"

"You'll do just as well."

The captain wrapped one hand about Sophie's arm.

Instinctively, she tried to pull away. "Unhand me, sir! What on earth do you believe can come of this?"

"Money, my dear Miss Winterton. Lots of money."

Sophie remembered his scheme. "You appear to have overlooked something, Captain. I am not an heiress."

"No," Gurnard acknowledged. "You're something even better. You're the woman Lester's got his eye on."

"What's that supposed to mean?" Sophie carefully tested the captain's hold.

"It means," Gurnard sneered, convincing her his grip was unbreakable by shaking her, "that Lester will pay and pay handsomely to have you returned to him. And he'll pay even more to ensure you're…unharmed, shall we say?"

Sophie recoiled as Gurnard thrust his face close to hers. "It seems Lester's windfall is to be *my* gain." With an abrupt laugh, he turned and dragged her towards the door. "Come on."

Dredging up every ounce of her courage, Sophie went rigid and pulled back. Her full weight served only to slow the captain, but it was enough to make him turn with a snarl.

Sophie lifted her chin, refusing to be cowed. "There is, as I said, something you appear to have overlooked, Captain. I am *not* going to marry Mr. Lester."

"Gammon," said Gurnard, and tugged her on.

"But I'm *not!*" Sophie placed her free hand over her heart. "I swear on my mother's grave that Mr. Lester has not asked for my hand."

"It's not my fault if he's backward." They had almost reached the top of the steps.

Sophie lost her temper. "You imbecile! I'm trying to make it plain to you that I am *not going to marry Jack Lester!*"

Gurnard stopped and turned to her, fury in every line of his large frame. "You," he began, pointing a finger at her.

"Should learn to accept Fate graciously."

There was a split second of silence, then Gurnard turned.

Only to meet a left jab that had a great deal more power behind it than the one he'd met earlier.

The result was the same. The captain's head hit the marble with a resounding thump.

Sophie glared down at him, prostrate at her feet. "Of all the unmitigated scoundrels," she began.

Jack shook his head and sighed. "Are you and your cousin so lost to all sensibility that you can't even swoon at the sight of violence?"

Sophie blinked at him, then humphed. "If you must know, I'm feeling quite violent myself. Did you know he intended to—"

"I heard." Jack reached for her and drew her to him. "But you don't need to worry about him any more."

Sophie readily went into his arms. "But shouldn't we—"

"It's already taken care of." Jack looked down at Gurnard, then prodded him with the toe of his boot. His victim groaned. "I sincerely hope you're listening, Gurnard, for I'm only going to say this once. I've had a word with an acquaintance of mine, the Earl of Melcham. He was most upset to hear of the method you'd selected to raise the wind. He doesn't approve—not at all. And I'm sure you know what happens to those of whom Melcham disapproves."

There was a stunned silence, then Gurnard groaned again.

Grimly satisfied, Jack turned Sophie towards the steps. "And now, my dear, I think it's time we left." Tucking her hand in his arm, he led her down onto the gravelled walk.

Sophie went readily, her mind seething with questions. "What happened to Clarissa? Did she go to the temple?"

Jack glanced down at her. "She did."

Sophie glared at him. "What happened?"

Jack smiled and told her, adding that Horatio had approved their scheme. "If Clarissa had simply not shown up, Gurnard would have assumed she'd been prevented from doing so, not that she wouldn't go to meet him. He'd have tried again to get her alone, and perhaps we wouldn't have learned of his intentions in time to foil him. It was best to make the situation as clear as possible."

"But what if he turns to some other young lady?"

"He won't have time. As of tomorrow, courtesy of Melcham, to whom Gurnard is deeply in debt, the captain will have entirely too much on his mind to think of persuading any other young lady to his rescue."

Sophie pondered his revelations, her feet following his lead. "So Ned floored the captain?"

"He seems to have floored Clarissa as well." Jack's lips curved in fond reminiscence. He slanted a glance at Sophie. "We all thought the opportunity too good to miss to advance Ned's standing with your cousin."

For an instant, Sophie stared into his smugly satisfied face. Then she burst out laughing. "Oh, dear. Was that supposed to be Ned's great scene—so that Clarissa would think him her hero and respond suitably?"

Frowning, Jack nodded.

"Oh, poor Ned." Sophie could not stop smiling. She glanced confidently up at Jack. "Just for your information, Clarissa settled on Ned some weeks ago, not all that long after we'd come up to town. She's been trying to nudge him along for the past two weeks at least. I'm not at all surprised to hear she flung herself into his arms. After all, what better opportunity she could hope for?"

Jack looked down at her through narrowed eyes. "Remind me," he said, "to tell Ned just what he's getting into, marrying a Webb female."

Sophie pressed her lips tightly together. When she was sure her voice was under control, she said, "I'm related to the Webbs; does that make me a 'Webb female', too?"

Jack's glance was supercilious. "I haven't yet decided."

It was then, when he stood back to usher her through the watergate, that Sophie realized that they had been walking in the wrong direction. A leafy lane stretched before them. Not far ahead, the lane ended by the banks of the Thames. Sophie halted. "Ah...Jack...?"

Jack looked down at her and held out his hand. "Your uncle's returned. He spoke to you, didn't he?"

"Yes." Eyes wide, Sophie studied his face. "He told me there's no reason we can't marry."

"Precisely." Jack smiled, closing his hand about the fingers she had automatically surrendered. He drew her closer and tucked her hand into the crook of his arm. "Which is to say that by common consent, general agreement and the blessing of Fate, my wait is, at long last, over."

"But shouldn't we..?" Sophie glanced back at the dark shrubbery of the Gardens, slowly receding in their wake.

Jack cast her a reproving glance. "Really, my dear. You don't seriously imagine that *I*, such as I am, could consider Vauxhall a suitable venue for a proposal, do you?"

There seemed no sensible answer to that.

But Sophie had no time to ponder the implications. They had reached the water's edge. She glanced about, somewhat surprised at the bustling scene. A stone wharf lined the river and extended out in a jetty where a small flotilla of pleasure craft bobbed gently at their moorings.

"If habits linger, he'll be at the end."

A most peculiar sensation started to creep along Sophie's nerves. She clung to Jack's arm as they wended their way between Garden patrons haggling with the boatmen, and others embarking for a slow ride home. The craft were of a variety of sizes, some holding no more than a couple, while others could comfortably carry a small party. Still others had canopies erected over their bows under which lovers could pursue their acquaintance in privacy, screened by drapes which let down about the sides.

It was towards one of these last that Jack led her.

"Rollinson?"

Sophie suddenly felt quite light-headed.

The beefy boatman in charge of the largest and most opulent craft turned from desultory conversation with his crew to peer up at Jack. "There you be, Mr. Lester!" He grinned, displaying a row of decidedly haphazard teeth, and tipped his felt hat to Sophie. "Got your message. We're here and ready, sir."

"Very good," Jack replied.

Sophie found it hard to follow the rest of their conversation, at least half of which was conducted in boatman's cant. She glanced about, trying to interest herself in the scene, rather than dwell on what their presence here probably meant. If she thought of that, she might feel obliged to protest.

As it was, she was not to escape making some part of the decision on her fate. Their itinerary agreed upon, Jack leapt down to the wooden planking of the boat's hull, which floated a good yard below the jetty.

He then turned to study Sophie, one brow rising. "Well, my dear?" With a graceful gesture, he indicated the boat and the curtain cutting off the bow. His slow, slightly crooked smile twisted his lips. "Will you trust yourself to me tonight?"

For an instant, Sophie stared down at him, oblivious of those about them, of the sly yet careful glances cast her by the boatmen. All she could see was Jack, waiting for her, a very definite glint in his eyes. For an instant, she closed her own. What he was suggesting was perfectly scandalous. Drawing in a deep breath, she opened her eyes and, with a soft smile, stepped to the edge of the jetty.

The familiar feel of Jack's hands about her waist was reassuring, soothing the peculiar jitteriness that, all of a sudden, had afflicted her. He set her down beside him, one arm slipping about her to steady her as he helped her across the rowing benches. Parting the heavy damask curtain that screened the bow, he ushered her through.

Sophie entered a private and very luxurious world of moonlight glinting on water. The curtain fell closed behind them, sealing them in. With a slight lurch, the boat got under way. Jack's arm came to urge her to a seat as the boat nosed out onto the river. Once clear of the craft by the jetty, the boat pulled smoothly, powerfully, upstream.

As her eyes adjusted to the deep shadows beneath the canopy, Sophie, fascinated, gazed about. She was seated amid a pile of huge silk cushions spread over a satin-draped platform, heavily padded, that was constructed to fit snugly across the bow. The platform all but filled the area behind the curtain, leaving barely enough room for a wine cooler, which, she noticed, contained a bottle, already open and chilling, and a small fixed buffet holding glasses and small dishes of unidentifiable delicacies. Jack turned from examining the buffet's offerings to look down at her.

"I think we'll leave the caviar for second course."

Sophie's eyes widened. She didn't need to ask what he fancied for the first. His eyes, even in the shadows, gleamed as they rested on her. Clearing her throat, suddenly dry, she asked, a trifle unsteadily, "You planned this?"

His smile was smugly triumphant. "To the last detail," Jack averred, coming to lounge on the cushions beside her. "It's customary, you know."

"Is it?" Sophie stared at him.

"Mmm-hmm." Jack leaned back, gazing upward to where the canopy overhead was drawn partially back, revealing the black velvet of the sky sprinkled with jewelled stars. "Seductions are never so satisfying as when they're well-planned."

Sophie bit her lip and eyed him warily.

His gaze on her face, Jack laughed and, reaching up, drew her down to lie among the cushions beside him. Sophie hesitated, then yielded to his gentle strength. Propped on one elbow, Jack smiled down into her wide eyes. Then he bent his head and kissed her, long and lingeringly, before whispering against her lips, "I'm not teasing, Sophie."

A thrill of desire raced through Sophie, all the way down to her toes. She opened her lips on a feeble protest—and Jack kissed her again. And kept kissing her until she had no breath left to speak.

"No, Sophie." Jack dropped soft kisses on her eyelids as his fingers deftly unbuttoned her gown. "I've had more than enough of wooing you, my love. You're mine, and I'm yours. And nothing else matters." His voice deepened at the last as he looked down at her breast, the firm ivory flesh filling his palm.

Sophie arched lightly as his thumb circled the rosy peak. Unable to speak, barely able to breathe, she watched him from beneath heavy lids as he caressed her. Then he lowered his head and she stopped breathing altogether, her fingers sinking into his shoulders as his tongue lightly teased, knowingly tantalized.

"Besides," Jack murmured against her soft skin. "We've only one thing left to discuss."

"Discuss?" The word came out weakly on a slow exhalation, the best Sophie could manage, her mind struggling against the drugging haze of his caresses.

"Hmm. We have to discuss what I'll accept as suitable recompense for my torture."

"Torture?" Sophie knew about torture. She was being tortured now, his hands touching her so skilfully she was gripped by an urgent longing. "What torture?"

"The torture of having to woo you, sweet Sophie."

Sophie stirred, consumed by the sweetest ache. "Was it torture?"

"Torture and worse," Jack vowed, his voice deep and raspy.

Sophie sighed. "What do you consider suitable recompense?" She just managed to get the words out before he stole her breath again with a caress so artful she thought she could faint. She didn't, but the sensations didn't stop, darting through her like lightning, spreading like warm fire beneath her skin.

Aeons filled with pleasure seemed to have passed before she heard his soft murmur.

"I know what I want as my reward for wooing you. Will you give it me?"

"Yes." Her voice was a soft whisper on the breeze.

Jack raised his head, a smile twisting his lips. "I haven't yet told you what I want."

Sophie returned his smile with one of her own. "It had better be me—for that's all I have to give you."

For the first time in his rakish career, Jack was lost for words. He looked down into her eyes, passion-filled and mysterious. "Sophie." His voice was hoarse, dark with his turbulent passions. "You're all I'll ever want."

"Then take me," Sophie murmured, wondering, very distantly, how she dared. She reached up and drew his lips to hers before her sane self could resurface and disturb the glorious moment.

Thereafter, her sanity or otherwise was not in question; desire caught her and held her until she glowed with its flame. Jack fed her fires, never letting her cool, until she ached for him to join her. When he did, it was as if the sun shone brightly out of the night-dark sky. Sophie surrendered to joy and delight and rapturous, delirious pleasure. For one timeless moment, she felt that she had flown so high she could touch the stars gleaming in the firmament. Then she softly drifted back to earth, safe, forever, in Jack's strong arms.

The gentle rocking of the boat, and Jack's heavy weight, drew her slowly back to reality.

Surprisingly, Sophie found her mind oddly clear, as if the sensations that had held her body in thrall had proved so overpowering that her wits had disengaged and retreated to a safe distance. She could feel the cool caress of the river breeze on her naked skin and her lover's touch as, propped now beside her, he gently stroked her hair from her face. She opened her eyes and looked up. He was a dark shadow as he hung over her, solid and comforting in the moonlight. Sophie listened for the shush of the water under the hull—and made a discovery. "We're not moving."

Jack's smile gleamed in the moonlight. "We're moored. Off a private park. The men left us nearly an hour ago." He reached up to spread out her curling hair, released from its moorings. "They'll come back later and take us home. My carriage will be waiting at the steps."

Sophie blinked. "You really did think of everything."

His smile grew broader. "I always aim to please." He shifted slightly, drawing her more comfortably into his arms and tucking a silk shawl tenderly about her. "And now that I've pleased you, how soon can we be wed?"

Still slightly dazed, Sophie stared up at him, marshalling her wandering wits.

"Not that I'm trying to rush you, my love, but there are any number of reasons why an early, if not immediate, wedding would suit us best.''

As he turned her hand over to press a kiss into her palm, and the touch of his lips stirred the embers that were only now dying within her, Sophie abruptly nodded. "I see your point." She stopped to clear her throat, amazed she could think at all. "My father's due back for a quick visit next month—can we wait until then?"

Jack raised his head to look down at her. "It might be hard." He smiled, his usual crooked smile. "But I suspect we can wait until then."

Sophie sighed, deeply content. She put up a hand to brush back the dark locks from his forehead. "You'll have to marry me; you've thoroughly compromised me. We've been away for far too long."

"I always intended to marry you. From the moment I first saw you in Lady Asfordby's ballroom."

Sophie studied his face in the moonlight. "Did you really?"

"From the moment I saw you dancing with that upstart Marston," Jack admitted. "I was smitten then and there."

"Oh, Jack!"

After the necessary exchange of affection brought on by that revelation, Sophie was the first to return to reality. "Dear Heaven," she exclaimed weakly. "We've been gone for hours."

Jack caught the hint of concern dawning in her voice. "Don't worry. Horatio knows you're with me."

Fascinated, Sophie stared at him. "Did you tell my aunt, too?"

"Good God." Jack shuddered. "What a horrible thought. If I had, I'd lay odds she'd have given me instructions. I don't think my pride could have stood it." Jack dropped a soft kiss on one delectable rosy peak. "Your aunt, my love, is just plain dangerous."

Privately, Sophie agreed but was far too distracted to find words to say so. Sometime later, her mind drifting in dazed consideration of the future he had spread before her, the home, the family—everything she had ever wanted—with him by her side, she returned to his point. "Speaking of marriage, sir, you have not yet asked me to marry you."

"I have—you quibbled and refused."

Sophie smiled into the night. "But you're supposed to ask me again, now that my uncle has given me permission to receive your addresses."

Jack sighed lustily, then shifted to move over her, one elbow planted on either side, his expression arrogantly commanding. His eyes, deep dark pools within which passion still smouldered, transfixed her.

"Very well, Miss Winterton. For the *very last time—will* you marry me? I realize, of course, that you are only a lady of expectations and not an heiress. However, as it transpires, I neither need nor want a wealthy bride. You, my beautiful, desirable Sophie—" Jack bent his head to do homage to her lips "—will do just wonderfully. You, my love, fulfil all *my* expectations." Another kiss stole her breath. "Every last one."

A soft smile curving her lips, her gaze misty with happiness, Sophie reached up to slide her arms about his neck. Her acceptance was delivered, not in words but in those actions which, to her mind, and Jack's spoke best.

AS THE WEBB CARRIAGE rocked into motion, leaving the shadows of Vauxhall behind, Lucilla sank back against the squabs. On the opposite seat, Jeremy and George yawned and closed their eyes, their faces wreathed in seraphic smiles. Behind, in the smaller carriage, Toby, Ned and Clarissa were doubtless still exclaiming over their exciting evening. Lucilla, however, was not impressed.

She had just been informed that Jack would be returning Sophie to Mount Street by a different route.

It was several long moments before she trusted herself to speak.

"And you told *me* not to meddle." With an audible humph, she cast a disgusted glance at her spouse.

Horatio was too wise to answer. He smiled serenely, glancing upriver as the carriage rattled over the bridge.

An Unwilling Conquest

Chapter One

"IS IT THE DEVIL we're running from, then?"

The question, uttered in the mildest of tones, made Harry Lester wince. "Worse," he threw over his shoulder at his groom and general henchman, Dawlish. "The matchmaking mamas—in league with the dragons of the *ton*." Harry edged back on the reins, feathering a curve at speed. He saw no reason to ease the wicked pace. His match greys, sleek and powerful, were quite content to keep the bits between their teeth. His curricle rushed along in their wake; Newmarket lay ahead. "And we're not running—it's called a strategic retreat."

"Is that so? Well, can't say I blame you," came in Dawlish's dour accents. "Who'd ever have thought to see Master Jack landed—and without much of a fight, if Pinkerton's on the up. Right taken aback, is Pinkerton." When this information elicited no response, Dawlish added, "Considering his position, he is."

Harry snorted. "Nothing will part Pinkerton from Jack—not even a wife. He'll swallow the pill when the time comes."

"Aye—p'raps. Still, can't say I'd relish the prospect of answering to a missus—not after all these years."

Harry's lips quirked. Realising that Dawlish, riding on the box behind him, couldn't see it, he gave into the urge to smile. Dawlish had been with him forever, having, as a fifteen-year-old groom, attached himself to the second son of the Lester household the instant said son had been put atop a pony. Their old cook had maintained it was a clear case of like to like; Dawlish's life was horses—he had recognised a master in the making and had followed doggedly in his wake. "You needn't worry, you old curmudgeon. I can assure you I've no intention, willingly or otherwise, of succumbing to any siren's lures."

"All very well to say so," Dawlish grumbled. "But when these things happen, seems like there's no gainsaying them. Just look at Master Jack."

"I'd rather not," Harry curtly replied. Dwelling on his elder brother's rapid descent into matrimony was an exercise guaranteed to shake his confidence. With only two years separating them, he and Jack had led much the same lives. They'd come on the town together more than ten years ago. Admittedly, Jack had less reason than he to question love's worth, nevertheless, his brother had been, as Dawlish had observed, a most willing conquest. The fact made him edgy.

"You planning on keeping from London for the rest of yore life?"

"I sincerely hope it won't come to that." Harry checked the greys for a slight descent. The heath lay before them, a haven free of matchmakers and dragons alike. "Doubtless my uninterest will be duly noted. With any luck, if I lay low, they'll have forgotten me by next Season."

"Wouldn't have thought, with all the energy you've put into raising a reputation like you have, that they'd be so keen."

Harry's lip curled. "Money, Dawlish, will serve to excuse any number of sins."

He waited, expecting Dawlish to cap the comment with some gloomy pronouncement to the effect that if the madams of society could overlook his transgressions then no one was safe. But no comment came; his gaze fixed unseeing on his leader's ears, Harry grudgingly reflected that the wealth with which he and his brothers, Gerald as well as Jack, had recently been blessed, was indeed sufficient to excuse a lifetime of social sins.

His illusions were few—he knew who and what he was—a rake, one of the wolves of the *ton*, a hellion, a Corinthian, a superlative rider and exceptional breeder of quality horseflesh, an amateur boxer of note, an excellent shot, a keen and successful huntsman on the field and off. For the past ten and more years, Society had been his playing field. Capitalising on natural talents, and the position his birth had bestowed, he had spent the years in hedonistic pleasure, sampling women much as he had the wines. There'd been none to gainsay him, none to stand in his path and challenge his profligate ways.

Now, of course, with a positively disgusting fortune at his back, they'd be lining up to do so.

Harry snorted and refocused on the road. The sweet damsels of the *ton* could offer until they were blue in the face—he wasn't about to buy.

The junction with the road to Cambridge loomed ahead. Harry checked his team, still sprightly despite their dash from London. He'd nursed them along the main road, only letting them have their heads once they'd passed Great Chesterford and picked up the less-frequented Newmarket road. They'd passed a few slower-moving carriages; most of the gentlemen intent on the week's racing would already be in Newmarket.

About them, the heath lay flat and largely featureless, with only a few stands of trees, windbreaks and the odd coppice to lend relief. There were no carriages approaching on the Cambridge road; Harry swung his team onto the hard surface and flicked the leader's ear. Newmarket—and the comfort of his regular rooms at the Barbican Arms—lay but a few miles on.

"To y'r left."

Dawlish's warning growl came over his shoulder in the same instant Harry glimpsed movement in the stand of trees bordering the road ahead. He flicked both horses' withers; as the lash softly swooshed back up the whip-handle, he slackened the reins, transferring them to his left hand. With his right, he reached for the loaded pistol he kept under the seat, just behind his right boot.

As his fingers closed about the chased butt, he registered the incongruity of the scene.

Dawlish put it into words, a heavy horse pistol in his hands. "On the king's highway in broad daylight—never-you-mind! What's the world a-coming to, I asks you?"

The curricle sped on.

Harry wasn't entirely surprised when the men milling in the trees made no attempt to halt them. They were mounted but, even so, would have had the devil of a time hauling in the flying greys. He counted at least five as they flashed past, all in frieze and heavily muffled. The sound of stifled cursing dwindled behind them.

Dawlish muttered darkly, rummaging about re-stowing his pistols. "Stap me, but they even had a wagon backed up in them trees. Right confident of their haul they must be."

Harry frowned.

The road curved ahead; he regathered the slack reins and checked the greys fractionally.

They rounded the curve—Harry's eyes flew wide.

He hauled back on the reins with all his strength, slewing the greys across the road. They came to a snorting, stamping halt, their noses all but in the low hedge. The curricle rocked perilously, then settled back on its springs.

Curses turned the air about his ears blue.

Harry paid no attention; Dawlish was still up behind him, not in the ditch. Before him, on the other hand, was a scene of disaster.

A travelling carriage lay on its side, not in the ditch but blocking most of the road. It looked as if one of the back wheels had disintegrated; the ponderous contraption, top-heavy with luggage, had toppled sideways. The accident had only just occurred—the upper wheels of the carriage were still slowly rotating. Harry blinked. A young lad, a groom presumably, was struggling to haul a hysterical girl from the ditch. An older man, the coachman from his attire, was hovering anxiously over a thin grey-haired woman, laid out on the ground.

The coach team was in a flat panic.

Without a word, Harry and Dawlish leapt to the ground and ran to calm the horses.

It took a good five minutes to soothe the brutes, good, strong coach horses with the full stubbornness and dim wits of their breed. With the traces finally untangled, Harry left the team in Dawlish's hands; the young groom was still helplessly pleading with the tearful girl while the coachman dithered over the older woman, clearly caught between duty and a wish to lend succour, if he only knew how.

The woman groaned as Harry walked up. Her eyes were closed; she lay straight and rigid on the ground, her hands crossed over her flat chest.

"My ankle—!" A spasm of pain twisted her angular features, tight under an iron-grey bun. "Damn you, Joshua—when I get back on my feet I'll have your hide for a footstool, I will." She drew her breath in in a painful hiss. "*If* I ever get back on my feet."

Harry blinked; the woman's tones were startlingly reminiscent of Dawlish in complaining mode. He raised his brows as the coachman lumbered to his feet and touched his forehead. "Is there anyone in the carriage?"

The coachman's face blanked in shock.

"*Oh my God!*" Her eyes snapping open, the woman sat bolt upright. "The mistress and Miss Heather!" Her startled gaze fell on the carriage. "Damn you, Joshua—what are you *doing*, mooning over me when the mistress is likely lying in a heap?" Frantically, she hit at the coachman's legs, pushing him towards the carriage.

"Don't panic."

The injunction floated up out of the carriage, calm and assured.

"We're perfectly all right—just a bit shaken." The clear, very feminine voice paused before adding, a touch hesitantly, "But we can't get out."

With a muttered curse, Harry strode to the carriage, pausing only to shrug out of his greatcoat and fling it into the curricle. Reaching up to the back wheel, he hauled himself onto the body. Standing on the coach's now horizontal side, he bent and, grasping the handle, hauled the door open.

Planting one booted foot on either side of the coach step, he looked down into the dimness within.

And blinked.

The sight that met his eyes was momentarily dazzling. A

woman stood in the shaft of sunshine pouring through the doorway. Her face, upturned, was heart-shaped; a broad forehead was set beneath dark hair pulled severely back. Her features were well defined; a straight nose and full, well-curved lips above a delicate but determined chin.

Her skin was the palest ivory, the colour of priceless pearls; beyond his control, Harry's gaze skimmed her cheeks and the graceful curve of her slender neck before coming to rest on the ripe swell of her breasts. Standing over her as he was, they were amply exposed to his sight even though her modish carriage dress was in no way indecorous.

Harry's palms tingled.

Large blue eyes fringed with long black lashes blinked up at him.

For an instant, Lucinda Babbacombe was not entirely sure she hadn't sustained a blow on the head—what else could excuse this vision, conjured from her deepest dreams?

Tall and lean, broad-shouldered, slim-hipped, he towered above her, long, sleekly muscled legs braced on either side of the door. Sunlight haloed his golden locks; with the light behind him she could not make out his features yet she sensed the tension that held him.

Lucinda blinked rapidly. A light blush tinged her cheeks; she looked away—but not before she registered the subdued elegance of his garments—the tightly-fitting grey coat, superbly cut, style in every line, worn over clinging ivory inexpressibles, which clearly revealed the long muscles of his thighs. His calves were encased in gleaming Hessians; his linen was crisp and white. There were, she noted, no fobs or seals hanging at his waist, only a single gold pin in his cravat.

Prevailing opinion suggested such severe attire should render a gentleman uninteresting. Unremarkable. Prevailing opinion was wrong.

He shifted—and a large, long-fingered, extremely elegant hand reached down to her.

"Take my hand—I'll pull you up. One of the wheels is shattered—it's impossible to right the carriage."

His voice was deep, drawling, an undercurrent Lucinda couldn't identify sliding beneath the silken tones. She glanced up through her lashes. He had moved to the side of the door and had gone down on one knee. The light now reached his face, illuminating features that seemed to harden as her gaze touched them. His hand moved impatiently; a black sapphire set in a gold signet glimmered darkly. He would need to be very strong to lift her out with one arm. Subduing the thought that her rescue might well prove a greater threat than her plight, Lucinda reached for his hand.

Their palms met; long fingers curled about her wrist. Lucinda brought her other hand up and clasped it about his—and she was airborne.

She drew in a swift breath—an arm of steel wrapped about her waist; her diaphragm seized. She blinked—and found herself on her knees, held fast in his embrace, locked breast to chest with her unnerving rescuer.

Her eyes were on a level with his lips. They were as severe as his clothes, chiselled and firm. His jaw was distinctly squared, the patrician line of his nose a testimony to his antecedents. The planes of his face were hard, as hard as the body steadying hers, holding her balanced on the edge of the carriage doorframe. He had released her hands; they had fallen to lie against his chest. One of her hips was pressed against his, the other against his muscled thigh. Lucinda forgot about breathing.

Cautiously, she lifted her eyes to his—and saw the sea, calm and clear, a cool, crystalline pale green.

Their gazes locked.

Mesmerised, Lucinda drowned in the green sea, her skin lapped by waves of warmth, her mind suborned to sensation. She felt her lips soften, felt herself lean into him—and blinked wildly.

A tremor shook her. The muscles surrounding her twitched, then stilled.

She felt him draw breath.

"Careful," was all he said as he slowly rose, drawing her

up with him, holding her steady until her feet could find purchase on the carriage.

Lucinda wondered just what danger he was warning her against.

Forcing his arms from her, Harry struggled to shackle his impulses, straining at their leash. "I'll have to lower you to the ground."

Peering over the carriage side, Lucinda could only nod. The drop was six feet and more. She felt him shift behind her; she jumped as his hands slipped beneath her arms.

"Don't wriggle or try to jump. I'll let go when your coachman has hold of you."

Joshua was waiting below. Lucinda nodded; speech was beyond her.

Harry gripped her firmly and swung her over the edge. The coachman quickly grasped her legs; Harry let go—but could not prevent his fingers from brushing the soft sides of her breasts. He clenched his jaw and tried to eradicate the memory but his fingertips burned.

Once on *terra firma*, Lucinda was pleased to discover her wits once more at her command. Whatever curious influence had befuddled her faculties was, thank Heaven, purely transitory.

A quick glance upwards confirmed that her rescuer had turned back to render a like service to her stepdaughter. Reflecting that at barely seventeen Heather's susceptibility to his particular brand of wizardry was probably a good deal less than her own, Lucinda left him to it.

After one comprehensive glance about the scene, she marched across to the ditch, leaned over and dealt Amy, the tweeny, a sharp slap. "Enough," she declared, as if she was speaking of nothing more than kneading dough. "Now come and help with Agatha."

Amy's tear-drenched eyes opened wide, then blinked. "Yes, mum." She sniffed—then shot a watery smile at Sim, the groom, and struggled up out of the thankfully dry ditch.

Lucinda was already on her way to Agatha, prone in the

road. "Sim—help with the horses. Oh—and do get these stones out of the road." She pointed a toe at the collection of large, jagged rocks littering the highway. "I dare say it was one of these that caused our wheel to break. And I expect you'd better start unloading the carriage."

"Aye, mum."

Halting by Agatha's side, Lucinda bent to look down at her. "What is it and how bad?"

Lips compressed, Agatha opened iron-grey eyes and squinted up at her. "It's just my ankle—it'll be better directly."

"Indeed," Lucinda remarked, getting down on her knees to examine the injured limb. "That's no doubt why you're white as a sheet."

"Nonsense—oooh!" Agatha sucked in a quick breath and closed her eyes.

"Stop fussing and let me bind it."

Lucinda bade Amy tear strips from her petticoat, then proceeded to bind Agatha's ankle, ignoring the maid's grumbles. All the while, Agatha shot suspicious glances past her.

"You'd best stay by me, mistress. And keep the young miss by you. That gentleman may be a gentleman, but he's a one to watch, I don't doubt."

Lucinda didn't doubt either but she refused to hide behind her maid's skirts. "Nonsense. He rescued us in a positively gentlemanly manner—I'll thank him appropriately. Stop fussing."

"Fussing!" Agatha hissed as Lucinda drew her skirts down to her ankles. "You didn't see him move."

"Move?" Frowning, Lucinda stood and dusted her hands, then her gown. She turned to discover Heather hurrying up, hazel eyes bright with excitement, clearly none the worse for their ordeal.

Behind her came their rescuer. All six feet and more of him, with a lean and graceful stride that conjured the immediate image of a hunting cat.

A big, powerful predator.

Agatha's comment was instantly explained. Lucinda concentrated on resisting the urge to flee. He reached for her hand—she must have extended it—and bowed elegantly.

"Permit me to introduce myself, ma'am. Harry Lester—at your service."

He straightened, a polite smile softening his features.

Fascinated, Lucinda noted how his lips curved upwards just at the ends. Then her eyes met his. She blinked and glanced away. "I most sincerely thank you, Mr Lester, for your assistance—yours and your groom's." She beamed a grateful smile at his groom, unhitching the horses from the coach with Sim's help. "It was immensely lucky you happened by."

Harry frowned, the memory of the footpads lurking in the trees beyond the curve intruding. He shook the thought aside. "I beg you'll permit me to drive you and your…" Brows lifting, he glanced from the younger girl's bright face to that of his siren's.

She smiled. "Allow me to introduce my stepdaughter, Miss Heather Babbacombe."

Heather bobbed a quick curtsy; Harry responded with a slight bow.

"As I was saying, Mrs Babbacombe." Smoothly Harry turned back and captured the lady's wide gaze with his. Her eyes were a soft blue, partly grey—a misty colour. Her carriage gown of lavender blue served to emphasise the shade. "I hope you'll permit me to drive you to your destination. You were headed for…?"

"Newmarket," Lucinda supplied. "Thank you—but I must make arrangements for my people."

Harry wasn't sure which statement more surprised him. "Naturally," he conceded, wondering how many other ladies of his acquaintance, in like circumstances, would so concern themselves over their servants. "But my groom can handle the details for you. He's familiar with these parts."

"He is? How fortunate."

Before he could blink, the soft blue gaze had left him for Dawlish—his siren followed, descending upon his servitor like a galleon in full sail. Intrigued, Harry followed. She summoned her coachman with an imperious gesture. By the time Harry joined them, she was busily issuing the orders he had thought to give.

Dawlish shot him a startled, distinctly reproachful glance.

"Will that be any trouble, do you think?" Lucinda asked, sensing the groom's distraction.

"Oh—no, ma'am." Dawlish bobbed his head respectfully. "No trouble at all. I knows the folks at the Barbican right well. We'll get all seen to."

"Good." Harry made a determined bid to regain control of the situation. "If that's settled, I suspect we should get on, Mrs Babbacombe." At the back of his mind lurked a vision of five frieze-coated men. He offered her his arm; an intent little frown wrinkling her brows, she placed her hand upon it.

"I do hope Agatha will be all right."

"Your maid?" When she nodded, Harry offered, "If she'd broken her ankle she would, I think, be in far greater pain."

The blue eyes came his way, along with a grateful smile.

Lucinda glanced away—and caught Agatha's warning glare. Her smile turned into a grimace. "Perhaps I should wait here until the cart comes for her?"

"No." Harry's response was immediate. She shot him a startled glance; he covered his lapse with a charming but rueful smile. "I hesitate to alarm you but footpads have been seen in the vicinity." His smile deepened. "And Newmarket's *only* two miles on."

"Oh." Lucinda met his gaze; she made no effort to hide the consideration in hers. "Two miles?"

"If that." Harry met her eyes, faint challenge in his.

"Well…" Lucinda turned to view his curricle.

Harry waited for no more. He beckoned Sim and pointed to the curricle. "Put your mistresses' luggage in the boot."

He turned back to be met by a cool, distinctly haughty blue glance. Equally cool, he allowed one brow to rise.

Lucinda suddenly felt warm, despite the cool breeze that

heralded the approaching evening. She looked away, to where Heather was talking animatedly to Agatha.

"If you'll forgive the advice, Mrs Babbacombe, I would not consider it wise for either you or your stepdaughter to be upon the road, unescorted, at night."

The soft drawl focused Lucinda's mind on her options. Both appeared dangerous. With a gentle inclination of her head, she chose the more exciting. "Indeed, Mr Lester. Doubtless you're right." Sim had finished stowing their baggage in the curricle's boot, strapping bandboxes to the flaps. "Heather?"

While his siren fussed, delivering a string of last-minute instructions, Harry lifted her stepdaughter to the curricle's seat. Heather Babbacombe smiled sunnily and thanked him prettily, too young to be flustered by his innate charms.

Doubtless, Harry thought, as he turned to view her stepmother, Heather viewed him much as an uncle. His lips quirked, then relaxed into a smile as he watched Mrs Babbacombe glide towards him, casting last, measuring glances about her.

She was slender and tall—there was something about her graceful carriage that evoked the adjective "matriarchal." A confidence, an assurance, that showed in her frank gaze and open expression. Her dark hair, richly brown with the suspicion of red glinting in the sun, was, he could now see, fixed in a tight bun at the nape of her neck. For his money, the style was too severe—his fingers itched to run through the silken tresses, laying them free.

As for her figure, he was having great difficulty disguising his interest. She was, indeed, one of the more alluring visions he had beheld in many a long year.

She drew near and he lifted a brow. "Ready, Mrs Babbacombe?"

Lucinda turned to meet his gaze, wondering how such a soft drawl could so easily sound steely. "Thank you, Mr Lester." She gave him her hand; he took it, drawing her to the side of the carriage. Lucinda blinked at the high step—the next instant, she felt his hands firm about her waist and she was lifted, effortlessly, to the seat.

Stifling her gasp, Lucinda met Heather's gaze, filled with innocent anticipation. Sternly suppressing her fluster, Lucinda settled herself on the seat next to her stepdaughter. She had not, indeed, had much experience interacting with gentlemen of Mr Lester's standing; perhaps such gestures were commonplace?

Despite her inexperience, she could not delude herself that her position, as it transpired, could ever be dismissed as commonplace. Her rescuer paused only to swing his greatcoat—adorned, she noted, with a great many capes—about his broad shoulders before following her into the curricle, the reins in his hands. Naturally, he sat beside her.

A bright smile firmly fixed on her lips, Lucinda waved Agatha goodbye, steadfastly ignoring the hard thigh pressed against her much softer limb, and the way her shoulder perforce had to nestle against his back.

Harry himself had not foreseen the tight squeeze—and found its results equally disturbing. Pleasant—but definitely disturbing. Backing his team, he asked, "Were you coming from Cambridge, Mrs Babbacombe?" He desperately needed distraction.

Lucinda was only too ready to oblige. "Yes—we spent a week there. We intended to leave directly after lunch but spent an hour or so in the gardens. They're very fine, we discovered."

Her accents were refined and untraceable, her stepdaughter's less so, while those of her servants were definitely north country. The greys settled into their stride; Harry comforted himself that two miles meant less than fifteen minutes, even allowing for picking their way through the town. "But you're not from hereabouts?"

"No—we're from Yorkshire." After a moment, Lucinda added, a smile tweaking her lips, "At the moment, however, I suspect we could more rightly claim to be gypsies."

"Gypsies?"

Lucinda exchanged a smile with Heather. "My husband died just over a year ago. His estate passed into his cousin's hands, so Heather and I decided to while away our year of mourning in travelling the country. Neither of us had seen much of it before."

Harry stifled a groan. She was a widow—a beautiful widow newly out of mourning, unfixed, unattached, bar the minor encumbrance of a stepdaughter. In an effort to deny his mounting interest, to block out his awareness of her soft curves pressed, courtesy of Heather Babbacombe's more robust figure, firmly against his side, he concentrated on her words. And frowned. "Where do you plan to stay in Newmarket?"

"The Barbican Arms," Lucinda replied. "I believe it's in the High Street."

"It is." Harry's lips thinned; the Barbican Arms was directly opposite the Jockey Club. "Ah—have you reservations?" He slanted a glance at her face and saw surprise register. "It's a race week, you know."

"Is it?" Lucinda frowned. "Does that mean it'll be crowded?"

"Very." With every rakehell and womaniser who could make the journey from London. Harry suppressed the thought. Mrs Babbacombe was, he told himself, none of his business. Very definitely none of his business—she might be a widow and, to his experienced eye, ripe for seduction, but she was a *virtuous* widow—therein lay the rub. He was too experienced not to know such existed—indeed, the fleeting thought occurred that if he was to plot his own downfall, then a virtuous widow would be first choice as Cupid's pawn. But he had recognised the trap—and had no intention of falling into it. Mrs Babbacombe was one beautiful widow he would do well to leave untouched—unsampled. Desire bucked, unexpectedly strong; with a mental curse, Harry shackled it—in iron!

The first straggling cottages appeared ahead. He grimaced. "Is there no acquaintance you have in the district with whom you might stay?"

"No—but I'm sure we'll be able to find accommodation

somewhere.'' Lucinda gestured airily, struggling to keep her mind on her words and her senses on the late afternoon landscape. ''If not at the Barbican Arms, then perhaps the Green Goose.''

She sensed the start that shot through him. Turning, she met an openly incredulous, almost horrified stare.

''*Not* the Green Goose.'' Harry made no attempt to mute the decree.

It was received with a frown. ''Why not?''

Harry opened his mouth—but couldn't find the words. ''Never mind why—just get it into your head that you cannot reside at the Green Goose.''

Intransigence flowed into her expression, then she put her pretty nose in the air and looked ahead. ''If you will just set us down at the Barbican Arms, Mr Lester, I'm sure we'll sort things out.''

Her words conjured a vision of the yard at the Barbican Arms—of the main hall of the inn as it would be at this moment—as Harry had experienced it at such times before. Jampacked with males, broad-shouldered, elegant *ton*nish gentlemen, the vast majority of whom he would know by name. He certainly knew them by nature; he could just imagine their smiles when Mrs Babbacombe walked in.

''No.''

The cobbles of the High Street rang beneath the greys' hooves.

Lucinda turned to stare at him. ''What on earth do you mean?''

Harry gritted his teeth. Even with his attention on his horses as he negotiated the press of traffic in the main street of the horse capital of England, he was still aware of the surprised glances thrown their way—and of the lingering, considering looks bent on the woman by his side. Arriving with him, being seen with him, had already focused attention on her.

It was none of his business.

Harry felt his face harden. ''Even if the Barbican Arms has

rooms to spare—which they will not—it's not suitable for you to stay in town while a race meeting's on.''

''I beg your pardon?'' After a moment of astonished surprise, Lucinda drew herself up. ''Mr Lester—you have most ably rescued us—we owe you our gratitude. However, I am more than capable of organising our accommodation and stay in this town.''

''Gammon.''

''What?''

''You don't know anything about staying in a town during a race-meet or you wouldn't be here now.'' Lips set in a thin line, Harry shot her an irritated glare. ''Devil take it—look around you, woman!''

Lucinda had already noticed the large number of men strolling the narrow pavements. As her gaze swept the scene, she noted that there were many more on horseback and in the sporting carriages of every description thronging the thoroughfare. Gentlemen everywhere. Only gentlemen.

Heather was leaning close, shrinking against her, not used to being stared at and ogled. She raised hazel eyes filled with uncertainty to Lucinda's face. ''Lucinda…?''

Lucinda patted her hand. As she raised her head, she encountered a boldly appraising stare from a gentleman in a high-perch phaeton. Lucinda returned his scrutiny with a frosty glance. ''Nevertheless,'' she maintained. ''If you will set us down at…''

Her words trailed away as she glimpsed, hanging above a broad archway just ahead, a signboard depicting a castle gateway. In that instant, the traffic parted; Harry clicked his reins and the curricle shot forward—straight past the archway.

Lucinda swivelled to peer at the sign as they moved steadily down the street. ''That's it—the Barbican Arms!'' She turned to look at Harry. ''You've passed it.''

Grim-faced, Harry nodded.

Lucinda glared at him. ''Stop,'' she ordered.

''You can't stay in town.''

''I can!''

"Over my dead body!" Harry heard his snarl and inwardly groaned. He closed his eyes. What was happening to him? Opening his eyes, he glared at the woman beside him. Her cheeks were becomingly flushed—with temper. A fleeting thought of how she would look flushed with desire shot through his unwilling mind.

Something of his thoughts must have shown in his face— her blue eyes narrowed. "Are you proposing to kidnap us?" Her voice held the promise of a long and painful death.

The end of the High Street appeared; the traffic thinned. Harry flicked his leader's ear and the greys surged. As the sound of hooves on cobbles died behind them, he glanced down at her and growled, "Consider it forcible repatriation."

Chapter Two

"*FORCIBLE REPATRIATION?*"

Harry shot her a narrow-eyed glare. "You don't *belong* in a race-town."

Lucinda glared back. "I belong wherever *I* choose to stay, Mr Lester."

His face set in uncompromising lines, Harry looked back at his team. Lucinda looked ahead, frowning direfully.

"Where are you taking us?" she eventually demanded.

"To stay with my aunt, Lady Hallows." Harry glanced at her. "She lives a little way out of town."

It had been many years since she'd allowed anyone to order her life. Nose in the air, Lucinda held to dignified disapproval. "How do you know she won't already have visitors?"

"She's a widow of long standing and lives quietly." Harry checked his team and turned onto a side road. "She has a whole Hall to spare—and she'll be delighted to make your acquaintance."

Lucinda sniffed. "You can't know that."

The smile he bent on her was infinitely superior.

Resisting the urge to gnash her teeth, Lucinda pointedly looked away.

Heather had perked up the instant they'd quit town; she smiled when Lucinda glanced her way, clearly restored to her usual sunny humour and unperturbed by the unexpected alteration to their plans.

Feeling distinctly huffy, Lucinda looked ahead. It was, she suspected, pointless to protest—at least, not until she'd met Lady Hallows. Until then, there was nothing she could do to ιegain the ascendancy. The infuriating gentleman beside her had the upper hand—and the reins. Her gaze flicked sideways, to where his hands, covered by soft doeskin gloves, dextrously managed the ribbons. Long slim fingers and slender palms. She'd noted that earlier. To her horror, the memory evoked a shiver—she had to fight to quell it. With him so close, he would very likely feel it—and, she suspected, would unhesitatingly guess its cause.

Which would leave her feeling embarrassed—and even more deeply disturbed. He evoked a most peculiar response in her— it had yet to fade, despite her irritation at his autocratic interference. It was a distinctly novel feeling—one she wasn't at all sure she appreciated.

"Hallows Hall."

She looked up to discover a pair of imposing gateposts which gave onto a shady avenue lined with elms. The gravelled drive wound gently along a slight ridge, then dipped to reveal a pleasant vista of rolling lawns surrounding a reed-fringed lake, the whole enclosed by large trees.

"How pretty!" Heather looked about in delight.

The Hall, a relatively recent structure in honey-coloured stone, sat on a rise above the drive, which wound past the front steps before curving around the corner of the house. A vine stretched green fingers over the stone. There were roses in abundance; ducks clacked from the lake.

An ancient retainer came ambling up as Harry drew his team to a halt.

"Thought as we'd see you this week, young master."

Harry grinned. "Good evening, Grimms. Is my aunt at home?"

"Aye—that she is—and right pleased she'll be to see you. Evening, miss. Miss." Grimms doffed his cap to Lucinda and Heather.

Lucinda's answering smile was distant. Hallows Hall stirred long-forgotten memories of life before her parents had died.

Harry descended and helped her down. After helping

Heather to the ground, he turned to see Lucinda looking about her, a wistful expression on her face. "Mrs Babbacombe?"

Lucinda started. Then, with a half-grimace and a frosty glance, she placed her hand on his arm and allowed him to lead her up the steps.

The door was flung open—not by a butler, although a stately personage of that persuasion hovered in the shadows—but by a gaunt, angular-featured woman a good two inches taller than Lucinda and decidedly thinner.

"Harry, m'boy! Thought you'd be here. And who's this you've brought?"

Lucinda found herself blinking into dark blue eyes, shrewd and intelligent.

"But what am I about? Come in, come in." Ermyntrude, Lady Hallows, waved her guests into the hall.

Lucinda stepped over the threshold—and was immediately enveloped in the warm, elegant yet homey atmosphere.

Harry took his aunt's hand and bowed over it, then kissed her cheek. "As elegant as ever, Em," he said, scanning her topaz gown.

Em's eyes opened wide. "Flummery? From you?"

Harry pressed her hand warningly as he released it. "Allow me to present Mrs Babbacombe, Aunt. Her carriage broke a wheel just outside town. I had the honour of driving her in. She had some idea of staying in town but I prevailed upon her to change her mind and give you the benefit of her company."

The words tripped glibly from his tongue. Rising from her curtsy, Lucinda shot him a chilly glance.

"Capital!" Em beamed and took Lucinda's hand. "My dear, you don't know how bored I sometimes get, stuck out here in the country. And Harry's quite right—you can't possibly stay in town during a meet—not at all the thing." Her blue eyes switched to Heather. "And who's this?"

Lucinda made the introduction and Heather, smiling brightly. bobbed a curtsy.

Em put out a hand and tipped Heather's chin up the better to view her face. "Hmm—quite lovely. You'll do well in a year or two.'' Releasing her, Em frowned. "Babbacombe, Babbacombe…'' She glanced at Lucinda. "Not the Staffordshire Babbacombes?''

Lucinda smiled. "Yorkshire.'' When her hostess only frowned harder, she felt compelled to add, "I was a Gifford before my marriage.''

"Gifford?'' Em's eyes slowly widened as she studied Lucinda. "*Great heavens!* You must be Melrose Gifford's daughter—Celia Parkes was your mother?''

Surprised, Lucinda nodded—and was promptly enveloped in a scented embrace.

"Good gracious, child—I knew your father!'' Em was in transports. "Well—I was a bosom-bow of his elder sister, but I knew all the family. Naturally, after the scandal, we heard very little of Celia and Melrose, but they did send word of your birth.'' Em wrinkled her nose. "Not that it did much good—stiff-necked lot, your grandparents. On both sides.''

Harry blinked, endeavouring to absorb this rush of information. Lucinda noticed, and wondered how he felt about rescuing the outcome of an old scandal.

"Just fancy!'' Em was still in alt. "I never thought to set eyes on you, m'dear. Mind you, there's not many left but me who'd remember. You'll have to tell me the whole story.'' Em paused to draw breath. "Now then! Fergus will get your luggage and I'll show you up to your rooms—after a dish of tea—you *must* be in need of refreshment. Dinner's at six so there's no need to hurry.''

Together with Heather, Lucinda found herself hustled towards an open doorway—a drawing-room lay ahead. On the threshold she hesitated and glanced back, as did Em behind her.

"You're not staying, are you, Harry?'' Em asked.

He was tempted—sorely tempted. His gaze not on his aunt but on the woman beside her, Harry forced himself to shake his head. "No.'' With an effort he shifted his gaze to his aunt's face. "I'll call sometime during the week.''

Em nodded.

Prompted by she knew not what, Lucinda turned and re crossed the hall. Their rescuer stood silently and watched her approach; she steadfastly ignored the odd tripping of her heart. She halted before him, calmly meeting his green gaze. "I don't know how to thank you for your help, Mr Lester. You've been more than kind."

His lips slowly curved; again, she found herself fascinated by the movement.

Harry took the hand she held out to him and, his eyes on hers, raised it to his lips. "Your rescue was indeed my pleasure, Mrs Babbacombe." The sudden widening of her eyes as his lips touched her skin was payment enough for the consequent hardships. "I'll ensure that your people know where to find you—your maids will arrive before nightfall, I'm sure."

Lucinda inclined her head; she made no effort to retrieve her fingers from his warm grasp. "Again, you have my thanks. sir."

"It was nothing, my dear." His eyes on hers, Harry allowed one brow to rise. "Perhaps we'll meet again—in a ballroom, maybe? Dare I hope you'll favour me with a waltz if we do?"

Graciously, Lucinda acquiesced. "I would be honoured. sir—should we meet."

Belatedly reminding himself that she was a snare he was determined to avoid, Harry took a firm grip on his wayward impulses. He bowed. Releasing Lucinda's hand, he nodded to Em. With one last glance at Lucinda, he strolled gracefully out of the door.

Lucinda watched the door shut behind him, a distant frown in her eyes.

Em studied her unexpected guest, a speculative glint in hers

AGATHA'S BEEN WITH ME forever," Lucinda explained. "She was my mother's maid when I was born. Amy was an under-maid at the Grange—my husband's house. We took her with us so that Agatha could train her to act as maid for Heather."

"Just as well," Heather put in.

They were in the dining-room, partaking of a delicious meal

prepared, so Em had informed them, in honour of their arrival. Agatha, Amy and Sim had arrived an hour ago, conveyed by Joshua in a trap borrowed from the Barbican Arms. Joshua had returned to Newmarket to pursue the repairs of the carriage. Agatha, taken under the wing of the portly housekeeper, Mrs Simmons, was resting in a cheery room below the eaves, her ankle pronounced unbroken but badly sprained. Amy had thus had to assist both Lucinda and Heather to dress, a task at which she had acquitted herself with honours.

Or so Em thought as she looked down the table. "So," she said, patting her lips with her napkin then waving Fergus and the soup tureen away. "You may start at the beginning. I want to know all about you since your parents died."

The sheer openness of the request robbed it of any rudeness. Lucinda smiled and laid aside her spoon; Heather was dipping into the tureen for the third time, much to Fergus's delight. "As you know, what with both families disowning my parents, I hadn't had any contact with my grandparents. I was fourteen at the time of the accident. Luckily, our old solicitor hunted up my mother's sister's address—she agreed to take me in."

"Now let's see." Em's eyes narrowed as she surveyed the past. "That would be Cora Parkes that was?"

Lucinda nodded. "If you recall, the Parkes family fortunes had taken a downturn sometime after my parents married. They'd retired from Society and Cora had married a mill-owner in the north—a Mr Ridley."

"*Never* say so!" Em was enthralled. "Well, well—how the mighty did fall. Your aunt Cora was one of the most intransigent when it came to any question of reconciliation with your parents." Em lifted her thin shoulders. "Fate's revenge, I dare say. So you lived with them until your marriage?"

Lucinda hesitated, then nodded.

Em noticed; her eyes sharpened, then flicked to Heather. Lucinda saw—and hastened to explain. "The Ridleys weren't exactly happy to have me. They only agreed to house me, thinking to use my talents as governess to their two daughters and then to broker my marriage as soon as maybe."

For a moment, Em stared. Then she snorted. "Doesn't surprise me. That Cora was ever out for her own gain."

"When I was sixteen, they arranged a marriage with another mill-owner, a Mr Ogleby."

"Ugh!" Heather looked up from her soup to shudder artistically. "He was a horrible old toad," she blithely informed Em. "Luckily, my father heard about it—Lucinda used to come and give me lessons. So *he* married Lucinda instead." Having done her bit for the conversation, Heather returned to her soup.

Lucinda smiled affectionately. "Indeed, Charles was my saviour. I only recently learned that he bought off my relatives in order to marry me—he never told me."

Em snorted approvingly. "Glad to hear they've *some* gentlemen in those parts. So you became Mrs Babbacombe and lived at…the Grange, was it?"

"That's right." Heather had finally relinquished the soup; Lucinda paused to serve herself from the platter of turbot Fergus offered. "To all appearances Charles was a well-to-do gentleman of moderate estate. In reality, however, he owned a considerable collection of inns up and down the country. He was really very wealthy but preferred a quiet existence. He was close to fifty when we married. As I grew older, he taught me all about his investments and how to manage them. He was ill for some years—the end was a relief when it came—but because of his foresight, I was able to handle most of the work for him."

Lucinda looked up to find her hostess staring at her.

"Who owns the inns now?" Em asked.

Lucinda smiled. "We do—Heather and I. The Grange, of course, went to Charles's nephew, Mortimer Babbacombe, but Charles's private fortune wasn't part of the entail."

Em sat back and regarded her with frank approval. "And that's why you're here—you own an inn in Newmarket?"

Lucinda nodded. "After the will was read, Mortimer asked us to vacate the Grange within the week."

"The blackguard!" Em glared. "What sort of a way is that to treat a grieving widow?"

"Well," Lucinda held up a hand. "I did offer to leave as soon as he wished—although I hadn't thought he'd be in such a hurry. He'd never even visited before—not really."

"So you found yourselves out on your ears in the snow?" Em was incensed.

Heather giggled. "It really turned out most fortuitously in the end."

"Indeed." Lucinda nodded, pushing her plate away. "With nothing organised, we decided to remove to one of our inns— one a little way away from the Grange, a place we weren't known. Once there, I realised the inn was far more prosperous than I would have guessed from the accounts our agent had recently presented. Mr Scrugthorpe was a new man—Charles had been forced to appoint a new agent a few months before he died when our old Mr Matthews passed on." Lucinda frowned at the trifle Fergus placed before her. "Unfortunately, Charles interviewed Scrugthorpe on a day he was in great pain and I had to be in town with Heather. To cut a long story short, Scrugthorpe had falsified the accounts. I called him in and dismissed him."

Lifting her gaze to her hostess's face, Lucinda smiled. "After that, Heather and I decided that travelling the country getting to know our inns was an excellent way to see out our year of mourning. It was exactly the sort of enterprise of which Charles would have approved."

Em snorted—this snort clearly signified her appreciation of Charles's good sense. "Seems to have been a very able man— your father, miss."

"He was a dear." Heather's open face clouded and she blinked rapidly, then looked down.

"I've appointed a new agent—a Mr Mabberly." Lucinda smoothly covered the awkward moment. "He's young but extremely efficient."

"And goes in awe of Lucinda," Heather offered, looking up to help herself to a second scoop of trifle.

"As he should," Em replied. "Well, Miss Gifford as was—

you've certainly done your parents proud thus far. A capable
lady of independent means at what—twenty-six?''

"Twenty-eight." Lucinda's smile was crooked. There were
times, such as today, when she suddenly wondered if life had
passed her by.

"A very fair achievement," Em declared. "I don't hold with
women being helpless." She eyed Heather's at last empty
plate. "And if you've finally finished, miss, I suggest we retire
to the drawing-room. Do either of you play the pianoforte?"

They both did and gladly entertained their hostess with various airs and sonatas, until Heather fell to yawning. At Lucinda's suggestion she retired, passing the tea trolley in the
doorway.

"Indeed, we've had an adventuresome day." Lucinda sat
back in an armchair by the fire and sipped the tea Em had
dispensed. Lifting her gaze, she smiled at Em. "I can't thank
you enough, Lady Hallows, for taking us in."

"Nonsense," Em replied with one of her snorts. "And you
could please me by dropping all the ladyships and just calling
me Em, like everyone else in the family. You're Melrose's
daughter and that's close enough for me."

Lucinda smiled, a trifle wearily. "Em, then. What's it a con-
traction for? Emma?"

Em wrinkled her nose. "Ermyntrude."

Lucinda managed to keep her lips straight. "Oh?" she said
weakly.

"Indeed. My brothers delighted in calling me all the con-
tractions you might imagine. When my nephews came along,
I declared it was Em and nothing else."

"Very wise." A companionable silence settled as they sa-
voured their tea. Lucinda broke it to ask, "Do you have many
nephews?"

From under heavy lids, Em's eyes glinted. "Quite a few.
But it was Harry and his brothers I had to guard against. A
rapscallion lot."

Lucinda shifted. "He has a lot of brothers?"

"Only two—but that's quite enough. Jack's the eldest," Em

blithely rattled on. "He's—let me see—thirty-six now. Then comes Harry, two years younger. Then there's quite a gap to their sister Lenore—she married Eversleigh some years back— she must be twenty-six now, which makes Gerald twenty-four. Their mother died years ago but my brother still hangs on." Em grinned. "Dare say he'll manage to cling to life long enough to see a grandson to carry on the name, the cantankerous old fool." The last was said affectionately. "But it was the boys I had most to do with—and Harry was always my favourite. Blessed by the angels and the devil both, of course, but such a good boy." Em blinked, then amended, "Well—a good boy *at heart*. They all were—are. I see most of Harry and Gerald these days—what with Newmarket so close. Harry runs the Lester stud which, even if 'tis I who say so—and Heaven knows I know next to nothing about horses—such a boring subject—is hailed as one of the premier studs in the land."

"Really?" There was not the slightest trace of boredom in Lucinda's face.

"Indeed." Em nodded. "Harry usually comes to watch his runners perform. Dare say I'll see Gerald this week, too. Doubtless he'll want to show off his new phaeton. Told me when last he was up that he was going to buy one, now the family coffers are full and overflowing."

Lucinda blinked.

Em didn't wait for her to find a subtle way to ask. One hand waving, she airly explained, "The Lesters have traditionally been strapped for cash—good estates, good breeding, but no money. The present generation, however, invested in some shipping venture last year and now the whole family's rolling in an abundance of the ready."

"Oh." Lucinda readily recalled Harry Lester's expensive elegance. She couldn't imagine him any other way. Indeed, his image seemed to have fixed in her mind, oddly vivid, strangely enthralling. Shaking her head to dispel it, she delicately smothered a yawn. "I'm afraid I'm not very good company, Lady— Em." She smiled. "I suspect I'd better follow Heather."

Em merely nodded. "I'll see you in the morning, m'dear."
Lucinda left her hostess staring into the fire.

Ten minutes later, her head pillowed in down, Lucinda
closed her eyes—only to find Harry Lester on her mind. Tired,
adrift, her memories of the day replayed, her interactions with
him claiming centre stage. Until she came to their parting—
which left one question to plague her. How would it feel to
waltz with Harry Lester?

A MILE AWAY, in the tap of the Barbican Arms, Harry sat
elegantly sprawled behind a corner table, moodily surveying
the room. A smoky haze wreathed a forest of shoulders; gentlemen mingled freely with grooms and stablemen, tipsters
wrangled with bookmakers. The tap was all business this evening; the first races, those for non-bloodstock, would commence the next day.

A barmaid came up, hips swaying. She set a tankard of the
inn's finest on the table, smiling coyly, one brow rising as
Harry flipped a coin onto her tray.

Harry caught her eye; his lips curved but he shook his head.
Disappointed, the girl turned away. Harry lifted the foaming
tankard and took a long sip. He'd abandoned the snug, his
habitual refuge, where only the cognescenti were permitted,
driven forth by the all-but-incessant questioning as to his delectable companion of the afternoon.

It seemed as if all in Newmarket had seen them.

Certainly all his friends and acquaintances were keen to learn
her name. And her direction.

He'd given them neither, steadfastly returning their bright-
eyed enquiries with a blank look and the information that the
lady was an acquaintance of his aunt's he'd simply been escorting to her door.

Those facts proved sufficient to dampen the interest of most;
the majority who frequented Newmarket knew of his aunt.

But he was definitely tired of covering the lovely Mrs Babbacombe's tracks, particularly as he was trying his damnedest
to forget her. And her loveliness.

With an inward growl, Harry immersed himself in his tankard and tried to focus his mind on his horses—usually an enthralling subject.

"There you are! Been looking all over. What're you doing
out here?" Dawlish slumped into the chair beside him.

"Don't ask," Harry advised. He waited while the barmaid,
with a fine show of indifference, served Dawlish before asking,
"What's the verdict?"

Dawlish shot him a glance over the rim of his tankard.
"Odd," came mumbling from behind it.

Brows lifting, Harry turned his head to stare at his henchman. "Odd?" Dawlish had gone with the coachman, Joshua,
to fetch the wainwright to the carriage.

"Me, Joshua and the wainwright all thinks the same." Dawlish set down his tankard and wiped the froth from his lip.
"Thought as how you should know."

"Know what?"

"That the cotter-pin on that wheel was tampered with—half-
sawed through, it was—*before* the accident. And the spokes
had been got at, too."

Harry frowned. "Why?"

"Don't know as how you noticed, but there were a curious
lot of rocks strewn about that stretch of road where the carriage
went over. None before—and none after. Just along that stretch.
No way a coachman could miss all of 'em. And they were just
round a corner so he couldn't see them in time to pull up."

Harry's frown was intense. "I remember the rocks. The boy
cleared them away so I didn't have to drive over them."

Dawlish nodded. "Aye—but the carriage couldn't avoid
them—and as soon as that wheel hit, the cotter would have
snapped and the spokes after that."

A chill swept Harry's nape. Five mounted men in frieze, with
a wagon, hiding in the trees, moving towards the road just after
the carriage went down. And if it hadn't been a race-week, that
particular stretch of road would almost certainly have been deserted at that time of day.

Harry lifted his gaze to Dawlish's face.

Dawlish looked back at him. "Makes you think, don't it?"

Grim-faced, Harry slowly nodded. "It does indeed." And he didn't like what he thought at all.

Chapter Three

"I'LL HAVE Y'R TEAM OUT in a jiffy, sir."

Harry nodded absentmindedly as the head-ostler of the Barbican Arms hurried off towards the stables. Pulling on his driving gloves, he strolled away from the inn's main door to await his curricle in a vacant patch of sunshine by the wall.

Before him, the courtyard was busy, many of the inn's guests departing for a day at the track, hoping to pick a few winners to start the week off on the right note.

Harry grimaced. He wouldn't be joining them. Not, at least, until he'd satisfied himself on the score of one Mrs Babbacombe. He had given up telling himself she was none of his business; after the revelations of yesterday, he felt compelled to brave her dangers—long enough to assure himself of her safety. She was, after all, his aunt's guest—at his insistence. Two facts which undoubtedly excused his interest.

"I'll get along and see Hamish then, shall I?"

Harry turned as Dawlish came up. Hamish, his head-stableman, should have arrived yesterday with his string of thoroughbred racers; the horses would be settling into their stables beyond the racetrack. Harry nodded. "Make sure Thistledown's fetlock's sufficiently healed—I don't want her entered unless it is."

Dawlish nodded sagely. "Aye. Shall I tell Hamish you'll be along shortly to see it?"

"No." Harry studied the fit of his gloves. "I'll have to rely on your combined wisdom this time. I've pressing matters elsewhere."

He felt Dawlish's suspicious glance.

574 AN UNWILLING CONQUEST

"More pressing than a prime mare with a strained fetlock?" Dawlish snorted. "I'd like to know what's higher on y'r list than that."

Harry made no effort to enlighten him. "I'll probably look in about lunchtime." His imaginings were very likely groundless. It could be no more than coincidence, and two likely females travelling without major escort, that had focused the attention of the men in frieze on the Babbacombe coach. "Just make sure Hamish gets the message in time."

"Aye," Dawlish grumbled. With a last keen glance, he headed off.

Harry turned as his curricle appeared, the head-ostler leading the greys with a reverence that bespoke a full appreciation of their qualities.

"Right prime 'uns, they be," he averred as Harry climbed to the box.

"Indeed." Harry took up the reins. The greys were restive, sensing the chance of freedom. With a nod for the ostler, he backed the curricle preparatory to making a stylish exit from the yard.

"Harry!"

Harry paused, then, with a sigh, drew in his impatient steeds. "Good morning, Gerald. And since when do you arise at this ungodly hour?"

He had spied his younger brother amongst the crowds in the tap the night before but had made no effort to advertise his presence. He turned to watch as Gerald, blue-eyed and dark-haired as was his elder brother Jack, strode up, grinning broadly, to place a familiar hand on the curricle's front board.

"Ever since I heard the story of you escorting two excessively likely looking females who, according to you, are connections of Em's."

"Not connections, dear brother—*acquaintances*."

Faced with Harry's languidly bored mask, Gerald lost a little of his assurance. "You mean they really are? Acquaintances of Em's, I mean?"

"So I discovered."

Gerald's face fell. "Oh." Then Dawlish's absence registered. Gerald shot a keen glance at his brother. "You're going to Em's now. Mind if I hitch a ride? Should say hello to the old girl—and perhaps to that dark-haired delight you had up beside you yesterday."

For an instant, Harry was shaken by the most absurd impulse—Gerald was his younger brother after all, of whom he was, beneath his dismissive exterior, distinctly fond. He concealed the unexpected emotion behind his ineffable charm—and sighed. "I fear, dear brother, that I must puncture your delusions—the lady's too old for you."

"Oh? How old is she?"

Harry raised his brows. "Older than you."

"Well—perhaps I'll try for the other one then—the blonde."

Harry looked down on his brother's eager countenance—and inwardly shook his head. "She, if anything, is probably too young. Just out of the schoolroom, I suspect."

"No harm in that," Gerald blithely countered. "They have to start sometime."

Feeling distinctly put-upon, Harry heaved a disgusted sigh. "Gerald…"

"Dash it all, Harry—don't be such a dog-in-the-manger. You're not interested in the younger chit—let me take her off your hands."

Harry blinked at his brother. It was undoubtedly true that any discussion of Mrs Babbacombe's situation would proceed a great deal more openly in the absence of her stepdaughter. "Very well—if you insist." Within Em's purlieu, Gerald could be relied on to keep within acceptable bounds. "But don't say I didn't warn you."

Almost gleefully, Gerald swung up to the curricle's seat. The instant he was aboard, Harry clicked his reins. The greys shot forward; he had to exert all his skills to thread them through the traffic thronging the High Street. He let them stretch their legs once free of the town; Em's leafy drive was reached in record time.

A stableboy came hurrying to take charge of the curricle.

Together, Harry and Gerald mounted the steps to Em's door. The oak door was set wide open, not an uncommon occurrence. The brothers wandered in. Harry tossed his gloves onto the ormolu table. "Looks like we'll have to go hunt. I expect my business with Mrs Babbacombe will take no more than half an hour. If you can keep Miss Babbacombe occupied until then, I'll be grateful."

Gerald cocked an eyebrow. "Grateful enough to let me tool your greys back to town?"

Harry looked doubtful. "Possibly—but I wouldn't count on it."

Gerald grinned and looked about him. "So where do we start?"

"You take the gardens—I'll take the house. I'll call if I need help." With a languid wave, Harry set off down one corridor. Whistling, Gerald turned and went out of the main door.

Harry drew a blank in the morning room and the parlour. Then he heard humming, punctuated by the click of shears, and remembered the small garden room at the end of the house. There he found Em, arranging flowers in a huge urn.

At his languid best, he strolled in. "Good morning, Aunt."

Em turned her head—and stared in stunned surprise. "Devil take it—what are you doing *here?*"

Harry blinked. "Where else should I be?"

"In town. I was sure you'd be there."

After a moment's hesitation, Harry conceded with the obvious. "Why?"

"Because Lucinda—Mrs Babbacombe—went into town half an hour ago. Never been there before—wanted to get her bearings."

A chill caressed Harry's nape. "You let her go alone?"

Turning back to her blooms, Em waved her shears. "Heavens, no—her groom accompanied her."

"Her groom?" Harry's voice was soft, urbane, its tone enough to send chills down the most insensitive spine. "The young tow-headed lad who arrived with her?"

He watched as a tell-tale blush spread over his aunt's high cheekbones.

Disconcerted, Em shrugged. "She's an independent woman—it doesn't do to argue overmuch." She knew perfectly well she should not have let Lucinda go into Newmarket this week without more tangible escort, but there was a definite purpose to her ploy. Turning, she surveyed her nephew. "*You* could try, of course."

For an instant, Harry couldn't believe his ears—surely not *Em?* His eyes narrowed as he took in her bland expression; this was the last thing he needed—a traitor in his own camp. His lips thinned; with a terse nod, he countered, "Rest assured I will."

Turning on his heel, he strode out of the room, down the corridor, out of the door and around to the stables. The stable-boy was startled to see him; Harry was merely glad the horses were still harnessed.

He grabbed the reins and leapt up to the seat. His whip cracked and the horses took off. The drive back to town established a new record.

Only when he was forced to slow by the press of traffic in the High Street did Harry remember Gerald. He cursed, regretting the loss of another to aid in his search. Taking advantage of the crawling pace, he carefully studied the crowded pavements from behind his habitually unruffled mien. But no dark head could he see.

He did, however, discover a large number of his peers—friends, acquaintances—who, like himself, were too experienced to waste time at the track today. He entertained not the slightest doubt that each and every one would be only too willing to spend that time by the side of a certain delectable dark-haired widow—not one would consider it time wasted.

Reaching the end of the street, Harry swore. Disregarding all hazards, he turned the curricle, missing the gleaming panels of a new phaeton by less than an inch, leaving the slow-top in charge of the reins in the grip of an apoplectic fit.

Ignoring the fuss, Harry drove quickly back to the Barbican

Arms and turned the greys into the loving hands of the head-ostler. The man confirmed that Em's gig was in residence. Harry surreptitiously checked the private parlour and was relieved to find it empty; the Arms was the favourite watering-hole of his set. Striding back to the street, he paused to take stock. And to wonder what ''getting her bearings'' meant.

There was no lending library. He settled on the church, some way along the street. But no likely looking widow haunted its hallowed precincts, nor trod the paths between the graves. The town's gardens were a joke—no one came to Newmarket to admire floral borders. Mrs Dobson's Tea Rooms were doing a brisk trade but no darkly elegant widow graced any of the small tables.

Returning to the pavement, Harry paused, hands on hips, and stared across the street. Where the devil was she?

A glimmer of blue at the edge of his vision had him turning his head. Just in time to identify the dark-haired figure who sailed through the street door of the Green Goose, a tow-headed boy at her back.

PAUSING JUST INSIDE the inn's door, Lucinda found herself engulfed in dimness. Musty dimness. As her eyes adjusted to the gloom, she discovered she was in a hall, with the entrance to the tap on her left, two doors which presumably led to private parlours on her right and a counter, an extension of the tap's bar, directly ahead, a tarnished bell on its scratched surface.

Suppressing the urge to wrinkle her nose, she swept forward. She had spent the last twenty minutes examining the inn from outside, taking due note of the faded and flaking whitewash, the clutter in the yard and the down-at-heel appearance of the two customers who had crossed its threshold. Extending one gloved hand, she picked up the bell and rang it imperiously. At least, that was her intention. But the bell emitted no more than a dull clack. Upending it, Lucinda discovered the clapper had broken.

With a disgusted grimace, she replaced the bell. She was wondering whether to tell Sim, waiting by the door, to raise his voice in summons when a large shadow blocked out what little light penetrated from the inn's nether regions. A man entered, burly, brawny—very big. His face was heavy-featured but his eyes, sunk in folds of fat, appeared merely uninterested.

"Aye?"

Lucinda blinked. "Are you Mr Blount?"

"Aye."

Her heart sank. "You're the innkeeper?"

"Nay."

When no more was forthcoming, she prompted, "You're Mr Blount, but you're not the innkeeper." There was hope yet. "Where is the Mr Blount who *is* the innkeeper?"

For a long moment, the burly individual regarded her stoically as if his brain was having difficulty digesting her question. "You want Jake—m'brother," he eventually offered.

Lucinda heaved an inward sigh of relief. "Precisely—I wish to see Mr Blount, the innkeeper."

"Wha'for?"

Lucinda opened her eyes wide. "That, my good man, is a matter for your brother and myself."

The hulking brute eyed her measuringly, then humphed. "Wait 'ere—I'll fetch 'im." With that, he lumbered off.

Leaving Lucinda praying that his brother took after the other side of the family. Her prayers were not answered. The man who replaced the first was equally burly, equally overweight and, apparently, only fractionally less dim-witted.

"Mr Jake Blount—the keeper of this inn?" Lucinda asked, with no real hope of contradiction.

"Aye." The man nodded. His small eyes swept her, not insolently but with weary assessment. "But the likes of you don't want to take rooms 'ere—try the Barbican or the Rutland up the road."

He turned away, leaving Lucinda somewhat stunned. "Just a minute, my good man!"

Jake Blount shuffled back to face her but shook his head. "Yer not the sort for this inn, see?"

Lucinda felt the breeze as the inn door opened. She saw Mr

Blount's eyes lift to the newcomer but was determined to retain his attention. "No—I do not see. What on earth do you mean—'not the sort for this inn'?"

Jake Blount heard her but was more concerned with the gentleman who now stood behind her, hard green eyes on him. Gold hair, gently waved at the ends, cut in the latest style, a well-cut coat of light brown worn over buckskin breeches and Hessians so highly polished you could see your face in them, all added up to a persona Blount recognised very well. He didn't need the many-caped greatcoat that swung from the gentleman's broad shoulders, nor the patrician features and hooded eyes nor yet the tall, lean and well-muscled frame, to tell him that one of the bloods of the *ton* had deigned to enter his humble inn. The fact made him instantly nervous. "Aaah…" He blinked and looked back at Lucinda. "Not the sort who takes rooms 'ere."

Lucinda stared. "What *sort* of lady takes rooms here?"

Blount's features contorted. "*That*'s wha' I mean—*no* ladies. Just *that* sort."

Increasingly certain she had wandered into a madhouse, Lucinda stubbornly clung to her question. "What sort is that?"

For an instant, Jake Blount simply stared at her. Then, defeated, he waved a pudgy hand. "Lady—I don't knows wha' you want wi' me but I got business to see to."

He lifted his gaze pointedly over her shoulder; Lucinda drew in a portentious breath.

And nearly swallowed it when she heard a drawling voice languidly inform the recalcitrant Blount, "You mistake, Blount. My business here is merely to ensure you deal adequately with whatever the lady desires of you."

Harry let his eyes meet the innkeeper's fully. "And you're perfectly correct—she is not *that* sort."

The particular emphasis, delivered in that sensual voice, immediately made clear to Lucinda just what "sort had been the subject of her discussion. Torn between unaccustomed fluster, mortification and outrage, she hesitated, a light blush tinging her cheeks.

Harry noticed. "And now," he suavely suggested, "if we could leave that loaded topic, perhaps we might proceed to the lady's business? I'm sure you're breathlessly waiting to discover what it is—as am I."

Over her shoulder, Lucinda shot him a haughty glance. "Good morning, Mr Lester." She gifted him with a restrained nod; he stood behind her right shoulder, large and reassuring in the dingy dimness. He inclined his head gracefully, his features hard-edged and severe, suggesting an impatience to have her business aired.

Inwardly grimacing, Lucinda turned back to the innkeeper. "I believe you were visited recently by a Mr Mabberly, acting for the owners of this inn?"

Jake Blount shifted. "Aye."

"I believe Mr Mabberly warned you that an inspection of your premises would shortly take place?"

The big man nodded.

Lucinda nodded decisively back. "Very well—you may conduct me over the inn. We'll start with the public rooms." Without pause, she swept about. "I take it this is the tap." She glided towards the door, her skirts stirring up dust eddies.

From the corner of her eye, she saw Blount stare, open-mouthed, then come hurrying around the counter. Harry Lester simply stood and watched her, an inscrutable expression on his face.

Lucinda swept on—into the gloomy, heavily shuttered room. "Perhaps, Blount, if we were to have those shutters wide I might be able to see well enough to form an opinion?"

Blount cast her a flustered glance, then lumbered to the windows. Seconds later, sunshine flooded the room, apparently to the discomfort of its two patrons, one an old codger wrapped in a rumpled cloak, hugging the inglenook, the other a younger man in the rough clothes of a traveller. They both seemed to shrink inwards, away from the light.

Lucinda cast a shrewd glance around the room. The interior of the inn matched its exterior, at least in the matter of neglect. The Green Goose was fast living up to Anthony Mabberly's

description as the very worst of the Babbacombe inns. Grimy
walls and a ceiling that had seen neither brush nor mop for
years combined with a general aura of dust and slow decay to
render the tap a most unwelcoming place. "Hmm." Lucinda
grimaced. "So much for the tap."

She slanted a glance at Harry, who had followed her in.
"Thank you for your assistance, Mr Lester—but I'm perfectly
capable of dealing with Mr Blount."

The green gaze, which had been engaged in a survey of the
unwholesome room, switched to her face. His eyes were less
unreadable than his features, but other than distinct disapproval
and a species of irritation, Lucinda couldn't be sure what their
expression portended.

"Indeed?" His brows lifted fractionally; his languid tone
was barely polite. "But perhaps I should remain—just in case
you and the good Blount run into any further... communication
difficulties?"

Lucinda suppressed the urge to glare. Short of ordering him
out of her inn, hardly supportive of her ploy to conceal her
ownership, she could think of no way to dispense with his
attentive presence. His green gaze was acute, perceptive; his
tongue, as she already knew, could be decidedly sharp.

Accepting fate's decree with a small shrug, Lucinda returned
her attention to Blount, hovering uncertainly by the bar.
"What's through that door?"

"The kitchens."

Blount looked shocked when she waved him on. "I'll need
to see those, too."

The kitchen was not as bad as she had feared, a fact she
attributed to the buxom but worn-down woman who bobbed
respectfully when introduced as "the missus". The Blounts'
private quarters gave off the large, square room; Lucinda dis-
avowed any desire to inspect them. After closely examining the
large open fireplace and engaging in a detailed discussion with
Mrs Blount on the technicalities of the draw and the overall
capacity of the kitchen, which, by their impatient expressions,

passed over both Blount's and Harry Lester's heads, she consented to be shown the parlours.

Both parlours were shabby and dusty but, when the shutters were opened, proved to have pleasant aspects. Both contained old but serviceable furniture.

"Hmm, mmm," was Lucinda's verdict. Blount looked glum.

In the back parlour, which looked out over a wilderness that had once been a garden, she eyed a sturdy oak table and its attendant chairs. "Please ask Mrs Blount to dust in here immediately. Meanwhile, I'll see the rooms above stairs."

With a resigned shrug, Blount went to the door of the kitchen to deliver the order, then returned to lead the way up the stairs. Halfway up, Lucinda paused to test the rickety balustrade. Leaning against it, she was startled to hear it crack—and even more startled to feel an arm of steel wrap about her waist and haul her back to the centre of the treads. She was released immediately but heard the muttered comment, "Damned nosy woman!"

Lucinda grinned, then schooled her features to impassivity as they reached the upper corridor.

"All the rooms be the same." Blount swung open the nearest door. Without waiting to be asked, he crossed to open the shutters.

The sunlight played on a dreary scene. Yellowing whitewash flaked from the walls; the ewer and basin were both cracked. The bedclothes Lucinda mentally consigned to the flames without further thought. The furniture, however, was solid—oak as far as she could tell. Both the bed and the chest of drawers could, with a little care, be restored to acceptable state.

Pursing her lips, Lucinda nodded. She turned and swept out of the door, past Harry Lester, lounging against the frame. He straightened and followed her along the corridor. Behind them, Blount shot out of the room and hurried to interpose himself between Lucinda and the next door.

"This room's currently taken, ma'am."

"Indeed?" Lucinda wondered what sort of patron would make do with the sad amenities of the Green Goose.

As if in answer, a distinctly feminine giggle percolated through the door.

Lucinda's expression grew coldly severe. "I see." She shot an accusing glance at Blount, then, head high, moved along the corridor. "I'll see the room at the end, then we'll return downstairs."

There were no further revelations; it was as Mr Mabberly had said—the Green Goose was sound enough in structure but its management needed a complete overhaul.

Descending once more to the hall, Lucinda beckoned Sim forward and relieved the lad of the bound ledgers he'd been carrying. Leading the way into the back parlour, she was pleased to discover the table and chairs dusted and wiped. Setting her ledgers on the table before the chair at its head, she placed her reticule beside them and sat. "Now, Blount, I would like to examine the books."

Blount blinked. "The books?"

Her gaze steady, Lucinda nodded. "The blue one for incomings and the red one for expenditures."

Blount stared, then muttered something Lucinda chose to interpret as an assent and departed.

Harry, who had maintained his role of silent protector throughout, strolled across to shut the door after him. Then he turned to his aunt's unexpected acquaintance. "And now, my dear Mrs Babbacombe, perhaps you would enlighten me as to what you're about?"

Lucinda resisted the urge to wrinkle her nose at him—he was, she could tell, going to be difficult. "I am doing as I said—inspecting this inn."

"Ah, yes." The steely note was back in his voice. "And I'm to believe that some proprietor has seen fit to engage you— employ you, no less—in such a capacity?"

Lucinda met his gaze, her own lucidly candid. "Yes."

The look he turned on her severely strained her composure.

With a wave, she put an end to his inquisition; Blount would soon be back. "If you must know, this inn is owned by Babbacombe and Company."

The information arrested him in mid-prowl. He turned a fascinated green gaze upon her. "Whose principals are?"

Folding her hands on her ledgers, Lucinda smiled at him. "Myself and Heather."

She did not have time to savour his reaction; Blount entered with a pile of ledgers in his arms. Lucinda waved him to a seat beside her. While he sorted through his dog-eared tomes, she reached for her reticule. Withdrawing a pair of gold-rimmed half-glasses, she perched them on her nose. "Now then!"

Beneath Harry's fascinated gaze, she proceeded to put Blount through his financial paces.

Appropriating a chair from the table—one that had been dusted—Harry sat by the window and studied Lucinda Babbacombe. She was, undoubtedly, the most unexpected, most surprising, most altogether intriguing woman he'd ever met.

He watched as she checked entry after entry, adding figures, frequently upside-down from Blount's ledgers. The innkeeper had long since abandoned all resistance; out of his depth, faced with a totally unforeseen ordeal, he was now eager to gain approval.

As she worked through the ledgers, Lucinda came to the same somewhat reluctant conclusion. Blount wasn't intentionally neglectful; he hadn't meant to run the inn into the ground. He simply lacked direction and the experience to know what to do.

When, after an hour, she reached the end of her inquiries, Lucinda took off her glasses and fixed Blount with a shrewdly assessing glance. "Just so we are clear, Blount, it is up to me to make a recommendation on whether Babbacombe and Company should retain your services." She tapped her closed ledger with one arm of her glasses. "While your figures are unimpressive, I will be reporting that I can find no evidence of malpractice—all seems entirely above board."

The burly innkeeper looked so absurdly grateful Lucinda had to sternly suppress a reassuring smile. "I understand you were appointed to your present position on the death of the former landlord, Mr Harvey. From the books it's clear that the inn had ceased to perform well long before your tenancy.''

Blount looked lost.

"Which means that you cannot be held to blame for its poor base performance.'' Blount looked relieved. "However,'' Lucinda continued, both tone and glance hardening, "I have to tell you that the *current* performance, for which you must bear responsibility, is less than adequate. Babbacombe and Company expect a reasonable return on their investment, Blount.''

The innkeeper's brow furrowed. "But Mr Scrugthorpe—he's the one as appointed me?''

"Ah, yes. Mr Scrugthorpe.''

Harry glanced at Lucinda's face; her tone had turned distinctly chilly.

"Well, Mr Scrugthorpe said as how the profit didn't matter so long as the inn paid its way.''

Lucinda blinked. "What was your previous position, Blount?''

"I used to keep the Blackbird's Beak, up Fordham way.''

"The Blackbird's Beak?''

"A hedge-tavern, I suspect,'' Harry put in drily.

"Oh.'' Lucinda met his gaze, then looked back at Blount. "Well, Blount, Mr Scrugthorpe is no longer Babbacombe and Company's agent, largely because of the rather odd way he thought to do business. And, I fear, if you wish to remain an employee of the company, you're going to have to learn to manage the Green Goose in a more commercial fashion. An inn in Newmarket cannot operate on the same principles as a hedge-tavern.''

Blount's forehead was deeply creased. "I don't know as how I rightly follow you, ma'am. Tap's a tap, after all.''

"No, Blount. A tap is not a tap—it is the principal public room of the inn and as such should possess a clean and welcoming ambience. I do hope you won't suggest that that,'' she pointed in the direction of the tap, "is clean and welcoming?''

The big man shifted on his seat. "Dare say the missus could do a bit of a clean-up.''

"Indeed." Lucilla nodded. "The missus and you, too, Blount. And whoever else you can get to help." She folded her hands on her ledgers and looked Blount in the eye. "In my report, I am going to suggest that, rather than dismiss you, given you've not yet had an opportunity to show the company of what you're capable, the company reserves judgement for three months and then reviews the situation."

Blount swallowed. "What exactly does that mean, ma'am?"

"It means, Blount, that I will make a list of all the improvements that will need to be done to turn this inn into one rivalling the Barbican Arms, at least in profit. There's no reason it shouldn't. Improvements such as a thorough whitewashing inside and out, all the timber polished, present bedding discarded and fresh bought, all furniture polished and crockery replaced. And the kitchen needs a range." Lucinda paused to meet Blount's eye. "Ultimately, you will employ a good cook and serve wholesome meals continuously in the tap, which will be refurbished accordingly. I've noticed that there are few places at which travellers staying in this town can obtain a superior repast. By providing the best fare, the Green Goose will attract custom away from the coaching houses which, because of their preoccupation with coaching, supply only mediocre food."

She paused but Blount only blinked at her. "I take it you are interested in keeping your position here?"

"Oh—yes, ma'am. Definitely! But…where's the blunt coming from for all that?"

"Why, from the profits, Blount." Lucinda eyed him straitly. "The profits before your wages are deducted—and before the return paid to the company. The company considers such matters as an investment in the inn's future; if you're wise, you'll consider my suggestions in light of an investment in your future."

Blount met her gaze; slowly he nodded. "Yes, ma'am."

"Good!" Lucinda rose. "I will make a copy of the improvements I'll be suggesting to the company and have my groom drop it by tomorrow." She glanced at Blount as he struggled to his feet; his expression suggested he was still reeling. "Mr Mabberly will look in on you in a month's time, to review your progress. And now, if there's nothing else, I will bid you good day, Blount."

"Yes, ma'am." Blount hurried to open the door. "Thank you, ma'am." He was clearly sincere.

Lucinda regally nodded and sailed from the room.

Reluctantly impressed, Harry followed close behind. Still inwardly amazed, he waited until they were back on the pavement, she gliding along with her nose in the air as if she had not just taken on Goliath and won, before catching her hand, neatly trapping it on his sleeve. Her fingers fluttered, then stilled. She cast him a quick glance, then studiously looked ahead. Her groom followed two paces behind, her ledgers clutched in his arms.

The young traveller who had been slouching in the tap slipped out of the inn door in their wake.

"My dear Mrs Babbacombe," Harry began in what he hoped was an even tone. "I do hope you're going to satisfy my curiosity as to why a gently reared female, however well-equipped for the task, goes about interrogating her company's employees?"

Unabashed, Lucinda met his gaze; aggravation showed clearly in the green. "Because there is no one else."

Harry held her gaze. His lips thinned. "I find that hard to believe. What about this Mr Mabberly—your agent? Why can he not take on the challenge of such as Blount?"

Lucinda's lips quirked. "You must admit he was a definite challenge." She slanted a deliberately provocative glance his way. "I feel quite chuffed."

Harry snorted. "As you well know, you performed a minor miracle. That man will now work himself to the bone—which will be a distinct improvement in itself. But that," he continued, his tone hardening, "is not the point."

"But it is, you see." Lucinda wondered why she was allowing him to put in his oar. Perhaps because it had been a long time since anyone had tried? "Mr Anthony Mabberly is all of twenty-three. He's an excellent man with the accounts and is scrupulously honest and fair—a far cry from Scrugthorpe.''

''Ah, yes. The undesirable Scrugthorpe.'' Harry cast her a quick glance. ''Why was he so undesirable?''

''Fraud. He was appointed by my husband just before his death—on one of his bad days, I'm afraid. After Charles's death, I by chance learned that the books as they were being presented to me did not reflect the actual figures generated by the inns.''

''What happened to Scrugthorpe?''

''I dismissed him, of course.''

Harry noted the righteous satisfaction that underlaid her tone. Clearly, Lucinda Babbacombe had not approved of Mr Scrugthorpe. ''So until recently the agent took responsibility for negotiating with your tenants?''

Lucinda lifted a haughty brow. ''Until I reorganised the company's procedures. Mr Mabberly would not know where to start with such as Blount—he's of a somewhat timid disposition. And I consider it appropriate that both Heather and myself are familiar with the inns that form our legacy.''

''Laudable though such sentiments might be, Mrs Babbacombe, I do hope—'' Harry broke off as she stopped and looked consideringly across the street. ''What is it?''

''Hmm?'' Absent-mindedly, Lucinda glanced up. ''Oh—I was just wondering if there was time left to do the Barbican Arms today.'' She glanced back at the busy inn across the street. ''But it looks rather crowded. Perhaps tomorrow morning would be better?''

Harry stared at her, an unwelcome suspicion slowly crystallising in his brain. ''Very much better,'' he averred. ''But tell me, Mrs Babbacombe—how many inns do you and your step-daughter own?''

She looked up at him, an unlikely innocence in her powder-blue eyes. ''Fifty-four,'' she replied. Then added, as if in afterthought, ''Up and down the country.''

Harry closed his eyes and struggled to suppress a groan. Then, without another word, with no more than a single speak-

ing glance, he escorted her into the yard of the Barbican Arms
and, with heartfelt relief, handed her up to Em's gig and
watched her drive away.

"SO SHE'S STAYING in Newmarket?"

Mr Earle Joliffe drew a riding crop back and forth through
his fingers. A thickset man of undistinguished mien, he sat back
in his chair, his pale gaze, as pale as his pasty complexion,
fixed on the young roughneck he'd sent into town to track their
quarry down.

"As to that, I ain't sure." The youngster took a swig from
his tankard.

They were in a rundown cottage three miles from Newmarket, the best they'd been able to rent at short notice. Four men
sat about the deal table—Joliffe, the youngster whose name
was Brawn and two others—Mortimer Babbacombe and Ernest
Scrugthorpe. The latter was a hulking man, rough despite the
severe clothes of a clerk; he sat silently glowering into his beer.
Mortimer Babbacombe, a slight figure in the attire of a would-
be dandy, shifted restlessly; he clearly wished himself elsewhere.

"She got into a gig and drove out eastwards. I couldn't follow."

Scrugthorpe grunted. "See? Told you she'd go to the Green
Goose. Couldn't keep away, meddling witch."

He spat contemptuously on the floor; the action made Mortimer even more uncomfortable.

"Ye-es, well." Joliffe transferred his gaze to Scrugthorpe.
"Might I remind you that she should, by now, have been in
our hands? That but for your lack of foresight, she would be?"

Scrugthorpe scowled. "How was I to know it were a race-
week? And that gentlemen would be using that road? Everything went perfect, elsewise."

Joliffe sighed and raised his eyes heavenwards. Amateurs—
they were all the same. How had he, who had spent his life
thus far successfully extracting a living from the rich, descended to the company of such? Lowering his gaze, his glance

fell on Mortimer Babbacombe. Joliffe's lips curled in a contemptuous sneer.

"Ought to mention," Brawn put in, surfacing from his tankard. "She was walking the street with a swell today—right chummy—looked like the same swell as wot rescued them."

Joliffe's eyes narrowed and he sat forward. "Describe this swell."

"Fair hair—like gold. Tall, looked like he'd strip to advantage. One of them bloods with a fancy cape." Brawn grimaced. "They all look the same to me."

Not so to Joliffe. "This blood—was he staying at the Barbican Arms?"

"Seemed so—the ostlers and all seemed to know him."

"Harry Lester." Joliffe tapped a pensive nail on the table. "I wonder…"

"Wonder what?" Mortimer looked at his erstwhile friend and most urgent creditor, his expression that of a man well out of his depth. "Would this man Lester help us?"

Joliffe snorted. "Only to the hangman's noose. But his peculiar talents bear consideration." Leaning forward, Joliffe placed both elbows on the table. "It occurs to me, my dear Mortimer, that we may be involving ourselves unnecessarily here." Joliffe smiled, an empty gesture that made Mortimer shrink. "I'm sure you'd be most agreeable to any way of achieving our aim without direct involvement."

Mortimer swallowed. "But how can Lester help us—if he won't?"

"Oh—I didn't say he won't—just that we needn't ask him. He'll help us entirely for the fun of it. Harry Lester, dear Mortimer, is the rake supreme—a practitioner extraordinaire in the gentle art of seduction. If, as seems possible, he's got your uncle's widow in his sights, then I wouldn't like to bet on her chances." Joliffe's smile grew. "And, of course, once she's demonstrably no longer a virtuous widow, then you'll have all the reason you need to legally challenge her guardianship of your cousin." Joliffe's gaze grew intent. "And once your pretty cousin's legacy's in your hands, you'll be in a position to pay me, won't you, Mortimer?''

Mortimer Babbacombe swallowed—and forced himself to nod.

"So what do we do now?" Scrugthorpe drained his tankard.

Joliffe considered, then pronounced, "We sit tight and watch. If we get a chance to lay hands on the lady, we will—just like we planned."

"Aye—far as I'm concerned, that's how we should do it—no sense in leaving anything to chance."

Joliffe's lip curled. "Your animosity is showing, Scrugthorpe. Please remember that our primary aim here is to discredit Mrs Babbacombe—not satisfy your lust for revenge."

Scrugthorpe snorted.

"As I was saying," Joliffe went on. "We watch and wait. If Harry Lester succeeds—he'll have done our work for us. If not, we'll continue to pursue the lady—and Scrugthorpe here will have his chance."

At that, Scrugthorpe smiled. Lecherously.

Chapter Four

WHEN LUCINDA DROVE into the yard of the Barbican Arms the next morning, Harry was waiting, shoulders against the wall, arms crossed over his chest, his boot against the wall for balance. He had plenty of time to admire the artless picture of mature womanhood seated beside Grimms in his aunt's gig. Elegantly gowned in a cornflower blue carriage dress, her dark hair restrained in a severe chignon thus revealing the delicate bones of her face, Lucinda Babbacombe predictably turned the heads of those still dawdling in the yard. Thankfully, the thoroughbred races were to commence that morning; most of Harry's contemporaries were already at the track.

Grimms brought Em's gig to a neat halt in the centre of the yard. With an inward snort, Harry pushed away from the wall.

Lucinda watched him approach—his graceful stride forcefully reminded her of a prowling tiger. A very definite thrill coursed through her; she avoided smiling her delight, contenting herself with a mild expression of polite surprise. "Mr Lester." Calmly, she extended her hand. "I hadn't expected to see you this morning—I thought you were here for the races."

His brows had risen sceptically at her first remark; on her second, his green eyes glittered. He grasped her hand—for an instant, as his eyes held hers, Lucinda wondered why she was playing with fire.

"Indeed," Harry replied, his habitual drawl in abeyance. He helped her from the carriage, steadying her on the cobbles. "I own to surprise on that score myself. However, as you are my aunt's guest, and at my instigation, I feel honour-bound to ensure you come to no harm."

Lucinda's eyes narrowed but Harry, distracted by the absence of groom or maid—Grimms had already disappeared into the stables—did not notice.

"Speaking of which, where's your groom?"

Lucinda allowed herself a small smile. "Riding with your brother and Heather. I have to thank you for sending Gerald to us—he's entertaining company for Heather—I dare say she would otherwise grow bored. And, of course, that leaves me free to tend to business without having to worry my head over her."

Harry didn't share her confidence—but he wasn't, at this point, concerned with her stepdaughter. His expression hardened as he looked down at her. He was still holding her hand; tucking it into his arm, he turned her towards the inn door. "You should at least have a groom with you."

"Nonsense, Mr Lester." Lucinda slanted him a curious glance. "Surely you aren't suggesting that at my age I need a chaperon?"

Looking into her eyes, softly blue, their expression openly independent, challenging yet oddly innocent, Harry inwardly cursed. The damned woman didn't need a chaperon—she needed an armed guard. Just why he had elected himself to the post was not a point he was willing to pursue. He contented himself with repressively stating, "In my opinion, Mrs Babbacombe, women like you should not be allowed out alone."

Her eyes twinkled; two tiny dimples appeared in her cheeks. "Actually, I'd like to see the stables." She turned to the archway leading from the main yard.

"The stables?"

Her gaze ranging their surroundings, Lucinda nodded. "The state of the stableyard frequently reflects the quality of the inn's management."

The state of the stables suggested the innkeeper of the Barbican Arms was a perfectionist; everything was neat, clean and in its place. Horses turned their heads to stare as Lucinda picked her way over the cobbles, still wet with dew, forced more than once to lean heavily on Harry's arm.

When they reached the earthen floor of the stables, she determinedly straightened. Regretfully withdrawing her fingers
from the warmth of his sleeve, she strolled along the row of
loose boxes, stopping here and there to acknowledge their curious occupants. She eventually reached the tack room and
peered in.

"Excuse me, ma'am—but you shouldn't be in here." An
elderly groom hurried out.

Harry stepped out of the shadows. "It's all right, Johnson.
I'll see the lady safe,"

"Oh!—it's you, Mr Lester." The groom touched his cap.
"That's all right and tight, then. Ma'am." With another tug of
his cap, the groom retreated into the tack room.

Lucinda blinked, then shot a glance at Harry. "Is it always
so ordered? So…" She waved at the loose boxes, each with
their half-doors shut. "So exact?"

"Yes." Harry looked down at her as she stopped beside him.
"I stable my carriage horses here—you may rest assured of
the quality in that respect."

"I see." Deeming all queries on the equine side of business
satisfied, Lucinda turned her attention to the inn proper.

Ushered through the main door, she looked with approval
on half-panelled walls, well-polished and glowing mellowly.
Sunshine reflected from crisply whitewashed walls; stray beams
danced across the flagged floor.

Mr Jenkins, the innkeeper, a neat, rotund person of genial
mien, bustled up. Harry performed the introductions, then stood
patiently by while Lucinda explained her purpose. Unlike
Blount, Mr Jenkins was all gratified helpfulness.

Lucinda turned to Harry. "My business with Mr Jenkins will
keep me busy for at least an hour. I wouldn't for the world
impose on your kindness, Mr Lester—you've already done so
much. And I can hardly come to harm within the inn."

Harry didn't blink. For her, the Arms played host to a panoply of dangers—namely his peers. Meeting her innocent gaze
with an impenetrable blandness, he waved a languid hand. "Indeed—but my horses don't run until later."

Which comment, he noted, brought a flash to her eyes. She hesitated, then, somewhat stiffly, acquiesced, inclining her head before turning back to Mr Jenkins.

Wearing patience like a halo, Harry followed his host and his aunt's guest about the old inn, through rambling passageways and storerooms, to bedchambers and even to the garrets. They were returning down an upper corridor when a man came blundering out of a room.

Lucinda, opposite the door, started; glimpsing the man from the corner of her eye, she braced herself for a collision. Instead, she was bodily set aside; the chubby young gentleman ran full tilt into a hard shoulder. He bounced off, crumpling against the door frame.

"Ouf!" Straightening, the man blinked. "Oh—hello, Lester. Slept in, don't y'know. Can't miss the first race." He blinked again, a puzzled frown forming in his eyes. "Thought you'd be at the track by now."

"Later." Harry stepped back, revealing Lucinda.

The young man blinked again. "Oh—ah, yes. Terribly sorry, ma'am—always being told I should look where I'm going. No harm done, I hope?"

Lucinda smiled at the ingenuous apology. "No—none." Thanks to her protector.

"Good-oh! I'd best be on my way, then. See you at the track, Lester." With an awkward bow and a cheery wave, the youthful sprig hurried off.

Harry snorted.

"Thank you for your assistance, Mr Lester." Lucinda slanted him a smile. "I'm really most grateful."

Harry took full note of the quality of her smile. Coolly, he inclined his head and waved her on in Jenkins's wake.

By the end of her tour, Lucinda was impressed. The Barbican Arms, and Mr Jenkins, were a far cry from the Green Goose and Jake Blount. The inn was spick and span throughout; she had found nothing remotely amiss. Her inspection of the books was a mere formality; Mr Mabberly had already declared the Arms a model of good finance.

She and her host spent a few minutes going over the plans for an extension to the inn. "For we're full to overflowing during race-meets and more than half full at other times."

Lucinda gave her general approval and left the details for Mr Mabberly.

"Thank you, Mr Jenkins," she declared, pulling on her gloves as they headed for the door. "I must tell you that, having visited all but four of the fifty-four inns owned by Babbacombe and Company, I would rank the Barbican Arms as one of the best."

Mr Jenkins preened. "Very kind of you to say so, ma'am. We do strive to please."

With a gracious nod, Lucinda swept out. Once in the courtyard she paused. Harry stopped beside her; she looked up at his face. "Thank you for your escort, Mr Lester—I'm really most grateful considering the other demands on your time."

Harry was too wise to attempt an answer to that.

Lucinda's lips twitched; she looked quickly away. "Actually," she mused, "I was considering viewing this race-meet." She brought her eyes back to his face. "I've never been to one before."

Harry looked down at her ingenuous expression. His eyes narrowed. "Newmarket race-track is no place for you."

She blinked, taken aback—Harry glimpsed real disappointment in her eyes. Then she looked away. "Oh."

The single syllable hung in the air, a potent testimony to crushed anticipation. Fleetingly, Harry closed his eyes, then opened them. "However, if you give me your word you will not stray from my side—not to admire some view, some horse or a lady's bonnet—" He looked down at her, his jaw setting. "I will engage to escort you there."

Her smile was triumphant. "Thank you. That would be very kind."

Not kind—foolish. It was, Harry was already convinced, the most stupid move he'd ever made. An ostler came running in answer to his curt gesture. "I'll have my curricle. You can tell

Grimms to take Lady Hallows's gig back; I'll see Mrs Bab-bacombe home.''

"Yessir."

Lucinda busied herself with the fit of her gloves, then meekly allowed herself to be lifted to the curricle's seat. Settling her skirts, and her quivering senses, she smiled serenely as, with a deft flick of the reins, Harry took the greys onto the street.

The race-track lay west of the town on the flat, grassy, largely tree-less heath. Harry drove directly to the stables in which his string of racers were housed, a little way from the track proper, beyond the public precincts.

Lucinda, drinking in the sights, could not miss the glances thrown their way. Stableboy and gentleman alike seemed disposed to stare; she was unexpectedly grateful when the stable walls protected her from view.

The horses were a wonder. Lifted down from the curricle, Lucinda could not resist wandering down the row of loose boxes, patting the velvet noses that came out to greet her, admiring the sleek lines and rippling muscles of what, even to her untutored eyes, had to be some of the finest horses in England.

Engaged in a brisk discussion with Hamish, Harry followed her progress, insensibly buoyed by the awed appreciation he saw in her gaze. On reaching the end of the row, she turned and saw him watching her; her nose rose an inch but she came back, strolling towards him through the sunshine.

"So all's right with entering the mare, then?''

Reluctantly, Harry shifted his gaze to Hamish's face. His head-stableman was also watching Lucinda Babbacombe, not with the appreciation she deserved but with horrified fascination. As she drew nearer, Harry extended his arm; she placed her fingertips upon it without apparent thought. "Just as long as Thistledown's fetlock's fully healed.''

"Aye." Hamish bobbed respectfully at Lucinda. "Seems to be. I told the boy to just let her run—no point marshalling her resources if it's still weak. A good run's the only way to tell.''

Harry nodded. "I'll stop by and speak to him myself.''

Hamish nodded and effaced himself with the alacrity of a man nervous around females, at least those not equine in nature.

Suppressing a grin, Harry lifted a brow at his companion. "I thought you agreed not to be distracted by horses?"

The look she bent on him was confidently assured. "You shouldn't have brought me to see yours, then. They are truly the most distractingly beautiful specimens I've ever seen."

Harry couldn't suppress his smile. "But you haven't seen the best of them. Those on that side are two-and three-year-olds—for my money, the older ones are more gracious. Come, I'll show you."

She seemed only too ready to be led down the opposite row of boxes, dutifully admiring the geldings and mares. At the end of the row, a bay stallion reached confidently over the half-door to investigate Harry's pockets.

"This is old Cribb—a persistent devil. Still runs with the best of them though he could retire gracefully on his accumulated winnings." Leaving her patting the stallion's nose, Harry went to a barrel by the wall. "Here," he said, turning back. "Feed him these."

Lucinda took the three dried apples he offered her, giggling as Cribb delicately lipped them from her palm.

Harry glanced up—and saw Dawlish outside the tack-room, standing stock-still, staring at him. Leaving Lucinda communing with Cribb, Harry strolled over. "What's up?"

Now that he was beside him, it was clear Dawlish was staring at his companion, not him.

"*Gawd's truth*—it's happened."

Harry frowned. "Don't be ridiculous."

Dawlish turned a pitying eye on him. "Ridiculous, is it? You do realize, don't you, that that's the first female you've ever shown your horses?"

Harry lifted a supercilious brow. "She's the first female ever to have shown an interest."

"Hah! Might as well hang up your gloves, gov'nor—you're a goner."

Harry cast his eyes heavenwards. "If you must know, she's never been to a race-meet before and was curious—there's nothing more to it than that."

"Ah-hah. So *you* says." Dawlish cast a long, defeated look at the slight figure by Cribb's box. "All *I* says is that you can justify it any ways you want—the conclusions still come out the same."

With a doleful shake of his head, Dawlish retreated, muttering, back into the tack-room.

Harry wasn't sure whether to laugh or frown. He glanced back at the woman, still chatting to his favourite stallion. If it wasn't for the fact they would shortly be surrounded by crowds, he might be inclined to share his henchman's pessimism. But the race-track, in full view of the multitudes, was surely safe enough.

"If we leave now," he said, returning to her side, "we can stroll to the track in time for the first race."

She smiled her acquiescence and laid her hand on his arm. "Is that horse you were talking of—Thistledown—running in it?"

Smiling down into her blue eyes, Harry shook his head. "No—she's in the second."

Lucinda found herself trapped in the clear green of his eyes; she studied them, trying to gauge what he was thinking. His lips twitched and he looked away. Blinking as they emerged into the bright sunshine, Lucinda asked, "Your aunt mentioned you managed a stud?"

His fascinating lips curved. "Yes—the Lester stud." With ready facility, prompted by her questions, he expiated at length on the trials and successes of his enterprise. What he didn't say but Lucinda inferred, it being the logical deduction to make from his descriptions, was that the stud was both a shining achievement and the very core of his life.

They reached the tents surrounding the track as the runners for the first race were being led to the barrier. All Lucinda could see was a sea of backs as everyone concentrated on the course.

"This way—you'll see better from the stands."

A man in a striped vest was guarding a roped arena before a large wooden stand. Lucinda noted that while he insisted on seeing passes from the other latecomers ahead of them, he merely grinned and nodded at Harry and let them by. Harry helped her up the steep steps by the side of the planks serving as seats—but before they could find places a horn blew.

"They're off." Harry's words echoed from a hundred throats—about them, all the patrons craned forward.

Lucinda turned obediently and saw a line of horses thundering down the turf. From this distance, neither she nor anyone else could see all that much of the animals. It was the crowd that enthralled her—their rising excitement gripped her, making her breathe faster and concentrate on the race. When the winner flashed past the post, the jockey flourishing his whip high, she felt inordinately glad.

"Well raced." Harry's gaze was on the horses and riders as they slowed and turned back to the gates.

Lucinda grasped the moment to study him. He was intent on observation, green eyes keenly assessing, shrewdly calculating. For an instant, she saw him clearly, his features unguarded. He was a man who, despite all other distractions in his life, was totally devoted to his chosen path.

He turned his head at that moment. Their eyes met, their gazes locked. He was standing on the step below her so her eyes were almost level with his. For a moment, he said nothing, then his lips twisted wrily.

Lucinda suppressed a delicate shiver.

With a gesture, Harry indicated the crowded lawns before them. "If you truly want to experience a race-meet, then you have to promenade."

Her own lips curving, Lucinda inclined her head. "Lead on, Mr Lester—I'm entirely in your hands."

She saw his brow quirk but pretended ignorance. On his arm, she descended the steps and exited the private enclosure.

"The Jockey Club maintains the stand for the use of its members," Harry informed her when she glanced back.

Which meant he was a well-known member. Even Lucinda had heard of the pre-eminence of the Jockey Club. "I see. The races are run under their auspices, I take it?"

"Correct."

He led her on a slow perambulation through the milling crowds. Lucinda felt distinctly round-eyed—she wanted to see everything, understand the fascination that drew so many gentlemen to Newmarket.

The same fascination that drove Harry Lester.

He showed her the bookmakers, each surrounded by knots of punters eager to lay their bets. They paraded before the tents and pavilions; again and again they were stopped by some acquaintance of Harry's, keen to exchange a few words. Lucinda was prepared to be on her guard, but she encountered nothing but polite deference in the glances thrown her way; all those who stopped to talk were disarmingly correct. Nevertheless, she felt no impulse to withdraw her hand from the security of her escort's elbow, where he had tucked it, drawing her close. In the press of male bodies, it was unquestionably comforting to have Harry Lester by her side. There were, she discovered, some ladies present. "Some have a real interest in the sport— usually the older ones." Relaxed, in his milieu, Harry glanced down at her. "Some of the younger ladies have a vested interest; their families, like mine, have a long-standing connection with the turf."

Mouthing an "oh", Lucinda nodded. There were other ladies, too, whom he had not seen fit to comment upon, who, she suspected, held dubious right to the title. The race-track, however, was an overwhelmingly male domain—every sub-category of the male population was certainly represented. Lucinda was quite sure she would have neither the courage nor the inclination to attend again—not unless Harry Lester was her escort.

"It's nearly time for the next race. I must speak to Thistle-down's jockey."

Lucinda nodded, conveying with a glance her intention of staying with him.

Harry threw her a brief smile then concentrated on forging a path to the mounting yard.

"She seems very lively, sir," the jockey vouchsafed as he settled in the saddle. "But the competition's stiff—Jonquil—that mare out of Herald—is a starter. And Caught by the Scruff, too. And some of them others are experienced racers—it'll be a miracle if she wins, what with her fetlock just come good an' all."

Harry nodded. "Just let her go—let her set her own pace. We'll consider this a trial, nothing more. Don't cram her—and no whip."

Lucinda left his side to pat the mare's velvet muzzle; a huge, dark brown eye invited her understanding. Lucinda grinned. "Hopeless, aren't they?" she crooned. "But you don't want to listen to them—men are notoriously hopeless at judging women. They should never so presume." From the corner of her eye, she saw Harry's lips lift; he exchanged a glance with the jockey, who grinned. "You just go out there and win the race—then see how they react. I'll see you in the winner's circle."

With a last pat for the mare, she turned and, with divine disregard for the expression on Harry Lester's face, allowed him to lead her back to the stands.

He secured seats in the third row, almost opposite the post. Lucinda leaned forward, eagerly scanning the horses trotting towards the barrier. She waved when Thistledown appeared.

Harry, watching her, laughed.

"She'll win—you'll see." With smug confidence, Lucinda sat back.

But when the horn sounded and the barrier was dropped, she leant forward again, eyes keenly searching the thundering charge for Harry's colours of green and gold. So intent was she that she didn't even notice she rose to her feet, in company with all the other spectators, as the horses rounded the bend. As they entered the straight, a gap appeared in their ranks—Thistledown shot through.

"There she is!" Lucinda grabbed Harry's arm. Only deeply

entrenched decorum kept her from jigging up and down.
"She's winning!"

Harry was too riveted to answer.

But Thistledown was indeed showing the field a clean pair
of heels. Halfway down the straight, her stride lengthened even
more—she appeared to be flying when she flashed past the
post.

"She won! She won!" Lucinda grasped both Harry's arms
and all but danced. "I *told* you she would!"

Rather more accustomed to the delights of victory, Harry
looked down at her face, wreathed in smiles and lit by the same
joy he still felt every time one of his horses came home first.
He knew he was smiling, as delighted as she if rather more
circumspect in showing it.

Lucinda turned back to locate Thistledown, now being led
from the course. "Can we go and see her now?"

"Indeed we can." Harry took her hand and tucked it tightly
in his arm. "You promised to meet her in the winner's circle,
remember?"

Lucinda blinked as he steered her out of the crowded stand.
"Is it permissible for ladies to enter the winner's circle?"

"There's no rule against it—in fact—" Harry slanted a
glance at her "—I suspect the Head of the Committee will be
delighted to see you." When she shot him a suspicious glance,
he laughed and urged her on. Once out of the enclosure and
free of those members keen to press their congratulations, a
path cleared before them, leading directly to the roped arena
where Thistledown, shiny coat flickering but clearly untired by
her dash, waited patiently.

As soon as Lucinda emerged from the crowd, the mare
pushed her head forward, dragging on the reins to get to Lucinda's side. Lucinda hurried forward, crooning her praises.
Harry looked on indulgently.

"Well, Lester! Another trophy for your mantel—surprised it
hasn't collapsed."

Harry turned as the President of the Jockey Club, present

Head of the Race Committee, appeared at his elbow. In his hands, he held a gold-plated statuette in the shape of a lady.

"Remarkable run—truly remarkable."

Shaking hands, Harry nodded. "Particularly as she's just recovered from a strained fetlock—I wasn't sure I'd race her."

"Just as well you did." The President's eye was on the horse and the woman apparently chatting to the beast. "Nice conformation."

Harry knew very well that Lord Norwich was not referring to the mare. "Indeed." His tone was dry; Lord Norwich, who had known him from the cradle, lifted a brow at him.

Glancing at the statuette, Harry confirmed that the lady was indeed decently garbed, then nodded at Lucinda. "It was Mrs Babbacombe who delivered the inspirational address prior to the race. Perhaps she should accept the award on my behalf?"

"Excellent idea!" Beaming, Lord Norwich strode forward.

Shielded by her brimming happiness, the aftermath of fulfilled excitement, Lucinda had succeeded in blithely ignoring the avid interest of the spectators. Lord Norwich, however, was impossible to ignore. But Harry strolled forward to stand by their side, quieting her uncertainties.

Lord Norwich gave a short speech, praising the mare and Harry's stables, then gallantly presented the statuette—to her.

Surprised, Lucinda looked at Harry—he smiled and nodded.

Determined to rise to the occasion, she graciously thanked his lordship.

"Quite, quite." His lordship was quite taken. "Need to see more game fillies at the track, what?"

Lucinda blinked at him.

Harry reached for her elbow and drew her to his side. He nodded at his strapper. "Take her back to the stables."

With a last lingering look for Lucinda, Thistledown was led away. Lord Norwich and the rest of the crowd turned away, already intent on the next race.

Still conscious of the fading thrill, Lucinda looked around, then cast a glance upwards.

Harry smiled. ''And you have my heartfelt thanks, too, my dear. For whatever magic you wove.''

Lucinda met his eyes—and stopped breathing. ''There was no magic.'' She felt his fingers on hers; she watched as he raised her hand and brushed his lips across the backs of her fingers. A long shiver traced its path down her spine, leaving an odd warmth in its wake. With an effort she veiled her eyes, breaking his spell. Catching her breath, she made a bid for her usual confidence; she raised the statuette and presented it to him, defiantly meeting his eyes.

He took it in his other hand, his gaze steady on hers.

Time lost its meaning; they stood, largely forgotten, in the centre of the winner's circle. Men crowded about, jostling each other but not touching them. They stood close, so close the small ruffle on Lucinda's bodice brushed the long lapel of Harry's coat. He sensed its flutter as her breathing grew more rapid but he was lost in her eyes, in a world of misty blue. He watched them widen, darken. Her lips softened, parted. Her bodice made contact with his coat.

His head had begun its slow descent when sanity awoke—and frantically hauled on his reins.

Great heavens! They were in the winner's circle at New-market!

Shaken to the depths of his soul, Harry dragged in a quick breath. He tore his gaze from her face, from the consternation that was filling her eyes, and the soft blush that had started to tinge her cheeks, and looked about them. No one, thank heaven, had seen.

His heart pounding, he took a firm grip of her elbow—and took refuge in action. ''If you've seen enough of the racing, I should get you back to Em's—she'll be wondering where you are.''

Lucinda nodded—the faintly bored drawl left her no choice. She felt—she didn't know what—shaken, certainly, but re-gretful, and resentful, too. But she couldn't argue with his wish to be gone from here.

But they still had the gamut of well-wishers to run—they

were stopped constantly, more than one gentleman wishing to make an offer for the mare.

Harry faced the hurdles with what patience he could, conscious that all he wished to do was escape. With her. But that was impossible—she was his danger, his Waterloo.

From now on, every time he looked into her face would be like looking down the barrel of a loaded gun. A weapon that could land him in painful slavery.

If he was wise, he wouldn't look too frequently.

Lucinda sensed his withdrawal although he cloaked it well. His urbane charm came to the fore—but he would not meet her eyes, her puzzled glances.

They finally escaped the crowds and walked back, in silence, to the stables. He lifted her to his curricle and swung up beside her, his expression closed.

He drove back to Hallows Hall without a word, his apparent concentration on his horses a wall Lucinda made no attempt to breach.

But when he drew up before the steps and secured the reins, then came around and lifted her down, she held her position in front of him even though his hands fell immediately from her. "Thank you for a most…instructive morning, Mr Lester."

His eyes flicked to hers; he took a step back. "A pleasure, Mrs Babbacombe." He bowed with innate grace. "And now I must bid you adieu."

Surprised, Lucinda watched as he swung up to the curricle's seat. "But won't you stay for luncheon? Your aunt would be delighted, I'm sure."

The reins in his hands, Harry drew in a deep breath—and forced himself to meet her gaze. "No."

The word hung between them—an unconditional denial. Harry saw the understanding in her eyes, sensed the sudden catch in her breathing as his rejection bit home. But it was better this way—to nip it in the bud before it could flower. Safer for her as well as for him.

But her eyes showed no comprehension of that, of the dangers he could see so clearly. Soft and luminous, they looked at him in hurt surprise.

He felt his lips twist in bitter self-mockery. "I can't."

It was all the explanation he could give. With a crack of his whip, he set his horses down the drive—and drove away.

Chapter Five

THREE DAYS LATER, Lucinda was still not satisfied that she understood what had happened. Seated in a wicker chair in a patch of sunlight in the conservatory, she idly plied her needle while her thoughts went round and round. Heather was out riding with Gerald, Sim in close attendance; her hostess was somewhere in the gardens, supervising the planting of a new border. She was alone, free to pursue her thoughts—little good though that seemed to be doing her.

She knew she was inexperienced in such matters, yet deep within lay an unshakeable conviction that something—something eminently to be desired—had sprung to life between herself and Harry Lester.

He had almost kissed her in the winner's circle.

The moment was etched in her memories, frustratingly incomplete, yet she could hardly fault him for drawing back. But he had then retreated, so completely it had left her feeling unexpectedly vulnerable and inwardly bruised. His parting words confounded her. She could not misconstrue the implications of that "No"—it was his "I can't" that truly baffled her.

He had not appeared since; courtesy of Gerald, who now haunted the house, she had learned he was still in Newmarket. Presumably, she was supposed to believe he was so immensely busy with his racers that he had no time for her.

With an inward snort, Lucinda jabbed her needle into the canvas. She was, she supposed, now too much the businesswoman to enjoy being shortchanged. But time was slipping away; she couldn't remain at Hallows Hall forever. Clearly, if she wanted to know just what might be possible, she was going to have to take an active hand.

But how?

Five minutes later, Em entered through the garden door, the hem of her old gardening gown liberally splattered with earth, a pair of heavy gloves in one hand.

"Phoof!" Sinking into the other armchair, separated from Lucinda's by a small matching table, Em pushed back wisps of browny-grey hair. "That's done!" She slanted a glance at her guest. "You look very industrious—quite wifely, in fact."

Lucinda smiled but did not look up.

"Tell me," Em mused, her sharp gaze belying her idle tone. "Have you ever considered remarrying?"

Lucinda's needle halted; she looked up, not at her hostess but through the long windows at the garden. "Not until recently," she eventually said. And returned to her needlework.

Em studied her downbent head, a definite glint in her eye. "Yes—well, it takes one like that. Suddenly pops into your mind—and then won't get out." With an airy wave of her gardening gloves, she continued, "Still, with your qualifications I hardly think you need worry. When you get to London you'll have a goodly selection of beaux lining up to put a ring on your finger."

Lucinda slanted her a glance. "My qualifications?"

Em's wave became a flourish. "Your breeding for one—nothing wrong with that, even if your parents were disowned. Your grandparents could hardly change the blood in their veins—as far as Society's concerned that's what counts." As if just struck by the fact, Em added, "In fact, the Giffords are as well connected as the Lesters."

"Indeed?" Lucinda eyed her warily.

Blithely, Em continued, "And there's your fortune, too—that legacy of yours would satisfy the most demanding. And you're hardly an antidote—you've got style, that indefinable something—noticed it straight off. Once the Bruton Street *mesdames* get a look at you they'll be vying for your custom, mark my words."

"I am, however, twenty-eight."

The blunt comment brought Em to a blinking halt. Turning her head, she stared at her guest. "So?"

Lucinda grimaced and looked down at her work. "Twenty-eight, I suspect, is somewhat long in the tooth to be attractive to town beaux."

For an instant longer, Em stared at her, then hooted with laughter. "*Rubbish*, my dear! The *ton*'s awash with gentlemen whose principal reason for avoiding matrimony is that they cannot stomach the bright-eyed young misses." She snorted. "More hair than wit, most of them, believe me." She paused to study Lucinda's face, half-averted, then added, "It's very common, my dear, for men to prefer more experienced women."

Lucinda glanced up—and met Em's eye. A light blush slowly spread across her cheeks. "Yes, well—that's another thing." Her gaze flicked to the green vistas beyond the window as she dragged in a determined breath. "I'm not. Experienced, I mean."

Em stared. "Not?"

"My marriage wasn't really a marriage at all—it was a rescue." Lucinda frowned, her gaze dropping to her tapestry. "You must remember I was only sixteen at the time—and Charles was nearing fifty. He was very kind—we were good friends." Her voice low, she added, "Nothing more." Straightening her shoulders, she reached for her scissors, "Life, I fear, has passed me by—I've been put back on the shelf without having been properly off it in the first place."

"I...see." Em blinked owlishly at the tips of her half-boots, peeking from beneath her dirtied hem. A broad smile slowly broke across her face. "You know—your...er, inexperience is not really a handicap, not in your case. In fact," she continued, her old eyes lighting, "it could well be a positive advantage."

It was Lucinda's turn to look puzzled.

"You see, you have to think of it from your prospective husband's point of view." Eyes wide, Em turned to face her. "What *he*'ll see is a mature and capable woman, one of su-

perior sense who can manage his household and family while
at the same time providing more—'' she paused to gesture
''—*satisfying* companionship than a young girl ever could. If
you make no show of your innocence, but allow him to—''
she gestured again as she groped for words ''—*stumble* on it
in good time, I'm sure you'll find he'll be only too delighted.''
With a last shrewd glance at Lucinda's face, Em added, ''I'm
sure Harry would be.''

Lucinda's eyes narrowed. She favoured her impossible hostess with a long stare. Then, looking down to tidy her needlework, she asked, ''Has he ever shown any interest in marrying?''

''Harry?'' Em sat back, a smile on her lips. ''Not that I ever
heard. But then, he's never had need to—there's Jack before
him and Gerald behind. Jack's about to marry—I just got a
summons to the wedding. So Harry's thoughts are unlikely to
turn to gold rings and white icing—not, that is, unless he's
given an incentive to pursue the subject.''

''Incentive?''

''Hmm. Often the case with gentlemen in that particular
mould—won't have a bar of marriage until the benefits become
so blatantly obvious that even they, with their blinkered vision,
can see it.'' Em snorted. ''It's all the fault of the light-skirts,
of course. Lining up to give them anything they want—whatever their lusts desire—without any strings attached.''

''I suspect,'' Lucinda said, her expression guarded, Harry's
''No'' echoing in her ears, ''that it would take a
fairly...powerful incentive to make Harry actively desire to be
wed.''

''Naturally—Harry's all male to his toes. He'll be as reluctant as the best of them, I don't doubt. He's lived a life of
unfettered hedonism—he's hardly likely to volunteer to
change.'' Em brought her gaze back to Lucinda's face. ''Not,
of course that that should deter *you*.''

Lucinda's head came up; she met Em's old eyes and saw in
them a wealth of understanding. She hesitated for only a moment. ''Why not?''

"Because, as I see it, you've got the most powerful weapon in your hands already—the only one that'll work." Em sat back and shrewdly regarded Lucinda. "Question is, are you game enough to use it?"

For a long moment, Lucinda stared at her hostess—then shifted her gaze to the gardens. Em sat patiently watching her—slim, dark-haired, fingers clasped in her lap, her expression calm and uninformative, a faraway look in her soft blue eyes.

At length, the blue eyes slowly turned back to Em. "Yes," Lucinda stated, calm and determined. "I'm game."

Em grinned delightedly. "Good! The first thing you'll need to understand is that he'll resist for all he's worth. He'll not come to the idea meekly—you can't expect it of him."

Lucinda frowned. "So I'll have to put up with more of this…" It was her turn to gesture as she sought for words. "This uncertainty?"

"Undoubtedly," Em averred. "But you'll have to hold firm to your purpose. And your plan."

Lucinda blinked. "Plan?"

Em nodded. "It'll take a subtle campaign to bring Harry to his knees."

Lucinda couldn't help but smile. "His knees?"

Em gave her a haughty look. "Of course."

Head on one side, Lucinda eyed her unpredictable hostess. "What do you mean by 'subtle'?"

"Well." Em settled in her chair. "For instance…"

"GOOD EVENING, Fergus."

"Good evening, sir."

Harry allowed his aunt's butler to relieve him of his great-coat, then handed him his driving gloves. "Is my brother here?" Harry turned to the mirror hanging above the ormolu table.

"Master Gerald arrived half an hour ago. In his new phaeton."

Harry's lips twitched. "Ah, yes—his latest achievement."

He made an almost imperceptible adjustment to the folds of his crisply white cravat.

"Your aunt will be delighted to see you, sir."

Harry met Fergus's eyes in the mirror. "No doubt." He let his lids fall, veiling his eyes. "Who else is here?"

"Sir Henry and Lady Dalrymple, Squire Moffat and Mrs Moffat, Mr Butterworth, Mr Hurst and the Misses Pinkerton." When Harry stood stock still, green eyes hooded, his expression utterly blank, Fergus added, "And Mrs Babbacombe and Miss Babbacombe, of course."

"Of course." Regaining his equilibrium, momentarily shaken, Harry resettled the gold pin in his cravat. Then, turning, he strolled towards the drawing-room door. Fergus hurried to open it.

Announced, Harry entered.

Her eyes met his immediately—she wasn't experienced enough to cloak her spontaneous reaction. She'd been speaking with Mr Hurst, a gentleman farmer whom Em, Harry suspected, had long had in her matchmaking sights. Harry paused just inside the door.

Lucinda smiled across the room—an easy, politely welcoming smile—and turned back to Mr Hurst.

Harry hesitated, then, languidly urbane, strolled to where his aunt sat ensconced in regal purple on the end of the *chaise*. "Dear Aunt," he said, bowing elegantly over her hand.

"Wondered if you'd come." Em grinned her triumph.

Harry ignored it. He nodded to the lady sharing the *chaise*. "Mrs Moffat." He was acquainted with all those Em had deigned to invite—he simply hadn't expected her to invite them. Tonight was the last night of the race-meet; tomorrow, after the final races in the morning, all the gentlemen would head back to town. His aunt's summons to dinner was not unusual, yet he had thought long and hard before accepting. Only the certainty that Mrs Babbacombe would shortly be returning to Yorkshire, well beyond his reach, while he intended to retire to Lester Hall in Berkshire, had persuaded him to do so. That, and the desire to see her again, to look into her misty blue eyes—one last time.

He had expected to share a table with his aunt, his brother, his aunt's houseguests—and no one else. Theoretically, the current situation, with so many distractions, should have reassured him. In fact, it did the opposite.

With a nod, and a swift glance at Mrs Babbacombe's dark head, he left the *chaise*, drifting to where Sir Henry Dalrymple stood chatting with Squire Moffat. Gerald was near the windows, Heather Babbacombe beside him, both conversing easily with Lady Dalrymple. The Misses Pinkerton, determined spinsters in their thirties, chatted with Mr Butterworth, Sir Henry's secretary.

Harry's gaze lingered on Lucinda, clad in delicate blue watered silk and talking animatedly with Mr Hurst; if she felt it, she gave no sign.

"Ah, Lester—up for the races, I presume?" Sir Henry beamed a welcome.

Squire Moffat snorted good-humouredly. "Precious little else to bring you this way."

"Indeed." Harry shook hands.

"Saw that filly of yours win in the second—great run." Sir Henry's faraway gaze said he was reliving the moment. Then he abruptly refocused. "But tell me, what do you think about Grand Larrikin's chances in the Steeple?"

The ensuing discussion on the Duke of Rutland's latest acquisition took up no more than half of Harry's mind. The rest was centred on his siren, apparently oblivious on the other side of the room.

Lucinda, perfectly aware of the sideways glances he occasionally sent her way, doggedly adhered to Em's strictures and studiously ignored him, prattling on about she knew not what to the loquacious Mr Hurst. He, thankfully, seemed so taken with the sound of his voice—a soothing baritone—that he didn't notice her preoccupation.

Struggling to focus her mind on his words, Lucinda steadfastly denied the increasing compulsion to glance at Harry Les-

616 AN UNWILLING CONQUEST

ter. Since the moment he'd appeared in the doorway, clad in severe black and white, his hair gleaming guinea gold in the candlelight, every elegant, indolent line screaming his position in the *ton,* her senses had defied her.

Her heart had leapt—Em had warned her that her summons wouldn't bring him if he didn't want to come. But he had arrived; it felt like she'd won, if not the first battle, then at least the opening skirmish.

She was so excruciatingly aware of him that when he left Squire Moffat and Sir Henry to languidly stroll her way, she had to clench her fists hard to stop herself from turning to greet him.

Approaching from behind her, Harry saw the sudden tension in her shoulders, bared by her gown. Beneath his heavy lids, his green eyes glinted.

As he drew abreast of her, he ran his fingertips down her bare forearm to capture her hand. Her eyes widened, but when she turned to smile at him there was no hint of perturbation in her face.

"Good evening, Mr Lester."

Harry smiled down into her eyes—and slowly raised her hand to his lips. Her fingers quivered, then lay passive. "I sincerely hope so, Mrs Babbacombe."

Lucinda accepted the salute with stalwart calm but withdrew her tingling fingers the instant he eased his grip. "I believe you're acquainted with Mr Hurst?"

"Indeed. Hurst." Harry exchanged nods with Pelham Hurst, who he privately considered a pompous ass. Hurst was a year older than he; they'd known each other since childhood but mixed as much as oil and water. As if to confirm he'd changed little with the years, Hurst launched into a recital of the improvements he had made to his fields; Harry dimly wondered why, with a vision like Lucinda Babbacombe in the vicinity, Pelham thought he'd be interested.

But Pelham rambled on.

Harry frowned. It was wellnigh impossible to keep his gaze on Lucinda Babbacombe's face while Hurst kept bombarding him with the details of crop rotation. Grasping a rare moment when Pelham paused for breath, he turned to Lucinda. "Mrs Babbacombe——"

Her blue eyes came his way—only to slide past him. She smiled in welcome. "Good evening, Mr Lester. Mr Butterworth."

Harry momentarily closed his eyes, then, opening them, forced himself to step back to allow Gerald and Nicholas Butterworth to make their bows. Together with Heather Babbacombe they joined their circle.

Any chance of detaching his quarry was lost.

Mentally gritting his teeth, Harry held to his position by her side. He knew he should go and chat to the Misses Pinkerton; he excused his lapse on the grounds that, being what he was, he made them nervous.

The thought gave him pause.

Lucinda felt very like Daniel in the lion's den—not at all sure of her safety. When the first trickle of heat slid down her nape, she didn't immediately register its cause. But when, but moments later, she felt the skin above her breasts tingle, she shot a frowning glance sideways.

Harry met it with a blank green stare—slightly questioning, all innocence. Lucinda raised her brows and pointedly turned back to the conversation. Thereafter, she steadfastly ignored all her senses—as best she could. She greeted Fergus's arrival and his stately pronouncement that dinner was served with considerable relief.

"If you would allow me to escort you in, Mrs Babbacombe?" Pelham Hurst, ineradicably convinced of his self-worth, offered a heavily creased sleeve.

Lucinda smiled and was about to accept when a drawling voice cut off her escape.

"I'm afraid, Hurst, that I'm before you." Harry smiled at his childhood acquaintance, the gesture in no way softening the expression in his eyes. "By days."

On the words, Harry shifted his green gaze to Lucinda's face—and dared her to contradict him.

Lucinda merely threw him an equable smile. "Indeed." She gave Harry her hand and allowed him to place it on his sleeve, turning as he did so to inform Mr Hurst, "Mr Lester has been of great assistance while we've been in Newmarket. I don't know how we would have escaped our upturned carriage if he hadn't happened along."

The remark, of course, led Pelham to enquire in deeply solicitous vein as to their accident. As the Misses Pinkerton had already wandered into the dining-room eschewing all male escort, Hurst was free to stroll on Lucinda's other side as Harry guided her into the dining-room.

By the time he took his seat beside the lovely Mrs Babbacombe, Harry's temper was straining at its leash.

But there were more trials in store. Lady Dalrymple, a motherly soul who had long deplored his unmarried state, took the seat to his left. Even worse, the Pinkerton sisters settled in opposite, warily eyeing him as if he was some potentially dangerous beast.

Harry wasn't sure they were wrong.

Ignoring all distractions, he turned to his fair companion. "Dare I hope you're satisfied with the outcome of your visit to Newmarket, Mrs Babbacombe?"

Lucinda fleetingly met his eyes, confirming that the question was, indeed, loaded. "Not entirely, Mr Lester. I can't help but feel that certain interests must regrettably be classed as unfinished business." Again she met his gaze and allowed her lips to curve. "But I dare say Mr Blount will manage."

Harry blinked, breaking the intensity of his gaze.

With a gentle smile, Lucinda turned away as Mr Hurst claimed her attention. She resisted the compulsion to glance to her right until the second course was being removed. Ineffably elegant, apparently relaxed, Harry was engaged in idly entertaining Lady Dalrymple.

At that moment, Mrs Moffat called upon Lady Dalrymple to confirm some report. Harry turned his head—and met Lucinda's determinedly mild gaze.

Resigned, he lifted a brow at her. "Well, my dear—what's

it to be? The weather is singularly boring, you know nothing about horses and as for what I'd prefer to discuss with you— I'm quite certain you'd rather I didn't.''

Attack—with a vengeance. There was no mistaking the light in his eyes. Lucinda inwardly quivered—outwardly she smiled. "Now there you are wrong, Mr Lester." She paused for an artful second before continuing, her gaze holding his, "I'm definitely interested in hearing about Thistledown. Is she still in town?"

He sat so perfectly still Lucinda found she couldn't breathe. Then one brow slowly rose; his eyes were jewel-like, crystalline and hard, sharp and brilliant. "No—she's on her way back to my stud."

"Ah, yes—that's in Berkshire, is it not?"

Harry inclined his head, not entirely trusting himself to speak. At the edge of his vision, the Pinkertons, oddly sensitive to atmospherics, were tensing, casting glances at each other, frowning at him.

Lady Dalrymple leaned forward to speak around him. "I'm so sorry you won't be here for my little gathering next week, Mrs Babbacombe. Still, I dare say you're quite right in heading to town. So much to do, so much to see—and you're young enough to enjoy the social whirl. Will you be bringing your stepdaughter out?"

"Possibly," Lucinda answered, ignoring the sudden tension that had laid hold of the body between them. "We'll make the decision once we're in town."

"Very wise." Lady Dalrymple nodded and turned back to Em.

"London?"

The question was quiet, his tone flat.

"Why, yes." Calmly, Lucinda met his green gaze. "I have four more inns to inspect, remember?"

For a pregnant moment, Harry's eyes held hers. "Which are?"

Again his voice was soft, steel cloaked in silk. Very thin silk.

"The Argyle Arms in Hammersmith, the Carringbush in Barnet, the Three Candles in Great Dover Street and the Bells at Wanstead."

"What's that about the Bells?"

Lucinda turned her head as Pelham Hurst butted in.

"An excellent inn—I can recommend it to you, Mrs Babbacombe. Often stay there myself. Don't like to risk my cattle in town, don't y'know."

Harry ignored him completely. Luckily, as a large apple tart was placed in front of him at that moment, Pelham didn't notice. Harry grasped the opportunity as the diners sat up and looked over the dessert course to lean closer to Lucinda. He spoke in a steely whisper. "You're out of your senses! Those are four of the busiest inns in England—they're all coaching inns on the major roads."

Lucinda reached for a jelly. "So I've been told."

Harry gritted his teeth. "My dear Mrs Babbacombe, your little act of being an inspector might work in country inns—" he broke off to thank Lady Dalrymple for passing the cream which he immediately set down "—but it'll get you nowhere in town. Aside from that, you cannot visit any of those inns alone."

"My dear Mr Lester." Lucinda turned to face him, her eyes wide. "Surely you're not trying to tell me my inns are dangerous?"

He was trying to tell her just that.

But Pelham Hurst, hearing only snippets, put in his oar. "Dangerous? Not a bit of it! Why, you'll be as safe as…as here, at the Bells. Highly recommend it, Mrs Babbacombe."

Glimpsing the goaded expression in Harry's green eyes, Lucinda kept her lips straight and made haste to assure Mr Hurst, "Indeed, sir. I'm sure that wasn't what Mr Lester meant."

"Mr Lester, as you well know, meant that you have as much experience as a green girl and rather less chance of surviving one of your 'inspections' at any of those inns without receiving at least three propositions and a *carte blanche*." Having deliv-

ered this clarification through clenched teeth, Harry attacked
the custard that had appeared before him.

"Would you care for some cream?" Lucinda, having helped
herself to a generous dollop, caught a drip on her fingertip. Her
eyes, innocently blue, met Harry's as she lifted her finger to
her lips.

For a blind instant, as she lowered her hand, Harry could
see nothing beyond her lips, ripe and luscious, begging to be
kissed. He heard nothing, was blissfully unaware of the gaggle
of conversation about him. Abruptly, he grabbed hold of his
reins, fast disappearing. He lifted his gaze and met hers. His
eyes narrowed. "No, thank you."

Lucinda simply smiled.

"It's fattening," Harry added but she only smiled more. She
looked very like the cat who had found the right jug.

Stifling a curse, Harry applied himself to his dessert. It was
no business of his if she insisted on swanning into danger. He'd
warned her. "Why can't Mabberly do those inns? Let him earn
his keep."

"As I told you before, Mr Mabberly does not have the right
qualifications for conducting an inquisition." Lucinda kept her
voice low, grateful that Heather had distracted Mr Hurst.

She waited for the next comment—but her neighbour merely
snorted and fell silent.

His disapproval lapped about her in waves.

Harry endured the rest of the evening outwardly urbane, inwardly brooding. The gentlemen did not linger over their port,
which was just as well for he was no good company. But when
they repaired to the drawing room, he discovered that, rather
than the general chatty atmosphere which was the norm for
Em's dinners, and which he'd been determined to exploit for
his own ends, tonight, they were to be entertained by the Babbacombes, Mrs and Miss.

With no good grace, Harry sat on a chair at the back of the
room, unmoved by what he recognised as an exemplary performance. The tea trolley appeared as the applause died.

His temper sorely strained, he was one of the last to come forward for his cup.

"Yes, indeed," Em said as he strolled up, nodding to Lady Dalrymple. "We'll be there—I'll look for you. It's going to be such fun to go the rounds again."

Harry froze, his hand half-outstretched.

Em looked up—and frowned. "Here you are!"

Harry blinked—and took the cup, Em's frown reflected in his eyes. "Are you contemplating going up to town, dear Aunt?"

"Not contemplating." Em threw him a belligerent glance. "I'm going. As Lucinda and Heather are set to visit there, we've decided to go together. Much the best thing. I've sent for them to open Hallows House—Fergus is going up tomorrow. It'll be wonderful, being in the swing again. I'll introduce Lucinda and Heather to the *ton*. Marvellous distraction—just what I need to give me new life."

She actually had the gall to smile at him.

Harry forced himself to utter the expected platitudes—under Lady Dalrymple's mild gaze he could hardly give his aunt the benefit of his true conclusions.

After that he beat a hasty retreat—even Squire Moffat and the intricacies of the local drainage system were preferable to farther contemplation of the web he now found himself in. The only one he could be open with was his brother.

"Em's insane. They all are," he growled as he joined Gerald by the window. Heather Babbacombe was chatting to Mrs Moffat. Harry noticed Gerald's smiling gaze rarely left the girl.

"Why? No harm in them going up to London. I'll be able to show Heather all the sights."

Harry snorted. "While London's rakes are attempting to show Mrs Babbacombe their etchings, no doubt."

Gerald grinned. "Well—you can take care of that. None of the others will come near if you hover at her shoulder."

The look Harry bent on him spoke volumes. "In case it's escaped your admittedly distracted intelligence, brother dear, I am currently the principal Lester target in the matchmakers' sights. Having lost Jack to Miss Winterton, they'll redouble their efforts and turn all their guns on yours truly.''

"I know." Gerald shot him an insouciant grin. "You've no idea how grateful I am that you're there for them to aim at—with any luck, they won't remember me. Good thing—I haven't a bean of your experience."

He was clearly sincere. Harry swallowed the sharp words that rose to his tongue. Lips compressed, he retired to the safety of Sir Henry's conversation, studiously avoiding any further contact with his fate. His siren. She who would lure him onto the rocks.

The guests left in concert. Harry and Gerald, as family, stood back to let the others take their leave. Em stepped onto the porch to wave farewell; Gerald and Heather were dallying by the drawing-room door. In the shadows by the front door, Harry found himself beside his temptation.

His aunt, he noticed, was in no rush to return.

"Will we see you in London, Mr Lester?"

She cast him an artless glance—Harry couldn't decide whether it was real or not. He looked down at her face, up-turned to his, blue eyes wide. "I have no plans to come up again this Season."

"A pity," she said, but her lips curved. "I had thought to repay my debt to you, as we'd agreed."

It took him a moment to recall. "The waltz?"

Lucinda nodded. "Indeed. But if you will not be in town, then this is goodbye, sir."

She held out her hand; Harry took it, shook it, but didn't release it. Eyes narrowing, he studied her open expression, those eyes he would swear could not lie.

She was saying goodbye. Perhaps, after all, escape was still possible?

Then her lips curved slightly. "Rest assured I'll think of you while waltzing through the London ballrooms."

Harry's fingers closed hard about hers—and clenched even harder about his gloves. The eruption that shook him—of anger, and sheer, possessive desire—very nearly broke his con-

trol. She looked up, eyes flaring, her lips slightly parted. It was
no thanks to her, and the soft, tempting look in her eyes, that
he managed to mask his reaction. He forced himself to release
her hand; his face felt stiff as he bowed. "I will bid you good
night, Mrs Babbacombe."

With that, he walked out, missing the disappointment that
clouded Lucinda's gaze.

From the top of the steps, she watched him drive away—
and prayed that Em was right.

Chapter Six

SHE WAS STILL PRAYING ten days later when, flanked by Em and Heather, she strolled into Lady Haverbuck's ballroom. Her ladyship's ball was the first of the major gatherings they had attended. It had taken them four days to successfully transfer to Hallows House in Audley Street; the following days had been taken up with the necessary visits to modistes and the fashionable emporia. The previous evening, Em had hosted a select party to introduce both her guests to the *ton*. The acceptances had gratified Em; it had been many years since she had been in the capital. But there had been one who had not responded to the white, gilt-edged card.

Lucinda herself had penned it and directed it to Harry's lodgings in Half Moon Street. But she had looked in vain for his golden head.

"You'll have to let him go if you want him to come back," Em had declared. "He's like one of his horses—you can lead him to the pond but you can't make him drink."

So she had let him go—without a murmur, without the slightest hint that she wanted him.

He had yet to return.

Now, elegantly clad in shimmering blue silk the colour of cornflowers, her dark hair artfully coiffed to fall in soft curls about her brow and temples, Lucinda stood on the edge of the ballroom floor and looked about her.

They were neither early nor late; the room was already well filled but not yet crowded. Elegant gentlemen conversed with fashionable matrons; dowagers and chaperons lined the walls. Their charges, mostly young girls making their come-out, were

readily identified by the pale pastel hues of their gowns. They
were everywhere, the bolder ones chatting with youthful
swains, others, more bashful, clinging to each other's company.

"Oh—look!" Heather clutched Lucinda's gloved arm.
"There's Miss Morley and her sister." Heather glanced up at
Lucinda. "May I join them?"

Lucinda smiled across the room at the cheery Misses Morley
"Certainly. But look for us when you've done."

Heather flashed her an excited smile.

Em snorted. "We'll be over there." Wielding a lorgnette,
she pointed to a *chaise* by the wall.

With a bob, Heather slipped away, a vision in palest turquoise muslin, her golden curls dressed high.

"A most fetching gown—even if 'twas I who chose it," Em
declared. She led the way to the *chaise*.

Lucinda followed. She was about to copy Em's descent onto
the brocaded seat when young Mr Hollingsworth appeared by
her elbow, an older, infinitely more elegant gentleman beside
him.

"I say, Mrs Babbacombe—delighted to see you again." Mr
Hollingsworth all but jigged with excitement.

Lucinda murmured a polite greeting; they had met Mr Hollingsworth at Hatchard's the day before.

"Beg you'll allow me to present my cousin, Lord Ruthven."

The elegant gentleman, dark-haired and handsome, bowed
gracefully. "I am indeed honoured to make your acquaintance.
Mrs Babbacombe."

Curtsying, Lucinda glanced up and met his eye; she suppressed a grimace as she recognised the speculative glint
therein.

"A rose amongst so many peonies, my dear." With a languid wave, Ruthven dismissed the youthful beauties about
them.

"Indeed?" Lucinda raised her brows sceptically.

Lord Ruthven was undeterred. And, as she quickly discovered, his lordship was not the only gentleman desirous of more
mature company. Others, largely of similar ilk, strolled up, un-

hesitatingly claiming Ruthven's good offices to perform the introductions. His lordship, indolently amused, obliged. Remembering her duties, Lucinda tried to retreat, only to have Em snort—indulgently amused—and wave her away.

"I'll keep an eye on Heather. You go and enjoy yourself—that's what *ton* balls are for."

Thus adjured, and reflecting that Em knew rather more about watching over young girls at *ton* balls than she did, Lucinda inwardly shrugged and smiled on her would-be court. In a very short time, she found herself surrounded—by a collection of gentlemen she mentally categorised as Harry Lester's contemporaries. They were, one and all, ineffably charming; she could see no harm in enjoying their company.

Then the music started, lilting strains wafting over the bright heads.

"Dare I claim your first cotillion in the capital, my dear?"

Lucinda turned to find Lord Ruthven's arm before her. "Indeed, sir. I would be delighted."

A smile curved his lips. "No, my dear—it is *I* who am delighted. You will have to find another adjective."

Lucinda met his eyes. She raised her brows. "My mind is a blank, sir. What would you suggest?"

His lordship was perfectly prepared to oblige. "Devastated with joy? In alt? Over the moon with happiness?"

Lucinda laughed. As they took their places in the set, she arched a brow at him. "How about—'so impressed I am unable to find words to express it'?"

Lord Ruthven grimaced.

As the evening progressed, Lucinda found herself much in demand. As she was ranked among the matrons, she did not have a dance-card but was free to bestow her hand on whomever she chose from amongst her assiduous court. Indeed, their assiduousness triggered her innate caution; while Ruthven appeared too good-humoured and indolent to be dangerous, there were others whose eyes held a more intent gleam.

One such was Lord Craven, who strolled into the ballroom late, surveyed the field from the top of the steps, then beat a disguised but determined path to her side. Dragooning Mr Satterly into providing an introduction, his lordship was bowing over Lucinda's hand when the unmistakable strains of a waltz filled the room.

"My dear Mrs Babbacombe, dare I hope you'll take pity on a latecomer and grant me the honour of this waltz?"

Lucinda met Lord Craven's dark hooded eyes—and decided her pity would be more wisely bestowed elsewhere. She let her eyes widen and swept a questioning glance at the gentlemen surrounding her.

They instantly came to her rescue, dismissing Lord Craven's claim as outrageous, presumptuous and unfair and plying her with any number of alternatives. Laughing lightly, Lucinda withdrew her fingers from Lord Craven's clasp. "I fear you must take your chance amongst the competition, my lord."

His lordship's expression turned distinctly stiff.

"Now, let's see." Lucinda smiled at her cavaliers and was about to bestow her favour upon Mr Amberly, who, despite the appreciation in his eyes, was another more inclined to amusement than seduction, when she felt a stir beside her.

Long, strong fingers encircled her arm, sliding over the bare skin just above her glove.

"My waltz, I believe, Mrs Babbacombe."

Lucinda's breath caught. She swung to face Harry; their eyes met—his were very green, his gaze sharp, oddly intent. Elation swept Lucinda. She struggled to hide it.

Harry's lips curved, their ends lifting in a smile, which turned to a grimace, hidden as he bowed.

When he straightened, his features were impassive.

"I say, Lester! This is dashed unfair." Mr Amberly all but pouted. Others muttered in similar vein.

Harry merely lifted a supercilious brow, his now-hooded glance shifting to rest on Lucinda's face. "As I recall, my dear, you owe me a waltz. I've come to claim it."

"Indeed, sir." Savouring the sound of his deep drawl, Lucinda gave up her fight and smiled her delight. "I always pay my debts. My first waltz in the capital is yours."

Harry's lips twitched but he stilled them. With an elegant gesture he claimed her hand and settled it on his sleeve.

Lucinda slanted a quick, triumphant glance at Em, but her mentor was hidden by her court. "Gentlemen." With a sunny smile and a nod for her disappointed cavaliers, who were shooting disgruntled glances at her unexpected partner, she allowed him to lead her to the floor.

Harry held his tongue until they reached the dance floor but as soon as he had whirled them into the swirling throng, he looked down and trapped Lucinda's blue gaze. "I realise, Mrs Babbacombe, that your experience does not extend to the vagaries of the *ton*. I fear I should warn you that many of the gentlemen presently intent on your smiles should be treated with extreme caution."

More concerned with adequately following his assured lead than with her redundant court, Lucinda frowned. "That's obvious."

Harry's brows slowly rose.

Lucinda's frown grew distracted. "I'm rather more than seven, you know. As far as I can see, there's no reason I shouldn't enjoy myself in their company—I'm hardly so green as to be taken in by their charms."

At that, Harry snorted. For a full minute, he considered the possibility of scaring her with a more explicit warning, then mentally shook his head. She wasn't, he realised, recalling Jake Blount and the Green Goose, easily scared. But he could hardly countenance her court.

Glancing down at her face, he saw she was still frowning, but in an abstracted way. "What's wrong?"

She started—and cast an irritated glance up at him.

"Well?"

"If you must know," Lucinda said. "I'm not terribly experienced at waltzing. Charles didn't, of course. I've had lessons—but it's rather different on a crowded floor."

Harry couldn't stop his slow grin. "Just relax."

The look she sent him suggested that she found his humour ill-conceived.

Harry chuckled—and drew her closer, tightening his arm about her so she could more easily sense his intentions.

Lucinda held her breath—then slowly let it out. Their new positions were just this side of decent but she felt immeasurably more secure. When Harry twirled her through a complicated set of turns as they negotiated the end of the room, she followed without faltering. Reassured, she relaxed—only to find her wits almost overwhelmed by her senses. His hard thighs brushed hers as they progressed down the room; she could feel the heat of his large body reaching for her, enveloping her, his strength effortlessly whirling her about. A strange tension gripped her, making breathing difficult. It was matched by the tension in the arm locked about her. From beneath her lashes, Lucinda glanced up. Her gaze found his lips. As she watched, they firmed into a straight line.

It was an uphill battle but Harry strove to push aside all distractions—like the enthralling curves encased in blue silk nestling in his arms, the womanly softness of those curves and the supple planes of her back, like the subtle scent of her that rose to tease his senses, and the graceful curve of her neck exposed by her new hairstyle—and remind his wandering wits just why he had returned to London. "When are you planning to visit your inns?"

Lucinda blinked, and shifted her gaze to his eyes. "Actually, I'd thought to start with the Argyle Arms at Hammersmith tomorrow."

Harry didn't bother asking if she'd arranged a suitable escort. The damned woman was so irrationally sure of herself, so ignorant of the true dangers, so determinedly wilful... His lips thinned. "I'll call for you at nine."

Lucinda's eyes opened wide.

Harry noticed—and frowned at her. "You needn't fear— we'll go in my curricle and I'll have Dawlish along. Perfectly proper, I assure you."

Lucinda swallowed her happy laugh. Em's strictures replayed in her head. She eyed him consideringly, then gracefully acquiesced. "Thank you, sir. Your company will, I'm sure, make the drive more interesting."

Harry narrowed his eyes, but could make nothing of her serene expression. Stifling a humph, he drew her a fraction closer—and set his mind to enjoying the rest of the waltz.

At its end, he strolled back with her to where her court waited, impatient and eager. Harry read the anticipation in their eyes. He stiffened. Instead of yielding his fair partner up with a flourish and an elegant bow, the prescribed procedure, he covered her hand, resting on his sleeve, with his. And remained, thus anchored, by her side.

Lucinda pretended not to notice. She chatted gaily, ignoring the intrigued glint in Lord Ruthven's perceptive eye and Mr Amberly's disapproving expression. Harry, she noted, made no attempt whatever to contribute to the conversation; she longed to look at him but standing so close, she could not. Not without making her interest obvious. She was somewhat relieved when Mrs Anabelle Burnham, a young matron ambling past on the arm of Mr Courtney, decided to join them.

"I declare, it's going to be yet another crush." Mrs Burnham fluttered her lashes at Lord Ruthven before turning her laughing brown eyes on Lucinda. "You'll grow used to them, my dear. And you have to admit these larger gatherings are... entertaining."

Another laughing glance went Lord Ruthven's way.

Lucinda struggled to keep her lips straight. "Indeed." Nothing loath, she slanted a glance up at her silent partner. "And the entertainment takes so many varied forms, too. Don't you find it so?"

Anabelle Burnham blinked, then her teasing smile brightened. "Oh, definitely, my dear Mrs Babbacombe. Definitely!"

She bestowed another arch glance on Lord Ruthven, then turned her sights on Mr Amberly.

Lucinda didn't notice—she was trapped in Harry's green gaze. The planes of his face were hard, sculpted, his expression impassive yet growing more forbidding by the second. She saw his eyes narrow slightly; his lips were a thin line. Breathing was suddenly very difficult.

The squeak of the violins saved her—she didn't know from what.

"Mrs Babbacombe—I declare you must, positively you must, bestow this quadrille on my poor self."

With a mental curse, Lucinda glanced to where Mr Amberly stood watching her, entreaty in his eyes. She blinked—and realized that he was begging her to rescue him. She couldn't help but smile.

She glanced up at Harry; gently she withdrew her hand from under his. For an instant, his fingers tensed—then he released her. "I haven't thanked you for my waltz, sir." Lucinda lifted her eyes to his. "It was most enjoyable."

His features were granite. He said nothing but bowed, effortlessly elegant in his severe black and white.

With an inclination of her head, Lucinda turned away and placed her hand on Mr Amberly's sleeve.

To her intense disappointment, Harry was no longer present when, at the conclusion of the quadrille, Mr Amberly returned her to the small group close by Em's chaise. Under cover of the conversation, Lucinda scanned the surrounding shoulders but could not find the ones she sought. She saw Heather, bright-eyed and clearly enjoying herself hugely. Her stepdaughter waved, then turned back to her set—Gerald Lester, the Morley sisters and two other young gentlemen. Feeling distinctly deflated, Lucinda forced herself to pay attention to her cavaliers. The circle around her, which had earlier thinned, now pressed in on her. She could understand why these events were labelled crushes. At least Mrs Burnham hadn't deserted her.

But her enjoyment in the evening had waned; it was an effort to conjure a bright smile and a witty response to the constant flow of repartee.

Somewhat later, the lilting strains of another waltz drifted from the musicians' dais at the other end of the room. Lucinda blinked. She had already danced with all those of her court she considered reasonably safe—she hadn't anticipated another waltz.

She glanced up—to find Lord Ruthven's eyes upon her, a curious glint in their depths. "Well, my dear?" he drawled. "Which one of us will you favour with a second dance?"

Lucinda raised her brows haughtily. And scanned those she had yet to favour at all. Three promptly pressed their claims— one, a rakish dandy a few years older than herself but infinitely more experienced, held the greatest promise. He might have impropriety on his mind but he was, Lucinda judged, manageable. With a serene smile, and a cool glance for Ruthven, she extended her hand. "Mr Ellerby?"

To give him his due, Mr Ellerby behaved with all due decorum on the dance floor. By the end of the dance, Lucinda was congratulating herself, not only on her increasing confidence in the waltz itself but on her accurate assessment of her partner, when Mr Ellerby abruptly reverted to type.

"Quite stuffy in here, don't you find, Mrs Babbacombe?"

Lucinda glanced up and smiled. "Indeed—one could hardly find it not. The room is certainly very crowded."

So crowded she could no longer see Em's *chaise*, concealed by the milling throng. The waltz had landed them at the other end of the room.

"This window leads to the terrace. And Lady Haverbuck's gardens are extensive. Perhaps a stroll through them would cool your cheeks, Mrs Babbacombe?"

Lucinda turned to stare at her erstwhile partner. The gleam in his eyes was unmistakable.

"Wouldn't want you to feel faint, would we?" Mr Ellerby leaned closer on the words, pressing her fingers meaningfully.

Lucinda stiffened. She drew a steady breath and opened her lips, fully intending to advise her importunate partner that her temper rarely induced faintness, when she was saved the necessity.

"I don't think Mrs Babbacombe needs a stroll on the terrace just now, Ellerby."

The drawled yet steely words sent a frisson of excitement through Lucinda; they turned Mr Ellerby sulky.

"Just a suggestion." He waved the point aside, then offered Lucinda his arm, all but glowering at Harry. "It's suppertime, Mrs Babbacombe."

"Indeed," came from beside her.

Lucinda glanced up and saw Harry's green gaze grow coldly challenging. His fingers feathered down her arm, then firmed about her wrist. She quelled a shiver.

Harry looked down at her. "If you wish, Mrs Babbacombe, I'll escort you in."

He lifted her hand and settled it on his sleeve. Lucinda met his eyes—then turned to coolly dismiss Mr Ellerby. "Thank you for an enjoyable waltz, sir."

Mr Ellerby looked as if he wished to argue—then he met Harry's gaze. With a grumpy air, he bowed. "My pleasure, ma'am."

"I'm sure it was," Harry muttered beneath his breath as he turned Lucinda towards the supper room.

"I beg your pardon?" Lucinda blinked up at him.

"Nothing." Harry's lips compressed. "Couldn't you chose a more suitable partner than Ellerby? You had enough real gentlemen about you—or can't you tell the difference?"

"Of course I can." Suppressing her smile, Lucinda put her nose in the air. "But I'd already danced with all of them. I didn't want to appear to be encouraging them."

Harry resisted the urge to grind his teeth. "Believe me, Mrs Babbacombe, you would do better to encourage the gentlemen and avoid the rakes altogether."

Lucinda copied one of Em's snorts. "Nonsense. I was in no danger."

She glanced up to see Harry's face turn to stone.

"Mrs Babbacombe, I have severe difficulty believing you would recognise danger if you fell over it."

Lucinda had to purse her lips to stop her smile. "Bosh!" she eventually returned.

Harry sent her a severe glance—and determinedly steered

her to a table. Not one of the small, intimate tables for two in the corners of the large supper-room, but a table to accommodate a small army set close to the buffet in the room's centre. Taking the seat he held for her, Lucinda cast him a puzzled glance.

She was even more puzzled when her court tentatively descended, and Harry forbore to bite. He sat beside her, leaning back in the chair, a champagne flute in one long-fingered hand, and silently monitored the conversation. His brooding presence acted as a most efficient damper, ensuring the jocularity remained strictly within acceptable bounds. Anabelle Burnham, joining them, cast one awed glance at Harry, then caught Lucinda's eye and raised her glass in a silent toast. Lucinda risked a quick grin, then let her gaze slide to Harry's face.

He was watching her, not the others, his lips set in a line she was coming to know well, his green gaze jewel-like and impenetrable.

Lucinda quelled a shiver. Turning back to the table, she forced herself to focus on her less interesting admirers.

As HE HAD PROMISED, Harry was waiting for her in the hall of Hallows House at precisely nine o'clock the next morning.

Descending the stairs with a dark blue half-cape draped over her bluebell-hued carriage dress, Lucinda watched as his gaze skimmed knowledgeably over her. When she reached the hall and came forward, her hand extended, his gaze lifted to her face.

Harry saw the feminine smugness in her eyes—and frowned. "At least you shouldn't freeze." He took her hand and bowed over it—then considered the sight of her small, slim hand nestling in his much larger one. "Don't forget your gloves."

Lucinda lifted a brow—and drew her gloves from her reticule. "I'll be back for luncheon, Fergus." Dutifully drawing on her gloves, she glanced at Harry. "Will you join us, Mr Lester?"

"No—please convey my regrets to my aunt." Harry grasped her arm and steered her to the door. Em's house was probably safe enough but his clubs would be safer; he no longer trusted his aunt. "I have other engagements."

Lucinda stopped on the top of the steps and glanced up at him. "I do hope I'm not inconveniencing you by claiming your escort to my inns?"

Harry looked down at her, his eyes narrowing. She was an inconvenience unlike any he'd ever encountered. "Not at all, my dear. If you recall, I wished this on myself." Why, he refused to consider. "But it's time we were away."

He led her down the steps, then lifted her to his curricle's seat. Avoiding Dawlish's eye, he retrieved the reins. He waited only until his henchman's weight tipped the carriage before giving his horses the office.

Lucinda thoroughly enjoyed her drive through the morning streets, not yet crowded. She saw orange-sellers plying their wares; she heard strawberry girls calling housewives to their doors. The city seemed different, clean and pristine beneath the morning's dew, the dust yet to be stirred by the traffic. The varied greens of the trees in the Park shifted like a kaleidoscope. Harry drove them briskly along the gravelled carriageway, then out of a distant gate. Once they were bowling along the road to Hammersmith, Lucinda turned her mind to business. Harry answered her questions on the inns they passed, occasionally referring to Dawlish. Lucinda noted that Harry's groom seemed uncommonly morose; his dour tones suggested a death in the family.

But she forgot Dawlish and his patent misery when they pulled into the yard of the Argyle Arms.

The Argyle Arms proved to have much in common with the Barbican Arms. The innkeeper, a Mr Honeywell, after one glance at Harry, deferentially escorted her over the large inn, which extended over three interconnecting wings. They were on the ground floor of one of the wings heading back towards the main entrance when Lucinda heard laughter behind a door she had assumed led to a bedchamber.

Visions of the Green Goose flitted through her mind. It had, however, been male laughter. She halted. "What's behind that door?"

Mr Honeywell remained impassive. "A parlour, ma'am."

"A parlour?" Lucinda frowned and looked about her. "Ah, yes—this was a separate house at one time, wasn't it?"

Mr Honeywell nodded and gestured for her to proceed.

Lucinda stood stock-still and stared at the closed parlour door. "That makes four parlours—does the inn's custom necessitate so many?"

"Not directly," Mr Honeywell admitted. "But we're so near town we often rent rooms to groups for meetings."

Lucinda pursed her lips. "I would like to inspect this extra parlour, Honeywell."

Mr Honeywell's expression grew wary. "Ah—this one's currently occupied, ma'am, but there's another just like it in the other wing. If you'd like to see that?"

"Indeed." Lucinda nodded but her eyes remained on the closed door. "Who is currently using this one?"

"Er…a group of gentlemen, ma'am."

Lucinda's brows rose; she opened her mouth.

"But—" Mr Honeywell smoothly interposed his stout frame between Lucinda and the door *"—*I really wouldn't advise you to interrupt them, ma'am."

Taken aback, Lucinda allowed her brows to rise higher; for a silent moment, she looked down on Mr Honeywell. When she spoke, her tone was chilly. "My dear Mr Honeywell—"

"Who's in there, Honeywell?"

Lucinda blinked. It was the first time in an hour that Harry had spoken.

Mr Honeywell cast an imploring glance at him. "Just a group of young bloods, sir. You'll know the sort."

"Indeed." Harry turned to Lucinda. "You can't go in."

As frigidly imperious as any dowager, Lucinda slowly turned and met his gaze. "I beg your pardon?"

Harry's lips twisted slightly but his gaze did not waver. "Let me put it this way." His tone was peculiarly soft, silky, with an undercurrent that threatened all manner of danger. "You're not going in there."

If Lucinda had had any doubt as to the reality behind the unsubtle threat, it was laid to rest by the look in his eyes, the set of his jaw and the tension that slowly infused his large frame. Despite her rising temper, she was assailed by an instinctive urge to step back—and a totally maniacal impulse to call his bluff just to see what he would do. Ignoring the shiver that squirmed down her spine, she sent him a seething glance, then transferred her gaze, now icy, to Mr Honeywell. "Perhaps you could show me this other parlour?"

The innkeeper's sigh was almost audible.

Shown the second parlour, repeatedly assured that it was virtually identical to the other, Lucinda gave her haughty approval. Stripping off her gloves, she nodded at Honeywell. "I'll examine the books now. You may bring them in here."

Honeywell departed to fetch his ledgers.

Leaving her gloves and reticule on the table, Lucinda slowly walked down the room. Halting by the window, she drew in a steadying breath and swung to face Harry. He had followed in her wake; she watched as he drew near, stopping directly before her, one brow lifting, a challenging look in his eye.

Lucinda returned it in full measure. "It may interest you to know, Mr Lester, that I had no intention of—" she gestured dismissively "—barging into a private meeting. A fact I was about to make clear to Mr Honeywell when you chose to intervene."

The arrested, suddenly defensive expression that flickered in Harry's eyes was balm to Lucinda's temper. She immediately pressed her advantage. "I merely wished to enquire as to the bona fides of the customers using my inn—a right I'm sure even *you* will agree is mine." She waggled a finger under his nose. "Neither you nor Mr Honeywell had any justification for jumping to such a conclusion—as if I was a child unaware of the proprieties! And *you*, sir, had no right to threaten me as you did." Turning aside and folding her arms, Lucinda elevated her chin. "I wish to hear an apology, sir, for your un-gentlemanly behaviour."

Silence greeted her demand. Harry studied her face, his gaze clear and steady. Then his lips twisted. "I suggest, my dear, that you refrain from holding your breath. My behaviour throughout this morning has been gentlemanly in the extreme."

Lucinda's eyes flew wide. *"Gentlemanly?"* Her arms dropped as she rounded on him.

Harry held up a hand. "I'll admit that both Honeywell and I might have jumped to unwarranted conclusions." His eyes met hers, his expression fleetingly rueful. "For myself, for that, I apologise unequivocally. For the rest, however..." His face hardened. "I fear you must excuse it on the grounds of extreme provocation."

"Provocation?" Lucinda stared at him. "What provocation was that, pray tell?"

The provocation of keeping her safe, shielded, the undeni-able, instinctive impulse that had him in its grip. The truth echoed in Harry's head; he struggled to shut his mind against it. He looked into her eyes; softly blue, they searched his, then widened. He dropped his gaze to her lips, full, blush red—a potent temptation. As he watched, they parted fractionally. About them, silence reigned; between them, the tension grew. Compelled, as aware of her increased breathing as he was of the deepening thud in his veins, Harry lifted a finger and, with the lightest of touches, traced her lower lip.

The shudder his touch evoked in her reverberated deep in his marrow.

His breath caught; if he met her gaze, he would be lost.

Desire welled, unexpectedly strong; he fought to shackle it. He tried to draw breath, tried to step away, and could not.

Distant footsteps drew near; in the corridor a board creaked.

Swiftly, Harry bent his head and touched his lips to hers in a caress so brief he barely registered the gentle movement of her lips beneath his.

When the door opened and Honeywell came in, he was standing by the fireplace, some yards from Lucinda. The innkeeper noticed nothing amiss; he placed the heavy ledgers on the table and looked hopefully at Lucinda.

Harry glanced her way but her back was to the window, hiding her expression.

Lucinda hesitated, just long enough to marshall her thoroughly disordered wits. Then she swept forward, plastering an expression of such haughtiness on her face that Mr Honeywell blinked. "Just the figures for this year, I think, Mr Honeywell."

The innkeeper hurried to do her bidding.

Immersed in figures, Lucinda struggled to soothe her tingling nerves, inflamed by that too-fleeting kiss and further abraded by Harry's lounging presence. For one instant, she had felt as if the world had spun wildly; determinedly, she put the memory aside and concentrated on Mr Honeywell's accounts. By the time she was satisfied, half an hour had passed, leaving her once more in control. Quite capable of maintaining a steady flow of artless prattle all the way back to Audley Street.

Other than bestowing on her one, long, unnervingly intent look, Harry made no particular comment, replying readily to any questions, but leaving the conversational reins in her hands. When they drew up at Em's steps, Lucinda felt she had handled them with laudable skill.

She chose the moment when Harry lifted her down to say, "I'm really most grateful for your escort, Mr Lester." With what she considered commendable fortitude, she refrained from further comment.

"Indeed?" Harry arched one brow.

Lucinda fought against a frown. "Indeed," she returned, meeting his gaze.

Harry looked down at her face, at her wonderfully blue eyes, gleaming with feminine defiance—and wondered how long he could hold her, his hands firm about her waist, before she became aware of it. "In that case, tell Fergus to inform me when you wish to inspect your next inn." She felt warm, vibrant, supple and alive between his hands.

Lucinda knew perfectly well where his hands were; she

could feel his fingers burning through her gown. But that kiss, so quick it was over almost before it had begun, had been her first intimation that victory was truly possible; despite the unnerving cascade of emotions the fleeting caress had evoked, she was determined not to back down. If she had, albeit unknowingly, breached his walls once, she could do it again. Battling breathlessness, she dropped her gaze to where her fingers rested against his coat. "But I couldn't so impose on your time, Mr Lester."

Harry frowned. He could see her eyes glinting through her lashes. "Not at all." He paused, then added, native caution returning, "As I told you before, given you're my aunt's guest, at my insistence, I feel it's the least I can do."

He thought he heard a disgusted humph. Suppressing a smile, he glanced up—and met Dawlish's deeply commiserating gaze.

All expression draining from his face, Harry dropped his hands. Stepping back, he offered his aunt's guest his arm, then gallantly, in open contempt of his henchman's foreboding, escorted her up the steps.

While waiting for Fergus to open the door, Lucinda glanced up—and intercepted an exchange of glances between Harry and Dawlish. "Dawlish seems very dismal—is anything amiss?"

Harry's features hardened. "No. He's just unused to getting up so early."

Lucinda blinked. "Oh?"

"Indeed." The door opened; beaming, Fergus held it wide. Harry bowed. "*Au revoir*, Mrs Babbacombe."

Crossing the threshold, Lucinda looked over her shoulder and threw him a smile—a soft, alluring, siren's smile. Then she turned and slowly headed for the stairs. Utterly mesmerised, Harry stood and watched her go, her hips swaying gently as she crossed the tiled hall.

"Sir?"

Harry came to himself with a start. With an abrupt nod to Fergus, he turned and descended the steps. Climbing into the curricle, he fixed Dawlish with a warning glance.

Then gave his attention to his horses.

Chapter Seven

A WEEK LATER, Harry sat at his desk in the small library of his lodgings. The window gave onto a leafy courtyard; outside, May bustled towards June while the *ton* worked itself into a frenzy of betrothals and weddings. Harry's lips twisted cynically; *he* was intent on other things.

A tap on the door brought his head up. The door opened; Dawlish looked in.

"Ah—there you be. Thought as how you'd want to know that they're bound for Lady Hemminghurst's this evening."

"Damn!" Harry grimaced. Amelia Hemminghurst had a soft spot for rakes—the fraternity would be well represented amongst her guests. "I suppose I'll have to attend."

"That's what I thought. You going to walk or should I bring the carriage around?"

Harry considered, then shook his head. "I'll walk." It would be twilight by then; the short stroll to Grosvenor Square would help ease the restlessness his self-imposed restrictions seemed to be creating.

With a humph and a nod, Dawlish retreated.

Idly toying with a pen, Harry reviewed his strategy. On quitting Newmarket, he had stubbornly adhered to his plans and gone home to Lester Hall. There he had found his brother Jack, along with his soon-to-be bride, Miss Sophia Winterton and her guardians, her uncle and aunt, Mr and Mrs Webb. While he had nothing against Miss Winterton, with whom his brother was openly besotted, he had not appreciated the considering light that had lit Mrs Webb's silver blue eyes, nor the contemplative expression with which she had regarded him. Her in-

terest had made him edgy. He had ultimately concluded that
London, and the dragons he knew, might well be safer than
Lester Hall.

He had arrived in town a day in advance of his aunt and her
company. Knowing Em, reared in a more dangerous age, travelled nowhere without outriders, he couldn't conceive that Mrs
Babbacombe might face any danger on the trip. Besides, the
incident on the Newmarket road had to have been due to mere
opportunism. Guarded by Em and her servants, Lucinda Babbacombe was safe enough.

Once they had settled in town, however, that had no longer
been the case. He had laid low as long as he could, avoiding
any unnecessary appearances, hoping thus to leave the dragons
and the matchmakers in ignorance of his presence. By spending
most of his days at his clubs, at Manton's or Jackson's or
similar all-male venues, eschewing the Park during the fashionable hours and driving himself everywhere rather than risk
strolling the pavements, a prey to dowagers and fond mamas,
he had largely achieved his objective.

And with Dawlish spending most of his time in the kitchens
at Hallows House, he had been able to emerge into the bright
lights only when absolutely necessary.

Like tonight. He had thus far succeeded in protecting the
damned woman from importunate inn-dwellers and rakes alike,
to the total confusion of the *ton*. And with his appearances
amongst their gilded flowers thus restricted, and so very patently centred on Lucinda Babbacombe, the dragons and matchmakers had had few opportunities to exploit.

Harry's lips twisted; he laid aside his pen. He knew better
than to bask in triumph—the Season had yet to end. Rising, he
frowned. He was, he hoped, as capable as the next of behaving
like a gentleman until then.

He pondered the point, then grimaced. Squaring his shoulders, he went up to change.

"TELL ME, Mr Lester—are you enjoying the Season's entertainments?"

The question took Harry by surprise. He glanced down at his partner's face, composed in polite enquiry, then looked up to whirl them around the end of Lady Hemminghurst's ballroom. He had arrived to find her already surrounded—by a crop of the most eligible rakes in town. He had wasted no time in extricating her and gathering her into his arms.

"No," he answered. The realisation gave him mental pause.

"Then why are you here?" Lucinda kept her eyes on his face and hoped for a straight answer. The question had grown increasingly important as day followed day and he made not the smallest move to fix her interest. Em's likening him to a horse appeared increasingly apt—he might have followed her to London, but he seemed determined not to pursue her.

He had escorted her to all four Babbacombe inns, remaining by her side throughout her inspections, but he had thereafter shown no interest in driving her elsewhere. All comments about the Park, about the delights of Richmond or Merton, fell on studiously deaf ears. Talk of a visit to the theatre had simply made him tense.

As for his behaviour in the ballrooms, she could only describe it as dog-in-the-manger. Some, like Lord Ruthven, found the situation immensely amusing. Others, like herself, were beginning to lose patience.

Harry glanced down and met her unwavering gaze. He frowned intimidatingly.

Lucinda raised her brows. "Am I to take it you'd rather be with your horses?" she enquired sweetly.

Goaded, Harry narrowed his eyes. "Yes." A mental picture leapt to mind. "I would infinitely prefer to be at Lestershall."

"Lestershall?"

His gaze growing distant, Harry nodded. "Lestershall Manor—my stud. It's named after the village, which in turn derives its name from my family's principal estate." The old manor house was in dire need of repairs. Now he had the money, he would put it to rights. The rambling, half-timbered house had the potential to be a wonderfully comfortable home; when he married, he would live there.

When he married? Harry clenched his jaw and forced his gaze back to his partner's face.

Lucinda captured it with a challenging glance. "Why, then, aren't you there?"

Because it's empty. Incomplete. The words leapt to Harry's conscious mind before he could shut them out. Her misty blue eyes lured him to the brink; the words burned his tongue. Mentally gritting his teeth, he smiled one of his more practiced smiles. "Because I'm here, waltzing with you."

There was nothing seductive in his tone. Lucinda kept her eyes innocently wide. "Dare I hope you're enjoying it?"

Harry's lips thinned. "My dear Mrs Babbacombe, waltzing with you is one of the few compensations my current lifestyle affords."

Lucinda allowed herself a sceptical blink. "Is it such a grind, then, your current life?"

"Indeed." Harry shot her a narrow glance. "My current round is one no rake should ever be forced to endure."

Gently, her eyes on his, Lucinda raised her brows. "Then why are you enduring it?"

Harry heard the final bars of the waltz; automatically, he whirled them to a halt. Her question echoed in his ears; the answer echoed deep within him. Her eyes, softly blue, held him, beckoning, inviting—open and reassuring. It took an effort of will to draw back, to find and cling to the cynicism which had kept him safe for so long. His features hardening, he released her and offered her his arm. "Why indeed, Mrs Babbacombe? I fear we'll never know."

Lucinda refrained from gnashing her teeth. She placed her hand on his sleeve, reflecting that a single waltz, which was all he ever claimed, was never long enough to press his defences. Why he was so intent on denying what they both knew to be fact was a point that increasingly bothered her. "Your aunt was quite surprised to see you in town—she said you would be…pursued by ladies wishful to have you marry their daughters." Did he, perhaps, see marriage as a trap?

"I dare say," Harry replied. "But London during the Season

has never been safe for well-born, well-heeled gentlemen." His eyes met hers. "Regardless of their reputations."

Lucinda raised her brows. "So you view the...pursuit as nothing more than a fact of life?"

"As inescapable as spring, although a dashed sight more inconvenient." Harry's lips twisted; he gestured up the room. "Come—I'll return you to Em."

"Ah..." Lucinda glanced about—and saw the gently billowing drapes hanging beside the long windows open to the terrace. Beyond lay the garden, a world of shadow and starlight. "Actually," she said, slanting a glance at him. "I feel rather warm."

The lie brought a helpful blush to her cheeks.

Harry's eyes narrowed as he studied hers. She was a hopeless liar; her eyes clouded over whenever she so much as prevaricated.

"Perhaps," Lucinda continued, trying for an airy tone, "we could stroll the terrace for a while." She pretended to peer through the windows. "There are some others outside—perhaps we could investigate the walks?"

It was at times like this that she most felt the deficiencies of her upbringing. Being married at sixteen had ensured she had not the smallest clue how to flirt or even encourage a man. When her escort made no response, she warily peeked up at him.

Harry was waiting to capture her attention, his expression that of a deeply irate man aware of the need to remain civil. "My dear Mrs Babbacombe, it would please me immensely if you could get it fixed in your pretty head that I am here, in London, braving all manner of dangers, for one—and only one—reason."

Her eyes genuinely wide, Lucinda blinked at him. "Oh?"

"Indeed." With restrained calm, Harry turned her up the room and started to stroll. His fingers, curled about her elbow, ensured she accompanied him. "I am here to ensure that, despite my inclinations, your inclinations and certainly despite those of your besotted court, you end this Season as you began it." He turned his head to capture her gaze. "As a virtuous widow."

Lucinda blinked again, then stiffened. "Indeed?" Looking forward, she lifted her chin "I wasn't aware, Mr Lester, that I had appointed you to the post of protector of my virtue."

"Ah—but you did, you see."

She glanced at him, denial on her lips—and met his green gaze.

"When you took my hand and let me pull you out of your carriage on the Newmarket road."

The moment leapt to her mind, that instant when she had knelt on the side of the carriage, locked in his arms. Lucinda quelled a shiver—and tilted her nose higher. "That's nonsense."

"On the contrary." The rake beside her appeared unperturbed. "I recall reading somewhere that if a man rescues another, then he takes on the responsibility for that rescued life. Presumably the same holds true if the one saved is a woman."

Lucinda frowned. "That's an eastern philosophy. You're English to your bones."

"Eastern?" Harry raised his brows. "From one of those countries where they cover their women in shrouds and keep them behind locked doors, no doubt. I've always put such eminently sensible notions down to the fact that such civilisations have apparently existed so much longer than ours."

On the words, they reached her court. Lucinda fought the urge to grind her teeth. If she heard one more of his glib excuses for being by her side she would, she felt sure, embarrass herself and Em and everyone else by screaming in fury. She plastered a bright smile on her lips—and let the admiration of her court and their subtle compliments soothe her abraded pride.

Harry stood it for five minutes, then silently relinquished his position by her side. He prowled the room but at no great distance, exchanging a few words with a number of acquaintances before retreating to a convenient alcove from where he could keep his self-imposed burden in view.

His very presence in the room was enough to keep the dangerous blades from her skirts. Those about her were all gentlemen at heart—they wouldn't pounce without an invitation. His interest, of course, was an added deterrent; he was prepared to wager that not one soul amongst all the *ton* understood what he was about.

With a somewhat grim grin, he settled his shoulders against the wall and watched as Lucinda gave Frederick Amberly her hand.

Taking the floor in yet another waltz, an apparent fixation of Lady Hemminghurst's, Lucinda fitted her steps to Mr Amberly's strides, distinctly shorter than Harry's, and let the music take hold.

Three revolutions later, she met her partner's somewhat concerned expression—and sternly reminded herself to smile. Not a spontaneous gesture.

She was distinctly irritated.

Rakes were supposed to seduce women—widows, particularly. Was she really so hopeless she couldn't break down Harry's resistance? Not that she wished to be seduced but, given his natural flair—and her status—she had to face the fact that, for them, that might well be the most sensible first step. She prided herself on her pragmatism; there was no point in not being realistic.

He had come to London; he was dancing attendance on her. But that clearly wasn't enough. Something more was required.

They were coming up the room for the third time when Lucinda's gaze refocused on Mr Amberly. Presumably if, at her advanced age, she wanted to learn how to encourage a rake, she was going to have to arrange lessons.

The waltz, most conveniently, left them at the other end of the room. Lucinda grasped her fan, dangling by its ribbon from her wrist. Opening it, she waved it to and fro. "The room is quite warm, don't you think, Mr Amberly?"

"Indeed, dear lady."

Lucinda watched as his gaze slid to the terrace windows.

Hiding a smile, she gently suggested, "There's a chair over there. If I wait there, could you fetch me a glass of lemonade?"

Her cavalier blinked and hid his disappointment. "Of course." He solicitously helped her to the chair, then, with an injunction not to move, disappeared into the crowd.

With an inward smile, Lucinda sat back, languidly waving her fan, and waited for her first lesson.

Mr Amberly duly reappeared, bearing two flutes of suspiciously tinted liquid. "Thought you'd prefer champagne."

With an inward shrug, Lucinda accepted a glass and took a delicate sip. Harry usually brought her champagne with her supper; it didn't affect her faculties. "Thank you, sir." She cast her escort a smile. "I was in dire need of refreshment."

"Hardly to be wondered at, my dear Mrs Babbacombe. Yet another crush." With an idle wave, Mr Amberly indicated the throng about them. "Don't know what the hostesses see in it, myself." His gaze dropped to Lucinda's face. "Reduces the opportunities to chat, don't y'know?"

Lucinda took due note of the gleam in Mr Amberly's eyes and smiled again. "Indubitably, sir."

Without further encouragement, Mr Amberly chatted on, interspersing remarks on the weather, the *ton* and events forthcoming with gently loaded comments. Lucinda found no difficulty in turning these aside. At the end of fifteen minutes, having politely declined an invitation to go driving to Richmond, she drained her glass and handed it to her escort. He placed it on a passing footman's tray and turned back to help her to her feet.

"I'm desolated, dear lady, that my projected excursion fails to tempt you. Perhaps I might yet stumble on a destination that finds greater favour in your eyes?"

Lucinda's lips twitched. She stifled a giggle. "Perhaps." Her smile felt oddly wide. She took a step, leaning heavily on Mr Amberly's arm. Suddenly, she felt distinctly flushed. Far warmer than she had before her drink.

"Ah..." Mr Amberly's eyes sharpened. "Perhaps, my dear Mrs Babbacombe, a breath of fresh air might be wise?"

Lucinda turned her head to consider the long windows—and forced herself to straighten. "I think not." She might wish to learn a few tricks but she had no intention of damaging her reputation. Turning back, she blinked as a glass appeared before her.

"I suggest you drink this, Mrs Babbacombe," came in clipped accents.

The tone suggested she had better do so if she knew what was good for her.

Obligingly, Lucinda took the glass and raised it to her lips, simultaneously raising her eyes to Harry's face. "What is it?"

"Iced water," Harry replied. He transferred his gaze to Frederick Amberly's innocent visage. "You needn't linger, Amberly. I'll escort Mrs Babbacombe back to my aunt."

Mr Amberly's brows rose, but he merely smiled gently. "If you insist, Lester." Lucinda held out her hand and he took it, bowing elegantly. "Your servant always, Mrs Babbacombe."

Lucinda bestowed a perfectly genuine smile. "Thank you for a most…delightful interlude, sir."

Mr Amberly's departing look suggested she was learning.

Then she glanced up at Harry's face. He was eyeing her narrowly.

"My dear Mrs Babbacombe, has anyone ever explained to you that remaining a virtuous widow is conditional on not encouraging rakes?"

Lucinda opened her eyes wide. "Encouraging rakes? My dear Mr Lester, whatever do you mean?"

Harry returned no answer but his lips thinned.

Lucinda grinned. "If you mean Mr Amberly," she continued ingenuously, "we were just chatting. Indeed," she went on, her smile widening again, "I have it on excellent authority that I'm *incapable* of encouraging rakes."

Harry snorted. "Rubbish." After a moment, he asked, "Who told you that?"

Lucinda's smile lit up the room. "Why, you did—don't you remember?"

Looking down into her very bright eyes, Harry inwardly

groaned. And hoped Amberly hadn't noticed just how thin the lovely Mrs Babbacombe's skull was. Taking the empty glass from her fingers, he deposited it on a passing tray, then took her hand and placed it on his sleeve. "And now, Mrs Babbacombe, we are going to perambulate, very slowly, around the room."

Bright blue eyes quizzed him. "Very slowly? Why?"

Harry gritted his teeth. "So you don't stumble." Into another rake's arms.

"Ah." Lucinda nodded sagely. A delighted, distinctly satisfied smile on her lips, she let him lead her, very slowly, into the crowd.

LUCINDA'S HEAD was throbbing when she followed Em into the carriage. Heather tumbled in after them and promptly curled up on the opposite seat.

Settling her skirts, Lucinda decided that, despite her minor discomfort, her evening had been a success.

"Damned if I know what Harry's about," Em stated as soon as Heather's breathing subsided into the soft cadence of sleep. "Have you made any headway with him yet?"

Lucinda smiled into the gloom. "Actually, I think I've at last found a chink in his armour."

Em snorted. "'Bout time. The boy's too damned stubborn for his own good."

"Indeed." Lucinda settled her head against the squabs. "However, I'm unsure how long this chink might take to develop into a breach, nor yet how potentially difficult it might prove to pursue. I don't even know whether, ultimately, it will work."

Em's next snort was one of pure frustration. "Anything's worth a try."

"Hmm." Lucinda closed her eyes. "So I think."

ON MONDAY, she danced twice with Lord Ruthven.

On Tuesday, she went driving in the Park with Mr Amberly.

On Wednesday, she strolled the length of Bond Street on Mr Satterly's arm.

By Thursday, Harry was ready to wring her pretty neck.

"I suppose this campaign has your blessing?" Harry looked down at Em, settled in majestic splendour on a *chaise* in Lady Harcourt's ballroom. He made no attempt to hide his barely restrained ire.

"Campaign?" Em opened her eyes wide. "What campaign?"

Harry gave her one of her own snorts—the one that signified incredulous disbelief. "Permit me to inform you, dear Aunt, that your protégée has developed a potentially unhealthy taste for living dangerously."

Having delivered himself of that warning, he stalked away. Not, however, to join the crowd about Lucinda Babbacombe. He propped the wall nearby, far enough away so that she wasn't likely to see him, and, eyes glittering greenly, watched her.

He was thus engaged when a hearty clap on the shoulder very nearly sent him sprawling.

"There you are, brother mine! Been looking all over. Didn't think to see you here."

Resuming his languid pose, Harry studied Jack's blue eyes; he decided his brother had yet to hear of his preoccupation. "It passes the time. But why are you back in town?"

"The arrangements, of course. All set now." Jack's blue gaze, which had been idly drifting the room, returned to Harry's face. "Next Wednesday at eleven at St. George's." Jack's slow grin surfaced. "I'm counting on your support."

Harry's lips twisted in a reluctant grin. "I'll be there."

"Good. Gerald, too—I haven't found him yet."

Harry looked over the sea of heads. "He's over there—beside the blonde ringlets."

"Ah, yes. I'll catch him in a minute."

Harry noted that his brother's eyes, glowing warmly, rarely left the slender blonde dancing with Lord Harcourt. Their host appeared captivated. "How's Pater?"

"Fine. He'll live to be eighty. Or at least long enough to see us all wed."

Harry bit back his instinctive response; Jack had heard him disparage marriage often enough. But not even his brother knew the reason for his vehemence; *that* had always remained his secret.

Following Jack's gaze, Harry studied his elder brother's chosen bride. Sophia Winterton was a charming, utterly open and honest woman whom Harry was certain Jack could trust. Harry switched his gaze to Lucinda's dark head; his lips twisted. She might serve him some tricks, as she was presently doing, but her motives would always be transparent. She was open and direct, uncommonly so; she would never seriously lie or cheat—she simply wasn't that sort of woman.

A sudden longing welled within him, followed immediately by the old uncertainty. Harry shifted his gaze, looking once more at Jack. Once he had found his particular Golden Head, Jack had moved very swiftly to claim her. As usual, his brother had been totally confident, assured in his decision. Studying Jack's smile, Harry felt an unexpected twinge of emotion—and recognized it as jealousy.

He straightened from the wall. "Have you seen Em?"

"No." Jack glanced about. "Is she here?"

Harry strolled with him through the crowd until he could point out their aunt, then left Jack to forge his way to her. Then, shackling his temper, he let his feet have their way. They took him to Lucinda's side.

From the opposite side of the large ballroom, Earle Joliffe watched Harry take his place in the select circle about Lucinda. "Odd. Very odd," was his judgement.

"What's odd?" Beside him, Mortimer Babbacombe inserted a pudgy finger beneath his neckcloth and eased the stiff folds. "Dashed warm in here."

Joliffe's glance was contemptuous. "What's odd, my dear Mortimer, is that, if there was ever a rake guaranteed to gain the entrée into your aunt-by-marriage's boudoir, it would be

Harry Lester.'' Joliffe glanced again across the room. "But as I read it, he's holding off. That's what's odd."

After a moment, Joliffe went on, "A disappointment, Mortimer. But it seems he's disappointed her, too—she's looking over the field, no doubt about that." Joliffe's gaze grew distant. "Which means that all we have to do is wait for the first whispers—these things always percolate from under even the most tightly closed doors. Then we'll get a little hard proof—it shouldn't be too difficult. A few eye-witnesses of comings and goings. Then we'll have your sweet cousin—and her even sweeter legacy—in our hands."

It was a reassuring prospect. Joliffe was over his ears in debt, although he'd been careful to conceal his desperation from Mortimer. His erstwhile friend was reduced to a shivering jelly just knowing he owed Joliffe five thousand pounds. The fact that Joliffe had pledged the money on, with interest, and to one against whom it was never wise to default, would turn Mortimer to a quivering wreck. And Joliffe needed Mortimer, hale and hearty, sound in mind and reputation, if he was ever to save his neck.

If he failed to help Mortimer to Heather Babbacombe's legacy, he, Earle Joliffe, man about town, would end life as a beggar in the Spitalfield slums. If he was lucky.

Joliffe's gaze rested on Lucinda's dark head. Once he had seen her, he had felt a great deal more confident. She was precisely the sort of widow who attracted the most dangerous of rakes. His hard eyes lighting, Joliffe squared his shoulders and turned to Mortimer. "Mind you, Scrugthorpe will have to forgo his revenge." Joliffe's lips lifted. "But then, nothing in life is ever quite perfect. Don't you agree, Mortimer?"

"Er—ah—yes."

With a last worried glance at his aunt-by-marriage, Mortimer reluctantly followed Joliffe into the crowd.

At that moment, the opening strains of a waltz percolated through the room. Lucinda heard it; her nerves, already taut, quivered. It was the third waltz of the evening, almost certainly the last. Relief had swept her when, only moments ago, Harry had, at last, materialised by her side. She had not seen him until then although she had felt his gaze. Breath bated, she had welcomed him with a soft smile. As usual, he had not joined in the conversation but had stood, his features hard, his expression remote, beside her. She had slanted a glance up at him; he had met it with an impenetrable look. Now, a smile on her lips as she graciously acknowledged the usual clamour of offers for the dance, she waited, buoyed with anticipation, to hear Harry's softly drawled invitation.

In vain.

The still silence on her left was absolute.

A deathly moment of awkward silence ensued.

Lucinda stiffened. With considerable effort, she kept her smile unaffected. She felt hollow inside but she had her pride. She forced herself to scan those desirous of partnering her. Her gaze came to rest on Lord Craven.

He had not appeared in her circle since that first evening two weeks ago. Tonight, he had been most assiduous.

Smiling brittlely, Lucinda held out her hand. "Lord Craven?"

Craven smiled, a coolly superior gesture, and bowed elegantly. "It will be a pleasure, my dear." As he straightened, he met her eyes. "For us both."

Lucinda barely heard; automatically, she inclined her head. With a gentle smile she acknowledged those she had disappointed but by not so much as a flicker of an eyelash did she acknowledge Harry. Outwardly serene, she allowed Lord Craven to lead her to the floor.

Behind her, she left an uncomfortable silence. After a moment, Lord Ruthven, cool and suddenly as remote as Harry, with no hint of his habitual good-humoured indolence in his eyes, lifted a brow. "I do hope, Lester, that you know what you're about?"

His eyes like green ice, Harry met his lordship's challenging stare and held it, then, without a word, looked away to where Lucinda was taking the floor in Lord Craven's arms.

At first, his lordship tried to hold her too close; Lucinda

frowned and he desisted. Thereafter, she paid him little heed, answering his polished sallies at random, their underlying tone barely registering. By the time the last chords sounded and his lordship whirled her to an elegant halt, her inner turmoil had calmed.

Enough to leave her prey to an enervating sense of defeat.

The emotion was not one she could approve. Straightening her shoulders and lifting her head, Lucinda reminded herself of Em's words: Harry would be no easy conquest but she had to hold firm to her plan.

So...here she was at the far end of the ballroom on Lord Craven's arm. His hand held hers trapped on his sleeve.

"Perhaps, Mrs Babbacombe, we should grasp the opportunity to become better acquainted?"

Lucinda blinked; his lordship gestured to a nearby door, set ajar.

"It's so noisy in here. Perhaps we could stroll the corridor?"

Lucinda hesitated. A corridor did not sound particularly secluded—and it was certainly crowded in the ballroom; her temples were starting to ache. She glanced up—and met Lord Craven's dark eyes and his faintly superior stare. She wasn't entirely sure of him but he was here, offering yet another potential prod to Harry's possessive nature.

She let her senses reach out, and felt the heat of Harry's gaze. He was watching over her; she cast a glance about but, in the dense crowd, could not find him.

Turning back, she met his lordship's gaze. Lucinda drew in a breath. She had told Em she was game. "Perhaps just a quick turn about the corridor, my lord."

She was quite certain her strategy was sound.

Unfortunately, this time, she had chosen the wrong rake.

Unlike Lord Ruthven, Mr Amberly and Mr Satterly, Lord Craven was not a familiar of Harry's and therefore lacked their insights into the game she was playing. They, one and all, had determined to assist her in whatever way they could, intrigued by the prospect of removing Harry from their paths. Lord Craven, however, had concluded that her flittering progress from rake to rake was merely a reflection of dissatisfaction with the distractions offered. Having seen how far the gentle touch had got his peers, he had determined on a more forceful approach.

With brisk efficiency, he whisked Lucinda through the doorway.

On the other side of the room, Harry swore, startling two dowagers gracing a nearby *chaise*. He wasted no time on apologies or speculation but started into the crowd. Aware of Craven's reputation, he had kept a close watch on his lordship and his burden but had momentarily lost them at the end of the dance, sighting them again just before Lucinda cast a glance about—then allowed Craven to lead her from the room. Harry knew very well what that glance had signified. The damned woman had been looking for him—to him—for rescue.

This time, she might need it.

The crowd, dispersing after the dance, milled aimlessly. Harry had to fight an impulse to push people out of his way. He forced himself to rein in his strides; he didn't want to focus any attention on his goal.

He finally broke free of the clinging crowd and gained the garden corridor. He didn't pause but went straight to its end where a door gave onto the terrace. Lady Harcourt had frequently bemoaned the fact that her ballroom did not open onto terrace and gardens, as was the fashionable norm. Silently, Harry stepped onto the flagstones. The terrace was deserted. His features hardening, he reined in his building rage and, hands on hips, scanned the deeply shadowed garden.

Muffled sounds drifted to his ears.

He was running when he rounded the corner of the terrace.

Craven had Lucinda backed against the wall and was trying to kiss her. She had ducked her head, frustrating his lordship's intent; her small hands on his chest, she was trying to push him away, incoherent in her distress.

Harry felt his rage claim him.

"Craven?"

The single word had Craven lifting his head and looking wildly about just as Harry caught his shoulder, spinning him into a punishing left cross that lifted his lordship from his feet and left him sprawled in an untidy heap against the stone balustrade.

Lucinda, her hand at her breast, swallowed a sob—and flung herself into Harry's arms. They closed about her; he hugged her fiercely; Lucinda felt his lips on her hair. His body was hard, rigid; she sensed the fury that possessed him. Then he shifted her to his side, keeping her within the protection of one arm. Her cheek against his coat, Lucinda glanced at Lord Craven.

Somewhat shakily, his lordship clambered to his feet. He worked his jaw, then, blinking, warily eyed Harry. When Harry made no move, Craven hesitated, then resettled his coat and straightened his cravat. His gaze shifted to Lucinda, then returned to Harry's face. His features studiously impassive, he raised his brows. "I appear to have misread the situation." He bowed to Lucinda. "My most humble apologies, Mrs Babbacombe—I pray you'll accept them."

Lucinda ducked her head, then hid her burning cheeks in Harry's coat.

Lord Craven's gaze returned to Harry's face. Something not at all civilised stared back at him. "Lester." With a curt nod, his lordship strolled carefully past and disappeared around the corner.

Leaving silence to enfold the two figures on the terrace.

Harry held himself rigid, every muscle clenched, his emotions warring within him. He could feel Lucinda trembling; the need to comfort her welled strong. He closed his eyes, willing himself to resistance, to impassivity. Every impulse he possessed impelled him to take her into his arms, to kiss her, possess her—to put an end to her silly game. A primitive male desire to brand her inescapably his rocked him to his core. Equally strong was his rage, his dislike of being so manipulated, so exposed by his own feelings, so vulnerable to hers.

Mentally cursing her for being the catalyst of such a scene, Harry struggled to suppress passions already too long denied.

The moment stretched, the tension palpable.

Trapped within it, Lucinda couldn't breathe; she couldn't move. The arm about her didn't tighten, but it felt like iron, inflexible, unyielding. Then Harry's chest swelled; he drew in an unsteady breath.

"Are you all right?"

His deep voice was flat, devoid of emotion. Lucinda forced herself to nod, then, drawing on her courage, stepped back. His arm fell from her. She drew in a deep breath and glanced up; one look at his face, at his utterly blank expression, was enough. His eyes showed evidence of some turbulent emotion, glittering in the green; what, she couldn't tell but she sensed his accusation.

Her breath tangling in her throat, she glanced away. His arm appeared before her.

"Come. You must return to the ballroom."

His face like stone, a graven façade masking turbulent feelings, Harry braced himself against the moment when her fingers settled on his sleeve.

Through the simple contact, Lucinda could sense his simmering anger, and the control that left his muscles twitching, shifting restlessly beneath her hand; for an instant, her feelings threatened to overwhelm her. She wanted him to comfort her, yearned to feel his arms about her once again. But she knew he was right—she had to reappear in the ballroom soon. Dragging in a shaking breath, she lifted her head. With the slightest of nods, she allowed him to lead her back, into the cacophany of conversation and laughter, back to the bright lights and bright smiles.

Her own smile appropriately bright if brittle, she gracefully inclined her head as, with a curt nod, Harry deposited her at the end of Em's *chaise*. He immediately turned on his heel; Lucinda watched him stride away, into the crowd.

Chapter Eight

"GOOD AFTERNOON, Fergus. Is Mrs Babbacombe in?"

Harry handed his gloves and cane to his aunt's butler. His expression stonily impassive, he glanced towards the stairs.

"Mrs Babbacombe is in the upstairs parlour, sir—she uses it as her office. Her ladyship's laid down upon her bed. These late nights are greatly tiring at her age."

"I dare say." With decisive stride, Harry headed for the stairs. "I won't disturb her. You needn't announce me." His lips thinned. "I'm quite sure Mrs Babbacombe is expecting me."

"Very good, sir."

The upstairs parlour was a small room at the back of the house. Tall windows looked onto the garden at the rear; two armchairs and a *chaise* plus an assortment of side-tables graced the floral rug by the fireplace while a large daybed filled the space before the windows. An escritoire stood against one wall; Lucinda, a vision in soft blue muslin, was seated before it, pen in hand, when Harry opened the door.

She glanced around, an abstracted smile on her lips—and froze. Her smile faded, replaced by a polite mask.

Harry's expression hardened. He stepped over the threshold and closed the door.

Lucinda rose. "I didn't hear you announced."

"Probably because I wasn't." Harry paused, his hand on the doorknob, and studied her haughty expression. She was going to hear him out, come what may; he wasn't in the mood to tolerate interruptions. His fingers closed about the key; the lock slid noiselessly into place. "This isn't a social call."

"Indeed?" One brow rising, Lucinda lifted her chin. "To what, then, do I owe this honour, sir?"

Harry's smile was a warning. "Lord Craven."

As he stalked towards her, his eyes boring into hers, Lucinda had to quell a weak impulse to retreat behind her chair.

"I've come to demand an assurance from you, Mrs Babbacombe, that you will, as of this moment, cease and desist in this little game of yours."

Lucinda stiffened. "I beg your pardon?"

"As well you might," Harry growled, coming to a halt directly before her, his eyes, glittering green, holding hers. "That little scene on Lady Harcourt's terrace was entirely your own fault. This ridiculous experiment of yours, this habit you've formed of encouraging rakes, has to stop."

Lucinda summoned a haughty glance. "I don't know what you mean. I'm merely doing what many ladies, situated similarly, would do—looking for congenial company."

"Congenial?" Harry lifted a supercilious brow. "I would have thought last night would have been sufficient demonstration of how 'congenial' the company of rakes can be."

Lucinda felt a blush tinge her cheeks. She shrugged and swung aside, stepping away from the desk. "Lord Craven was clearly a mistake." She glanced back to add, "And I have to thank you most sincerely for your aid." Deliberately, she met Harry's gaze, then calmly turned and drifted towards the windows. "But I really must insist, Mr Lester, that my life is my own to live as I please. It's no business of yours should I choose to develop a..." Lucinda gestured vaguely "...a relationship with Lord Craven or anyone else."

A tense silence greeted her statement. Lucinda paused, fingers lightly trailing the high back of the daybed, her gaze fixed, unseeing, on the prospect beyond the windows.

Behind her, Harry closed his eyes. Fists clenched, his jaw rigid, he fought to shackle his response to what he knew to be deliberate provocation, to suppress the clamorous impulses her words had evoked. Behind his lids, a fleeting image took shape—of her, struggling in Lord Craven's arms. Abruptly, Harry opened his eyes.

"My dear Mrs Babbacombe." He bit the words out as he stalked after her. "It's clearly time I took a hand in your education. No rake in his right mind is interested in a relationship—other than of an extremely limited sort."

Lucinda glanced over her shoulder and saw him coming. She turned to meet him—and abruptly found herself backed against the wall.

Harry's eyes trapped hers. "Do you know what we are interested in?"

Lucinda took in his predatory smile, his glittering eyes, heard the undercurrent in his silky voice. Deliberately, she tilted her chin. "I'm not a complete innocent."

Even as the lie left her lips, her breathing seized. Harry moved closer, crowding her against the wall, stopping only when she could retreat no further, her soft skirts caressing his thighs, brushing his boots.

His lips, so fascinating, were very close. As Lucinda watched, they twisted.

"Perhaps not. But when it comes to the likes of Craven and the others—or me—you're hardly experienced, my dear."

Her expression intransigent, Lucinda met his gaze. "I'm more than capable of holding my own."

His eyes flared. "Are you?"

Harry felt barely civilised. She kept prodding the demon within him; he felt barely sane. "Shall we put that to the test?"

He framed her face with his hands and deliberately moved one inch nearer, pressing her against the wall. He felt her draw in a quick breath; a quiver shivered through her. "Shall I show you what we *are* interested in, Lucinda?" He tilted her face to his. "Shall I show you what's on our—" his lips twisted in self-mockery "—*my* mind every time I look at you? Waltz with you?"

Lucinda didn't answer. Eyes wide, she stared into his, her breathing shallow and rapid, her pulse skittering wildly. His brows rose mockingly, inviting her comment; his eyes burned.

Then his gaze dropped from hers; Lucinda watched as he focused on her lips. She couldn't suppress the impulse to run the tip of her tongue over the smooth curves.

She felt the shudder that rippled through him, heard the groan he tried to suppress.

Then his head swooped and his lips found hers.

It was the caress she had longed for, planned for, plotted to attain—yet it was like nothing she had dreamed. His lips were hard, forceful, commanding. They captured hers, then tortured them with subtle pleasures, ravishing her senses until she submitted. The kiss caught her up, conquered and willing, and skilfully swept her free of reality, into a place where only his will prevailed. He demanded—she surrendered. Completely.

When he asked, she gave, when he wanted more, she unhesitatingly yielded. She sensed his need—and wanted, deeply desired, his satisfaction. She kissed him back, thrilled to feel the surge of unleashed passion that answered her. The kiss deepened, then deepened again, until she could sense nothing beyond it and the wild longing that swelled within her.

What deep-seated alarm it was that hauled Harry to his senses he did not know. Perhaps the urgent clamouring of rampant desires and the consequent need to arrange their fulfilment? Whatever it was, he suddenly realised the danger. It took every last ounce of his strength to draw back.

When he lifted his head, he was shaking.

Searching for sanity, he stared at her face—her lids slowly rose, revealing eyes so blue, so soft, so glowing with a siren's allure that he couldn't breathe. Her lips, kiss-bruised, gleaming red, ripe and, as he could now testify, so very sweet, drew his gaze. He felt himself falling under her spell again, leaning closer, his lips hungry for hers.

He dragged in a painful breath—and lifted his gaze to her eyes.

Only to see, in the soft blue depths, an awakening intelligence, superseded by a very feminine consideration.

The sight shook him to the core.

Her gaze dropped to his lips.

Harry shuddered; fleetingly, he closed his eyes. "Don't."

It was the plea of a defeated man.

Lucinda heard and understood. But if she didn't press her advantage now, she would lose it. Em had said he'd be thrilled—but he was so stubborn, if she didn't play that card now, he might not give her another chance.

She lifted her gaze to his. Slowly, she drew her hands from between them and pushed them up over his shoulders. She saw the consternation that filled his eyes; his muscles were locked tight, paralysed. He was unable to deny her.

Harry knew it; restraining his all-but-overpowering desire took all his strength. He couldn't move, could only watch his fate draw near as her arms tightened about his neck and she stretched upwards against him.

When her lips were an inch from his, she raised her eyes and met his tortured gaze. Then her lids fell and she pressed her lips to his.

His resistance lasted all of two heartbeats, as long as it took for desire, shackled, suppressed for so long it had grown to ungovernable proportions, to sear through him, cindering every last one of his good intentions, his rational reasons, his logical excuses.

With a groan that was ripped from deep within him, he drew her into his arms and engulfed her in his embrace.

With all restraint shattered, he kissed her deeply, caressed her, let his desire ignite and set fire to them both. She kissed him back, her hands clinging, her body wantonly enticing.

Desire rose between them, wild and strong; Lucinda abandoned herself to it, to the deep surge of their passions, fervently hoping to thus disguise any false move, any too-tentative response. If he sensed her innocence, all would come to nought—of that she was sure.

His caresses were magic, the response they drew so shattering she would be shocked—if she let herself think. Luckily, coherent thought was beyond her, blocked out by heated clouds of desire. Her senses whirled. His hands on her breasts provoked an urgent, building compulsion unlike any she'd ever experienced.

When one hand dropped low and he drew her hips hard against him, moulding her to him, flagrantly demonstrating his desire, Lucinda moaned softly and pressed closer.

Burgeoning passion left them frantic, hungry for each other, so desperate Harry's head was spinning as he backed her to the daybed. He refocused his will on salvaging some modicum of his customary expertise, bringing it to bear as he divested her of her gown and petticoats, brushing her fluttering hands aside, content enough that she was too befuddled to sensibly assist. Desire urged them on, riding them both; clad only in her chemise, Lucinda flung his cravat to the floor, then fell on the buttons of his shirt with a singlemindedness as complete as his. She seemed fascinated by his chest; he had to pick her up and put her on the daybed so he could sit and tug off his boots.

Lucinda was fascinated—by him, by the sense of rightness that gripped her, by the warm desire flowing in her veins. She felt free, unrestrained by any tenets of modesty or decorum, sure that this was how it should be. He stripped and turned towards her; she wrapped her arms about him, revelling in the feel of his warm skin, burning to her touch. Their lips met; urgency welled, heating her through and through. He drew off her chemise; as their bodies met, she shivered and closed her eyes. They kissed deeply, then Harry pressed her back against the soft cushions. Caught up in the spring tide of their loving, Lucinda lay back and drew him to her.

He lay beside her and loved her but their spiralling need soon spelled an end to such play. Eyes closed, Lucinda knew nothing beyond a deep and aching emptiness, the overwhelming need he had brought to life and only he could assuage. Relief and expectation flooded her when he shifted and his weight pinned her to the bed. She tried to draw breath, to steel herself; his hand slipped beneath her hips and steadied her— with one smooth flexion of his powerful body he joined them.

Her soft gasp echoed in the room. Neither of them moved, both stunned to stillness.

Slowly, his heart thudding in his ears, Harry raised his head and looked down at her face. Her eyes were shut, a frown tangling her brows, her lower lip caught between her teeth. Even as he watched, she relaxed a little beneath him, her features easing.

He waited for his emotions to catch up with the facts. He expected to feel angry, tricked, deceived.

Instead, a shattering feeling of possessiveness, untouched by lust, driven by some far more powerful emotion, welled within him, thrusting out all regrets. The sensation grew, joyously swelling, strong and sure.

Harry didn't question it—or how it made him feel.

Lowering his head, he brushed her lips with his. "Lucinda?"

She snatched in a breath then her lips clung to his. Her fingers fluttered against his jaw.

Harry brought up a hand to gently smooth away clinging tendrils of her hair from her face.

Then, with infinite tenderness, he taught her how to love.

SOME CONSIDERABLE TIME LATER, when Lucinda again made contact with reality, she discovered herself wrapped in Harry's arms, her back against his chest as he half-sat, propped against the raised head of the daybed. She sighed long and lingeringly, the glory dimming yet still glowing within her.

Harry bent over her; she felt his lips at her temple.

"Tell me of your marriage."

Lucinda's brows half-rose. With one fingertip, she drew whorls in the hair on his forearm. "To understand, you need to realise that I was orphaned at fourteen. Both my parents had been disowned by their families." Using the minimum of words, she explained her past history, one hand moving slowly back and forth along Harry's arm, snug about her, all the while. "So, you see, my marriage was never consummated. Charles and I were close, but he didn't love me in that way."

Harry kept his doubts to himself, rendering silent thanks to Charles Babbacombe for keeping her safe, for loving her enough to leave her untouched. His lips in her hair, the subtle scent of her filling him, Harry made a silent vow to her late husband's shade that, as the recipient of his legacy, he would keep her safe for evermore.

"You'll have to marry me." He spoke the words as they occurred to him, thinking aloud.

Lucinda blinked. The joy that had filled her faded. After a quiet moment, she asked, "*Have* to marry you?"

She felt Harry straighten as he looked down at her.

"You were a virgin. I'm a gentleman. The prescribed outcome of our recent activity is a wedding."

His words were definite, his accents clipped. Lucinda closed her eyes; she didn't want to believe her ears. The last vestige of lingering afterglow evaporated, the promise of the long, inexpressibly tender moments they had shared vanished.

Lucinda stifled a sigh; her lips firmed into a determined line. Opening her eyes, she turned in Harry's arms and looked him straight in the eye. "You want to marry me because I was a virgin—is that correct?"

Harry frowned. "It's what's expected."

"But is it what you want?"

"It doesn't matter what I want," Harry growled, his eyes narrowing. "The matter, thank heaven, is simple enough. Society has rules—we'll follow them—to the general satisfaction of all concerned."

For a long moment, Lucinda studied him, her thoughts chaotic. It was an offer—of sorts—from the man she wanted.

But it wasn't good enough. She didn't just want him to marry her.

"No."

Stunned, Harry watched as she scrambled out of his arms and off the daybed. She found her chemise and pulled it on.

He sat up. "What do you mean—'No'?"

"No—I will not marry you." Lucinda struggled into her petticoats.

Harry stared at her. "Why not, for heaven's sake?" She started towards her gown and nearly tripped over his breeches.

He heard a stifled curse as she bent to untangle her feet. Then she flung the breeches at him and continued towards her gown.

With a muttered curse of his own, Harry grabbed the breeches and hauled them on, then pulled on his boots. He stood and stalked over to where Lucinda was pushing her arms through the sleeves of her gown.

Hands on hips, he towered over her. "Damn it—I seduced you! You *have* to marry me."

Eyes ablaze, Lucinda shot him a furious glance. "*I* seduced *you*, if you recall. And I most certainly do not *'have to marry you'*!"

"What about your reputation?"

"What of it?" Lucinda tugged her gown up over her shoulders. Turning to face him, she jabbed a finger in his chest. "No one would ever believe that *Mrs* Lucinda Babbacombe, *widow,* had been a virgin until you came along. You've got no lever to use against me."

Looking up, she met his eyes.

And abruptly changed tack. "Besides," she said, looking down to do up the buttons of her bodice, "I'm sure it's not accepted practice for rakes to offer marriage to every woman they seduce."

Harry ground his teeth. "Lucinda…"

"And I have *not* made you free of my name!" Lucinda glared at him. She wouldn't let him use it—he'd whispered it, coupled with every conceivable endearment, as he'd made love to her.

Love—the emotion she knew he felt for her but was determined to deny.

It wasn't good enough—it would *never* be good enough.

She whirled on her heel and marched to the door.

Harry swore. Buttoning his shirt, he started after her. "This is crazy! I've offered for you, you demented woman! It's what you've been after ever since I hauled you out of that damned carriage!"

Lucinda had reached the door. She swung around. "If you're

so adept at reading my mind, then you'll understand perfectly why I'm throwing you out!''

She gripped the doorknob, turned it and yanked. Nothing happened. She stared at the door. "Where's the key?"

Thoroughly distracted, Harry automatically reached into his breeches pocket. "Here."

Lucinda blinked, then grabbed the key and rattled it into the keyhole.

Harry watched her in disbelief. "Damn it—I've given you a proposal—what more do you want?"

Her hand on the knob, Lucinda drew herself up and turned to face him. "I *don't* want to be offered for because of some social technicality. I don't want to be rescued, or…or protected or married out of pity! What I *want*—" Abruptly, she halted and dragged in a deep breath. Then she lifted her eyes to his and deliberately stated, "What I want is to be married for love."

Harry stiffened. His face hardened. "Love is not considered an important element for marriage within our class."

Lucinda pressed her lips together, then succinctly stated, "Balderdash." She flung open the door.

"You don't know what you're talking about!" Harry ran his fingers through his hair.

"I know *very well* what I'm talking about," Lucinda averred. None better—she loved him with all her heart and soul. Glancing about, she spied his coat and cravat by the daybed. She flew across the room and pounced on them.

Harry turned to face her, blocking the doorway as she bustled back.

"There." Lucinda crammed the expensive coat and cravat into his arms. "Now get out!"

Harry drew in a steadying breath. "Lucinda—"

"*Out!*"

Without warning, Lucinda pushed hard in the middle of his chest. Harry staggered back, over the threshold.

Lucinda grabbed the door. "Goodbye, Mr Lester! Rest assured I'll bear your instructions as to the interests of your set in mind in the coming weeks!''

With that, she slammed the door and locked it.

The fury that had sustained her abruptly drained. Slumping back against the door, she covered her face with her hands.

Harry glared at the white-painted panels. He considered forcing his way back in—then he heard a stifled sob. His heart wrenched—racked by frustration, he stuffed it back behind his inner door and slammed that shut as well. His lips set in a grim line, he turned on his heel and marched down the corridor. He caught sight of himself in a mirror. Abruptly, he halted and shrugged on his coat, then draped the creased cravat about his throat.

It took him three tries before he could achieve anything remotely resembling decency. With a snort, he turned and headed for the stairs.

He had made an offer. She had refused.

The damned woman could go to hell by herself.

He was finished with being her protector.

He was finished with her.

DISCOVERED, two hours later, with dark shadows under swollen red eyes, Lucinda could hardly deny Em her confidence.

Her hostess was stunned. "I can't understand it. What the devil's wrong with him?''

Lucinda sniffed and dabbed her eyes with a lace-edged square. "I don't know." She felt like wailing. Her lips set in a mulish line. "But I *won't* have it."

"Quite right, too!" Em snorted. "Don't worry—he'll come about. Probably just took him by surprise."

Lucinda considered, then wearily shrugged.

"Seems to me that there must be something we don't know," Em mused. "Known him all his life—he's always the predictable one—always good reasons and logical arguments behind his actions—he's not an impulsive man." She grinned, her gaze distant. "Quite the opposite—Jack's impulsive.

Harry's cautious." A frown slowly settled over her face. "Has been for a long time, now I think of it."

Lucinda waited, hoping for some reassuring insight, but her hostess remained sunk in thought.

Then Em snorted and shook herself, her stiff bombazine rustling. "Whatever it is, he'll just have to come to terms with it and offer for you properly."

Lucinda swallowed and nodded. "Properly"—by which she meant he would have to tell her he loved her. After today, and all they had shared, she would settle for nothing less.

THAT EVENING, Em took charge and insisted Lucinda remain at home, there to have an early night and recover her composure and her looks.

"The last thing you want to do is show him or the *ton* a face like that."

Having thus overcome Lucinda's half-hearted resistance, Em left the redoubtable Agatha ministering with cold cucumber compresses and, with the effervescent Heather under her wing, strode forth to do battle at Lady Caldecott's ball.

She spied Harry in the throng, but was not the least surprised when her errant nephew showed no disposition to come within firing range. But it was not him she had come to see.

"Indisposed?" Lord Ruthven's cool grey eyes reflected honest concern. "I do hope it's nothing serious?"

Well—it is and it isn't." Em lifted a brow at him. "You're one who's far more awake than you appear, so I dare say you've noticed that she's been endeavouring to bring a certain recalcitrant to heel. Never an easy task, of course. A difficult road to travel—prone to find potholes in one's path. She's a bit moped at present." Em paused to glance again at his lordship. "Dare say, when she reappears tomorrow, she could do with a little encouragement, don't y'know?"

Lord Ruthven studied Harry's aunt with wary fascination. "Ah—indeed." After a moment, in which he recalled the numerous times Harry had cut him out when they'd both had the same ladybird in their sights, he said, "Pray convey my most earnest wishes for a speedy recovery to Mrs Babbacombe. I will, of course, be delighted to welcome her back to our midst—I look forward to her return with uncommon anticipation.''

Em grinned. "Dare say you do.''

With a regal wave, she dismissed him. Lord Ruthven bowed gracefully and withdrew.

Fifteen minutes later, Mr Amberly stopped by her *chaise*. The instant the formalities were over, he asked, ''Wondered if you'd be so good as to convey my regards to Mrs Babbacombe? Understand she's under the weather tonight. She's a distraction sorely missed by us poor bachelors. Wanted to assure her of my continuing support when she once again graces our halls.''

Em smiled her approval. ''I'll make certain to pass your kind words on, sir.''

Mr Amberly bowed and drifted away.

To Em's satisfaction, her evening was punctuated by a succession of similar encounters as, one after another, Harry's close friends stopped by to pledge their aid in furthering Lucinda's cause.

Chapter Nine

LADY MOTT'S DRUM BADE FAIR to being the most horrendous crush of the Season. Or so Lucinda thought as she inched through the crowd on Lord Sommerville's arm. About them, the *ton* milled *en masse;* it was difficult to see more than five feet in any direction.

"Phew!" Lord Sommerville threw her an apologetic glance. "Pity the dance landed us so far from your companions. Normally enjoy wandering the room—but not like this."

"Indeed." Lucinda tried to keep her smile bright, no mean effort when she felt like wilting. The heat was rising about them; bodies hemmed them in. "I must confess that I've yet to divine why *such* a crowd, beyond the bounds of sense, should be considered so desirable."

Lord Sommerville nodded sagely.

Lucinda hid a weak grin. His lordship was close to her own age, yet she felt immeasurably older. He was still striving for a position amongst the rakes of the *ton;* in her opinion, he had some developing yet to do before he would rival some she could name.

Harry's image rose in her mind; with an effort, she banished it. There was no point in bemoaning what was well and truly spilt milk.

Ever since she had flung his offer in his teeth, she'd been plagued by doubts—doubts she did not wish to countenance. She hadn't seen him since; he had not returned to go down on bended knee. Presumably, he had yet to see the error of his ways. Or else, despite her firm conviction—and what did she know of the matter, after all?—he did not truly love her.

She kept telling herself that if that was so, then it was all for the best—when he had forced her to put her thoughts into words, she had realised just how much a marriage built on love now meant to her. She had everything else she could want of life—except that—a loving husband with whom she could build a future. And what use was all the rest without that?

She'd been right—but her heart refused to lift, hanging like a leaden weight in her breast.

Lord Sommerville craned his neck to peer forward. "Looks like the crowd thins just ahead."

Her smile growing weaker, Lucinda nodded. The couple immediately in front of them paused to acknowledge an introduction. Trapped, they halted. Lucinda glanced to her left—directly at a gold pin in the shape of an acorn, nestling in the snowy folds of a cravat tied with mathematical precision. She knew that pin—she had pulled it free a little over twenty-four hours before.

A vice tightened about Lucinda's chest. She looked up.

Clear green eyes, the colour of a storm-tossed sea, met hers. Her heart in her mouth, Lucinda searched but could read nothing in his shadowed gaze. His expression was hard, impassive, the planes of his face an impenetrable mask. Defeated there, Lucinda looked at his lips.

Only to see them firm, thinning into a severe line.

Puzzled, she glanced up—and caught a fleeting glimpse of uncertainty in his eyes. She sensed his hesitation.

Five feet and two pairs of shoulders separated them.

His eyes returned to hers; their gazes locked. He shifted, his lips twisted, quirking up at the ends.

"Ah—there we are. At last!" Lord Sommerville turned and bowed, gesturing before them.

Distracted, Lucinda looked ahead and discovered the crowd had eased, leaving a path forward. "Ah—yes."

She glanced at Harry.

Only to see him turn aside to greet an imposing matron with a simpering young girl in tow. He acknowledged the introduction to the chit with a restrained bow.

Battling the constriction in her chest, Lucinda drew in a deep breath and turned away, forcing herself to listen to Lord Sommerville's patter with some semblance of interest.

From the corner of his eye, Harry watched her move away; he clung to the sight of her until she was swallowed up by the crowd. Only then did he give his attention to Lady Argyle.

"Just a *little* soirée—a select few only." Lady Argyle beamed. "So you younger folk can chat and get to know each other better. Not something one can readily accomplish in this crowd, is it?"

Her ladyship's protruberant eyes invited him to agree. Harry was far too old a hand to fall for the trick. His expression coldly impassive, he looked down on her from a very great distance. "I'm afraid, Lady Argyle, that I'm otherwise engaged. Indeed," he continued, languid boredom threatening, "I don't look to spend much time in the ballrooms this Season." He caught her ladyship's suspicious eye. "Pressing matters elsewhere," he murmured. With a smooth bow, he took advantage of a break in the surrounding throng to slip away, leaving Lady Argyle unsure just what, exactly, he had been telling her.

Once free, Harry hesitated, then followed in Lucinda's wake. His declaration that he was finished with her rang mockingly in his ears; he shut off the sound. After trying a number of tacks, he finally located her, at the centre of her inevitable court. Ruthven was there, as were Amberly and Satterly. Harry's eyes narrowed.

Amberly was at Lucinda's side, chatting with his usual facility; he gestured hugely and everyone laughed, Lucinda included. Then it was Satterly's turn; Hugo leaned forward and smiled, clearly retelling some *on dit* or recounting some incident. Ruthven, on Lucinda's other side, glanced down at her. He was watching her face closely. Harry's lips compressed.

Concealed by the crowd, he focused on Lucinda. She smiled at Satterly's tale yet the gesture lacked the warmth Harry knew it could hold. The conversation became general; she laughed and returned some comment but without the assured gaiety she normally displayed. The dangerous tension that had gripped him eased.

She was subdued—very possibly unhappy beneath her calm veneer.

Guilt welled; ruthlessly, Harry stifled it. Serve the damned woman right—he'd offered; she'd refused.

He'd escaped a dangerous situation. Logic suggested he remove himself from further temptation. Harry hesitated, and saw Ruthven offer Lucinda his arm.

"Might I suggest a short stroll about the terrace, m'dear?" Concerned by the wan, haunted look in Lucinda's eyes, Ruthven could think of nothing else that might bring her some ease. Her gaze, dark and shadowed, constantly roamed the crowd. "Some fresh air will help you forget this stuffy ballroom."

Lucinda smiled, aware her brightness had dimmed. "Indeed," she said, glancing around. "The atmosphere is too close for my comfort, but…" She hesitated, then glanced up at his lordship. "I'm really not sure…"

She let the words trail away, unable to put her uncertainty into words.

"Oh—don't worry about that." Mr Amberly waved expansively. "Tell you what—we'll all go." He smiled encouragingly at Lucinda. "Nothing *anyone* could make of that, what?"

Lucinda blinked—and glanced at Lord Ruthven and Mr Satterly.

"Capital notion, Amberly." His lordship again offered her his arm, this time with a gallant flourish.

"Just the ticket." Mr Satterly nodded and stepped back, waving her on.

Lucinda blinked again. Then, realising they were all watching her, waiting, genuine thoughtfulness their only motivation, she smiled gratefully, and even more gratefully relaxed. "Thank you, gentlemen, that would indeed be most kind of you."

"Only too happy," came from Mr Satterly.

"A pleasure, m'dear," from Mr Amberly.

Lucinda glanced up and found Lord Ruthven's eyes ruefully twinkling. His lips twisted in a wry smile.

"Nothing too good for a friend, you know."

More reassured than she had been all evening, Lucinda smiled back.

From the depths of the crowd, Harry watched the little cavalcade head off, Ruthven steering Lucinda in Satterly and Amberly's wake. As the realisation that Ruthven's goal was one of the long windows opening onto the terrace crystallised in his brain, tension gripped Harry anew. He took a step forward—then stopped short.

She was no longer any business of his.

Satterly and Amberly stood aside for Lucinda and Ruthven to pass through the window—then followed. Harry blinked. For an instant, he stared, eyes slowly narrowing, at the gently billowing drapes through which all four had disappeared.

Then his lips curved cynically. With such cavaliers, the lovely Mrs Babbacombe had no need of further protection.

Somewhat stiffly, he turned on his heel and headed for the cardroom.

"AURELIA WILCOX ALWAYS DID give the best parties." Em rustled her silks in the dark of the carriage as it rolled down Highgate Hill. After a moment, she diffidently added, "Didn't see Harry tonight."

"He wasn't there." Lucinda heard the weariness in her voice and was glad Heather, curled on the seat opposite, wasn't awake to hear it. Her stepdaughter was thoroughly enjoying her taste of the *ton* in a wholly innocuous, innocent way. If it hadn't been for Heather's undoubted enjoyment, she would be seriously considering removing from the capital, regardless of the fact that such a move would clearly signal defeat.

She felt defeated. Tuesday night had just come and gone, with no sign of Harry. She hadn't seen him since Lady Mott's ball on Saturday evening; since then, he had not even been present at the balls and parties they had attended. His presence was not something she would miss—his gaze had always triggered a certain sensation, quite unique, within her.

A sensation she now missed—dreadfully.

"Perhaps he's already left London?" Her tone was uninflected, yet the words embodied her deepest fear. She had played her cards and lost.

"No." Em stirred on the seat beside her. "Fergus mentioned that Dawlish is still haunting the kitchens." Softly, Em snorted. "The Almighty only knows to what purpose."

After a moment, Em went on, her voice low, "It was never going to be easy, y'know. He's as stubborn as a mule—most men are over matters like this. You have to give him time to get used to the idea—to let his resistance wear itself out. He'll come around in the end—just wait and see."

Wait and see. As the carriage rattled on over the cobbles, Lucinda laid her head back against the squabs and reviewed her recent actions. No matter how she tried, she could not regret any of them—faced with the same situation, she would act as she had again. But neither dwelling on the past—nor idling through the present—was advancing her cause. But she could hardly seduce Harry again if he didn't come near her.

Worse—he was no longer concerned for her safety, even though Lord Ruthven, Mr Amberly and Mr Satterly had been particularly assiduous in their attentions. Indeed, if it hadn't been for their enthusiastic if totally platonic support, she doubted she could have held her head up over these past nights. The balls, which she had initially found fascinating, had lost their attraction. The dances were boring, the waltzes trials. As for the promenading, the incessant visiting, the constant appearances demanded by the *ton*, she increasingly saw them as a waste of time; her business persona re-emerging, no doubt. If she told true, she now viewed the time she spent in *ton*nish endeavours as a very poor investment.

It was unlikely to render her the return she sought.

Unfortunately, she had no idea what new tack to take, how to realign her strategies to bring her goal back in sight.

Her goal, in this case unfortunately not inanimate, had taken matters into his own hands—which left her with nothing to do but wait—a scenario she found intensely irksome.

Lucinda stifled a snort—Em's habit was catching.

But Em was very likely right—again. She would have to wait—she had played her cards.

It was Harry's turn now.

SOME TWELVE HOURS LATER, Harry lounged in his customary pose, propping the wall in the long ballroom of the Webb residence in Mount Street, idly watching the crowd gathered to celebrate his brother's nuptials. His father, of course, was there, sitting in his chair at the other end of the room. Beside him sat Em, resplendent in deep blue silk. Her principal houseguest had not attended.

Not, of course, that he needed to worry his head over where she was or what she was doing. Not with the way his friends were behaving. Over the past five days, they had taken to squiring her everywhere while coolly regarding him with a pointedly critical air. Ruthven, indeed, with a sublime disregard for the cryptic, had felt moved to tell him he was "being a damned fool". Ruthven—who was six months older than Harry, but had yet to show the slightest sign of bestirring himself enough to find a wife. Ruthven—who had a title to keep in the family. Disgusted, Harry had snorted—and informed his erstwhile friend that if he was so enamoured of the lady then *he* could pay her price.

Ruthven had blinked, then had looked a trifle abashed.

Eyes hooded, Harry took a soothing sip of brandy, the glass cradled in one hand.

Only to be thumped on the shoulder at the most critical moment.

Harry choked. Recovering his breath, he swung to face his assailant. "Damn it—I hope your wife aims to teach you some manners!"

Jack laughed. "Probably—but none, I suspect, that will apply to you." Deep blue eyes twinkling, he raised his brows at

Harry. "She thinks you're dangerous. In severe need of the right woman to blunt your lethal edge."

"Indeed?" Harry replied, repressively chill. He took another sip of his brandy and looked away.

Jack was undeterred. "As I live and breathe," he affirmed. "But she's of the opinion it'll take a brave woman—a Boadicea, I gather—to successfully take you on."

Harry rolled his eyes—but couldn't stop his mind supplying an image of Lucinda, half-naked, bedaubed with blue paint, driving a chariot. "Your wife is clearly blessed with a typically extravagant feminine imagination."

Jack chuckled. "I'll let you know after the honeymoon. We're off to Rawling's Cottage for a week. Nice and quiet up in Leicestershire just now."

Harry shook his head, a half-smile on his lips as he took in his brother's bright eyes. "Just don't lose anything vital—like your wits."

Jack laughed. "I think I'll manage—just." His slow grin surfaced as his gaze found his wife at the centre of a crowd near the door. He turned to Harry and put out his hand. "Wish me luck?"

Harry met his gaze. He straightened—and took Jack's hand. "You know I do. And your Golden Head as well."

Jack grinned. "I'll tell her." Poised to leave, Jack slid Harry a sidelong glance. "Take care yourself." With a last nod, he headed for his future.

Leaving Harry to wonder just how much of his current predicament showed in his face.

Fifteen minutes later, at the top of the steps outside the Webbs' house, he watched as the carriage carrying Jack and his bride rounded the corner into South Audley Street and disappeared from view. The assembled throng turned with a sigh and shuffled back indoors. Harry hung back, avoiding Em and his father. He re-entered the hall at the rear of the crowd.

The butler had just returned with his gloves and cane when a cool, calm voice enquired, "But surely you'll stay for just a little while, Mr Lester? I feel we've hardly had a chance to become acquainted.''

Harry turned to view Mrs Webb's delicate features—and her silver-blue eyes which, he was quite positive, saw far too much for his comfort. "Thank you, ma'am, but I must away." He bowed elegantly.

Only to hear her sigh as he straightened.

"I really do hope you make the *right* decision."

To Harry's intense discomfort, he found himself trapped in her silver-blue stare.

"It's quite easy, you know—no great problem, even though it always feels as if it is. One just has to decide what one wants *most* of life. Take my word for it." She patted his arm in a motherly fashion, quite at odds with her supremely elegant appearance. "It's quite easy if you put your mind to it."

For the first time in a very long while, Harry was rendered speechless.

Lucilla Webb smiled up at him, utterly ingenuous, then fluttered a delicate hand. "I must return to my guests. But do try *hard* to get it right, Mr Lester. And good luck."

With an airy wave, she glided back to the drawing-room.

Harry escaped.

On reaching the pavement, he hesitated. His lodgings? Brook's? Manton's? Frowning, he shook his head and started walking.

Unsummoned, the image of Boadicea returned. Harry's frown faded; his lips twitched, then curved. A fanciful notion. But was he really such a dangerous figure that a woman needs must put on armour to deal with him?

The rake within him was not averse to the analogy; the man wasn't so sure of the compliment. He was sure, however, having had the point proved repeatedly, that Lucinda Babbacombe was not the sort of woman to *recognise* danger, much less actively consider it. She, he imagined, would simply have looked the Roman commanders in the eye and calmly pointed out that they were trespassers. Then waited, arms folded, toe tapping, for them to remove themselves from her land.

Very likely, they would have gone.

Just as he—

Abruptly, Harry shook himself free of his thoughts. Drawing in a breath, he lifted his head—and found he was nearing the end of South Audley Street. Ahead, the leafy precincts of Green Park beckoned.

Without allowing himself to consider, he strode on, then crossed Piccadilly to amble beneath the trees. There were few of the fashionable in sight—it was early yet and most would go to Hyde Park nearby. The gentle lawns about him played host to nursemaids and children, an odd couple or two strolling, like himself, aimlessly down the paths.

He strolled slowly on, letting the peace sink into him, keeping his mind purposely blank.

Until a cricket ball hit him on the side of the knee.

Harry stifled a curse. He stooped and picked up the ball, then hefted it in one palm as he looked about for its owner.

Or owners, as it happened to be.

There were three of them, one slightly older but even he was barely seven. They sidled around a tree and approached with great caution.

"I—I'm most fearfully sorry, sir," the eldest piped up. "Did it hurt terribly?"

Harry sternly quelled an impulse to laugh. "Horrendously," he replied, lending the word maximum weight. All three faces fell. "But I dare say I'll survive." They recovered—and eyed him hopefully, large eyes fringed with long lashes, faces as innocent as the dawn.

As his fingertips found the ball's seam, Harry gave up the struggle and let his lips lift. He squatted, coming down to their height, and held out the ball, spinning it so that it whizzed like a top between his fingers.

"Oh—I say!"

"How d'you do that?"

They gathered about him, polite reticence forgotten. Harry showed them the trick, a facility learned over the long summers of his childhood. They oohed and aahed and practised themselves, eagerly seeking advice.

"James! Adam? Where on earth have you got to? Mark?"

The three looked guiltily about.

"We have to go," the ringleader said. Then smiled—a smile only a young boy could master. "But thanks so much, sir."

Harry grinned. He stood and watched them hurry around the tree and over the lawns to where a rotund nurse waited impatiently.

He was still grinning when Mrs Webb's words floated through his head. "One just has to decide what one wants *most* of life."

What he most wanted—he hadn't thought of it for years. He had once, more than ten years ago. He had been very sure, then, and had pursued his goal with what had been, at that time, his usual confident abandon. Only to find himself—and his dreams—betrayed.

So he had put them away, locked them in the deepest recess of his mind, and never let them out again.

Harry's lips twisted cynically. He turned away and resumed his stroll.

But he couldn't turn his mind from its path.

He knew very well what he most wanted of life—it was the same now as it had been then; despite the years, he hadn't changed inside.

Harry stopped and forced himself to draw in a deep breath. Behind him, he could hear the piping voices of his late companions as together with their nurse they quit the park. About him, youngsters cavorted and played under watchful eyes. Here and there, a gentleman strolled with his wife on his arm, their children ranging about them.

Harry let out the breath trapped in his chest.

Other lives were full—his remained empty.

Perhaps, after all, it was time to re-examine the possibilities. Last time had been a disaster—but was he really such a coward he couldn't face the pain again?

HE ATTENDED THE THEATRE that night. For himself, he cared
little for the dramatics enacted on the stage—and even less for
the histrionics played out in the corridors, the little dramas of
*ton*nish life. Unfortunately, the lovely Mrs Babbacombe had
voiced her wish to experience Edmund Kean; Amberly had
been only too happy to oblige.

Concealed in the shadows by the wall of the pit, opposite
the box Amberly had hired, Harry watched the little party settle
into their seats. The bell had just rung; the whole theatre was
abustle as society's blessed took their seats in the tiers of boxes,
the girls and ladies ogled by the bucks in the pit, while the less
favoured looked on from the galleries above.

Hugging the deep shadows cast by the boxes above him,
Harry saw Amberly sit Lucinda with a flourish. She was
dressed in blue as usual, tonight's gown of a delicate lavender
hue, the neckline picked out with silver thread. Her dark hair
was dressed high over her pale face. Settling her skirts, she
looked up at Amberly and smiled.

Harry watched, a chill slowly seeping into his soul.

Amberly laughed and spoke, bending closer so she did not
have to strain to hear.

Abruptly, Harry swung his gaze to the other members of the
party. Satterly was chatting to Em, who had taken the seat
beside Lucinda. Heather Babbacombe plumped down in the
seat beyond Em; Harry spied Gerald standing behind her, his
stance clearly proclaiming how he viewed his fair charge.

Momentarily taken aback, Harry frowned. Gerald's expression was easy for him to read, even at this distance. His brother
looked far too intent. He was midway through making a mental
note to have a quiet word in his baby brother's ear, when he
pulled himself up short. Heather Babbacombe might be young
but she was, to his reading, an intensely carefree and honest
young girl. Who was he to speak against her?

His gaze drifted back to Lucinda. His lips twisted, more in
self-mockery than in humour.

Who was he to argue with love?

What other reason could he give for being here—other than

a deep need for reassurance? Even Dawlish had taken to eyeing him with something perilously close to pity. When he had, somewhat irritably, demanded, "What the devil's the matter?" his dour henchman had rubbed his chin, then opined, "It's just that you don't exactly seem to be enjoying yourself—if you know what I mean."

He had glared and stalked into the library—but he knew very well what Dawlish had meant. The last week had been sheer hell. He had thought that cutting Lucinda Babbacombe out of his life, given she had only just entered it, would be easy enough. He was, after all, a past master at leaving women behind him; avoiding relationships was part of a rake's stock-in-trade.

But putting the lovely Mrs Babbacombe out of his thoughts had proved impossible.

Which left him with only one alternative.

As Mrs Webb had so succinctly put it—what he wanted most.

But did she still want him?

Harry watched as Amberly rattled on, gesticulating elegantly. He was a wit of sorts, and a polished raconteur. The possibility that Lucinda, having rejected his proposal, might have set him aside in her heart, decided he was not worth the trouble and turned instead to someone else for comfort, was not a particularly reassuring thought.

Even less reassuring was the realisation that, if she had, he would get no second chance—had no right to demand another, nor to interfere with his friend's pursuit.

A vice closed around Harry's chest. Amberly gesticulated again and Em laughed. Lucinda looked up at him, a smile on her lips. Harry squinted, desperate to see the expression in her eyes.

But she was too far away; when she turned back to the front of the box, her lids veiled her eyes.

The fanfare sounded, erupting from the musician's pit before the stage. It was greeted with noisy catcalls from the pit and polite applause from the boxes. The house lamps were doused as the stage lamps flared. The performers in the farce made their entrance; all eyes were riveted on the stage.

All except Lucinda's.

Eyes adjusting to the darkness, Harry saw she was looking down, not at the stage, apparently staring at her hands, possibly playing with her fan. She kept her head up, so no one in the box behind her would suspect her attention was not focused on the play, as was theirs. The flickering light played over her features, calm but hauntingly sad, reserved but eloquently expressive.

Harry drew in a deep breath and straightened away from the wall. Some of the tightness in his chest melted away.

Abruptly, Lucinda lifted her head and looked around—not at the stage but at the audience, uncaring of who might notice her distraction. Harry froze as her gaze scanned the boxes above him, then shifted further along.

Even in the poor light, he could see the hope that lit her face, that invested her whole body with sudden animation.

He watched it slowly fade.

She blinked, then slowly settled back in her chair, her face composed yet inexpressibly sadder than before.

Harry's heart twisted painfully. This time, he didn't try to shut it away, to blot out the emotion. But as he turned and moved silently to the door along the wall, he acknowledged the joy that came in its wake.

He hadn't been wrong about Lucinda Babbacombe. The damned woman was so ridiculously sure of herself she hadn't even considered the danger in loving him.

Stepping out of the darkness of the pit, he smiled.

Two floors above, in the crowded gallery, Earle Joliffe was very far from smiling. In fact, he was scowling—at Lucinda, and the party in Amberly's box.

"Deuce take it! What the devil's going on?" he hissed.

Beside him, Mortimer Babbacombe returned an uncomprehending look.

Disgusted, Joliffe gestured at the box opposite. "What's she *doing* to them? She's turned a whole gaggle of the worst wolves in London into pussycats!''

Mortimer blinked. "Pussycats?"

Joliffe all but snarled. "Lap-dogs, then! She *is* a damned witch—just like Scrugthorpe said.''

"Quiet there!"

"Ssh!" came from all around them.

For a moment, Joliffe contemplated a mill with positive glee. Then sanity intruded; he forced himself to stay in his seat. But his eyes remained fixed on his sacrificial lamb—who had transmogrified into a wolf-tamer.

After a moment, Mortimer leaned closer. "Perhaps they're softening her up—pulling the wool over her eyes. We can afford to give them a little time—it's not as if we're that desperate for the money.''

Joliffe stared at him—then sank his chin in his hands. "Rakes don't behave as they are to your aunt-by-marriage when they're hot on a woman's trail," he explained through clenched teeth. His jaundiced gaze rested on Amberly and Satterly. "They're being *nice,* for heaven's sake! Can't you see it?''

Frowning, Mortimer looked across the theatre, studying the silent tableau.

Joliffe swallowed a curse. As for not being desperate—they were—very desperate. An unexpected meeting with his creditor last night had demonstrated to him just how desperate they truly were. Joliffe quelled a shiver at the memory of the odd, disembodied voice that had floated out of the carriage, stopping him in his tracks on the mist-shrouded pavement.

"Soon, Joliffe. Very soon." A pause had ensued. Then, "I'm not a patient man.''

Joliffe had heard tales enough of the man's lack of patience—and what usually transpired because of it.

He was desperate all right. But Mortimer had too weak a head to be entrusted with the news.

Joliffe concentrated on the woman seated across the dark-

ened pit. "We'll have to do something—take an active hand."
He spoke more for himself than Mortimer.

But Mortimer heard. "What?" He turned to Joliffe, a
shocked, somewhat stupid expression on his face. "But... I
thought we'd agreed there was no need to be openly involved—to actually *do* anything ourselves!"

His voice had risen.

"*Shh!*" came from all sides.

Exasperated, Joliffe grabbed Mortimer's coat and hauled him
to his feet. "Let's get out of here." He sent a venomous glance
across the theatre. "I've seen enough."

He pushed Mortimer ahead of him to the exit.

Immediately they gained the corridor, Mortimer turned on
him, clutching his coat. "But you said we wouldn't need to
kidnap her."

Jollife eyed him in disgust. "I'm not talking about kidnap-
ping," he snapped, wrenching his coat free. He looked ahead,
his features hardening. "For our purposes, there's a better
way."

He glanced at Mortimer, contempt in his eyes.

"Come on—there's a certain party we need to see."

Chapter Ten

BY THE TIME Em took her seat at the breakfast table on Friday morning, she was considering visiting Harry herself. Not that it would do any good—but she felt so helpless every time she looked at Lucinda's face. Calm and pale, her guest sat toying with a piece of cold toast, her expression distant.

Em swallowed her snort. Feeling dejected herself, she poured a cup of tea.

"Are we going anywhere today?" Heather, seated further down the table, fixed big hazel eyes almost pleadingly on Em.

Em slanted a glance at Lucinda. "Perhaps we'll just have a quiet day today. A drive in the Park in the afternoon. We've Lady Halifax's ball tonight."

Lucinda's smile was perfunctory.

"Greenwich was such fun." Heather struggled to invest her words with conviction. Lord Ruthven had arranged an outing yesterday to the Observatory, hoping to lift Lucinda's spirits. He and Mr Satterly, who had made one of the party, had battled valiantly but to no avail.

Lucinda shifted in her chair. "It was very kind of Lord Ruthven to arrange it. I must send a note around to thank him."

Em doubted Ruthven would appreciate it. The poor man had pulled out all stops but it was clear Lucinda barely saw him. Not that she made reference to what was occupying her mind. Her composure was faultless; those who did not know her would detect nothing amiss. Those who did saw the superficiality of her smiles, which no longer reached her eyes, mistier than ever and distressingly remote. She was naturally reserved;

now, despite going amongst them, she seemed to have with-drawn from real contact.

"Perhaps," Heather ventured, "we could go to the museum? We haven't seen Lord Elgin's marbles yet. You said you'd like to."

Lucinda tilted her head. "Perhaps."

Helpless, Heather glanced at Em.

Em shook her head. She had originally thought Heather too young, too immature, to sense Lucinda's silent woe. Over the last few days, she had realised that Heather both saw and un-derstood, but with the confidence of youth had imagined mat-ters would work themselves out somehow. Now, even Heather's confidence was flagging. She was as concerned as Em, which worried Em all the more.

The door opened; Fergus appeared at Em's side and pre-sented a silver salver.

"The mail, ma'am. And there's a letter just hand-delivered for Mrs Babbacombe. The boy didn't wait for a reply."

Em picked up the white, sealed packet, painfully aware of the sudden tension that had gripped Lucinda. One glance at the scrawled direction was enough to tell her it wasn't from Harry. Helpless to do otherwise, she handed it over without comment, trying not to watch as, the seal broken, the expectation that had momentarily lit Lucinda's face died.

Lucinda frowned as she read the short missive, then, gri-macing, laid it aside. She looked down at her toast, now stone-cold. With a tiny sigh, she reached for the teapot.

Em was beyond social niceties. "Well?"

Lucinda glanced at her, then shrugged. "It's an invitation to some houseparty in the country."

"Whose?"

Lucinda frowned. "I can't immediately recall the lady." She sipped her tea, glancing down at the note. "Lady Martindale of Asterley Place."

"Martindale?" Em started to frown, then her face cleared. "Oh—that'll be Marguerite. She's Elmira, Lady Asterley's daughter. She must be helping out. But that's wonderful!" Em turned to Lucinda. "*Just* the thing! Some fresh air and genteel fun is precisely what you need. Elmira is one of my oldest friends although we haven't met in ages. She'll be getting on, now. When's this party to be?"

Lucinda hesitated, then grimaced. "It starts later today—but the invitation's just for me."

Em blinked. "Just for…?" Then she blinked again, her face clearing. "Ah—I see!"

Lucinda looked up. "What is it?"

Em straightened. "Just remembered. Harry's a close friend of Elmira's son—Alfred, Lord Asterley. Been thick as thieves since they were at Eton together."

She watched as Lucinda reached again for the note.

"Oh?"

"Indeed." Em's eyes glazed as she considered the possibilities. "Always hand-in-glove in mischief. Got sent down together any number of times." For a moment, she remained sunk in thought, then flicked a glance at Lucinda, busy scrutinising the invitation. "You know," Em said, sitting back in her chair, "it's probably not surprising that the invitation's just for you. I can see how it would have been—Elmira had a last-minute cancellation and asked Alfred if he could suggest someone suitable to fill the gap." Em hesitated, then added, "And Alfred and Harry *are* very close."

The more Em thought of it, the more convinced she was that Harry was behind the unexpected invitation. It would be just like him to manoeuvre to get Lucinda into the country, free of mentors, admirers and step-daughters, so he could make amends for his behaviour away from all interested eyes. Very Harry indeed.

Em snorted.

The atmosphere around the breakfast table had altered dramatically. Instead of resignation bordering on the morose, speculation now tinged the air. Varying degrees of calculation and decision were reflected in the ladies' expressions.

Pushing her plate aside, Heather put their thoughts into words. "You *have* to go."

"Absolutely," Em agreed. "Heather and I are more than capable of entertaining each other for a few days."

Lucinda, reanimated but still frowning, looked up from the invitation. "You're sure it's acceptable for me to go alone?"

"To Asterley Place? Of course!" Em dismissed the point with a wave. "It's not as if you were a young girl making her come-out. And you'll find plenty there you've already met, I don't doubt. Very fashionable, Elmira's parties."

"*Do* go." Heather leaned over the table. "I'd love to hear all about it. Maybe we'll all be invited next time."

Lucinda glanced at Heather's eager young face. Her hesitation was pure prevarication; if there was any possibility Harry had organised the invitation then she had no choice but to go

She straightened and drew in a breath—a surge of revivifying hope came with it. "Very well. If you're sure you can manage without me?"

Em and Heather vociferously assured her they could.

AFTER LUNCHEON, Em retired to the morning room, her mood one of pleasant expectation. Sinking onto the *chaise,* she cast a contented glance about her, then relaxed against the cushions and, slipping off her slippers, swung her feet up. Propping her head on a cushion, she closed her eyes and sighed deeply.

And wondered if it was too early to feel smug.

She was deep in dreams of white tulle and confetti when the click of the door latch had her blinking awake.

What was Fergus thinking of?

Prepared to take umbrage, she turned her head—and saw Harry enter.

Em blinked again. She opened her mouth—then caught sight of the white flower in Harry's buttonhole.

He *never* wore buttonholes—except at weddings.

Harry saw her arrested expression and inwardly grimaced; he should have left the buttonhole off. But he had dressed with inordinate care—it had seemed the right touch at the time.

He was determined to do this right. If they'd had the sense to stay at home yesterday, the ordeal would be over by now.

Reining in his impatience, he closed the door and turned to face his aunt just as she managed to catch her breath.

"Ah…"

"Precisely," Harry said, no trace of the languid in his tones. 'If you don't mind, Aunt, I'd like to see Mrs Babbacombe." He met Em's slightly protruberant eyes. "Alone."

Em blinked. "But she's left."

"Left?" All expression drained from Harry's face. For a moment, he couldn't breathe. "Left to where?"

Em put a hand to her spinning head. "But…to Asterley, of course." Eyes widening, she sat up. "Aren't you going?"

His wits reeling, Harry stared at her. "I've got an invitation," he admitted, somewhat cautiously.

Em flopped against the cushions, a hand at her breast. "Thank heaven for that. Only reason she went." Recalling the point, she turned to glare at Harry. "Not, of course, that that'll prove any use—it's plain as a pikestaff *you* didn't organise to have her invited."

"Organise…?" Harry stared at her as if she'd run mad. "Of course I didn't!" He paused, then asked, "Why the devil did you think I did?"

Lips prim, Em shrugged. "Well, there's no reason you couldn't have—I'm quite sure Alfred could have got another name on Elmira's lists if you'd asked him."

"Elmira?"

Em waved. "I know Marguerite issued the invitations but it'll still be Elmira's party."

Fists clenched, Harry closed his eyes—and stifled the explosive anger building within him. His father was older than Em—and suffered from the same, oddly selective memory. Em clearly recalled his connection with Alfred but had totally forgotten that his mother, Elmira, had been dead some eight years.

The parties at Asterley Place were, these days, rather different from those Em recalled.

Harry drew in a deep breath and opened his eyes. "When did she leave?"

Em frowned somewhat petulantly. "About eleven." She

glanced at the clock on the mantelshelf. "She'll be halfway there by now."

Grim-faced, Harry turned on his heel.

Em stared. "Where are you going?"

Harry glanced back, his hand on the knob, his expression hard and unyielding. "To rescue Boadicea from a gaggle of lecherous Romans."

With that, he departed, shutting the door behind him, leaving Em staring in bemusement at the uninformative panels.

"Boadicea?"

HARRY STRODE THROUGH the door of his lodgings, ripping the white gillyflower from his lapel and tossing it onto the hall table. "Dawlish! Where the devil are you?"

"I'm right here," came in mumbles from down the corridor. Dawlish appeared, an apron over his street clothes, silver spoons and a polishing rag in his hands. "Now what's yer trouble? I thought as how you'd gone to settle it?"

Harry ground his teeth. "I had—but apparently I should have made an appointment. The damned woman's gone off for a quiet sojourn in the country—to Asterley Place."

He had rarely seen Dawlish so dumbfounded.

"Asterley?"

"Precisely." Harry shrugged off his greatcoat. "And, no, she hasn't changed her lifestyle. The damned female has no idea what she's blithely heading into."

Dawlish's eyes grew round. "Gawd help her." He took the coat from Harry.

"I sincerely doubt he can." Harry stripped off his gloves and threw them onto the table with the gillyflower, then turned to the stairs. "Come on—stop standing there like a gawp. We'll need the greys—she's got more than a two hours' start on us."

As Harry pounded upstairs, Dawlish blinked, then shook himself. "With you fired up and the greys in their usual mood, we should be able to cut that in half easily."

Harry didn't hear. He strode into his bedroom; it was the work of a few minutes to throw a selection of clothes into a bag. Dawlish came in as he was shrugging into a bottle-green coat; he had already changed his ivory inexpressibles for buckskin breeches.

"No need to kill y'rself," Dawlish advised, picking up the bag. "We'll make it on her heels."

Frowning, Harry led the way out. "We'll get there a full hour after her," he growled.

An hour in which she, a total innocent, would have to fend for herself in a house full of wolves, all of whom would assume she was willing prey.

LUCINDA DESCENDED from her carriage before the steps of Asterley Place and looked around. The house bore a relatively recent façade, Ionic columns supporting the porch roof, classic geometric lines delineating the long windows. It stood in a large park, directly before a long sloping lawn leading down to the shores of a lake. Glimpses of gardens tantalised on both sides; the subtle scent of roses wafted over a brick wall. Wide stone steps led up to the porch; as footmen came running to assist with the baggage, Lucinda unhurriedly ascended to find her host, hostess and their major-domo waiting.

"Welcome to Asterley Place, my dear Mrs Babbacombe. Can't say how delighted I am to see you here." Lord Asterley, a gentleman of average height with a tendency to corpulence, severely restrained, bowed, then shook Lucinda's hand.

Lucinda smiled in return, recalling now that she had met his lordship during her earlier weeks in the capital. "I must thank you for your invitation, my lord. It was most…opportune—and appreciated." She couldn't suppress the hope that welled within her; anticipation lit her eyes and her smile.

Lord Asterley noticed—and was instantly smitten. "Indeed? Very pleased to hear it, m'dear." He patted her hand, then turned to the lady beside him. "Allow me to present my sister, Lady Martindale. She acts as my hostess at these little gatherings, y'know."

Lucinda turned and was engulfed in a warm smile.

Lady Martindale shook hands, a smile wreathing her pretty

face. "Please call me Marguerite. Everyone else who stays does." Her ladyship was some years Lucinda's senior, a buxom blonde, as transparently good-natured as her brother. "I do hope you enjoy yourself whilst here—don't hesitate to let me know if there's anything the least amiss."

Lucinda could feel herself relaxing. "Thank you."

"The others are gathering in the conservatory—once you've had a chance to refresh yourself, do please join them." Marguerite gestured to the house, gathering Lucinda as she turned towards it. "I dare say there are others you already know but we pride ourselves on informality here." She leaned closer to add, "You may be sure there are none present who don't know *precisely* how to behave, so you need have no worries other than deciding with whom you wish to pass the time."

Lucinda returned her smile.

"Now then—we've put you in the Blue Room." Her ladyship glanced at Lucinda's cambric carriage dress. "Clearly an inspired choice. Melthorpe here will show you the way and see your maid and baggage sent up. We dine at six."

Lucinda thanked her again, then followed in the major-domo's wake. He was a small man, shrunk within his dark clothes, his long nose and hunched shoulders giving him a crow-like appearance.

As they gained the top of the wide main staircase, Lucinda caught his eye. He gestured along one corridor; she followed as he started down it. And inwardly frowned. Why on earth should Melthorpe regard her so severely? He stopped before a door at the end of the corridor, opening it and standing back so she could precede him; Lucinda took a closer look at his face as she passed.

Casting a professionally assessing glance around the room, she approved it with a nod. "Thank you, Melthorpe. If you would send my maid up immediately?"

"As you wish, ma'am."

She watched as, with a frigid air that barely avoided incivility, Melthorpe bowed and withdrew. Lucinda frowned at the door as it shut behind him.

There was little possibility she had misread his manner—she had too many years' experience of servants and underlings. The man had looked at her, treated her, as if... It was a moment before she could correctly place his behaviour. When she did, she was dumbstruck.

The door opened and Agatha appeared, a footman with Lucinda's case immediately behind. Lucinda watched as her maid, dourly severe as only she could be, instructed the footman to place the case by the dressing-table, then closed the door behind him.

"Well!" Agatha turned to face her.

Lucinda noted the speculation in Agatha's old eyes, but did not respond. From experience, she knew she would get more information if she let Agatha deliver it in her own fashion. And she was suddenly very curious about Asterley Place.

Stripping off her gloves, she threw them on the bed—a wide four-poster with a tasselled canopy. Her bonnet followed. Then she spread her skirts and considered them. "Hmm—too crushed. I'll change into my new tea gown, just until dinner."

Agatha humphed as she bent to the case buckles. "I haven't seen much of them yet, but they do seem a stylish lot. A goodly gaggle of snooty gentlemen's gentlemen in the kitchens as I passed—and from the looks of some of the lady's maids I reckon there'll be fights over the curling tongs before nightfall. Best let me do your hair up, too."

"Later." Lucinda glanced at her reflection in the mirror over the dressing table. "There'll be time before dinner."

"Six, they said. Midway between country and town." Agatha pulled an armful of dresses from the case. "Did hear one of them mention that they have it that way so there'll be more of the evening for 'their little games', whatever that might mean."

"Games?" Perhaps the Asterley household amused themselves with the usual country house parlour games? Lucinda frowned. The vision of Lord Asterley and the buxom Marguerite presiding over such entertainments wasn't convincing. Lips firming, Lucinda stood. "Come—help me change. I want to meet the other guests before dinner."

As she'd been told, they were in the conservatory. It was an unusually large version built on at the back of the house and filled with potted palms to create a leafy grotto. There was a tiled pool at its centre; the guests were gathered about it, some in wicker chairs, others standing chatting in groups.

One glance made Lucinda very glad she had changed. They were indeed a stylish lot, confident, gaily plumed birds nestling within the greenery. She nodded to Mrs Walker, an elegant widow, and Lady Morcombe, a dashing matron, both of whom she had met in town.

"My dear Mrs Babbacombe." Marguerite rustled forward. "Pray let me introduce you to Lord Dewhurst—he's only just returned from Europe and so has yet to meet you."

Lucinda calmly returned Lord Dewhurst's greetings while inwardly gauging her companions. She could detect nothing odd to account for her flickering nerves. "Indeed," she replied to Lord Dewhurst's query. "I've quite enjoyed my time in town. But the balls are becoming a trifle…" She gestured. "Overdone—don't you find it so? So crowded one can hardly hear one's self think. And as for breathing…"

His lordship laughed, a smooth, suave sound. "Indeed, my dear. Little gatherings such as this are much more *convenable*."

The subtle emphasis he placed on the last word had Lucinda glancing up at him. His lordship looked down at her, a warm light in his eyes.

"I'm sure you'll discover, my dear, that at Asterley Place, it's very easy to find both time and place to…think."

Lucinda stared at him. Before she could gather her wits, he took her hand and bowed low.

"Should you find yourself wishful of company, my dear, pray don't hesitate to call on me. I can be exceedingly thoughtful, I assure you."

"Ah—yes. That is," desperate, Lucinda wrestled her wits

into order, "I'll bear your offer in mind, my lord." She inclined her head, somewhat stiffly.

She waited while his lordship bowed again then gracefully strolled away. Then dragged in a quick breath—and cast another, much more critical, look about her.

And wondered how she could have been so blind. Every one of the ladies present was undoubtedly that, but they were all either widowed or married, all of unquestionable breeding yet of an age when, it might be imagined, they might have a very real interest in indulging in discreet liaisons.

As for the gentlemen, they were each and every one of a type she recognised all too well.

Before she had time to think further, Lord Asterley strolled up.

"My dear Mrs Babbacombe—can't tell you how thrilled I was to learn of your interest in our little gatherings."

"My interest?" Lucinda swallowed her amazement and politely if coolly raised her brows.

Lord Asterley smiled knowingly; she half-expected him to wink and nudge her elbow. "Well—perhaps not especially in *our* gatherings, but in the type of entertainment we all find so..." his lordship gestured expansively "...fulfilling." He looked down at her. "I do hope, my dear, that, should you feel so inclined, you won't hesitate to call on me—to help enliven your stay here?"

Clinging to polite form, Lucinda inclined her head; as she could find no suitable words in which to answer his lordship, she left him to think what he would.

He beamed and bowed; to her chagrin, Lucinda found it very hard to feel indignant with one so openly cheery. She nodded and drifted to the pool. There was a seat vacant beside Mrs Allerdyne, a *ton*nish widow who, Lucinda now realised, was probably not quite as virtuous as she appeared.

Mrs Allerdyne turned as Lucinda subsided onto the wicker seat.

"Good afternoon, Mrs Babbacombe—or can I dispense with formality and call you Lucinda?"

Lucinda blinked at Henrietta Allerdyne's charmingly gentle
face. "Yes, of course." Feeling as if her eyes had just been
opened to yet another aspect of *ton*nish life, Lucinda, somewhat
dazedly, glanced about her again.

"This is your first time here, isn't it?" Henrietta leaned
closer. "Marguerite mentioned it," she explained when Lucinda switched her gaze back. "No need to feel awkward about
it." Henrietta patted Lucinda's hand. "We're all friends here,
of course. The very last whisper in discretion—no need to fear
any comments once you're back in town." Henrietta glanced
around with the air of one entirely at her ease. "It's been like
that for years, ever since Harry started it."

"Harry?" Lucinda's breath stuck in her throat. "Harry Lester?"

"Mmm." Henrietta was exchanging none-too-idle glances
with an elegant gentleman across the room. "As I recall, Harry
was the one who thought of the idea. Alfred simply imple-
mented it to Harry's directions."

Harry—who had sent her here.

For an instant, Lucinda felt as if she would faint—the room
receded into a dark mist; a chill spread through her. She swallowed; clenching her fists in her lap, she fought back the diz-
ziness. When she could, she murmured, "I see." Henrietta,
engrossed with her gentleman, had not noticed her difficulty—
nor her sudden pallor. Her cheeks felt icy; Lucinda grasped the
moment to recoup, to let her senses settle. Then, with what
nonchalance she could, she asked, "Does he often attend?"

"Harry?" Henrietta smilingly nodded to her gentleman and
turned back. "Occasionally—he's perennially invited but one
never knows if he'll show." Henrietta's smile turned affectionate. "Not one to run in anyone's harness, Harry."

"No, indeed!" Lucinda ignored the questioning look her
tartness invoked. A rage unlike any she had ever experienced
was rising within her.

Was her invitation here Harry's way of showing her how he
now viewed her? That she had become one with these ladies,
dallying with any gentleman who took their fancy? Had he sent

her here to experience the "congenial company" she had assured him she was seeking?

Or had he sent her here to teach her a lesson—and was planning to arrive just in time to rescue her from the consequences?

Her jaw set, her hands clenched, Lucinda abruptly stood. She felt like screaming, pacing the floor—*throwing things!*—she wasn't sure which of his possible motives enraged her the most. She dragged in a deep breath. "I hope he comes," she breathed through clenched teeth.

"Lucinda?" Henrietta leaned forward to peer up into her face. "Are you quite well?"

Rigid, Lucinda plastered a smile on her lips. "Perfectly, thank you."

Henrietta didn't look convinced.

Luckily, the gong sounded, sending them to their rooms. Lucinda reined in her impatience enough to accompany Henrietta to her door—then briskly strode down the corridor to the Blue Room.

"What have you heard?" she demanded of Agatha the instant the door shut behind her.

Agatha looked up from the navy blue silk gown she was laying out on the bed. She took one look at Lucinda's face—and answered directly. "Not much—but nothing good. Lots of innuendo 'bout what the nobs get up to o'nights. Doors opening and closing at all hours." Agatha sniffed. "An' such like."

Lucinda sat at the dressing table and started pulling pins from her hair. She shot her maid a severe look. "*What* else?"

Agatha shrugged. "Seems like it's the expected thing here—not just the odd couple or so, like happens anywhere." The maid grimaced. "Did hear one of the footmen liken it to a set of coaching inns—one coach pulls in as the last's pulling out."

Lucinda sat back and stared at Agatha in the mirror. "Great heavens," she finally said, somewhat weakly. Then she rallied—no matter what the general practice, she was confident that not one of the gentlemen present would force his attentions on an unwilling lady.

Her gaze fell on the navy silk gown. "Not that one." Her eyes narrowed. "The silk gauze."

Agatha straightened, hands on her hips. "The gauze?"

In the mirror, Lucinda raised haughty brows.

Agatha snorted. "'Tis barely decent."

"For my purposes tonight, it'll be perfect." Lucinda drew out the last word to a literal purr. She wasn't the one who would learn a lesson tonight.

Grumbling beneath her breath, Agatha put away the navy silk and drew out the shimmering silk gauze, its colour a silvery sky blue. Laying it carefully on the bed, she sniffed disapprovingly, then came up and started on Lucinda's laces.

Lucinda tapped her comb on the table. "This is a horrendous coil." She frowned. "Have you asked after Lady Asterley?"

Agatha nodded. "There isn't one. The last—her as was Lord Asterley's mother—died years ago."

"Oh." Lucinda blinked, then, drawing in a breath, squared her shoulders. "Well—tonight can't be helped—but we'll be leaving tomorrow."

"Aye—so I thought."

Lucinda heard the relief in Agatha's voice. She hid an affectionate grin. "Don't worry—despite all indications to the contrary, they are entirely gentlemen at heart."

Agatha humphed. "So you say—but gentlemen can be very persuasive at times."

Lucinda rose and let her gown fall to the floor. Stepping out of it, she allowed Agatha to help her into the sheath of shimmering blue silk. Only when she was finally ready to descend to the drawing-room did she deign to acknowledge Agatha's last comment.

"As I should hope you know by now," she said, fixing Agatha with a haughty glance, "I'm more than capable of managing any gentleman who might darken my horizon. So just tidy up in here—and let Joshua know that we'll be departing in the morning." Lucinda glided to the door—then paused to look back at her maid. "And don't *worry*, you old curmudgeon!"

With that, she turned and, a scintillating vision in shimmering silver blue, glided out of the door.

The drawing-room quickly filled, the guests eager for each other's company. Now sure of her footing, Lucinda found no difficulty in strolling through the crowd, acknowledging the compliments and the open admiration in the gentlemen's eyes, artfully turning aside their subtle suggestions. She was once more in control—but her nerves were taut, her whole being on edge.

The moment she'd been waiting for finally arrived.

Harry walked into the room, creating, she noticed, an immediate stir. He must have arrived while they were changing; he was dressed in his usual severe black and white, his fair hair gleaming in the candlelight. Marguerite broke off her conversation to sweep forward and greet him—with a peck on the cheek, Lucinda noted. Lord Asterley came up to wring his hand. Other gentlemen nodded and called greetings; many of the ladies prinked and preened, smiling in gracious welcome.

Abruptly finding herself the object of a piercing green stare, Lucinda didn't smile at all. Her heart stuttered, then accelerated; a vice slowly closed about her chest. Her expression studiously remote, she inclined her head fractionally and turned back to Mr Ormesby and Lady Morcombe.

And waited for him to come to her.

He didn't—nor was he about to. That much was made plain within ten minutes. Excruciatingly aware of his gaze, dwelling on her shoulders, bare above the abbreviated neckline of her gown, and on her upper breasts, likewise revealed, Lucinda gritted her teeth and inwardly cursed. What the devil was he up to now?

Cursing her, as it happened—Harry could barely restrain the urge to cross the room, lay hold of one delicate wrist and haul her away. What the deuce did she mean by appearing in such a gown? Of the sheerest silk gauze, it shimmered and glimmered, tantalised and teased. The soft material clung wherever it touched, outlining then concealing her slender form, artfully displaying the graceful curves of hips and thighs and the smooth planes of her back. As for her breasts, they were barely concealed at all—the square neckline had been cut by a miser. Gritting his teeth, he forced his feet to remain still. As all the gentleman were openly captivated, at least he didn't need to disguise his interest.

"Harry, old chap! Didn't think to see you here. Thought you might be looking to take a leaf out of Jack's book, what?"

Harry bent a look of intense irritation on Lord Cranbourne. "Not my style, Bentley. But who have you got your eye on?"

Lord Cranbourne grinned. "Lady Morcombe. She's a ripe little plum—that old codger of a husband of hers doesn't appreciate her as he ought."

"Hmm." Harry sent another penetrating glance about the room. "Just the usual crowd, is it?"

"All except the lovely Mrs Babbacombe—but you know all about her, as I recall?"

"Indeed." Harry's gaze rested again on Lucinda. Again he quelled the urge to go to her side.

"Your interest lie that way this evening?"

Harry shot Lord Cranbourne a quick glance, but his lordship's question was clearly an idle one. "Not as you mean it."

With a nod, he strolled away—before a puzzled Lord Cranbourne could ask for clarification.

With studied nonchalance, Harry circled the room, watching, assessing. His interest was certainly centred on Lucinda—but his first concern was to determine who had placed her name on the invitation list.

He'd been halfway to Asterley before his mind had cleared enough to see the point. *He* hadn't suggested her—so who had? And why?

He prowled the room, carefully studying, not only Lucinda, but all who approached her, intent on discovering which, of his fellow rakes, felt he had first claim.

By the time dinner was announced, by Melthorpe in sepulchural vein, Lucinda had come to the conclusion that Harry was waiting for something—presumably disaster—to befall her, so that he could come to her aid and take charge of her again. Vowing it would never be so, she smiled graciously on Mr Ormesby as he offered her his arm. "Do you come here often, sir?"

Mr Ormesby gesticulated airily. "Now and then. A peaceful interlude away from the bustle of town, what?"

"Indeed." From the corner of her eye, Lucinda saw Harry frown. Then Marguerite stopped beside him and claimed his arm. Lucinda turned a bright smile on Mr Ormesby. "I will rely on you, sir, if I may, to guide me in Asterley's ways."

Mr Ormesby looked thoroughly chuffed. "A pleasure, my dear."

Lucinda blinked, and hoped she wasn't raising any false expectations. "Tell me—are the dinners very elaborate?"

Tonight's wasn't, but neither was it less than an elegant sufficiency with four full courses and two removes. The conversation, to Lucinda's relief, remained general throughout, with much exchanging of the latest gossip and *on dits,* accompanied by considerable merriment, all in the best of taste.

Indeed, if it hadn't been for the subtle undercurrent, borne on glances and the occasional whispered word, her enjoyment would have been unreserved.

"My dear Mrs Babbacombe." Lord Dewhurst, on Lucinda's left, leaned closer to claim her attention. "Have you heard of the treasure hunt Marguerite has organised for tomorrow?"

"Treasure hunt?" Aware of the growing warmth in his lordship's gaze, Lucinda dimly wondered if such an enterprise, in this company, could possibly be innocent.

"Indeed—and we play a version of Fox and Geese that will, I'm sure, delight you. Needless to say, there's no board involved." His lordship smiled. "We, ourselves, represent the pieces."

Lucinda could just imagine. But she kept her smile serene, grasping the offer of a custard to turn aside without comment. In doing so, she caught Harry's eye. He was seated across the table, some way along. Despite the distance, she could sense his simmering irritation, there in the odd tenseness that invested his apparently relaxed frame, and in the way his long fingers

gripped his wine glass. Lucinda summoned a radiantly ingenuous smile—and turned it on Mr Ormesby.

Harry felt the muscle in his jaw ripple; his teeth were
clenched tight. He forced his jaw to relax, turning aside as
Marguerite waved at him from the end of the table.

Lucinda had hoped to catch her breath, to rest her wits and
strengthen her defences, when the ladies retired to the drawing-
room. But at Asterley, port was the last thing on the gentlemen's minds; they followed in the ladies' wake, not even
glancing at the decanters on the sideboard.

"We generally take things quietly on the first evening," Mr
Ormesby informed Lucinda as he joined her by the hearth.
"Let people…get to know one another, if you take my mean-
ing."

"Exactly!" Lord Asterley followed hard on Mr Ormesby's
heels. "Tomorrow, of course, things will liven up a trifle." He
rubbed his hands together and looked over the assembled company. "We'd thought to start by punting on the lake, then move
on to the Treasure Hunt. Marguerite's got it all organised—to
be held in the gardens, of course." He turned a perfectly innocent smile on Lucinda. "Plenty of quiet nooks to find treasure in."

"Oh?" Lucinda endeavoured to look politely vague.

"Nothing starts till after noon, of course. We generally all
meet in the breakfast parlour about then. Gives everyone a
chance to catch up on their sleep, don't y'know."

Lucinda nodded, making a mental note to be on the road
shortly after ten. Quite how she was to excuse herself, and on
what grounds, she did not know—but she'd think of something
by tomorrow morning.

Lord Cranbourne and Lady Morcombe joined them; the conversation revolved about the expected entertainments of the
next few days—the communal ones. As for the others, those
that remained unspecified, Lucinda was increasingly aware of
the speculative glances cast her way, by Mr Ormesby, Lord
Asterley and Lord Dewhurst in particular.

For the first time since entering Asterley Place, she began to

feel truly uneasy. Not out of fear for her virtue, but from dislike
of the potentially embarrassing situations she might soon find
herself in. Mr Ormesby and Lord Asterley showed no disposition to leave her side; to Lucinda's relief, they were both
summoned by Marguerite to help pass the teacups. She grasped
the opportunity to fill a vacant chair by the *chaise*. On its end
sat a pretty woman much of an age with herself; Lucinda
vaguely recalled being introduced at Almack's.

"Lady Coleby—Millicent." The woman smiled and nodded
as she passed a teacup. "Always a pleasure to welcome another
to our circle."

Lucinda's answering smile was a trifle weak. She hid it behind her cup. She was beginning to wonder if she should have
braved the fuss and left three hours ago.

"Have you made your choice yet?" Over the rim of her cup,
Lady Coleby raised a questioning brow.

Lucinda blinked. "Choice?"

Her ladyship gestured about her. "From amongst the gentlemen."

Lucinda looked blank

"Oh—I forgot. You're new." Lady Coleby lowered her cup
and leaned closer. "It's all very simple. One just decides which
of the gentlemen one likes the best—one, two or more if your
taste runs that way—then one lets them know—discreetly, of
course. You don't need to do anything more; it's all miraculously well-organised."

Faced with an unwaveringly enquiring gaze, Lucinda swallowed a mouthful of tea. "Ah—I'm not sure."

"Well, don't leave it too long or the best will be taken."
Lady Coleby touched Lucinda's sleeve. "I'm after Harry Lester, myself," she confided, nodding to where Harry stood on
the opposite side of the room. "He's not attended in an age—
not since I've been coming anyway, which is more than a year.
But all that excessive elegance, all that lethal grace—" Lady
Coleby broke off with a delicate shiver. "Deep waters hold
dangerous currents, so they say." Her gaze fixed on Harry, she
took a sip of her tea. "I never would have believed brash,

impetuous Harry would turn out like that. It just goes to show. He's nothing like the fresh-faced young gentleman who offered for me all those years ago.''

Lucinda froze. Then, slowly, she set her cup back on her saucer. ''He offered for you?''

''Oh, yes! Not officially—it never came to that. Ten and more years ago it was.'' Her ladyship affected a dewy-eyed look, then giggled. ''He was most *terribly* enamoured—well, you know how young men can be.'' She waved her hand. ''Utterly over the moon. Wild, impassioned declarations—it was all so thrilling for he was very handsome, even then.''

Lucinda studied Lady Coleby's face as her ladyship studied Harry, engaged in a discussion with a Mr Harding. ''But you didn't accept him?''

''Heavens, no! Poor as church mice, the Lesters. Or they were. Mind you…'' a speculative glint lit her ladyship's brown eyes ''…now that Coleby's dead and gone and the Lesters have suffered a windfall—'' Lady Coleby broke off to state, ''Positively *enormous,* my dear, so I've heard. Well—'' she turned back to survey Harry, anticipation lighting her face ''—I really do believe I should renew old acquaintances.''

At that moment, Harry and Mr Harding parted. Harry directed a piercing glance across the room.

Her ladyship smiled delightedly and rose, laying aside her teacup. ''And it appears there'll be no better time. Do excuse me, my dear.''

Lucinda forced herself to incline her head. Picking up both cups, she carried them to where Marguerite sat by the tea trolley, all the while keeping her gaze firmly fixed on her hostess.

Harry's gaze was fixed on her. He hesitated, frowning, his lips set in a firm line. No gentlemen had pressed her; none had displayed any proprietary interest. Three, if not four, were seriously enamoured; another few were watching closely. But none seemed to consider they had first claim—they were all vying for her favours as if she had swanned into their orbit on her own account.

Which left him with the puzzle unsolved. With an inward

grimace, he put it aside until the morning. He was about to cross the room, to head off what he knew would be an embarrassing and confusing confrontation, when he felt a touch on his sleeve.

"Harry!" Millicent, Lady Coleby, uttered the word on a long breathy exhalation. She opened wide brown eyes at him, her delicately tinted cheeks aglow.

Briefly, Harry nodded. "Millie." His head rose again as he looked for Lucinda; she was still chatting to Marguerite.

"Dear Harry." Engrossed in artlessly studying his cravat, Millie didn't notice his interest was elsewhere. "I've always carried a torch for you—you do know that, don't you? I had to marry Coleby—you must see that. You're so much older now—you understand the ways of our world." Millie let a knowing smile curve her lips. "I've heard you understand the ways very well, Harry. Perhaps we might…travel a few avenues together tonight?"

Millie glanced up—just as Lucinda nodded to Marguerite and headed for the door. Harry, about to move, was forced to focus on Millie, standing directly in front of him.

"Excuse me, Millie. I've business elsewhere."

With that, he nodded and sidestepped, then halted, his gaze on Lucinda—and the three gentlemen who had intercepted her. Concentrating, he could just make out their words.

"My dear Mrs Babbacombe." Alfred was the first to gain her side. "Dare I hope you've found the evening to your taste?"

"You've proved a most welcome addition to our ranks, ma'am." Ormesby was close behind. "I do hope we can entice you to spend more time with us—I, for one, can think of little I'd like better."

Lucinda blinked; before she could answer, Lord Dewhurst joined them.

He took her hand and bowed low. "Enchanted, my dear. Dare I hope for some time to further our acquaintance?"

Lucinda met his lordship's calm but distinctly warm gaze—

and wished herself elsewhere. Heat tinged her cheeks—then, from the corner of her eye, she saw Harry. Watching.

Drawing in a steadying breath, Lucinda smiled at her three would-be *cicisbei*. With what she hoped they understood as a pointed disregard for all they had hinted at, if not said, she calmly stated, "If you'll excuse me, gentlemen, I believe I will retire early."

With a benedictory smile, she swept them a curtsy; they immediately bowed low. Rising, Lucinda headed straight for the door. Confident she had avoided a potential quagmire, head high, she glided from the room.

Harry stared after her.

Then uttered a single, pungent expletive and spun on his heel. He exited the room by the windows to the terrace. At speed.

Millie simply stared—then lifted her shoulders in a baffled shrug—and glided after Mr Harding.

Lucinda climbed the stairs and traversed the corridors, engrossed, not with the details of her imminent departure nor yet imaginings of what she had escaped. Lady Coleby's revelations of Harry's long-ago disappointment filled her mind.

She could imagine, very clearly, how it must have been, how, with the impetuosity of youth, he had laid his love at his chosen one's feet, only to see it spurned. It must have hurt. A great deal. The fact explained many things—why he was now so cynical of love, not marriage itself, but the love needed to support it, the intensity he now harnessed, that certain something which made so many women view him as dangerous—excitingly but definitely so—and his emotionally cautious nature.

Reaching her room, Lucinda shut the door firmly behind her. She looked for a key, grimacing resignedly when she discovered there wasn't one.

Thanks to Lady Coleby, and her lack of what Lucinda felt was any proper feeling, she could now understand why Harry was as he was. That, however, did not excuse his behaviour in engineering her present predicament.

Eyes narrowing as she considered his perfidy, Lucinda glided across the room, lit by a single candelabra on the dressing table, and gave the bell pull a definite tug.

The door opened. Her hand still clutching the embroidered pull, Lucinda turned.

To see Harry slip around the door.

He scanned the room and found her. "There's no point ringing for your maid—the house rules forbid servants the upper corridors after ten."

"What?" Lucinda stared. "But what are you doing here?"

Harry closed the door and looked around again.

Lucinda had had enough. Eyes narrowing, she sailed across the room to confront him. "However, as you *are* here, I have a bone to pick with you!"

Reassured they were alone, Harry brought his gaze to her face as she halted, slender and straight, before him. "Indeed?"

"As you well know!" Lucinda glared up at him. "How *dare* you organise to have me invited to such a gathering as this? I realise you might be somewhat irritated because I did not accept your proposal—" She broke off as the thought occurred that she, like Lady Coleby, might be said to have rejected him. "But the circumstances were nothing like those of Lady Coleby. Or whoever she was then." With an irritated wave, she dismissed Lady Coleby. "Whatever your feelings in the matter, I have to tell you that I view your behaviour in this instance as *reprehensible!* Utterly callous and without justification! It is totally inconceivable to me why you—"

"I didn't."

The steel beneath the words cut through her denunciation.

Arrested in mid-tirade, Lucinda blinked up at him. "You didn't?"

His jaw set, his lips a thin line, Harry regarded her through narrowed eyes. "For a woman of superior sense, you frequently indulge the most remarkable notions. *I* didn't arrange to have you invited. On the contrary." His tone turned conversational, his accents remained clipped; the undercurrent was positively lethal. "When I discover who did, I'm going to wring his neck."

"Oh." Lucinda backed a step as he closed the distance between them. Her eyes met his; abruptly, she stiffened and stood her ground. "That's all very well—but what are you doing here now?"

"Protecting you from your latest folly."

"Folly?" Lucinda coolly raised her brows—and her chin. "What folly?"

"The folly of the invitation you just, all unwittingly, issued." Harry glanced at the bed, then the fireplace. The fire was lit, a smallish blaze but there was plenty of wood by the hearth. An armchair sat before it.

Lucinda frowned. "What invitation?"

Harry's gaze came back to her face; he merely raised his brows at her.

Lucinda snorted. "Nonsense. You're imagining things. I issued no invitation—I did nothing of the sort."

Harry gestured to the armchair. "Let's just wait and see, shall we?"

"No—I want you out of here." Lucinda couldn't tilt her chin any higher. "Your presence is totally improper."

Harry's eyes glittered. "Naturally—that's the purpose of these parties, in case you hadn't realised." His gaze fell to her breasts. "And speaking of improper—who the devil told you that gown was decent?"

"A whole *host* of appreciative gentlemen," Lucinda informed him, belligerently planting her hands on her hips. "And I hardly need you to tell me what the purpose of this little gathering is *but*, for your information, I plan to have nothing to do with it."

"Good—we agree on that much."

Lucinda narrowed her eyes. Harry met her gaze with a stubbornness as unwavering as her own.

A knock came on the door.

Harry smiled coldly. He pointed a finger at Lucinda's nose. "Wait here."

Without waiting for any agreement, he swung on his heel and retraced his steps. He opened the door. "Yes?"

Alfred jumped. "Oh—ah!" He blinked wildly. "Oh—it's you, Harry. Er—I didn't realise."

"Obviously."

Alfred shifted his weight from one foot to the other, then gestured vaguely. "Right-ho! Er...I'll call later, then."

"Don't bother—the reception will be the same."

The words were a dire warning. Harry shut the door on his old schoolfriend's face, before he could think of doing anything else with the vacuously good-natured features.

He swung back—to find Lucinda staring at the door in utter disbelief. "*Well!* What cheek!"

Harry smiled. "I'm so glad you now see my point."

Lucinda blinked, then gestured at the door. "But he's gone now. You told him not to come back." When Harry merely raised his brows, she folded her arms and lifted her chin. "There's no reason you can't leave now."

Harry's smile turned feral. "I can give you two very good reasons."

They came knocking an hour or so apart.

Lucinda gave up blushing after the first.

She also stopped urging Harry to leave; this was not the sort of houseparty at which she felt comfortable.

When the hour after midnight passed and no one else came creeping to knock on the panels of her door, Lucinda finally relaxed. Curled up against the pillows on her bed, she looked across at Harry, eyes closed, head back, sprawled in the big armchair before the fire.

She didn't want him to go.

"Get into bed—I'll stay here."

He hadn't moved or opened his eyes. Lucinda could feel her heart thudding. "There?"

His lips twisted. "I'm perfectly capable of spending a night in a chair for a good cause." He shifted, stretching his legs out before him. "It's not too uncomfortable."

Lucinda considered, then nodded. His eyes looked closed.

"Do you need any help with your lacings?"

She shook her head—then realised and answered, "No."

"Good." Harry relaxed. "Good night, then."

"Good night."

Lucinda watched him for a moment, then settled down amid the covers, drawing them over her. Although it was a four-poster, there were no hangings on the bed; there was no screen behind which she could change. She lay back against the pillows; when Harry made no sound, did not move, she shifted onto her side.

The soft flickering firelight touched his face, lighting the hollows, throwing the strong bone structure into relief, shading his heavy lids, etching the firm contours of his lips.

Lucinda's eyes slowly closed and she drifted into sleep.

Chapter Eleven

WHEN SHE AWOKE the next morning, the fire had died. The chair before it was empty.

Lucinda let her lids fall and snuggled down beneath the covers. Her lips curved in a lazy smile; a deep contentment pervaded her. Idly, she searched for the cause—and remembered her dream.

The time, as she recalled, had been very late, deep in the long watches of the night. The house had been silent when she'd supposedly woken—and seen Harry sprawled in the chair before the dying fire. He had shifted restlessly and she had remembered the blanket left on a chair by the bed. She had slipped from beneath the covers, her shimmering gown slithering over her limbs. On silent feet, she had retrieved the blanket and approached the chair by the fire.

She had halted six feet away, stopped by some sixth sense. His eyes had been closed, long brown lashes gilded at the tips almost brushing his high cheekbones. She had studied his face, the angles and planes, austere in repose, the carved jaw and sculpted lips. Her gaze had travelled on, down his long, graceful body, loose-limbed in sleep, the subtle tension that normally invested it in abeyance.

A little sigh had caught in her throat.

And she had felt the touch of his gaze.

Raising her eyes, she had seen his were open, his gaze, heavy-lidded, on her face. He had studied her, not broodingly but with a gentle pensiveness that had held her still.

She had sensed his hesitation, and the instant he put it aside. Lifting one hand, he had held it out, palm upwards, to her.

Indecision had held her, poised, quivering. He said nothing; his hand hadn't moved. She had drawn in a long, deep breath— and placed her hand in his. His fingers had closed gently but firmly about hers, then he had drawn her slowly towards him.

The blanket had fallen from her grasp to lie on the floor, forgotten. He had drawn her nearer, then reached for her, pulling her gently onto his lap.

She had gone very readily, her heart soaring as she felt his heat enfold her, his thighs hard beneath hers. Then his arms had closed about her and she had raised her face for his kiss.

When they had first come together, desire had propelled them into intimacy, leaving no time for the gentler side of passion. In her dream last night they had explored that aspect fully, spending hours before the fire, wrapped in passion's web.

Beneath the covers, Lucinda closed her eyes tight; a long delicious shiver rippled through her.

In her imagination, she could feel Harry's hands upon her, the long fingers experienced, so knowing, his palms hard and calloused from frequent handling of the reins. He had opened the door to a wonderland of sensation—and conducted her through it, educating her senses until they had been filled with pleasure—and him.

He had stripped her gown from her in tantalising stages after his lips, artfully following the neckline, had made her long to rid herself of it. He had gently eased it down, revealing her breasts, on which he had lavished untold attention. In her mind, she felt again the touch of his hair, soft as silk on her heated skin.

How long she had lain, naked in his arms as he loved her, the dying firelight gilding her in bronze and gold, she couldn't recall. But it had felt like hours before he had lifted her and carried her to the bed.

He had drawn down the covers and laid her on the sheets, then rekindled the candles in the candelabra and placed it on the table by the bed. She had blushed and reached for the covers.

"No. Let me look at you."

His voice had been low, soft and deep. Deep currents, indeed, but these weren't turbulent, dangerous, but deeper still, slow, steady and infinitely strong. They had swept aside her inhibitions, leaving her with no reservations; held in his green gaze, she had lain as he had left her and watched while he undressed.

Then he had joined her on the bed and desire had flared; this time, he had held it harnessed and showed her how to manage the reins. The power was no less strong but, this time, she had appreciated it fully, felt its quality in each long-drawn moment, in each subtle movement, each lingering caress.

The end had been just as glorious but had left a deeper sense of peace, a more shattering realisation of how strong the power that held them now was.

There had been tears in her eyes when, after it was over, she had lifted her lids and looked up into his face.

And had seen therein what she had almost given up hope of ever seeing—resignation, perhaps, but acceptance, too. It had been there in his eyes, glowing beneath his heavy lids, there in the gentler cast of his features. And there most especially in his mobile lips, no longer so hard and severe, but softer, more pliable. He had met her gaze—and hadn't tried to hide his reaction, nor draw back from the reality.

Instead, he had lowered his head and kissed her, long, deeply, lingeringly, then lifted from her and wrapped her in his arms.

A dream—nothing more, her dream, the embodiment of all her hopes, her deepest desires, the answer to her most secret needs.

Lucinda shut her eyes tight, clinging to the deep sense of peace and contentment, even if it was only illusory.

But the day had dawned; light, streaming through the open shutters, played on her lids. Reluctantly, she lifted them—and saw the blanket, half-folded still, sitting on the floor before the hearth.

Her eyes widened. Blinking, she noted the candelabra—on the table beside the bed. Slowly, hardly daring to breathe, she started to turn over. She only got halfway onto her back before she registered the chaos of the covers. Lucinda swallowed, and turned flat on her back. She slanted a glance sideways—and let out the breath she'd been holding. The bed beside her was empty. But the pillow beside hers was deeply dented.

As a final, incontrovertible piece of evidence, a sunbeam, bobbing in, highlighted two fine gold hairs, reposing on the white lawn of the pillowcase.

Lucinda groaned and shut her eyes.

The next instant, she sat bolt upright and flung the covers from her. Only then did she recall she was naked. Grabbing the covers back, she rummaged amid their confusion and discovered the nightgown Agatha had laid out the night before. Muttering curses, Lucinda struggled into it, then leapt from the bed.

She crossed the room with determined strides and yanked violently on the bell pull.

She was leaving. Now.

IN THE LIBRARY on the ground floor, Harry paced back and forth before the windows. He had dispatched an intrigued Melthorpe to rout out his master, wherever he might be, with a message that his presence was urgently required.

The door latch clicked; Harry swung about as Alfred entered, nattily attired in a check coat over country breeches and high boots. Harry himself was dressed for travelling in his bottle-green coat and buckskins.

"There you are!" With a smile unimpaired by having been summarily summoned from someone else's bed, Alfred strolled forward. "Melthorpe didn't say what the problem was, but you look in fine fettle. Dare say your night was a great deal more exciting than mine, what? Mrs Babbacombe looks set to take the title of most delectable widow of the year—particularly if she can keep *you* entertained, happy as a grig, all night long—"

The last word ended on a strangled note as Harry's fist made contact with Alfred's face.

Harry groaned and put a hand to his brow. "Sorry—sorry."

His expression openly apologetic, he extended his hand to Alfred, who was now measuring his length on the rug. "I didn't *mean* to hit you." Harry's jaw hardened. "But you'd be well advised to mute your comments on the subject of Mrs Babbacombe."

Alfred made no move to take his hand, or get up. "Oh?" He was clearly intrigued.

Disgusted with himself, Harry waved him up. "It was just instinctive. I won't hit you again."

"Ah, well." Alfred sat up and gingerly felt his left cheekbone. "I know you didn't *mean* to hit me—nothing's broken, so you must've pulled the punch. Very grateful you did, mind—but if it's all the same to you, I'll just remain here until you tell me what this is all about—just in case, with my usual babble, I inadvertently trigger any more of your instincts."

Harry grimaced. Hands on hips, he looked down at Alfred. "I think someone's been using us." He gestured about him. "The Asterley Place house-parties."

Unexpected intelligence seeped into Alfred's eyes. "How?"

Harry compressed his lips, then stated, "Lucinda Babbacombe should never have been invited. She's a thoroughly virtuous female—take it from me."

Alfred's brows rose. "I see." Then he frowned. "No, I don't."

"What I want to know is who suggested you invite her?"

Alfred sat up and draped his arms over his knees. He blinked up at Harry. "You know, I don't think I like being used. It was a chap named Joliffe—brushed up against him a couple of times at some hell or other but he's generally about town—Ernest, Earle, something like that. Ran across him on Wednesday night at that hell in Sussex Place. He happened to mention that Mrs Babbacombe was looking for a little entertainment and he'd promised he'd mention her to me."

Harry was frowning. "Joliffe?" He shook his head. "Can't say I've had the pleasure."

Alfred snorted. "Wouldn't exactly call it a pleasure. Bit of a loose fish."

Harry's gaze abruptly focused. "You took the word of a loose fish on the subject of a lady's reputation?"

"Of course not." Alfred hurriedly leaned back out of reach, his expression distinctly injured. "I checked—you know I always do."

"Who with?" Harry asked. "Em?"

"*Em?* Your aunt Em?" Alfred blinked. "What's she got to do with it? Old tartar she is—was. Used to pinch my cheeks every time she came visiting."

Harry snorted. "She'll do more than pinch your cheeks if she finds out what you invited her protégée to."

"*Her protégée?*" Alfred looked horrified.

"You obviously didn't check too hard," Harry growled, swinging away to pace once more.

Alfred squirmed. "Well, you see, time was tight. We had this vacancy; Lady Callan's husband came back from Vienna sooner than she'd expected."

Harry humphed. "So who *did* you check with?"

"The lady's cousin or something by marriage. Mortimer Babbacombe."

Harry frowned and stopped pacing. The name came floating back to him from his first memories of Lucinda. "Mortimer Babbacombe?"

Alfred shrugged. "Innocuous sort, a bit weak, but can't say I've heard anything against him—other than that he's a friend of Joliffe's."

Harry prowled over to stand directly before Alfred. "Let me get this straight—Joliffe suggested Mrs Babbacombe was looking for an invitation to the entertainment here and Mortimer Babbacombe confirmed she liked living life on the racy side?"

"Well, not in so many words. Couldn't expect him to come right out and *say* such a thing of a female relative, what? But you know how it goes—I made the suggestions and gave him plenty of time to deny them. He didn't. Seemed clear enough to me."

Harry grimaced. Then nodded. "All right." He looked down at Alfred. "But she's leaving."

"When?" Alfred struggled to his feet.

"Now. As soon as possible. Furthermore, she's never been here."

Alfred shrugged. "Naturally. *None* of the ladies are here."

Harry nodded, grateful for his own past deviousness. It was his fertile mind that had devised these parties, where married ladies and widows of the *ton* could enjoy a little illicit dalliance without running the risk of any social repercussions. Total discretion was an absolute requirement—all the ladies who attended had the same secret to hide. As for the gentlemen, honour and their peers—and the likelihood of future invitations—were more than sufficient to ensure their silence.

So the damned woman, despite all, was safe—yet again.

Harry frowned.

"Come on—let's have breakfast." Alfred turned towards the door. "Might as well reap the rewards of being so early—we can snaffle two helpings of kedgeree."

Still frowning, Harry followed him to the door.

An hour later, Lucinda swept down the main staircase, Agatha, dourly protective, three steps behind. An incipient frown tangled Lucinda's brows, put there by Melthorpe, who had knocked on her door while they had been packing with a breakfast tray and a message that his lordship would hold himself in readiness to take leave of her whenever she was ready. Then, a few minutes ago, when Agatha had opened her door, it was to discover a footman patiently waiting to carry her bag to the carriage.

For the life of her, she couldn't understand how they had known she was leaving.

It was all most confusing, a situation not helped by the skittering, totally uncharacteristic panic that had laid siege to her confidence.

As she set foot on the last flight of stairs, Lord Asterley strolled out of the dining-room. Harry followed in his wake, a sight that made Lucinda inwardly curse. She switched her gaze to her gloves, tugging them on; when she lifted her face, it was set in determined lines. "Good morning, my lord. I'm afraid I must depart immediately."

"Yes, of course—I quite understand." Alfred waited by the bottom of the stairs, his most charming smile in place.

Lucinda struggled not to frown. "I'm so glad. I have enjoyed my stay, but I'm sure it's for the best if I leave this morning." She avoided looking at Harry, standing behind his host.

Alfred offered her his arm. "We're quite devastated to have you leave, of course, but I've had your carriage brought around."

Beginning to feel distinctly distracted, Lucinda put her hand on his sleeve. "How kind of you," she murmured. From beneath her lashes, she glanced at Harry but could make nothing of his urbane expression.

"A pleasant day for a drive—hope you reach your destination without any fuss."

Lucinda allowed his lordship—expatiating in similar, totally inconsequential vein—to lead her down the steps.

As he had said, her carriage awaited, Joshua on the box. Lucinda paused on the last step, turning to her host as Agatha slipped past. Calmly, she held out her hand. "Thank you, my lord, for a most interesting stay—even if it was so short."

"Delighted, m'dear, delighted." Alfred bowed extravagantly over her hand. "Dare say I'll see you shortly in London." As he straightened, his gaze met Harry's over Lucinda's shoulder. "In the ballrooms," he hastily added.

Lucinda blinked. Then she turned to the carriage, and discovered Agatha, her expression thoroughly disapproving, up beside Joshua on the box.

"Here—allow me."

Before she could do anything about her maid's unexpected position, Lucinda found herself handed into the carriage. Deciding that rapid departure was undoubtedly her wisest course, she took her seat by the window and settled her skirts. She could get Agatha down once they were clear of the drive.

Lord Asterley spoke through the window. "Do hope you enjoyed your stay. We'll look to see you again next—"

Abruptly he caught himself up, a comical look on his face. "Ah—no. Not again."

"Quite," came in clipped accents from behind him.

His lordship quickly stepped back. Lucinda, features rigidly impassive, drew breath to farewell her predatory protector—only to see Harry nod to his lordship and calmly climb into the carriage.

Lucinda stared at him.

Harry smiled a touch grimly, saying, *sotto voce*, as he moved past, "Smile sweetly at Alfred—or he'll be even more confused."

Lucinda did as she was told, plastering an utterly fatuous smile on her lips. Lord Asterley stood on the steps and waved until the curve of the drive hid them from sight.

As soon as it did, Lucinda rounded on Harry. "*What* do you think you're doing? Is this another of your forcible repatriations?"

Harry settled his shoulders against the seat. "Yes." He turned his head to look at her, brows rising arrogantly. "You aren't going to tell me you belonged at Asterley Place—are you?"

Lucinda blushed, and changed tack. "Where are we going?" She had not left Asterley Place in an unfashionable rush solely because of the activities of its guests. After last night, she had no idea how Harry now viewed her, despite what she had sensed, despite what she now hoped. Undermining her confidence was the realisation, the cast-iron certainty, that if he wanted her, she would go to him—without any marriage vows—without any vows at all. She had intended to rush back to the safety of Em's side, where her own weakness would be bolstered by Em's staunch propriety.

She had never before run from anything or anyone—but what she felt for Harry was not something she could fight.

Her heart thumping uncomfortably, she watched, eyes wide, as he sat back, laid his head against the squabs and stretched his long legs before him, crossing his booted ankles. He closed his eyes. "Lester Hall."

"Lester Hall?" Lucinda blinked—not Lestershall, his own house, but Lester Hall, his family home.

Harry nodded, settling his chin in his cravat.

"Why?"

"Because that's where you've been since yesterday. You left town in your carriage and drove there, with your maid and coachman. I followed several hours later in my curricle. Em and Heather will be following in Em's carriage this morning— Em was indisposed yesterday. That's why they didn't accompany you."

Lucinda blinked again. "Why did I go and leave them behind?"

"Because my father was expecting you last night and you didn't want to disappoint him."

"Oh." After a moment's hesitation, Lucinda asked, "*Is* he expecting me?"

Harry opened one eye, studied the delightful picture she made in her blue cambric carriage dress, her hair neatly caught in a chignon, her bonnet framing her face—the whole made distinctly more entrancing by the uncertainty he could see in her misty blue eyes and her slightly stunned expression—then closed his eye again. "He'll be delighted to see you."

Lucinda thought long and hard about that. "Where's your curricle?" she eventually asked.

"Dawlish drove it back last night with a message for Em. You needn't worry—she'll be there by the time we arrive."

There didn't seem anything more to say. Lucinda sat back— and tried to make sense of what she'd learned.

Some miles later, Harry broke the silence. "Tell me about Mortimer Babbacombe."

Hauled from deep contemplation, Lucinda frowned. "Why do you want to know about him?"

"Is he a cousin of your late husband's?"

"No—he's Charles's nephew. He inherited the Grange and the entailed estate when Charles died."

Eyes still closed, Harry frowned. "Tell me about the Grange."

Lucinda shrugged. "It's a small property as such things go. Just the house and enough fields to support it. Charles's wealth derived from the Babbacombe Inns, which he'd bought with the fortune he'd inherited from his maternal grandfather."

Half a mile had passed before Harry asked, "Was Mortimer Babbacombe familiar with the Grange?"

"No." Lucinda let her gaze wander over the lush fields through which they were passing. "It was one of the things I found particularly strange—that having barely set foot in the place—I believe he had visited for a day the year before Charles and I married—he was so very keen to take up residence."

Another long silence ensued; again, Harry broke it. "Do you know if Mortimer was aware of Charles's wealth?"

Lucinda frowned. It was some moments before she answered. "If you mean did he know Charles was personally wealthy, then yes, I think he must have known. Although he didn't visit while I lived at the Grange, he did appeal to Charles for financial relief. Basically on an annual basis. Charles used to look on it as a pension for his heir, but the sums were often quite large. The last two were for two and three thousand pounds. However..." Lucinda paused to draw breath. She glanced at Harry. His eyes were now open, narrowed and fixed on the carriage seat opposite as he pondered her words. "If you mean did Mortimer know the details of Charles's fortune, then I can't be sure he did. Certainly, in the past ten years, Charles made no effort to communicate such matters." She shrugged. "They were, after all, none of Mortimer's business."

"So he might not have known that Charles's money did not derive from the estate itself?"

Lucinda humphed. "I would have thought any fool could have seen that the Grange could not possibly generate anything like the amounts Charles regularly sent to Mortimer."

Not from London. And they had no guarantee that Mortimer Babbacombe was not, in fact, just such a fool. But Harry kept such observations to himself. He closed his eyes and listened to the rumble of the wheels as his mind juggled the facts.

Someone, he was now convinced, was taking an unwarranted interest in Lucinda's affairs—but to what end he couldn't fathom. Mischief, pure and simple, was impossible to rule out, yet instinct warned him that alone was insufficient reason. On the face of it, Mortimer Babbacombe seemed the most likely candidate, but it was impossible to ignore the fact that he was not Lucinda's heir—her aunt in Yorkshire stood nearest in line. And anyway, why send her to Asterley?

Who could possibly benefit by her enjoying a discreet liaison?

Harry inwardly shook his head—and let the matter slide. Time enough to bend his mind to it when they headed back to London. Until then, she was going to be under his eye every minute of the day—and very close, and safe, every minute of the night. Lester Hall and its surrounding acres were the safest place on earth for a Lester bride.

Her eyes on the greenery sliding past the windows, Lucinda decided that she should feel reassured, not only by Harry's manner, but by his efforts to protect her name. She cast a sideways glance at him; he appeared to be asleep. Recalling how he had spent the night, she could hardly feel surprise. She was physically tired herself but too keyed up to relax.

But as the wheels went around and the miles rumbled past and she had more time to dwell on their state, it occurred to her that she had no guarantee Harry had actually altered his stance.

The carriage hit a rut; a strong arm shot out and saved her from falling to the floor.

Lucinda righted herself; Harry's hand fell away. She turned to him—and glared at his still shut eyes. "Lady Coleby was speaking to me yesterday."

Languidly, his brows rose. "Oh?"

Despite his tone, he had tensed. Lucinda pressed her lips together and forged on. "She told me you had once been in love with her."

She could feel her heart thudding in her chest, in her throat. Harry opened his eyes. Slowly, he turned his head until his eyes, very green, met hers. "I didn't—then—know what love was."

His eyes held hers for a long moment, then he turned forward and closed them again.

The wheels rolled on; Lucinda stared at him. Then, slowly, she drew in a deep breath. A smile—of relief, of welling hope—broke across her face. Her lips still curved, she settled her head against the squabs—and followed Harry's example.

Chapter Twelve

THREE DAYS LATER, Harry sat in a garden chair under the spreading branches of the oak at the bottom of the Lester Hall lawn, squinting through the early afternoon sunshine at the blue-clad figure who had just emerged onto the terrace.

She saw him; she raised her hand, then descended the steps and headed his way. Harry smiled.

And watched his intended stroll towards him.

Her gown of cerulean blue muslin clung to her figure as she walked. Her face was shaded by a villager hat, three blue daisies decorating its band. He had put them there himself, first thing this morning, when their petals had still sparkled with dew.

Harry's smile deepened; contentment swept through him. *This* was what he wanted—what he was determined to have.

A shout, greeted by gay laughter, drew his attention to the lake. Gerald was punting Heather Babbacombe about. Face alight, Heather was laughing up at Gerald, smiling down at her from his place in the stern.

Harry raised his brows, resigned to what he strongly suspected was the inevitable. But Heather was still very young, as was Gerald; it would be some years yet before they realised just what this Season had begun.

He hadn't been at all surprised to see his younger brother drive up to the Hall a bare hour after he and Lucinda had arrived. As he had foreseen, Em and Heather had reached the Hall before them; Em had already had the household in hand.

Other than casting him a curious, almost wary look, Em had forborne to comment on his arrangements. To his considerable satisfaction, after the debacle of Asterley Place, it appeared his aunt was content to run in his harness.

Just as his intended, albeit suspiciously, was doing.

Harry rose as she approached, his smile openly welcoming.

Returning his smile, Lucinda put a hand to her hat as a gentle breeze whipped her skirts about her. "It's such a lovely afternoon, I'd thought to stroll the grounds."

"An excellent idea." The breeze died; Harry claimed her hand and with a calmly proprietorial air, tucked it in his arm. "You haven't explored the grotto at the end of the lake, have you?"

Lucinda dutifully admitted ignorance and allowed him to steer her onto the path skirting the lake's edge. Heather saw them and waved; Gerald hallooed. Lucinda smiled and waved back, then let silence fall.

And waited.

As she'd been waiting for the past three days.

Her sojourn at Lester Hall was proving far more pleasant than her projected stay at Asterley Place could ever have been. From the moment Harry had led her into the drawing-room and introduced her to his father, his intentions had been plain. Everything—every glance, every touch, every little gesture, every single word and thought that had passed between them since— had underscored the simple fact. But not once during their twilight strolls on the terrace, throughout their ambling rides through woods and fields, through all the hours they had spent together out of the past seventy-two, had he said one single word to the point.

He hadn't kissed her either—a fact which was fuelling her impatience. Yet she could hardly fault his behaviour—it was gentlemanly in the extreme. The suspicion that he was wooing her—traditionally, according to all the accepted precepts, with all the subtle elegance only one of his experience could command—had taken firm root in her mind.

Which was all very well, but...

With one hand on the crown of her hat, Lucinda tipped her head up and studied the sky. "The sunshine's been so constant one forgets the days are winging past. I fear we should return to London soon.''

"I'll escort you back to town tomorrow afternoon.''

Lucinda blinked. "Tomorrow afternoon?''

Harry raised his brows. "As I recall, we're all promised to Lady Mickleham on the following evening. Em, I suspect, will need the rest.''

"Yes, indeed." Lucinda had forgotten Lady Mickleham's ball entirely. After a moment's hesitation, she continued, "I sometimes wonder if Em is overtiring herself in our cause. Heather and I would never forgive ourselves if she ran herself aground because of us.''

Harry's lips twisted in a reluctant grin. "Fear not. She's a seasoned campaigner; she knows how to pace herself. Moreover, I can assure you the prospect of playing hostess to you both for the rest of the Season is currently providing her with expectations of untold enjoyment." That, he knew, was the unvarnished truth.

Lucinda shot him a glance from beneath her lashes, then looked ahead. "I'm relieved you think so, for I must confess I'm looking forward to rejoining the throng. It seems an age since I was swirling around a ballroom, held in a gentleman's arms.''

The look Harry sent her was distinctly dry. "Indeed—I'm quite looking forward to your return to the ballrooms myself.''

"Oh?" Lucinda bestowed on him a smiling glance. "I hadn't thought you so enamoured of the balls.''

"I'm not.''

Wide-eyed, Lucinda looked up at him. "What, then, lures you there?''

A siren. Harry looked down into her soft blue eyes—and raised his brows. "I dare say you'll understand once we're part of the crush again.''

Lucinda's answering smile was weak. She looked forward— and concentrated on not gnashing her teeth. It was all of a piece—she wondered if he was actually trying to drive her to some rash act. Like visiting his room late tonight.

It was a measure of her frustration that she actually considered the idea before, regretfully, setting it aside. The initiative was no longer hers; he had claimed it when he'd brought her here. She wasn't at all sure how to wrest it from him—and even less certain that he would let it go.

"Here we are."

Harry gestured ahead to where the path apparently disappeared into a hedge of greenery. They approached; he put out a hand and held aside a curtain of vines and creepers—blooming honeysuckle among them—to reveal white marble steps leading upward into a cool, dimly lit cave.

Enchanted, Lucinda ducked under his arm and went ahead, climbing the steps to emerge onto the tassellated floor of a mock-temple, formed by four marble pillars separating a rock-face on one quadrant, with the lake on the other three. The pillars supported a domed ceiling, covered in blue and green tiles, highly glazed, reflecting the sunshine glancing in off the lake in myriad hues from turquoise to deep green. Leafy vines and the apricot blooms of honeysuckle wreathed the arches looking onto the lake, the gentle breeze stirring their shadows.

The temple was built out over the water, the central arch giving onto steps which led down to a small stone jetty. Wide-eyed, Lucinda halted in the very centre of the temple—and discovered one of its secrets. Each of the three open arches gave onto a different vista. The one to her right led the eye over a short stretch of lake then straight down a glade thick with ferns and shrubs. To her left lay a view over a long arm of the lake to a distant shore lined with willows and beech. Straight ahead lay the most charming vista of all—Lester Hall itself lay perfectly framed within the arch, glinting water in the foreground, manicured lawns leading up to the imposing façade, flanked by the shrubbery and wilderness to the left, the rose garden, just coming into bloom, and the formal gardens on the right.

"It's beautiful." Lucinda went to stand by one of the pillars to better appreciate the view.

Harry hung back in the shadows, content to watch the play

of sunlight across her face. When she leaned back against the pillar and sighed contentedly, he strolled forward to stand beside her. After a moment, he asked, "Have you enjoyed your Season? Do you look to become a devotee—enamoured of the *ton* in all its glory, the crushes, the never-ending carousel of balls, parties and yet more balls?"

Lucinda half turned to look into his face. She searched his eyes, but neither they nor his expression gave any hint of his feelings. She considered, then answered, "By and large, I find the *ton* and its entertainments amusing." Her lips curved in a self-deprecating smile, her eyes reluctantly twinkling. "But you will have to remember that this is my first exposure to 'the carousel'—I'm still enjoying the novelty." Her expression growing serious, she put her head on one side the better to study him. "But the *ton* is your milieu—have you not enjoyed the balls this Season?"

Harry's gaze touched hers, then he looked down. He took one of her hands in his. Small, slender, her hand nestled in his much larger palm, confidently trusting. Harry closed his fingers about hers, his lips twisting. "There have been… compensations."

His lids rose; he met Lucinda's gaze.

Slowly, she raised her brows. "Indeed?" When he offered nothing more but simply looked away across the lake, she followed his gaze to Lester Hall, basking in the afternoon sun. As at Hallows Hall, Lucinda felt the tug of old memories. She sighed. "However, to answer your question, despite my fascination, I seriously doubt I could stomach a never-ending round of *ton*nish life. I fear I would need a steady diet of country peace to enable me to brave the Season on a regular basis." She slanted a glance at Harry and found him watching her. Her lips quirked. "My parents lived very retired in a rambling old house in Hampshire. When they died, I removed to the Yorkshire moors, which, of course, is as retired as it's possible to be."

Harry's features relaxed, subtly but definitely. "So you're a country miss at heart?" He lifted one brow. Slowly, his eyes on hers, he raised her hand. "Naïve?" He brushed his lips across her fingertips, then turned her hand in his. "Innocent?" His lids fell as he pressed a kiss to her palm.

Lucinda shuddered; she made no effort to hide it. She couldn't breathe, could barely think as Harry's lids rose and his eyes, green and direct, met hers.

His lips twisted; he hesitated, then shifted closer and bent his head to hers.

"And mine?"

He breathed the question against her lips, then captured them in a long, commanding kiss.

Lucinda answered in the only way she could—she turned to him, sliding her arms up and wrapping them about his neck, then kissed him back with a fervour to match his own.

Instinct prompted Harry to edge back, drawing her around the pillar to where the shadows shielded them from inadvertent eyes.

Silence filled the small pavilion. The breeze idly played with the honeysuckle, wafting perfume through the air; a drake hooted from some distant reed-fringed shore. The shadows shifted gently over the figures entwined in the pillar's lee. Spring had blossomed; summer stood in the wings, eager for its day.

"Oh! How lovely—a Grecian temple! Can we go and see?"

Heather's high-pitched tones carried easily across the water, hauling Harry and Lucinda back to their senses. Harry's chest swelled as he drew in a deep breath—then looked down. Lucinda's eyes slowly filled with comprehension; Harry felt his lips firm as he saw his frustration mirrored in misty blue.

Muttering a curse, he bent his head to taste her lips one last time, then drew his hand from her breast and quickly, expertly, rearranged her bodice, doing up the tiny buttons with a dexterity equal to that with which he had undone them.

Blinking, struggling to subdue her harried breathing, Lucinda straightened his collar and brushed back the heavy lock of hair she'd disarranged. She had shifted his cravat; her hands fluttered uncertainly.

Harry abruptly stepped back, long fingers reaching for the starched folds. "Your skirts."

Lucinda looked down—and swallowed a gasp. She shot an indignant glare at Harry, which he met with an arrogantly raised brow, then shook the clinging muslin down, smoothing the folds so that the skirts once more hung free. She spied her hat lying on the floor; she swiped it up and set it in place, tangling the ties in her haste.

"Here—let me." Harry deftly separated the ribbons, then tied them in a neat bow.

Putting up a hand to check on his efforts, Lucinda threw him a haughty glance. "Your talents are quite astonishing."

Harry's smile was a touch grim. "And extremely useful, you'll admit."

Lucinda tilted her chin, then, turning, plastered a bright smile on her lips as Gerald's voice floated up from the bottom of the steps.

"Take care! Wait till I make fast."

Lucinda strolled forward into the sunshine at the top of the steps. "Hello—did you have a pleasant time on the lake?"

Gerald looked up at her and blinked. When Harry appeared from the shadows behind her, Gerald's expression turned wary.

But Harry only smiled, albeit a touch coolly. "Just in time, Gerald. Now we can take the punt and you can show Miss Babbacombe around the temple then stroll back."

"Oh, yes! Let's do that." Heather could barely wait for Gerald to assist her from the bobbing craft. "It's such a lovely spot—so secluded."

"Usually," Harry murmured, so low only Lucinda heard.

She shot him a warning glance but her smile didn't waver. "The tiles on the ceiling are quite splendid."

"Oh?" Heather trod up the steps and into the temple without further encouragement.

Gerald, meanwhile, was staring, mesmerised, at Harry's gold acorn pin, the one his excessively precise brother used to anchor his cravat. The pin was askew. Blinking in bemusement Gerald raised his eyes to Harry's, only to be met by a languid distinctly bored green gaze—which he knew very well meant he'd be well advised to quit his brother's presence forthwith. "Ah—yes. We'll walk back."

His expression studiously blank, Gerald nodded to Lucinda and hurried after Heather.

"Mrs Babbacombe?"

Lucinda turned to find Harry, the long pole in one hand, steadying the boat, as he held his other hand out to her. She put her fingers in his; he helped her into the punt. Once she had settled her skirts on the cushions in the prow, he stepped into the stern and poled off.

The dark water glided past the hull; reclining against the cushions, Lucinda trailed her fingertips in the lake—and filled her sight with Harry. He avoided her gaze, concentrating, to all appearances, on their surroundings.

With a small, disbelieving sniff, Lucinda switched her gaze to the shores slipping past.

The ends of Harry's lips lifted; his gaze, falling to her profile, was unusually soft but cynical, too. Hands on the pole, he propelled them through the water; not even the most inveterate rake could seduce a woman while poling a punt. He hadn't planned their recent close brush with intimacy—for once, he was truly grateful for his younger brother's interruption. He had reason enough to marry his siren, and too many excuses he had yet to convince her he no longer needed. Their night at Asterley had only added to the list, lending weight to the social pressures she might imagine had influenced him. Social pressures he himself had foolishly raised in order to hide the truth.

Harry lifted his gaze to the vista before them—the façade of Lester Hall—Jack's home now, no longer his. His gaze grew distant; his jaw firmed.

She had made it plain that it was important for her to know the truth of why he wished to wed her; during the past days, he had realised it was important to him to know that she did. So before they were done, before he again asked her to be his bride, they would have it all clear between them.

His siren would know the truth—and believe it.

LUCINDA OPENED HER EYES the next morning to discover a dusky pink rose unfurling on her pillow. Enchanted, she took the delicate bloom into her hand, cradling it gently. The dew on the petals fractured the sunshine.

Her smile wondering, delighted, she sat up and pushed the covers back. Every morning she had spent at Lester Hall, she had woken to find just such a tribute waiting somewhere in her room.

But on her pillow...?

Still smiling, she rose.

Fifteen minutes later, her expression serene, she glided through the breakfast parlour doors, the rose between her fingers. As usual, Harry's father was not present—he was a semi-invalid and did not stir before noon; Em adhered to town hours so would not rise until eleven. As for Heather and Gerald, they had the night before announced their intention of riding to a distant folly; they would, Lucinda judged, be well on their way by now. Which left Harry alone, seated at the table's head, long legs stretched out before him, his fingers crooked about the handle of a cup.

Lucinda felt his gaze as she entered; with every appearance of unconsciousness, she considered her lover's token, then, with a softly distant smile, tucked it lovingly into her cleavage, making great show of nestling the velvet petals against the curves of her breasts.

She looked up to see Harry transfixed. His fingers had tightened about the handle of his cup, a stillness, like that of a predator about to pounce, had settled over his long frame. His gaze was riveted on the rose.

"Good morning." Lucinda smiled sunnily and went forward to take the seat the butler held for her.

Harry tried to speak, then had to clear his throat. "Good morning." He forced his gaze to Lucinda's; it sharpened as he read her expression. He shifted in his seat. "I'd thought to visit the stud before we head back to town. I wondered if you'd care to accompany me—and perhaps renew your acquaintance with Thistledown."

Lucinda reached for the teapot. "Thistledown's here?"

Harry nodded and took a long sip of coffee.

"Is it far?"

"Only a few miles." He watched as Lucinda spread a muffin with jam. She leant both elbows on the table, the muffin held with both hands, and took a bite; a minute later, the tip of her tongue went the rounds of her lips. Harry blinked.

"Will we ride?" Lucinda didn't think to voice her agreement formally; he had known from the first she would go.

Harry stared at the rose nestling between her breasts. "No—we'll take the gig."

Lucinda smiled at her muffin—and took another bite.

Twenty minutes later, still clad in her lilac walking dress, the dusky pink rose in pride of place, she sat beside Harry as he tooled the gig down a narrow lane. "So you don't spend much time in London?"

Harry raised his brows, his attention on the bay between the shafts. "As little as possible." He grimaced. "But with a venture like the stud, it's necessary to remain visible amongst the *cognescenti,* which is to say, the gentlemen of the *ton.*"

"Ah—I see." Lucinda nodded sagely, the wide brim of her villager hat framing her face. "Contrary to all appearances, you care nothing for the balls, the routs, the parties—and less for the good opinion of the feminine half of the *ton.* Indeed—" she opened her eyes wide "—I cannot understand how you have come by the reputation you bear. Unless—" She broke off to look enquiringly up at him. "Perhaps it's all a hum?"

Harry's attention had left the bay gelding; it was focused on Lucinda, the light in his eyes enough to make her shiver. "My reputation, my dear, was not gained in the *ballrooms.*"

Lucinda kept her gaze wide. "Oh?"

"No," Harry stated—more in answer to the hopeful expression in her eyes than her question. His expression severely reproving, he clicked the reins, setting the horse to a trot.

Lucinda grinned.

The stud was soon reached. Harry tossed the reins of the gig to a groom, then lifted Lucinda down. "I need to talk to my head-stableman, Hamish MacDowell," he said as they strolled towards the stable complex. "Thistledown should be in her box. It's in the second yard."

Lucinda nodded. "I'll wait for you there." The stables were a massive conglomerate of buildings—stables proper, as well as tackrooms and barns housing training gigs as well as what appeared to be quite enormous quantities of fodder. "Did you start it up—or was it already in existence?"

"My father established the stud in his youth. I took over after his accident—about eight years ago." Harry's gaze swept over the stud—the neat, cobbled yards and stone buildings before them, the fenced fields on either side. "Whenever I'm home I offer to drive him over—but he never comes." He looked down, then added, "I think seeing it all—the horses—reminds him of his inability. He was a bruising rider until a fall put him in that chair of his."

"So you're the son who takes after him most in the matter of horses?"

Harry's lips twitched. "In that regard—and, some might argue, his other most consuming passion."

Lucinda glanced at him, then away. "I see," she replied, her tone repressive. "So is this now all yours?" Her gesture took in the whole complex. "Or is it a family concern?"

She looked up at Harry, light colour in her cheeks, but made no attempt to excuse the question.

Harry smiled. "Legally, it's still my father's. Effectively—" He halted, lifting his head to sweep his surroundings, before looking down to meet her gaze. "I'm master of all I survey."

Slowly, Lucinda raised her brows. "Indeed?" If he was her master, did that make her his mistress? But no—she knew very well that was not his aim. "I believe you said Thistledown was in the second yard?" When Harry nodded, she inclined her head regally. "I'll await you there."

Nose in the air, she headed through the archway into the second yard. Inwardly, she humphed dejectedly. What *was* his reason for delay?

She located Thistledown by the simple expedient of standing

in the middle of the square yard and looking about until an excitedly bobbing head caught her eye.

The mare seemed overjoyed to see her, pushing her nose against her skirts. Lucinda hunted in her pockets and located the sugar lumps she'd stolen from the breakfast table; her offering was accepted with every evidence of equine pleasure.

Folding her arms on the top of the stall door, Lucinda watched as the mare lapped water from a bucket. "Can it really be so very difficult to simply ask me again?"

Thistledown rolled a dark eye enquiringly.

Lucinda gestured. "Women are notoriously changeable—in all the novels *I've* ever read, the heroines always said no when first asked."

Thistledown harrumphed and came to nudge her shoulder.

"Precisely." Lucinda nodded and absent-mindedly stroked the mare's nose. "I'm entitled to a chance to change my mind." After a moment, she wrinkled her nose. "Well—at least revise my decision in the light of fresh developments."

For she very definitely hadn't changed her mind. She knew what she knew—and Harry knew it, too. It was simply a matter of the damned man admitting it.

Lucinda humphed; Thistledown whinnied softly.

From the shadows by the tack room, Harry watched the mare shake her head and nudge Lucinda. He smiled to himself—then turned as Dawlish came lumbering up.

"Seen Hamish, have you?"

"I have. That colt of Warlock's looks promising, I agree."

"Aye—he'll win a pot before he's done, I reckon." Dawlish followed Harry's gaze to Lucinda. He nodded in her direction. "P'raps you should introduce the lady to him—get her to have a little chat to him like she did with the mare?"

In mock surprise, Harry stared at his henchman. "Is that approval I detect? From you—the arch-misogynist?"

Dawlish frowned. "Don't know as how I know what a misogynist is, rightly, but at least you've had the sense to find one as the horses like—and who might actually come in handy to boot." Dawlish snorted. "What I wants to know is why you can't get a move on—so's we can all get back to knowing where we are?''

Harry's gaze clouded. "There are a few loose ends I'm presently tying up."

"Is that what you calls them these days?"

"Apropos of which," Harry continued imperturbably, "Did you get that message to Lord Ruthven?"

"Aye—his lordship said as he'd see to it."

"Good." Harry's gaze had returned to Lucinda. "We'll leave about two. I'll take the curricle—you can go with Em."

He didn't wait for Dawlish's grumbling grunt but sauntered after Lucinda. She had left the mare and wandered along the loose boxes to stop at the end where a grey head had come out to greet her.

She looked around as Harry drew near. "Did he win at Newmarket?"

Harry grinned and stroked Cribb's nose. "He did." The horse nudged his pockets but Harry shook his head. "No apples today, I'm afraid."

"When's he racing next?"

"Not this year." Harry took Lucinda's arm and steered her towards the gate. "The Newmarket win took him to the top of his class; I've decided to retire him at his peak, so to speak. He'll stand for the rest of this season. I might give him a run next year, but if the present interest in him as a stud continues, I'd be a fool to let him waste his energies on the track."

Lucinda's lips quirked; she struggled to suppress her grin.

Harry noticed. "What is it?"

Colouring slightly, Lucinda shot him a glance from beneath her lids.

Harry raised his brows higher.

Lucinda grimaced. "If you must know," she said, switching her gaze to the horizon. "I was simply struck by the fact that managing a stud is a peculiarly apt enterprise for…er, one with your qualifications."

Harry laughed, an entirely spontaneous sound Lucinda realised she had not before heard.

"My dear Mrs Babbacombe!" His green eyes quizzed her. "What a thoroughly shocking observation to make."

Lucinda glared, then put her nose in the air.

Harry chuckled. Ignoring her blushes, he drew her closer. "Strangely enough," he said, his lips distinctly curved, "you're the first to ever put it into words."

Lucinda fell back on one of Em's snorts—the one that signified deep disapproval. Disapproval gave way to hope when she realised Harry was not leading her back to the gig but towards a small wood bordering the nearest field. A path led between the trees, cut back to permit easy strolling.

Perhaps…? She never finished the thought, distracted by the discovery that the wood was in reality no more than a windbreak. Beyond it, the path was paved as it ambled about a small pond where water lilies battled with reeds. "That needs clearing."

Harry glanced at the pond. "We'll get to it eventually."

Lucinda looked up and followed his gaze—to the house. Large, rambling, with old-fashioned gables, it was made of local stone with a good slate roof. On the ground floor, bow windows stood open to the summer air. A rose crept up one wall to nod pale yellow blooms before one of the upstairs windows. Two large, leafy oaks stood one to each side, casting cool shade over the gravelled drive which wound from some gateway out of sight down a long avenue to end in a sweep before the front door.

She glanced at Harry. "Lestershall?"

He nodded, his eyes on the manor house. "My house." Briefly, his lips twisted. "My home." With a languid wave, he gestured ahead. "Shall we?"

Suddenly breathless, Lucinda inclined her head.

They strolled on to where their path debouched onto the lawn, then crossed the grassy expanse and ducked beneath the low branches of one of the oaks to join the drive. As they approached the shallow stone steps, Lucinda noticed the front door stood ajar.

"I've never really lived here." Harry steadied her as they

scrunched across the gravel. "It had fallen into disrepair, so
I've had a small army through to set it to rights."

A burly individual in a carpenter's leather apron appeared in
the doorway as they set foot on the steps.

"Mornin', Mr Lester." The man ducked his head, his cheery
face lit by a smile. "It's all coming together nicely—as I think
you'll find. Not much more to do."

"Good morning, Catchbrick. This is Mrs Babbacombe. If it
won't inconvenience you and your men, I'd like to show her
around."

"No inconvenience at all, sir." Catchbrick bowed to Lucinda, bright eyes curious. "Won't be no trouble—like I said,
we're nearly done."

So saying, he stood back and waved them on into the hall.

Lucinda crossed the threshold into a long and surprisingly
spacious rectangular hall. Half-panelling in warm oak was sur-
mounted by plastered walls, presently bare. A mound draped
in dust covers in the centre of the floor clearly contained a
round table and a large hall stand. Light streamed in from the
large circular fanlight. Stairs, also in oak with an ornately
carved balustrade, led upwards, the half-landing sporting a long
window which, Lucinda suspected, looked out over the rear
gardens. Two corridors flanked the stairs, the left ending in a
green baize door.

"The drawing-room's this way."

Lucinda turned to find Harry standing by a set of handsome
doors, presently set wide; a boy was polishing the panels in-
dustriously.

The drawing-room proved to be of generous proportions,
although on far smaller a scale than at the Hall. It boasted a
deep bow window complete with window seat and a long low
fireplace topped by a wide mantel. The dining-room, now shap-
ing to be an elegant apartment, had, as had the drawing-room,
a large mound of furniture swathed in dust cloths in its midst.
Lucinda couldn't resist lifting one corner of the cloth.

"Some pieces will need to be replaced but most of the furniture seems sound enough.'' Harry's gaze remained on her face.

"Sound enough?'' Lucinda threw back the cover to reveal the heavy top of an old oak sideboard. "It's rather more than that. This is a very fine piece—and someone's had the sense to keep it well-polished.''

"Mrs Simpkins. She's the housekeeper,'' Harry supplied in answer to Lucinda's raised brows. "You'll meet her in a moment.''

Dropping the dustsheet, Lucinda went to one of the pair of long windows, presently propped open, and looked out. The windows gave onto a terrace which ran down the side of the house and disappeared around the corner to run beneath the windows of the parlour, which itself gave off the dining-room, as she next discovered.

Standing before the parlour windows, looking out across the rolling lawns, ringed by flowerbeds, presently a colourful riot of spring and early summer blooms, Lucinda felt a deep sense of certainty, of belonging, as if she was putting down roots where she stood. This, she knew, was a place she could live and grow and blossom.

"These three reception-rooms open one into the other.'' Harry waved at the hinged panels separating the parlour from the dining room "The result's quite large enough to host a hunt ball.''

Lucinda blinked at him. "Indeed?''

His features impassive, Harry nodded and waved her on. "The breakfast parlour's this way.''

So was the morning room. As he led her through the bright, presently empty and echoing rooms, lit by the sunshine streaming in through the diamond-paned windows, Lucinda noted the dry plaster walls waiting to be papered, the woodwork and panelling already polished and gleaming.

All the furniture she saw was old but lovingly polished, warm oak, most of it.

"There's only the decorating left to do,'' Harry informed her as he led her down a short corridor running beside the large room he had described as his study-cum-library. There, the bookshelves had been emptied and polished to within an inch of their lives; piles of tomes stood ready to be returned to their places once the decorating was done. "But the firm I've hired won't be in for a few weeks yet—time enough to make the necessary decisions."

Lucinda eyed him narrowly—but before she could think of any probing comment, she was distracted by what lay beyond the door at the end of the corridor. An elegantly proportioned room, it overlooked the side garden; roses nodded at the wide windows, framing green vistas.

Harry glanced about. "I haven't yet decided what this room should be used for."

Looking around, Lucinda found no pile of shrouded furniture. Instead, her gaze was drawn to new shelves, lining one wall. They were wide and open, just right for stacking ledgers. She glanced about; the windows let in good light, an essential for doing accounts and dealing with correspondence.

Her heart beating in a very odd cadence, Lucinda turned to look at Harry. "Indeed?"

"Hmm." His expression considering, he gestured to the door. "Come—I'll introduce you to the Simpkins."

Suppressing a snort of pure impatience, Lucinda allowed him to steer her back down the corridor and through the baize-covered door. Here she came upon the first evidence of established life. The kitchens were scrupulously clean, the pots gleaming on their hooks on the wall, a modern range residing in the centre of the wide fireplace.

A middle-aged couple were seated at the deal table; they quickly got to their feet, consternation in their faces as they gazed at Lucinda.

"Simpkins here acts as general factotum—keeping an eye on the place generally. His uncle is butler at the Hall. Mrs Babbacombe, Simpkins."

"Ma'am." Simpkins bowed low.

"And this is Mrs Simpkins, cook and housekeeper—without whom the furniture would never have survived."

Mrs Simpkins, a buxom, rosy-cheeked matron of imposing girth, bobbed a curtsy to Lucinda but fixed Harry with a baleful eye. "Aye—and if you had only thought to warn me, Master Harry, I would have had tea and scones ready and waiting."

"As you might guess," Harry put in smoothly, "Mrs Simpkins was once an undernurse at the Hall."

"Aye—and I can remember you in short coats quite clearly, young master." Mrs Simpkins frowned at him. "Now you just take the lady for a stroll and I'll pop a pot on. By the time you come back I'll have your tea laid ready in the garden."

"I wouldn't want to put you to—"

Harry's pained sigh cut across Lucinda's disclaimer. "I hesitate to break it to you, my dear, but Martha Simpkins is a tyrant. It's best to just yield gracefully." So saying, he took her hand and led her towards the door. "I'll just show Mrs Babbacombe the upstairs rooms, Martha."

Lucinda turned her head to throw a smile back at Mrs Simpkins, who beamed delightedly in reply.

The stairs led to a short gallery.

"No family portraits, I'm afraid," Harry said. "Those are all at the Hall."

"Is there one of you?" Lucinda looked up at him.

"Yes—but it's hardly a good likeness. It was done when I was eighteen."

Lucinda raised her brows but, recalling Lady Coleby's words, made no comment.

"This is the master suite." Harry threw open a pair of panelled doors at the end of the gallery. The room beyond was large, half-panelled, the warm patina of wood extending to the surrounds of the bow window and its seat. A carved mantel framed the fireplace, unusually large; a very large structure stood in the centre of the floor, screened by the inevitable dustcovers. Lucinda glanced at it curiously, but obediently turned as Harry, a hand at her back, conducted her through the adjoining dressing-rooms.

"I'm afraid," he said, as they returned to the main chamber, "that Lestershall doesn't run to separate bedrooms for husband

and wife." Lucinda glanced up at him. "Not, of course," he continued imperturbably, "that that should concern you."

Lucinda watched as he leaned a shoulder against the window frame. When he merely returned her expectant look with one of the blandest innocence, she humphed and turned her attention to the large, shrouded mound.

"It's a four-poster," she decided. She crossed to lift a corner of the dustcover and peer under. A dark cave lay before her. With thick, barley-sugar posts, the bed was fully canopied and draped with matching brocades. "It's enormous."

"Indeed." Harry watched her absorption. "And has quite a history, too, if the tales one hears are true."

Lucinda looked up from her study. "What tales?"

"Rumour has it the bed dates from Elizabethan times, as does the house. Apparently, all the brides brought back to the house have used it."

Lucinda wrinkled her nose. "That's hardly surprising." She dropped the covers and dusted her hands.

Harry's lips slowly curved. "Not in itself, perhaps." He pushed away from the window and strolled to where Lucinda stood waiting. "But there are brass rings set into the headboard." His brows rose; his expression turned pensive. "They quite excite the imagination." Taking Lucinda's arm, he turned her towards the door. "I must remember to show them to you sometime."

Lucinda opened her mouth, then abruptly closed it. She allowed him to lead her back into the corridor. She was still considering the brass rings when they reached the end of the hall, having looked in on a set of unremarkable bedchambers along the way.

"These stairs lead to the attics. The nursery is there, as well as the Simpkins's rooms."

The nursery proved to take up one entire side of the commodious space beneath the rafters. The dormer windows were set low, just right for youngsters. The suite comprised five interconnecting rooms.

"Bedrooms for the head nurse and tutor on either end, bedrooms for their charges, male and female and this, of course, is the schoolroom." Harry stood in the centre of the large room and looked around, a certain pride showing in his expression.

Lucinda eyed it consideringly. "These rooms are even larger, relatively speaking, than your bed."

Harry raised his brows. "I had rather thought they would have need to be. I'm planning on having a large family."

Lucinda stared into his clear green eyes—and wondered how he dared. "A large family?" she queried, refusing to retreat in disorder. "Taking after your father in that respect, too?" She held his gaze for an instant longer, then strolled to look out of a window. "Three boys, I assume, is your goal?"

Harry's gaze followed her. "And three girls. To preserve a reasonable balance," he added in reply to Lucinda's surprised glance.

Annoyed at her reaction, and the fluttery feeling that had laid siege to her stomach, Lucinda snorted. And glanced about again. "Even with six, there's room enough to spare."

She had thought that would be the end of that particular conversation but the reprobate teasing her hadn't finished.

"Ah—but I'd thought to leave sufficient space for the odd few who might not come in the correct order, if you take my meaning. Begetting boy or girl is such a random event, after all."

Lucinda stared into impassive green eyes—and longed to ask if he was joking. But there was something in the subtle tension that held him that left the distinct impression he wasn't.

Feeling a quiver—no longer odd but decidedly familiar—ripple through her, Lucinda decided she'd had enough. If he could talk about their children then he could put his mind to the first of the points that came before. She straightened and lifted her head, her gaze holding his.

"Harry—"

He shifted, turning to look out of the window. "Mrs Simpkins has our tea and scones waiting. Come—we can't disappoint her." With an innocent smile, he took Lucinda's arm and turned her towards the door. "It's nearly noon, too—I suspect we should get back immediately after our impromptu feast. We don't want to be late getting on the road this afternoon.''

Lucinda stared at him in disbelief.

Harry smiled. "I know how much you're looking forward to getting back to town—and waltzing in gentlemen's arms.''

Frustration filled Lucinda, so intense it made her giddy. When Harry merely raised his brows, all mild and innocent, she narrowed her eyes and glared.

Harry's lips twitched; he gestured to the door.

Lucinda drew in a deep, steadying breath. If she wasn't a lady...

Setting her teeth against the urge to grind them, she slid her hand into the crook of his arm. Lips set in a thoroughly disapproving, not to say disgruntled line, she allowed him to lead her downstairs.

Chapter Thirteen

"SO—DO YOU have it clear?" Seated behind the desk in his library, Harry drew an unnibbed pen back and forth between his fingers, his gaze, very green, trained on the individual in the chair before him.

Plain brown eyes regarded him from an unremarkable countenance; the man's attire proclaimed him not of the *ton* but his occupation could not be discerned from the drab garments. Phineas Salter could have been anything—almost anyone—which was precisely what made him so successful at his trade.

The ex-Bow Street Runner nodded. "Aye, sir. I'm to check up on the gentlemen—Mr Earle Joliffe and Mr Mortimer Babbacombe—with a view to uncovering any reason they might have to wish a Mrs Lucinda Babbacombe—the said Mortimer's aunt-by-marriage—ill."

"*And* you're to do it without raising a dust." Harry's gaze became acute.

Salter inclined his head. "Naturally, sir. If the gentlemen are up to anything, we wouldn't want to tip them the wink. Not before we're ready."

Harry grimaced. "Quite. But I should also stress that we do not wish, at any time, for Mrs Babbacombe herself to become aware of our suspicions. Or, indeed, that there might be any reason for investigation at all."

Salter frowned. "Without disrespect, sir, do you think that's wise? From what you've told me, these villains aren't above drastic action. Wouldn't it be better if the lady's forewarned?"

"If it were any other lady, one who would be predictably shocked and content thereafter to leave the matter in our hands,

I'd unhesitatingly agree. However, Mrs Babbacombe is not one such.'' Harry studied his newest employee; when he spoke his tone was instructive. "I'd be willing to wager that, if she were to learn of Babbacombe's apparent involvement with her recent adventures, Mrs Babbacombe would order her carriage around and have herself driven to his lodgings, intent on demanding an explanation. Alone."

Salter's expression blanked. "Ah." He blinked. "A bit naïve, is she?"

"No." Harry's tone hardened. "Not particularly. She's merely incapable of recognising her own vulnerability but, conversely, has infinite confidence in her ability to prevail." The planes of his face shifted, his expression now mirroring his tone. "In this case, I would rather not have her put it to the test."

"No, indeed." Salter nodded. "From what little I've heard tell, this Joliffe's not the sort for a lady to tangle with."

"Precisely." Harry rose; Salter rose, too. The ex-Runner was a stocky man, broad and heavy. Harry nodded. "Report back to me as soon as you have any word."

"I will that, sir. You may depend on me."

Harry shook Salter's hand. Dawlish, who, at Harry's intimation, had silently witnessed the interview, straightened from his position by the door and showed Salter out. Turning to the windows, Harry stood idly flicking the pen between his fingers, gazing unseeing at the courtyard beyond.

Salter was well-known to the intimates of Jackson's saloon and Cribb's parlour. A boxer of some skill, he was one of the few not of the *ton* with a ready entrée to those *ton*nish precincts. But it was his other skills that had led Harry to call him in. Salter's fame as a Runner had been considerable but clouded; the magistrates had not approved of his habit of, quite literally, using thieves to catch thieves. His successes had not ameliorated their disapproval and he had parted company from the London constabulary by mutual accord. Since then, however, he had established a reputation among certain of the *ton*'s gentlemen as a reliable man whenever matters of questionable, possibly illegal, behaviour needed to be investigated with absolute discretion.

Such a matter, in Harry's opinion, was Mortimer Babbacombe's apparent interest in Lucinda's well-being.

He would have handled the matter himself but was at a loss to understand Mortimer's motives. He could hardly let the matter rest and, given his conviction that it was linked with the incident on the Newmarket road, he had opted for caution, to whit, the discretion and skill for which Salter was renown.

"Well, then!" Dawlish returned and shut the door. "A fine broiling, altogether." He slanted a glance at Harry. "You want me to keep an eye on her?"

Slowly, Harry raised his brows. "It's an idea." He paused, then asked, "How do you think her coachman—Joshua, isn't it?—would take the news?"

"Right concerned, he'd be."

Harry's eyes narrowed. "And her maid, the redoubtable Agatha?"

"Even more so, unless I miss my guess. Right protective, she is—after you took them away from Asterley and organised to cover the lady's tracks, she's revised her opinion of you."

Harry's lips twitched. "Good. Then recruit her as well. I have a feeling we should keep as many eyes on Mrs Babbacombe as possible—just in case."

"Aye—no sense in taking any risks." Dawlish headed for the door. "Not after all your hard work."

Harry's brows flew up. He turned—but Dawlish had escaped.

Hard work? Harry's lips firmed into a line. His expression resigned, he turned back to the greenery outside. The truly hard part was yet to come but he had charted his course and was determined to stick to it.

When next he proposed to his siren, he wanted no arguments about love.

"Oh!" Dawlish's head popped back around the door. "Just remembered—it's Lady Mickleham's tonight. Want me to organise the carriages and all when I see Joshua?"

Harry nodded. The skies outside were a beautiful blue. "Before you go, have the greys put to."

"You going for a drive?"

"Yes." Harry's expression turned grim. "In the Park."

Fergus opened his aunt's door to him fifteen minutes later. Harry handed him his gloves and shrugged off his greatcoat. "I assume my aunt is resting?"

"Indeed, sir. She's been laid down this hour and past."

"I won't disturb her—it's Mrs Babbacombe I wish to see."

"Ah." Fergus blinked, his expression blanking. "I fear Mrs Babbacombe is engaged, sir."

Harry slowly turned his head until his gaze rested on Fergus's impassive countenance. "Indeed?"

He waited; Fergus, to his relief, deigned to answer his unvoiced question without insisting on an embarrassing prompt.

"She's in the back parlour—her office—with a Mr Mabberly. A well-spoken young gentleman—he's her agent, I understand."

"I see." Harry hesitated, then, quite sure Fergus understood only too well, dismissed him with a nod. "No need to announce me." With that, he mounted the stairs, reining in his impatience enough to make the ascent at least appear idle. But when he gained the upper corridor, his strides lengthened. He paused with his hand on the parlour doorknob; he could hear muted voices within.

His expression distinctly hard, he opened the door.

Lucinda was seated on the *chaise,* an open ledger on her lap. She looked up—and broke off in mid-sentence to stare at him.

A youngish gentleman, precise and soberly dressed, was hovering by her shoulder, leaning over to look at the figures to which she was pointing.

"I wasn't expecting you," Lucinda said, shaking her wits into order.

"Good afternoon," Harry replied.

"Indeed." Lucinda's glance held a definite warning. "I believe I've mentioned Mr Mabberly to you—he's my agent. He assists me with the inns. Mr Mabberly—Mr Lester."

Mr Mabberly somewhat hesitantly put out his hand. Harry regarded it for an instant, then shook it briefly. And immediately turned to Lucinda. "Will you be long?"

Lucinda looked him in the eye. "At least another half-hour."

Mr Mabberly shifted, casting a nervous glance from Lucinda to Harry and back again. "Er...perhaps—"

"We have yet to do the Edinburgh accounts," Lucinda declared, shutting the heavy ledger and lifting it from her lap. Mr Mabberly hastened to relieve her of it. "It's that book there—the third one." As Mr Mabberly hurried across the room to retrieve the required tome, Lucinda raised limpid eyes to Harry's face. "Perhaps, Mr Lester—"

"I'll wait." Harry turned, walked two paces to the nearest chair, and sat down.

Lucinda watched him impassively—she didn't dare smile. Then Anthony Mabberly was back and she turned her attention to her three Edinburgh inns.

As Lucinda checked figures and tallies and rates, comparing the present quarter with the last and that of the year before, Harry studied Mr Mabberly. Within five minutes, he had seen enough to reassure him; Mr Mabberly might regard his employer as something of a goddess, but Harry was left with the distinct impression that his admiration was occasioned more by her business acumen than by her person. Indeed, inside of ten minutes, he was ready to swear that Mr Mabberly's regard was entirely intellectual.

Relaxing, Harry stretched out his legs—and allowed his gaze to settle on his principal concern.

Lucinda sensed the easing of his tension—not a difficult feat as it had reached her in waves—with a measure of relief. If he refused to accept she would need to deal with such as Anthony Mabberly, that regardless of all else she had a business to run, then they would face serious hurdles all too soon. But all appeared serene. While waiting for Mr Mabberly to fetch the last ledger, she glanced at Harry to find him regarding her with nothing more unnerving than very definite boredom in his eyes.

He lifted a brow at her but offered no word.

Lucinda turned back to her work—and quickly completed it.

Mr Mabberly did not dally but neither did he run. He very correctly took his leave of Lucinda, then bowed punctiliously to Harry before departing, promising to carry out Lucinda's commissions and report as usual the next week.

"Humph!" Harry remained standing, watching the door close behind Mabberly.

After one glance at his face, Lucinda remarked, "I do hope you're not about to tell me there is any impropriety in my seeing my agent alone?"

Harry bit his tongue; he swung to face her, his gaze distinctly cool. As he watched Lucinda's gaze shifted, going past him.

"After all," she continued, "he could hardly be considered a danger."

Harry followed her gaze to the daybed before the windows. He looked back at her, and surprised an expression of uncertainty, mixed with a readily identifiable longing. They were, once again, very much alone; his inclinations, he knew, matched hers. Harry cleared his throat. "I came to persuade you to a drive in the Park."

"The Park?" Surprised, Lucinda looked up at him. Em had told her Harry rarely drove in the Park during the hours of the fashionable promenades. "Why?"

"Why?" Harry looked down at her, his expression momentarily blank. Then he frowned. "What sort of a ridiculous question is that?" When Lucinda's gaze turned suspicious, he waved a languid hand. "I merely thought you might be bored and could do with the fresh air. Lady Mickleham's balls are notoriously crowded."

"Oh." Lucinda slowly rose, her eyes searching his face but with no success. "Perhaps a drive would be a good idea."

"Indubitably." Harry waved her to the door. "I'll wait downstairs while you get your coat and bonnet."

Ten minutes later, Lucinda allowed him to lift her into his curricle, still not at all sure she understood. But he was here—she could see no reason to deny herself his company. Reflecting that after yesterday, when he had driven her all the way from

Lester Hall to Audley Street in his curricle, she should have had a surfeit of his dry comments, she blithely settled her skirts and looked forward to a few more.

He didn't disappoint her.

As they passed through the heavy wrought-iron gates and on into the Park, bowling along the shaded drive, Harry slanted her a glance. "I regret, my dear, that as my horses are very fresh, we won't be stopping to chat—you'll have to make do with waves and smiling glances."

Engaged in looking about her, Lucinda raised her brows. "Indeed? But if we aren't to chat, why are we here?"

"To see and be seen, of course." Again Harry diverted his attention from his leader, who was indeed very skittish, to glance her way. "That, I have always understood, is the purpose of the fashionable promenades."

"Ah." Lucinda smiled sunnily back at him, not the least perturbed. She was quite content to sit beside him in the sun and watch him tool about the gravel drives, long fingers managing the reins.

He met her gaze, then looked back at his horses. Still smiling, Lucinda looked ahead to where the drive was lined by the barouches and landaus of the matrons of the *ton*. The afternoon was well advanced; there were many who had reached the Park before them. Harry was forced to rein in his horses as the traffic increased, curricles and phaetons of all descriptions wending their way between the carriages drawn up by the verge. Lady Sefton, holding court in her barouche, waved and nodded; Lucinda noticed that she appeared somewhat startled.

Lady Somercote and Mrs Wyncham likewise greeted her, then Countess Lieven favoured them with a long, dark-eyed stare before inclining her head graciously.

Harry humphed. "She's so stiff-necked I keep waiting to hear the crack."

Lucinda smothered a giggle as, rounding the next curve, they came upon Princess Esterhazy. The Princess's large eyes opened wide, then she beamed and nodded delightedly.

Lucinda smiled back; inwardly, she frowned. After a moment, she asked, "Do you frequently drive ladies in the Park?"

Harry clicked his reins; the curricle shot through a gap between a swan-necked phaeton and another curricle, leaving both the other owners gasping. "Not recently."

Lucinda narrowed her eyes. "*How* recently?"

Harry merely shrugged, his gaze fixed on his horses' ears.

Lucinda regarded him closely. When he offered not a word, she ventured, "Not since Lady Coleby?"

He looked at her then, his green glance filled with dire warning, his lips a severe line. Then he looked back at his horses. After a moment, he said, his tone exceedingly grudging, "She was Millicent Pane then."

Harry's memory flitted back through the years; "Millicent Lester" was what he'd been thinking then. His lips twisted wrily; he should have noticed that didn't sound right. He glanced down at the woman beside him, in blue, as usual, her dark hair framing her pale face in soft curls, the whole enchanting picture framed by the rim of her modish bonnet. "Lucinda Lester" had a certain balance, a certain ring.

His lips curved but, her gaze abstracted, she didn't see. She was, he noted, looking decidedly pensive.

The drive ahead cleared as they left the area favoured by the *ton*. Harry reined in and joined the line of carriages waiting to turn back. "Once more through the gauntlet, then I'll take you home."

Lucinda shot him a puzzled glance but said nothing, straightening and summoning a smile as they headed back into the fray.

This time, heading in the opposite direction, they saw different faces—many, Lucinda noted, looked surprised. But they were constantly moving; she got no chance to analyse the reactions the sight of them seemed to be provoking. Lady Jersey's reaction, however, needed no analysis.

Her ladyship was in her barouche, languidly draped over the cushions, when her gimlet gaze fell on Harry's curricle, approaching at a sedate walk. She promptly sat bolt upright.

"Merciful heavens!" she declared, her strident tones dramatic. "I never thought to see the day!"

Harry shot her a malevolent glance but deigned to incline his head. "I believe you are acquainted with Mrs Babbacombe?"

"Indeed!" Lady Jersey waved a hand at Lucinda. "I'll catch up with you next Wednesday, my dear."

Her ladyship's glance promised she would. Lucinda kept her smile gracious but was relieved when they passed on.

She slanted a glance at Harry to discover his face set in uncompromising lines. As soon as the traffic thinned, he clicked the reins.

"That was a very short drive," Lucinda murmured as the gates of the Park hove in sight.

"Short, perhaps, but quite long enough for our purposes."

The words were clipped, his accents unencouraging. Lucinda's inner frown deepened. "Our purposes". What, precisely, were they?

SHE WAS STILL WONDERING WHEN, gowned in hyacinth-blue watered silk, she descended the stairs that evening, ready for Lady Mickleham's ball. Being in constant expectation of an offer was slowly sapping her patience; there was no doubt in her mind that Harry intended making her another, but the when and the why of his reticence were matters that increasingly worried her. She descended most of the stairs in an abstracted daze, glancing up only as she neared their foot. To have her gaze lock with one of clear green.

Eyes widening, Lucinda blinked. "What are you doing here?"

Her astonished gaze took in his severely, almost austerely cut evening clothes, black and stark white as always. The gold acorn pin in his cravat winked wickedly.

She watched his lips twist in a wry grimace.

"I'm here," Harry informed her, his accents severely restrained, "to escort you—and Em and Heather—to Lady Mickleham's ball.'' He strolled to the end of the stairs and held out a commanding hand.

Lucinda looked at it, a light blush staining her cheeks. She was glad there were no servants about to witness this exchange. As her fingers, of their own volition, slid into his, she raised her eyes to his face. "I wasn't aware you considered it necessary to escort us to such affairs."

His features remained impassive, his eyes hooded, as he drew her down to stand before him.

The door at the end of the hall swung open; Agatha strode through, Lucinda's evening cloak over her arm. She checked when she saw Harry, then merely nodded at him, severe as ever but with less hostility than was her wont, and came on. Harry held out a hand; Agatha readily surrendered the cloak, then turned on her heel and retraced her steps.

Lucinda turned; Harry placed the velvet cloak about her shoulders. Raising her head, she met his gaze in the mirror on the wall. In the corridor above a door opened and shut; Heather's voice drifted down, calling to Em.

If she clung to polite phrases, he would fence and win. Lucinda drew in a quick breath. "Why?"

For a moment, his gaze remained on hers, then dropped to her throat. She saw his lips quirk, in smile or grimace she couldn't tell.

"Circumstances," he began, his voice low, "have changed." He raised his head and his eyes met hers. His brows rose, faintly challenging. "Haven't they?"

Lucinda stared into his eyes and said nothing at all; she wasn't about to gainsay him. But had things truly changed? She was no longer so sure of that.

Heather came skipping down the stairs, followed, more circumspectly, by Em. Amid the bustle of finding cloaks and gloves, Lucinda had no further chance to question Harry's new tack. The short trip to Mickleham House in Berkeley Square was filled with Heather's bright prattle and Em's reminiscences. Lucinda remained silent; Harry sat in the shadows opposite, equally quiet.

The ordeal of the crowded stairway left no opportunity for private converse. Lucinda smiled and nodded to those about them, aware of the curious glances thrown their escort. For his part, Harry remained impassively urbane but as they neared their host and hostess, he bent his head to murmur, very softly, in her ear, "I'll take the supper waltz—and I'll escort you into supper."

Her lips setting, Lucinda shot him a speaking glance. *Take* the supper waltz, indeed! She inwardly humphed, then turned to greet Lady Mickleham.

As Harry had foretold, her ladyship's rooms were full to overflowing.

"This is ridiculous," Lucinda muttered as they forged a path towards one side of the ballroom, hoping to find a *chaise* for Em.

"It's always this bad at the end of the Season," Em returned. "As if building to a frenzy before summer sends everyone home to the country."

Lucinda stifled a sigh as thoughts of the country—the grotto by the Lester Hall lake, the peace and serenity of Lestershall Manor—returned to her.

"Well—there's only a few weeks left to go," put in Heather. "So I suppose we should make the most of them." She glanced at Lucinda. "Have you decided where we'll spend the summer?"

Lucinda blinked. "Ah…"

"I dare say your stepmother feels such decisions are a trifle premature," Harry drawled.

Heather's lips formed an innocent "O"—she seemed perfectly content to accept the uninformative statement.

Lucinda let out a slow breath.

Em found a place on a *chaise* with Lady Sherringbourne; the two ladies promptly fell to exchanging revelations on the alliances forged that year.

Lucinda turned—to find herself all but engulfed by her court, who, as she was rapidly informed, had been awaiting her reappearance with bated breath.

"A whole week you've been away, m'dear. Quite desolate, we've been." Mr Amberly smiled benignly.

"Not that I can't understand it," Mr Satterly remarked. "The crushes are becoming far too real for my liking. Drive anyone away." His gaze rose to Harry's face, his expression utterly bland. "Don't you think so, Lester?"

"Indeed," Harry replied, casting a steely glance about them. With him on one side and Ruthven, equally large, on the other, Lucinda was at least assured of space enough to breathe. The rest of her court gathered before them, creating an enclosure of relative sanity for which, he was sure, they were all rendering silent thanks.

"And where did you go to recoup, my dear Mrs Babbacombe? The country or the seaside?"

It was, predictably, Lord Ruthven who voiced the inevitable question. He smiled encouragingly down at Lucinda; she sensed the subtle teasing behind his smile.

"The country," she vouchsafed. Then, prompted by some inner devil, released, she knew, by the repressive presence on her left, she added, "My stepdaughter and I accompanied Lady Hallows on a visit to Lester Hall."

Ruthven blinked his eyes wide. "Lester Hall?" Slowly, he lifted his gaze to Harry's face. Entirely straightfaced, his lordship raised his brows. "Noticed you were absent from town this week, Harry. Took some time from the frantic whirl to recuperate?"

"Naturally," Harry drawled, clinging to his usual imperturbability, "I escorted my aunt and her guests on their visit."

"Oh, naturally," Ruthven agreed. He turned to Lucinda. "Did Harry show you the grotto by the lake?"

Lucinda regarded his lordship with as bland an expression as she could manage. "Indeed—and the folly on the hill. The views were quite lovely."

"The views?" Lord Ruthven looked stunned. "Ah, yes. The views."

Harry ground his teeth but was too wise to react—at least

not verbally. But his glance promised retribution—only Ruthven, one of his oldest friends, was prepared to ignore it.

To Lucinda's relief, his lordship's teasing, although in no way openly indelicate, was cut short by the musicians. It took a moment or two before it became clear that Lady Mickleham had decided to open her ball with a waltz.

The realisation brought the usual clamour of offers. Lucinda smiled graciously—and hesitated. The room was very crowded, the dance floor would be worse. In cotillion or quadrille, with sets and steps fixed, demanding a certain space, there was little chance of unexpected intimacy. But the waltz? In such cramped conditions?

The thought brought in its wake a certainty that her circumstances had indeed changed. She did not wish to waltz close with anyone but Harry. Her senses reached for him; he was standing, very stiff, intensely contained, beside her.

Harry saw her glance up, unconscious appeal in her eyes. His reaction was immediate and quite impossible to restrain. His hand closed over hers; he lifted it to place her fingers on his sleeve. "My waltz, I believe, my dear."

Relief flooded Lucinda; she remembered to incline her head, and smile fleetingly at her court as Harry led her from their midst.

On the ballroom floor, she relaxed into Harry's arms, allowing him to draw her close with no attempt at dissimulation. She glanced up at him as they started to slowly twirl; his eyes met hers, his expression still aloof but somehow softer. Their gazes held; they communicated without words as they slowly revolved down the room.

Then Lucinda lowered her lashes; Harry's arm tightened about her.

As she had foreseen, the floor was crowded, the dancers cramped. Harry kept her safe within the circle of his arms; she was very aware that if anything threatened, she had only to step closer and he would protect her. His hard body was no threat—she had never seen it as such. He was her guardian in the oldest sense of the word—he to whom she had entrusted her life.

The waltz ended too soon; Lucinda blinked as Harry's arms fell from her. Reluctantly, she stepped away and placed her hand on his arm, then let him steer her back through the throng.

Harry glanced at her face, his features impassive, concern in his eyes. As they neared her court, he leaned closer to murmur, "If you don't care to waltz, simply plead fatigue." Lucinda glanced up at him; he felt his lips twist. "It's the latest fashionable ploy."

She nodded—and straightened her shoulders as they rejoined her court.

Lucinda was inexpressibly grateful for that piece of advice— her supposed fatigue was accepted without a blink; as the evening wore on, she began to suspect that her earnest court were no more enamoured of dancing in such cramped surrounds than she.

Immovable, repressively silent, Harry remained by her side throughout the long evening. Lucinda greeted the supper waltz with a certain measure of relief. "I understand Mr Amberly, Mr Satterly and Lord Ruthven are particular friends of yours?"

Harry glanced fleetingly down at her. "Of a sorts," he reluctantly conceded.

"I would never have guessed." Lucinda met his sharp glance with wide eyes. Harry studied her innocent expression, then humphed and drew her closer.

At the end of the waltz, he led her directly to the supper room. Before she could gather her wits, Lucinda found herself installed at a secluded table for two, shaded from much of the room by two potted palms. A glass of champagne and a plate piled high with delicacies appeared before her; Harry lounged gracefully in the seat opposite.

His eyes on hers, he took a bite of a lobster patty. "Did you notice Lady Waldron's wig?"

Lucinda giggled. "It nearly fell off." She took a sip of champagne, her eyes sparkling. "Mr Anstey had to catch it and jiggle it back into place."

To Lucinda's delight, Harry spent the entire half-hour regaling her with anecdotes, *on dits* and the occasional dry observation. It was the first time she had had him to herself in such a mood; she gave herself up to enjoying the interlude.

Only when it ended and he led her back to the ballroom did it occur to her to wonder what had brought it on.

Or, more specifically, why he had put himself out to so captivate her.

"Still here, Ruthven?" Harry's drawl hauled her back to the present. He was eyeing his friend with a certain, challenging gleam in his eye. "Nothing else here to interest you?"

"Nothing, I fear." Lord Ruthven put his hand over his heart and quizzed Lucinda. "Nothing as compares with the joys of conversing with Mrs Babbacombe."

Lucinda had to laugh. Harry, of course, did not. His drawl very much in evidence, he took charge of the conversation. As the languid, distinctly bored accents fell on her ear, Lucinda realised that he never, normally, drawled at her. Nor Em. When he spoke to them, his accents were clipped. Apparently, he reserved the fashionable affectation for those he kept at a distance.

With Harry holding the reins, the conversation predictably remained in stultifyingly correct vein. Lucinda, smothering a yawn, considered an option that might, conceivably, assist her cause while at the same time rescuing her poor court.

"It's getting rather warm, don't you find it so?" she murmured, her hand heavy on Harry's arm.

He glanced down at her, then lifted his brows. "Indeed. I suspect it's time we left."

As he lifted his head to locate Em and Heather, Lucinda allowed herself one, very small, very frustrated snort. She had intended him to take her onto the terrace. Peering through the crowd, she saw Em deep in discussion with a dowager; Heather was engaged with a party of her friends. "Ah...perhaps I could manage for another half-hour if I had a glass of water?"

Mr Satterly immediately offered to procure one and ploughed into the crowd.

Harry looked down at her, a faint question in his eyes. "Are you sure?"

Lucinda's smile was weak. "Positive."

He continued to behave with dogged correctness—which, Lucinda belatedly realised, as the crowds gradually thinned and she became aware of the curious, speculative glances cast their way, was not, in his case, the same as behaving circumspectly.

The observation brought a frown to her eyes.

It had deepened by the time they were safely in Em's carriage, rolling home through the now quiet streets. From her position opposite, Lucinda studied Harry's face, lit by the moonlight and the intermittent flares of the streetlamps.

His eyes were closed, sealed away behind their heavy lids. His features were not so much relaxed as wiped clean of expression, his lips compressed into a firm, straight line. Seen thus, it was a face that kept its secrets, the face of a man who was essentially private, who revealed his emotions rarely if ever.

Lucinda felt her heart catch; a dull ache blossomed within.

The *ton* was his milieu—he knew every nuance of behaviour, how every little gesture would be interpreted. He was at home here, in the crowded ballrooms, as she was not. As at Lester Hall, here, he was in control.

Lucinda shifted in her seat. Propping her chin in her palm, she stared at the sleeping houses, a frown drawing down her fine brows.

Free of her scrutiny, Harry opened his eyes. He studied her profile, clear in the moonlight. His lips curved in the slightest of smiles. Pressing his head back against the squabs, he closed his eyes.

AT THAT MOMENT, in Mortimer Babbacombe's lodgings in Great Portland Street, a meeting was getting underway.

"Well—did you learn anything to the point?" Joliffe, no longer the nattily attired gentleman who had first befriended Mortimer, snarled the question the instant Brawn ambled through the door. Heavy-eyed from lack of sleep, his colour high from the liquor he had consumed to calm his nerves, Joliffe fixed his most junior accomplice with a dangerous stare.

Brawn was too young to heed it. Dropping into a chair at the parlour table about which Joliffe, Mortimer and Scrugthorpe were already seated, he grinned. "Aye—I learned a bit. Chatted up the young maid—no mor'n a bit of a thing. She told me a few things before that groom—yeller-haired lot—came and fetched her orf. Heard him giving her what for "bout talking to strangers, so I don't think I'll get any more by that road." Brawn grinned. "Pity—wouldn't ha' minded—"

"Damn you—get on!" Joliffe roared, his fist connecting with the table with enough force to set the tankards jumping. *"What the devil happened?"*

Brawn shot him a look more puzzled than frightened. "Well—the lady did go orf to the country that day—just like you'd planned. But seemingly she went to some other house— a place called Lester Hall. The whole household went up the next day—the maid said as she thought it'd been planned."

"Damn!" Joliffe swilled back a mouthful of porter. "No wonder I couldn't get any of the crew who'd gone up to Asterley to say they'd seen her. I thought they must've been practising discretion—but the damned woman hadn't gone!"

"Seems not." Brawn shrugged. "So what now?"

"Now we stop playing and kidnap her." Scrugthorpe lifted his face from his tankard. "Like I said from the first. It's the only way of being sure—all this trying to get the rakes to do our job for us has got us precisely *nowhere.*" He spat the last word, his contempt bordering on the open.

Joliffe held his eye; eventually, Scrugthorpe looked back at his mug.

"That's what I say, anyway," Scrugthorpe mumbled as he took another swallow.

"Hmm." Joliffe grimaced. "I'm beginning to agree with you. It looks like we'll have to take an active hand ourselves."

"But...I thought..." Mortimer's first contribution to the conversation died away as both Joliffe and Scrugthorpe turned to look at him.

"Ye-es?" Joliffe prompted.

Mortimer's colour rose. He put a finger to his cravat, tugging at the floppy folds. "It's just that…well—if we do do anything direct—well—won't she know?"

Joliffe's lip curled. "Of *course* she will—but that's not to say she'll be in any hurry to denounce us—not after Scrugthorpe here has his revenge."

"Aye." Scrugthorpe's black eyes gleamed. "Jus' leave her to me. I'll make sure she ain't in no hurry to talk about it." He nodded and went back to his beer.

Mortimer regarded him with mounting horror. He opened his mouth, then caught Joliffe's eye. He visibly shrank, but muttered, "There must be another way."

"Very likely." Joliffe drained his tankard and reached for the jug. "But we don't have time for any more convoluted schemes."

"Time?" Mortimer looked confused.

"Yes, *time!*" Snarling, Joliffe turned on Mortimer. Mortimer paled, his eyes starting like a frightened rabbit's. With an effort, Joliffe reined in his temper. He smiled, all teeth. "But don't you worry your head over it. Just leave everything to Scrugthorpe and me. You do your bit when asked—and everything will work out just fine."

"Aye." Brawn unexpectedly chipped in. "I was thinking as you'd better get a different plan. From what the maid told me, seems like the lady's in expectation of 'receivin' an offer,' as they says. I don't know as I understand these things rightly, but seems pretty useless making her out to be a whore if she's going to marry a swell."

"*What?*" Joliffe's exclamation had all of them starting. They stared at their leader as he stared—in total stupefication—at Brawn. "She's about to *marry?*"

Warily, Brawn nodded. "So the maid said."

"*Whom?*"

"Some swell name of Lester."

"Harry Lester?" Joliffe calmed. Frowning heavily, he eyed

Brawn. "You sure this maid got it right? Harry Lester's not the marrying kind."

Brawn shrugged. "Wouldn't know about that." After a moment, he added, "The girl said as this Lester chap had called this afternoon to take the lady for a drive in the Park."

Joliffe stared at Brawn, all his certainties fading. "The Park," he repeated dully.

Brawn merely nodded and cautiously sipped his beer.

When Joliffe next spoke, his voice was hoarse. "We've got to move soon."

"Soon?" Scrugthorpe looked up. "How soon?"

"Before she's married—preferably before she even accepts an offer. We don't need any legal complications."

Mortimer was frowning. "Complications?"

"Yes, damn you!" Joliffe struggled to mute his snarl. "If the damned woman marries, the guardianship of her stepdaughter passes into her husband's hands. If Harry Lester takes the reins, we can forget getting a farthing out of your lovely cousin's estate."

Mortimer's eyes widened. "Oh."

"Yes—oh! And while we're on the subject, I've a little news for you—just to strengthen your backbone." Joliffe fixed his eyes on Mortimer's wan countenance. "You owe me five thousand on a note of hand. I passed that vowel on, with one of my own, to a man who charges interest by the day. Together, we now owe him a cool twenty thousand, Mortimer—and if we don't pay up soon, he's going to take every pound out of our hides." He paused, then leaned forward to ask, "Is that clear enough for you, Mortimer?"

His face a deathly white, his eyes round and starting, Mortimer was so petrified he could not even nod.

"Well, then!" Scrugthorpe pushed his empty tankard away. "Seems like we'd best make some plans."

Joliffe had sobered dramatically. He tapped the tabletop with one fingernail. "We'll need information on her movements." He looked at Brawn but the boy shook his head.

768 AN UNWILLING CONQUEST

"No good. The maid won't talk to me again, not after the roasting that groom gave her. And there's no one else."

Joliffe's eyes narrowed. "What about the other women?"

Brawn's snort was eloquent. "There's a few o'them all right—but they're all as sour as green grapes. Take even you till next year to chat 'em up—and they'd likely refuse to talk even then."

"Damn!" Joliffe absentmindedly took a sip of his porter. "All right." He set the tankard down with a snap. "If that's the only way then that's the way we'll do it."

"How's that?" Scrugthorpe asked.

"We watch her—all the time, day and night. We make our arrangements and keep all in readiness to grab her the instant fate gives us a chance."

Scrugthorpe nodded. "Right. But how're we going to go about it?"

Joliffe sent an intimidating glance at Mortimer.

Mortimer swallowed and shrank in his chair.

With a contemptuous snort, Joliffe turned back to Scrugthorpe. "Just listen."

Chapter Fourteen

FIVE NIGHTS LATER, Mortimer Babbacombe stood in the shadows of a doorway in King Street and watched his aunt-by-marriage climb the shallow steps to Almack's unprepossessing entrance.

"Well." Heaving a sigh—of relief or disappointment he was not quite sure—he turned to his companion. "She's gone in—no point in watching further."

"Oh, yes, there is." The words came in a cold hiss. In the past five days, Joliffe's polite veneer had peeled from him. "You're going to go in there, Mortimer, and keep a careful eye on your aunt. I want to know everything—who she dances with, who brings her lemonade—*everything!*" Joliffe's piercing gaze swung to fix on Mortimer's face. "Is that clear?"

Mortimer hugged the doorframe, his relief rapidly fading. Glowering glumly, he nodded. "Can't think what good it'll do," he grumbled.

"Don't think, Mortimer—just do as I bid you." In the shadows, Joliffe studied Mortimer's face, plain and round, the face of a man easily led—and, as was often the case with such, prone to unhelpful stubbornness. Joliffe's lip curled. "Do try to recapture a little of your earlier enthusiasm, Mortimer. Remember—your uncle overlooking your claim to be your cousin's guardian and appointing a young woman like your aunt instead is an insult to your manhood."

Mortimer shifted, pulling at his fleshy lower lip. "Yes, it is."

"Indeed. Who is Lucinda Babbacombe, anyway, other than a pretty face smart enough to take your uncle in?"

"Quite true." Mortimer nodded. "And, mind, it's not as if I've any bone to pick with her—but anyone would have to admit it was dashed unfair of Uncle Charles to leave all the ready to her—and just the useless land to me."

Joliffe smiled into the night. "Quite. You're merely seeking redress for the unfair actions of your uncle. Remember that, Mortimer." He clapped Mortimer on the shoulder and waved towards Almack's. "I'll wait at your lodgings for your news."

Mortimer nodded. Straightening his rounded shoulders, he headed for the sacred portal.

Deep within the hallowed halls, Lucinda nodded and smiled, responding to the chatter with confident ease while her mind trod an endless trail of conjecture and fact. Harry had driven her in the Park on the past five afternoons, albeit briefly. He had appeared every evening, unheralded, simply there, waiting when she descended the stairs to escort them to the balls and parties, remaining by her side throughout but saying not a word as to his purpose.

She had gone beyond impatience, even beyond chagrin—she was now in the grip of a deadening sense of the inevitable.

Lucinda summoned a smile and gave her hand to Mr Drumcott, a not-so-young gentleman who had recently become betrothed to a young lady in her first Season.

"I beg you'll do me the honour of dancing this quadrille with my poor self, Mrs Babbacombe."

Lucinda acquiesced with a smile but as they took their places she caught herself scanning the crowd—and inwardly sighed. She should, of course, be glad Harry had not arrived this evening to escort them here—that, she was convinced, would have been the last straw.

That he intended making her his bride was patently clear—his likely motive in underscoring that fact publicly was what was dragging her heart down. The memory of his first proposal—and her refusal—haunted her. She hadn't known, then, of Lady Coleby and her earlier rejection of Harry's love. Her own refusal had been driven by the simple belief that he loved her and would, if pushed, acknowledge that love. To hear the words on his lips was something she craved, something she needed. But not, she was increasingly certain, something Harry needed.

She couldn't rid herself of the idea that he was painting her into a corner, that his present behaviour was designed to render a second rejection impossible. If, after all his studied performances, she refused him again, she would be labelled cruel-hearted, or, more likely, as Sim would put it, "dicked in the nob".

Lucinda grimaced—and had to hurriedly cover the expression with a smile. As they embarked on the final figures of the quadrille, Mr Drumcott blinked at her in concern; she forced another smile—a travesty considering her true state. If Harry kept on as he was, when next he proposed, she would have to accept him, regardless of whether he offered his heart along with his hand.

The quadrille ended; Lucinda sank into the final, elaborate curtsy. Rising, she straightened her shoulders and determinedly thanked Mr Drumcott. She was not, she told herself, going to dwell on Harry's motives any longer. There must be some other explanation—if only she could think what it was.

At that precise moment, the object of her thoughts sat at the desk in his library attired in long-tailed black evening coat and black knee-breeches, garments he considered outmoded in the extreme.

"What have you learned?" Harry leaned both arms on the blotter and pinned Salter with a steady green gaze.

"Enough to make my nose quiver." Salter settled himself in the chair before the desk. Dawlish, who had shown him in, closed the door; folding his arms, he leaned back against it. Salter pulled out a notebook. "First—this Joliffe chap is more of a bad egg than I'd thought. A real sharp—specialises in 'befriending' flats, preferably those who come fresh on the town, gullible and usually young, though, these days, as he's no spring chicken himself, his victims also tend to be older. Quite a history—but nothing, ever, that could be made to stick. Lately, however, quite aside from his usual activities, Joliffe's taken to deep play—and not in the hells either. Word has it he's heavily in debt—not to his opponents—he's paid them off—but the total sum amounts to a fortune. All evidence points to Joliffe being in the clutches of a real bloodsucker—a certain individual who works out of the docks. Don't have any information on him except that he's not one to keep dangling too long. A mistake that often turns fatal, if you take my meaning.''

He lifted his gaze to Harry's face; his expression grim, Harry nodded.

''Right then—next up is Mortimer Babbacombe. A hopeless case—if Joliffe hadn't picked him up one of the other Captain Sharps would have. Born a flat. Joliffe took him under his wing and underwrote his losses—that's the usual way these things start. Then, when the flat gets his hands on whatever loot is coming his way, the sharps take the major cut. So when Mortimer came into his inheritance, Joliffe was sitting on his coattails. From then, however, things went wrong.''

Salter consulted his notebook. ''Like Mrs Babbacombe told you, it seems Mortimer had no real understanding of his inheritance—but Charles Babbacombe had paid off his debts annually, to the tune of three thousand at the last. Seems certain Mortimer assumed the money came from his uncle's estate and the estate was therefore worth much more than it is. My people checked—the place can't make much more than expenses. It's apparently common knowledge up that way that Charles Babbacombe's money came from Babbacombe and Company.''

Shutting his book, Salter grimaced. ''That's all right and tight—and a nasty surprise it must have been for Joliffe. But what I can't see is why he's gone after Mrs Babbacombe—knocking her on the head isn't going to benefit them. Joliffe's more than experienced enough to work that out—some old aunt of hers is her nearest kin. Yet they're keeping constant watch on Mrs Babbacombe—and not as if they've got anything cordial on their minds.''

Harry stiffened. ''They're watching her?''

''And my people are watching them. Very closely.''

Harry relaxed. A little. He frowned. ''We're missing something.''

''Precisely my thought.'' Salter shook his head. ''Operators like Joliffe don't make too many mistakes—after his first disappointment with Mortimer, he wouldn't have hung around unless there's a chance of some really rich pickings in the wind.''

''There's money all right,'' Harry mused. ''But it's in the business. As you know, Charles Babbacombe willed that to his widow and his daughter.''

Salter frowned. ''Ah, yes—this daughter. A young chit, barely seventeen.'' His frown deepened. ''From all I've seen, Mrs Babbacombe's no easy mark—why pick on her rather than the daughter?''

Harry blinked, somewhat owlishly, at Salter. ''Heather,'' he said, his tone oddly flat. After a moment, he drew in a long breath and straightened. ''That must be it.''

''What?''

Harry's lips twisted. ''I've often been told that I've a devious mind—perhaps, for once, it can be of real use. Just hear me out.'' His gaze grew distant; absent-mindedly, he reached for his pen. ''Heather is the one they *could* use to milk the business of cash—*but*—what if Lucinda is Heather's guardian, as well as Heather's mentor? In either role, Joliffe and company would have to *get rid* of Lucinda to get to Heather.''

Slowly, Salter nodded. ''That's possible—but why try that ramshackle business of sending Mrs Babbacombe to that fancy orgy palace, then?''

Harry hoped Alfred never heard of his ancestral home referred to in such vein. He tapped the blotter with the pen. ''That's what makes me so certain Heather's guardianship must be the key—because in order to get rid of Lucinda for such purposes, showing her as unfit to be guardian of a young girl would be sufficient for Mortimer, who is Heather's next of kin, to apply to overturn Lucinda's guardianship in favour of himself. Once that's done, they could simply cut all contact between Heather and Lucinda—and use Heather to draw funds from her half of the investment."

Gazing into space, Salter nodded. "You're right—that must be it. Roundabout but it makes sense."

"And now they've failed to paint the lady scarlet," put in Dawlish, "they're planning to snatch her up and do away with her."

"True enough," agreed Salter. "But my people know what to do."

Harry refrained from asking just who Salter's "people" were.

"Even so," Dawlish continued, "they can't keep a-watching her forever. And seems to me this Joliffe character's one as should be behind bars."

Salter nodded. "You're right. There's been a few unexplained 'suicides' in Joliffe's past that the magistrates were never convinced about."

Harry repressed a shudder. The thought of Lucinda mixed up with such characters was not to be borne. "At this instant, Mrs Babbacombe is safe enough—but we need to make sure our conjecture's true. If it's not, we could be following the wrong scent—with potentially serious consequences. It strikes me that there might well be a second guardian, which would render our hypothesis unlikely."

Salter lifted a brow. "If you know the lady's legal man, I could make some discreet inquiries."

"I don't. And he's very likely in Yorkshire." Harry thought—then looked at Dawlish. "Mrs Babbacombe's maid and coachman have been with the family for years. They might know."

Dawlish straightened from the door. "I'll ask."

"Couldn't you just ask the lady herself?" Salter asked.

"No." Harry's reply was unequivocal. His lips twisted in a grimace. "At the moment, the very last thing I want to do is ask Mrs Babbacombe about her legal affairs. The question of Heather's guardianship can't be all that hard to answer."

"No. And I'll tip my people the wink to yell the instant they sniff any shift in the wind." Salter got to his feet. "As soon as we know for sure what these jackals are about, we'll devise a way to trip them up nicely."

Harry didn't reply. He shook hands with Salter, the thought in his mind that if tripping up Joliffe involved placing Lucinda in any danger at all, it simply wouldn't happen.

When Dawlish returned from showing the ex-Runner out, Harry was standing in the centre of the room, strapping his gloves on his palm.

"Well!" Dawlish opened his eyes wide. "There you be—all tricked out and not at the party. Best I drive you there, then."

Harry looked down, casting a long-suffering glance at breeches he had long ago sworn never again to don. His expression grimly resigned, he nodded. "Best you do."

His knock on Almack's door very nearly prostrated old Willis, the porter. "*Never* did I think to see *you* here again, sir!" Willis raised his shaggy brows. "Something in the wind?"

"You, Willis, are as fervent a gossip as any of your mistresses."

Unrepentant, Willis grinned. Harry gave him his gloves and cloak and sauntered into the ballroom.

To say his entrance caused a stir would be a gross understatement. It caused a flutter, a ruffling of feathers, and, in some, a mild panic akin to hysteria, all fuelled by the intense speculation that rose in feminine breasts as he strolled, gracefully but entirely purposefully, across the room.

Her emotions aswirl, Lucinda watched his approach with unwilling fascination. Her heart started to soar, her lips lifted—then her earlier thoughts engulfed her. A tightness gripped her lungs, squeezing slowly. Candlelight gleamed on his golden

hair; in the old-fashioned attire, he looked less suave and deb-
onair but, if anything, even more the rake than before. As she
felt the touch of a hundred eyes, her lips firmed. He was ex-
ploiting them all, manipulating the whole *ton*—shamelessly.

As he neared, she held out her hand, knowing he would
simply take it if she didn't. "Good evening, Mr Lester. How
very surprising to see you here."

Her gentle sarcasm did not escape Harry; he raised his brows
as he raised her fingers to his lips and gently brushed a kiss
across their tips.

He had done it so often Lucinda had forgotten it was no
longer the accepted mode of greeting. The collective gasp that
seemed to fill the ballroom reminded her of the fact. Her smile
remained in place but her eyes flashed.

The reprobate before her merely smiled. And tucked her
hand in his arm. "Come, my dear, I rather think we should
stroll." With a nod, he excused them from the two gentlemen
who had been passing the time by Lucinda's side. "Gibson.
Holloway."

They had barely taken two steps before Lady Jersey appeared in their path. Harry promptly bowed, so elaborately it
was almost a joke, so gracefully it was impossible to take of-
fense.

Sally Jersey humphed. "I had meant to ask Mrs Babbacombe
for news of you," she informed Harry without a blink. "But
now you're here, I need hardly enquire."

"Indeed," Harry drawled. "I'm positively touched, Sally
dear, that you should think to take an interest in my poor self."

"Your self isn't so poor anymore, if you recall."

"Ah, yes. A twist of fate."

"One which has brought you once more within the sights
of the ladies here. Take care, my friend, else you slip and get
tangled in their nets." Lady Jersey's eyes twinkled. She turned
to Lucinda. "I would congratulate you, my dear—but I fear
he's quite incorrigible—utterly irreclaimable. But if you seek

revenge, all you have to do is take him to the furthest point from the door and cut him loose—then watch him flounder.''

Her expression serene, Lucinda raised her brows. ''I'll bear the point in mind, ma'am.''

With a regal nod, Sally Jersey swept on.

''Don't you dare,'' Harry murmured as they strolled on, his drawl instantly evaporating. His hand rose to cover hers where it lay on his sleeve. ''You couldn't be so hard-hearted.''

Again Lucinda lifted her brows; her eyes, no longer laughing, met his. ''No?''

Harry's eyes searched hers; Lucinda saw them narrow slightly.

Suddenly breathless, she squeezed his arm and forced a smile to her lips. ''But you hardly need me to protect you.''

Determinedly, she looked ahead, still smiling, her expression as serene as before.

A short silence ensued, then Harry's voice sounded in her ear, low and completely expressionless, ''You're wrong, my dear. I need you—very much.''

Lucinda couldn't risk looking at him; she blinked rapidly and nodded to Lady Cowper, beaming from a nearby *chaise*. Were they talking of protection from the matchmaking mamas—or something else?

She got no chance to clarify the point—the mamas, the matrons and the dragons of the *ton* descended *en masse*.

To Harry's irritation, his evening at Almack's proved even more trying than he had imagined. His transparent obsession with the woman on his arm, which he had been at such pains to advertise, had, as he had known it would, doused all hope that he might be struck by lightning and forget himself enough to smile on one of the matrons' young darlings. They had got the point; unfortunately, they had all taken it into their heads to be first with their congratulations.

The very first of these thinly veiled felicitations came from the indefatigable Lady Argyle, her pale, plain daughter still in tow. ''I can't say how pleased I've been to see you at our little entertainments again, Mr Lester.'' She bestowed an arch glance before turning her gimlet gaze on Lucinda. "You must make sure he continues, my dear." She tapped Lucinda's arm with her fan. "*Such* a loss when the most handsome gentlemen cling to their clubs. Don't let him backslide."

With another arch glance and a flutter of her fingers, her ladyship departed, silent daughter in her wake. Harry idly wondered if the girl actually spoke.

Then he glanced down—and saw Lucinda's face. No one else would have noticed anything amiss, but he was now too used to seeing her relaxed, happy. She was neither, now, her features tense, her lips without the full softness they normally displayed.

They sustained two more delighted outpourings in rapid succession, then Lady Cowper caught them. Her ladyship was her usual, kind-hearted self, quite impossible to curtail. Harry bore her soft smiles and gentle words—but as soon as she released them, he took a firm grip on Lucinda's arm and steered her towards the refreshment-room. "Come—I'll get you a glass of champagne."

Lucinda glanced up at him. "This is Almack's—they don't serve champagne."

Harry looked his disgust. "I'd forgotten. Lemonade, then." He looked down at her. "You must be parched."

She didn't deny it or make any demur when he handed her a glass. But even in the refreshment-room the avalanche of felicitations he'd unwittingly triggered continued. There was, Harry quickly discovered, no escape.

By the time the next dance, a waltz, the only one of the evening, let them seek refuge on the floor, he had realised his error. He grasped the moment as he drew Lucinda into his arms to apologise. "I'm afraid I miscalculated." He smiled down into her eyes—and wished he could see in. They were more than misty, they were cloudy. The sight worried him. "I'd forgotten just how competitive the matrons are." He couldn't think of any acceptable way to explain that, when it came to a prize such as he now was, the matrons would rather accept someone like Lucinda, an outsider albeit one of their class, than see an archrival triumph.

Lucinda smiled, apparently at ease, but her eyes did not lighten. Harry drew her closer and wished they were alone.

When the dance ended, he looked down at her face, making no attempt to hide the frown in his eyes. "If you like we'll go and find Em. I dare say she'll have had enough of this."

Lucinda acquiesced with a nod, her expression rigidly serene.

Harry's prediction proved true—Em had also been beseiged. She was very ready to depart.

"A bit like running under fire," she grumpily informed Lucinda as Harry handed her into the carriage. "But it's a dashed sight too much when they start angling for invitations to the wedding." Her snort was eloquent.

Harry glanced at Lucinda, already seated in the carriage; a shaft of light from the doorway illuminated her face. Her eyes were huge, her cheeks pale. She looked tired, worn down— almost defeated. Harry felt his heart lurch—and felt a pain more intense than any Millicent Pane had ever caused.

"Now don't forget!" Em tapped him on the sleeve. "Dinner's at seven tomorrow—we'll look to see you before that."

"Ah. Yes." Harry blinked. "Of course." With a last glance at Lucinda, he stepped back and closed the door. "I'll be there."

He watched the carriage roll away, then, frowning, turned towards his club, just a few steps around the corner. But when he reached the lighted door he paused, then, still frowning, continued on to his rooms.

An hour later, sunk in her feather mattress, Lucinda stared up at the canopy of her bed. Tonight had clarified matters— unequivocally, incontrovertibly. She'd been wrong—no other explanation existed for Harry's actions, other than the obvious. The only thing *she* now needed to decide was what she was going to do about it.

She watched the moonbeams cross her ceiling; it was dawn before she slept.

HARRY DIDN'T LEAVE his rooms the next morning, alerted by a message from Salter and disappointing information from Dawlish.

"They don't know," Dawlish repeated for Salter's benefit when they gathered in Harry's library at eleven. "Both are sure Mrs Babbacombe's Miss Heather's guardian but whether there's another they can't say either way."

"Hmm." Salter frowned. He looked at Harry. "Word came in from some of my people. Joliffe's hired a carriage with four strong horses. No particular destination and he didn't hire any boys with it—paid a goodly deposit to take it without."

Harry's fingers tightened about his pen. "I think we can conclude that Mrs Babbacombe is in danger."

Salter grimaced. "Perhaps—but I've been thinking about what your man here said. You can't go watching them for forever—and if they don't take one, they might take the other. The stepdaughter's still their ultimate goal."

It was Harry's turn to grimace. "True." He stood poised to remove Lucinda from all danger but it was undoubtedly true that, if Joliffe was desperate enough, such a move would expose Heather as Joliffe's next target.

"I've been thinking," Salter continued, "that this matter of the carriage is probably for the best. It means he's planning a move soon. We're alerted—something Joliffe doesn't know. If we can sort out the facts about this guardianship, meanwhile keeping a close watch on Joliffe and his crew, then before they can make their move, we can tie them up with a warrant. My sources are sure Mortimer Babbacombe will talk readily enough. Seems he's in over his head."

Harry drew his pen back and forth through his fingers, his gaze distant as he considered the next twenty-four hours. "If you need the information about the guardianship to obtain a warrant, then we'll have to investigate further." His gaze shifted to Dawlish. "Go and see Fergus—ask if he knows where to contact a Mr Mabberly of Babbacombe Inns."

"Ah—no need." Salter held up a large finger. "Leave that to me. But what shall I tell Mr Mabberly?"

Harry's lips compressed. "He's Mrs Babbacombe's agent—she trusts him, I gather—so you may tell him whatever you must. But he'll very likely know the answer. Or at least know who does."

"Still no thoughts of just asking the lady?"

Slowly, Harry shook his head. "But if we haven't got the answer by tomorrow evening, I'll ask her."

Salter accepted the deadline without comment. "Need any help keeping an eye on the pair of them?"

Again Harry shook his head. "They won't be leaving Hallows House today or tonight." He looked at Salter, his expression resigned. "My aunt is holding a soirée."

IT WAS THE BIGGEST SOIRÉE Em had held in years and she was determined to enjoy it to the full.

Lucinda said as much as, side by side, she and Harry ascended the stairs to the ballroom. "She's positively wound tight. You could almost believe it was she making her come-out."

Harry grinned. The exceedingly select dinner Em had organised to precede her "little entertainment" had been a decided success; the company had been such as to gratify the most ambitious hostess. "She's enjoyed herself tremendously these last few months. Ever since you and Heather joined her."

Lucinda met his eyes briefly. "She's been very good to us."

"And you've been very good for her," Harry murmured as they reached the head of the staircase.

Em was already there, taking up her position to greet the first of the guests who were even now milling in the hall.

"Don't forget to compliment her on the décor," Lucinda whispered. "It's all her own effort."

Harry nodded. When Em waved insistently, summoning Lu-

cinda to her side, he bowed and strolled on into the ballroom.
It was indeed a sight—garlanded with purple and gold—Em's
favourite colours—lightened here and there with a touch of
blue. Cornflowers stood in urns on tables by the side of the
room; blue bows tied back the curtains about the long windows.
Harry smiled and paused to glance back at the trio at the door—
Em in heavy purple silk, Heather in pale gold muslin with a
hint of blue at neckline and hem, and Lucinda—his siren—
stunning in a gown of sapphire silk trimmed with fine golden
ribbons.

Harry decided that sincerely complimenting his aunt would,
in this instance, be easy. He strolled the room, chatting with
acquaintances, even steeling himself to converse with the few
ageing relatives Em had seen fit to invite. But he did not lose
sight of the welcoming party; when Em finally quit her position, he was already at Lucinda's side.

She smiled up at him, unaffectedly open, the gesture warm
yet with a lingering sense of…Harry gazed down into her
softly blue eyes, even softer now, and realised with a jolt that
what he could sense was melancholy.

"If the crowds keep rolling in as they are, Em's soirée will
be declared the very *worst* crush of the Season." Lucinda
placed her hand on his arm and laughed up at him. "I might
very well have to plead fatigue from the first."

Harry returned her smile but his gaze remained acute. "Lady
Herscult is one of Em's oldest friends; she's charged me most
straitly to bring you directly to her."

With a serene smile and an inclination of her head, Lucinda
allowed him to lead her into the growing crowd.

As they passed through the throng, people stopped them to
chat, all beaming. They discovered Lady Herscult on a *chaise;*
she twitted Harry and Lucinda both before letting them escape.
Throughout, Harry watched Lucinda carefully; with unshakeable serenity, she turned aside any questions too probing, her
smile calmly assured.

The first waltz interrupted their meanderings—Em had chosen to enliven her soirée with three dances, all waltzes.

As, without seeking any permission, Harry drew Lucinda, unresisting, into his arms, he arched a brow. "A novel arrangement."

A gurgle of laughter came to his ears.

"She said," Lucinda explained, "that she could see no point in wasting time with quadrilles and cotillions when what everyone really wanted was waltzes."

Harry grinned. "Very Em."

Lucinda smiled as he whirled her through the turn, her ease on the dance floor a far cry from her first excursion. She felt supple in his arms, fluidly matching her steps to his, following effortlessly, not, he suspected, even conscious that he held her so close. She would probably notice if he didn't.

His lips curved; she noticed.

"Now why are you smiling?"

Harry couldn't stop his slow smile from breaking. His eyes caught hers—he felt he could lose himself in the blue. "I was just thinking what a good job I've made of teaching you to waltz."

Lucinda raised her brows. "Indeed? Can I not claim some small achievement for myself?"

Harry's smile went crooked. He drew her a fraction closer, his eyes a brilliant green. "You've achieved a great deal, my dear. On the floor—and off."

Her brows rose higher. She held his gaze, her expression serene, her smile soft, her lips eminently kissable. Then she lowered her lids and looked away, leaning her head fleetingly against his shoulder.

When they weren't playing waltzes, the musicians had been instructed to entertain Em's guests with gentle airs and sonatas, all pleasing to the ear. As they wandered the crowds, engaging in the usual banter and occasional repartee, without question or, indeed, thought, remaining by each other's side, Harry realised that his siren was indeed calmer, more her usual self than she had been at Almack's the night before.

His relief was telling; he had, he realised, been harbouring a deep concern. Presumably, last night, it had merely been the unexpected gush of semi-congratulations that had shaken her; tonight, she seemed at ease, assured, typically confident.

If he could only discover the cause of the strange hint of sorrow that lay, deep but present, beneath her serene veneer—and eradicate it—he'd be happier than any man, he felt, had any right to be.

She was perfect, she was his—as he had always sensed she could be. All he wanted of life was here, with her, within his grasp; time was all that now stood in his path.

But tomorrow would come—it wasn't what he'd originally planned but he wasn't going to wait any longer. He had completed all the important acts—she would simply have to believe him.

The supper waltz came and went, as did supper itself, an array of delicacies Em's old cook had, Lucinda assured him, been up the past three nights producing. Filled with laughter and repartee, the hours fled past until, at the last, the musicians laid bow to string once more and the strains of the last waltz rose above the sea of glittering heads.

The third waltz.

Close by the edge of the floor, Harry and Ruthven were deep in discussions of a distinctly equine nature while beside them Mr Amberly and Lucinda pursued a shared interest in landscapes. As the music swelled, Harry turned to Lucinda—just as she turned to him. Their gazes locked; after a moment, Harry's lips twisted wryly.

His eyes on hers, he offered her, not his arm but his hand.

Lucinda glanced at it, then looked into his green eyes. Her heart accelerated, pulsing in her throat.

Harry's brows slowly rose. "Well, my dear?"

Her gaze steady on his, Lucinda drew in a breath. Her smile soft and oddly fragile, she placed her hand in his.

Harry's fingers closed tight over hers. He bowed elegantly; Lucinda's smile grew—she sank into a curtsy. Harry raised her, a light in his eyes she had not before seen. He drew her into his arms, then, with consummate skill, whirled them onto the floor.

Lucinda let herself flow with his stride. His strength surrounded her; he was protection and support, lover and master, helpmate and friend. She searched the hard planes of his face, chiselled, austere; with him, she could be what she wished—what she wanted to be. Her gaze softened, as did her lips. He noticed; his gaze fell to her lips, then rose again to capture hers, a subtle shift in the green raising a slow heat beneath her skin, a warmth that owed nothing to the crowds and everything to what lay between them.

With inherent grace, they swirled down the long room, seeing no one, aware of nothing beyond their shared existence, trapped by the waltz and the promise in each other's eyes.

Lord Ruthven and Mr Amberly looked on, smugly satisfied smiles on their faces.

"Well—I think we can congratulate ourselves, Amberly." Lord Ruthven turned and held out his hand.

"Indeed." Mr Amberly beamed and shook it. "A job well done!" His eyes lifted to the couple circling the floor. His smile grew broader. "No doubt about it."

Lord Ruthven followed his gaze—and grinned. "Not a one."

As she leaned back against Harry's arm and let the magic of the moment take her, Lucinda knew that was true. Even while a small part of her sorrowed, she felt elation sweep her. He would ask her very soon—and she knew how she would answer. She loved him too much to deny him again, even should he deny her. Deep inside, her conviction that he loved her had never waned—it never would, she was sure. She could draw on that for strength as she had hoped to draw on his acknowledgement of his love. If it was not to be, it wasn't; she was too prosaic a creature to rail against a much-desired fate.

With the last ringing chord of the waltz, the evening was declared over.

As family, Harry hung back, allowing the other guests to depart. Gerald finally headed downstairs, leaving Harry with Lucinda at their head. His hand found hers in the folds of her gown; twining his fingers through hers, he drew her to face him. Ignoring Em leaning against the balustrade on Lucinda's other side, Harry raised Lucinda's hand to brush a kiss across her knuckles, then shifting his hold, his gaze steady on hers, he tipped her fingers back to place a kiss on her inner wrist.

Lucinda, trapped in his gaze, suppressed a delicious shiver.

Harry smiled—and traced her cheek with one long finger. "We'll talk tomorrow."

The words were soft, low—they went straight to Lucinda's heart. She smiled softly; Harry bowed, first to her, then to Em. Then, without a backward glance, he descended the stairs—to the very last, the very picture of the elegant rake.

Outside Hallows House, lurking in the shadows on the opposite side of the street, unremarkable amid the small gathering of urchins and inveterate watchers who congregated outside any ball or party, Scrugthorpe kept his eyes fixed on the lighted doorway and muttered beneath his breath.

"Just wait till I get my hands on you, bitch. Once I'm done with you, no high-stickler of a gentleman will want to sully himself with you. Damaged goods, you'll be—well and truly damaged." He cackled softly, gleefully and rubbed his hands. In the shadows, his eyes gleamed.

A link-boy, waiting to pick up any likely trade, strolled past, casting Scrugthorpe an incurious glance. A few paces on, the boy passed a street-sweeper, leaning on his broom, his face obscured by an ancient floppy hat. The link-boy grinned at the sweeper, then ambled on to prop against a nearby lamppost.

Scrugthorpe missed the exchange, intent on the last stragglers emerging from Hallows House.

"You'll be mine very soon," he leered. "Then I'll teach

you not to give a man lip. Too hoity by half.'' His grin turned feral. ''I'll bring you back to earth right quick.''

A thin, tuneful whistle floated across Scrugthorpe's senses, distracting him from his plotting. The tune continued—a popular air; Scrugthorpe stiffened. Alert, he scanned the shadows for the whistler. His gaze settled on the link-boy. The tune continued; Scrugthrope knew it well, even down to the curious lilting catch the whistler put at the end of each verse.

Scrugthorpe cast a last glance at the empty doorway across the road, then, with every evidence of unconcern, headed off down the street.

The sweeper and link-boy watched him go. Then the link-boy nodded to the sweeper and slipped into the shadows in Scrugthorpe's wake.

Chapter Fifteen

THE NEXT MORNING, Harry was flat on his stomach deep in dreams, his arms wrapped about his pillow, when a large hand descended on his bare shoulder.

His response was instantaneous—half-rising, eyes wide, muscles tensed, fists clenching.

"Now, now!" Dawlish had wisely backed out of reach. "I wish as you'd get out of that habit—there ain't no angry husbands 'round here."

Eyes glittering, Harry hauled in a breath then expelled it irritably. Propping himself on one arm, he raked his hair out of his eyes. "What the devil's the time?"

"Nine," Dawlish replied, already at the wardrobe. "But you've got visitors."

"At *nine?*" Harry turned over and sat up.

"Salter—and he's brought that agent of the missus's—Mr Mabberly."

Harry blinked. Draping his arms over his knees, he stared at Dawlish. "I haven't married the damned woman yet."

"Just getting in some practice, like." Dawlish turned from the robe with a grey coat over his arm. "This do?"

Ten minutes later, Harry descended the narrow staircase, wondering if Lucinda would prefer a grander place when they stayed in town. He hoped she wouldn't—he'd been renting these rooms for the past ten years; they felt comfortable, like a well-worn coat.

He opened the door to his study and beheld his visitors,

Salter standing by the desk, Mabberly, looking thoroughly uncomfortable, perched on the chair before it.

At sight of him, Mabberly rose.

"Good morning, Mabberly." Harry nodded and shut the
door. "Salter."

Salter returned his nod but refrained from comment, his lips
compressed as if holding the words back.

Stiff as a poker, Mr Mabberly inclined his head fractionally.
"Mr Lester. I hope you'll forgive this intrusion but this gentleman—" he glanced at Salter "—is most insistent that I provide answers to questions regarding Mrs Babbacombe's affairs
that I can only describe as highly confidential." Decidedly
prim, Mr Mabberly brought his gaze back to Harry's face. "He
tells me he's working for you."

"Indeed." Harry waved Mr Mabberly back to his chair and
took his own behind the desk. "I'm afraid we are in pressing
need of the information Mr Salter has requested of you, in a
matter pertaining to Mrs Babbacombe's safety." As Harry had
expected, the mention of Lucinda's safety stopped Mr Mabberly in his tracks. "That is," Harry smoothly continued, "assuming you do, in fact, know the answers?"

Mr Mabberly shifted, eyeing Harry somewhat warily. "As
it happens, I do—it's necessary for one in my position, acting
as the company's representative, to be absolutely certain just
whose interests I'm representing." He shot a glance at Salter,
then brought his gaze back to Harry. "But you mentioned Mrs
Babbacombe's safety. How can the information you requested
be important?"

Succinctly, Harry told him, detailing no more than the bare
bones of the presumptive plot; Mr Mabberly was businessman
enough to readily follow their hypothesis. As the tale unfolded,
his open features reflected shock, outrage—and, eventually, a
dogged determination.

"The cads!" Slightly flushed, he glanced at Harry. "You
say you intend taking out a warrant against them?"

Salter answered. "We've cause enough for a warrant *pro-*

vided we can find evidence on this guardianship business—without that, their motive's uncertain.''

"So." Harry fixed Mr Mabberly with a flat green gaze. "The question is will you help us?"

"I'll do anything I can," Mr Mabberly vowed, his voice ringing with fervour. Even he heard it. A trifle shocked, he hurried to excuse it. "Mrs Babbacombe's been very good to me, you understand—there aren't many who would appoint someone as relatively young as myself to such an important position."

"Of course." Harry smiled, endeavouring to make the gesture as unthreatening as he could at that hour of the morning. "And, as a loyal employee of Babbacombe and Company, you would naturally be anxious to assist in ensuring your principals' personal safety."

"Indeed." Obviously more comfortable, Mr Mabberly sat back. "Mrs Babbacombe is indeed Miss Babbacombe's sole legal guardian." Again, a slight flush rose in his cheeks. "I'm perfectly sure because, when I first took up my position, I was uncertain as to the point—so I asked. Mrs Babbacombe's always a model of business etiquette—she insisted I see the guardianship deed."

Salter straightened, his expression lightening. "So—not only do you *know* she's the sole guardian—you can swear to it?"

Mr Mabberly nodded, swivelling to look at Salter. "Certainly. I naturally felt obliged to read the document and verify the seal. It was unquestionably genuine."

"Excellent!" Harry looked at Salter—the big man's face was alight, his frame suddenly thrumming with harnessed energy. "So we can get that warrant without further delay?"

"If Mr Mabberly here will come with me to the magistrate and swear to Mrs Babbacombe's status, I can't see anything that'll stop us. I've already got friends in the force standing by—they'll do the actual arrest but I, for one, definitely want to be there when they take Joliffe into custody."

"I'm prepared to come with you immediately, sir." Mr

Mabberly stood. "From the sounds of it, the sooner this Joliffe person is a guest of His Majesty's government the better."

"I couldn't agree more." Harry stood and offered Mr Mabberly his hand. "And while you two are tying up Joliffe and his crew, I'll keep Mrs Babbacombe under my eye."

"Aye—that'd be wise." Salter shook hands with Harry and they all turned to the door. "Joliffe's got the makings of a fairly desperate character. It wouldn't hurt to keep the lady close—just until we've got him safely stowed. I'll send word the instant we've got the blackguards in custody, sir."

"Send word to me at Hallows House," Harry told him.

After seeing his guests to the hall, Harry returned to the study and quickly glanced through his letters. He looked up as Dawlish entered with a cup of coffee. "Here you are." Dawlish set the cup down on the blotter. "So—what's the sum of it, then?"

Harry told him.

"Hmm—so that clerk fellow's not so useless after all?"

Harry took a sip of his coffee. "I never said he was useless. Gormless. And I'm willing to accept that I might have misjudged him."

Dawlish nodded. "Good! Last day of this ramshackle business, then. Can't say I'm sad."

Harry snorted. "Nor I."

"I'll get breakfast on the table." Dawlish glanced at the long-case clock in the corner. "We've still an hour to go before we're due at Hallows House."

Harry set down his cup. "We'd best use the time to get all tidy here—I expect to leave for Lester Hall later this evening."

Dawlish looked back from the door, brows flying. "Oh-ho! Finally going to take the plunge, are you? 'Bout time, if you ask me. Mind—wouldn't have thought you'd choose a family picnic to do it at—but it's your funeral."

Harry lifted his head and glared but the door had already closed.

LATER THAT AFTERNOON, Harry recalled Dawlish's observation with grim resignation. Not in his wildest dreams had he imagined playing the most important scene of his life on such a stage.

They were seated on colourful coach rugs on a long grassy slope leading down to the gently rippling River Lea. Some miles north of Islington, not far from Stamford Hill, the woods and meadows close by the river provided a pleasant spot for young families and those seeking a draught of country peace. Although some way down the low escarpment, their position afforded them an uninterrupted view over the river valley, meadows giving way to marshland, water glinting in the sun. Roads meandered through the marshes, leading to Walthamstow, just beyond the valley. Oaks and beeches at their backs shielded them from the sun; the haze of a glorious afternoon surrounded them. Bees buzzed, flitting from fieldflower to hedgerow bloom; doves cooed overhead.

Harry drew in a deep breath—and shot a considering glance at Lucinda, stretched out beside him. Beyond her reclined Em, her hat over her face. On a neighbouring rug sat Heather and Gerald, engrossed in animated discourse. Beyond them, at a suitable distance, perched on and about a collection of fallen logs, sat Agatha and Em's even more severe dresser, together with Em's coachman, Dawlish, Joshua, Sim and the little maid Amy. In their dark clothes, they looked like so many crows.

Harry grimaced and looked away. Fate had chosen a fine moment to turn fickle.

The instant he had realised that it was Heather's guardianship that was Joliffe and Mortimer Babbacombe's goal, he had determined to come between them and Lucinda with all possible speed. By marrying her, he would assume legal responsibility in all such matters—automatically, without question. It was the one, absolutely guaranteed way of protecting her, of shielding her from their machinations.

But her yesterday had been filled with preparations for the soirée; the household had been at sixes and sevens. He hadn't liked his prospects of finding a quiet moment, let alone a quiet corner to propose.

As for today, they had organised this outing a week ago as a quiet relaxation away from the *ton* after the excitement of the soirée. They had come in two carriages, Em's and Lucinda's, the menservants riding atop; Agatha and Amy had shared Lucinda's carriage with their mistress and himself. They had lunched surrounded by sunshine and peace. Now Em looked set for her postprandial nap; it would probably be at least an hour before hunger again prodded Heather and Gerald to a more general awareness.

So, since learning of her danger, this was his first chance to remove her from it. Hiding his determination behind an easy expression, Harry got to his feet. Lucinda looked up, putting up her hand to shield her eyes. Harry smiled reassuringly down at her before lifting his gaze to her drab watchdogs. With a slight movement of his head, he summoned Dawlish, then strolled back towards the trees. When he was out of earshot of his intended and his aunt, he stopped and waited for Dawlish to reach him.

"Something wrong?"

Harry smiled politely. "No. I just thought I'd let it be known that, when I take Mrs Babbacombe for a stroll in a few moments, we won't need an escort." When Dawlish screwed up his eyes, as if considering arguing, Harry continued, his tone growing steely, "She'll be perfectly safe with me."

Dawlish humphed. "Can't say as I blame you. Cramp anyone's style, it would, having to go down on your knees before an audience."

Harry raised his eyes heavenwards in a mute gesture of appeal.

"I'll tell the others."

Harry hurriedly lowered his gaze but Dawlish was already stomping back through the trees. Muttering a curse, Harry did the same, returning to the rugs on the grass.

"Come for a walk."

Lucinda glanced up at the soft words—which cloaked what sounded like a command. Beside her, Em was gently snoring; Heather and Gerald were in a world of their own. She met Harry's eyes, very green; he raised a brow and held out his hand. Lucinda studied it for an instant, savouring the thrill of anticipation that shot through her, then, with studied calm, laid her fingers in his.

Harry drew her to her feet. Tucking her hand in his arm, he turned her towards the leafy woods.

The woods were not extensive, merely stands of trees separating fields and meadows. They strolled without words, leaving the others behind, until they came to a large field left fallow. The meadow grasses and flowers had taken over; the ground was carpeted in a shifting sea of small bright blooms.

Lucinda sighed. "How lovely." She smiled up at Harry.

Engaged in scanning their surroundings, he glanced back at her in time to return her smile. The trees screened them from their companions and any others strolling the river banks; they were not isolated but as private as, in the circumstances, it was probably wise to be. He gestured ahead; by unvoiced agreement, they strolled to the centre of the field where a large rock, weathered to smoothness, created a natural seat.

With a swirl of her blue muslin skirts, Lucinda sat. Harry noticed that her gown matched the cornflowers scattered through the grass. She had worn a new bonnet but had let it fall to dangle by its ribbons on her back, leaving her face unshadowed. She lifted her head and her gaze met his.

Stillness held them, then her delicate brows arched slightly, in query, in invitation.

Harry scanned her face, then drew in a deep breath.

"Ah-hem!"

They both turned to see Dawlish striding across the field. Harry bit back a curse. "What *now?*"

Dawlish cast him a sympathetic glance. "There's a messenger come—'bout that business this morning."

Harry groaned. "Now?'

Dawlish met his eye. "Thought as how you might think it better to get that matter all tied and tight—before you get... distracted, like."

Harry grimaced—Dawlish had a point.

"Set on seeing you specifically, this messenger—said as that was his orders." Dawlish nodded back at the trees. "Said he'd wait by the stile yonder."

Swallowing his irritation, Harry shot a considering glance at Lucinda; she met it with an affectionate smile. Spending five minutes to acknowledge the end of Joliffe's threat would leave him free to concentrate on her—wholly, fully, without reservation. Without further interruption. Harry looked at Dawlish. "Which stile?"

"It's along the fence a little way."

"We didn't pass a fence."

Dawlish frowned and surveyed the woods through which he'd come. "It's that way—and around to the left, I think." He scratched his head. "Or is it the right?"

"Why don't you just show Mr Lester the way?"

Harry turned at Lucinda's words. She had plucked some blooms and started to plait them. He frowned. "I'll find the stile. Dawlish will stay here with you."

Lucinda snorted. "Nonsense! You'll take twice as long." She picked a cornflower from her lap, then tilted her face to look up at him, one brow arching. "The sooner you get there, the sooner you'll be back."

Harry hesitated, then shook his head. Joliffe might be behind bars but his protective instincts still ran strong. "No. I'll—"

"Don't be absurd! I'm perfectly capable of sitting on a rock in the sunshine for a few minutes alone." Lucinda lifted both arms to gesture about her. "What *do* you imagine could happen in such a sylvan setting?"

Harry glared, briefly, aware she would very likely be perfectly safe. Hands on hips, he scanned the surrounding trees. There was open space all around her; no one could creep up and surprise her. She was a mature and sensible woman; she would scream if anything untoward occurred. And they were all close enough to hear.

And the sooner he met with Salter's messenger, the sooner he could concentrate on her, on them, on their future.

"Very well." His expression hard, he pointed a finger at her. "But stay there and don't move!"

Her answering smile was fondly condescending.

Harry turned and strode quickly across the field; the damned woman's confidence in herself was catching.

Like many countrymen, Dawlish could retrace his steps to anywhere but could never describe the way. He took the lead; within a matter of minutes, they found the fence line. They followed it to a small clearing in which stood the stile—surrounded by a small army of people.

Harry halted. "What the devil...?"

Salter pushed through the crowd. Harry caught sight of Mabberly and three representatives of Bow Street among a motley crew of ostlers, grooms and stablelads, link-boys, jarveys, street urchins, sweepers—basically any likely looking scruffs to be found on the streets of London. Obviously Salter's "people".

Then Salter stood before him, his face decidedly grim. "We got the warrant but when we went to serve it, Joliffe and his crew had done a bunk."

Harry stiffened. "I thought you were watching them?"

"We were." Salter's expression grew bleaker. "But someone must have tripped up somewhere—we found our two watchers coshed over the head this morning—and no sign of our pigeons anywhere."

Harry's mind raced; chill fingers clutched his gut. "Have they taken the coach?"

"Yep," came from one of the ostlers. "Seems like they left 'bout ten—just afore the captain here came with his bill."

Mr Mabberly stepped forward. "We thought we should warn you to keep an especially close eye on Mrs Babbacombe—until we can get this villain behind bars."

Harry barely heard him. His expression had blanked. *"Oh, my God!"*

He whirled and raced back the way he'd come, Dawlish on his heels. The rest, galvanised by Harry's fear, followed.

Harry broke from the trees and scanned the field—then came to a skidding halt.

Before him the meadow grasses swayed in the breeze. All was peaceful and serene, the field luxuriating in the heat. The sun beat down on the rock in its centre—now empty.

Harry stared. Then he strode forward, his expression like flint. A short chain of blue cornflowers had been left on the rock—laid down gently, not flung or mauled.

Breathing rapidly, Harry, hands on hips, lifted his head and looked about. "Lucinda?"

His call faded into the trees—no one answered.

Harry swore. "They've got her." The words burned his throat.

"They can't have got far." Salter gestured to his people. "It's the lady we're after—tallish, dark-haired—most of you've seen her. Name of Mrs Babbacombe."

Within seconds, they were quartering the area, quickly, efficiently, calling her name, threshing through undergrowth. Harry headed towards the river, Dawlish beside him. His throat was already hoarse. His imagination was a handicap—he could conjure visions far too well. He had to find her—he simply had to.

LEFT IN THE PEACE of the meadow, Lucinda smiled to herself, then settled to convert the cornflowers growing in abundance around the base of the rock into a blue garland. Beneath her calm, she was impatient enough, yet quite confident Harry would shortly be back.

Her smile deepened. She reached for a bright dandelion to lend contrast to her string.

"Mrs Babbacombe! Er—Aunt Lucinda?"

Blinking, Lucinda turned. She searched the shadows beneath

the trees and saw a slight, shortish gentleman waving and beckoning.

"Good lord! Whatever does *he* want?" Laying aside her
garland, she crossed to the trees. "Mortimer?" She ducked
under a branch and stepped into the cool shade. "What are you
doing here?"

"A-waiting for you, bitch," came in a growling grating
voice.

Lucinda jumped; a huge paw wrapped about her arm. Her
eyes widened in incredulous amazement as she took in its
owner. "*Scrugthorpe!* What the devil do you think you're doing?"

"Grabbing you." Scrugthorpe leered, then started to drag
her deeper into the trees. "Come on—the carriage's waiting."

"What carriage? Oh, for goodness' sake!" Lucinda was
about to struggle in earnest when Mortimer took her other elbow.

"This is all most distressing—but if you'll only listen—it's
really nothing to do with you, you know—simply a matter of
righting a wrong—fixing a slight—that sort of thing." He
wasn't so much helping to drag her along as clinging to her
arm; his eyes, a weak washy blue, implored her understanding.

Lucinda frowned. "What on earth is all this about?"

Mortimer told her—in disjointed phrases, bits and pieces,
dribs and drabs. Totally engrossed in trying to follow his tale,
Lucinda largely ignored Scrugthorpe and his dogged march forward, absent-mindedly letting him pull her along, shifting her
attention only enough to lift her skirts over a log.

"Damned hoity female!" Scrugthorpe kicked at her skirts.
"When I get you alone, I'm going to—"

"And then, you see, there was the money owed to Joliffe—
must pay, y'know—play and pay—honour and all that—"

"And after that, I'll tie you up good—"

"So it turned out to be rather a lot—not impossible but—
had to find it, you see—thought I'd be right after Uncle Charles

died—but then it wasn't there—the money, I mean—but I'd already spent it—owed it—had to raise the wind somehow—''

"Oh, I'll make you pay for your sharp tongue, I will. After I've done, you'll—"

Lucinda shut her ears to Scrugthrope's ravings and concentrated on Mortimer's babblings. Her jaw dropped when he revealed their ultimate goal; their plan to reach it was even more astonishing. Mortimer finally concluded with, "So, you see—all simple enough. If you'll just make the guardianship over to me, it'll all be right and tight—you do see that, don't you?"

They had reached the edge of the river; a narrow footbridge lay ahead. Abruptly, Lucinda hauled back against Scrugthrope's tow and stood her ground. Her gaze, positively scathing, fixed on Mortimer.

"*You ass!*" Her tone said it all. "Do you really believe that, just because you're so weak and stupid as to get…?" Words momentarily failed her; she wrenched her elbow from Mortimer's grasp and gestured wildly. "Gulled by a sharp." Eyes flashing, she transfixed Mortimer; he stood rooted to the spot, his mouth silently opening and shutting, his expression that of a terrified rabbit facing the ultimate fury. "That I will meekly hand over to you my stepdaughter's fortune so you can line the pockets of some cunning, immoral, inconsiderate, rapacious, fly-by-night excuse for a man?" Her voice had risen, gaining in commanding volume. "You've got *rocks* in your head, sir!"

"Now see here." Scrugthrope, somewhat dazed by her vehemence, shook her arm. "That's enough of that."

Mortimer was exceedingly pale. "But Uncle Charles owed me—"

"Nonsense! Charles owed you *nothing!* Indeed, you got more than you deserved. What you have to do, Mortimer," Lucinda jabbed him in the chest, "is get back to Yorkshire and get your affairs in order. Talk to Mr Wilson in Scarborough—he'll know how to help. Stand on your own feet, Mortimer—believe me, it's the only way." Struck by a thought, Lucinda asked, "Incidentally, how is Mrs Finnigan, the cook? When we left she had ulcers, poor thing—is she better?"

Mortimer simply stared at her.

"*Enough,* woman!" Scrugthorpe, his face mottling, swung Lucinda about. Opting for action rather than words, he grabbed her by the shoulders and pulled her to him. Lucinda uttered a small shriek and ducked her head—just in time to avoid Scrugthorpe's fleshy lips. He grunted; she felt his fingers grip her shoulders tightly, bruising her soft flesh. She struggled, rocking to keep him off balance. Her gaze directed downwards, she saw his feet, clad in soft leather shoes, shuffling to gain greater stability. Lucinda lifted her knee, inadvertently striking Scrugthorpe in the groin. She heard his sharp intake of breath—and brought her boot heel down with all the force she could muster, directly onto his left instep.

"*Ow!* You *bitch!*" His voice was crazed with pain.

Lucinda jerked her head up—her crown connected with Scrugthorpe's chin with a most satisfying crack. Scrugthorpe yowled. He put one hand to his foot and the other to his chin—Lucinda was free. She whisked herself away—and Mortimer grabbed her.

Furious, she beat at his hands, his face; he was no Scrugthorpe—she broke free easily enough, pushing Mortimer into a bush in the process. Gasping, dragging much needed air into her lungs, Lucinda picked up her skirts and fled onto the bridge. Behind her, Scrugthorpe, swearing foully, hobbled in pursuit.

Lucinda cast a quick glance behind—and ran faster.

She looked ahead and saw a gentleman striding onto the other end of the bridge. He was dressed neatly in riding breeches and top coat and wore Hessians. Lucinda thanked her stars and waved. "Sir!" Here, surely, was one who would aid her.

To her surprise, he stopped, standing with his feet apart, blocking the exit to the bridge. Lucinda blinked, and slowed. She halted in the centre of the bridge.

The man had a pistol in his hand.

It was, Lucinda thought, as she slowly watched it rise, one of those long-barrelled affairs gentlemen were said to use when duelling. The sun struck its silver mountings, making them gleam. Beneath her, the river gurgled onwards to the sea; in the wide sky above, the larks swooped and trilled. Distantly, she heard her name called but the cries were too weak to break the web that held her.

A chill spread over her skin.

Slowly, the pistol rose, until the barrel was level with her chest.

Her mouth dry, her heart pounding in her ears, Lucinda looked into the man's face. It was blank, expressionless. She saw his fingers shift and heard a telltale click.

A hundred yards downstream, Harry broke through the woods and gained the river path. Panting, he looked around—then glanced up at the bridge. He froze.

Two heartbeats passed as he watched his future, his life, his love—all he had ever wanted—face certain death. Salter and some of his men were on the opposite bank, closing fast, but they would never reach Joliffe in time. Still others were rushing for this end of the bridge. Harry saw the pistol level—saw the slight upward adjustment necessary to bring the aim to true.

"Lucinda!"

The cry was wrenched from him, filled with despair and rage—and something more powerful than both. It sliced through the mesmeric daze that held Lucinda.

She turned, her hand on the wooden rail—and saw Harry on the nearby shore. Lucinda blinked. Safety lay with Harry. The rail was a simple one, a single wooden top-rail supported by intermittent posts. Before her, the area below the rail was empty, open. She put both hands on the rail and let herself drop through.

She plummeted to the river as the shot rang out.

Harry watched her fall. He had no idea whether she'd been hit or not. She entered the river with a splash; when it cleared, there was no sign of her.

Cursing, Harry raced forward, scanning the river. Could she swim? He reached the bank just short of the bridge and sat down. He was tugging off one boot when Lucinda surfaced. Pushing her hair out of her eyes, she looked about and saw him. She waved, then, as if she went swimming in rivers every day, calmly stroked for shore.

Harry stared. Then, his expression hardening, he slammed his foot back in his boot. He rose and strode to the river's edge. His emotions clashing wildly, swinging from elation to rage with sufficient intensity to make him dizzy, he stood on the bank and waited for her to reach him.

He had lost Dawlish somewhere in the woods; those of Salter's people who had been near, seeing him waiting, wisely left him to it. He was distantly aware of the commotions engulfing both ends of the bridge but he didn't even spare them a glance. Later, they learned that Mr Mabberly had distinguished himself by laying Mortimer Babbacombe low while Dawlish had taken great pleasure in scientifically darkening the daylights of the iniquitous Scrugthorpe.

Gaining the shallows, Lucinda stood and glanced back at the bridge. Satisfied that her attackers were being dealt with as they deserved, she reached behind her and caught hold of her dripping hat. Tugging the wet ribbons from about her neck, she stared in dismay at the limp creation. "It's ruined!" she wailed.

Then she looked down. "And my dress!"

Harry couldn't take anymore. The damned woman had nearly got killed and all she was concerned with was the fate of her hat. He strode into the shallow water to stand towering by her side.

Still mourning her headgear, Lucinda gestured at it. "It's beyond resurrection." She looked up at him—in time to see his eyes flare.

Harry slapped her wet bottom—hard enough to leave his palm stinging.

Lucinda jumped and yelped. "Ow!" She stared at him in stunned surprise.

"The next time I tell you to stay where I leave you and *not* to move you will do precisely *that*—do I make myself clear?" Harry glared down at her, into eyes that, even now, held a hint of mutinous determination. Then his gaze fell to her breasts. He blinked. "Good lord! Your dress!" Immediately, he shrugged off his coat.

Lucinda sniffed. "Precisely what I said." With injured dignity, she accepted the coat he placed about her shoulders—she even allowed him to do up the buttons, closing it loosely about her.

"Come—I'm taking you home immediately." Harry took her elbow and helped her onto the bank. "You're soaked—the last thing I need is for you to take a chill."

Lucinda tried to look back at the bridge. "That was Mortimer back there, you know."

"Yes, I know." Harry drew her into the woods.

"You do?" Lucinda blinked. "He had some strange idea that Charles had done him out of his rightful inheritance, you know, that—"

Harry let her fill his ears with an account of Mortimer's justification of his deeds as he steered her through the woods. It was infinitely reassuring to hear her voice. His fear that she might suffer from delayed shock receded, lulled by her calm and logical recital, her unflustered observations. She was, he had to grudgingly, somewhat astonishingly concede, totally unaffected by her ordeal. *He* was a nervous wreck. He led her directly to the carriages.

Lucinda blinked when they appeared before them. "But what about the others?"

Harry hauled open the door of her carriage as Joshua and Dawlish hurried up. "We can leave a message for Em and Heather—Mabberly can explain."

"Mr Mabberly?" Lucinda was astonished. "Is he here?"

Harry cursed his loose tongue. "Yes. Now get in." He didn't wait for her to do so—he picked her up and put her in. Joshua was already climbing to the box; Harry turned to Dawlish. "Go

back and explain everything to Em and Miss Babbacombe—
assure them Mrs Babbacombe's taken no hurt other than a
soaking.''

From inside the carriage came a definite sniff. Harry's palm
tingled. He put a foot on the carriage step. ''I'm taking her
back to Hallows House—we'll wait for them there.''

Dawlish nodded. ''All the rest's taken care of.''

Harry nodded. He turned back to the carriage, remembering
to grab his greatcoat, left on the rack atop, before he ducked
through the door. Dawlish shut it behind him and slapped the
coach's side. It lurched into motion; heaving a heavy sigh,
Harry subsided onto the seat and shut his eyes.

He remained thus for a full minute; Lucinda watched him
somewhat warily. Then he opened his eyes, tossed his greatcoat
onto the opposite seat, and reached out and systematically let
down all the blinds. The sun still penetrated the thin leather,
suffusing the interior with a golden glow.

''Ah...'' Before Lucinda could decide what to say, Harry
sat back, reached for her and hauled her onto his lap.

Lucinda opened her lips on a token protest—he captured
them in a long, searing kiss, his lips hard on hers, demanding,
commanding, ravishing her senses until her thoughts melted
away and took her wits with them. She kissed him back with
equal fervour, perfectly willing to take all he offered.

When he finally consented to raise his head, she lay against
his chest, dazedly blinking up at him, with not two thoughts to
her name.

The sight filled Harry with a certain satisfaction. With an
approving grunt, he closed his eyes and let his head fall back
against the squabs. ''If you ever do anything like that again,
you'd better be prepared to eat standing up for the following
week. At least.''

Lucinda threw him a darkling glance and reached a hand to
her abused posterior. ''It still hurts.''

Harry's lips lifted. He raised his lids enough to look down
at her. ''Perhaps I should kiss it better?''

Her eyes flew wide—then she looked intrigued.

Harry caught his breath. "Perhaps we'd better leave that until later."

Lucinda raised a brow. She held his gaze, then shrugged and snuggled closer. "I didn't plan to be set upon, you know. And who were all those people?"

"Never mind." Harry juggled her around so she was sitting on his knees facing him. "There's something I want to say—and I'm only going to say it once." His eyes met hers. "Are you listening?"

Lucinda drew in a breath—and couldn't let it out. Her heart in her mouth, she nodded.

"I love you."

Lucinda's face lit up. She leaned towards him, her lips parting—Harry held up a restraining hand.

"No—wait. I haven't finished." He held her with his eyes. Then his lips twisted. "Such words from a man such as I can hardly be convincing. You know I've said them before—in reams. And they weren't true—not then." His hand found hers where it rested on his chest; he raised her fingers to his lips. "Before you came along, I didn't know what the words meant—now I do. But I couldn't expect you to find the words convincing, when I wouldn't myself. So I've given you all the proof that I can—I've taken you to visit with my father, shown you my ancestral home." Lucinda blinked—Harry continued with his list. "You've seen the stud and I've shown you the house that I hope we'll make our home." He paused, eyes glinting, lips lifting at the ends as he met Lucinda's gaze. "And I *was* joking about the six children—four will do nicely."

Breathless, dazed, giddy with happiness, Lucinda opened her eyes wide. "Only four?" She let her lids fall. "You disappoint me, sir."

Harry shifted. "Perhaps we can settle on four to begin with? I wouldn't, after all, wish to disappoint you."

Lucinda's rare dimple appeared in her cheek.

Harry frowned. "Now where was I? Ah, yes—the proofs of

my devotion. I accompanied you back to London and drove you in the Park, I danced attendance on you in every conceivable way—I even braved the dangers of Almack's.'' His eyes held hers. ''All for you.''

''Is *that* why you did it—to convince me you loved me?'' Lucinda felt as if her heart would burst. She had only to look into his eyes to know the truth.

Harry's lips twisted in a self-deprecatory grin. ''Why else?'' He gestured expansively. ''What else could move me to prostrate myself at your feet?'' He glanced at them—and frowned. ''Which, incidentally, are very wet.'' He reached down and eased off her sodden boots. That done, he pushed up her wet skirts and started on her garters.

Lucinda smiled. ''And you danced three waltzes with me—remember?''

''How could I forget?'' Harry returned, busy rolling down her stockings. ''A more public declaration I cannot imagine.''

Lucinda giggled and wriggled her chilled toes.

Harry straightened and met her eyes. ''So, Mrs Lucinda Babbacombe—after all my sterling efforts—do you believe me when I say I love you?''

Lucinda's smile lit her eyes. She reached up both hands to frame his face. ''Silly man—you had only to say.'' Gently, she touched her lips to his.

When she drew back, Harry snorted disbelievingly. ''And you'd have believed me? Even after my *faux pas* that afternoon you seduced me?''

Lucinda's smile was soft. ''Oh, yes.'' Her dimple came back. ''Even then.''

Harry decided to leave it at that. ''So you agree to marry me without further fuss?''

Lucinda nodded once, decisively.

''Thank heaven for that.'' Harry closed his arms about her. ''We're getting married in two days at Lester Hall—it's all arranged. I've got the licence in my pocket.'' He glanced down and saw the damp patches on his coat, close about her. He

frowned and lifted her back so she was once more sitting upright on his knee. "I hope you haven't got it wet enough for
the ink to run." He undid the coat buttons and lifted the garment from her.

Lucinda laughed, so delirious with happiness she couldn't
contain it. She reached out and drew his head to hers and kissed
him longingly. The kiss deepened, then Harry disengaged.

"You're very wet. We should get you out of these things."

Siren-like, Lucinda raised her brows, then obediently turned
so he could undo her laces. He eased her from her gown, dropping it to the floor where it landed with a soft splat.

Her chemise, drenched and all but transparent, clung like a
second skin. A soft blush rose beneath it; Lucinda let her lids
veil her eyes, watching Harry's hands from beneath her lashes
as, gently yet deliberately, he peeled the delicate material from
her.

Harry sensed the heat rising within her, heard the sudden
shallow intake of her breath as he drew the last shred of concealment from her. She shivered—but he didn't think it was
due to being cold. Drawing in a deep breath, she raised her
eyes to his.

Lucinda looked into eyes brilliantly green, screened by
heavy lids; nothing could hide the desire that burned in their
peridot depths.

She sat naked on his lap. His hands moved gently over her,
over her back, over her arms, languidly stroking, caressing. He
leaned forward and pressed kisses to the bruises Scrugthorpe
had left on her shoulders. Lucinda shuddered. Unbidden, entirely unexpected, a long-forgotten conversation drifted through
her mind. Eyes agleam, she chuckled softly.

Harry stared at her hungrily, the siren who had lured him to
his doom. Clinging to sanity, he raised a brow in the nearest
he could get to languid enquiry.

Lucinda laughed. She caught his eyes with hers, then, leaning closer, let her lids screen her eyes. "Em once said," she
murmured, "that I should aim to get you on your knees."

Fleetingly, she lifted her eyes to his, her lips gently curved. "I don't think she meant it in quite this way."

The body beneath her was hard, rigid, powerful but harnessed.

"Ah, yes. An eminently wise old lady, my aunt." Gently, Harry lifted Lucinda, settling her so she was straddling his knees, her knees on the seat on either side of his hips. "But she tends to forget that—sometimes—it's very hard for a rake to—er—change his spots."

Lucinda wasn't at all sure about her change in position. "Ah, Harry?"

"Hmm?" Harry wasn't interested in further conversation.

Lucinda realised as much when he urged her towards him and his lips closed gently about one tightly furled nipple. Her breath caught. "Harry—we're in a carriage."

Her protest was breathless. His lips left her; he put out his tongue and rasped her sensitised flesh. Lucinda shuddered and closed her eyes; his hands on her hips held her steady—every time she caught her breath, he stole it away. "You can't be serious," she eventually managed to gasp. She paused—then sucked in a quick breath. "Not here? In a moving carriage?"

His answering chuckle sounded devilish. "Perfectly possible, I assure you." His hands shifted. "The rocking's part of the fun—you'll see."

Lucinda struggled to draw her mind from the sensual web he had so skilfully woven. "Yes, but—" Abruptly, her eyes flew open. "*Dear heaven!*" After a stunned moment, her lids fell. She whispered, a soft catch in her voice, "Harry?"

A long moment of breathy silence ensued, then Lucinda sighed—deeply. "Oh, *Harry!*"

AN HOUR LATER, as the carriage slowly rolled into the leafy streets of Mayfair, Harry looked down at the woman in his lap. She was curled snugly in his greatcoat, dry and warm—he was prepared to swear no chill could have survived the fire that had recently claimed them. Her clothes lay in a sodden heap on the floor; his coat and breeches would keep Dawlish occupied for hours. Harry didn't care—he had all he most wanted of life.

He glanced down—and dropped a kiss on her curls.

He'd been a most unwilling conquest but he was ready to admit he was well and truly conquered.

Tipping his head, he looked into his siren's face, blissful in repose.

She stirred, then snuggled closer against him, one hand on his chest, over his heart.

Harry smiled, closed his eyes—and closed his arms about her.

Some secrets are better left buried...

Yesterday's Scandal by **WILKINS**

A mysterious stranger has come to town...

Former cop Mac Cordero was going undercover one last time to
find and exact revenge on the man who fathered, then abandoned
him. All he knew was that the man's name was McBride—a name,
that is synonymous with scandal.

...and he wants her!

Responsible, reliable Sharon Henderson was drawn to the sexy-as-
sin stranger. She couldn't help falling for him hard and fast. Then
she discovered that their love was based on a lie....

YOU WON'T WANT TO MISS IT!

On sale September 2000 at your favorite retail outlet.

HARLEQUIN®
Makes any time special ™

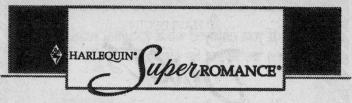

HARLEQUIN *Super* **ROMANCE**

Here's what small-town dreams are made of!

BORN IN A SMALL TOWN

is a special 3-in-1 collection featuring

New York Times bestselling author
Debbie Macomber's brand-new *Midnight Sons*
title, *Midnight Sons and Daughters*

Judith Bowen's latest *Men of Glory* title—
The Glory Girl

Janice Kay Johnson returns to
Elk Springs, Oregon with *Patton's Daughters*
in *Promise Me Picket Fences*

Join the search for romance in three small towns
in September 2000.

Available at your favorite retail outlet.

HARLEQUIN®
Makes any time special ™

Visit us at www.eHarlequin.com

HSRBORNR